S.C. 813.3 SIMM   c.3

Simms, William Gilmore, 1806
-1870.

Katharine Walton

DATE	ISSUED TO	
14NOV 03	Marilyn Bowman	38 8957

Katharine Walton

The Revolutionary War Novels
of
William Gilmore Simms

1. *Joscelyn*
2. *The Partisan*
3. *Mellichampe*
4. *Katharine Walton*
5. *The Scout*
6. *The Forayers*
7. *Eutaw*
8. *Woodcraft*

Revolutionary War Novels

4

Katharine Walton

by

William Gilmore Simms

With Introduction and Explanatory Notes

Published for the Southern Studies Program
University of South Carolina

THE REPRINT COMPANY, PUBLISHERS
SPARTANBURG, SOUTH CAROLINA
1976

This volume was reproduced from an 1854 edition.

Introduction and Notes Copyright © Southern Studies Program 1976.

Reprinted: 1976
The Reprint Company, Publishers
Spartanburg, South Carolina

ISBN 0-87152-238-1
Library of Congress Catalog Card Number: 76-8888
Manufactured in the United States of America on long-life paper

Library of Congress Cataloging in Publication Data

Simms, William Gilmore, 1806-1870.
    Katharine Walton : or, The rebel of Dorchester.

    (Simms Revolutionary War novels ; v. 4)
    Reprint of the ed. published by Redfield, New
York.
    1.   South Carolina——History——Revolution, 1775-1783
——Fiction. I. Title.
PZ3.S592Si vol. 4 [PS2848]   813'.3   76-8888
ISBN 0-87152-238-1

Contents

Acknowledgments   vii
Introduction   ix
Katharine Walton   following page xiv
Explanatory Notes   477

Acknowledgments

The cooperative efforts of a number of organizations and individuals made possible this publication of Simms' eight novels of the Revolution in South Carolina. It had been originally planned to include them in the Centennial Edition of the Writings of William Gilmore Simms, published by the University of South Carolina Press. However, a textual study of the novels indicated that a new edition, newly set in type, would be desirable for only one of them, *Joscelyn*. Accordingly, the Editorial Board of the Centennial Edition, consisting of James B. Meriwether, General Editor; Keen Butterworth, Textual Editor; and Mary C. Simms Oliphant, John C. Guilds, and Stephen Meats, decided to omit the remaining seven novels from the edition and to seek another publisher to bring them out with new introductory and explanatory matter, but with their texts reproduced by photo-offset from the Redfield edition of Simms' works, originally published in the 1850's.

Joscelyn, with an introduction and notes by Professor Meats and its text established by Professor Butterworth, was published in October 1975 by the University of South Carolina Press as volume XVI of the Centennial Edition, with the Seal, as an Approved Text, of the Center for Editions of American Authors. When Thomas E. Smith of The Reprint Company agreed to undertake the publication of the Revolutionary novels as a set, the University of South Carolina Press agreed to license the reissue of *Joscelyn* (without its textual apparatus) so that all eight novels might, for the first time, be brought out together.

The Southern Studies Program of the University of South Carolina, of which Professor Meriwether is Director, agreed to provide appropriate historical notes and introductory matter for the set. The preparation of the notes was carried out as a collaborative project by graduate students in the Southern Studies Program, under the direction of Professor Meriwether and Professor Meats. A grant to the Southern Studies Program by the South Carolina Committee for the Humanities, in support of a series of public seminars on Simms and the Revolution, directed by Professor Meats, aided greatly in the work upon the notes for the set.

When planning for publication had been completed, the South Carolina American Revolution Bicentennial Commission gave the project its endorsement and agreed to purchase 150 sets to be used for educational purposes within the State of South Carolina. Special thanks are due to John Hills, Director, and to Bradley Morrah and Sam P. Manning, Chairman and Vice Chairman, respectively, of the Commission, for their interest in and assistance with this project.

In the preparation of the historical notes for these volumes, the assistance of E. L. Inabinett, Director of the South Caroliniana Library, and of his staff was invaluable. Thanks are also due to Charles Lee, State Archivist of South Carolina, and to his staff; and to Professors George C. Rogers, Robert Weir and David Chesnutt, of the History Department of the University of South Carolina. Editorial assistance on the notes was provided by Elisabeth Muhlenfeld and Dianne Anderson of the Southern Studies Program, and by Margaret C. Thomas of The Reprint Company. Special thanks are due to Mrs. Oliphant for making available her great store of knowledge concerning her grandfather's life and work.

James B. Meriwether
Stephen Meats

Introduction

William Gilmore Simms was South Carolina's and the South's leading man of letters in the 19th century. He was born in Charleston on 17 April 1806 and died there on 11 June 1870. During his long literary career, which began in 1825 with the publication of his first separate work, *Monody on the Death of Gen. Charles Cotesworth Pinckney*, Simms wrote and published twenty-seven novels or romances, five collections of short fiction, eighteen volumes of poetry, two of drama, four volumes of history and geography, four of biography, and five volumes of reviews and miscellaneous prose, a total of sixty-five volumes. Probably an equal or greater amount of material was furnished to various periodicals and annuals during his career, including four novels that appeared serially in magazines between 1863 and 1869. As an editor, he brought out three volumes of the works of other authors and four miscellaneous anthologies, and was associated editorially with a substantial number of significant periodicals, among which were such South Carolina newspapers as the Charleston *Courier* and the Charleston *Mercury*, and such journals as *The Magnolia*, the *Southern Literary Gazette*, the *Southern and Western Magazine and Review* and *The Southern Quarterly Review*. As his many published addresses attest, he was also a popular lecturer on a variety of subjects, and he left a number of works, including one of his finest short stories, in manuscript at his death.

As a student of history, Simms' interests ranged over nearly every stage of the development of western civilization, beginning with ancient Greece and Rome and carrying through to European history of the age of Napoleon and after, but he was most interested in the history of the western hemisphere, particularly in the way the early Spanish, French and English settlements evolved into the nations of his own time. Evidence in his correspondence and in his published reviews and notices indicates his extensive knowledge of contemporary and older accounts of these eras and events. In his historical writings about most places and periods, he shows himself to be only a student of history rather than a historian—that is, he depended for his knowledge entirely on the previous researches and writings of the real historians in these fields. But his study of the American Revolution, particularly in South Carolina and the South, was quite a different matter. In these areas he possessed the historian's knowledge of primary sources—personal and official correspondence, legal documents, diaries, eye-witness accounts, and other records—as well as being thoroughly familiar with all the published histories, biographies, memoirs, records, and volumes of correspondence available. He owned a large archive of Revolutionary War manuscripts himself and had access to other extensive private collections. Although his own manuscripts were predominantly of Southern and South Carolina interest, they did not concentrate exclusively on these areas. His collection also contained considerable numbers of the letters and other papers of prominent civilian and military figures of the Revolution from nearly every one of the original thirteen states, including, among others, large collections of the correspondence of General Washington, General Greene, Henry Laurens while President of the Continental Congress, John Laurens while Washington's aide-de-camp, and the Baron DeKalb, as well as smaller numbers of letters by Patrick Henry, John Adams, John Jay, General Horatio Gates, Governor Jonathan Trumbull, and Samuel A. Otis. Simms was also intensely interested in the local legends and traditions of the Revolution in South Carolina and spent nearly a lifetime collecting such materials in his travels around his native state and in his correspondence with local historians and antiquarians.

Simms put his extensive knowledge of the Revolution to use in a wide variety of article- and book-length works over a period of nearly forty-five years. Among his most notable non-fictional publications on the Revolution are *The History of South Carolina* (1840), which devotes nearly two-thirds of its length to the Revolution; full-length biographies of General Francis Marion (1844) and General Nathanael Greene (1849); *South-Carolina in the Revolutionary War* (1853), a book defending the importance of the state's contributions to the conflict; a volume of the war correspondence of Colonel John Laurens for which Simms wrote a biographical memoir of Laurens; extensive articles on such prominent Revolutionary figures as Governor John Rutledge and the Baron DeKalb; biographical sketches of nearly a dozen Revolutionary soldiers and civilians for various biographical and historical works; a substantial number of lectures on topics ranging from particular battles to individual men; and many book reviews in which he uses his own primary knowledge of the Revolution to support, expand upon, or to refute the work he is evaluating. Simms was also instrumental in encouraging other amateur historians to write down the results of their researches by publishing their works in some of the journals he edited, particularly in *The Magnolia* and *The Southern Quarterly Review*.

But Simms made the most extensive use of his knowledge of the history, legends and traditions of the Revolution in the series of eight Revolutionary War novels which constitute the most ambitious treatment of the conflict by an American author of the 19th century. Concentrating on the progress of the war in South Carolina, these novels were written and published in the following order:

1835 *The Partisan: A Tale of the Revolution.* 2 volumes. New York: Harper & Brothers. Revised edition, entitled *The Partisan: A Romance of the Revolution*, New York: Redfield, 1854.

1836 *Mellichampe A Legend of the Santee.* 2 volumes. New York: Harper & Brothers. Revised edition, New York: Redfield, 1854.

1841 *The Kinsmen: or the Black Riders of Congaree. A Tale.* 2 volumes. Philadelphia: Lea and Blanchard. Revised edition, entitled *The Scout or The Black Riders of Congaree,* New York: Redfield, 1854.

1850 *Katharine Walton: or, the Rebel of Dorchester. An Historical Romance of the Revolution in Carolina.* Philadelphia: A. Hart, 1851. Revised edition, entitled *Katharine Walton or The Rebel of Dorchester,* New York: Redfield, 1854. A shorter version was first published serially in *Godey's Lady's Book* (February-December, 1850) with the title "Katharine Walton: or, the Rebel's Daughter. A Tale of the Revolution."

1852 *The Sword and the Distaff; or, "Fair, Fat and Forty," A Story of the South, at the Close of the Revolution.* Charleston: Walker, Richards & Co. Revised edition, entitled *Woodcraft or Hawks about the Dovecote A Story of the South at the Close of the Revolution,* New York: Redfield, 1854. First published serially in semi-monthly supplements to the *Southern Literary Gazette* (February-November, 1852).

1855 *The Forayers or The Raid of the Dog-Days.* New York: Redfield.

1856 *Eutaw A Sequel to The Forayers, or the Raid of the Dog-Days A Tale of the Revolution.* New York: Redfield.

1867 *Joscelyn A Tale of the Revolution.* Columbia, S.C.: University of South Carolina Press, 1975. Volume 16 of *The Centennial Edition of the Writings of William Gilmore Simms.* First published serially in *The Old Guard* (January-December, 1867).

Because the order in which the eight novels were published does not follow the chronology of the Revolution itself, they should be read in this sequence in order to follow Simms' narrative of the conflict: *Joscelyn; The Partisan; Mellichampe; Katharine Walton; The Scout; The Forayers; Eutaw;* and *Woodcraft.*

Joscelyn portrays the civil war in the back country in the late summer and fall of 1775. This was the first open warfare of the Revolution in the South, involving the citizens of South Carolina and Georgia who took either the whig (American) or loyalist (British) side. The next three volumes of the series are closely linked and can be considered a trilogy. With the first of them, *The Partisan*, the action of the series skips to June 1780, immediately after the fall of Charleston in May. Simms uses several representative though fictionalized characters to show the development of partisan resistance to British occupation. The main historical event of this novel is the Battle of Camden (August 1780) in which the crushing defeat of the Southern Continental Army threw the entire responsibility of resistance on the irregular volunteer forces under Francis Marion and other partisan commanders. *Mellichampe*, the second volume of the trilogy, centers its narrative around a different set of fictional characters in following the activities of Marion's band in its struggle with loyalist and British forces in the Santee River area in the fall of 1780. The third novel in the trilogy, *Katharine Walton*, picks up the narrative involving the fictional characters of *The Partisan* in September 1780 and describes the impact of the war on their family fortunes over a period of several months. Much of the novel portrays the social life of the British garrison in Charleston and the participation of various civilians in the American war effort. *The Scout* opens in May 1781 not long after the Battle of Hobkirk's Hill and ends in June after the British abandonment of the star-fort at Ninety Six. This novel concentrates on the struggle between partisan forces and the outlaw bands that operated under British authority in plundering the central portion of the state around the Congaree and Wateree River areas. The retreat of British forces toward Orangeburg and from there to

Charleston due to their inability to maintain their outpost at Ninety Six is the subject of *The Forayers* and its sequel, *Eutaw*. The central historical event of these two novels is the Battle of Eutaw Springs (September 1781) which virtually ended British domination in South Carolina. The final novel, *Woodcraft*, begins just as the British are evacuating Charleston in December 1782, and portrays the difficulties experienced by soldiers and civilians of South Carolina in making the transition from the lawless disorder of the late stages of the war to a condition of relative peace and civil order. Most of the action of the novel occurs on a ruined low country plantation on the Ashepoo River.

KATHARINE WALTON

Although it had been planned much earlier, the actual writing of Simms' fourth novel of the Revolution, *Katharine Walton*, apparently was not begun until the fall of 1849. Publication of the serial version in *Godey's Lady's Book* in 1850 was followed by book publication in August 1851 by the Philadelphia firm of A. Hart.

Simms revised the novel for publication, in June 1854, in the Redfield collected edition of his works. It was many times reprinted, first by Redfield and later by a number of other publishers, but without further revision or correction by the author. The text of the present volume was reproduced by offset from a copy of the first impression of the Redfield edition. The type page has been enlarged to 115% of the size of the original.

Darley-fecit

KATHARINE WALTON

OR

THE REBEL OF DORCHESTER

BY W. GILMORE SIMMS, Esq.

AUTHOR OF "THE YEMASSEE," "THE PARTISAN," "MELLICHAMPE," THE
SCOUT," "WOODCRAFT," "GUY RIVERS," ETC.

"Every minute now
Should be the father of some stratagem."
KING HENRY IV.

NEW AND REVISED EDITION

REDFIELD
110 AND 112 NASSAU STREET, NEW YORK.
1854.

STEREOTYPED BY C. C. SAVAGE.
13 Chambers Street, N. Y.

TO THE

HON. EDWARD FROST,

OF SOUTH CAROLINA.

———✦———

MY DEAR FROST:

ESCAPED from official responsibilities — from the cares of one of the most exacting, if not the most harassing of all professions — and settled down comfortably to the grateful employments of agricultural life — I assume you to be in the full possession of that calm of mood and temper, favorable equally to happiness and thought, in which all the human faculties rise to their most perfect excellence ; —

> " Content to breathe your native air,
> In your own ground,"

and pleased to contemplate, at easy distance, the prolonged struggles of that world, from the oppressive and exhausting excitements of which you are measurably free. Beneath your eye the cotton fields bloom and blow ; and over the sunny plains, whitened with noble harvests, you gaze at the spires of the distant city, pleasantly reminded of its bustling swarms, in a situation which finds you unvexed by its complaints. Here, in the enjoyment of freedom, ease, a grateful prospect, and that repose which constitutes the vital blessing of security, you find books a genial substitute for society, and in foregoing the struggles with the present, feel yourself more than compensated by the consoling possessions of the past. In such a scene and situa-

1

tion, I do not scruple to challenge your regards, for that art, in fiction, which, while you were upon the bench, among the big-wigged gentry, would have been very much out of place, occupying any share of your consideration, and certainly not to be held for a moment of any authority in the formation of your solemn judgments. Now, you may luxuriate in the treasures of romance, without endangering the dignity of law—now, you may feed upon song and story without rendering suspicious the ultimate decrees of justice. No one now, of all the Burleighs of society, will chide you with rewarding the muse too extravagantly; or throw up hand and eyes, in holy horror, to find you poring over the pages of Scott and Cooper, instead of the better-authorized, and more musty volumes of Bracton and Fleta, Littleton and Sir Edward Coke—to enumerate no other of those grave monsters of great profundity—I will not say dullness lest I ruffle your lingering veneration—whom " even to name," by one who has utterly renounced their authority, "would be unlawful." You may now, in brief, recover all your natural tastes, without disturbing the peace of society, or vexing the sensibilities of convention—recover all the tastes which the legal profession expects you to surrender, and with an eye newly opening to art, and a soul growing daily more and more sensible to the truth in fiction, acquire a better sense of the sweet in humanity, and the beguiling and blessing which always compensate (no matter what the cost) in the higher regions of the ideal. Nay, even though you put down the books of Scott and Cooper to take up mine, it will somewhat reconcile you to the rebuke of taste, when you reflect that I summon to my aid the muse of local History—the traditions of our own home—the chronicles of our own section—the deeds of our native heroes—the recollections of our own noble ancestry.

"Katharine Walton," the romance which I now venture to inscribe with your name, constitutes a sequel to " The Partisan," and is the third of a trilogy, designed especially to illustrate an important period, in our parish country, during the progress of the Revolution. You are quite as familiar with the scene occupied by the action in these stories as myself, and quite as well taught in the general characteristics of the actors. Of my handling of these subjects, it becomes me to say nothing. But while I forbear all remark upon the plan and conduct of these romances, I may be permitted to say that they were, when originally published, so many new developments and discoveries to our people. They opened the way to historical studies among us—they suggested clews to the historian—they struck and laid bare to other workers, the veins of tradition which everywhere enriched our territory—they showed to succeeding laborers—far abler than myself—what treasures of *materiel*, lay waiting for the shaping hands of future genius. When I first began these fictions, no one dreamed of the abundance of our possessions of this sort—that a scene or story, picture or statue, had been wrought out of the crude masses which lay buried in our soil. My friends denounced my waste of time upon scenes, and situations, and events, in which they beheld nothing latent —nothing which could possibly (as they thought) reward the laborer. *Now*, South Carolina is regarded as a very storehouse for romance. She has furnished more materials for the use of art and fiction, than half the states in the Union. Regarding myself as nearly at the end of my labors and career, I may be permitted to suggest this comparison, with a natural feeling of pride and satisfaction.

A few words more. While " The Partisan," and " Mellichampe," occupied ground in the interior, scenes at the head of the Ashley, and along the Santee and Wateree, " Katharine Walton" brings us to the city ; and a large proportion of the work, and much of its interest, will be found to consist in the delineation of the social world of Charleston, during the Revolutionary period. These delineations are so many careful studies, pursued through a series of many years, and under the guidance of the most various and the best authorities. The matter, in fact, is mostly historical, even when merely social. The portraits are mostly of real persons. The descriptions of life, manners, customs, movements, the social aspects in general, have all been drawn from sources as unquestionable as abundant. The social reunions, in many instances, as described in the story, were real occurrences. The anecdotes, the very repartees, though never before in print, are gathered from tradition and authority. I have, in a great part of the story, contented myself with simply framing the fact; preferring to render my materials unique, rather than to put them upon record as bold and casual reminiscences.

The trilogy contemplated when I began "The Partisan," is now complete with "Katharine Walton," though it will be found that certain of the *dramatis personæ* of this series, have a prolonged existence, in another romance, yet to follow, which opens at the moment when the war of the Revolution closes; and is designed to show the effects of that conflict upon the condition of the country, the fortunes of its people, and the general *morale* of society. But of this, nothing need be spoken now. Enough for the present, and for the volume in your hands. I do not ask, my dear Frost, that this book shall take the place with you, or with any of your ancient brethren, of the fathers in the law; but shall be quite satisfied, if when the Bigwigs are fairly shelved, or under the table—out of sight and mind—you closet yourself for an hour with my heroine of the Ashley; a woman drawn, I honestly think, after our best models of good manners, good taste, good intellect, and noble, generous sensibilities; frank, buoyant, and refined; yet superior to mere convention.

> "A spirit, yet a woman too!
> Her household motions light and free,
> And steps of virgin liberty!—
> A creature not too bright nor good
> For human nature's daily food;
> For transient sorrows, simple wiles,
> Praise, blame, love, kisses, tears, and smiles."

Yielding you now to the lady, while the south wind sweeps in from the sea, bringing you perfumes of orange from the groves of Hayti and the Cuban, I leave you, my dear Frost, to the most genial embraces of the summer.

Very faithfully, your friend, &c.

W. GILMORE SIMMS.

WOODLAND, *April*, 1854.

KATHARINE WALTON.

CHAPTER I.

OLD SOLDIERS.

OUR story opens early in September, in the eventful year of American revolutionary history, one thousand seven hundred and eighty. Our scene is one destined to afford abundant materials for the purposes of the future romancer. It lies chiefly upon the banks of the Ashley, in South Carolina, a region which, at this period, was almost entirely covered by the arms of the foreign enemy. In previous narratives, as well as in the histories, will be found the details of his gradual conquests, and no one need be told of the events following the fall of Charleston, and terminating in the defeat of General Gates at Camden, by which, for a season, the hopes of patriotism, as well as the efforts of valor which aimed at the recovery of the country from hostile domination, were humbled, if not wholly overthrown. The southern liberating army was temporarily dispersed, rallying slowly to their standards in the wildernesses of North Carolina; few in number, miserably clad, and almost totally wanting in the means and appliances of war. The victory of the British over Gates was considered complete. It was distinguished by their usual sacrifices. Many of their prisoners were executed upon the spot, mostly upon the smallest pretexts and the most questionable testimony. These sacrifices were due somewhat to the requisitions of the loyalists, to the excited passions of the conquerors, and, in some degree, to their own scorn of the victims. But one of those decreed for sacrifice had made his escape, rescued, in the moment of destined execution, by a most daring and unexpected onslaught of a small body of partisans, led by a favorite leader. Colonel Richard Walton, a gentleman of great personal worth, of considerable wealth, and exercising much social influence, had, under particular circumstances, and when the state was believed to be utterly lost to the confederacy, taken what was entitled "British protection." This was a parole, insuring him safety and shelter beneath the protection of the conqueror, so long as he preserved his neutrality. It was some reproach to Colonel Walton that he had taken this protection; but, in the particular circumstances of the case, there was much to extenuate his offence. With his justification, however, just at this moment, we have nothing to do. It is enough that the violation of the compact between the citizen and the conqueror was due to the British commander. In the emergency of invasion, at the approach of the continental arms, the securities of those who had taken protection were withdrawn by proclamation, unless they presented themselves in the British ranks and took up arms under the banner of the invader. Compelled to draw the sword, Colonel Walton did so on the side of the country. He fell into the hands of Cornwallis at the fatal battle of Camden; and, steadily refusing the overtures of the British general to purge himself of the alleged treason by taking a commission in the service of the conqueror, he was ordered to execution at Dorchester, in the neighborhood of his estates, and as an example of terror to the surrounding country. He was rescued at the foot of the gallows, from the degrading death which had been decreed him. By a well-planned and desperate enterprise, led by Major Singleton, a kinsman, he was plucked from the clutches of the executioner; and the successful effort was still farther distinguished by the almost total annihilation of the strong guard of the British, which had left the garrison at Dorchester to escort the victim to the fatal tree.

The beautiful hamlet of Dorchester was partially laid in ashes during the short but sanguinary conflict; and, before reinforcements could arrive from the fortified post at the place, the partisans had melted away, like so many shadows, into the swamps of the neighboring cypress, carrying with them, in safety, their enfranchised captive. The occurrence had been one rather to exasperate the invader than to disturb his securities. It was not less an indignity than a hurt; and, taking place, as it did, within twenty miles of the garrison of Charleston, it denoted a degree of audacity, on the part of the rebels, which particularly called for the active vengeance of the invader, as an insult and a disgrace to his arms.

But if the mortification of Major Proctor, by whom the post at Dorchester was held, was great, still greater was the fury of Colonel Balfour, the commandant of Charleston. The intelligence reached him, by express, at midnight of the day of the affair, and roused him from the grateful slumbers of a life which had hitherto been fortunate in the acquisition of every desired indulgence, and from dreams holding forth the most delicious promise of that *otium cum dignitate* which was in the contemplation of all his toils. To be aroused to such intelligence as had been brought him, was to deny him both leisure and respect — nay, to involve him in possible forfeiture of the possession of place and power, which, he well knew, were of doubtful tenure only, and easily determined by a run of such disasters as that which he was now required to contemplate. Yet Balfour, in reality, had nothing with which to reproach himself in the affair at Dorchester. No blame, whether of omission or performance, could be charged upon him, making him liable to reproach for this misfortune. He had no reason to suppose that, with Rawdon in command at Camden, and Cornwallis, but recently the victor over Gates, with the great body of the British army covering every conspicuous point in the country, that any small party of rebels should prove so daring as to dart between and snatch the prey from the very grasp of the executioner. Marion had, however, done this upon the Santee, and here now was his lieutenant repeating the audacious enterprise upon the Ashley. Though really not to blame, Balfour yet very well knew how severe were the judgments which, in Great Britain, were usually visited upon the misfortunes or failures of British captains in

America. He had no reason to doubt that in his case, as commonly in that of others, his superiors would be apt to cast upon the subordinate the responsibilities of every mischance. It is true that he might offer good defence. He could show that, in order to strengthen his army against Gates, Cornwallis had stripped the city of nearly all its disposable force, leaving him nothing but invalids, and a command of cavalry not much more than sufficient to scour the neighborhood, bring in supplies, and furnish escorts. Dorchester had been shorn of its garrison for the same reason by the same officer. The reproach, if any, lay at the door of Cornwallis. Yet who would impute blame to the successful general, who offers his plea while yet his trumpets are sounding in every ear with the triumphal notes of a great victory? Success is an argument that effectually stops the mouth of censure. To fasten the reproach upon another, by whom no plea of good fortune could be offered, was the policy of Balfour; and his eye was already turned upon the victim. But this, hereafter. For the present, his task was to repair, if possible, the misfortune; to recover the freed rebel; to put Dorchester in a better state to overawe the surrounding country, and make himself sure in his position by timely reports of the affair to his superiors; by which, showing them where the fault might be imputable to themselves, while studiously imputing it to another, he should induce them to such an adoption of his views as should silence all representations which might be hurtful to his own security.

All these meditations passed rapidly through the brain of Balfour, as he made his midnight toilet. When he came forth, his plans were all complete. As we are destined to see much more of this personage in the progress of our narrative, it will not be unwise, in this place, to dwell somewhat more particularly upon the mental and moral nature of the man. At the period of which we write, he was in the vigor of his years. He had *kept* well, to borrow the idiom of another people, and was altogether a very fine specimen of physical manhood. With an erect person, fully six feet in height, broad-chested, and athletic; with cheeks unwrinkled, a skin clear and florid; eyes large, blue, and tolerably expressive; and features generally well-chiseled, he was altogether a person to impose at a glance, and almost persuade, without further examination, to the conviction of generous impulses, if not a commanding intellect, as the natural concomitants of so much that is prepossessing in the exterior. But Balfour was a man of neither mind nor heart. In ordinary affairs, he was sufficiently shrewd and searching. It was not easy, certainly to delude him, where his selfish interests were at all at issue. In the mere details of business, he was methodical and usually correct; but he neither led nor planned an enterprise; and, while able in civil matters to carry out the designs of others, it is not seen that he ever counselled or conceived an improvement. His passions were more active than his mind, yet they never impelled him to courageous performance. He was a carpet knight, making a famous figure always on parade, and, in the splendid uniform of his regiment, really a magnificent person — in the language of a lady who knew him well, "as splendid as scarlet, gold lace, and feathers, could make a man." But he never distinguished himself in action. Indeed, the record is wanting which would show that he had ever been in action. That he should have risen to his high station, as second in command of the British army in South Carolina — for such was his rank — might reasonably provoke our surprise, but that the record which fails to tell us of his achievements in battle, is somewhat more copious in other matters. His method of rising into power was among the reproaches urged against him. His obsequious devotedness to the humors and pleasures — we may safely say vices — of Sir William Howe, first gained him position, and finally led to his present appointment. In the capacity of commandant at Charleston, his arrogance became insufferable. His vanity seems to have been in due degree with the servility which he had been forced to show in the acquisition of his objects. He could enact the opposite phases in the character of his countryman, Sir Pertinax MacSycophant, without an effort at transition — *boo* without shame or sense of degradation, and command without decency or sense of self-respect. In counsel, he was at once ignorant and self-opinionated. In the exercise of his government, he absorbed all the powers of the state. "By the subversion," says

Ramsay, " of every trace of the popular government, without
any proper civil establishment in its place, he, with a few co-
adjutors, assumed and exercised legislative, judicial and executive
powers over citizens in the same manner as over the common
soldiery." He was prompt to anger, obdurate in punishment,
frivolous in his exactions, and bloated with the false consequences
of a position which he had reached through meanness and exercised without dignity. Feared and hated by his inferiors,
despised by his equals, and loved by few, if any, he was yet
one of that fortunate class of persons whom an inordinate but
accommodating self-esteem happily assures and satisfies in every
situation. Gratifying his favorite passions at every step in his
progress, he probably found no reason to regret the loss of affections that he had never learned to value and never cared to win.
Utterly selfish, his mind had nevertheless never risen to the appreciation of those better treasures of life and of the heart which
the noble nature learns to prize beyond all others, as by a natural instinct. His sympathies were those only of the sensual
temperament. His desires were those of the voluptuary. He
was an unmarried man, and his habits were those of any other
gay Lothario of the army. The warm tints upon his cheek
were significant of something more than vulgar health ; and the
liquid softness of his eye was indicative of habits such as were
admitted not to be among the worst traits of that passionate
Roman whose world was lost probably quite as much by wine as
love. Balfour was not the person to forfeit *his* world through
either of these passions, though he too freely and frequently
indulged in both. He possessed yet others which Mark Antony
does not seem to have shared, or not in large degree ; and his
avarice and lust of power were the rods, like those of Aaron,
which kept all others in subjection. But we have lingered
sufficiently long upon his portrait. Enough has been said and
shown to furnish all the clews to his character. Let us now see
to his performances.

In a short period after receiving his advices from Dorchester
Balfour was prepared for business. His secretary was soon in
attendance, and his aids were despatched in various quarters in
search of the officers whom he had summoned to his morning

conference. He occupied, as "Headquarters," that noble old mansion, still remaining in the lower part of King street, Charleston, known as number *eleven*. At that period it belonged to the estate of Miles Brewton. Subsequently, it became the property of Colonel William Allston, in whose family it still remains. But with Balfour as its tenant, the proprietorship might fairly be assumed to be wholly in himself; determinable only in the event, now scarcely anticipated by the invader, of the state ever being recovered by the arms of the Americans. With his secretary seated at the table, his pen rapidly coursing over the sheets under the diction of his superior, Balfour trod the apartment—the southeast chamber in the second story— in evident impatience. At times, he hurried to the front windows, which were all open, and looked forth, as any unusual sounds assailed his ears. Returning, he uttered sentence after sentence of instruction, and paused only to approach the sideboard and renew his draught of old Madeira, a bottle of which had been freshly opened before the secretary came. At length, to the relief of his impatience, the sound of a carriage was heard rolling to the door, and the soldier in attendance looked in to announce

"Colonel Cruden."

"Show him in," was the reply; and, the next moment, the person thus named made his appearance, and was welcomed in proper terms by the commandant, who, turning to the secretary, hastily examined what he had written, as hastily attached his seal and signature, and, in lower tones than was his wont, gave him instructions in what manner to dispose of the papers.

"Leave us now," said Balfour, "but be not far; I may need you shortly. No more sleep to-night; remember that. You may help yourself to some of the wine; it may assist you in sustaining your vigil."

The young man did not scruple to employ the privilege awarded him. He drank the wine, and, with a bow, retired.

"Let us drink, also, Cruden," was the speech of Balfour, the moment the youth had gone. "This early rising renders some stimulus necessary, particularly when the matter is as annoying as troublesome. Come, this Madeira is from the cellar of old

Laurens, some time president of Congress. He had a truer taste for Madeira than politics. There is no better to be found in all the city. Come."

"But what is this business which calls us up at this unseasonable hour?"

"Something in your way, I fancy. But first let me congratulate you on your appointment. As agent for sequestrated estates, you should soon be a millionaire."

"There certainly ought to be good pickings where rebellion has been so fruitful," said the other.

"Surely; and in possession of the fine mansion of that premature rebel, Cotesworth Pinckney—decidedly the finest house in Carolina—you are already in the enjoyment of a pleasant foretaste of what must follow. The house, of course, will remain your own."

"I suppose so, if the state is not reconquered."

"And have you any fears of this, after the defeat of that sentimental hero, Gates, at Camden? That affair seems to settle the question. These people are effectually crushed and cowed, and Congress can never raise another army. The militia of the Middle states and the south are by no means numerous, and they want everything as well as arms. The New-Englanders no longer take the field, now that the war has left their own borders; and, come what may, it is very clear that the Carolinas, Georgia, and Florida, must still remain the colonies of Great Britain. In that event, a peace which even yields independence to the more northern provinces, will give nothing to these: and my faith in the *uti-posidetis* principle makes me quite easy with regard to my possessions."

And he looked round upon the pleasant apartment which he occupied with the air of a man perfectly satisfied with the architectural proportions of his building.

"I am glad to hear you in this pleasant vein. From your impatient summons, I had thought the devil was to pay."

"And so he is," said the commandant, suddenly becoming grave; "the devil to pay, indeed; and I am sorry to tell you that your kinsman, Proctor, is in danger of sharp censure, if not a loss of his commission."

"Ha!"

" He has nearly suffered the surprise of his post; suffered this malignant Walton to be snatched from his clutches on the way to execution, half of his men to be cut to pieces, and Dorchester burnt to ashes."

" You confound me!"

" It is too true. There is his own despatch, which, of course, makes the best of it."

He pointed to the table where lay a couple of letters with the seals both broken; and Cruden was about to place his hand on one of them, when his grasp was prevented, rather precipitately, by that of Balfour.

" Stay; that is not the despatch. Here it is," giving the one letter, and carefully thrusting the other into his pocket. But Cruden had already seen the superscription, which bore the Dorchester stamp also. He made no comment, however, on the circumstance, and forbore all inquiry, while he proceeded to read the despatch of Major Proctor, to whom the post at Dorchester and the contiguous country had been confided.

" This is certainly a most unfortunate affair; but I do not see how Proctor is to blame. He seems to have done everything in his power."

"That is to be seen. I hope so, for your sake no less than his. But it is a matter of too serious a kind not to demand keen and searching inquiry."

" Proctor had no more than seventy men at the post. Cornwallis stripped him of all that could be spared; and more, it seems, than it was safe to spare."

" My dear friend, you are just in the receipt of a handsome appointment from Cornwallis. How can you suppose, that he should err in a military calculation of this sort? How suppose that the king of Great Britain can be persuaded of his error at the very moment which brings him advices of so great a victory? It is impossible! Come, let us replenish;" and he again filled the glasses. Cruden drank, but deliberately; and while the goblet was yet unfinished, paused to say —

" I see, Balfour, my kinsman is to be sacrificed."

"Nay, not so; we shall give him every opportunity of saving

himself. On my honor, he shall not be pressed to the wall. But you see for yourself that the affair is an unlucky one—a most unlucky one—just at this juncture."

"And Proctor such a good fellow—really a noble fellow."

"Admitted; and yet, between us, Cruden, he has been particularly unfortunate, I fear, in allowing his affections to be ensnared by the daughter of this very rebel, Walton; who is not without attractions, considering her vast estates. She is more than good-looking, I hear—indeed, Kitty Harvey tells me that she was quite a beauty a year ago. Moll is not willing to go so far, but says she was very good-looking. Now, these charms, in addition to some two or three hundred slaves, and a most baronial landed estate, have proved too much for your nephew; and the fear is that he has shown himself quite too indulgent—indeed, a little wilfully careless and remiss; and to this remissness the rebel owes his escape."

"This is a very shocking suspicion, Balfour; and not to be reported or repeated without the best of testimony. John Proctor is one of the most honorable men living. There does not seem to have been any remissness. These partisans of Singleton were surely unexpected; and when Proctor sends out half of his disposable force to escort the rebel to execution, one would think he had furnished quite as large a guard as was requisite."

"So, under ordinary circumstances, it would seem; and yet where would this party of rebels, though led by a notoriously daring fellow, find the audacity to attack such a guard within sight of the fortress, in midday, unless secretly conscious that the chances favored him in an extraordinary manner? Mind you, now, I say nothing of my own head. I give you only the conjectures, the mere whisperings of others, and beg you to believe that I keep my judgment in reserve for more conclusive evidence."

"I don't doubt that Proctor will acquit himself before any court. But have you any farther advices—no letters?"

"None that relate to this affair," was the rather hesitating reply.

"And what is it, Balfour, for which you want me now?"

"A cast of your office, *mon ami*. I wish to afford you an opportunity of exercising yourself in your new vocation. You must accompany me to Dorchester this very day. Here is a memorandum of particulars. Take your secretary with you. The estates of this rebel Walton are to be sequestered. You shall take them in charge and administer them. Lands, negroes, house, furniture, man-servant and maid-servant, ox and ass, and such an equipage as you will scarcely find any where in the colonies. I am told that the Madeira in Walton's garrets is the oldest in the country. Remember, there must be a fair division of *that* spoil. I have not insisted upon your merits to Cornwallis to be denied my reward. Besides, the stud of this rebel is said to be a magnificent one. I know that Tarleton itched to find a plea for laying hands upon his blooded horses. We must share them also, Cruden. I am by no means satisfied with my stock, and must recruit and supply myself. There are two or three hundred negroes, an immense stock of plate, and a crop of rice just about to be harvested. You will be secure of most of this treasure, anyhow, even should you find an heir for it in your nephew."

This last sentence was said with a smile, which Cruden did not greatly relish. There was much in what Balfour had spoken to disquiet him as well as give him pleasure. Cruden, like the greater number of his fellow-soldiers, was anxious to spoil the Egyptians. His avarice was almost as blind and devouring as that of Balfour, and his love of show not less; but he had affections and sympathies, such as are grateful to humanity. He was proud of his nephew, whose generous and brave qualities had done honor to their connection; and he was not willing to see him sacrificed without an effort. This he clearly perceived was Balfour's present object. Why, he did not care to know. It was enough that he resolved to do what was in his power to defeat his purpose.

We need not follow the farther conference of these good companions. It was of a kind to interest themselves only. With the first glimpses of the gray dawning, Cruden took his departure to hasten his preparations for the contemplated journey; while Balfour, having given all his orders, threw himself upon a sofa, and soon slept as soundly as if he had only just retired for the night.

CHAPTER II.

SOCIAL STABBING.

THE blare of trumpets beneath his windows, announcing the readness of his cavalry to march, found Balfour at the conclusion of a late breakfast. He was soon in the saddle, and accompanied by his friend Cruden, followed by some inferior officers. This party rode on slowly, while the major in command of the brigade proceeded on the march, drawing up only as they reached the great gate of the city. The stranger who at this day, shall find himself gazing upon the southern front of the stately pile called the "Citadel," in Charleston—a building of the state, devoted to the purposes of military education—will stand at no great distance from what was then the main entrance to the city. Along this line ran the fortifications, extending from the river Cooper to the Ashley, and traversing very nearly what is now the boundary line between the corporate limits of Charleston and its very extensive suburb. At that early period, the fortifications of the place were at some distance from the settlement. The surface occupied by the city scarcely reached beyond a fourth of the present dimensions, and in the north and west, was distinguished only by some scattered and inferior habitations. "Up the path" was the phrase used by which to distinguish the region which had been assigned to the defences and beyond.

Without, the region lay partially in woods, broken only by an occasional farmstead and worm fence, which, when the British took possession of the "Neck" for the purpose of the leaguer, soon disappeared, either wholly or in part, beneath the fire and the axe. The gate of the city stood a little to the east of

King street—not quite midway, perhaps, between that and Meeting street. It was covered within by a strong *horn-work* of masonry, originally built by the besieged, and afterward improved by the enemy. It was a work of considerable strength in that day, fraised, picketed, and intended as a citadel. The British, after the fall of the city, greatly strengthened and increased these fortifications; though even in their hands, the lines remained what are called field-works only.

Beyond them, at the moment when we request the reader's attention, were still perceptible the traces of the several footholds, taken by the enemy when the leaguer was in progress. You could see the *debris* of the redoubts, under the cover of which they had made their approaches; the several parallels—though thrown down in part, and the earth removed, with the view to strengthening the fortifications—still showing themselves upon the surface, and occasionally arresting the eye by an unbroken redoubt, or the mound which told where the mortar-battery had been erected. Farms and fences had been destroyed: trees had been cut down for pickets and abbatis; and even that noble avenue, leading from the city, called the "Broadway," which old Archdale tells us was "so delightful a road and walk of a greath breadth, so pleasantly green, that I believe no prince in Europe, by all their art, can make so pleasant a sight for the whole year," even this had been shorn of many of its noblest patriarchs, of oak and cedar, for the commonest purposes of fuel or defence. It was still an avenue, however, to compel the admiration of the European. All was not lost of its ample foliage, its green umbrage, its tall pines, fresh and verdant cedars, and ancient gnarled oaks: and, as the splendidly uniformed cavalry of the British, two hundred in number, filed away beneath its pleasant thickets, the spectacle was one of a beauty most unique, and might well persuade the spectator into a partial forgetfulness of the fearful trade which these gallant troopers carried on. On each hand, from this nearly central point, might glimpses be had of the two rivers, scarce a mile asunder; beneath which, on the most gradual slope of plane, the city of Charleston rises, the Ashley on the west, the Cooper on the east, both navigable for a small distance—streams of ample breadth, if not of depth; and in fact rather arms of the sea than arteries of the land.

The British detachment, about to leave the garrison, its objects not known, nor its destination, was necessarily a subject of considerable interest to all parties. Whig and loyalist equally regarded its movements with curiosity and excitement. The recent defeat of the Americans at Camden; the sudden and startling event, so near at hand, in the rescue at Dorchester, and the partial conflagration of that hamlet, were all now known among the citizens. The question with the one party was that of the dethroned sovereign of England on the ominous appearance of Gloster, "What bloody scene hath Roscius now to act?" — while the other looked forward to new progresses, ending in the acquisition of fresh spoils from new confiscations, and the punishment of enemies whom they had learned to hate in due degree with the appreciation of their virtuous patriotism, which persevered, under all privations, in a manly resistance to the invader. Groups of these, of both parties, separated naturally by their mutual antipathies, had assembled in the open space contiguous to the citadel, and were now anxiously contemplating the spectacle. Among these, scattered at plays that had an earnest signification, were dozens of sturdy urchins, already divided into parties according to the influence of their parental and other associations. These, known as the "Bay Boys" and the "Green Boys," were playing at soldiers, well armed with cornstalks, and hammering away at each other, in charging and retreating squadrons. The "Bay Boys" were all loyalists, the "Green Boys" the Whigs, or patriots: and in their respective designations, we have no inadequate suggestion of the influences which operated to divide the factions of their elders in the city. The "Bay Boys" represented the commercial influence, which, being chiefly in the hands of foreigners, acknowledged a more natural sympathy with Britain than the "Green Boys," or those of the suburban population, most of whom were the agricultural aristocracy of the low country, and with whom the revolutionary movement in Carolina had its origin.

The appearance of Balfour and his suite dispersed these parties, who retired upon opposite sides, leaving a free passage for the horses, which were driven forward with but small regard for the safety of the crowds that covered the highway. The men turned away with as much promptitude as the boys; neither Whig nor loyalist having much assurance of consideration from a ruler so arrogant and capricious as Balfour, and so reckless of the comfort of inferiors. A few women might be seen, as if in waiting, mostly in gig or chair—then the most commonly used vehicle—though one or more might be seen in carriages, and a few on horseback, followed by negro servants. Those were all prepared to leave the city, on brief visits, as was customary, to the neighboring farms and plantations along one or other of the two rivers. They were destined to disappointment, Balfour sternly denying the usual permit to depart from the city, at a moment when there was reason to suppose that stray bodies of Marion's parties were lurking in the neighborhood. The precaution was a proper one; but there was no grace or delicacy in the manner of Balfour's denial.

"Get home, madam," was the rude reply to one lady, who addressed him from the window of her carriage; "and be grateful for the security which the arms of his majesty afford you within the walls of the city. We will see after your estates."

"My concern is, sir, that you will prove yourself only too provident," answered the high-spirited woman, as she bade her coachman wheel about to return.

"There is no breaking down the spirit of this people," muttered Balfour to Cruden as they rode forward. "That woman always gives me the last word, and it is never an unspiced one."

"They who lose the soup may well be permitted to enjoy the pepper," said Cruden. "It ruffles you, which it should not."

"They shall bend or break before I am done with them," answered the other. To the major commanding in his absence, he gave strict injunctions that no one should be allowed to leave the city under any pretence.

"Unless General Williamson, I suppose?" was the inquiry, in return.

"Has he desired to go forth to-day?"

"To-morrow, sir."

"Well, let him be an exception;" and he rode off; "though"

—continuing, as if speaking to himself—"were he wise, he
should hug the city walls as his only security. His neck would
run a sorry chance were he to fall into the hands of his ancient
comrades."

"I do not see that his desertion of the enemy has done us
much service," was the remark of Cruden.

"You mistake : his correspondence has been most efficient.
He has brought over numbers in Ninety-Six and along the Con-
gares. But these are matters that we can not publish."

At the "Quarter's House," between five and six miles, the
party came to a halt. This was a famous place in that day for
parties from the city. The long low building, still occupying
the spot, might be almost esteemed a *fac-simile* of the one which
covered it then. It received its name, as it was the officers'
quarters for the old field range contiguous, which is still known
as "Izard's Camp." It was now a region devoted to festivity
rather than war. Hither the British officers, of an afternoon,
drove out their favorite damsels. Here they gamed and drank
with their comrades; and occasionally a grand hop shook the
rude log foundations of the fabric, while the rafters gleamed with
the blaze of cressets, flaming up from open oil vessels of tin.
Though not yet midday, Balfour halted here to procure refreshments; and Mother Gradock, by whom the place was kept, was
required to use her best skill—which was far from mean in this
department of art—in compounding for her sensual customer a
royal noggin of milk punch; old Jamaica rum being the potent
element which the milk was vainly expected to subdue. A
lounge of half an hour in the ample piazza, and the party resumed their route, following after the march of the brigade at a
smart canter. A ride of four hours brought them to Dorchester,
where, apprised of their approach, the garrison was drawn out to
receive them.

The spectacle that met the eyes of Balfour, in the smoking
ruins of the village, was well calculated to impress him with a
serious sense of the necessity of a thorough investigation into the
affair. He shook his head with great gravity as he said to Cruden—

"It will be well if your kinsman can acquit himself of the
responsibility of this affair. Proctor is a good officer; is quick,

sensible, and brave; but I fear, Cruden, I very much fear, that he has been somewhat remiss in this business. And then the awkward relations which are said to have existed between this rebel's daughter and himself——"

"Stay," said Cruden; "he approaches."

The next moment, Major Proctor joined the party, and offered the proper welcome. He was a young man, not more than twenty-eight or thirty in appearance; and more than ordinarily youthful to have arrived at the rank which he held in the service. But he had been fortunate in his opportunities for distinction; and, both in the conquest of New York and of Charleston, had won the special applause of his superiors for equal bravery and intelligence. His person was cast in a very noble mould. He was tall, erect, and graceful, with a countenance finely expressive; lofty brow, large and animated eyes; and features which, but for a stern compression of the lips, might have appeared effeminately handsome. At this time, his face was marked by an appropriate gravity. He conducted his visiters through the village, pointing out the scene of every important transaction with dignity and calmness. But his words were as few as possible; and every reference to the subject, naturally so painful, was influenced chiefly by considerations of duty to his superior.

When his examination of the field was ended, they made their way toward the fortress, at the entrance of which they found an officer in waiting, to whom Balfour spoke rather eagerly, and in accents much less stately than those which he employed in dealing with subordinates. Captain Vaughan—for such was the name and title of this officer—met the eye of Proctor at this moment, and did not fail to observe the dark scowl which overshadowed it. A sudden gleam of intelligence, which did not seem without its triumph, lighted up his own eyes as he beheld it; and his lip curled with a smile barely perceptible to a single one of the party. Balfour just then called the young officer forward, and they passed through the portals of the fortress together. Proctor motioned his kinsman Cruden forward also, but the latter, twitching him by the sleeve, held him back as he eagerly asked the question in a whisper—

"For God's sake, John, what is all this? How are you to blame?"

"Only for having an enemy, uncle, I suppose."

"An enemy? I thought so. But who?"

Proctor simply waved his hand forward in the direction of Vaughan, whose retiring form was still to be seen following close behind Balfour.

"You will soon see."

"Vaughan! But how can he hurt you? Why should he be your enemy?"

"I am in his way somewhat; and—but not now, uncle. Let us go forward."

They were soon all assembled in Proctor's quarters, where dinner was in progress. Balfour had already renewed his draughts, enjoying with a relish, the old Jamaica, of which a portly square bottle stood before him. His beverage now was taken without the milk; but was qualified with a rather small allowance of cool water. The conversation was only casual. It was tacitly understood that, for the present, the subject most in the mind of all parties was to be left for future discussion. Proctor did the honors with ease and grace, yet with a gravity of aspect that lacked little of severity. Captains Vaughan and Dickson were of the company—officers both belonging to the station—and Cruden contrived to examine, at intervals, the features of the former, of whom he knew but little, with the scrutiny of one who had an interest in fathoming the character of him he surveyed. But Vaughan's face was one of those inscrutable ones—a dark fountain, which shows its surface only, and nothing of its depths. He was not unaware of Cruden's watch—that circumspect old soldier, with all his shrewdness and experience, being no sort of match for the person, seemingly a mere boy, small of features, slight of figure, and with a chin that appeared quite too smooth to demand the reaping of a razor—whom he sought to fathom. Yet those girlish features, that pale face, and thin, effeminate, and closed lips, were the unrevealing representatives of an intense ambition, coupled with a cool, deliberate, almost icy temper, which seldom betrayed impatience, and never any of its secrets. His eyes smiled only, not his lips, as he noted the furtive scrutiny which Cruden maintained.

At length, dinner was announced, and discussed. Balfour was at home at table. He was a person to do the honors for the *bon vivant;* and here, perhaps, lay some of the secret of his influence with Sir William Howe. Fish from the Ashley, which glided beneath the walls of the fortress, and venison from the forests which spread away on every hand within bowshot, formed the chief dishes of the feast; and the Jamaica proved an excellent appetizer and provocative. Wines were not wanting; and the commandant of Charleston very soon showed symptoms which acknowledged their influence. Before the cloth had been removed, his forbearance was forgotten; and, rather abruptly, the affair of Walton's rescue was brought upon the table.

"I'll tell you what,.Proctor, this affair is decidedly unfortunate. Here you have seventy-six men in garrison, good men, not including invalids, and you send out a detachment of thirty only to escort this rebel Walton to the gallows. I must say, you might almost have expected what followed."

"Really, Colonel Balfour, I see not that. I send out half of my force, or nearly so, to superintend the execution of a single man. One would suppose such a force sufficient for such a purpose. Was I to abandon the garrison entirely? Had I done so, what might have been the consequences? Instead of the mere rescue of the prisoner, the post might have been surprised and captured with all its stores, and the garrison cut to pieces."

"Scarcely, if the reported force of the rebels be true. They do not seem to have had more than twenty men in all."

"You will permit me to ask, sir, how you arrived at this conclusion? I am not conscious of having made any definite report of the number of the rebels in this assault."

"No, Major Proctor; and this, I an sorry to observe, is a most unaccountable omission in your report. You had the evidence of a worthy loyalist, named Blonay, who distinctly told you that they numbered only twenty men."

"The deficiencies of my report, Colonel Balfour, seem to have been particularly supplied by other hands," was the ironical remark of Proctor, his eye glancing fiercely at Vaughan as he spoke; "but your informant is scarcely correct himself, sir, and has been too glad to assume, as a certainty, a report which was only

conjectural. Blonay stated distinctly that there were twenty
men *and more.* These were his very words. He did not say
how many. His whole account was wretchedly confused, since
his mind seems to have been distracted between the difficulty of
rescuing his mother from the feet of the horse, by which she
was really trampled to death, and the desire of taking revenge
upon a single enemy, upon whom alone his eyes seem to have
been fixed during the affair. This Blonay, sir, instead of being
a worthy loyalist, is a miserable wretch, half Indian, and of no
worth at all. He has an Indian passion for revenge, which, on
this occasion, left him singularly incapable of a correct observation on any subject which did not involve the accomplishment
of his passion. But, allowing that the rebels made their assault
with but twenty men, it must be remembered that they effected
a surprise——"

"Ah! that was the reproach, Major Proctor; there was the
error, in allowing that surprise."

" But, Balfour," said Cruden, " this seems to be quite unreasonable. A detachment of thirty men from the post, leaving but
forty in charge of it, seems to be quite large enough."

" That depends wholly on circumstances, Cruden," was the
reply of Balfour, filling his glass.

" Exactly, sir," resumed Proctor; " and these circumstances
were such as to call for a guard for the prisoner no stronger
than that which I assigned it. But a few days had elapsed
since Earl Cornwallis totally defeated the rebel army at Camden. Were we to look for an effort of the rebels, in his rear,
of this description? Did we not know that Marion, with his
brigade, had joined himself to the force of Gates; and had we
not every reason to suppose that he had shared its fate? The
whole country was in our possession. Lord Rawdon held Camden; Colonel Stuart was at Ninety-Six; Orangeburg, Motte's,
Watson's, Monk's Corner, Quimby—all posts garrisoned by
ourselves; and our scouts brought no tidings of any considerable force of rebels embodied in any quarter."

" But the *inconsiderable,*" answered Balfour.

" They were surely provided against in a force of thirty men,
led by a competent officer, who sealed his devotion with his life."

"Why did you not take command of the escort yourself?" queried Balfour.

For a moment, an expression of strong disgust spread over the face of Proctor. But he replied, calmly—

"It might be a sufficient answer to say, that such was not my duty. The command of the post at Dorchester involved no obligation to assume the duties of a subordinate. But I will express myself more frankly. I could not have assumed this duty without violating some of the most precious feelings of humanity. I had enjoyed the hospitality of Colonel Walton; had shared his intimacy; and cherished a real esteem for the noble virtues of that gentleman, which his subsequent unhappy rebellion can not obliterate from my mind. I could not have taken part in the terrible event of that day, I preferred, sir, as my duty allowed it, to withdraw from so painful a spectacle."

"Ah! that was the error—the great error. The soldier, sir, has obligations to his king superior to those of mere sentiment. I am sorry, Major Proctor—very sorry—not less for your sake, than because of the deep sympathy which I have with my friend, Cruden."

"But, Balfour," said Cruden, "it strikes me that John's course has been quite justifiable. With his force, he could not have detached from the garrison more than he did, as an escort for the rebel's execution. And, under the circumstances of the country, with Cornwallis so completely triumphant over Gates, and with our troops everywhere overawing every conspicuous point, there could be no reason to anticipate such a surprise as this. Now"—

"My dear Cruden, all this sounds very well; and were these things to be considered by themselves I have no doubt the defence would be properly urged. But I am afraid that an evil construction may be placed upon the deep sympathy which our young friend seems to have felt for the family of this rebel. He seems to have been a frequent visiter at Walton's plantation."

"Only, sir, when Colonel Walton was understood to be a friend of my king and government."

"That he never was."

"He was admitted in our roll of friends among the people of

2

the country; and I have Lord Cornwallis's especial instructions to treat him with great courtesy and favor, in the hope of winning him over to active participation in our cause."

"Very true, sir; that *was* our object; but how long is it since this hope was abandoned? Could you have entertained it, my dear major, for a moment after your fruitless attempt to capture Singleton, the lieutenant of Marion, harbored by this very rebel —nay, rescued by Walton from your grasp, at the head of an armed force, which put you at defiance? Nay, I am not sure that the curious fact, that Walton suffered you to escape, though clearly in his clutches, will not make against you. Even since these events, it is understood that you have more than once visited the daughter of this rebel, alone, without any attendants, returning late in the evening to your post."

Proctor smiled grimly, as he replied—

"It will be something new, I fancy, to the officers of his majesty in Charleston and elsewhere, if it be construed into a treasonable affair when they visit a rebel damsel. But really, Colonel Balfour, this conversation assumes so much the appearance of a criminal investigation, that I see no other course before me than to regard it as a sort of court of inquiry. Perhaps, sir, I had better tender my sword, as under arrest. At all events, sir, permit me to demand a court of inquiry for the full examination of this affair."

He unbuckled his sword as he spoke, and laid it upon the table.

"What are you about, John? What need of this?" demanded Cruden. "I am sure that Balfour means nothing of the kind."

"Perhaps it is just as well, Cruden," answered Balfour, "that our young friend should so determine. I like to see young men fearless of investigation. Better he should invite the court than have it forced upon him; and you will see, from what I have said, that there is much of a suspicious nature in this affair which it is proper for him to clear up. But remember, my friends, what I have said has been said in a friendly spirit. I have too much regard for both of you to suffer you to be taken by surprise. You now see what points are to be explained, and what doubts discussed and settled."

This was all said very coolly; we shall not say civilly.

"I am deeply indebted to your courtesy, Colonel Balfour," answered Proctor, "and will be glad if you will still further increase my acknowledgments, by suffering me to know the sources of that information which, I perceive, has followed my footsteps as a shadow."

"Nay, now, my young friend, you must really excuse me. I should be happy to oblige you; but the nature of the affair, and the caution which is due to my situation, will not suffer me to comply with your desires. Excuse me. Let us have a glass all round."

"Stay," said Cruden; "am I to understand that John is deprived of his command at this post?"

"Most certainly," interposed Proctor, himself. "Until purged of these suspicions, I can certainly hold no station of trust in the service of his majesty."

"Your nephew has a right notion of these matters, Cruden," remarked Balfour; "but it will not be long. He will soon purge himself of these suspicions, and be in a situation to resume all his trusts."

"And to whom," said Cruden, "will you confide the post, meanwhile?"

"Who?—ay!" looking round. "I had thought of requesting our young friend, Vaughan, here, to administer its duties, and to take charge of the precincts of Dorchester."

Vaughan bowed his head quietly and respectfully, and in a few calmly-expressed words, declared his sense of the compliment. The keen eye of Proctor was fastened upon him with a stern and scornful glance, and, a moment after he left the apartment, followed by his uncle.

"This is a most abominable affair, John," was his remark; "a most abominable affair!"

"Do you think so, sir? There would be nothing abominable about it, were there not a villain in the business."

"And that villain—"

"Is Vaughan! the servile tool of Balfour; the miserable sycophant, who fancies that ambition may be served by falsehood. But I shall crush him yet. His triumph is for the moment only."

CHAPTER III.

NATIVE PRINCESS.

THE sun was still an hour high when Balfour gave instructions to prepare his horses and a small escort, proposing a visit to the plantation called " The Oaks," the domain of the famous rebel, Colonel Walton.

" You will, of course accompany me, Cruden. Your duties begin in this quarter. It is just as well that we should have this estate within our clutches as soon as possible, and before the alarm is taken. We will quarter ourselves upon the young lady to-night, and see how the land lies. Should she prove as beautiful as they describe, we shall make her a ward of the king, and dispose of her accordingly."

" In that event, you had best take her to the city."

" I shall most surely do so."

" I shall certainly be better pleased to take charge of the plantation in her absence. Our authority might otherwise, conflict. With the dawn, we must proceed to gather up the negroes, and for this purpose I shall need your assistance. You will have a sufficient detachment with you ?"

" Twenty men will do. There are some three hundred slaves, I understand of all classes ; and the fewer soldiers we employ in bringing these into the fold, the less heavy will be the assessment on the estate."

This was said with a grin, the meaning of which was perfectly understood by his associate.

" Does my nephew accompany us, Balfour ?"

" If he chooses."

" I may need his assistance in the matter."

" You have brought your secretary ?"

"Yes; but John is a ready fellow at accounts—as quick with the pen as with the sword;—besides, he knows something of the estate already, and may give some useful hints in respect to plate, horses, and other property, which these rebel women are apt to conceal."

"The plate generally finds its way into the cellar, or under some great oak-tree in the woods; but I have long been in possession of a divining rod, which conducts me directly to the place of safe-keeping. We have only to string up one of the old family negroes, and, with a tight knot under the left ear, and a little uneasiness in breathing, he soon disgorges all his secrets. But, in truth, these women seldom hide very deeply. It is usually at the very last hour that they consent to put away the plate, and then it is rather hurried out of sight than hidden. I have sometimes detected the hoard by the ears of a silver milk-pot, or the mouth of a coffee-urn, or the handle of a vase, sticking up unnaturally beside an old chimney in the basement. But see your nephew, and let us ride."

Cruden proceeded to Proctor's room; but, on the expression of his wish, was met by a firm and prompt refusal.

"How can you ask me, Colonel Cruden, to take part in this business? It is your duty, as the proper officer of the crown, and that is *your* apology. I should have none."

"I am afraid, John, you are quite too deeply interested in this beauty."

"Stop, sir; let us have nothing of this. Enough, that Miss Walton can never be to me more than she is. She is one always to command my respect, and I beg that she will yours. For my sake, sir, administer this unpleasant duty, upon which you go, with all possible tenderness and forbearance."

"I will, John, for your sake. To be sure I will."

And they separated—Balfour clamoring without, impatiently, for his companion, who soon after joined him. An easy ride of an hour brought them to the noble avenue, "The Oaks," which conducted, for half a mile, to the entrance of Colonel Walton's dwelling—a stately, sombre wood—the great, venerable trees arching and uniting completely over the space between, while their bearded mosses drooped to the very ground itself. The

mansion was in a style of massive grandeur to correspond with
so noble an entrance. The approach of the British party was
known to the inmates, even before it had entered upon the avenue. These inmates consisted, now, only of Colonel Walton's
maiden sister, Miss Barbara—a lady of that certain age which
is considered the most uncertain in the calendar—when, in fact,
the spinster ceases to compute, even as she ceases to grow—
and Katharine, the only daughter of the fugitive rebel himself.
Katharine was still a belle and a beauty, and youthful accordingly. She might have been nineteen; and, but for the majestic
and admirable form, the lofty grace of her carriage, the calm and
assured expression of her features, the ease and dignity of her
bearing—the fresh sweetness of her face, and the free, luxuri-
ant flow of her long, ungathered locks, simply parted from her
forehead, and left at freedom upon her neck and shoulders—
would have occasioned a doubt whether she was quite sixteen.
An obsequious negro, who rejoiced in the name of Bacchus,
without making any such exhibition of feature or conduct as
would induce the suspicion that he was a worshipper at the
shrine of that jolly divinity, received the British officers at the
entrance, and ushered them into the great hall of the mansion.
Their escort, having had previous instructions, was divided into
two bodies, one occupying the front avenue, the other that which
led to the river, in the rear of the building. But two persons
entered the house with Balfour and Cruden—Captain Dickson,
of the garrison, and one who knew the Walton family, and the
secretary of Colonel Cruden.

It was not long before the ladies made their appearance.
Though by no means disposed to waive any proper reserves of
the sex, they were yet prepared to recognise the policy which
counselled them to give no undue or unnecessary provocations
to those to whose power they could offer no adequate resistance. *Mrs.* Barbara Walton—the old maid in those days being
always a *mistress*, through a courtesy that could no longer regard her as a *miss*—led the way into the hall, dressed in her
stateliest manner, with a great hoop surrounding her as a sort of
chevaux de frize—a purely unnecessary defence in the present
instance—and her head surmounted by one of those towers of

silk, gauzes, ribands, and pasteboard, which were so fashionable
in that day, and which reminded one of nothing more aptly than
of the rude engravings of the Tower of Babel in old copies of
the Bible, done in the very infancy of art. Poor Mrs. Barbara
was a tame, good-natured creature, nowise decided in her character, upon whom a foolish fashion could do no mischief, but who
was always playing the very mischief with the fashions. They
never were more military in character than in her hands—
leading to conquest only by the absolute repulsion of all assailants. Whether, at forty-five, this good creature fancied that it
was necessary to put her defences in the best possible array
against such a notorious gallant as Balfour, we may not say;
but certainly she never looked more formidable on any previous
occasion. Her very smiles were trenches and pitfalls for the
invader—and every motion of her person, however gracefully
intended, seemed like a "warning to quit"—with a significant
hint of "steel traps and spring guns" in waiting for trespassers.

Doubtless, the venerable maiden might have largely compelled the consideration of the British officers, but for the bright
creature that appeared immediately behind her; and who, without any appearance of timidity or doubt, quietly advanced and
welcomed the strangers, as if performing the most familiar office
in the world. Balfour absolutely recoiled as he beheld her. So
bright a vision had not often flashed across his eyes.

"By Jove," he muttered at the first opportunity, to Cruden,
"she *is* a beauty! What a figure!—what a face! No wonder
your kinsman neglected his duties for his love."

"It is yet to be seen that he has done so," was the grave
aside of Cruden.

"Having seen her," whispered Balfour, "I can believe it
without further testimony."

We need not follow these asides. Katharine did the honors
of the reception with an ease and dignity, which, while making
the visiters at home, made it sufficiently evident that she felt
quite as much what was due to her condition as to their claims.
She wore the appearance of one who was conscious of all the
cares, the responsibilities, and the dangers of her situation; yet
without yielding to any of the fears or weaknesses which might

he supposed, in one of her sex, to flow from their recognition.
Her schooling had already been one of many trials and terrors.
Her guests knew something of the training through which she
had gone, and this rendered her bearing still more admirable in
their sight. But her beauty, her virtue, her dignity, and character did not suffice, after the 𝑓𝑖st impressive effect produced by
her appearance, to disarm her chief visiter of any of his purposes. The usual preliminaries of conversation—such common-
places of remark as belong to the ordinary encounters of persons
in good society—having been interchanged as usual, and Balfour seized the opportunity of a pause, when his fair hostess,
indeed, appeared to expect something from him in the way of a
revelation, to break ground in regard to the ungracious business
on which he came.

"It would greatly relieve me, Miss Walton," said he, with a
manner at once seemingly frank as seemingly difficult, "if I
could persuade myself that you, in some degree, anticipate the
painful affair which brings me to your dwelling."

"That it is painful, sir, I must feel; and, without being able
to conjecture what will be the form of your business, I can
easily conceive it to be such as can be agreeable to none of the
parties. To me, at least, sir, and to mine, I can very well conjecture that you bring penalty and privation at least."

"Nay, nay! These, I trust, are not the words which should
be used in this business. In carrying out the orders of my
superior, and in prosecuting the service which is due to my
sovereign, I shall certainly be compelled to proceed in a manner materially to change your present mode of life; but that
this will involve penalty and privation is very far from probable.
The conduct of your father—his present attitude in utter defiance to the arms and authority of his majesty, and in total
rejection of all the gracious overtures made to him, as well by
Earl Cornwallis as by Sir Henry Clinton, leaves it impossible
that we should extend to him any indulgence. As a rebel in
arms—"

"Stay, sir!—you speak of my father. It is not necessary
that you should say anything to his daughter's ear, save what
is absolutely necessary that she should know. If I conceive

rightly your object in this visit, it is to visit upon my father's property the penalty of my father's offence."

"'Pon my soul," whispered Cruden, "the girl speaks like a very Portia. She comes to the point manfully."

"You relieve me, Miss Walton; and, in some measure, you are correct," answered Balfour, interrupting her speech. "It could not be supposed that his majesty should suffer Colonel Walton to remain in possession of his property, while actually waging war against the British standard. Colonel Cruden, here, is commissioned by Lord Cornwallis to sequestrate his estates — their future disposal to depend wholly upon the final issues of the war."

Here Cruden interposed, by reciting the general terms of the British regulation in regard to the confiscated or sequestrated estates of the rebels — enumerating all the heads of the enactment, and proceeding to details which left no doubt unsatisfied, no ambiguity which could lead to doubt, of the universal liability of the estate of the offender. Lands, houses, slaves; furniture and horses; plate and jewelry — "Of course, Miss Walton, the personal ornaments of a lady would be respected, and"—

Katharine Walton smiled quietly. This smile had its explanation, when the commissioner commenced his operations next day — but, though he was very far from conjecturing its signification, it yet struck him as something mysterious. Balfour, also, was impressed with the smile of Katharine, which seemed quite unnatural under the circumstances.

"You smile, Miss Walton."

"Only, perhaps, because one who anticipates the worst needs no such details as Colonel Cruden has bestowed on me. You are the masters here, I know. For myself, you see I wear no jewels. I had some toys, such as rings, brooches, chains, and watches, but I thought it unseemly that I should wear such ornaments, when the soldiers of my people wanted bread and blankets, and they all found their way, long since, to the money-chest of Marion."

"The devil!" muttered Cruden, in tones almost audible, though meant as an aside to Balfour. "It is to be hoped that the family plate has not taken the same direction."

"We shall see at supper, perhaps," was the whisper of Balfour.

Katharine Walton was seen again to smile. She had possibly heard the apprehensions of Cruden. At least, she might reasonably have conjectured them. She resumed —

"And now, Colonel Balfour, that I am in possession of your determination, you will permit me to retire for awhile, in order that I may properly perform the duties of a hostess. For this night, at all events, I may reasonably be expected to act in this capacity, let to-morrow bring forth what it may."

"Stay — a moment, Miss Walton — I am not sure that you conceive all that we would say — all, in fact, that is appointed us to execute."

"Well, sir ?"

"Lord Cornwallis has left it to my discretion to decide whether, as a ward of the crown, you should be left exposed to a dangerous propinquity with rebellion — whether, in short, it would not be advisable that one so lovely, and so worthy of his guardianship, should not be placed in safety within the walls of the city."

"Ha ! that, indeed, is something that I had not anticipated. And this, sir, is left to your individual discretion ?"

"It is, indeed, Miss Walton," replied the commandant, turning his eyes very tenderly upon hers, and throwing into his glance as much softness as could well consist with the leer of a satyr.

"Well, sir, I suppose that even this claim can challenge nothing but submission. As I have said already, you are the master here."

She retired with these words.

"'Pon my soul, Cruden, the girl is a princess. With what a grace she yields ! She seems nowise stubborn; and so beautiful ! It ought not to be very difficult to thaw the heart of such a woman. That she has not been won before, is because they have never suffered her to come to the city."

"But, by ——, should the plate have followed the jewels, Balfour ?"

"The question is a serious one. We shall see at supper. Your kinsman might have said something of this matter, if he pleased. He must have seen, in his frequent visits, whether any display of plate was made."

" He did not visit frequently," said Cruden.

" Ah! but he did; too frequently for his good;—but here comes that gentlemanly negro; Bacchus, they call him. Such a name seems particularly suited to a butler. I think, Cruden, you had better send him to me. I like the fellow's manners. He has evidently been trained by a gentleman. Well, my man?"

" My lady begs to tell you, gentlemen, that supper waits."

"Very well—show the way. Did you hear that, Cruden?— my lady! How these Provincials do ape nobility!"

CHAPTER IV.

THE RANGER.

THE business of the feast had scarcely been begun, when it
was interrupted by a heavy tread without, as of more than one
iron-shod person; and, the door being thrown open by Bacchus,
a dull-faced lieutenant, having charge of the escort of Balfour,
showed himself at the entrance, and begged a hearing.

"What's the matter, Fergusson? Can't it keep till after
supper?" was the somewhat impatient speech of Balfour.

He was answered by a strange voice; and a little bustle followed, in which a person, totally unexpected, made his appearance upon the scene. The stranger's entrance caused the commandant's eyes to roll in some astonishment, and occasioned no
small surprise in all the assembly. He was a tall young man,
of goodly person, perhaps twenty-eight or thirty years of age,
but habited in a costume not often seen in the lower country.
He wore one of those hunting-shirts, of plain blue homespun,
fringed with green, such as denoted the mountain ranger. A
green scarf was wrapped about his waist, with a belt or baldric
of black, from which depended a very genteel cut-and-thrust.
On his shoulder was an epaulette of green fringe also; and he
carried in his hand, plucked from his brows as he entered the
apartment, a cap of fur, in which shone a large gay button;
behind which may have been worn a plume, though it carried
none at present. The costume betrayed a captain of loyalist
riflemen, from the interior, and was instantly recognised as such
by the British officer. But the stranger left them in no long
surprise. Advancing to the table, with the ease of a man who

had been familiar with good society in his own region all his life, yet with a *brusqueness* of manner which showed an equal freedom from the restraints of city life, he bowed respectfully to the ladies, and then addressed himself directly to Balfour.

"Colonel Balfour, I reckon?"

"You are right, sir; I am Colonel Balfour."

"Well, colonel, I'm right glad I met you here. It may save me a journey to the city, and I'm too much in a hurry to get back to lose any time if I can help it. I'm Captain Furness, of the True Blue Rifles, of whom, I reckon, you've heard before. I've ridden mighty hard to get to you, and hope to get the business done as soon as may be, that I come after. Here's a letter from Colonel Tarleton. I reckon you hain't heard the news of the mischief that's happened above?"

"What mischief?"

"You've heard, I reckon, that Lord Cornwallis gave Saratoga Gates all blazes at Rugely's Mills?"

"Yes, yes; we know all that."

"Well, but I reckon you don't know that just when Cornwallis was putting it to Gates in one quarter, hard-riding Tom was giving us ginger in another?"

"And who is hard-riding Tom?"

"Why, Tom Sumter, to be sure—the game-cock, as they sometimes call him; and, sure enough, he's got cause enough to crow for a season now."

"And what has he been doing above?"

"Well, he and Tom Taylor broke into Colonel Carey's quarters, at Camden Ferry, and broke him up, root and branch, killing and capturing all hands."

"Ha! indeed! Carey?"

"Yes. And that isn't all. No sooner had he done that than he sets an ambush for all the supplies that you sent up for the army; breaks out from the thicket upon the convoy, kills and captures the escort to a man, and snaps up the whole detachment, bag and baggage, stores, arms, spirits, making off with a matter of three hundred prisoners."

"The devil! Forty wagons, as I live! And why are you here?"

"Me? Read the letter, Colonel. Lord Cornwallis has sent Tarleton after Sumter, and both have gone off at dead speed; but Tarleton has sent me down to you with my lord's letter and his own, and they want fresh supplies sent after them as fast as the thing can be done. I'm wanting some sixty-five rifles, and as many butcher-knives, for my own troop, and a few pistols for the mounted men. Colonel Tarleton told me you would furnish all."

Balfour leaned his chin upon both hands, and looked vacantly around him, deeply immersed in thought. At the pause in the dialogue which followed, Katharine Walton asked the stranger if he would not join the party at the supper-table. He fastened a keen, quick, searching glance upon her features; their eyes met; but the intelligence which flashed out from his met no answering voice in hers. He answered her civilities gracefully, and, frankly accepting them, proceeded to place himself at the table—a seat having been furnished him, at the upper end, and very near to her own. Balfour scowled upon the stranger as he beheld this arrangement; but the latter did not perceive the frown upon the brow of his superior. He had soon finished a cup of the warm beverage put before him; and, as if apologizing for so soon calling for a fresh supply, he observed, while passing up his cup—

"I've ridden mighty far to-day, miss, and I'm as thirsty as an Indian. Besides, if you *could* make the next cup a shade stronger, I think I should like it better. We rangers are used to the smallest possible quantity of water, in the matter of our drinks."

"The impudent backwoodsman!" was the muttered remark of Balfour to Cruden, only inaudible to the rest of the company. The scowl which covered his brow as he spoke, and the evident disgust with which he turned away his eyes, did not escape those of the Ranger; and a merry twinkle lighted upon his own as he looked in the direction of the fair hostess, and handed up his cup. Had Balfour watched him a little more closely, it is possible that he might have remarked something in his manner of performing this trifling office which would have afforded new cause of provocation. The hand of the Ranger lingered near

the cup until a ring, which had previously been loosened upon
his little finger, was dropped adroitly beside the saucer, and
beyond all eyes but hers for whom it was intended. Katharine
instantly covered the tiny but sparkling messenger beneath her
hands. She knew it well. A sudden flush warmed her cheek;
and, trusting herself with a single glance only at the stranger,
he saw that he was recognised.

CHAPTER V.

LESSONS IN MANNERS.

THE evening repast, in the good old times, was not one of
your empty shows, such as it appears at present. It consisted
of goodly solids of several descriptions. Meats shared the place
with delicacies; and tea or coffee was the adjunct to such grave
personages as Sir Loin, Baron Beef, and Viscount Venison.
Balfour and Cruden were both strongly prepossessed in favor of
all titled dignitaries, and they remained in goodly communion
with such as these for a longer period than would seem reasonable now to yield to a supper-table. Captain Dickson naturally
followed the example of his superiors; and our loyalist leader,
Furness, if he did not declare the same tastes and sympathies
in general, attested, on this occasion, the sharpness of an appetite
which had been mortified by unbroken denial throughout the
day. But the moment at length came which offered a reasonable pretext to the ladies for leaving the table. The guests no
longer appealed to the fair hostess for replenished cups; and,
giving the signal to her excellent, but frigid and stately aunt,
Mrs. Barbara, Katharine Walton rose, and the gentlemen made
a like movement. She approached Colonel Balfour as she did
so, and laid the keys of the house before him.

"These, sir, I may as well place at once in your keeping. It
will satisfy you that I recognise you as the future master here.
I submit to your authority. The servant, Bacchus, will obey
your orders, and furnish what you may require. The wines and
liquors are in that sideboard, of which you have the keys. Good-
night, sir; good-night, gentlemen."

The ease, grace, and dignity, with which this communication

was made surprised Balfour into something like silence. He could barely make an awkward bow and a brief acknowledgment as she left the apartment, closely followed by her aunt. The gentlemen were left to themselves : while Bacchus, at a modest distance, stood in respectful attendance.

"By my life," said Cruden, "the girl carries herself like a queen. She knows how to behave, certainly. She knows what is expected of her."

"She *is* a queen," replied Balfour, with quite a burst of enthusiasm. "I only wish that she were mine. It would make me feel like a prince, indeed. I should get myself crowned King of Dorchester, and my ships should have the exclusive privilege of Ashley river. 'The Oaks' should be my winter retreat from the cares of royalty, and my summer palace should be at the junction of the two rivers in Charleston. I should have a principality—small, it is true; but snug, compact, and with larger revenues, and a territory no less ample than many of the German princes."

"Beware!" said Cruden half seriously. "You may be brought up for *lèse-majesté*."

"Pshaw! we are only speaking a vain jest, and in the presence of friends," was the reply of Balfour, glancing obliquely at Captain Furness. The latter was amusing himself, meanwhile, by balancing his teaspoon upon the rim of his cup. A slight smile played upon his mouth as he listened to the conversation, in which he did not seem to desire to partake. Following the eye of Balfour, which watched the loyalist curiously, the glance of Cruden was arrested rather by the occupation than the looks of that person. His mode of amusing himself with the spoon was suggestive of an entirely new train of thought to the commissioner of sequestrated estates.

"By the way, Balfour, this looks very suspicious. Do you observe ?"

"What looks suspicious ?"

"Do you remember the subject of which we spoke before supper ?—the plate of this rebel Walton ? It was understood to be a singularly-extensive collection—rich, various, and highly valuable. You remark none of it here—nothing but a beggarly collection of old spoons. The coffee-pot is tin or pewter; the tea-service, milk-pot, and all, of common ware. I am afraid the plate has followed the jewels of the young lady, and found its way into the swamps of Marion."

A scowl gathered upon the brow of Balfour, as he glanced rapidly over the table. The next moment, without answering Cruden, he turned to Bacchus, who stood in waiting with a face the most inexpressive, and said—

"Take the keys, Cupid, and get out some of the best wines. You have some old Jamaica, have you not?"

The reply was affirmative.

"See that a bottle of it is in readiness. Let the sugar-bowl remain, and keep a kettle of water on the fire. This done, you may leave the room, but remain within call."

He was promptly obeyed. The conversation flagged meanwhile. Cruden felt himself rebuked, and remained modestly silent, but not the less moody on the subject which had occasioned his remark. Balfour referred to it soon after the disappearance of Bacchus.

"It is as you say, Cruden; there is certainly no display before us of the precious metals. I had really not observed the absence of them before. In truth, everything was so neatly arranged and so appropriate, that I could fancy no deficiencies. Besides, my eyes were satisfied to look only in one direction. The girl absorbed all my admiration. That she has not herself gone into the camp of Marion, is my consolation. I shall compound with you cheerfully. You shall have the plate, all that you may find, and the damsel comes to me."

The cheeks of the loyalist captain, had they caught the glance, at that moment, of the commandant of Charleston, would have betrayed a peculiar interest in the subject of which he spoke. They reddened even to his forehead, and the spoon slid from his fingers into the cup. But he said nothing, and the suffusion passed from his face unnoticed.

"I am afraid than you would get the best of the bargain. But it may be that the plate is still in the establishment. It would scarcely be brought out on ordinary occasions."

"Ordinary occasions! Our visit an ordinary occasion!" exclaimed Balfour. "Lay not that flattering unction to your soul, my good fellow. These Carolinians never allow such occasions to escape them of making a display. The ostentation of the race would spread every available vessel of silver at the entrance of stranger guests of our rank. Nothing would be wanting to make them glorious in our eyes, and prompt us to proper gratitude in theirs. They would certainly crowd sideboard and supper-table with all the plate in the establishment."

"Ay, *were* we guests, Balfour; but that were no policy, if we came as enemies. Would they tempt cupidity by ostentatious exhibitions of silver? Scarcely! They would be more apt to hide away."

"As if they knew not that we are as good at seek as they at hide! No, no, my dear fellow; I am afraid that your first conjecture is the right one. If the woman gives her jewels, it is probable that the plate went before. But we shall see in season. Meanwhile, I am for some of the rebel's old Madeira. Come, Captain Furness, let us drink confusion to the enemy."

"Agreed, sir," was the ready answer. "I am always willing for that. I am willing to spoil the Egyptians in any way. But to see how you do things here below, makes one's mouth water. We have mighty little chance in our parts, for doing ourselves much good when we pop into an enemy's cupboard. There's monstrous small supply of silver plate and good liquor in our country. The cleaning out of a rebel's closet in 'Ninety-Six' won't give more than a teaspoon round to the officers of a squad like mine; and the profits hardly enough to reconcile one to taking the pap-spoon out of a baby's jaws, even to run into Spanish dollars. But here, in these rich parts, you have such glorious pickings, that I should like greatly to be put on service here."

"Pickings!" exclaimed Balfour, lifting his eyes, and surveying the loyalist from head to foot, as he held the untasted goblet suspended before his lips — "pickings! Why, sir, you speak as if the officers honored with the commission of his majesty, could possibly stoop to the miserable practice of sharing selfishly the confiscated possessions of these rebels."

"To be sure, colonel; that's what I suppose. Isn't it so, then?" demanded the loyalist, not a whit abashed.

"My good sir, be a little wiser; do not speak so rashly. Let me enlighten you."

"Pray do; I'll thank you, colonel."

"To distress the enemy, to deprive them of the means to be mischievous, alone causes the sequestration of their goods and chattels. These goods and chattels must be taken care of. It may be that these rebels will make proper submission hereafter, will make amends for past errors by future service; and, in such cases, will be admitted to his majesty's favor and receive their possessions at his hands again, subject only to such drawbacks as flow necessarily from the expense of taking care of the property, commissions on farming it, and unavoidable waste. These commission are generally derived from mere movables, silver and gold, plate and jewels, which, as they might be lost, are at once appropriated, and the estate credited with the appropriation against the cost and trouble of taking care of it. That the officers in his majesty's commission should employ this plate, is simply that his majesty's service may be sufficiently honored and may command due respect. Selfish motives have no share in the transaction. We have no 'pickings,' sir—none! *Appropriations*, indeed, are made; but, as you see, solely for the equal benefit of the property itself, the service in which we are engaged, and the honor of his majesty. Do you comprehend me, my young friend?"

"Perfectly, sir; perfectly. I see. Nothing can be clearer."

"Do not use that vulgar phrase again, I pray you, in the hearing of any of his majesty's representatives. 'Pickings' may do among our loyalist natives. We do not deny them the small privileges of which you have spoken. You have emptied in your experience, I understand, some good wives' cupboards in Ninety-Six. You have grown wealthier in tea and pap-spoons. It is right enough. The laborer is worthy of his hire. These are the gifts with which his majesty permits his loyal servants to reward themselves. But, even in your case, my young friend, the less you say about the matter the better. Remember, always, that what is appropriated is in the name, and, consequently, for the uses of his majesty. But no more 'pickings,' if you love me."

An air of delicate horror always accompanied the use of the offensive phrase. The loyalist captain professed many regrets at the errors of his ignorance.

"I see, I see; 'appropriations' is the word, not 'pickings' There is a good deal in the distinction, which did not occur to me before. In fact, I only use the phrase which is common to us in the up country. Our people know no better; and I am half inclined to think that, were I to insist upon 'appropriations,' instead of 'pickings,' they would still be mulish enough to swear that they meant the same thing."

Balfour turned an inquisitive glance upon the speaker; but there was nothing in his face to render his remark equivocal. It seemed really to flow from an innocent inexperience, which never dreamed of the covert sneer in his answer. He tossed off his wine as he finished, and once more resumed his seat at the table. So did Cruden. Not so, Balfour. With his arms behind him, after a fashion which Napoleon, in subsequent periods, has made famous, if not graceful, our commandant proceeded to pace the apartment, carrying on an occasional conversation with Cruden, and, at intervals, subjecting Furness to a sort of inquisitorial process.

"What did you see, Captain Furness, in your route from the Congarees? Did you meet any of our people? or did you hear anything of Marion's?"

"Not much, colonel; but I had a mighty narrow escape from a smart squad, well-mounted, under Major Singleton. From what I could hear, they were the same fellows that have been kicking up a dust in these parts."

"Ha! did you meet them?" demanded Cruden. "How many were there?"

"I reckon there may have been thirty or thirty-five—perhaps forty all told."

"You hear?" said Cruden.

"Yes, yes!" rather impatiently was the reply of Balfour. "But how knew you that they were Singleton's men?"

"Well it so happened that I got a glimpse of them down the road, while I was covered by the brush. I pushed into the woods out of sight, as they went by, and found myself suddenly upon a man, a poor devil enough, who was looking for a hiding-place as well as myself. He knew all about them; knew what they had been after, and heard what they had done. His name was Cammer; he was a Dutchman, out of the Forks of Edisto."

" What route did they pursue ?"

" Up the road, pushing for the east, I reckon."

" And you want rifles and sabres, eh ?"

" And a few pistols, colonel."

" Do you suppose that you have much work before you, after this annihilation of Gates at Camden ?"

" Well, I reckon there was no annihilation, exactly. The lads run too fast for that. They are gathering again, so they report, pretty thick in North Carolina, and are showing themselves stronger than ever in our up-country. The fact is, colonel, though Lord Cornwallis has given Gates a most famous drubbing, it isn't quite sufficient to cool the rebels. The first scare, after you took the city, is rather wearing off; and the more they get used to the sound of musket bullets, the less they seem to care about them. The truth is, your British soldiers don't know much about the use of the gun, as a shooting iron. They haven't got the sure sight of our native woodsmen. They are great at the push of the bayonet, and drive everything before them : but at long shot, the rebels only laugh at them."

" Laugh, do they ?"

" That they do, colonel, and our people know it; and though they run fast enough from the bayonet, yet it's but reasonable they should do so, as they have nothing but the rifle to push against it. If they had muskets with bayonets, I do think they'd soon get conceited enough to stand a little longer, and try at the charge too, if they saw a clever opportunity."

" That's your opinion, is it ?"

" Not mine only, but his lordship, himself, says so. I heard him, with my own ears, though it made Colonel Tarleton laugh."

" And well he might laugh ! Stand the bayonet against British soldiers. I wonder that his lordship should flatter the scoundrels with any such absurd opinion."

"Well now, colonel, with due regard to your better judgment, I don't see that there's anything so very absurd in it. Our people come of the same breed with the English, and if they had a British training, I reckon they'd show themselves quite as much men as the best. Now, I'm a native born American myself, and I *think* I'm just as little likely to be scared by a bayonet as any man I know. I'm not used to the weapon, I allow; but give me time and practice, so as to get my hand in, and I warrant you, I'd not be the first to say 'Back out, boys, a hard time's coming.' People fight more or less bravely, as they fight with their eyes open, knowing all the facts, on ground that they're accustomed to, and having a weapon that's familiar to the hand. The rifle is pretty much the weapon for our people. It belongs, I may say, to a well-wooded country. But take it away from them altogether, and train them every day with musket and bayonet, with the feel of their neighbor's elbow all the while, and see what you can make of them in six months or so."

"My good friend, Furness, it is quite to your honor that you think well of the capacities of your countrymen. It will be of service to you, when you come to confront our king's enemies in battle; but you are still a very young man—"

"Thirty-two, if I'm a day, colonel."

"Young in experience, my friend, if not in years. When you see and hear more of the world, you will learn that the bayonet is the decreed and appointed weapon for a British soldier over all nations. He may be said to be born to it. It was certainly made for him. No people have stood him with it, and take my word for it no people will."

"Unless, as I was saying, a people of the same breed—a tough, steady people, such as ours—that can stand hard knocks, and never skulk 'em when they know they're coming. I've seen our people fight, and they fight well, once they begin—"

"As at Camden."

"There they did'nt fight at all; but there was reason—"

"Let us take a glass of wine together, Captain Furness. I feel sure that you will fight well when the time comes. Meanwhile, let us drink. Come, Cruden, you seem drowsing. Up with you, man. Our rebel, Walton, had a proper relish for

Madeira. This is as old as any in the country. What would they say to such a bottle in England ?"

"What! can't they get it there ?" demanded the loyalist captain, with an air of unaffected wonderment.

"No, indeed, Furness. You have the climate for it. You see, you have yet to live and learn. Our royal master, George the Third, has no such glass of wine in his cellar. Come, fill, Cruden, shall I drink without you ?"

"I'm with you! Give us a sentiment."

"Well! Here's to my Altamira, the lovely Katharine Walton; may she soon take up arms with her sovereign! Hey! You don't drink my toast, Captain Furness ?"

"I finished my glass before you gave it, colonel."

"Fill again! and pledge me! You have no objections to my sentiment ?"

"None at all! It don't interfere with a single wish of mine. I don't know much about the young lady; but I certainly wish, in her case, as in that of all other unmarried young women, that she may soon find her proper sovereign."

"I see you take me. Ha! ha! You are keen, sir, keen. I certainly entertain that ambition. If I can't be master over Dorchester and the Ashley, at all events, I shall aim to acquire the sovereignty over her. Cruden, my boy, you may have the ancient lady—the aunt. She is a gem, believe me—from the antique! Nay, don't look so wretched and disgusted. She is an heiress in her own right, has lands and negroes, my friend, enough to make you happy for life."

"No more of that, Nesbitt. The matter is quite too serious for jest."

"Pshaw! drink! and forget your troubles. Your head is now running on that plate. What if it is gone, there are the lands, the negroes, and a crop just harvesting—some nine hundred barrels of rice, they tell me!"

A sly expression passed over the features of the loyalist captain, as Balfour enumerated the goods and chattels still liable to the grasp of the sequestrator; but he said nothing. Balfour now approached him, and putting on an air of determined business, remarked abruptly—

" So, Captain Furness, you desire to go with me to Charleston for arms ?"

" No, indeed, colonel; and that's a matter I wish to speak about. I wish the arms, but do not wish to go to Charleston for them, as I hear you've got the small-pox and yellow fever in that place."

" Pshaw! They never trouble genteel people, who live decently and drink old Madeira."

" But a poor captain of loyalists don't often get a chance, colonel, of feeding on old Madeira."

" Feeding on it! By Jove, I like the phrase! It is appropriate to good living. One might fatten on such stuff as this without any other diet, and defy fever and the ague. Afraid of small-pox? Why, Captain Furness, a good soldier is afraid of nothing."

" Nothing, colonel, that he can fight against, to be sure; but dealing with an enemy whom you can't cudgel, is to stand a mighty bad chance of ever getting the victory. We folks of the back country have a monstrous great dread of small-pox. That was the reason they could get so few of the people to go down to Charleston when you came against it. They could have mustered three thousand more men, if it hadn't been for that."

" It's well they didn't. But there's no need of your going to the city if you don't wish it. You can stay here with Cruden, or in Dorchester, till I send on the wagons."

" That'll do me, exactly; and now, colonel, if you have no objections, I'll find my way to a sleeping place. I've had a hard ride of it to-day—more than forty-five miles—and I feel it in all my bones."

" We can spare you. Ho, there!—Jupiter!—Cupid!"

" Bacchus, I think they call him," said the loyalist.

" Ay! How should I forget when the Madeira is before us. Come, sir, captain, let us take the night-cap; one, at least. I mean to see these bottles under the table before I leave it."

Furness declined; and, at that moment Bacchus made his appearance.

" Find a chamber for this gentleman," said the commandant;

3

and, bidding the British officers good night, Furness left the apartment under the guidance of the negro. When they had emerged into the passage-way, the loyalist captain, to the great surprise of the former, put his hand familiarly upon his shoulder, and in subdued tones, said—

"Bacchus, do you not know me?"

The fellow started and exclaimed—

"Mass Robert, is it you?—and you not afear'd?"

"Hush, Bacchus; not a word, but in a whisper. Where am I to sleep?"

"In the blue room, sir."

"Very good: let us go thither. After that, return to these gentlemen, and keep an eye on them."

"But you're going to see young missis?"

"Yes; but I must do it cautiously."

"And you a'n't afear'd to come here! Perhaps you got your people with you, and will make a smash among these red-coats?"

"No. But we must say as little as possible. Go forward, and I will tell you further what is to be done."

The negro conducted the supposed loyalist—passing through the passage almost to its extremity, and thence ascending a flight of steps to the upper story. Here another passage, corresponding in part with that below, opened upon them, which, in turn, opened upon another avenue conducting to wings of the building. In one of these was the chamber assigned to Furness. To this they were proceeding, when a door of one of the apartments of the main building was seen to open. The loyalist paused, and, in a whisper, said—

"Go, Bacchus, to my chamber with the light. Cover it when you get there, so that it will not be seen by the soldiers from without. Meanwhile, I will speak to your mistress."

The negro disappeared, and Katharine Walton in the next moment, joined the stranger.

"Oh, Robert, how can you so venture? Why put your head into the very jaws of the lion?"

"Let us follow this passage, Kate. We shall be more secure. Balfour and his companions sleep in the chamber below, I suppose?"

" Yes."

" Come, then, and I will try to satisfy all your doubts, and quiet all your fears."

And the speaker folded his arms tenderly about the waist of the maiden, as he led her forward through a passage that seemed equally familiar to both the parties.

CHAPTER VI.

LOVE PASSAGES.

"And now, Robert," said Katharine Walton, "tell me the reason of this rashness. Why will you so peril yourself, and at a moment when the memory of that dark and terrible scene in which you rescued my father from a base and cruel death still fills my eyes and heart ? What do you expect here ? What would you do ?—which prompts you to incur this danger ?"

"Ah, Kate," replied her companion, fondly clasping her to his bosom, "were it not a sufficient answer to boast that my coming provokes such a sweet and tender interest in you ? The gentle concern which warms the bosom of the beloved one is surely motive enough to stimulate the adventure of a soldier; and I find a consolation from all toils and perils, I assure you, in a moment of meeting and satisfaction so precious as this. If you will censure my rashness, at least give credit to my fondness.

"Do I not, Robert ? And is not this further proof of your attachment, added to so many, which I never can forget, as dear to me as any hope or treasure that I own ? But there is some other motive, I am sure, for your presence now. I know that you are not the person, at a season when your services are so necessary to the country, to bestow any time even upon your best affections, which might better be employed elsewhere. Surely, there is a cause which brings you into the snares of our enemies, of a nature to justify this rashness."

"There is—there is, dear Kate; and you are only right in supposing that, precious as it is to me to enjoy your presence, and clasp you in fond embrace, even this pleasure could not have beguiled me now from the duties of the camp."

"But how have you deceived these people?"

"How did I deceive you, Kate? You did not see through my disguise; you who know me so well, any more than Balfour and Cruden, to whom I am so utterly unknown."

"True—true; and yet, that I did not detect you, may be owing to the fact that I scarcely noted your entrance or appearance. I took for granted that you were one of the enemy, and gave you scarce a look. When I knew you, I wondered that I had been deceived for a moment. Had I not been absorbed by my own anxieties, and prepossessed against your appearance, I should have seen through your disguise without an effort."

"Yet Bacchus knew me as little as yourself."

"For the same reasons, doubtless. But what is the history of this disguise, Robert? And is there a real Captain Furness?"

"There is. We surprised him yesterday on his way to the city, and soon after I had separated from your father. His letters and papers suggested the deception; and I did not scruple to employ the contents of his saddle-bags in making my appearance correspond with his. We are not unlike in size, and there is something of a likeness in the face between us. A *ruse de guerre* of considerable importance depends upon my successful prosecution of the imposture. We shall procure a supply of arms and ammunition, which is greatly wanted in camp; and possibly effect some other objects, which I need not detail to you."

"But the peril, Robert."

"You have become strangely timid and apprehensive, Kate, all on a sudden. Once you would have welcomed any peril, for yourself as well as me, which promised glorious results in war or stratagem. Now—"

"Alas! Robert, the last few days have served to show me that I am but a woman. The danger from which you saved my father brought out all my weakness. I believe that I have great and unusual strength for one of my sex; but I feel a shrinking at the heart, now, that satisfies me how idly before were all my sense and appreciation of the great perils to which our people are exposed. Robert, dear Robert, if you love me, forego this adventure. You surely do not mean to visit the city?"

"Not if I can help it. The small-pox furnishes a good excuse, which Balfour is prepared to acknowledge. But heed not me. At all events, entertain no apprehension. I am not so unprepared for danger as you think. I have a pretty little squad in the Cypress, and can summon them to my side in an hour. True, they are not equal to any open effort against such a force as is now at Dorchester. But let Balfour disappear, and your father but get the recruits that he expects, and we shall warm the old tabby walls for them with a vengeance."

"Whither has my father gone?"

"To the southward—along the Edisto. He may probably range as far as the Savannah. He has ten of my followers with him, which straitens me somewhat. But for this, I had been tempted to have dashed in among these rascals here, and taken off the commandant of Charleston, with his mercenary commissioner of sequestration. If you only had heard their discussion upon the division of your plate and jewels! the beasts!"

"You must have laughed, surely?"

"Knowing, as I did, to what market the plate and jewels went, it was certainly hard to keep from laughing outright."

"Alas! Robert, this reminds me that the evil so long anticipated, has come at last. You hear that I am to be dispossessed. 'The Oaks' must know a new proprietor, and the servants— that is the worst thought—they will be scattered; they will be dragged off to the city, and made to work at the fortifications, and finally shipped to the West Indies."

"I can laugh at them there too, Kate;" and her companion could not entirely suppress a chuckle.

"How?"

"Never mind; better that you should know nothing. You will know all in the morning."

"Can it be that you have got the negroes off, Robert?"

"Ah! you will suffer me to have no secrets. They will all be off before daylight. Many of them are already snug in the Cypress, and a few days will find them safe beyond the Santee. The house servants alone are left, and such of the others as our British customers will be scarcely persuaded to take. Our venerable 'Daddy Bram' is here still, with his wool whiter than the moss; and Scipio, who was an old man, according to his own showing, in the Old French War; and Dinah, who is the Mrs. Methusaleh of all the Ashley, and a dozen others of the same class. Balfour's face will be quite a study as he makes the discovery. But this is not all. We have taken off the entire stud —every horse, plough, draught, or saddle, that was of any service, leaving you the carriage horses only, and a few broken-down hackneys."

"This must have been done last night?"

"Partly; but some of it this very day, and while Balfour was dawdling and drinking at Dorchester."

"Were you then here last night, Robert?"

"Ay, Kate, and with an eye upon you as well as your interests. You had a visiter from Dorchester, Kate."

"Yes; Major Proctor, he came in the afternoon—

"And is disgraced for coming! Your charms have been too much for him. It is already over Dorchester that he has been superseded in his command for neglect of duty, and is to be court-martialed for the affair of your father's rescue."

"Ah! I am truly sorry for him! He was an amiable and courteous gentleman, though an enemy."

"What! would you make me jealous? Am I to be told that he is a fine-looking fellow also—nay, positively handsome?"

"And what is it to me?"

"No woman, Kate, thinks ill of a man for loving her—no sensible woman, at least; and pity is so near akin to love, that the very disgraces that threaten this gentleman make me a little dubious about his visits."

"He will probably pay no more."

"What! do you mean to say, Kate, that you have given him reason to despair?"

"No, Robert, not so"—with a blush which remained unseen —"but this disgrace of his removes him from Dorchester, and carries him to Charleston—"

"Whither you go also?"

"Not if I can help it."

"Why, what do you propose to do?"

"To fly with you to the Santee, if I can not remain here."

"Impossible, Kate! Who is to receive you on the Santee? Was it not thence that my poor sister hurried to find refuge with you in the last moments of her precious life? Our plantation was harried, and our dwellings burnt by the tories, before I sent her hither. Besides, how would you escape hence—how travel, if you did succeed in making your escape—and in what security would you live in a region over which the ploughshare of war will probably pass and repass for many weary months?"

"And do you counsel me to go to the city—to place myself in the custody of these mercenaries?"

"You are in their custody now. You can do no better. The city is, at all events, secure from assault. Were the French to help us with an efficient fleet, and could our army be rallied under an efficient general, we might do something against it; but of this there is little present prospect. The same degree of security could attend you nowhere else in the South at present. Our war must be a Fabian war—irregular, predatory, and eccentric in regard to the region in which it will prevail. No, Kate, however much I would rejoice to bear you away with me, even as the knight of olden time carried off his mistress from the very castle of her tyrant sire, I love you too much to make such an attempt now, when I know not whither I could bear you to place you in even partial security."

"The mountains of North Carolina?"

"But how get there? We cannot hope that you should travel as we are constrained to do; for days without food; riding sometimes day and night to elude the enemy, or to find friends: with neither rest, nor food, nor certainty of any kind, and with the constant prospect of doing battle with an enemy as reckless and more faithless than the savage. You must submit, Kate, with the best possible grace, to the necessity which we can not conquer."

A deep sigh answered him.

"You sigh, Kate; but what the need? Apart from the security which the city affords, and which was always doubtful here, you will find yourself in the enjoyment of society, of luxuries, gay scenes, and glorious spectacles; the ball, the rout, the revel, the parade—"

"Robert Singleton!" was the reproachful exclamation. It was a moody moment with our hero, such as will sometimes deform the surface of the noblest character, as a rough gust will deface the gentle beauties of the most transparent water.

"You will achieve new conquests, Kate. Your old suitor, Proctor, will be again at your feet; you will be honored with the special attentions of that inimitable *petit maitre*, the gallant Harry Barry;* 'Mad Campbell' and 'Fool Campbell,'† who, in spite of their nicknames, are such favorites with the tory ladies, will attach themselves to your train; and you will almost forget, in the brilliancy of your court, the simple forester, whose suit will then, perhaps, appear almost presumptuous in your sight."

"I have not deserved this, Robert Singleton."

"You have not, dearest Kate; and I am but a perverse devil thus to disquiet you with suspicions that have really no place within my own bosom. Forgive something to a peevishness that springs from anxiety, and represents toil, vexation, disappointment, and unremitting labors, rather than the thought that always esteems you, and the heart that is never so blessed as when it gives you all its love. It is seldom that I do you injustice; never, dearest cousin, believe me when I think of you *alone*, and separate from all other human considerations. It is then, indeed, that I love to think of you; and in thinking of you thus, Kate, it is easy to forget that the world has any other beings of worth or interest."

"No more, Robert—no more."

But, as she murmured these words, her head rested happily upon his bosom. With all around her apprehension and trouble, and all before her doubt, if not dismay, the moment was one of unmixed happiness. But she started suddenly from his fond embrace, and, in quick accents, resumed —

"I know not why it is, Robert, but my soul has been shrinking, as if within itself, under the most oppressive presentiments of evil. They haunt me at every turning. I can not shake off the feeling, that something crushing and dreadful is about to

---

* A small wit in the British garrison.
† Nicknames of well-known British officers in Charleston.

happen to me; and, since the decree of this commandant of Charleston, I associate all my fears with my visit to that city. This it is that makes me anxious to escape—to fly anywhere for refuge—even to the swamps of the Cypress; even to the mountains of North Carolina, making the journey, if you please, on horseback, and incurring all risks, all privations, rather than going to what seems *my fate* in Charleston. Tell me, Robert, is it not possible?"

"Do not think of it, Kate. It is *not* possible. I see the troubles, the dangers, the impossibilities of such an enterprise, as they can not occur to you. Dismiss these fears. This presentiment is the natural consequence of what you have undergone, the reaction from that intense and terrible excitement which you suffered in the affair at Dorchester. It will pass away in a few days, and you will again become the calm, the firm, the almost stoical spirit—certainly in endurance—which you have shown yourself already. In Charleston, your worst annoyance will be from the courtesies and gallantries of those you will despise. You will be dependent upon them for civilities, and will need to exercise all your forbearance. Balfour will be the master of your fortunes; but he will not presume to offend you. You will need to conciliate him, where you can— where it calls for no ungenial concessions. We have many friends in that city; and my venerable aunt, who is your kinswoman also, will support you by her steady sympathies and courageous patriotism. You will help to cheer some of our comrades who are in captivity. You will find full employment for *your* sympathies, and, in their exercise, gain solace. Fear nothing—be hopeful—our dark days will soon pass over."

"Be it so. And yet, Robert——"

"Stay! Hear you not a movement below?"

"The British officers retiring, perhaps. They sleep in chambers below, and will not come up stairs at all. Bacchus has his instructions."

"You were saying——"

"The case of my father, Robert——"

"Hush! My life! these feet are upon the stairs! What can it mean?"

"Heavens! there is no retreat to my chamber! The light ascends! Surely, surely, Bacchus can not have mistaken me! O, Robert, what is to be done? You can not cross to *your* chamber without being heard, nor I to mine without· being seen!"

"Be calm, Kate. Let us retire as closely as possible into this recess. Have no fears. At the worst, see, .I am armed with a deadly weapon that makes no noise!"

He grasped the hilt of a dagger, which he carried in his bosom : and they retired into a dark recess, or rather a minor avenue, leading between two small apartments into the balcony in the rear. Meanwhile the heavy steps of men—certainly those of Balfour and Cruden—were heard distinctly upon the stairs : while the voice of Bacchus, in tones somewhat elevated, was heard guiding them as he went forward with the light.

"Steps rather steep, gentlemen : have to be careful. This way, sir."

"Why do you speak so loud, Hector? Do you wish to waken up the house? Would you disturb the young lady—the queen of Dorchester—my—my——I say, Cruden, come along, old fellow, and take care of your steps!"

Katharine trembled like a leaf. Robert Singleton—for such was his true name—put her behind him in the passage as far as possible, and placed himself in readiness for any issue. At the worst, there were but two of the enemy within the house ; and our hero felt himself—occupying a certain vantage ground, as he did—more than a match for both. Let us leave the parties thus, while we retrace our steps, and return to the two whom we left fairly embarked on their carousals. Captain Dickson, it should not be forgotten, had gone back to Dorchester as soon as he had finished his supper.

CHAPTER VII.

CHOICE SPIRITS.

To us, even now in the midst of a wonderful temperance reform, with Father Matthew in the land to second the great moral progress, and to make its claims at once impressive and religious, for the contemplation of succeeding time as for the benefit of our own, it will be difficult to conceive the excesses which prevailed in the use of ardent and vinous beverages in the days of which we write. They had harder heads, probably, in those days than in ours: they could drink with more audacity, and under fewer penalties, physical and moral, in their debauches. Certainly, they were then far less obnoxious to the censure of society for the licentious orgies in which it was the delight of all parties to indulge; and, indeed, society seldom interfered, unless, perhaps, to encourage the shocking practice, and to goad the young beginner to those brutal excesses from which the natural tastes might have revolted. "He was a milk-sop," in proverbial language, "who could not carry his bottle under his belt." "Milk for babes, but meat for men," the language of the apostle, was the ironical and scornful phrase which the veteran toper employed when encountering a more abstemious companion than himself. Precept and example thus combined, it was scarcely possible for the youth to withstand the pernicious training; and the terrible results have ensued to our period, and still measurably hold their ground, in practices which it will need the continued labors of a generation of reformers wholly to obliterate. To drink deep, as they did in Flanders, was quite a maxim with the soldiers of the Revolution on both sides; and too many of the American generals, taught in the same school, were much more able to encounter their British adversaries over a bottle than in the trial and the storm of war. Scotch drinking was always as famous as Dutch or English. Indeed, it is, and has ever been, quite absurd to speak of the indulgence of the Irish as distinguishing them above their sister nations in a comparison of the relative degrees of excess which marked their several habits. The Scotch have always drank *more* than the Irish; but they drank *habitually*, and were thus less liable to betray their excesses.

Balfour was a fair sample of his countrymen in this practice. He had one of those indomitable heads which preserve their balance in spite of their potations. A night of intoxication would scarcely show any of its effects in the morning, and certainly never operated to embarrass him in the execution of his daily business. His appearance usually would seldom warrant you in suspecting him of any extreme trespasses over his wine. He would be called, in the indulgent phrase, as well of that day as our own, a generous or free liver—one who relished his Madeira, and never suffered it to worst his tastes or his capacities. Such men usually pay the penalty in the end; but we need not look so far forward in the present instance. Enough for us that, with the departure of the ladies and the supposed loyalist, and Captain Dickson, the worthy commandant of Charleston determined to make a night of it. In this he was measurably seconded by his companion. Cruden, however, had a cooler head and a more temperate habit. Besides, he had a master passion, which sufficed to keep him watchful of his appetites, and to guard against the moment of excess. Still he drank. What officer of the army, in those days, did not drink, who had served three campaigns in America, after having had the training of one or more upon the continent of Europe?

"The wine improves, Cruden," said Balfour. "I say, Mercury, how much of this wine have you in the cellar?"

"We don't keep wine in the cellar, master," replied the literal Bacchus, who showed himself at the entrance when summoned; "we keep it in the garret."

"Well, well, no matter where. Have you got much of this wine in the garret?"

"A smart chance of it, I reckon, sir."

"What an answer! But this is always the case with a negro. A smart chance of it—as if one could understand anything from such an answer. Have you got a thousand bottles?"

"Don't think, sir."

"Five hundred?"

"Can't say, general."

"Five, then?"

"Oh, more than five—more than fifty, sir."

"Enough for to-night, then, at all events. Go and bring us a few more bottles. This begins to thicken. I say, Cruden, I can respect even a rebel who keeps good liquors. Such a person must always possess one or more of the essentials of a gentleman. He may not be perfectly well bred, it is true, for that depends as much on good society as upon good wines; but he shows that, under other circumstances, something might have been made of him. But why do you not drink? You neither drink nor talk. Finish that glass now, and tell me if you do not agree with me that the man deserves respect whose wines are unimpeachable."

"I can readily acknowledge the virtues which I inherit."

"Good—very good. It is a phrase to be remembered so long as the work of sequestration goes on with such happy results. But good fortune does not seem to agree with you. You are moody, Cruden."

"It is the effect of the Madeira. Wine always makes me so. I like it, perhaps, as well as anybody; but it sours me for a season. I become morose, harsh, ungenial——"

"What an effect! It is monstrous. It is only because you stop short where you should begin. 'Drink deep,' was the counsel of the little poet of Twickenham. That's the only secret. Do you read poetry, Cruden? I could swear no!"

"No, indeed, it appears to me great nonsense."

"It comes to me—the taste for it, I mean—always with my liquor. I never think of it at other periods. I would keep a poet myself, if I could find a proper one. Poor André did some rhyming for me once, but it went like a broken-winded hackney. Harry Barry has a sort of knack at versemaking; but it is monstrous insipid, and only fit for his friend M'Mahon. 'Me and my friend M'Mahon!' 'Me and my friend Barry!' Are you not sick of the eternal speech of these two great-eared boobies, when they prattle of each other?"

"I never listen to them."

"You are right; but as I talk a great deal myself over my wine, I can't do less than listen to the brutes when I am sober."

"I say, Balfour, have you given any orders about the search of this place to-morrow? We should take it early."

"Oh, you are too impatient. Your avarice gets the better of you. Sufficient for the day is the plunder thereof. No cares to-night. Ha! Jupiter, you are there."

This was said to Bacchus, as he arranged half a dozen dusty bottles upon the sideboard.

"Draw one of those corks; put the bottle here; remove these skins, and prepare to answer."

He was obeyed.

"Now stand there, that we may have a good view of you. Your name is Brutus, you say?"

"Bacchus, master."

"Bacchus! Bacchus! Strange that I should always forget. Bacchus, you have a very beautiful young mistress."

The negro was silent.

"Do you not think so, fellow?"

"She always good to me, master."

"And that, you think, means the same thing. Well, we'll not dispute the matter. Now, Bacchus, do you think that your young mistress cares a copper for any of the young officers at Dorchester? Speak up, like a man."

"I don't know, general."

"You general me, you rascal! But you sha'n't out-general me. I tell you, you do know. Answer, sirrah—didn't they come here constantly after your young mistress? Wasn't that handsome fellow, Proctor, always here?"

"Balfour, Balfour," interposed Cruden, "do not forget, I beg you, that Proctor is my kinsman."

"Pshaw! Why will you be throwing your nephew constantly in my teeth? Isn't ours a common cause? Don't we stand or fall together? And if your kinsman is in our way, sha'n't we thrust him out of it? What's he to either of us when the accounts are to be made up?"

"My sister's child, Balfour."

"Pish, were he your own now! Don't interrupt the negro. I say, Neptune, wouldn't you like to see your young mistress well married?"

"If she have no objection, master."

"A judicious answer! Well, she can have no objection, surely, to being married to a governor. Eh?"

"I reckon, master."

"She shall have a governor for her husband, Jupiter; she shall—and you shall be his body servant. I mean to be governor here, Pluto, as soon as we've driven all these rebels out; and she shall be my wife. Do you hear, fellow?"

"Yes, sir."

"You're a sensible fellow, Bacchus, and know that a governor's something more than a major of foot, or dragoons either. He makes majors of foot and dragoons—ay and unmakes them too, when they're troublesome. I say, Cruden, this affair looks squally for Proctor; it does; and yet I'm sorry for the fellow, I am. I like him as much on his account as your own. Come, we'll drink his health. You won't refuse that?"

Cruden filled his glass moodily and drank. Balfour proceeded—

"You think, Cruden, that I am talking with too much levity? Don't deny it. I see it your face. You look as surly as Sir William, with the last touches from the tail of the gout—just beginning to be unmiserable. But, you shall see. I will conduct the rest of the good fellow's examination with due sobriety."

"If you have any more questions to ask, let him answer about the plate."

"Ay, to be sure; I meant to come to that. I see what troubles you. Ho, Pluto, your master was a gentleman; I know, from your manners. I can always tell a gentleman by his servants. They reflect his manners; they imitate them. That is to say, your master *was* a gentleman before he became a rebel. You are no longer his servant, and *you* continue a gentleman still. Your master was rich, eh?"

" I expect, sir,"

" He had lands and negroes, and, I feel certain, kept good wines. Now, Plutus, among the qualities of a gentleman who is rich, he must be in possession of a famous service of plate ; he must have urns of silver, punch-bowls, plates, vases, teapots, cream-pots, milk-pots, and a thousand things necessary to the table and the sideboard, made out of the bright metal, eh ?"

" Yes, sir ; I expect so."

" And, Juno, your master had them all, hadn't he ?"

" O yes, sir."

" Where are they, Bacchus ?" put in Cruden.

" I don't know, master."

" What ? Well ! Go on, Colonel Cruden, go on ; if you are not satisfied with my—ah !—with my mode of—of—making this little domestic inquisition, why, you are at perfect liberty to —to do it better, if you can."

Cruden sullenly apologized, as he perceived that there was no propriety in doing otherwise.

" Go on, Balfour ; I didn't mean to take the game out of your hands. No one could do it better."

" I flatter myself you're right, Colonel Cruden. I *do* think that I can—ah—examine this gentleman of a negro as—as— successfully as any gowned inquisitor of—of—Westminster. But you've put me out. I must have something stronger than Madeira to restore my memory. I say, Brutus—Bacchus— have you the water heated ?"

" Yes, sir—general."

" And did your master—that was—did he have the decency, fellow, to keep in his cellar any good old Scotch whiskey ?"

" I don't think, master ; but there is some particular fine old Jamaica."

" There is ? It will do. Jamaica is only an apology for old Scotch whiskey ; but it is such an apology, Cruden—I say, Cru- den, it is such an apology as any gentleman may accept. I must have some of it."

The bottle was already on the sideboard which contained the then favorite liquor of the South — Madeira being excepted al- ways—and Bacchus was soon engaged in placing the spirits, the sugars, and the boiling water under the hands of Balfour, who insisted upon uniting the adverse elements himself.

"How gloriously it fumes! There, Cruden; drink of that, old fellow, and bless the hand that made it. Bacchus, you shall have a draught yourself—you shall, you handsome old rascal—the better to be able—you hear—to answer my questions. There is mnch of this Jamaica?"

"Smart chance, geueral."

"Drink, fellow, and forget your old master in your new.

The negro showed some reluctance; and the commandant of Charleston, rising from his chair, seized the fellow by his wool with one hand, while he forced the huge goblet, with its smoking potation, into his mouth. Few negroes reject such a beverage, or any beverage containing spirits; and Bacchus, though a tolerably temperate fellow, swallowed the draught without much reluctance or suffering.

"And now for this plate, Cæsar?"

"Yes, sir."

"You say there was plate?"

"Yes, sir."

"Where was it kept?"

"In little room up stairs, sir."

"Have you the key to that room?"

"It's on the bunch, master."

"Show it me."

The negro pointed it out. Balfour grasped it firmly, and shook it free from the rest.

"And now, fellow, where's the key to your wine vaults—your cellar?"

"Garret, Bacchus?" interposed Cruden.

"I thank you, Colonel Cruden. But had you—I say, Cruden, in a moment more I should have used the word myself. *Garret*, fellow?"

"I left it in the door, master, last time I went up, thinking maybe you might want more of the Madeira."

"You did? You sensible fellow! Who shall say that a negro lacks forethought? Ah, Bacchus! you are the man for me. Come, Cruden, let us go."

"Whither? What do you mean?"

" To explore the wine-vaults—to look into the cellar—to see after the plate! Now or never. I must see the extent of our possessions, old boy, before I sleep to-night."

The curiosity of Cruden—his cupidity, rather—prevailed over his sense of propriety. He was quite as ready for the exploration of the plate-room as was Balfour for the wine-cellar; and the two started, without further delay, under the guidance of Bacchus, bearing the candle. It was only when they emerged from the dining-room into the great passage-way below stairs, that our lovers above were first apprized of the danger in which they stood of discovery. The voice of Bacchus first told them of the probable intrusion of the British officers into a portion of the dwelling not assigned to them, and in which their presence, at that hour of the night, was totally unexpected.

The alarm of Katharine Walton may be imagined. Her fears, with regard to the safety of her companion, were naturally mixed up with the apprehensive sense of female delicacy, which must suffer from any detection under such circumstances. Singleton shared in this apprehension, with regard to her, more than any with regard to himself. He felt few fears of his personal safety, for he was conscious that he possessed, in the last resort, a means for escape, in the conviction that he could, himself, easily deal with the two enemies, encountering him, as they would, unexpectedly. To feel that his pistols were ready to his grasp in his belt, that the dagger was in his gripe and free for use, was to reassure himself, and to enable him, with composed nerves, to quiet those of his fair companion.

Meanwhile, the two Britons, both somewhat unsteady, though not equally so, made their way up the stairs. The anxiety of Bacchus to give due warning to those above, prompted him more frequently than seemed necessary to Balfour, to insist, in loud tones, upon the necessity of the greatest caution in ascending a flight of steps which, he repeated, were more than ordinarily steep.

" Hold on to the banister, general," he cried, on seeing the commandant make a sweeping lurch against the wall; " these steps are mighty high and steep."

"Shut up, fellow, and go ahead ! Throw your light more behind you, that we may see the steepness. There, that will do. This is a large house, Cruden, eh? The proprietor contemplated a numerous progeny when he built. Solid, too : feel these banisters."

"All mahogany," was the answer.

"And carved. Old style, and magnificent. These provincials were ambitious of showing well, eh? An old house, eh? I say, Pluto, is this house haunted?"

"Haunted, master?"

"Yes, fellow. Don't you understand? Have you any ghosts about?"

"Why, yes, sir. The old lady walks, they say."

"What old lady?"

"The lady of the old landgrave."

"Landgrave?" exclaimed Cruden, inquiringly.

"Yes," answered Balfour. "You know that they had their nobles in this province : there were the landgravinoes, which is German for lord or baron, and their cassicoes, which is Indian for another sort of nobility; and their palatinos, which is a step higher than both, I'm thinking—a pretty little establishment for a court in the woods. It was a nice sort of fancy of Lord Shaftesbury, after whom they christened this river and its sister—Ashley and Cooper—and if the old fox hadn't had his hands full of other conceits, we might have had him here setting up as a sort of Prince Macklevelly, the Italian, on his own account."

All this was spoken as Balfour hung upon the banister, midway up the steps, steadying himself for a renewed effort, and balancing to and fro, with his eyes stretched upward to the dim heights of the lofty ceiling.

"Yes," said he, continuing the subject, "an old house, and a great one—not ill-planned for a palace; the family an old one, and of the nobility."

"An Indian nobility," said Cruden, somewhat contemptuously.

"Well, and why not? Nobility is nobility, whether savage or Saxon; and I'll marry into it when I can. Take my advice, and do the same. Is it not arranged between us that we are to divide the fair ladies of this establishment? I am to have the young one, Cruden, old fellow—being more suited, you know, by reason of my youth and good-fellowship, to her tender years. The stately and magnificent aunt, Mistress Barbara, who has a right to the quarterings of her great grandsire, and is an heiress in her own right, they tell me—she is the very fellow for you, Cruden. You will make a famous couple. She will preside like a princess in your Pinckney chateau; and the royal ships, as they enter the harbor, will be always sure to give you a salute. Yes, I yield to you the aunt; I do, Cruden, old fellow, without grudging; and I will content myself modestly with the young creature."

This was spoken at fits and starts, the tongue of our worthy commandant, by this time, having thickened considerably, to say nothing of frequent spasmodic impediments of speech, known as hiccoughs to the vulgar.

"You are disposed of in a somewhat summary manner, Kate," whispered Singleton to his companion, both of whom had heard every syllable that was spoken.

" The brute !" was the muttered reply.

"What would Aunt Barbara say to all this ?"

" If she be awake," said Katharine, " she hears it all. It will greatly provoke her."

" I can fancy her indignation ! How she tosses her head !"

" Hush, Robert; they advance."

" If we are to divide all our spoils, Balfour," was the slow reply of Cruden, " upon the principle you lay down, my share would be a sorry one."

"What! you won't take the antique ? Ha! ha! You go for tenderer spoils, do you ? but I warn you, no squinting toward my Bellamira. She is mine ! Look elsewhere, if the old lady don't suit you; but look not to the young one. Divide the spoils equally, to be sure ! 'Pickings' was the word of our backwoods captain—the unsophisticated heathen ! 'Pickings !' The rascal might as well have called it stealings at once. But here we are, landed at last. Hello, Brutus, whose portraits are these ? Lift your light, rascal. Ha! that's a pretty woman— devilish like our virgin queen. Who's that, Plutus ? Your young mistress ?"

"No, sir; that's her great grandmother, the landgravine."

"God bless her nobility! It's from her that my queen of Sheba inherits her beauty. I shall have no objection to marry into a family where beauty, wealth, and title, are hereditary. I shall love her with all my heart and all my strength. And this, Scipio?"

"That's master, the colonel, sir—Colonel Walton."

"The rebel! Fling it down from the wall, fellow! I'll have no rebel portraits staring me in the face—me, the representative here of his most sacred majesty, George the Third, king of England, Scotland, Ireland, defender of the Faith, and father of a hopeful family. I say, down with the rebel-rascal, fellow; down with it! We'll have a bonfire of all the tribe, this very night. They shall none escape me. I have burnt every effigy of the runagates I could lay hands on; and, by the blessed saints! I will serve this with the same dressing. Do you hear, Beelzebub? Down with it!"

Katharine Walton, in her place of hiding, her soul dilating with indignation, was about to dart forward to interpose, totally forgetful of her situation, when the arm of Singleton firmly wrapped her waist. In a whisper, he said—

"Do not move, Kate, dearest; they will hardly do what this drunken wretch requires. But even should they, you must not peril yourself for the portrait, however precious it may be to your sympathies. Subdue yourself, dear heart. We must submit for a season."

"O, were I but a man!" said the high-souled damsel, almost audibly.

"Hush, Kate! Believe me, I prefer you infinitely as you are."

"O, how can you jest, Robert, at such a moment?"

"Jest! I never was more serious in my life."

"But your tone?"

"Says nothing for my heart, Kate. It is better to smile, if we can; and *play* with words, at the moment when, though we feel daggers, we dare not use them."

Meanwhile, the negro made no movement to obey the orders of Balfour. He simply heard, and looked in stupid wonderment.

"Do you not hear me, fellow? Must I tear down the staring effigy myself?

He advanced as he spoke, and his hands were already uplifted to the picture, when Cruden interposed—

"Leave it for to-night, Balfour. You will alarm the household. Besides, you will give great offence to the young lady. I don't love rebels any more than you, and will help to give themselves as well as their effigies to the fire; but let it be done quietly, and after you've sent the girl to town. You wouldn't wish to hurt her feelings?"

"Hurt her feelings? No! how could you imagine such a vain thing? Of course, we'll leave the rebel for another season. But he shall burn in the end, as sure as I'm Nesbitt Balfour."

"Robert," whispered Katharine, in trembling accents, "that portrait must be saved from these wretches. It must be saved, Robert, at every hazard."

"It shall be, Kate, if I survive this night."

"*You* promise me;—that is enough."

CHAPTER VIII.

GHOSTLY PASSAGES.

THE lovers were suddenly hushed, in their whispered conversation, by the nearer approach of the British officers. Cruden had, at length, persuaded his companion to forget the rebel portraits for awhile, and to address himself earnestly to the more important object of their search. Under the guidance of the reluctant Bacchus, they drew nigh to the plate chamber, or the closet, in which, according to the negro, the silver of the household was usually kept. This apartment was placed at the extremity of the passage, closing it up apparently in this quarter, but with a narrow avenue leading beside it, and out upon a balcony in the rear of the building. It was in this narrow passage that Katharine and her lover had taken shelter. The outlet to the balcony was closed by a small door; and against this they leaned, in the depth of shadow. With the dim candlelight which guided the enemy, they might reasonably hope, in this retreat, to escape his notice—unless, indeed, the light were brought to bear distinctly upon their place of hiding. Here they waited, in deep silence and suspense, the approach of the British officers.

Bacchus might have saved the commandant and the commissary the trouble of their present search. He well knew that the silver of the household had all disappeared. It is true that he knew not positively what route it had taken; but his conjectures were correct upon the subject. He was prudently silent, however—rather preferring to seem ignorant of a matter in which a too great knowledge might have ended in subjecting him to some of the responsibility of the abstraction. They reached the door, and Balfour fumbled with the keys to the great impatience of his companion, who more than once felt tempted to offer his assistance; but forbore, from sufficient experience of the tenacious vanity of the commandant. At length the opening was effected, and the two darted in—Bacchus lingering at the entrance, prepared to make a hasty retreat should the discoveries of his superiors result in any threatening explosion. For a time their hopes were encouraged. They beheld several rows of broad shelves, almost covered with old boxes, some of which were fastened down. It required some time to examine these; but, at length, the unpleasant conviction was forced upon them that they had wasted their labor upon a beggarly account of empty boxes.

"Bacchus," said Cruden, "is there no other closet?"

"Bacchus, you beast, where's the plate, I say?"

"'Tain't here, general," humbly responded the trembling negro.

"Well, that's information for which we are grateful; but, you bloody villain, if you don't find it—if a spoon's missing, a cup, a tankard, a pot, a—a—I'll have you hung up by the ears, you villain, with your head downward, like Saint Absalom! Do you hear, Plutus? Do you know what hanging means, eh? Do you know how it feels? Do you know——"

"Ask him, Balfour, if there are not other closets."

"Poh! poh! Cruden; am I the man, at this time of day, to be taught how to put the question to a son of Ishmael? What do we want with closets? What have we got by looking into closets? It's the plate we want; the precious metals, the cream of Potosi—the silver, the ingots, the Spanish bars,. you sooty, black, Ethiopan, Beelzebub; and if they're not forthcoming— ay, to-night, this very hour—you shall have despatches tor your namesake and grandfather, you nefarious Pluto—head downward, you son of soot and vinegar! Do you hear? Head downward shall you swim the Styx, old Charon, with a fiftypound shot about your neck, by way of ballast for a long voyage. The plate, old villain, if you wish to be happy on dry land, and keep your honest Ethiopan complexion!"

Bacchus declared himself fully sensible of the dangerous dis-

4

tinction with which he was threatened; but declared himself, in good set terms, and with the most earnest protestations, totally ignorant of the whereabouts of the missing treasure.

"I'm a poor nigger, master; they never gave the silver to me to keep. The colonel or young missis always kept the keys."

"Tell us nothing, fellow," said Cruden. "We know perfectly well that you are the trusted servant of your rebel master; we know that you have helped to hide the plate away. Show us where you have hidden it, and you will be rewarded; refuse, or pretend not to know, and as certainly as the commandant swears it, you will be hung up to the nearest tree."

"Head downward!" muttered Balfour.

"If you will b'lieve a poor black man when he swears, master, I swear to you I never had any hand in hiding it."

"Swear, will you, old Pluto? And by what god will your reverence pretend to swear, eh?" was the demand of Balfour.

"I swear by the blessed Lord, master!"

"Poh! poh! that won't do, you old rapscallion. Would you be taking the name of the Lord in vain? Would you have me encourage you in violating the Ten Commandments? Besides, you irreverent Ichabod, such an oath will not bind such a sable sinner as you are. No, no; you shall swear by the Bull Apis, you Egyptian; you shall swear by the Horned Jupiter, by the Grand Turk, and by Mahomet and Pharaoh. Do you hear? Will you swear by Jupiter Ammon?"

"I never heard of such a person, master."

"You never did! Is it possible? You see, Cruden, how lamentably ignorant this rebellious rascal is. I shall have to take this Ethiopan into my own keeping, and educate him in the right knowledge. I will teach you, Busiris, and make you wise —that is, if I do not hang you. But hang you shall, by all the gods of Egypt—and that is an oath I never break—unless you show where you have hid this treasure."

"I never hid it, master: I swear by all them people you mention!"

"People! They are gods, fellow, gods! But he swears, Cruden; he swears."

"Yes," said the other; "and as he does not seem to know

about the hiding, let him conduct us to the other closets and close rooms. There are other rooms, Bacchus," continued Cruden, who ventured, upon the somewhat drowsy state of Balfour, to take a leading part in the examination.

" Some rooms down stairs, colonel," said the negro, eagerly.

"Down stairs? But are there no others above stairs? What is this opening here, for example? Whither does this avenue lead?" and, as he inquired, he approached the mouth of the passage, at the extremity of which Katharine Walton and her lover were concealed.

" Here, Bacchus, bring your light here! This place must lead somewhere—to some chamber or closet. Let us see. Your light! Ten to one this conducts us to the hiding-place of the treasure."

The hand of Katharine clasped convulsively the arm of Singleton, as she heard these suggestions. Her companion felt all the awkwardness of their situation; but he apprehended little of its dangers. He felt that he was quite a match for Cruden, even against the half-drunken Balfour; and he had no doubt that Bacchus would not wait for his orders or those of his mistress to join in a death-grapple with the enemy. He gently pressed the hand of the maiden, with the design to reassure her; then quietly felt the handle of his dirk. His breathing was painfully suppressed, however, as he waited for the movement or the reply of Bacchus. That faithful fellow was sufficiently prompt in the endeaver at evasion.

" That's only the passage into the open balcony, master; that just leads out into the open air;" and speaking thus, he resolutely bore the light in the opposite direction.

"Never you mind; bring the light here, fellow; let us see" —the very apparent reluctance of Bacchus stimulating the curiosity of Cruden.

" The open air!" said Balfour. " To be sure, I want a little fresh air. The balcony, too! That should give us a view of the prospect. The scene by starlight must be a fine one. We'll but look out for a moment, Cruden; and then give up the search for the night. I'm sleepy, and, after another touch of the tankard, will doff boots and buff, and to bed. This ignoramus

knows nothing. We'll find the plate in the cellar, or under some
of the trees, with a little digging. Don't be uneasy; I carry a
divining rod, which is pretty sure to conduct me to all hiding-
places. It only needs that the rod should be put in pickle for
awhile. Ha, fellow, do you know what is meant by a rod in
pickle ?"

"Don't let us forget the balcony, Balfour. Do you not wish
to look out upon the night ?"

"Ay, true ; to be sure."

"Here, fellow, Bacchus, your light here."

"Yes, sir," was the answer; and the heart of Katharine Walton bounded to her mouth as she heard the subdued reply, and
listened to the movement of feet in the direction of the passage.
But Bacchus had no intention of complying with a requisition
which he felt so dangerous to the safety of those whom he loved
and honored. The negro, forced to the final necessity, still had
his refuge in a native cunning. It was at the moment when he
turned, as if to obey the imperative commands of Cruden, that
Balfour wheeled about to approach him ; and Bacchus timed his
own movements so well, that his evolutions brought him into
sudden contact with the person of the commandant. The light
fell from his hand, and was instantly extinguished, while a cry
of terror from the offender furnished a new provocation to the
curiosity of the British officers.

"Lord ha' mercy upon me ! what is that ?"

"What's what, you bloody Ishmaelite ?" exclaimed Balfour,
in sudden fury. "You've ruined my coat with your accursed
candlegrease !"

"Lord ha' mercy ! Lord ha' mercy !" cried the negro, in well-
affected terror.

"What scares you, fool ?" demanded Cruden.

"You no see, master ? The old lady ! She walks ! I see
her jest as I was turning with the candle."

"What, the old landgrave's housekeeper ?" demanded Balfour.

"Pshaw !" cried Cruden ; "don't encourage this blockhead in
his nonsense. Away, fool, and relight your candle ; and may
the devil take you as you go !"

The commissioner of confiscated estates was now thoroughly roused. His disappointment, in the search after the missing plate, and the fear that it would prove wholly beyond his reach, had vexed him beyond endurance. He was really glad of an occasion to vent his fury upon the negro, since the temper of Balfour was such as to render it necessary that he should exhibit the utmost forbearance in regard to his conduct, which Cruden was nevertheless greatly disposed to censure a thousand times a day. It was with a heavy buffet that he sent Bacchus off to procure a light, following his departure with a volley of oaths, which proved that, if slow to provocation, his wrath, when aroused, was sufficiently unmeasured. Even Balfour found it proper to rebuke the violence which did not scruple at the quality of his curses.

"Don't swear, Cruden, don't; its a pernicious immoral practice; and here, in the dark, at midnight—for I heard the clock strike below just before old Charon dropped the candle—and with the possibility—I say possibility, Cruden—that we are surrounded by spirits of the dead, ghosts of past generations, venerable shades of nobility—for you must not forget that the ancestors of this rebel colonel were landgraves and landgravinoes—his grandmother, as you hear, being the first landgrave in the family—you saw her portrait on the wall, with an evident beard upon her chin, no doubt intended by the painter to denote the dignity and authority of her rank, as Michael Angelo painted Moses with a pair of horns; and there is a propriety in it, do you see; for ghosts—By the way, Cruden, you believe in ghosts, don't you?"

"Not a bit."

"You don't? Then I'm sorry for his majesty's service that it has such an unbelieving infidel in it. A man without faith is no better than a Turk. It's a sign that he has no reverence. And that's the true reason why these Americans became rebels. The moment they ceased to believe in ghosts and other sacred things, they wanted to set up for themselves. Don't you follow their example. But where are you going?"

Cruden was striding to and fro impatiently.

"Nowhere."

" Don't attempt to walk in this solid darkness," counselled the
moralizing Balfour, who gradually, and with some effort, holding
on to the wall the while, let himself down upon the floor, his
solid bulk, in spite of all his caution, giving it a heavy shake as
he descended. " Don't walk, Cruden; you may happen upon
a pitfall ; you may get to the stairway and slip. Ah ! did you
hear nothing, Cruden ?"

' Nothing !" somewhat abruptly.

" I surely heard a whisper and a rustling, as if of some ancient silken garment. Come near to me, Cruden, if you would
hear. I wish that fellow Bacchus would make haste with his
light. I surely heard a footstep ! Listen, Cruden."

"I hear nothing ! It's your fancy, Balfour ;" and the other
continued to stride away as he spoke, not seeming to heed the
repeated requests of Balfour to approach him, in order properly
to listen.

Balfour's senses, in all probability had not deceived him. The
moment that Bacchus had disappeared, Singleton whispered to
his trembling companion—

" Now is our time, Kate, if we would escape. Bacchus has
flung down his light only to give us the opportunity. Let us
use it."

" But they are at the entrance ?"

" I think not. Near it, I grant you; but on the side, and
with room enough for us to pass. Follow me."

It was lucky that the necessities of the service had long since
forced upon Singleton the use of moccasins. There were few
boots in the camp of Marion. The soft buckskin enabled our
partisan to tread lightly through the passage ; the heavy tread
of Cruden contributing greatly to hush all inferior sounds. Singleton grasped firmly, but gently, the wrist of his companion.
But she no longer trembled ; her soul was now fully nerved to
the task. Balfour had, however, in reality, settled down in part,
at the entrance of the passage. He was seeking this position of
humility and repose at the very moment when the two began
their movement. For the instant, it compelled them to pause ;
but when assured that he was fairly couched. they passed lightly
beside him ; and, had not his superstitious fancies been awakened

by the story of the ghostly landgravine, his suspicions might have been more keenly awakened by the supposed rustlings of the ancient silk. To steer wide of Cruden was an easy task for our fugitives, as his footsteps announced his whereabouts with peculiar emphasis. The great passage was traversed with safety, and the maiden paused at the door of her chamber. Fortunately, it had been left ajar when she joined Singleton, though this had been done without regard to any anticipations of the interruptions they had undergone. To push it open and enter occasioned no noise. Singleton detained her only for an instant, as he whispered—

"Be not alarmed, Kate, at anything that may take place to-night—at any uproar or commotion."

"What mean you? What——But go! I hear Bacchus. You have not a moment to lose."

He pressed her hand, and stole off to the stairway. The steps yielded and creaked as he descended ; but the heavy boots of Cruden still served as a sufficient diversion of the sound from the senses of the British officers. Our partisan passed on that side of the hall below which lay in shadow, being careful not to place himself within the range of the light carried by Bacchus, who crossed him in the passage. He had something to say to the negro, but deferred it prudently, nothing doubting that he would find his way to his chamber when all had become quiet in the house.

Let us once more ascend with the light, and see the condition of the enemy. Balfour was philosophizing. His drink had rendered him somewhat superstitious.

"I say, Cruden," said he, "if I have not felt the rustling of a ghost's petticoat to-night, may I be ——!"

"I see no necessity why even a female ghost should appear in petticoats."

"It would be a very improper thing to appear without them," was the decent reply. "But," continued our philosopher, "I certainly heard her footsteps."

"Really, Balfour, if I could conceive of ghosts at all, I should certainly have no reason to suppose that they needed to make any noise in walking. A ghost, with so much materiality about it as to make her footsteps heard, is one with whom any strong man might safely grapple."

"Cruden, Cruden, you are no better than a pagan. You have no faith in sacred things. I certainly heard a rustling as of silks, and the tread of a person as if in slippers—a dainty, light, female footstep, such as might reasonably be set down by an ancient lady of noble family. I am sure it was a ghost. I feel all over as if a cold wind had been blowing upon me. I must have a noggin; I must drink! I must sleep. Confound the plate, I say! I'd sooner lose it all than feel so cursed uncomfortable."

"I am afraid it *is* lost, Balfour," responded the other, in tones of more lugubrious solemnity than those which his companion had used in the discussion of the supernatural.

"No matter," was the reply of Balfour; "we'll talk the matter over in the daylight. I don't despair. There is the cellar yet, and the vaults. Vaults are famous places, as I told you, for hiding treasure. But the mention of vaults brings back that ghost again. Where are you, Cruden? Why do you walk off to such a distance? Beware! You'll tumble down the steps headlong, and I shall then have you haunting me for ever after."

"No fear. But here the negro comes with the light. Perhaps it is just as well that we should go to bed at once, and leave the search till the morning. It is not likely that we shall make much progress under present circumstances."

"Some of that liquor first, Cruden. My night-cap is necessary to my sleep. I thought I had taken quite enough already; but this cold wind has chilled me to the bones, and sobered me entirely. The ghost must have had something to do with it— one spirit acting upon another."

"The light now appeared, and Bacchus emerged from the stairhead; and with an evident grin upon his features as he beheld Cruden erect in the centre of the passage, as if doubtful where to turn, bewildered utterly in the dark; and Balfour at the extremity of it, his huge frame in a sitting posture, in which dignity did not seem to have been greatly consulted.

"Ha, Beelzebub," cried the commandant, the moment he beheld the visage of the negro, "you are here at last! This is a hanging matter, you scoundrel, to leave us here in the dark to be tormented by the ghosts of your old grandmother. I have hung many a better fellow than yourself for half the offence; and, were you a white man, you should never see another daylight. Look to it, rascal, and toe the mark hereafter, or even your complexion shall not save you from the gallows."

"I will look to it, general, jest as you tell me."

"See that you do. Here, Cruden, give me an arm; my limbs seem quite stiff and numbed. That infernal wind! It was surely generated in a sepulchre!"

Cruden did as he was desired, and the bulky proportions of the commandant were raised to an erect position on the floor. He stood motionless for a moment, having thrown off the arm that helped him up, as if to steady himself for further progress; but the ghost, or rather his superstitious fancies, had really done much to sober him. His hesitation was due less to any real necessity than to his own doubts of the certainty of his progress. While thus he stood, Cruden in the advance, and Bacchus between the two, aiming to divide the light with strict impartiality, for their mutual benefit, the eyes of Balfour rested upon the portraits against the wall. That of the ancient landgravine first compelled his attention.

"Hark you, Beelzebub; that, you say, is the venerable lady who still keeps house here at midnight? She is the proprietor of the ghost by which I have been haunted. It was her garment that rustled beside me, and her footsteps that I heard; and it was she that blew upon me with her ghostly breath, giving me cold and rheumatics. She shall burn as a witch to-morrow, with her rebel grandson. Do you hear, fellow? Let the fagots be collected after breakfast to-morrow. We shall have a bonfire that shall be a due warning to witch and rebel; and to all, you sooty rascal, that believe in them."

"Come, Balfour, let us retire."

Cruden was now at the head of the stairway.

"Let us drink, first. Advance the light, Beelzebub; and see that you bear it steadily. Drop it again, and I smite your head off where you stand, ghost or no ghost. It's not so sure, yet, that you shall escape from hanging. If there be but a single spot of grease on my regimentals to-morrow, Beelzebub—say your prayers suddenly. I shall give you very little time."

The party at length found themselves safely below. Scarcely had they disappeared, when Mistress Barbara Walton put her head out of her chamber door. She had overheard the progress from beginning to end. She had drank in, with particular sense of indignation, that portion of the dialogue which, as the two officers first ascended the stairs, had related to herself, and the cavalier disposition which it was proposed to make of her : and she felt that she was in some measure retorting upon the parties themselves when she could vent her anger on the very spot which had witnessed their insolence.

"The brutes !" she replied ; " the foreign brutes ! But I despise them from the bottom of my heart. I would not bestow my hand upon their king himself, the miserable Hanover turnip, let alone his hirelings. The drunken wretches ! Oh !" she exclaimed, looking up at the picture of the venerable landgravine threatened with the flames—" oh ! how I wish that her blessed spirit could have breathed upon them, the blasphemous wretches—breathed cramps upon their bones, the abominable heathens ! To speak of me as they have done ! Of me—the only sister of Richard Walton ! Oh, if he were here—if I could only tell him how I have been treated !"

The British officers suffered little from this burst of indignation. Balfour was soon comforted in the enjoyment of his night-cap ; and Cruden was not unwilling to console himself, under his disappointments, by sharing freely of the beverage. In a little while both of them were asleep—the former in full possession of such a sleep as could only follow from the use of such a night-cap.

CHAPTER IX.

RING THE ALARM-BELL.

It was not very long after the house had become quiet, that the faithful Bacchus might have been seen entering the chamber of Singleton, or, as we shall continue to call him for a time, the captain of loyalists. He remained some time in counsel with the latter; and, at length, the two emerged together from the room. But they came forth in utter darkness, invisible to each other, and only secure in their movements by their equal familiarity with the several localities of the house. We may mention that Furness had not sought his couch when he separated from Katharine Walton. He was now armed to the teeth, with sword and pistol; his hunting-horn suspended from his neck, and his whole appearance that of one ready for flight or action. Bacchus soon left his side, and our partisan awaited him in the great passage of the hall. But a little time had elapsed when the negro rejoined him. They then left the house together, and disappeared among the shade-trees which surrounded it on every side.

An hour might have elapsed after their departure, when the silence of midnight was broken by the single blast of a horn, apparently sounded at some distance. This was echoed by another that seemed to issue from the front avenue of the dwelling. Both avenues, front and rear, had been occupied, in part, by the detachment which had accompanied the commandant from Dorchester, and which was justly supposed fully equal to his protection and objects. But the force which, concentrated, would have been adequate to these purposes, was not sufficient to cover the vast extent of woods which encompassed

the dwelling; and his men, when scattered, were really lost
amidst the spacious forest-area of which "The Oaks" constituted
the centre. Distributed at certain points, as guards and sentinels, however well disposed, there were still long stretches of
space and thicket which the detachment failed to cover; through
the avenues of which a subtle scout, familiar with the region,
might easily pick his way, unseen and unsuspected, under cover
of the night. The Scotch officer on duty for the night, a Captain M'Dowell, was circumspect and vigilant; but he was ignorant of the neighborhood, and, without any inferiority of
intelligence or neglect of duty, had failed to dispose his little
force to the best advantage. But he was wakeful; and the
sound of the midnight and mysterious horn had aroused him to
every exercise of vigilance. Another signal followed from another quarter, which, after a brief pause, was echoed from a
fourth; and our worthy captain of the guard began to fancy
that his little force was entirely surrounded. He at once proceeded to array and bring his separate squads together; keeping them as much as possible *in hand*, and in preparation for
all events. We need not follow him in his operations, satisfied
that, awakened to a sense of possible danger, he is the man to
make the best disposition of his resources.

It was in the moment when Balfour's sleep was of the pro-
foundest character, that Cruden, followed by his white servant,
both armed, but very imperfectly dressed, bolted headlong into
the chamber of the sleeping commandant. He heard nothing of
the intrusion. He was in a world very far away from that in
which he was required to play his part — a world in which his
dreams of delight were singularly mixed with those of doubt;
in which visions of boundless treasures were opened to his sight
but denied his grasp — a pale, spectral form of an ancient lady
rejoicing in a beard, always passing between him and the object
of his desires. There were other visions to charm his eyes, in
which the treasure took the shape of a beautiful young woman;
while the obstacle that opposed his approach was that of a fierce
rebel, breathing rage and defiance, whom his fancy readily conceived to be no other than the insurgent father of Katharine
Walton. With a brain thus filled with confused and conflicting

objects, and not altogether free from the effects of that torpify-
ing nostrum upon which he had retired, the events in progress,
in his actual world, however startling, made little or no impression upon his senses. The noise that filled his ears was associated happily with the incidents in his dreaming experience, and
this failed entirely to arouse him to external consciousness.

"He sleeps like an ox," cried Cruden, as he held the candle
above the sleeper, and shook him roughly by the shoulder.

"Ha! ho! there! What would you be after? Will you
deny me? Defy me? Do you think that I will give it up—
that I fear your sword, you infernal rebel, or your——Eh!
what!"—opening his eyes.

The rough ministry of the commissioner of confiscated estates
at length promised to be effectual. The incoherent speech of
the dreamer began to exhibit signs of a returning faculty of
thought.

"What! Cruden! you! What the devil's the matter?"

"Do you not hear? The devil seems to be the matter indeed!"

"Hear! What should I hear?"

"What! do you *not* hear? There's uproar enough to rouse
all the seven sleepers, I should think."

"And so there is! What is it?"

"Rouse up, and get yourself dressed. There is a surprise, or
something like it."

With the aid of Cruden and his servant, the commandant was
soon upon his feet, rather submitting to be put into clothes and
armor than greatly succoring himself. His faculties were still
bewildered, but brightening with the rise and fall of the noises
from without. These were such as might naturally be occasioned
by the surprise of a post, at midnight, by an enemy—the rush
and shout of men on horseback, the blast of bugles, and occasionally the sharp percussion of the pistol-shot suddenly rising
above the general confusion.

It was not long before Balfour was ready. With sword and
pistol in hand, accompanied by Cruden similarly equipped, he now
made his way out of the chamber to the front entrance of the
house, in which quarter the greatest uproar seemed to prevail.

When there, and standing in the open air under the light of the stars, they could more distinctly trace the progress of the noise. It seemed to spread now equally away to the river, on the route below, and in the rear of the mansion, making in a westerly direction. They had not well begun making their observations, uncertain in which direction to turn their steps, when they suddenly beheld a lithe and active figure darting from the thicket in the rear, and making toward them. The stranger was at once challenged by Cruden, and proved to be our loyalist captain, Furness. He, too, carried sword and pistol ready in his grasp; and his voice and manner were those of one eager and excited by the fray. He seemed nowise surprised by their appearance, however much they may have been at his.

"Rather more scared than hurt, I reckon, colonel," was his frank and ready salutation. "How long have you been out?"

"Only this moment," was the answer of Balfour. "But what's the matter?"

"There's no telling exactly. Everything seems to have become wild without a reason. I was roused from as sweet a sleep as I ever tasted, by the ringing of a horn in my very ears —so it seemed to me. And then there was another horn answering to that; then, after a little while, there was a shout and a halloo, and the rush of one horse, and then another, and then a score of pistol-shots. With that, I put out to see what was the matter, and what was to be done, and followed in the direction of the noise; but I could find out nothing, got bewildered in the woods, and, in beating about for an opening, I heard a rush not far off. Now, says I, the enemy is upon me; and I braced myself up for a hard fight as well as I could. I heard the bush break suddenly just before me, and I called out. No answer; but, as the bush moved, I cracked away at it with a pistol-shot, and soon heard a scamper. It proved to be an old cow, who was evidently more alarmed than anybody else. She moved off mighty brisk after that; but it's ten to one she carries the mark of my bullet. I was so nigh to her that I could not well have missed."

"And this is all you know, Captain Furness?"

"Pretty much all! I have only seen two or three of the

troopers, and they seemed so much disposed to send their bullets at me, that I have tried to steer clear of them. They are gone out mostly somewhere to the west; but they know the country better than I do, for I've quite lost my reckoning where I am."

At this moment, the clatter of a horseman, at a hard gallop, awakened the curiosity of all parties anew. He emerged from the rear avenue to the dwelling, and soon alighted before Balfour. He was a sergeant, and a pretty old one, despatched by the captain of the guard to satisfy the doubts and inquiries of his superior. But his information was very meagre. It amounted only to this—that there had been an alarm; that the post had been apparently threatened on every side at different times; that bugles had been sounded, seemingly as signals, but that they had seen no human enemy, and had found nothing living within their circuit but themselves and a drove of milch cattle. Still, some of the men had reported the sound of horses' feet, as of a considerable party of mounted men; and, as they insisted upon the report, the captain had deemed it advisable to push the search in the direction which the enemy had been described as having pursued. This was all that he could say. He eyed our loyalist captain rather closely during the recital, and at length said—

"Was it you, sir, I met off here in the south, beating about the bushes?"

"I reckon it was, sergeant; and, if I hadn't been quick enough, your pistol-shot wouldn't have left me much chance of answering you now. 'Twas the narrowest escape I ever had."

"And why didn't you answer?"

"For the best of reasons. You asked me for the word, and I knew nothing about it. But I'll take good care never to volunteer again when there's a surprise, without getting proper information beforehand."

The sergeant looked for a moment steadily at the captain of loyalists. He was a shrewd, keen, almost white-headed soldier, and the gaze of his light blue eye was fixed and penetrating, as if he referred to this scrutiny as a last test for resolving his doubts; but the appearance of Furness was singularly composed and *nonchalant.* He did not appear to regard himself as an object of watch, or doubt, or inquiry at all. The soldier seemed at length satisfied; and, touching his cap reverently, said to Balfour—

"It's all right, colonel?"

"Yes, sergeant, that will do. Remount, and hurry back to Captain M'Dowell. Tell him to discontinue this chase. He may only find himself in some cursed ambush. Let him return, and resume his station. We shall hear his full report in the daylight."

The sergeant bowed, and cantered off in a moment.

"It seems you had a narrow escape, Captain Furness," said Balfour, with more of respectful consideration in his manner than had usually marked his deportment when addressing the loyalist.

"Yes, indeed, colonel; a much narrower escape than a man bargains for at the hands of his friends."

"But it was all a mistake, captain."

"True; but it's a mighty small consolation, with a bullet through one's brains or body, to be told that the shot was meant for a very different person."

"Never mind, captain—a miss, as your own people say, is as good as a mile. It is something gained for you that we have had such excellent proof of your vigilance and courage in his majesty's cause. Future favors will heal past hurts."

He was yet speaking—all the parties standing grouped, at the southern or chief entrance of the building, and partly within the hall—usually called, in the south, the passage, generally as, in large dwelling-houses, running through the centre of the building—when the door in the rear was heard to creak upon its hinges. Cruden, who at this moment was within the passage, though near the southern entrance and the rest of the group, turned instantly, and beheld a female figure which had just entered. He could distinguish no features, since the only light within the apartment was afforded by an unsnuffed candle, which had been set down by his servant on the floor when hurrying from Balfour's chamber—the light used by the party without, being a common lantern. At first, a vague remembrance of

Balfour's ghost of the Landgravine passed through Cruden's brain; but he was of an intellect too stolid to suffer him long to remain under the delusion of his fancies. He at once conjectured that this female must be Katharine Walton or her aunt; and, in either case, he associated her appearance, at this hour and under these circumstances, with the yet unaccounted for alarms of the night. His cupidity promptly suggested that the plate, which had been the object of his search already, was even now in course of hiding or removal; and, with this conjecture, his decision was as eager, and his performance as impetuous as that of the young lover hurrying his virgin favorite to the altar. With a bound, scarcely consistent with the dignity of his official station and the massive dimensions of his person, he darted across the passage, and grappled the stranger by the wrist.

"Ho! there! the light—bring the light. Balfour, I fancy I have captured your ghost."

Our commissioner of confiscated estates did not perceive that, just behind his captive, and about to enter the door after her was the sooty face of Bacchus. The darkness favored the escape of the negro, who, crouching quietly without, waited his opportunity to enter the hall unseen.

"What means this violence, Colonel Cruden?" was the calm inquiry made by Katharine Walton, in the most serene and gentle accents. Meanwhile, Balfour and our captain of loyalists had hastened to the group at the summons of the excited Cruden. It was with a difficult effort that Singleton could suppress his emotions, and subdue the feeling that prompted him to seize the commissioner by the throat and punish him for the brutal grasp which he had set upon the woman of his heart; but the peril of his situation compelled his forbearance, however unwilling, and stifled the passion working in his soul, however violent. But his hand more than once wrought as if working with his dagger; and, with clenched teeth, he found himself compelled repeatedly to turn away from the scene and pace the hall in an excitement which was scarcely to be repressed. Katharine Walton repeated her demand of her assailant, in accents, however, so firm and calm, as only to increase his indignation.

"What means this violence, madam, indeed? What means

this uproar, this alarm, madam, at this unseasonable hour of the night? Why are you here, let me ask you, and habited as if for a journey? Look! it is clear she has been abroad—her bonnet and clothes are wet with the dew. Answer, Miss Walton—what has carried you out at this hour? Where have you been? What have you been doing? Speak—you do not answer."

"And if you were to subject my neck, sir, to a grasp as vice-like as that which you hold upon my wrist, you should receive no answer from my lips, unless at my perfect pleasure," was the reply of the maiden.

"Ha! do you defy me?"

"I scorn you, sir! Release me, sir, if you would not subject yourself to the scorn of all those who hear of this indignity."

Singleton could no longer avoid interposition; but he maintained the character which he had assumed. Coming forward, he said—

"That's right, colonel; I don't see why a woman shouldn't be made to speak out, in war-times, just the same as a man. I've seen the thing tried before. There was a woman up in our parts that hid her husband away, and Major Tatem burnt a hole in her tongue to make her speak. If you want help now, colonel, just you say the word, and I reckon that both of us together can bring this young woman to her senses."

Cruden turned fiercely upon the speaker, as he rather flung the maiden from his grasp than released her. The offer of help in such a performance as that in which he was engaged, was a sufficient reflection—though apparently very innocently made —upon the brutality of the action.

"Your assistance will be asked when it is desired, sir," was the angry answer.

"O yes, I reckon; but, you see, I've been a sort of volunteer once already to-night, and I'm always ready to help his majesty's officers in time of trouble."

"Miss Walton," said Balfour, with a sort of severe courtesy, "you are aware that the circumstances in which you appear to-night are exceedingly suspicious."

"Certainly, sir; I am seen in full dress in my father's dwelling at midnight. Heretofore, sir, I have been accustomed to act my pleasure in this house. I am painfully reminded that I have other and less indulgent masters. It must not surprise you that I am slow to recognise or understand my new responsibilities."

"We are certainly in authority here, Miss Walton; but without any desire of subjecting you to any painful or personal restraint or coercion."

"The bonds of your colleague, sir, are an excellent commentary upon your forbearance. I confess they afford me no grateful ideas of the liberty which I am to enjoy in future. But, as I have said, you are the masters here. Am I permitted to retire?"

"Certainly, Miss Walton; but you will not think me unreasonable, if, in the morning, I shall ask you for an explanation of present appearances. This——"

He was interrupted by an exclamation from Cruden's servant, at the southern entrance. All parties turned at the interruption.

"There seems to be a great fire, colonel," said the servant. "Look away yonder in the south."

Balfour and Cruden hastily joined him, and a smile of intelligence was interchanged between the maiden and her lover. In the meantime, Bacchus seized the opportunity quietly to make his way into the hall. The party at the entrance was soon overwhelmed with conflicting speculations as to the conflagration which now spread out magnificently before their eyes.

"The woods are on fire," said Cruden.

"No," was the reply of Balfour; "it is a house rather. Miss Walton, pray oblige me—can you explain the nature of this fire?"

Katharine smiled playfully.

"I will give you no answer to any questions, Colonel Balfour, to-night—if only to satisfy myself that the coercion under which I labor does not extend to my thoughts or speech. I presume that, with another day, there will be no mystery about any of the events of this night."

With these words, she disappeared. The oath of vexation was only half uttered on the lips of Balfour, when his eye caught sight of Bacchus, stretching forward curiously in the rear of the loyalist.

"Ha! fellow, is it you? You, at least, shall answer. Look, sirrah — what does that fire mean?"

"I reckon it's the rice-stacks, master, that's a burning."

"The rice-stacks!" exclaimed Cruden, in horror. "The rice-stacks! the whole crop of rice — a thousand barrels or more! What malignity! And could this young woman have been guilty of such a crime? Has she, in mere hatred to his majesty's cause, wantonly set fire to a most valuable property of her own?"

"Impossible!" replied Balfour. "There has been an enemy about us : this was his object. The alarm was a real one. But we must see if anything can be saved, Captain Furness, you have already given proof of your zeal to-night in his majesty's cause. May I beg your further assistance? We will sound our bugles, and call in our squad. Meanwhile, let us hasten to the spot. The stacks are generally separate; while one or more burn we may save the rest?"

The idea was an absurd one, and proved sufficiently fruitless. The stacks were all on fire, and in great part consumed before the parties reached the spot. The hands that did the mischief left little to be done; and Cruden groaned in the agony of his spirit, at a loss of profits which almost made him forgetful of the missing plate. But day dawns while he surveys the spectacle; and the red flames, growing pale in the thickening light, play now only in fitful tongues and jets among the smouldering ashes of the ripened grain, gathered vainly from the sheaves of a bounteous harvest.

"We must have a thorough examination into this diabolical business," said Balfour, as he led the returning party to the dwelling.

CHAPTER X.

ALL SORTS OF SURPRISES.

WITH the return to the dwelling, Balfour and Cruden resumed the search into the secrets of the household, which, as we have seen, was begun with doubtful results during the previous night. The stores of wine proved satisfactory to the former; but the Flemish account, in most respects, which the exploration yielded, greatly increased the ill-humor of the latter. The plate was nowhere visible; and certain reports, made by the captain on duty, in respect to the affairs of the plantation, tended greatly to increase the gravity of both these persons. But we need not anticipate the gradual development of the various causes of grievance. Enough to remark, in this place, that, when descending the stairs from the attic, where he had been to examine into the condition of the Madeira, and passing through the great passage which was the scene of the most striking part of their labors the previous night, the eye of Balfour was arrested by the pictures upon the wall, or rather by the vacant panels which appeared among them. To his consternation, the portraits of both the rebel colonel and of the ghostly landgravine, which he had equally devoted to the flames, had disappeared from their places.

"The devil!" he exclaimed to Cruden, pointing to the deficiency; "we must have been overheard last night."

"How should it have been otherwise?" was the surly answer. "These chambers are occupied by the women, and you spoke as if you meant that they should hear everything. With a knowledge of your purpose they have defeated it, they have contrived to secrete the pictures."

"But I will contrive to find them!" was the angrily-expressed resolution of Balfour. "They shall not baffle me. They can not have carried them far, and they shall burn still. Prayers shall not save them."

"Let me counsel you first to send off the women to the city. Make no stir till you have got rid of them."

"You are right; but I shall take leave to examine them first, touching the events of last night."

"Say nothing of your own purposes while doing so," said Cruden. "We have probably already taught them quite too much. You might have burnt the portraits of the old woman and the rebel, without a word, but for that unnecessary threat last night."

"And would I have seen the portraits, or had any occasion to speak of them, but for your confounded impatience to look after the silver? In all probability, the occasion and the warning have been seized for carrying that away as well as the pictures "

"I am afraid it was gone long before. But that idea of burning the pictures might have taught these malignants what to do with the rice. But it is too late now for retort and recrimination; and here comes the captain of loyalists."

Furness came to the foot of the stairs and met them.

"The young lady tells me that breakfast is waiting for you, gentlemen."

"The young lady?" exclaimed Balfour, eying the partisan keenly. "So, you have been talking with her, eh?"

"Why yes," replied the other, with a manner of rare simplicity. "I somehow began to feel as if I could eat a bit after the run, and hurry, and confusion of the night; so I pushed into the dining-room, looking out for the commissary. I met the young woman there, and had a little talk with her; and breakfast was just then beginning to make its appearance."

"What had she to say about this affair of last night?" demanded Cruden.

"Mighty little: she seems rather shy to speak. But she don't look as if there had been any alarm. She's as cool as a cucumber if not so green."

"You are a wit, Captain Furness," grimly remarked Cruden, as the three walked together into the breakfast-room.

Here they found the excellent aunt and her niece, evidently waiting for their uninvited guests. In the rigid and contracted features of the former, so different from their amiable expression of the previous evening, might be traced the counter influences produced upon her mind by what she had heard, during their midnight conference, of the irreverent allusions to herself by the commandant of Charleston. But the face of Katharine was as placid as if she had enjoyed the most peaceful and unbroken slumbers — as if there had been nothing to affect her repose, her peace of mind, or to annoy her with apprehensions either of the present or the future. Indeed, there was a buoyant something in her countenance and manner which declared for a feeling of exhilaration, if not of triumph prevailing in her bosom. The breakfast-table exhibited the most ample cheer, and all was grace and neatness in the display. The ladies took their seats, after a brief salutation, and the guests immediately followed their example.

It was the purpose of Balfour to forbear all subjects of annoyance until after the repast; but he was not permitted to be thus forbearing. He had scarcely commenced eating, before the captain of the guard requested to see him at the entrance. Excusing himself, with some impatience, he went out; and returned, after a brief interval, with quite an inflamed countenance.

"Miss Walton," said he, "are you aware that all the negroes of your father have disappeared from the plantation?"

"I have heard so, sir," quietly replied the lady.

"Heard so, Miss Walton? And who could have presumed to carry them off without your permission?"

"No one, I fancy, sir, unless my father himself."

"Your father himself! What! do you know that he ordered their departure?"

"I presumed so, sir. They would hardly have gone unless he had done so."

"And whither have they gone?"

"Ah, now, sir, you demand much more than I can answer."

"And when did they leave the place?"

"Nor can I answer that, exactly. I have reason to think some hours before your arrival."

" You knew of our coming, then ?"

" Not a syllable. My father may have done so ; and I myself thought it not improbable."

" It was in anticipation of our visit, then, I am to understand, that you have conveyed away—your father, I mean—all the moveable valuables of your plantation and household; your negroes, horses; your plate, silver, and——"

The maiden answered with a smile :—

" Nay, sir, but your questions seem to lead to odd suspicions of the purpose of your visit. How should we suppose that the presence of his majesty's officers should be hurtful to such possessions ?"

" No evasion, Miss Walton, if you please," was the interruption of Cruden.

" It is not my habit, sir, to indulge in evasions of any sort. I rather comment on an inquiry than refuse to answer it. I note it as singular only, that his majesty's officers, high in rank and renowned in service, should suppose that their simple approach should naturally cause the riches of a dwelling to take wings and fly. In regard to ours, such as they are—our plate, money, and jewels—it gives me pleasure to inform you that they disappeared long before your presence was expected. My father, some time ago, adopted a very new and unusual sort of alchemy. He turned his gold and silver into baser metals—into iron and steel, out of which lances, and bayonets, and broadswords, have been manufactured ; and these have been circulating among his majesty's officers and soldiers quite as freely, if less gratefully, than if they had been gold and silver."

" Well," exclaimed the loyalist captain, with a rare abruptness, " if the young woman doesn't talk the most downright rebellion, I don't know what it is she means to say."

Balfour looked toward him with a ghastly smile, which had in it something of rebuke, however ; and the risible muscles of the fair Katharine could scarcely be subdued as she listened to the downright language of her lover ; and watched the countenance, expressive of the most admirable simplicity and astonishment, with which he accompanied his words. Balfour resumed :—

" My dear Miss Walton, you are a wit. His majesty's officers are indebted to you. But the business is quite too serious with us for jest, however amusing it may seem to you. We have too much at stake for fun——"

"And I have nothing at stake, sir, I suppose!" she abruptly replied, the moisture gathering in her eyes; "a homestead over-run with a foreign soldiery; a family torn asunder, its privacy invaded, its slaves scattered in flight, and the head of the house in exile, and threatened with butchery. Oh, sir, I certainly have more reason for merriment than can be the case with you?"

"I did not mean that, my dear young lady. I did not mean to give you pain. But you must see that I am here as the agent of my sovereign, and sworn that nothing shall divert me from my duties. I am compelled, however unwillingly, to ask you those questions, as I must report on all the facts to my superiors. I beg that you will not hold me accountable for the simple per-formance of a duty which I dare not avoid."

"Proceed, sir, with your questions."

"I'll thank you, ma'am, for another cup of that coffee," said the captain of loyalists, pushing the cup over to the stately aunt.

"Miss Walton, do you know by whose orders the rice-stacks were consumed last night, and who was the agent in the work?"

"I have reason to believe that my father ordered their de-struction. Of the particular hand by which the torch was ap-plied, I can tell you nothing."

"But you know?"

"No, sir, I do not."

"There were certain pictures removed from the walls of the gallery above stairs, during the night?"

"Which you had sentenced to the flames, sir?"

"You overheard us, Miss Walton."

"I did, and resolved that you should burn me as soon. _I_ had them removed, sir. For this, I only am responsible."

"You had? Pray, Miss Walton, who was your agent in this business?"

"I answer you, sir, the more willingly, as I rejoice to believe that he is now entirely beyond your reach. Sir—Colonel Bal-four—to spare you the necessity for further inquiries, let me as-sure you that the only person having any right to dispose of

5

Colonel Walton's property as has been done, was the very person who did exercise this right. It was by his act that our plate has disappeared, our negroes and horses withdrawn from the estate, the rice fired in the stack, and the pictures removed."

"You do not mean——"

"Yes, sir, I do mean that Colonel Walton himself had the rice fired last night; and it was by his direction, though at my entreaty, that the portraits were removed."

"But he did this through the hands of others. Miss Walton, you were abroad last night, in the very hour of confusion and alarm. I demand of you, as you hope for indulgence at the hands of his majesty, to declare what agent of your father did you see in the execution of these acts."

"No agent, sir. I saw my father himself! To *him* the portraits were delivered, and under his eye were the torches applied to the rice-stacks."

Balfour and Cruden both bounded from their seats, the former nearly drawing the cloth, cups, and breakfast, from the table. For a moment he regarded the features of Katharine Walton with a glance of equal rage and astonishment. She, too, had risen ; and her eyes met those of the commandmant with a calm smile, seasoned with something of triumph and exultation. The loyalist captain, meanwhile, continued his somewhat protracted occupation of draining his coffee-cup. "One stupid moment, motionless, stood" the British officer. In the next, Balfour cried aloud —

"Two hundred guineas for him who takes the rebel alive !"

With this cry, he rushed to the door of the house, where a sergeant was in waiting. Katharine almost crouched as she heard these words. She pressed her hand spasmodically to her heart, and an expression of keen agony passed over her face. It was but an instant, however. Cruden had followed Balfour to the door, and a single glance of intelligence between the maiden and her lover served to reassure her. In the next instant, our partisan had joined Balfour in the courtyard.

"Colonel," said he, "if you 're going to send out in pursuit of the rebel, I 'm your man as a volunteer. I 'd like to have the fingering of a couple of hundred of the real stuff as well as anything I know."

"Captain Furness, you will do honor to his majesty's service. I accept your offer."

In less than twenty minutes, the whole force of the British at the "Oaks" was in keen pursuit; the supposed captain of loyalists taking the lead, intrusted with a *quasi* command, and pursuing the chase with an eagerness which charmed all parties equally with his energy and zeal.

CHAPTER XI.

STRANGE RELATIONSHIPS.

THE purpose of Singleton, in taking part in the pursuit of Colonel Walton, may be readily conjectured. With his equal knowledge of his uncle's objects, and of the country through which he rode, it was easy, particularly as the region was little known by any of the pursuers, to shape and direct the chase unprofitably. It was maintained during the day, under many encouraging auguries, but was wholly without results; and the party returned to the "Oaks" about midnight in a condition of utter exhaustion.

The captain of loyalists had sufficiently proved his zeal, and Balfour was pleased to bestow upon him the highest commendations. They had long conferences together in regard to the interests of the common cause, particularly with reference to the state of feeling in the back country, and by what processes the spirit of liberty was to be subdued, and that of a blind devotion to his majesty's cause was to be inculcated and encouraged.

On all these matters Singleton was able to speak with equal confidence and knowledge. It was fortunate that a previous and very intimate acquaintance with these then remote regions had supplied our partisan with an abundance of facts, as well in regard to persons as to places. He showed very clearly that he knew his subjects thoroughly, and his report was comparatively a correct one; only so much varied, here and there, as more and more to impress the commandant with the importance of his own influence, and the necessity of giving it the fullest countenance. The particular purpose on which he came was in a fair way to be satisfied. Balfour promised him all the necessary supplies, perfectly delighted with his zeal, his shows of intelligence, however rudely displayed; for Singleton, with the assumption of the hardy character of the backwoodsman, was specially mindful of all those peculiarities of the character he had adopted which were likely to arrest the attention of the Briton. His letters to General Williamson, from certain well-known leaders among the mountain-loyalists, were all freely placed under Balfour's examination, and the latter was at length pleased to say that Williamson would meet with our partisan at the "Quarter" or the Eight-Mile House—contiguous places of resort on the road from Charleston—without the latter being required to expose himself to the dangers of the small-pox in that city; for which the supposed loyalist continued to express the most shuddering horror and aversion. These matters were all adjusted before the departure of the commandant for the capital—an event which followed the next day.

Katharine Walton, in the meantime, had already taken her departure, with the excellent Miss Barbara; travelling under an escort of a few dragoons, in the family carriage, drawn by the only horses of any value which had been left by Colonel Walton, or Singleton, upon the estate. It was during the pursuit of her father by her lover that she had been sent away to the city; and though her absence, on his return, had dashed his spirits with a certain degree of melancholy, yet he felt that it was really for the best; since, to have seen her under constraint, and subject to various annoyances, at the hands of their common enemy, without power to interfere, was only matter of perpetual mortification to himself. But when, again, he reflected upon the sudden, undisguised, and passionate admiration which Balfour had shown for her, a momentary chill seized upon his heart; but, to dispel this, it was only necessary to recall the high qualities, the superior tone, the known courage and devotion of his cousin, and his thorough conviction of her faith to himself, under all privations, to restore his equanimity and make him confident of the future. He saw Balfour depart the next day without apprehension. Cruden remained upon the plantation, having with him a small guard. He was joined by his nephew, Major

Proctor, whose assistance he needed in making a necessary inventory of all the effects upon the estate.

Singleton was, at first, rather shy of the acquaintance of one whom he knew to be a rival, though an unsuccessful one; and he was not entirely assured that the other had not enjoyed such a sufficient view of him on a previous and memorable occasion, when they were actually in conflict, as to recognise him through all his present disguises. But this doubt disappeared after they had been together for a little while; and, once relieved from this apprehension, our partisan freely opened himself to the advances of the other. Proctor was of a manly, frank, ingenuous nature, not unlike that of Singleton, though with less buoyancy of temper, and less ductility of mood. Though grave, and even gloomy at moments, as was natural to one in his present position of partial disgrace, the necessities of his nature led him to seek the society of a person who, like Singleton, won quickly upon the confidence. The young men rode or rambled together, and, in the space of forty-eight hours, they had unfolded to their mutual study quite enough of individual character, and much of each individual career, to feel the tacit force of an alliance which found its source in a readily-understood sympathy.

Youth is the season for generous confidences. It is then only that the heart seeks for its kindred, as if in a first and most necessary occupation. It was easy with our partisan to develop his proper nature, his moods, tastes, and impulses, without endangering his secret, or betraying any more of his history than might properly comport with his situation. And this was quite satisfactory to Proctor. It was enough for him that he found a generous and sympathizing spirit, who could appreciate his own and feel indignant at his humiliations; and he failed to discover that the revelations of Singleton were not of a sort to involve many details, or exhibit anything, indeed, of his outer and real life. He himself was less cautious. The volume of indignation, long swelling in his bosom, and restrained by constant contact with those only of whom he had just need to be suspicious, now poured itself forth freely in expression, to the great relief of his heart, when he found himself in the company of one whom he perceived to be genial as a man, and whose affinities, of a political sort, if they inclined him to the British cause, were yet but seldom productive of any social affinities between the parties. The provincials had been quite too long a subject of mock to the hirelings and agents of the crown, to respect them for anything but the power which they represented; and Proctor, who had long seen the error of the social policy of his countrymen, had always been among the few who had sought quite as much to conciliate as conquer. Still, the conversation of the two seemed studiously to forbear the subjects which were most interesting to both. They hovered about their favorite topics, and flew from them as eagerly as the lapwing from the nest which the enemy appears to seek.

It was at the close of the second day of their communion that the game was fairly started. The two dined with Cruden, and during the repast, the latter frequently dwelt upon Proctor's situation; the evident disposition of Balfour to destroy him, in spite of the ties of interest which had attached the uncle to himself; and the commissioner of confiscated estates finally lost himself in the bewildering conjectures by which he endeavored to account for the antipathy of the commandant. Singleton, of course, was a silent listener to all the conversation. It was one in which he did not feel himself justified in offering any opinions; but when Cruden had retired to his *siesta*—the afternoon being warm and oppressive—the two young men still lingered over their wine, and the conversation, freed from the restraining presence of one who could command their deference, but not their sympathies, at once assumed a character of greater freedom than before. Their hearts warmed to each other over the generous Madeira which had ripened for twenty years in the attic of "The Oaks," and all that was phlegmatic in the nature of Proctor melted before its influence and the genial tone of our partisan.

"You have heard my excellent uncle," he said, as he filled his beaker and passed the decanter to his companion. "He sees and avows his conviction that Balfour is preparing to destroy me, not through any demerits of mine, but in consequence of some secret cause of hostility; yet he says not a word of his readiness to take peril upon himself on my behalf, and is prepared, I perceive, to yield me to my fate—to suffer me to be disgraced for ever, rather than break with the selfish scoundrel whose alliance he finds profitable. One might almost doubt, from what he daily sees, if there be not something in the ties of kindred which makes most of the parties confound them with bonds, which the heart feels to be oppressive, because they are natural and proper. I have found it so always."

"Your indignation probably makes you unjust. Colonel Cruden evidently feels your situation seriously. The whole of his conversation to-day was devoted to it."

"Ay: but with how many reproaches intermingled, how many doubts as to the cause of offence which I have given, how many covert suspicions; all of which are meant to prepare the way to my abandonment. I see through his policy. I know him better than you. He would, no doubt, save me and help me, if he could do so without breaking with Balfour, or endangering his own interests; but he will take no risks of this or any sort. His whole counsel goes to persuade me to make my submission to Balfour—to follow his own example, and surrender my pride, my personal independence, and all that is precious to a noble nature, to a selfish necessity, whose highest impulses sound in pounds, shillings, and pence. This I can not and will not do, Furness. Let me perish first!"

"But how have you lost the favor of Balfour?"

"I never had it. I rose to my present rank in the army without his help. No one receives his succor without doing base service for it. I have withheld this service, and I presume this is one of the causes of his antipathy."

"Scarcely: or he would not have suffered you to hold position so long."

"There you mistake. As long as Cornwallis was in Charleston, or Clinton, I was secure. From the one I received the appointments and promotion which the other confirmed. Besides, Balfour needed some pretext before he could remove me, and time was necessary to mature this pretext. I am the victim of a conspiracy."

Proctor then proceeded to give a brief history of his career and command in Dorchester, and of that rescue of Colonel Walton at the place of execution, of which Singleton knew much more than himself.

"But this Captain Vaughan, of whom you have spoken," said Singleton, "what has prompted him to become the agent of Balfour in this business?"

"*Major* Vaughan!" retorted the other, bitterly. "He rises to my rank in the moment of my downfall. I am not sure that he is simply the agent of Balfour. I have reason to think that he has motives of hostility entirely his own. It might be a sufficient reason to suppose that to succeed to my place would be motive quite enough for a spirit at once base and ambitious. But, in the case of Vaughan, such a conjecture would not be entirely satisfactory. Vaughan really possesses character. He has courage, but without magnanimity. His pride, which is unrelieved by generosity, would perhaps discourage a baseness which had its root only in his desires to rise. Though ambitious enough, his ambition does not assume the character of a passion, and is anything but ardent and impetuous. Hate, perhaps—"

"Why should he hate you?"

"That is the question that I have vainly sought to answer. Yet I have the assurance that he *does* hate me with the most intense bitterness, and there is that in his deportment, during our whole intercourse, which tends to confirm this representation."

"From whom does your knowledge come on this subject?"

"Even that I cannot answer you. There is a mystery about it; but if you will go with me to my room, I will show you the sources of my information. Fill your glass—we have seen the bottom of the decanter, and I must drink no more. But if you—"

Singleton disclaimed any desire for a protracted sitting, and the two adjourned to Proctor's apartment. Here he produced from his trunk a packet of letters. From these he detached a couple of notes, delicately folded, and of small form, such as ladies chiefly delight to frame. These, according to their dates, he placed before the partisan.

"The first was received," he said, "a day before Vaughan was appointed to a post under me at Dorchester. Read it."

The note was brief, and ran thus:—

"Major Proctor will beware. In the person of Captain Vaughan he will find an enemy—a man who hates him, and who will seek or make occasion to do him evil. "A Friend.

" *Charleston,* May 10."

"Three weeks ago," said Proctor, "this followed it."
He himself read the second epistle, and then handed it to Singleton. Its contents were these:—

"Major Proctor has been heedless of himself. He has had the warning of one who knew his danger. He has not regarded it. The serpent has crept to his bosom. He is prepared to sting—perhaps his life, most certainly his honor. Let him still be vigilant, and something may yet be done for his security. But the enemy has obtained foothold; he has spread his snares; he is busy in them still. Captain Vaughan is in secret correspondence with Colonel Balfour; and Major Proctor is beloved by neither. Shall the warnings of a true friend and a devoted faith be uttered in his ears in vain?"

"These are in a female hand," said Singleton.

"Yes; but that does not prove them to be written by a female."

"Not commonly, I grant you; but in this instance I have no question that these notes were penned by a woman. The characters are natural, and such as men can not easily imitate. They betray a deep and loyal interest. It is evident that the heart speaks here in the letters, even if not in the language. That they are slightly disguised, is in proof only of what I say; since the disguise is still a feminine one. Have you no suspicion?"

"None."

"What says Colonel Cruden?"

"Would I show them to him? No—no! He could not comprehend the feeling which would make me, though I know nothing of the writer, shrink and blush to hear them ridiculed."

Singleton mused in silence for a while. Proctor continued:

"I have no sort of clew to the writer. I can form no conjectures. I know no handwriting which this resembles. I have racked my brain with fruitless guesses."

"Have you no female acquaintance in the city by whom they might have been written?"

"None," answered the major, somowhat hastily. "I formed few intimates in Charleston. The rebel ladies would have nothing to say to us, and the others did not seem to me particularly attractive."

"But you were in society?"

"But little : a few parties at private houses, a public ball of Cornwallis's, and some others, in which I walked the rooms rather as a spectator than as a guest. I am quite too earnest a man to feel much at home in mixed assemblages."

Singleton mused before he rejoined—

"You have, I should say, made more impression than you think for. These notes, I am confident, were written by a female. She is evidently warmly interested in your safety and success. She is apparently familiar with the affairs of Balfour, even those which are most secret; and that she has not conjectured idly, is proved by the correct result of her suggestions. You have verified the truth of her warnings. She is evidently, as she styles herself, a friend. The friendship of women means always something more than friendship. Her sympathies belong to the impulses, rather than the thoughts; to the policy or necessities, rather than the tastes of the individual : though these are necessarily a part of the influences which govern the policy. In plain terms, Proctor, you have made a conquest without knowing it."

"Scarcely. I can think of no one."

"That only proves that the lady has been less successful than yourself, and that your vanity has not been actively at work while you lounged through the fair assemblies of the city. But this aside. In the facts I have enumerated, are probably to be found all the clews to your mysterious informant. She is a woman; she has some mode of reaching the secrets of Balfour, and of fathoming the secret hostility which she evidently indicates as personal on the part of Vaughan. With these clews, can you make no progress?"

"None. I have invariably gone upon the presumption that the writer was of the masculine gender. I am not sure that I

should be nigher to a discovery were I to adopt your notion of
the other. And yet, the secrets of Balfour are much more
likely to be fathomed by a woman than a man. His character,
among the sex, you know; and there are some in Charleston
who have considerable power over him. But, woman or man,
the writer of these billets has spoken the words of sober truth.
I have experienced the importance of her warnings, and may
realize the fruits which she predicts and fears. The hate of
this man, Vaughan, has been long apparent to me. How he
works is the problem which I have yet to fathom. There is
one thing, however, which is certain, that I now feel for him as
fervent a hate as he can possibly entertain for me. There are
some passages already between us of an open character, of
which I can take notice; and, though our acquaintance is so
recent, I know no one upon whom I can more properly rely
than yourself to bring about an issue between us."

"A personal one?"

"Surely! The feeling that separates us once understood, I
am for an open rupture and the last extreme. I can not consent
daily to meet the man who hates, and who labors to destroy me,
wearing a pacific aspect, and forbearing the expression of that
hostility which is all the time working in my soul. Colonel
Cruden will leave 'The Oaks' in three days. I will linger behind him; and, if you will bear my message to Major Vaughan,
I shall consider it one of those acts of friendship to be remembered always."

"He will scarce accept your challenge now. His duties will
justify him in denying you."

"Perhaps; but for a season only. At all events, I shall have
relieved my breast of that which oppresses it. I shall have
declared my scorn and hate of my enemy. I shall have flung
in his teeth my gauntlet of defiance, and declared the only terms
which can in future exist between us. You will bear my message, Furness?"

"My dear Proctor, I am but a provincial captain of loyalists,
one whom your regular soldiery are but too apt to despise. Will
it not somewhat hurt your cause to employ me as your friend in

such a matter? Were it not better to seek some friend among your own countrymen in the garrison?"

"Do not desert—do not deny me!" exclaimed the young man, warmly and mournfully. "I have no friend in the garrison. It is filled with the tools of Balfour, or the tools of others; and scarcely one of them would venture, in the fear of the commandant's future hostility, to bear my message to his creature. I am alone! You see, my own kinsman prepares to abandon my cause at the first decent opportunity. Do not *you* abandon me. I have been won to you as I have been won to few men whom I have ever met. I have opened to you the full secrets of my heart. Say to me, Furness, that you will do me this service. Let me not think that I can not, on the whole broad face of God's earth, summon one generous spirit to my succor in this hour of my extremity."

"I will be your friend, Proctor; I will stand by you in the struggle, and see you through this difficulty," was the warm effusion of Singleton as he grasped the hand of his companion. "I take for granted that Vaughan cannot fight you while in command at Dorchester; but I concur with you that the more manly course is to let him understand at once the terms between you, and obtain from him a pledge to give you notice whenever he shall be at liberty to afford you redress. I will ride over to Dorchester to-morrow."

"Here's my hand, Furness; I have no spoken thanks. But you have lessened wondrously the sense of isolation here at my heart. I shall love you for this warmth and willingness for ever;" and he wrung the hand which he grasped with a passion almost convulsive.

He might well do so. He little knew the extent of the concession which had been made him; how many old and not quite dead and buried jealousies had to be overcome; nor in what various involvements the pliancy of the unsuspected American partisan might subject the counterfeit loyalist. Had he known! But he had no suspicions, and he now gave way to a buoyancy of mood that seemed to make him forgetful of all enemies.

"We must have a bumper together, my friend! What say you? Come! To the hall, once more; and then, if you please, for a canter. There are some lively drives in this neighborhood among these glorious old oaks, which I fear I shall seldom take again with the feelings and the hopes which possessed me once. You saw Miss Walton yesterday?"

The question was put abruptly. The blood suddenly flushed the face of the partisan; but he answered promptly and innocently —

"Oh yes; I saw her."

"A most noble creature! Ah, Furness, that is a woman whom a man might love and feel his dignity ennobled rather than depressed; and it should be properly the nature of the marriage tie always to produce such effects. But come! She is not for us, I fear, my dear fellow."

Singleton did not venture to answer; but he could not quite suppress the smile which would gleam out in his eyes and quiver on his lips, faintly, like an evening sunbeam on the leaves. It escaped the observation of his companion, who, putting his arm affectionately through that of his newly-found friend, hurried him back to the dining-room. They did not resume their seats at the table; but filled their glasses at the sideboard, and were just about to drink, when the trampling of a horse's feet was heard suddenly at the entrance. The door was opened a moment after, and who should appear before them but the identical Major Vaughan who had so greatly formed the subject of their recent deliberations.

CHAPTER XII.

THE BLADES CROSS.

THE parties did not readily distinguish each other. The window blinds had been drawn, to shut out the fierce glare of the evening sun, and the room was in that partial darkness which rendered objects doubtful except by a near approach. It was was only when Vaughan had advanced into the centre of the room, and within a few steps of the spot where Proctor stood, his glass still raised in his hand, but drained of its contents, that the latter perceived his enemy. To fling the goblet down upon the sideboard, and rapidly to confront the visiter, was with Proctor the work of an instant. His movements were quite too quick to suffer Singleton to interpose ; and, not having yet discovered who the stranger was, he did not in the slightest degree anticipate the movements or suspect the feelings of his companion. Nor was he aware, until this moment, that the Madeira which Proctor had drunk was rather more than his brain could well endure.

In those days, every man claiming the respect of his neighbors for even an ordinary amount of manhood, was supposed to be equal to almost any excess in drinking. Our young friends had, perhaps, really indulged to no excess beyond the more moderate practice of present times. Singleton, in fact, was as clear-headed and as cool at this moment as at any period of his life. He had drunk but little ; and though Proctor might have gone somewhat beyond him, the quantity taken by both would probably not have annoyed any veteran. But Proctor was one of those persons who suddenly fall a victim ; who will be perfectly sober, apparently, at one moment, and in the very next will show themselves unmanageable. Not knowing this, and not suspecting the cháracter of the new-comer, Singleton beheld the sudden movement of his companion without the slightest apprehension of the consequences. He was not left long in doubt upon either subject. In the twinkling of an eye, Proctor had confronted his enemy. Their persons were almost in contact— Vaughan drawing himself up quietly, but not recoiling, as Proctor approached him. The salutation of the latter, as well as his action, was of a sort to warn him of the open hostility which was henceforth to exist between them.

"You are come, sir! Oh! you are welcome! You come at the right moment! We have just been talking of you."

"I am honored, sir," was the cold response.

"Never a truer word from a false tongue?" was the savage reply.

"False!" exclaimed Vaughan; "false, sir!"

"Ay, ay, sir; false—false! I have said it, Captain Vaughan —pardon me, *Major* Vaughan. It were scarcely fair to deny you the price of your treachery. Judas *did* receive his thirty pieces of silver; and you have your promotion and the post of Dorchester. Major Vaughan, you are a scoundrel!"

Vaughan grew black in the face, and clapped his hand upon his sword. By this time, Singleton interposed.

"You are drunk," said Vaughan, very coolly, releasing the weapon from his grasp.

"Drunk!" was the furious response of Proctor; and the utmost efforts of Singleton could scarcely keep him, though totally unarmed, from taking his enemy by the throat.

"Drunk! By heavens, you shall answer for this among your other offences!"

"I am ready to do so at the proper season," said the other; "but it will be for me to determine when that season shall be. At present, I am on a duty which forbids that I prefer my personal affair to that of my sovereign. I would see Colonel Cruden."

"How many scoundrels shelter themselves from danger by that plea of duty! You come to see Colonel Cruden! You shall see him, must dutiful subject of a most generous sovereign;

but you shall first see me. You know me, Major Vaughan; you know that I am not one to be put off in the just pursuit of my redress. Do you deny, sir, that you have wronged me — that you have defamed me to our superiors — that you have secretly lied away my fame? Speak! Do you deny these things? And if you deny not, are you prepared to atone?"

"I have no answer for you, sir. You are not in a condition to merit or to understand an answer."

Singleton interposed.

"That *may* be true, Major Vaughan. My friend Major Proctor has suffered his indignation to get the better of his caution; but I believe that I am calm, sir; and, as he has confided to me, as his friend, the cause of his complaint against you, let me entreat you to a moment's private conference with me. Proctor, leave us for a little while. Go to your chamber. I will see to this business. Leave it in my hands."

Casting a wolfish glance at his enemy, Proctor, after a moment's hesitation, prepared to obey the suggestion of his friend; and had already half crossed the apartment in the direction of his chamber, when the reply of Vaughan to Singleton recalled him.

"And pray, sir, who are you?" was the inquiry of the British officer, in tones of the coolest insolence.

Singleton felt the sudden flush upon his face; but he had his faculties under rare command.

"I am one, sir, quite too obscure to hope that my name has ever reached the ears of Major Vaughan; but in the absence of other distinctions, permit me to say that my claims to his attention are founded upon an honorable, though obscure position, and a tolerable appreciation of what belongs to a gentleman. I am known, sir, as Captain Furness, of the loyalists."

"It is certainly something new that a British officer should seek his friend in a provincial. It would seem to argue something in his own position which denied him a proper agent among his own rank and order. But you will excuse me, Captain Furness, of the loyalists, if I refuse to listen to you in your present capacity. I need not inform a gentleman of so much experience as yourself that, charged as I am with the duties of the post of

Dorchester, I cannot so far forget myself as to suffer my personal affairs to take the place of those of my sovereign. What I may do or undertake hereafter, how far I may be persuaded to listen to the demands of Major Proctor, made in a different manner and under other circumstances, must be left to my own decision. For the present, sir, I must decline your civilities as well as his. Suffer me to leave you, if you please."

The whole manner of Vaughan was insupportably offensive, to say nothing of his language, which indirectly reflected upon the provincial character in a way to render Singleton almost as angry as Proctor. He inwardly resolved that the insolent Briton should answer to himself hereafter ; but with a strong will he restrained any ebullition of feeling, and put upon his temper a curb as severe as that with which Vaughan evidently subdued his own. He felt that, dealing with one who was clearly quite as dextrous as cool, nothing but the exercise of all his phlegm could possibly prevent the enemy from increasing the advantage which the wild passions of Proctor had already afforded him. His reply, accordingly, was carefully measured to contain just as much bitterness and sting as was consistent with the utmost deliberateness and calm of mood.

"Were you as solicitous, Major Vaughan, to forbear offence as you evidently are to avoid responsibility, I might give you credit for a degree of Christian charity which one scarcely concedes to a British soldier."

"Sir !"

"Suffer me to proceed. In affairs of honor, if I sufficiently understand the rules which regulate them, it is a new ground of objection which urges a provincial birthplace as an argument against the employment of a friend. The truly brave man, anxious to do justice and accord the desired redress, makes as few objections as possible to the mere auxiliaries in the combat. What you have said sneeringly in regard to our poor provincials, was either said by way of excusing yourself from the combat on the score of something disparaging in the relation between my principal and myself, or——"

"By no means," replied the other, quickly. "I am certainly willing to admit that a principal may employ whom he pleases, so that he be one to whom the social world makes no objection."

" On one point you have relieved me," replied Singleton quietly ; " but there is another. I was about to say that your language, in reference, to the employment of a provincial as his friend by my principal, was either meant to evade the conflict——"

" Which I deny."

" Or was designed as a gratuitous sarcasm upon the class of people to whom I have the honor to belong."

Vaughan was evidently annoyed. Singleton's cool, deliberate mode of speaking was itself an annoyance ; and the horns of the dilemma, one of which he had evaded without anticipating the other, left him without an alternative. Proctor, meanwhile, had hung about the parties, occasionally muttering some savage commentary upon the dialogue ; but, with a returning consciousness of propriety, without seeking to take any part in it. When, however, the conversation had reached the point to which Singleton had brought it, he could not forbear the remark—

" Something of a dilemma, I should think—the horns equally sharp, and the space between quite too narrow for the escape of a very great man. A poor devil might squeeze through, and nobody note the manner of his escape; but for your swollen dignitaries, your people who read Plutarch, and, ambitious like the son of Ammon, refuse the contest unless kings are to be competitors, escape from such horns is next to impossible, unless by a sudden shrinking of the mushroom dignities. Furness, why were you born a buckskin ?"

The fierce dark eyes of Vaughan, now singularly contracted by the closing of the brows above, were turned slowly and vindictively upon the speaker, the change in whose proceedings, tone, and manner, had been singularly great in the space of a few minutes. It would seem as if Proctor, now conscious of having blundered by his previous loss of temper, had by a resolute effort, subdued his passion into scorn, and substituted sarcasm for violence. At all events, the change was no less surprising to Singleton than to Vaughan, whose eyes now glanced from one to the other of the parties, with something of the expression of the wild boar about to be brought to bay. But he never lost

his composure. Indeed, he felt that it was his only security. Yet
his annoyance was not the less at the predicament to which Singleton had reduced him by his brief but sufficient examination
of his language. It would have been the shortest way to have
boldly defied his new assailant, to have continued to deal in the
language of scorn and sarcasm, and shelter himself under the
habitual estimate which the British made of the native loyalists;
but there were several reasons why he should not venture on
this course. To deal in the language of violence and defiance,
while pleading duty against the dangerous issues which it involved, was too manifest an inconsistency; and, at this juncture,
tutored by frequent and severe experience, to say nothing of the
necessities of the British cause, the positive instructions of the
royal commanders everywhere were to conciliate, by all possible
means, the sympathies and affections of such of the natives as
had shown, or were likely to show, their loyalty. Vaughan felt
the difficulties of his situation, which his pride of stomach necessarily increased. He found it easier to evade than to answer
the supposed loyalist.

"I see, sir, that your object is to force a quarrel upon me, at
the very moment when I tell you that the service of his majesty
denies that I shall answer your demands."

"Did I not tell you what an unprincipled knave it was?" said
Proctor.

"You are scarcely ingenuous, Major Vaughan," was the reply
of Singleton; "and I forbear now what I should say, and what
I will take occasion to say hereafter, in regard to the responsibilities which you plead. My *own* account with you must be
left to future adjustment; but, in this affair of my friend, you
can, at all events, leave us to hope that you will seek an early
period to give him the interview which you now deny. We accept your plea of *present* duty. We are willing to acknowledge
its force; and all that we now ask is that you give us your
pledge to answer to his requisition at the earliest possible moment."

"I will not be bullied, sir, into any promises," was the brutal
yet deliberate reply.

"Bullied, sir!" exclaimed Singleton.

"Ay, sir; I say bullied! I am here set upon by two of you, when I have no friend present, and at a moment which finds me unprepared; and will not be forced into pledges which it may be a large concession of my dignity and character to keep hereafter. Were I to consent to such a requisition as your principal makes, I should be only affording him an opportunity of bolstering up, at my expense, a reputation which is scarcely such, at this moment, as to deserve my attention. It will be——"

"Do you hear the scoundrel!" was the furious interposition of Proctor. "There is but one way, Furness, with a knave like this! Coward!" he cried, springing upon the other as he spoke, "if your sword will not protect your plumage, the subject of my reputation is out of place upon your lips!"

With these words, with a single movement, he tore the epaulet from the shoulders of his enemy. In an instant the weapon of Vaughan flashed in the air, and, almost in the same moment, Proctor tore down his own sword, which, with that of Singleton, was hanging upon the wall. The blades crossed with the rapidity of lightning, and, before our partisan could interfere, that of Vaughan had drawn blood from the arm of his opponent. Goaded as he had been, the commander of the post at Dorchester was still much the cooler of the combatants. His coolness was constitutional, and gave him a decided advantage over his more impetuous assailant.

But they were not permitted to finish as they had begun. In another moment, Colonel Cruden rushed into the apartment, still enveloped in his dressing-gown, but with his drawn sword in his hand. In the same instant, having possessed himself of his own weapon, Singleton beat down those of the combatants, and passed between them with the action and attitude of a master.

"How now!" cried Cruden, "would you butcher an officer of his majesty in my very presence? Two of you upon a single man!"

"You see!" said Vaughan, with bitter emphasis.

"You have lied!" was the instant, but quietly stern whisper of Singleton in his ears. The other started slightly, and his lips were closely compressed together.

"You show yourself too soon, my uncle," cried Proctor; "we

were engaged in the prettiest *passa-témpo*. I was teaching our young friend here, the new major in command at Dorchester, a new *stoccáta*, which is particularly important, by way of finish to his other accomplishments. You will admit that one so expert in stabbing with tongue and pen ought not to be wanting in the nobler weapon whose use may at least atone for the abuse of his other instruments."

"I will admit nothing! You are a rash young man, headstrong, and bent on your own ruin. I would have saved you in spite of yourself. But this conduct is too outrageous. This assault upon my guest, and a royal officer in the prosecution of his duties, cannot be passed over. I abandon you to your fate!"

"Said I not, Furness? The very words! I saw it all. Nevertheless, my uncle, you owe me thanks for so soon affording you an opportunity of satisfying your desire, and accomplishing your purpose."

"What purpose?"

"That of abandoning me to my fate."

"Go to! You are mad. Captain Furness, why do I see you in this quarrel?"

"You do *not* see me in this quarrel, Colonel Cruden, except as a mediator. My sword was only drawn to beat down their opposing weapons; though Major Vaughan, it seems, counselled perhaps only by his apprehensions, would make it appear that I was drawn against him."

Vaughan contented himself with giving Singleton a single look, in which malignity contended on equal terms with scorn and indifference. But the latter feelings were rather expressed than felt. The young men knew each other as enemies.

"Let me hear no more of this matter, gentlemen. As for you, John"—to Proctor—"this last outrage compels me to tell you that I will countenance you in none of your excesses. Do not look for my support or protection. That you should have broken through all restraints of reason, at the very moment when your friends were most anxiously revolving in what mode to save you from former errors, is most shameful and astonishing. I give you up. There is no saving one who is bent on destroying himself."

"Nay, uncle, do not sacrifice yourself in my behalf. I well know how ready you have been to do so on all previous occasions. Make no further sacrifice, I pray you. And pray entreat my friends not to suffer their anxieties to make them pale on my account. I would not have them lose an hour of sleep, however much I suffer. See to it, uncle: will yon? I am more concerned in respect to yourself than any of the rest."

"Come with me, Major Vaughan. These young men have been drinking. Let that be their excuse."

The two left the room together.

"Friends! Oh, friends!—excellent friends! Ha! ha! ha!"

The excited mood of Proctor spoke out in the bitterest mockery. Singleton remembered what he had said before on the subject of his uncle's selfishness, and his own isolation. He understood all the secret anguish that was preying on a generous nature in a false position, and denied all just sympathies. He felt too warmly for the sufferer not to forgive the rashness to which his secret sufferings had goaded him.

"Proctor, you bleed."

"Do I? Where?"

"In your arm."

"Is it possible I was hit? I never felt it."

"You would scarcely have felt it had the sword gone through your heart."

"I almost wish it had, Furness! The wound is there, nevertheless."

"Nay, nay! that will heal. Let me see to the arm. Experience and necessity have made me something of a surgeon."

With tenderness, and not a little skill, Singleton dressed the wound, which was slight, though it bled quite freely. This done, he said—

"Proctor, this man is more than a match for you."

"What! at the small-sword?"

"No; in point of temper. He is cool-headed and cold-hearted. His nerves are not easily shaken, and he has his blood under excellent command. He will always foil you— he will finally conquer in the struggle—unless you put yourself under a more severe training than any to which you have ever

subjected yourself. You will have to learn the lesson to subdue
yourself to your necessities. Till a man does this, he can do
nothing. I can readily conjecture that the subtlety of this man
has, in some way, enmeshed you. I have no doubt that you
are in his snares; and I foresee that, like a spider, confident in
the strength of his web, he will lie *perdu* until you exhaust
yourself in vain struggles, and when fairly exhausted and at his
mercy, he will then administer the *coup de grace.*"

"What! are you my friend, yet paint me such a humiliating
picture!"

"It is because I am your friend, and deeply sympathize with
you, that I have drawn this picture. It is necessary to make
you shudder at what you may reasonably apprehend, or you
will never learn the most important of all lessons in such a conflict—not to shrink or startle because you suffer; not to speak
out in passion because you feel; and never to show your weapon until you are fully prepared to strike. The subtlest scheme
of villany may be foiled, if we only bide our time, keep our
temper, and use the best wits that God has given us. For villany has always some weak place in its web. Find out *that*,
and there will be little difficulty in breaking through it. Do
you believe me?—do you understand me?"

"Ah, Furness! I would I had such a friend as you in the
city. It is there that the struggle must be renewed."

"I have a friend there, to whom I will commend you; a rare
person, and an old one. But of this hereafter. It is not too
late for our proposed canter. Let us ride, if for an hour only,
and get ourselves cool."

CHAPTER XIII.

SCOUTING AND SENTIMENT.

THE two friends rode together for an hour or more, until the night came down and counselled their return. They pursued the great road below, leading down the Ashley, and unfolding, at every mile in their progress, the noble avenues of oak conducting to those numerous stately abodes along the river, which rendered it, in that day, one of the most remarkable spots for wealth and civilization which was known in the whole country. Some of these places were still held by their owners, who had temporized with the invader, or, being females or orphans, had escaped his exactions. Others, like "the Oaks," were in the hands of the sequestrator, and managed by his agents. The mood of Proctor did not suffer him to pay much regard to the prospect, though, under auspices more grateful to his feelings, he had felt it a thousand times before. He had ridden along this very road in company with Katharine Walton, at a period when his heart fondly entertained a hope that he might find some answering sympathy in hers. He had been painfully disabused of this hope, in the conviction that she was now betrothed irrevocably to another; but his mind, which was in that state when it seems to find a melancholy pleasure in brooding upon its disappointments, now reverted to this among the rest.

"I am a fated person, Furness. You have heard of men whom the world seems solicitous to thwart; whom Fortune goes out of her way to disappoint and afflict; who fall for ever just when they appear to rise, and who drink bitter from the cup in which they fancy that nothing but sweets have been allowed to mingle? I belong to that peculiar family!"

"Pardon me, Proctor, but I have little faith in this doctrine of predestination. That Fortune distributes her favors unequally, I can understand and believe. This is inevitable, from the condition of the race, from its very necessities, which make it important to the safety and progress of all that all should not be equally favored; and from those obvious discrepancies and faults in training and education, which move men to persevere in a conflict with their own advantages. But that Fortune takes a malicious pleasure in seeking out her victims, and defeating perversely the best plans of wisdom and endeavor, I am not ready to believe. In your case, I really see no occasion for such a notion. Here, while still a very young man, you have attained a very high rank in the British army—an institution notoriously hostile to sudden rise, or promotion, unless by favor."

"And to what has it conducted me?" said the other, abruptly breaking in. "To comparative discredit; to temporary overthrow; and possibly, future shame. Certainly to an obscuration of hope and fortune."

"Let us hope not—let us try that such shall not be the case. This despondency of mood is really the worst feature in your affairs."

"Ah, you know not all! I hope to struggle through this affair of Dorchester. On that subject you have warned me to an effort which I had otherwise been scarcely prepared to make; and you have shown me clews which I shall pursue quite as much from curiosity as from any other feeling. If this affair were all! I asked you if you had seen Miss Walton? You will not be surprised to hear me say that I loved her from the first moment when I beheld her. I do not know that it will occasion any surprise when I tell you that I loved in vain."

It did *not ;* but of this Singleton said nothing.

"Pride, ambition, fortune, love, all baffled! Do you doubt that Fate has chosen me out as one of those victims upon whom she is pleased to exercise her experiments in malice? Yet all shone and seemed so promising at first."

"But you are still at the beginning of the chapter, my dear fellow. Your life has scarce begun. The way is a long one yet before you. It will be strange, indeed, if it should long continue clouded. You will recover position. You will detect and expose this Vaughan, and be restored to that rank in the army which you so eminently deserve. I say nothing of your *affaire de cœur*. The subject is, at all times, a delicate one. But is it so certain that your prospects with Miss Walton are entirely hopeless ?"

The curiosity which Singleton expressed in his latter question is not without its apology. It would seem to be natural enough to a lover, whatever might be his own certainties on the score of his affections.

" On that subject say no more. She is betrothed to another. More than that, she truly loves him. It is not a passion of the day when the young heart, needing an object about which to expand, rather seeks than selects a favorite. She has made her choice deliberately, bringing her mind to co-operate with her heart, and her attachment is inflexible. This I know. She is a remarkable woman. Not a woman in the ordinary sense of the term. Not one of the class who readily reconcile themselves to events, who can accommodate their affections to their condition, and expend just so much of them upon their object as to maintain external appearances. Her heart goes thoroughly with her decision, and her will only follows her affections. But I tire you. You cannot feel greatly interested in one whom you so little know."

" But I *am* interested in the character you describe. More than that, I am interested in *you*. Follow your bent, and suppose me a willing listener."

" Nay, on this subject I will say no more. It is one which has its annoyances. My admiration of Miss Walton only makes me feel how greatly I have been a loser, and gives such an edge to my despondencies as to make me resigned to almost any fate. But you spoke of the army, and of my restoration to rank. On this point let me undeceive you. I have no longer any military ambition. The recovery of position is only important to me as a recovery of reputation. The stain taken from my name, and I sheathe my sword for ever. I am sick of war and bloodshed—particularly sick of *this* war, which I am ashamed of, and the favorable result of which I deem hopeless."

"Ha! how?   Do you mean to the royal arms?"

"You are surprised.   But such is even my thought.   Great
Britain is destined to lose her colonies.   She is already almost
exhausted in the contest.   Her resources are consumed.   Her
debt is enormous.   Her expenses are hourly increasing.   She
can get no more subsidies of men from Germany, and her Irish
recruits desert her almost as soon as they reach America.   Her
ministers would have abandoned the cause before this, but for
the encouragement held out by the native loyalists."

"And they have taken up arms for the crown, only because
they believed the cause of the colonies hopeless against the
overwhelming power of the mother-country.   Could they hold
with you in our interior, the British cause would find no advo-
cates."

"They will hold with me as soon as the foreign supplies
cease.   Already they begin to perceive that they themselves
form the best fighting materials of our armies."

"Fighting with halters about their necks."

"Precisely; but the moment they discover fully our weakness, they will make terms with the Revolutionary party, which
will only be too ready to receive them into its ranks.   I foresee
all that is to happen, and the British ministry sees it also.
Nothing but pride of stomach keeps them even now from those
concessions which will prove inevitable in another campaign.
They must have seen the hopelessness of the cause the moment
that they found no party sufficiently strong, in any of the colonies, to control the progress of the movement.   No people can
be conquered by another, three thousand miles removed from
the seat of action, so long as they themselves resolutely *will* to
continue the conflict.   The vast tract of sea which spreads between this country and Europe, is itself sufficient security.   To
transport troops, arms, and provisions, across this tract is, in
each instance, equivalent to the loss of a battle.   There is no
struggle which could prove more exhausting in the end."

"You hold forth but poor encouragement to our loyalist
brethren," said Singleton, with a smile scarcely suppressed.

"Hear me, Furness; I would say or do nothing which could
injure the service in which I have hitherto drawn the sword.

My own loyalty, I trust, will always be unimpeachable; but, my friend, the regard which I feel for you prompts me to wish, for your own sake, that you had drawn the sword with your people rather than against them. The American loyalists must and will be abandoned to their fate. They will be the greatest losers in the contest. They will forfeit their homes, and their memories will be stained with reproach to the most distant periods. It is, perhaps, fortunate for them, as tending to lessen this reproach in the minds of all just persons, that the greater number of them, particularly in these southern colonies, are native Britons. It was natural that they should side with their natural sovereign. But, for the *natives* of the soil, there can be no such excuse. Abandoned by Great Britain, they will be doomed to an exile which will lack the consolations of those who can plead for their course, all the affinities of birth, and all the obligations of subjects born within the shadow of the throne. I would to God, for your sake, that you had been a foreigner, or had never drawn weapon against your people!"

How Singleton longed to grasp the hand of the speaker, and unfold to him the truth. But his secret was too precious to hazard, even in the hands of friendship; and quite too much depended on his present concealment to suffer him to give way to the honest impulse which would have relieved him of all discredit in the eyes of his companion.

"You have placed the subject under new lights before my eyes," was his answer. "It is something to be thought upon. That the British power has been weakened, that its capacity for conquest is greatly lessened, I have already seen; but I had no thought that such opinions were generally prevalent in your army."

"Nor do I say that they are. You will scarcely get Balfour to think as I do, even when the orders reach him for the evacuation of Charleston; and as for my excellent uncle, so long as his charge of confiscated estates increases, he will fancy that the game is just what it should be. But, to my mind, the event is inevitable. These colonies of Carolina and Georgia may be cut off from the confederacy; but even this estrangement must be temporary only. They, too, will be abandoned after a brief

experiment, and the independence of America will be finally
and fully acknowledged. The war must have ceased long ago,
and after a single campaign only, had it not been begun pre-
maturely by the Americans. The colonies were not quite ready
for the struggle. In a single decade more, the fruits would have
been quite ripe; and it would only have required a single shaking of the tree. Then they would not have needed a French
alliance. The native population would have been so greatly in
the ascendant, that the foreign settlers would not have dreamed
of any opposition to the movement."

"Our loyalists, according to your notions, have shown themselves unwise; but their fidelity, you will admit, is a redeeming
something, which ought to secure them honorable conditions and
against reproach."

"I am not so sure of that. The true loyalty is to the soil, or
rather to the race. I am persuaded that one is never more safe
in his principles than when he takes side with his kindred.
There is a virtue in the race which strengthens and secures our
own; and he is never more in danger of proving in the wrong
than when he resolutely opposes himself to the sentiments of his
people. At all events, one may reasonably distrust the virtue
in his principle when he finds himself called upon to sustain it
by actually drawing the sword against his kindred. But the
subject is one to distress you, Furness, and I have no wish to do
so. I have simply been prompted to speak thus plainly by the
interest I take in your fortunes. Were I you, I should seek
from Balfour an opportunity to exchange the service, and get a
transfer to some of the British regiments in the West Indies."

"I shall live and die on my native soil," said the other,
quickly. "If our cause fails I will perish with it."

"It *will* fail, Furness."

"Never! never!" was the emphatic reply.

"Let us change the subject," said the other. "Did you remark these pine woods as we passed them half an hour ago?
What a grateful and delicate tint they wore in the evening sun!
Can you conceive of anything more sombre than their gloomy
shadows, *now*, in the dusky folds of evening! They stand up
like so many melancholy spectres of glorious hopes which have

perished—gloomy memorials of joys and triumphs which the heart had dreamed in vain. Do you know that I could now, with a relish, penetrate these grim avenues, and lay myself down in the deepest part of the thicket, to muse, throughout the night, and night after night, with a sort of painful satisfaction!"

"I have mused and brooded under such shadows a thousand times, night and day, without a gloomy feeling—nay, with something of a joy that found its pleasure in due degree with the growth of its most melancholy emotions."

"The heart gives its character to the scene always. The genius of place is born always in the soul of the occupant. Mine is not a joyous spirit now, and I would embrace these shadows, if a thousand times more gloomy, as if they had been my kindred. But what is this that stirs? Ha! who goes there?"

At the challenge, a shadow dashed across the road; and Proctor, clapping spurs to his horse, with the old military feeling of suspicious watch and command, forced the animal forward in the direction of the fugitive; but he soon recoiled—with a sudden consciousness that he was totally unarmed—as he beheld, standing close by the road-side, and partly sheltered by a huge pine, the figure of a man with a musket already presented, and the eye of the stranger deliberately coursing along the barrel. At that moment, Singleton cried out—

"Hold up, my good fellow. Would you shoot us without giving the time of day?"

The stranger threw up his musket and brought the butt heavily upon the ground.

"There's no time of day," said he, with a chuckle, "when you are about to ride over a body."

The speaker came out from the shadow of the tree as he answered, with an air of unaffected confidence. He was dressed in the common blue homespun of the country; but his garments were of that mixed military and Indian character which denoted the forester or ranger of the period.

"Who are you?" demanded Proctor.

"My name's Futtrell, if that's what you want to know, and I'm from the Cypress. Have you seen, gentlemen, either on you, a stray sorrel nag, with a blaze in his face, and his left foreleg white up to his knees? He's a right smart nag, and a little wild, that got off from the lot now two days ago; and was tracked down as far as Bacon's bridge, an thar we lost him."

This inquiry seemed to anticipate all questions; and, by this time, Proctor, remembering that he was no longer in command, felt no disposition to ask anything further. Having answered the question of the stranger in the negative, he was disposed to ride on; but by this time Mr. Futtrell was curiously examining the horse of Singleton.

"That's a mighty fine beast of yourn, stranger," he said, stroking the animal's neck and forelegs.

"You wouldn't like to buy him?" said Singleton, good-humoredly.

"That I should, stranger," replied the other, "if buying a horse meant taking him with a promise to pay when the skies should rain golden guineas."

"We are in danger of no such shower for some time to come, or from any quarter," said Proctor. "Let us ride, Furness."

And, as he spoke, the steed of the speaker went slowly ahead. At this moment, the stranger seized his opportunity to thrust a scrap of paper into the hands of Singleton, who stooped down to him and whispered a single sentence; then rode away to join his companion, who had perceived none of these movements.

"Dang it!" muttered Futtrell, looking after the two, "our colonel's just as full of stratagems as an egg's full of meat. Proctor was always reckoned a real keen fellow for an Englishman, yet the colonel goes into him as if he had a key for all the doors in his heart. Well, we shall know all about it, I reckon, before the night's over."

With these words, the stranger disappeared within the shadows of the wood, which, from this point, spread away, in unbroken depth and density, to the west — a continuous wall of thicket almost encircling the plantation of Colonel Walton, and forming a portion only of his extensive domain. The spot where our companions encountered Futtrell was scarcely half a mile from the mansion-house. The two former, meanwhile, made their way to "The Oaks" without further interruption.

When they reached the entrance of the dwelling, it was found that the servant of Major Proctor was not present, as was his custom, to receive his master's horse. A negro came forward and took that of Singleton.

Proctor was impatient, and began to clamor loudly for his fellow; but the cry of "John—John! what ho! there—John!" had scarcely been sounded a second time, when the person summoned—a short, squat, sturdy Englishman, with a red face—made his appearance, in a run, out of breath, and seemingly somewhat agitated by his exhaustion or his apprehensions. Proctor did not perceive his discomposure, but contented himself with administering a sharp rebuke for his absence and neglect. Singleton's eye was drawn to the fellow, and something in his appearance rendered our partisan distrustful for a moment; but nothing was said, and he soon entered the dwelling with his companion.

Cruden was in waiting to receive them, and his manner was much more conciliatory and gracious than when they separated in the afternoon. He was governed by a policy, in this deportment, which will have its explanation hereafter. We need not bestow our attention upon the conversation which occupied the parties during the evening, as it was of that casual nature designed simply *pour passer le temps*, which need not employ ours. When Cruden retired, the young men were free to resume their conference, which, though it had regard to the subjects most interesting to them, and in some degree of interest to us, yet conducted to nothing more definite than we have already understood. They separated at a tolerably early hour, and Singleton retired to his chamber—but not to sleep. It will occasion no surprise when we find our partisan, at midnight, emerging stealthily from his apartment, and from the dwelling, and making his way secretly to the wood where he had encountered Futtrell. What he saw, whom he found, or what was done there, by himself or others, must be reserved for another chapter. We must not anticipate. It is sufficiently clear, however, that Singleton has not committed himself to the association with his enemies, without having friends at need, and within easy summons of his bugle.

6*

CHAPTER XIV

CAMP-FIRES.

WHEN General Greene was despatched to the south, after the defeat of Gates at Camden, to take charge of the southern army, he found himself in a region of the world so utterly different from everything in his previous experience, that he was fain to acknowledge himself bewildered by what he saw, if not at a loss as to what he should undertake. According to his letters, he was in a country in which a general was "never at any moment quite secure from a capital misfortune." The difficulty was certainly a bewildering one, particularly where the generalship was of that inflexible sort which could not readily accommodate its strategy to novel circumstances and conditions. This was the peculiar deficiency of Gates, who, for example, because he had achieved the capture of Burgoyne, in a hilly and rather densely-settled country, without the aid of cavalry, hurried to the conclusion that he was equally independent of such an arm in a perfectly level and sparsely-settled region, where, in truth, cavalry should have been his most necessary dependence. Greene was not so stubborn; but his genius was still too much lacking in flexibility. His embarrassment, in the scene of his new operations, arose from the immense forests, the impervious swamps by which they were relieved and intersected, and the wonderful security in which a lurking enemy might harbor, within sight of the very smokes of the camp, without being suspected of any such near neighborhood. This, which was particularly true of the region of country watered by the Pedee, the Congaree, the Santee, and other leading arteries of the interior, was, in a measure, true, also of the tracts lying along the Cooper and Ashley;

though portions of the lands which were watered by these streams had been, for a considerable space of time, under a high state of cultivation.

To those familiar with the country, even now, it will occasion no surprise to be told that the Carolina partisans were wont to penetrate with confidence between the several posts of the British throughout the colony, and to lie in wait for favorable opportunities of surprise and ambush, within the immediate vicinity of Charleston. A close thicket, a deep swamp skirting road or river, afforded, to a people familiar with these haunts, ample harborage even within five miles of the enemy's garrison; and the moment of danger found them quickly mounted on the fleetest steeds, and darting away in search of other places of refuge. We have seen with what audacity Colonel Walton ventured upon his own domain, though guarded by his foes, and under the very eye of the strong post of Dorchester. It will be easy to conceive that Singleton's troopers could find a secure place of hiding, indulging in a rational confidence, for days in this very neighborhood. Such was the case; and to one of these retreats we propose to conduct the reader, anticipating the approach of the commander of the party lying thus *perdu*.

About a mile west of the Ashley, and a few miles only below the British post at Dorchester, the explorer may even now penetrate to a little *bay*, or small bottom of drowned land, the growth of which, slightly interspersed with cypress and tupelo, is chiefly composed of that dwarf laurel called the *bay*, from which the spot, in the *parlance* of the country, derives its name. The immediate basin, or circuit of drowned land, retains to this moment its growth and verdure; but we look now in vain for the dense forest of oak, hickory, pine, ash, and other forest-trees, by which it was encircled, and under the shadows of which the partisans found their refuge in the days of the Revolution. These formed a venerable sanctuary for our foresters, and here, with an admirable *cordon* of videttes and sentries they made themselves secure against surprise, so long as they chose to keep their position. We need not describe the place more particularly. Most of our readers possess a sufficient general idea of the shadows and securities of such a spot; of its wild beauties, and the sweet

solemnity of its solitude. Let them take into view the near
neighborhood of streams and rivers, girdled by dense swamp
fastnesses, almost impenetrable, except by obscure and narrow
avenues, known only to the natives of the country, and they
will readily conceive the degree of security attainable by the
partisan warrior, who is alert in his movements, and exercises
an ordinary share of prudence and circumspection.

The spot which we now approach was quite familiar to the
party by whom it is occupied. Most of them were born in the
neighborhood, and accustomed from boyhood to traverse its
shadowy passages. This will account for the confidence which
they felt in making it their place of harborage, almost within
cannon shot of the fortress of the enemy. The squad which
Singleton had here placed in waiting was a small one, consisting
of twelve or fifteen persons only. At the hour when he left
" The Oaks" on foot, to visit them in their place of hiding, they
were in expectation of his coming. Futtrell had returned, and
apprized them of his whispered promise to that effect. A group
of gigantic oaks surrounded their bivouac, their great branches
glossily and always green, and draped with wide, waving streamers of venerable moss. The fires of the party were made up in
a hollow formed by the gradual sloping of the earth from three
several sides. This depression was chosen for the purpose, as
enabling them the better to conceal the flame which, otherwise,
gleaming through some broken places in the woods, might have
conducted the hostile eye to the place of refuge. In this hollow,
in sundry groups, were most of the party. Some sat or stood
engaged in various occupations. Some lay at length with their
feet to the fire, and their eyes, half shut, looking up at the green
branches, or the starlighted skies overhead. One might be seen
mending his bridle, close by the fire ; another was drawing the
bullet from his rifle, cleansing or burnishing it ; and others were
grouped, with heads together, in quiet discourse among themselves. Saddles lay close beneath the trees ; cloaks, and coats,
and bridles, depended from their branches ; and several blankets hung down from similar supports, the use of which was ob-
viously to assist in concealing the gleam of firelight from the
eyes of the stranger in the distance,

One object in this enumeration should not be suffered to escape our attention. This was a great pile of canes, or reeds, of which the river swamps and lowlands throughout the country furnished an abundance, and which two of the younger persons of the party were busy in trimming of their blades and plumes, fashioning them into arrows of a yard long, and seasoning in the warm ashes of the fire. Feathers of the eagle, the crane, the hawk, and common turkey, a goodly variety, indeed, were crowded into a basket between the lads thus employed. With these they fitted the shafts, when ready in other respects; and bits of wire, and nails of wrought iron, rounded and sharpened with a file, were, with considerable dexterity, fitted into the heads of the shafts. The employment afforded a commentary on the emergencies of our war of independence, though it is still a question, whether the implements of the Indian warrior did not possess some advantages over those of civilization, which tended to lessen greatly the disparity between the several weapons. Of this matter something will be learned hereafter. Sheaves of arrows already prepared for use, and rude bows, made of white oak and ash, might be seen placed away in safety beneath the trees, among other of the munitions of the encampment; all of which betokened a rude but ready regard to the exigencies of warfare.

At a little distance from these parties and their tools, and on the opposite side of the fire, was a group of four persons, of whom nothing has yet been said. These were busy in preparations of another sort. The carcass of a fine buck lay between them, and two of the party were already preparing to cut him up. One of these persons with arms bare to the elbows, flourished a monstrous *couteau de chasse,* with the twofold air of a hero and a butcher. This was a portly person of the most formidable dimensions, with an abdominal development that might well become an alderman. He had evidently a taste for the work before him. How he measured the brisket! how he felt for the fat! with what an air of satisfaction he heaved up the huge haunches of the beast! and how his little gray eyes twinkled through the voluminous and rosy masses of his own great cheeks!

"I give it up!" he exclaimed to his companions. "There is no wound except that of the arrow, and it has fairly passed through the body, and was broken by the fall. I give it up! I will believe anything wonderful that you may tell me. You may all lie to me in safety. I have no more doubts on any subject. Everything's possible, probable, true hereafter, that happens. But that you, such a miserable sapling of a fellow as you, Lance, should have sent this reed through such a beast — clean through — is enough to stagger any ordinary belief!"

The person addressed, a tall, slender lad, apparently not more than eighteen or nineteen, laughed good-naturedly, as, without other reply, he thrust forth his long, naked arm, and displayed, fold upon fold, the snaky ridges of his powerful muscles.

"Ay, I see you have the bone and sinew, and I suppose I must believe that you shot the deer, seeing that Barnett gives it up; but I suppose you were at butting distance. You had no occasion to draw bow at all. You used the arrow as a spear, and thrust it through the poor beast's vitals with the naked hand."

"Shot it, I swow, at full fifty-five yards distance! I stepped it off myself," was the reply of the person called Barnett.

"I give up! I will believe in any weapon that brings us such meat. Henceforth, boys, take your bows and arrows always. The Indian was a sensibler fellow than we gave him credit for. I never could have believed it till now; and when Singleton took it into his head to supply such weapons to our men, for the want of better, I thought him gone clean mad."

"Yet you heard his argument for it?" said Lance.

"No. I happen to hear nothing when I am hungry. I shouldn't hear you now, but for my astonishment, which got the better of my appetite for a few moments. I will hear nothing further. Use your knife, Lance; lay on, boy, and let's have a steak as soon as possible."

"Sha'n't we wait for the colonel?" said Lance.

"I wait for no colonels. I consider them when I consider the core *(corps)*. What a glorious creature! — fat an inch thick, and meat tender as a dove's bosom! Ah, I come back to the Cypress a new man! Here I am at home. The Santee did well enough; but there's a sweetness, a softness, a plumpness, a beauty about bird and beast along the Ashley, that you find in the same animals nowhere else. God bless my mother!"

" For what, in particular, lieutenant ?"

" That she chose it for my birthplace. I shouldn't have been half the man I am born anywhere else ; shouldn't have had such discriminating tastes, such a fine appetite, such a sense of the beautiful in nature."

And thus, talking and slashing, the corpulent speaker maintained the most unflagging industry, until the deer was fairly quartered, a portion transferred, in the shape of steaks, to the reeking coals, and the rest spread out upon a rude scaffolding to undergo the usual hunter-process of being cured, by smoking, for future use. The skin, meanwhile, was subjected to the careful cleansing and stretching of the successful hunter.

And then the whole party grouped themselves about the fire, each busy with his steak and hoe-cake. There was the rèdoubtable Lieutenant Porgy, and the youthful ensign, Lance Frampton, already known as the taker of the prey, and little Joey Barnett, and others, known briefly as Tom, Dick, and Harry ; and others still, with their *noms de guerre*, such as Hard-Riding Dick, and Dusky Sam, and Clip-the-Can, and Black Fox, and Gray Squirrel : a merry crew, cool, careless, good-humored, looking, for all the world, like a gipsy encampment. Their costume, weapons, occupation ; the wild and not ungraceful ease with which they threw their huge frames about the fire ; the fire, with its great, drowsy smokes slowly ascending, and with the capricious jets of wind sweeping it to and fro amidst the circle ; and the silent dogs, three in number, grouped at the feet of their masters, their great, bright eyes wistfully turned upward in momentary expectation of the fragment ; all contributed to a picture as unique as any one might have seen once in merry old England, or, to this day, among the Zincali of Iberia.

" Ah, this is life !" said Lieutenant Porgy, as he supplied himself anew with a smoking morsel from the hissing coals. " I can live in almost any situation in which man can live at all, and do not object to the feminine luxuries of city life, in lieu of a better ; but there is no meat like this, fresh from the coals, the owner of which hugged it to his living heart three hours ago. One feels free in the open air ; and, at midnight, under the trees, a venison steak is something more than meat. It is food for

thought. It provokes philosophy. My fancies rise. I could
spread my wings for flight. I could sing—I feel like it now—
and, so far as the will is concerned, I could make such music as
would bring the very dead to life."

And the deep, sonorous voice of the speaker began to rise,
and he would have launched out into some such music as the
buffalo might be supposed to send forth, happening upon a fresh
green flat of prairie, but that Lance Frampton interposed, in
evident apprehension of the consequences.

"Don't, lieutenant; remember we're not more than a mile
from the river road."

"Teach your grandmother to suck eggs! Am I a fool? Do
I look like the person to give the alarm to the enemy? Shut
up, lad, and be not presumptuous because you have shot a deer
after the Indian fashion. Do you suppose that, even were we
in safer quarters, I should attempt to sing with such a dry
throat? I say, Hard-Riding Dick, is there any of that Jamaica
in the jug?"

"It is a mere drop on a full stomach."

"Bring it forth. I like the savor of the jug."

And the jug was produced, and more than one calabash was
seen elevated in the firelight; and the drop sufficed, in not unequal division, to improve the humor of the whole party.

"The supper without the song is more endurable," was the
philosophy of Porgy, "than the song without the supper. With
the one before the other, the two go happily together. Now it
is the strangest thing in the world that, with such a desperate
desire to be musical, I should not be able to turn a tune. But
I can *act* a tune, my lads, as well as any of you; and, as we are
not permitted to give breath to our desires and delights, let us
play round as if we were singing. You shall observe me, and
take up the chorus, each. Do you understand me?"

"Can't say I do," said Futtrell. "Let's hear."

"You were always a dull dog, Futtrell, though you are a
singer. Now, look you, a good singer or a good talker, an orator
or a musician of any kind, if he knows his business, articulates
nothing, either in song or speech, that he does not *look*, even
while he speaks or sings. Eloquence, in oratory or in music,

implies something more than ordinary speech. It implies passion, or such sentiments and feelings as stir up the passions. Now every fool knows that, if we feel the passion, so as to speak or sing it, we must *look* it too. Do you understand me now ?"

" I think I do," was the slowly uttered response of Futtrell, looking dubiously.

" Very well. *I* take it that all the rest do, then, since you are about the dullest dog among us," was the complimentary rejoinder. " Now, then, I am going to sing. I will sing an original composition. I shall first begin by expressing anxiety, uneasiness, distress ; these are incipient signs of hunger, a pain- ful craving of the bowels, amounting to an absolute gnawing of the clamorous inhabitants within. This is the first part, continu- ed till it almost becomes despair ; the music then changes. I have seen the boys bringing in the deer. He lies beneath my knife. I am prepared to slaughter him. I feel that he is secure. I see that he will soon be broiling in choice bits upon the fire. I am no longer uneasy or apprehensive. The feeling of despair has passed. All is now hope, and exultation, and anticipation ; and this is the sentiment which I shall express in the second part of the music. The third follows the feast. Nature is paci- fied ; the young wolf-cubs within have retired to their kennels. They sleep without a dream, and a philosophical composure possesses the brain. I meditate themes of happiness. I specu- late upon the immortality of the soul. I enter into an analysis of the several philosophies of poets, prophets, and others, in relation to the employments and enjoyments of the future ; and my song subsides into a pleasant murmuring, a dreamy sort of ripple, such as is made by a mountain brooklet, when, after wearisome tumb- lings from crag to crag, it sinks at last into a quiet and barely lapsing watercourse, through a grove, the borders of which are crowded with flowers of the sweetest odor. Such, boys, shall be my song. You will note my action, and follow it, by way of chorus, as well as you can."

All professed to be at least willing to understand him, and our philosopher proceeded. Porgy was an actor. His social talent lay in the very sort of amusement which he now proposed to them. He has himself described the manner of his performance in the declared design. We shall not attempt to follow him; but may say that scarcely one of those wildly-clad foresters but became interested in his dumb show, which at length, became so animated that he leaped to his feet, in order the better to effect his action, and was only arrested in his performance by striding with his enormous bulk, set heavily down, upon the ribs of one of the unlucky dogs who lay by the fire. The yell that followed was as full of danger as the uttered song had been, and quite discomfited the performer. His indignation at the misplaced position of the dog might have resulted in the wilful application of his feet to the offending animal, but that, just then, the hootings of an owl were faintly heard rising in the distance, and answered by another voice more near.

"It is Moore," said Lance Frampton. "It is from above. We shall have the colonel here directly."

"Let him come," was the response of Porgy; but he is too late for the music. That confounded dog!"

CHAPTER XV.

WOODCRAFT.

THE object of the signal was rightly conjectured. It brought Singleton. Successive hoots of the owl—who was one of the scouts of the party—indicated the several points of watch by which the route from "The Oaks" to the place of refuge had been guarded; and our partisan had no reason to complain, among his people, of any neglect of duty. He was received with the frank welcome of those who regarded him with equal deference and affection, as a friend and comrade no less than a superior. Lance Frampton seized his extended hand with the fondness of a younger brother; and even the corpulent Porgy, in his salutation of welcome, expressed the warmth of a feeling of which he was nowise lavish on common occasions. Supper had been reserved for their superior: and the venison steak, cast upon the coals as he approached, now strenuously seconded, by its rich odors, the invitation of his followers to eat. But Singleton declined.

"Were it possible, I should certainly fall to, my good fellow; for, of a truth, the smokes of that steak are much more grateful to my nostrils than the well-dressed dishes of the fashionable kitchen. My tastes have become so much accommodated to the *wild flavor* of the woods, in almost everything, that, out of the woods, I seem to have no great appetite for anything. I eat and drink as a matter of course, and with too little relish to remark on anything. Had I not already eaten supper, I should need no exhortation beyond that of the venison itself. Besides, I have no time. I must hurry back to the settlement as soon as possible."

"You must certainly *taste* of the meat, colonel," was the response of Porgy, "if only because of the manner in which it was killed—with bow and arrow."

"Indeed! Who was the hunter?"

"Lance! You know I laughed when you spoke of bows and arrows for our men. I confess I thought it monstrous foolish to adopt such weapons. But I am beginning to respect the weapon. What put you in the notion of it, colonel?"

"We had neither shot nor powder, if you recollect. What was to be done? The Indians slew their meat, and fought fatal battles, with these. weapons before the coming of the white people. The French and Spanish narrative describes them as fighting fiercely, and frequently cutting off the whites with no other weapons. Of the effect of the arrow in good hands, history gave us numerous and wonderful examples. The English, in the time of Henry the Seventh, slew with the clothyard shaft at *four* hundred yards."

"Impossible!"

"True, no doubt. In the time of Henry the Eighth, it was considered an efficient weapon at two hundred and fifty yards. Fighting with the French and Spaniards, the Indians could drive an arrow through a coat of escaupil—stuffed cotton—so as to penetrate fatally the breast which it covered; and some of their shafts were even found efficient when aimed against a coat-of-mail. With such evidence of the power of the weapon, its use never should have been abandoned. Certainly, where we had neither shot nor powder, nor muskets, it was the proper weapon for our hands. There would then have been no reason for one half of our people to wait in the woods, during an action, until their comrades should be shot down, before they could find the means of doing mischief by possessing themselves of the weapons of the fallen men. Bows and arrows, well handled, would have been no bad substitutes for muskets. In the hands of our people, accustomed to take sure aim, they would have been much more efficient than the musket in the hands of the raw, unpractised Englishman; while spears, made of poles, well sharpened and seasoned in the fire, would have been, like the pikes of the Swiss, quite equal to the bayonet at any time. These are weapons with which we might always defend a country of such great natural advantages for war as ours."

" There's reason in it, surely."

" But the arguments in behalf of the bow and arrow are not exhausted. In the first place, you can never get out of ammunition. The woods everywhere abound in shafts; and, in a single night, a squad of sharp-shooters may prepare weapons for a week's campaign and daily fighting. Wet and storm never damage your ammunition. A shaft once delivered is not lost. It may be recovered and shot a dozen times; and it is less burdensome, as a load, to carry a bow and sixty arrows than a gun with as many bullets. The arrow is sped silently to its mark. It makes no report. It flies unseen, like the pestilence by night. It tells not whence it comes. Its flash serves not as a guide to any answering weapon. Against cavalry it is singularly efficient. The wound from an arrow, which still sticks in the side of the horse, will absolutely madden him, and he will be totally unmanageable, rushing, in all probability, on his own columns, deranging their order, and sending dismay among the infantry. In regard to the repeated use of the same arrow, I may remind you of the fact that the French in Florida, under Laudonniere, were compelled, in some of their bloodiest fights with the red men, to stop fighting, at every possible chance, in order to gather up and break the arrows which had been delivered. I need not say what an advantage such a necessity would afford to an assailing party."

" I begin to respect the weapon," said Porgy; " I shall practise at it myself. I already feel like a Parthian."

" The greatest secret," continued Singleton, " in the use of the bow, seems to consist in drawing the arrow to its head. This was the secret of the English, and must have been of all very remarkable bowmen. To do this, the arrow must be drawn to the right ear. It is then delivered with its greatest force, and this requires equally sleight and strength. The feebler nations of the East, the Italians, and the gentle, timid races of the island of Cuba, and of Peru, seem to have drawn the weapon, as the ladies do, only to the breast. This mode of shooting diminishes the force one half. But you must practise constantly, boys, all of you, when you have nothing more pressing on hands, so as to make sure of the butts at a hundred yards. That will answer for us. If this war is to last two years longer, as I suppose it will, we shall have no other ammunition to rely upon. We must take our bows from the savages, and our pikes from the Swiss."

There was some little more conversation, which, like that reported, forms no part of the absolute business of our narrative. But Singleton was not the person to waste much time. It was important, he thought, to raise the estimate of the bow and arrow among his followers, deeming it highly probable, not only that the weapon might be made very efficient even in modern warfare, but that it might be the only one left to them for future use. The partisans of Carolina, during the struggle for the recovery of the state, very seldom went into action with more than three rounds to the man.

"And now, Lance," said Singleton, "a few words with you."

He led him aside from the rest.

"Do you bring me any letters?"

"None, sir; the colonel had no time for writing, and no conveniences."

"Where did you leave him?"

"On the Edisto."

"West side?"

"Yes, sir."

"Had the negroes all come in?"

"All, sir, but one—a young fellow named Aaron, whom he thinks must have fallen into the hands of the enemy, or run off to them. He has sent them off for the Santee, under the charge of Lieutenant Davis, with an escort of ten men."

"How does he recruit?"

"Well, sir, he got nineteen men along the Edisto, and fifteen brought their own rifles. His force is now forty-five, not counting *our* people, who will soon join us. He had a brush with a party of tories, under Lem Waters; killed three, and took seven. He thinks of making a push for the Savannah, where there is one Major Fulton, with a party. He will then come back to the Edisto, and perhaps scout about the Ashley in hopes of picking up a train of wagons. He is mightily in want of powder and ball, and begs that you will send him all you have to spare."

"He must look to the bow and arrow, I am afraid, at least for a season. Still, I am in hopes to do something for him, if my present scheme turns out well. But everything is doubtful yet. Did you get any tidings along the route?"

"Nothing much, sir. The country's moving everywhere; now on one side, now on the other; and I hear something everywhere of small parties, gathering up cattle and provisions."

The examination was still further pursued; but enough has been said to show the whereabouts and the performances of Colonel Walton, which were the chief objects of Singleton. The two soon rejoined the rest; and, after some general instructions and suggestions, Singleton led Lieutenant Porgy aside to communicate his more private wishes.

"At twelve to-morrow," said he, "I expect to be in the neighborhood of the Eight-Mile and Quarter-House. At one or other of these places, God willing, I hope to be at that hour. I wish you to cross the river with your party, and shelter yourself in the swamp-forest along the banks. Send your scouts out with instructions to keep watch upon both the Quarter and Eight-Mile House. A couple of chosen men, quick and keen-sighted, must be within hearing, but close, in the thicket of Izard's camp. Should they hear a triple blast of my horn, with a pause of one, and then another blast, let them make, with all speed, to the point from which I sound. Let them carry their rifles as well as broadswords, and see that their pieces are fit for service. But on no account let them disturb any persons along the route."

"Suppose a convoy for Dorchester, under a small guard?"

"Let it pass without disturbance, and let them not show themselves, on any pretext, or with any temptation in their sight, unless they hear my signal."

"We are grievously in want of everything. A single full powder-horn, and half a dozen or a dozen bullets, to each man, is all that we can muster. Salt is wanted, and——"

"I know all your wants, and hope shortly to supply them; but I have objects in view of still more importance, and they must not be perilled even to supply our deficiencies. Let these instructions be closely followed, lieutenant, if you please. I shall probably find an opportunity of seeing and speaking with you, in the evening, on my return route to Dorchester."

"Do you venture there again?"

"There, or to 'The Oaks!'"

"Is there anything more, Colonel Singleton, in the way of instructions?"

"Nothing."

"Then let me have a word, colonel; and you will excuse me if I speak quite as much as a friend as a subordinate."

"My dear Porgy——"

"Ah, colonel——"

"Let me say, once for all, that I regard you as a comrade always, and this implies as indulgent a friendship as comports with duty."

"Do I not know it? I thank you! I thank you from the bottom of my heart!—and I have a heart, Singleton—by Apollo, I have a heart, though the rascally dimensions of my stomach may sometimes interfere with it. And now to the matter. I am concerned about you. I am."

"How?"

"As a soldier, and a brave one, of course you know that you are liable to be killed at any moment. A wilful bullet, a sweeping sword-stroke, or the angry push of a rusty bayonet, in bad hands, may disturb as readily the functions of the bowels in a colonel as in a lieutenant. For either of these mischances, the professional soldier is supposed, at all times, to be prepared; and I believe that we both go to our duties without giving much heed to the contingencies that belong to them."

"I am sure that *you* do, lieutenant."

"Call me Porgy, colonel, if you please, while we speak of matters aside from business. If I am proud of anything, it is of the affections of those whom I esteem."

"Go on, Porgy."

"Now, my dear colonel, that you should die by bullet, broadsword, or bayonet, is nothing particularly objectionable, considering our vocation. It may be something of an inconvenience to you, physically; but it is nothing that your friends should have reason to be ashamed of. But to die by the halter, Colonel Singleton—to wear a knotted handkerchief of hemp—to carry the knot beneath the left ear—throwing the head awkwardly on the opposite side, instead of covering with it the Adam's apple—to be made the fruit of the tree against the nature of the tree—to be hitched into cross-grained timbers, against the grain —to die the death of a dog, after living the life of a man—this, sir, would be a subject of great humiliation to all your friends, and must, I take it, be a subject of painful consideration to yourself."

"Very decidedly, Porgy," was the reply of the other, with a good-natured laugh.

"Why will you incur the dangers of such a fate? This is what your friends have a right to ask. Why put yourself, bound, as it were, hand and foot, in the keeping of these red-coated Philistines, who would truss you up at any moment to a swinging limb with as little remorse as the male alligator exhibits when he swallows a hecatomb of his own kidney. Why linger at Dorchester, or at 'The Oaks,' with this danger perpetually staring you in the face? There are few men at 'The Oaks,' and the place is badly guarded. The force at Dorchester itself is not so great but that, with Col. Walton's squadron, we might attempt it. Say the word, and, in forty-eight hours, we can harry both houses; and if swinging must be done by somebody, for the benefit of 'The Oaks' hereafter, why, in God's name, let it be a British or a Hessian carcass instead of one's own. I might be persuaded, in the case of one of these bloody heathens, to think the spectacle a comely one. But in your case, colonel, as I am living man, it would take away my appetite for ever."

"Nay, Porgy, you overrate the danger."

"Do I! Not a bit. I tell you these people are getting desperate. Their cruelties are beginning only; and for this reason, that they find the state unconquered. So long as there is a single squad like ours between the Pedee and the Savannah, so long is there a hope for us and a hate for them. Hear to me, colonel, and beware! There is deadly peril in the risks which you daily take."

7

146

KATHARINE WALTON.

"I know that there is risk, Porgy; but there are great gains depending upon these risks, and they must be undertaken by somebody. Our spies undertake such risks daily."

"A spy is a spy, colonel, and nothing but a spy. He was born to a spy's life and a spy's destiny. He knows his nature and the end of his creation, and he goes to his end as to a matter of obligation. He includes the price of the halter, and the inconvenience of strangulation, in the amount which he charges for the duty to be done. But we who get no pay at all, and fight for the fun and the freedom of the thing only—there's no obligation upon us to assume the duty of another, at the risk of making a bad picture, and feeling uncomfortable in our last moments. No law of duty can exact of me that I shall not only die, but die of rope, making an unhandsome corse, with my head awfully twisted from the centre of gravity, where only it could lie at ease! My dear colonel, think of this! Say the word! and fight, scout, or only scrimmage, we'll share all risks with you, whether the word be 'Oaks' or 'Dorchester!'"

"The peril will be soon over, Porgy. Three days will end it, in all probability; and, in that time, the same prudence which has kept me safe so long will probably prevail to secure me to the end. Have no fears—and do not forget that you can always strike in at the last moment. Your scouts see all that goes on, and, in a moment of danger, you know the signal."

"Be it so! we're ready! Still I could wish it otherwise. But, by the way, talking of what we see, there's something that Bostwick has to tell you. He was stationed between 'The Oaks' and 'Dorchester' during the afternoon, and came in soon after dark. Here, Bostwick!"—and as the fellow came out of the front to the place where the two had been conversing, Porgy continued:—

"The colonel wants to hear of you what took place between the commandant of the post of Dorchester, Major Vaughan, and the chunky red faced fellow, whom you did not know"

Bostwick told his story, which was briefly this. He had seen Vaughan ride toward "The Oaks," and saw him returning to Dorchester just before dark. When within a mile of "The Oaks," Vaughan drew up and dismounted, leading his horse aside from the road and close to the thicket in which Bostwick lay concealed. Here he was soon joined by a "chunky red-faced fellow," as Porgy had described him, and a conversation of several minutes took place between the two, a portion of which only was intelligible to the scout. The names of Proctor and Furness, however, were several times mentioned by both parties; and Vaughan was evidently much interested in the subject. And length, the stranger, whom he called "John," gave him two letters, or folded papers, which Vaughan opened and read eagerly. Bostwick heard him say, distinctly—

"These, John, are very important. I now see whence he gets his knowledge. Find me more of these papers, John. He must have others. These do not tell all, yet he knows all! Find the rest, and be on the watch when he receives a new one."

"You will give them back to me," said John, "now that you have read them."

"Yes, when I have copied them. You shall have them to-morrow. You say that he showed these papers to Captain Furness?"

"Not sure, your honor; but he had them on the bedside when they talked together. I saw them through the keyhole."

"With that," continued Bostwick, "the major took a piece of gold money from his pocket and dropped it beside him where he stood. The other stooped and picked it up, and offered it to the major, who said, 'Keep it for your honesty, John.' They had something more to say, but I couldn't make it out, though I listened hard, thinking it might consarn you, colonel. After that, the major mounted and put off, and I tracked the other back to 'The Oaks.' He got in jist when you returned from riding with Major Proctor."

"Thank you, Bostwick—it does, in some measure, concern me. You are a good fellow, and though I have no gold pieces to drop for your benefit, yet you shall also be remembered for your honesty."

The business despatched which brough. him to the encampment of his followers, the farewell of Singleton was no such formal leave-taking as distinguishes the military martinet. It was the affectionate farewell of comrades, who felt that they were parting with a friend rather than a superior.

CHAPTER XVI.

HOW TO PLAY WITH KNAVES.

Our partisan returned, without being discovered, to the mansion-house at "The Oaks," and reached his room in silence. He was soon asleep, for with a mind at ease, and habits of physical activity, sleep is never slow to bring us the needful succor. In the morning, he was up betimes, and soon made his way to the chamber of Proctor, who still slept—the unsatisfactory, uneasy sleep of anxiety and apprehension. Singleton had already thought of what he should do and say, in regard to the revelation which he felt that it was necessary to make to his new companion. There was some difficulty in accounting for the information he had acquired, touching the faithlessness of Proctor's servant, John; but our partisan had discussed the matter calmly in his own mind, and had come to the conclusion that Proctor should hear of the important fact, without being suffered to ask for an authority. This reservation, in the case of a man of character and good sense, like Singleton, was not a matter of difficulty.

The treacherous servant, knowing his master's habits of late rising, was absent. Singleton ascertained this fact before proceeding to Proctor's chamber. He thought it not improbable that John had gone to a meeting with Vaughan, with the view to the seasonable recovery of the letters; and, possibly to receive instructions for the future. It was important to avail himself of his absence, the better to effect his exposure. The British major was somewhat surprised to find Singleton in his chamber.

" Why, what's the matter, Furness ?   I'm devilish glad to see you ; but why so early ?"

" I shall leave you directly after breakfast, and had something to say to you in private, which I regard as of moment to yourself, particularly at this juncture."

" Ah ! but whither do you go ?"

" Below, to meet with General Williamson, at the Quarter House."

"And what's this business ?"

" I have made a little discovery, Proctor, but can not now inform you in what manner I have made it, nor who are my authorities. On this point, you must ask me no questions, for I shall certainly answer none. In fact, a little secret of my own is involved in the matter, and this must make you content with what I shall be willing to disclose. But you will lose nothing. All that is important to you shall be told, and it must satisfy you when I assure you solemnly that it comes from the most unquestionable sources. You may safely believe it all."

" Be it so ! On your own conditions, then. I have the utmost faith in your assurance."

" I thank you ;—and, first, can you let me see again those two letters of your anonymous correspondent ?"

" Certainly ;" and Proctor leaped out of bed, threw on his *robe de chambre*, and proceeded to search his *escritoir*. The letters were not forthcoming. His trunks were next overhauled, his dressing-case, the pockets of his coat—they were nowhere to be found.

"I am satisfied," said Singleton; " I feel sure that you look in vain."

" I must have taken them with me, and left them below stairs."

" No ! They are in the hands of Vaughan, your enemy !"

" How ! What mean you ?" demanded the other.

Singleton then related what he had heard of the interview between Vaughan and the fellow John, as Bostwick reported it, suppressing, of course, all the clews to his source of information ; but otherwise withholding nothing. Proctor was in a rage of indignation.

"Fool that I was! and I saw nothing; I suspected nothing; and this execrable scoundrel has been a spy upon my footsteps, Heaven knows how long! But I shall have the satisfaction, before I send him adrift, of reading him such a lesson with the horsewhip as shall be a perpetual endorsement to his back and character."

"You will do no such thing, Proctor," said Singleton, coolly, while going to the door and looking out upon the passage. It was clear, and he returned.

"Dress yourself at once, Proctor, and come with me to my chamber. It is more secure from eaves-droppers than this apartment. And first, let me entreat that you will bridle your anger; and, above all, suffer not this fellow to see or to suspect it. Let me exhort you to begin, from this moment, the labor of self-restraint. Your success in extricating yourself from the difficulty in which you stand, will be found in the adoption of that marble-like coldness of character which really confers so much strength upon your enemy. You must be cool, at least, and silent too. Come, hasten your dressing, for I have much to say, and shall have little time to say it in before breakfast."

Proctor already deferred to the prompt, energetic, and clear-headed character of Singleton. He stared at him a moment, and then proceeded to obey him. His toilet was as quickly made as possible, and they were soon in Singleton's chamber. The latter then renewed the subject, and continued his counsels in the following fashion : —

"You have lived long enough, my dear Proctor, in our southern country, to know something of the rattlesnake. If you have ever had occasion to walk into our woods of a summer night, and to have suddenly heard the rattle sounded near you, you can very well conceive the terror which such a sound will inspire in the bosom of any man. It is a present and a pressing danger, but you know not from what quarter to expect the blow. The ringing seems to go on all around you. You fancy yourself in a very nest of snakes; and you are fixed, frozen, expecting your death every moment, yet dread to attempt your escape —dread to lift a foot lest you provoke the bite which is mortal. It is the very inability to face the enemy, to see where he lies in ambush, that is the chief occasion of your terror. Could you see him — could you look on him where he lies — though coiled almost at your feet, head thrown back, jaws wide, fangs protruded, and eyes blazing, as it were, with a coppery lustre — you would have no apprehensions — he would, in fact, be harmless, and you could survey him at your leisure, and knock him quietly on the head as soon as you had satisfied your curiosity. Now, I regard it as particularly fortunate that you have discovered, in this instance, where your chief danger lies. You see your enemy. You know where he is. You know through what agency he works, and nothing is more easy thaৰ to keep your eye upon him, follow him in all his windings, and crush him with your heel at the most favorable moment. Your man John is the pilot to your rattlesnake. You are probably aware that the rattlesnake has his pilot, as the shark his, and the lion his?"

"Is it so?"

"Even so; and so far from showing yourself angry with this good fellow John, whose benevolence is such that he would serve two masters — so far from dismissing him with the horsewhip — your policy is not even to let him know what you have discovered. He will probably bring back these letters quietly, and you will find them, after your return from breakfast, in the proper place in your *escritoir;* and you will show yourself quite as unsuspicious as before."

"And keep the fellow still in my service?"

"To be sure, for the best of reasons! Through him you may be able to ascertain the game of his employer. By him you will probably trace out the windings of his master-snake. You will simply take care to put no important secrets in his way."

"But he has false keys, no doubt, to every trunk and *escritoir* that I have?"

"Most probably, and you will suffer him to *keep* them; only find some other hiding-place for your important matters to which you are secure that he carries no key, simply because of his ignorance of the hiding-place. Ordinary letters you will put away in the old places as before. Nay, as your enemy Vaughan seems to know this hand-writing — which you do not — you may amuse yourself by putting other choice specimens in his way.

Imitate the hand occasionally—write yourself a few billets-doux
now and then—and you may suggest little schemes for interviews between yourself and the unknown fair one, upon which
your excellent fellow John will maintain a certain watch; and
you can maintain your watch *on him.* It is now certain, from
what Vaughan has said, that the handwriting is known to him,
and that it is a woman's!"

"But the wearisome toil of such a watch—the annoying feeling that you have such a rascal about you."

"Very annoying, doubtless, and troublesome; but it is one
of those necessities which occur in almost every life—where a
man has to endure much, and struggle much, and exert all his
manhood to secure safety or redress, or vengeance."

"Ha! that is the word! vengeance! and I will have it!"

"It is an advantage to keep John, that you do know him.
Dismiss him, and you warn Vaughan and himself that he is suspected—possibly discovered. This makes your enemy cautious.
He still may employ John to your dis-service, though you employ him not. Should you get another servant are you better
sure of his fidelity? Is it not just as likely that he will be bought
and bribed also? Will you doubt him?—can you confide in
him? Neither, exactly—both, certainly to some extent! Why
not confide in John to the same extent? In other words, confide in neither. Seem not to suspect him, but leave nothing at
his mercy. This is simply a proper, manly vigilance where you
are surrounded by enemies, and where their strategems and
your incaution have already given them an advantage in the
campaign."

"Ah! Furness, had I your assistance?"

"You do not need it. Exert your own faculties and subdue
your passion until you are certain of your prey. If you be not
cool, patient, watchful, you are lost in the struggle. Are you a
man? Here is one of the most admirable of all opportunities to
assert and prove your manhood. Any blockhead, with the ordinary gentlemanly endowment of courage, can fight through
the enemy's ranks, or perish with honor. But it is the noblest
manhood, that in which courage is twinned with thought, to fight
only at your pleasure, and make your intellect the shield in the

struggle. Do not fear that I shall desert you, Proctor, when you need a friend."

"I thank you. You are right. I feel that I can do what you counsel, and I *will* do it. Let me have your further counsels.

We need not pursue those suggestions of Singleton, by which he advised the details in general terms, of that policy with which he sought to impress his companion. Proctor was by no means a feeble man—in fact, he was rather a strong one, capable of thought and possessed of latent energies which needed nothing but the spur of a will which had not yet been forced into sufficient activity. The superior will of Singleton finally stimulated his own. He acknowledged its superiority and tacitly deferred to it. The other was copious in his suggestions, and they were those of a vigilant mind, sharpened by practice, and naturally well endowed with foresight and circumspection. He took a comprehensive view of all the difficulties in the way of the British officer, and succeeded in pointing out to him where, and in what manner, he would most probably find the clews which would successfully lead him out from among his enemies. We need only give his closing counsels, as they somewhat concern us at present.

"Do not think of leaving 'The Oaks' just now, Proctor. Remain here, keeping the excellent John with you until your uncle departs. Busy yourself as his secretary. He needs your services. The young man he has with him can give him little help, and he knows it. He is disposed to conciliate you, and I would not show myself hostile or suspicious. It may serve you somewhat, as well as Cruden, to remain here as long as you can. Your policy is to gain time, and to be as near your enemy as possible, affording him all his present opportunities, as long as this can be done with propriety. For this, you have a reasonable excuse, so long as Cruden remains. While here, you may also serve this young lady, the daughter of Walton, in whom you appear to have an interest. Her affairs may well need the assistance of such a friend as yourself."

The call to breakfast brought John to the presence of his master. Proctor played his part successfully, and the fellow

7*

had no suspicions, though somewhat surprised to find the former up and dressed, and in the chamber of the loyalist, Furness. We may add that, when Proctor looked into his *escritoir*, an hour after Singleton's departure, he found the missing letters in the place where he kept them usually.   Our partisan left "The Oaks" soon after breakfast, his farewells being exchanged with Cruden and his nephew at the table.   A silent but emphatic squeeze of the hand, on the part of Proctor, spoke more impressively than words the warmth of that young man's feelings.

CHAPTER XVII.

SURPRISE.

RIDING slowly, and looking about him with a curious interest as he rode, Singleton did not reach his place of destination till nearly one o'clock. He was not unconscious, as he proceeded, of occasional intimations in the forest that his friends were already at the designated points of watch. At intervals, the hootings of the owl, or a sharp whistle, familiar to Marion's men, apprized him where to look for them in the moment of emergency. He himself was not without his weapons, though the small-sword at his side alone was visible. An excellent pair of pistols was concealed within the ample folds of his hunting-shirt, and a beautifully polished horn was slung about his neck. With a fleet and powerful steed of the best Virginia blood, well-trained, and accustomed to obey cheerfully the simplest word of his rider, Singleton felt as perfectly confident of his own security as it is possible for one to feel under any circumstances. He rode forward with coolness, accordingly, to the place of meeting, with a person, for whom, at that period, the patriots of South Carolina felt nothing but loathing and contempt.

General Williamson, the person thus regarded, was a Scotchman, who had probably entered the colonies some twelve or fifteen years before, and had acquired considerable social and political influence in the upper country—the region which he occupied being originally settled in great part by Europeans direct from the Old World, or immediately from Pennsylvania and New York. In the first dawning of the Revolutionary struggle, Williamson took sides with the *movement*, or patriotic party. It is probable that he was influenced in this direction, rather in consequence of certain local rivalries in the interior, and because of the judicious persuasions, or flatteries, of the leading men of the lower country—Drayton, Laurens, and others—than because of any real activity of his sympathies with the cause of colonial independence. He was an illiterate, but shrewd person; and, as a colonel first, and finally a general of militia, he behaved well, and operated successfully in sundry conflicts with the Indians of the frontier and the loyalists of his own precincts. The fall of Charleston, which temporarily prostrated the strength of the state, threw him into the arms of the enemy. He took what is commonly known as a "British protection," by which he professed to observe a neutrality during the progress of the war. In the condition of affairs—the utter overthrow of the army of the south, the belief that its resources were exhausted, and the growing opinion that Congress would be compelled, through similar exhaustion of resource, to yield to the British, at least the two colonies of Georgia and South Carolina, both of which were covered by the invading army—this measure, on the part of Williamson, was perhaps not so censurable. The same act had been performed by many others in conspicuous positions, who could offer no such apology as Williamson. He was a foreigner; originally a subject of the British crown; sprung from a people remarkable always for their loyalty, and whose affinities were naturally due to the cause of Britain. But Williamson's error was not limited to the taking of "protection." He took up his abode within the walls of Charleston, and it became the policy of the British to employ his influence against the cause for which he had so recently been in arms. In this new relation, it is doubtful if he exercised much influence with the borderers whom he deserted. It was enough that such were understood to be his new objects, by which he had secured, in especial degree, the favor of the British commandant at Charleston. The affair of Arnold, in the north, furnished a name to Williamson in the south; and when spoken of subsequently to the detection of Arnold's treason, he was distinguished as the "Arnold of Carolina." This summary will sufficiently serve as introductory to what follows. It was to confer with this person, thus odiously distinguished, that we find Colonel Singleton, of Marion's brigade, in the assumed character and costume of Captain Furness, of the loyalist rifles, on his way to the public hotel, some eight miles from Charleston.

Williamson had been, somewhat impatiently, awaiting his arrival in one of the chambers of the hotel, whence he looked forth upon the surrounding woods with the air of a man to whom all about him was utterly distasteful. A British dragoon sat upon a fallen tree, some thirty yards from the dwelling, his horse being fastened to a swinging limb, and ready saddled and bitted, awaiting in the shade.

There was something in what he saw to darken the brows of the general, who, wheeling away from the window, threw himself upon a seat in the apartment, and, though there was no fire on the hearth, drawing near to it and thrusting his heels against the mantel. He was a stout, well-built personage, on the wintry side of forty, perhaps, with large but wrinkled forehead, and features rather prominent than impressive. His head was thrown back, his eyes resting cloudily upon the ceiling, and his position at such an angle as simply preserved his equlibrium. His meditations were not of an agreeable character. His darkened brows, and occasional fragments of soliloquy, showed them to be gloomy and vexatious. He had many causes for discontent, if not apprehension. He had sacrificed good name, position, and property, and had found nothing compensative in the surrender. His former comrades were still in the field, still fighting, still apparently resolute in the cause which he had abandoned; the British strength was not increasing, their foothold less sure than before, and their treatment of himself, though civil and respectful, was anything but cordial—was wholly wanting in warmth; and there was no appearance of a disposition to confer upon him any such command as had been given to Arnold. Whether an appointment equal to that which he had enjoyed in the state establishment, would have reconciled him to his present relations, it is difficult to determine. No such proffer had been made him, nor have we any evidence that he was anxious for such an appointment. He was not a man of enterprise; but he could not deceive himself as to the fact that the British authorities had shown themselves disappointed in the amount of strength which his acquisition had brought to their cause. His desertion of the whigs had been followed by no such numbers of his former associates as, perhaps, his own assurances had led his present allies to expect. His labors were now chiefly reduced to a maintenance of a small correspondence with persons of the interior, whom he still hoped to influence, and to such a conciliation of the humors of Balfour—whose weaknesses the shrewd Scotchman had soon discovered—as would continue him in the moderate degree of favor which he enjoyed. This statement will serve to indicate the nature of that surly and dissatisfied mood under which we find him laboring.

He was thus found by Singleton—as Captain Furness, of the loyalists—whose presence was announced by a little negro, habited only in a coarse cotton shirt reaching to his heels. Of the slight regard which Williamson was disposed to pay to his visiter, or to his objects, or to those of his British employers, we may form a reasonable idea from the fact that he never changed his position in the seat which he occupied; but still, even on the entrance of the supposed loyalist, maintained his heels against the mantel, with the chair in which he sat properly balanced upon its hind legs. His head was simply turned upon his shoulders enough to suffer his eyes to take in the form of his visiter.

Singleton saw through the character of the man at a glance. He smiled slightly as their eyes encountered, and drew a rather favorable inference from the treatment thus bestowed upon a seeming loyalist. The auspice looked favorable to the interests of the patriotic party. He approached, but did not seek, by any unnecessary familiarity, to break down those barriers upon which the dignity of his superior seemed disposed to insist. At once putting on the simple forester, Singleton addressed him—

" You 're the general—General Williamson—I reckon ?"

" You are right, sir. I am General Williamson. You, I suppose, are Captain Furness, of the loyalist rifles ?"

" The same, general, and your humble servant."

" Take a seat, captain," was the response of Williamson, never once changing his position.

"Thank you, sir, and I will," said the other, coolly, drawing his chair within convenient speaking distance.

"You brought letters to me, Captain Furness, from Colonels Fletchall, Pearis, and Major Stoveall. You are in want of arms, I see. On this subject, I am authorized, by Colonel Balfour, to tell you that a train of wagons will set forth to-morrow from the city. One of these wagons is specially designed for your command, containing all your requisitions. It is that which is numbered eleven. The train will be under a small escort, commanded by Lieutenant Meadows, whom you are requested to assist in his progress. The route will be by Nelson's Ferry to Camden; and when you have reached Camden, your wagon will be detached and surrendered to your own keeping. You will order your command to rendezvous at that point. But here is a letter of instructions from Colonel Balfour, which contains more particular directions."

Singleton took the letter, which he read deliberately, and put away carefully in his bosom. A pause ensued. Williamson lowered his legs, finally, and said—

"There is nothing further, Captain Furness. You have all that you require."

"There were some letters, general, that I brought for you," was the suggestion of Singleton.

There was a marked hesitancy and dissatisfaction in the reply of his companion.

"Yes, sir: my friends seem to think that I ought to write despatches by you to certain persons, over whom I am supposed to exercise some influence. I do not know that such is the case; and, even if it were, I am not satisfied that I shall be doing a friendly act to the persons referred to by encouraging them, at this stage of the war, to engage in new and perilous enterprises, and form new relations directly opposite to those in which they are acting now."

"But, general, the cause of his majesty is getting quite desperate among us. We sha'n't be able to hold our ground at all, unless we can get out on our side such men as Waters, Caldwell, Roebuck, Thomas, Miller, and a few others."

"That is the very reason, Captain Furness, that I am unwilling to advise men, whom I so much esteem, to engage in an enterprise which may ruin them for ever."

"How, general? I don't see — I don't understand."

"Very likely, Captain Furness," said the other, quite impatiently. "You see, sir, though as much prepared as ever to promote the success of his majesty's arms and to peril myself, I do not see that it would be altogether proper for me, dealing with friends, to give them such counsel as would involve them in useless dangers, or encourage them in enterprises, the fruits of which may not be profitable to the cause I espouse, and fatal to themselves. In the first place, I doubt greatly if my recommendation would have any effect upon the persons you mention. It is true, they were my friends and followers when I served the whig cause; but I see no reason to think that, in changing sides, I continued to keep their respect and sympathy. In the next place, I am not satisfied that the officers of the crown, or the British government itself, are taking the proper course for pushing their conquests or securing the ground that they have won. They hold forth no encouragement to the people of the soil. They do not treat well the native champions who rise up for their cause. The provincials are not properly esteemed. They never get promotion; they are never intrusted with commands of dignity, or with any power by which they could make themselves felt. The war languishes. No troops, or very few, now arrive from Great Britain; and these, chiefly Irish, are better disposed to fight *for* the rebels than fight against them. In fact, sir, I see nothing to encourage our friends in risking themselves, at this late day, in the struggle. Those who are already committed, who have periled fame and fortune on the cause, who can not return to the ranks they have abandoned, they must take their chances, I suppose; but even these see no proper motive which should urge them to persuade persons whom they esteem into the field. I have already done all that I could. When I first left the ranks of the whigs, I wrote to these very persons, giving them the reasons which governed me in my conduct, and urging these reasons upon them as worthy of the first consideration. To these letters I have received no answer. What should prompt me to write them again? Of what possible avail these arguments, repeated now when their prospects are really improving and their strength is greater? A proper pride, Captain Furness, revolts at the humiliation of such a performance."

"I could have wished, General Williamson," replied Singleton, his tone and manner changing, "that you could have found a better reason than your pride for your refusal to do what is required."

"Why, who are you, sir?" demanded Williamson, drawing back his chair, and confronting the speaker for the first time.

A smile of Singleton alone answered this question, while he proceeded—

"I am better pleased, sir, to believe in another reason than that you have given for this forbearance. The decline of English power in the back country, and its weakness and bad management below, are certainly sufficient reasons to keep the patriots steadfast in *their* faith. But, sir, permit me to ask if you have suffered Colonel Balfour to suspect that you are likely to use this language to me, or to refuse these letters?"

An air of alarm instantly overspread the countenance of Williamson.

Again I ask, who are you?" was his reply to this question.

"I am not exactly what I seem, General Williamson; but my purpose here is not to inspire you with any apprehension."

"Are you not the son of my venerable friend, Ephraim Furness, of Ninety-Six?"

"I am not, sir; I will mystify you no longer. For certain purposes, I have borrowed the character of Captain Furness, who is in my hands a prisoner. I am, sir, Colonel Singleton, of Marion's brigade."

Williamson sprang in horror to his feet.

"Ha! sir! of Marion's brigade! What is your purpose with me?—what do you design? Do you know, sir, that you are in my power? that I have only to summon yonder dragoon, and your life, as a spy and a traitor, is in my hands?"

"Coolly, General Williamson; do not deceive yourself. It is *you* who are in *my* hands, your dragoon to the contrary notwithstanding! A single word from you, sir, above your breath, and I blow out your brains without a scruple."

He drew forth his pistols as he spoke. Williamson, meanwhile, was about to cross the room to possess himself of his small-sword that lay upon the table. Singleton threw himself in the way, as he proceeded thus : —

"I have not come here unadvisedly, General Williamson, or without taking all necessary precautions, not only for *my* safety, but for *yours.* I have only to sound this bugle, and the house is surrounded by the best men of Marion. You know *their* quality, and you have heard of *me!* I came here, expecting to find you in the very mood in which you show yourself—discontented —humbled to the dust by your own thoughts—conscious and repenting of error—dissatisfied with the British—dissatisfied with your new alliance, and anxious to escape all further connection with it, as equally satisfied that it is fatal to your future hopes and dishonorable to your name. But I came also prepared, if disappointed in these calculations, to make you my prisoner, and subject you, as a traitor to the American cause, to a summary trial, and a felon's death."

A blank consternation overspread the visage of Williamson. He was under the eye of a master—an eye that looked into his own with all the eager watch of the hawk or the eagle, and with all the stern confidence in his own strength which fills the soul of the tiger or the lion. The big sweat stood out in great drops upon the brow of the victim; he attempted to speak, but his voice failed him; and still he wavered, with an inclining to the window, as if he still thought of summoning the dragoon to his assistance. But the native vigor of his intellect, and his manhood, soon came to his relief. He folded his arms across his breast, and his form once more became steady and erect.

"You have your pistols, Colonel Singleton! Use them—you *shall* use them—you shall have my life, if that is what you desire; but I will never yield myself alive to the power of your people."

"You must not be suffered to mistake me, General Williamson. If I have been compelled to utter myself in the words of threatening, it was an alternative, which you have the power to avoid. We do not wish your death. We wish your services. We know, as well as yourself, that the power of the British is declining—that the days of their authority are numbered. We know the apology which can be made for your desertion of the American cause——"

"As God is my judge, Colonel Singleton, I never deserted it until it had deserted me! My officers recommended the protection—our troops were scattered—we had no army left. Beaufort was cut to pieces—our cavalry dispersed—Congress would, or could, do nothing for us—and, in despair of any success or safety, not knowing where to turn, I signed the accursed instrument which was artfully put before us at this juncture, and which offered us a position of neutrality, when it was no longer possible to offer defence."

"You could have fled, general, as hundreds of us did, to North Carolina and Virginia, to be in readiness for better times."

"So I might, sir; but so also might your kinsman, Colonel Walton."

Singleton was silenced for a moment by the retort; but he used it for the purposes of reply.

"Colonel Walton is now atoning, sword in hand, for his temporary weakness and error. He was too much governed, General Williamson, by considerations such as, no doubt, weighed upon you. He had great wealth, and a favorite daughter."

"Ah! there it is! That, sir, is the melancholy truth. Family and lands were the thoughts that made me feeble, as it made others."

There was an appearance of real mental agony in the speaker, in the utterance of these words, which moved the commiseration of Singleton. He proceeded more tenderly:—

"Undoubtedly, you had your apology, General Williamson, for much of this error; but not *for all!* Still, atonement *for all* is within your power; and I have not come hither unadvised of your situation, or of the capacity which you still possess to do service to the country. It is clear that, soon or late, the British must be expelled from the state. Unless you make terms with its future masters, your good name, which you would entail to your children, and your vast landed estates, are equally the forfeit. I *know* that these reflections are pressing upon you. I *know* that you yourself, or one whom I assume to be you—you alone can determine if I am right—have already initiated the steps for your return to the bosom of your old friendships and associations. Sir, I was in the tent of General Greene when Mrs. William Thompson and her daughter reached his presence from the city."

"Ah!"

"I saw a certain paper taken from the bosom of the unconscious child by the mother. It had been put into her bosom by an officer in Charleston, as she was about to leave the city—"

"Enough, sir, enough! And General Greene?"

"Look at this paper, General Williamson."

Unscrewing the hilt of his sword, Singleton drew forth a small, neatly-folded billet, without signature or address, which contained certain brief propositions.

"Read this paper, general. There is nothing explicit in it, nothing to involve any party. But it comes from General Marion, with the approbation of General Greene; it is designed for *you!* and you are entreated to recognise *me* as fully authorized to explain their views and to receive and report your own. You will be pleased to learn from me that your situation, your feelings, and your desires, are perfectly understood; and that they pledge themselves to use all their influence and power in procuring your honorable restoration to the confidence of the country, upon your taking certain steps, which I am prepared to explain, for putting yourself right once more in relation to the cause for which we are contending. It is with you to decide."

"Declare your objects, your wishes, Colonel Singleton. Say the word, and I throw myself at once among the squadrons of Greene, and offer my sword once more, in any capacity, in the service of my country."

This was said eagerly, and with quite as much earnestness of manner and feeling as was called forth by the terms of the declaration.

"I am afraid, General Williamson, that you could do us but little service by such a proceeding. You would only endanger yourself without serving our cause. To deal with you candidly, you have a penance to perform. You must approve yourself a friend by absolute and valuable services before you can be recognised as such. There is no injustice in this. You will remember your own answer, on your Cherokee expedition, in 1776, when Robert Cunningham came into your camp and offered his services. You objected that, however, willing yourself to confide in his assurances, the prejudices of your people could not be overcome with regard to him. His case then, is yours now. To show yourself among our troops would be to peril your life only. I could not answer for it."

"In the name of God, then, what am I to do? How can I serve you!"

"Where you are—in the camp—in the city of the enemy," answered Singleton, impressively resting his hand upon the wrist of his companion, "you may do us a service of the last importance, the results of which will be eminently great—the merits of which will wholly acquit you of all past weaknesses. Hear me, sir. We *know* that we have friends in Charleston, who are impatient of the miserable, the brutal, and degrading yoke of Nesbitt Balfour! We *know* that many are desperately inclined to rise in arms, and to seek, at all hazards, to rescue the city from the enemy. It needs but little help or encouragement from without; and *that* help General Greene is not disposed to withhold, whenever he can be satisfied of a reasonable prospect of success. The British garrison in Charleston is known to be weak and dispirited. Their cavalry is small. They have no enterprise. Supplies from Britain do not often arrive in season, and the commandant has already more than once meditated recruiting bodies of the blacks as troops for supplying their deficiencies, and meeting the emergencies which increase daily. Let them once be compelled to put that design into execution, and they not only stimulate all the patriots into renewed activity—arm many who have been hitherto inert—but drive from their ranks every loyalist who is a slaveholder. This is their peril—this shows their feebleness. Of this feebleness we propose to take advantage on the first specious showing of good fortune. For this purpose we desire, within the city, a friend who will promptly and truthfully convey intelligence—will ascertain our friends—inform us in regard to our resources—show where the defences are weakest, and keep us well advised of the plans, the strength, and the movements of the enemy. It is for you to determine whether you will act in this capacity—one nowise inconsistent with your present feelings and former principles, and one, I may add, by no means inconsistent with a sound policy, which must see that the days of British rule are numbered on this continent."

What need to pursue, through its details, the protracted conference between the parties? Let it suffice that the terms vouchsafed by Greene, through Singleton, were acceded to by Williamson. In some degree, he had been already prepared for this retransfer of his allegiance to his former faith. We must do him the justice, however, to add that he would greatly have preferred to have done his part, as heretofore, in the field of battle. But this was clearly impossible; and his own shrewd sense soon persuaded him of the truth and force of Singleton's reasoning. They separated with an understanding that they were to meet again at designated periods, and a cipher was agreed upon between them. It was quite dark when Singleton, after a smart canter, found himself once more at "The Oaks." We forego the details of a brief interview with his scouting party, on the route, as not necessary to our progress, and designed only to instruct his followers in respect to theirs.

CHAPTER XVIII.

THE REVEL.

IN the brief and hurried meeting which had taken place between Singleton and his men, on his return from the interview
with Williamson, he had given them such instructions as caused
their general movement. Their camps, on both sides of the
Ashley, were broken up that very night; and, lighted by a
friendly moon—having so arranged as to give a wide berth to
"The Oaks," as well as Dorchester—they were scouring away
by midnight, through well-known forest-paths, in the direction of
"The Cypress," at the head of the Ashley, where lay another
party of the band.

There was famous frolicking that night in the secure recesses
of the swamp. Here they might laugh and sport without apprehension. Here they might send up the wild song of the hunter
or the warrior, nor dread that the echoes would reach unfriendly
ears. Well might our fearless partisans give loose to their live-
lier impulses, and recompense themselves for the restraints of the
past in a cheerful hilarity and play. There was a day of respite
accorded to their toils, and their fires were gayly lighted, and
their venison steaks smoked and steamed upon the burning
coals, and their horns were converted into drinking cups; and
the dance enlivened their revels, under the great oaks and cypresses, towering over the islet hammocks of the deep morass.

"Shall all be toil and strife, and care and anxiety, my comrades?" was the cry of Porgy, as they surrounded the fire when
supper was concluded and listened to the oracular givings-forth
of that native epicurean. "We, who ride by midnight and
fight by day, who scout and scour the woods at all hours and

seasons, for whom there is no pay and as little promotion,
shall we not laugh and dance, and shout and sing, when occasion offers, and leave the devil, as in duty bound, to pay the piper? Hear our arrangements for the night. Give ear, boys,
and hearken to the duties assigned you. Half a dozen of you
must take the dogs and gather up a few coons and 'possums.
We must take care of the morrow, in spite of the apostle. Who
volunteers for the coon hunt?"

"If the lieutenant will go himself, I'm one to volunteer," said
Ben Mosely.

"Out upon thee, you young varmint! Do you mean me?
With such a person as mine—a figure made for state occasions
and great ceremonials only? Do you mean *me?*"

"To be sure I do," was the reply.

"Why, this is flat treason! It's a design against my life, as
well as my dignity. *I* hunt coons! *I* splash and plunge among
these hammocks, bestraddle fallen cypresses, rope myself with
vines, burrow in bogs, and bruise nose and shin against snags
and branches! Come closer, my son, that I may knock thee
upon the head with this lightwood knot."

"Thank you for nothing, lieutenant—I'm well enough at this
distance," said Ben, coolly.

"No—no, my children; the employment should always suit
the party. You are young and slight. You will pass through
avenues where I should stick, and leap bayous through which I
should have to flounder: my better plan is presiding at your
feasts, and giving dignity to your frolics. Call up your dogs,
Ben—you, Stokes, Higgins, Joe, Miller, Charley, Droze, and
Ike Waring—and put out without more delay. I know that
you can get us more coons than any others of the squad; and I
know that you like the sport. Be about it. We shall console
ourselves during your absence, as well as we can, with dance
and song, with a few games of old sledge, and with an occasional
draught from the jug of Jamaica, in honor of your achievements."

Some playful remonstrances from the party thus chosen were
urged against the arrangement, and no doubt one or more of
them would have preferred infinitely to remain behind; but

they were all young, and the supper and the rest of an hour, which they had enjoyed, had put them in the humor which makes men readily submissive to a superior, particularly when the labor takes something of the aspect of a frolic.

"But you will let us have a sup of the Jamaica, Uncle Porgy, before we set out?"

"Yes, yes. You are good children; and perhaps your only deficiency is in the matter of spirit. You shall embrace the jug."

"A sup all round," was the cry from some one in the background.

"What impudent fellow is that, yelping out from the darkness made by his own face? Let him come forward and get his deserts."

"If that's what you mean, uncle," said the speaker, coming forward, "I shall have the jug to myself."

"What! you, Pritchard!—the handle only, you dog! Why should you have a right to any?"

"The best right in the world. And now let me ask, Lieutenant Porgy, where this old Jamaica, for it *is* old Jamaica, came from?"

"Truly, I should like to have that question answered myself. It *is* *old* Jamaica, I avouch—very old Jamaica. We had not a drop when we went down to 'The Oaks,' and the gallon jug that Singleton sent out to us was soon emptied, dose it out as cautiously as we could. Where, then, did this come from?"

"It's a devil's gift, I reckon," said another, "since no one can tell anything about it."

"A devil's gift!—as if the devil gave good things at any time! But if a devil's gift, my children, for which of our many virtues has he bestowed this upon us?"

"And I say," cried Pritchard, "that it is an angel's gift, if I know anything about it. And I ought to know, since it was I who brought it here."

"Excellent young man!" cried Porgy.

"Say excellent young woman, too," was the response of Pritchard, "since, I reckon, you owe that jug to Miss Walton."

"The deuce we do! And here have I been loitering and hanging over the jug, and arguing about its origin and all that

8

sort of nonsense, without knowing by instinct whose health was to be first honored. Give me the cup here, one of you. Let me unseal. Kate Walton, boys, is a noble creature, whom we must treat with becoming reverence. I knew her when she was a child, and even then she was a calm, prim, thoughtful, but fond and generous little creature. God bless her! Boys, here's man's blessing upon woman's love!"

"Three times three!" was the cry, as the cup went round.

"We are mere blackguards now, boys. Nobody that sees us in these rags, begrimed with smoke, could ever suppose that we had been gentlemen; but, losing place and property, boys, we need not, and we do not, lose the sense of what we have known, or the sentiment which still makes us honor the beautiful and the good."

"Hem! After supper, lieutenant, I perceive that you are always sentimental," was the remark of Pritchard.

"And properly so. The beast is then pacified. There is then no conflict between the animal and the god. Thought is then supreme, and summons all the nobler agencies to her communion. But have ye drunk, ye hunters? Then put out. You have scarce two hours to daylight; and if you hope to take coon or 'possum, you must be stirring. Call up your dogs."

"Hee-up! Hee-up! Snap!—Teazer!—Bull!"

The dogs were instantly stirring, shaking themselves free from sleep, their eyes turned up to the hunters, and their long noses thrust out, while they stretched themselves at the summons of the horn.

"Here, dogs! Hee-up! hee-up! hee-up! Away, boys! Hee-up! hee-up, Snap! Teazer, there! Bull!"

And, with the cheering signals, the hunters gathered up their torches, some taking an axe, and others a bundle of lightwood (resinous pine), beneath the arm. Waving their lights across the darkness, they were soon away, the glimmer of the torches showing more and more faintly at every moment through the thick woods of the swamp. The dogs well knew the duties required of them, and they trotted off in silence, slow coursing with their noses to the earth.

This interruption lasted but a moment; and while some of

the party remaining in the camp were stretched about the fire, drowsing or talking, others drew forth from sainted wallets their well-thumbed packs of cards. A crazy violin began to moan in spasms from the end of a fallen tree on the edge of the hammock, against the decaying but erect branches of which the musician leaned, while his legs crossed the trunk; and other preparations were made for still other modes of passing the rest of the night, but few being disposed to give any heed to sleep. For that matter, there was little need of sleep to the greater number. They had slept, the scouts excepted, through the greater part of the day preceding, while in the woods near "The Oaks," and while waiting on the movements of Singleton during his conference with Williamson near Izard's camp. They were mostly bright, therefore, for the contemplated revels, of whatever sort. A wild dance, rather more Indian than civilized, exercised the fiddle of the younger man of the group, which ended finally in a glorious struggle to draw each other into the fire, around which they circled in the most bewildering mazes.— Such figures Taglioni never dreamed of.—Little heeding these rioters, Porgy had his circle busy in a rubber of whist; while yet another group was deeply buried in the mysteries of "seven-up," "old sledge," or, to speak more to the *card*, "all-fours."— We need not follow the progress of the gamesters, who, in the army, are usually inveterate. Enough that much *Continental* money, at its most exaggerated value, changed hands in the course of an hour's play; fortune having proved adverse to the philosopher, Porgy, leaving him minus fifteen hundred dollars —a sum which, according to the then state of the currency, would not have sufficed to buy for the winner a stout pair of negro shoes.

"Curse and quit!" cried the corpulent lieutenant. "There's no luck for a fat man after supper. And now tell us. Pritchard, how you got possession of that jug of Jamaica. We will try its flavor again while you tell your story. One better appreciates the taste of his liquor a full hour after supper, than just when he has finished eating—the palate then has no prejudices."

The party replenished their horns, after the Scandinavian fashion, and Pritchard replied—

" You must know that when the colonel and Miss Walton
came out to meet her father that night when we gave Balfour's
regulars such a scare and tramp, they went forward beyond the
rice-stacks, leaving me, Tom Leonard, and somebody else—Bill
Mitchell, I think it was, though I can't say"—

" No matter who—go ahead."

" Well, three of us were left in the little wood of scrubby
oaks between the stacks and the dwelling, as a sort of watch.
Who should come along, a little after the colonel and the lady
had passed, but Cesar, the negro! Him we captured, and he
made terms with us immediately, giving up his prog; and his
hands were full—this jug of Jamaica, a small cheese, and a bag
of smoked tongue."

" Smoked tongue and cheese! And you mean to say, Sergeant Pritchard, that you have suffered these most important
medicines to be lost? Smoked tongues and cheese! What
have you done with them? I have seen none of them."

" I knew better than that, lieutenant. We hadn't well got
possession of the negro and the provisions, before the cursed
bugle sounded. The negro dodged; Tom Leonard took the
back track to give the alarm; and where Bill Mitchell went—
if 'twas he—there's no telling; but the jug, the bag, and the
cheese lay at my feet. Was I to lose them—to leave them?"

" It would have been cowardice—nay, treason—had you
done so, Sergeant Pritchard."

" I knew *that*, lieutenant; and, gathering up the good things,
I pushed out for the great bay lying west of the mansion, and
had just time to hide myself and the jug"—

" The tongue and cheese? The tongue, the"—

" Oh, I hid them, too; and there they lay safely, in the hollow of a cypress, while I made my way, after the red coats had
passed, back to the camp. We took the circuit by the bay,
when we pushed for the cypress, and I then picked them up and
brought them off. I have them all here in safety."

" It is well that you have! Yet did you trifle terribly with
the safety of these valuable stores. Two days and nights hidden
in a cypress hole, and not a word said about them!"

" I knew that we had plenty of venison."

"But they might have been found by the enemy, Sergeant Pritchard. They might have gladdened the hearts of the Philistines!"

"I hid them too well for that."

"They might have been eaten up by the wood-rats!"

"I thrust them up the hollow, and put a crotch-stick up to sustain them."

"It is well that you took these precautions. Had they been lost, Pritchard, I would have brought you to the halberds. Good things, so necessary to our commissariat and medicine-chest, are not to be periled idly ; and when they are the gift of beauty, the trust becomes more sacred still. You may thank your stars, Pritchard, that the flavor of this Jamaica is so excellent"—smacking his lips after the draught—"I feel that I must forgive you."

"I should like a little sugar with mine," said one of the young fellows stretching out his horn.

"Sugar!" exclaimed Porgy. "What sacrilege! Young man, where did you receive your education? Would you spoil a cordial of such purity as this with any wretched saccharine infusion? Sugar, sir, for *bad* rum, not for good! Take it as it is ; drink it, however unworthy of it, but do not defile it. For such an offence against proper taste as this, were justice done, a fellow should have a baker's dozen on his bare back."

The youth was glad to receive the potion assigned him, and to swallow it, at a gulp, unsweetened.

"And now, boys"—they had now ceased dancing and playing, and had gathered around our epicurean—"and now, boys, it lacks a good hour to the morning," said Porgy, taking out a huge silver watch, almost as large and round as a Dutch turnip, and holding it up to the fire light. "There are no eyes present quite ripe for sleep. I am for a story or a song. Where's our poet?—where's Dennison? He has not had a sup of the creature. He must drink, and give us something. I know that, for the last three days, he has been hammering at his verses. Where is he? Bring him forward!"

The poet of the camp uncoiled from the ragged camlet under which he had been musing rather than drowsing—a slender youth of twenty-five, with long and massive hair, black and disordered, that rolled down upon his shoulders; and a merry dark eye that seemed to indicate the exuberance of animal life rather than thought or contemplation. He drank, though without seeming to desire the beverage, and was then assailed by Porgy for his song or story.

"You've been scribbing, I know, in your eternal book. Let's see what you've done."

The poet knew too well the party with whom he had to deal, and he indulged in no unnecessary affectation. He had become quite too well accustomed to the requisitions of the camp not to understand that, in moments like the present, each member had to make his contribution to the common stock of enjoyment. The hour had properly come for his. The animal excitement of the company had pretty well worked off, and the moods of nearly all—the physical man being somewhat exhausted—were prepared for more intellectual enjoyment. He professed his readiness, and the partisans flocked in to get proper places near the fire. They crowded close about the poet, some seated, others kneeling, and others in the background, who wished to see as well as hear, stretching themselves over the heads and shoulders of those more fortunate in having found places within the circle. Meanwhile, new lightwood brands were thrown upon the fire, and the flames blazed up gloriously, in singular contrast with the gloomy, but grotesque shadows of the surrounding forest. And thus, with an audience admirably disposed to be appreciative, nowise eager to be critical, and by no means persuaded that fault-finding is one of the most essential proofs of judgment, the poet of the partisans spun his yarn, in a rude, wild measure, well adapted to his audience and the times.

He gave them a mournful and exciting ballad, recounting one of the frequent events of the war, within their own experience —the murder of one of their most youthful comrades, while on his way to see his mistress, a beautiful girl of Black Mingo, who went by the name of the "Beauty of Britton's Neck." Her name was Britton, and that of her lover Calvert. As the ballad of our poet would occupy too much space to appear in these pages, we shall give the story in prose. Calvert left the camp, with Marion's permission. It was remembered, afterward, that Marion, on granting leave to the young ensign, who was barely of age, said to him with a grave smile, "Be on the look-out, Harry, for it is one danger to the youth who goes frequently to see his mistress, that he teaches the way to others." Calvert, perhaps, forgot the advice. He fell into an ambush prepared for him by one Martin, who was also the lover of the damsel, and who had discovered the route usually pursued by Calvert. Martin was the leader of a small band of tories. He brought them together with great secrecy, and succeeded in capturing his rival, whom he finally slew in cold blood. Then, riding to the house of Mrs. Britton, he rudely thrust his trophies before the damsel—the sword, cap, and pistols of her lover, which were all well known to her. The scarf which she had wrought for him with her own hands, still moist with his blood, was also spread before her; and, overawed by the threats of the desperado, the mother of the girl not only consented that he should have her, but proceeded to insist upon her daughter's immediate acceptance of the hand which had been so freshly stained with the blood of her betrothed.

Mary Britton seemed to consent; but, watching her opportunity, she contrived to steal away from sight, to select and saddle one of the best horses in the stable, and to ride away to the camp of Marion, but a few miles off, without awakening the apprehensions of the tories. The partisans were soon and suddenly brought down upon Martin's gang, who were surprised and made captive to a man—Martin himself having but a few moments for prayer, and suffering death upon the spot where Calvert's body had been found.

Such was the ballad of our forest poet, which was of a sort to satisfy the critical requisitions of most of his companions—Lieutenant Porgy alone, perhaps, excepted. Not that he refused to receive pleasure from the narrative. He was not unwilling to admit that his sensibilities were touched quite as keenly as any of the rest; but his tastes kept pace with his sensibilities; and, while his comrades were breathing sentiments of indignation against the tories, he contented himself with showing that the poet was not perfect.

"I was one, the Lord be praised," exclaimed Pritchard, "at the stringing up of that vile beast, Martin. He died like a coward, though he lived like a tiger."

"Pretty much the case always. I've seldom known a man who hadn't *heart*, who had courage. I suppose, Dennison, you're as near the truth in that story as you could be. You have all the facts, and yet you are not truthful."

"How so, lieutenant?" inquired the poet with an air of pique.

"You lack simplicity. You have too many big words, and big figures. Now, the essence of the ballad is simplicity. This is particularly necessary in a performance where the utmost fullness and particularity of detail are insisted upon. Here, you do not generalize. You compass the end aimed at by elaborate touches. The effect is reached in a dramatic way; and you are called upon to detail the particular look, the attitudes, and, as closely as possible, the very words of the speaker."

"Would you have had me introduce all the oaths of the outlaw?" demanded Dennison.

"No; but some of them are essential—enough to show him truthfully, and no more. What I mean to require throughout the ballad is that sort of detail which you have given us where you make the old lady take Mary Britton to the kitchen, to argue with her in favor of marrying Martin. When you make the poor girl say, 'You too against me, mother?' you reach the perfection of ballad writing. Had the whole story been written in this style, Dennison, I should have asked a copy at your hands, and should have preserved it in my wallet through the campaign."

"Along with his smoked venison and mouldy cheese," *sotto voce*, said the disappointed Dennison to one of his companions, as he turned away. A capacious yawn of Lieutenant Porgy was the fit finish of a criticism, of which we have given but a small specimen; and the party, following his example, dispersed to their several covers, seeking that sleep for which the poem and the critique had somewhat prepared them, just as the faintest streaks of morning were beginning to show themselves through the tops of the cypresses. With daylight the coon-hunters came in, bringing with them sundry trophies of their success; and were soon after followed by another party who had just left Colonel Walton. Among these was Walter Griffin, a person of no small importance in the eyes of young Lance Frampton. The reason of this interest we shall see hereafter. Lance had been on the *qui vive* for some time, and met·Griffin on his return, on the outskirts of the camp.

" And how is all, sir?" was the rather hesitating question.

" All well, Lance, and Ellen sends you these."

He took from his bosom, as he spoke, a pair of coarse cotton stockings, knitted recently, and handed them to the young man with a good-natured smile. The latter received them with a blush, and hurriedly thrust them into his own bosom. It was a curious gift from a maiden to her lover, but not less precious as a gift because of its homeliness. Let us leave the cypress camp to its repose for the next three hours. At noon, its inmates were all in motion, scouring fleetly across the country in a northerly direction.

8*

CHAPTER XIX.

SKRIMMAGE.

On the same day which witnessed the departure of our squad of partisans from the swamps of the Ashley Cypress, Singleton, otherwise Furness, took a friendly leave of his new acquaintance, Major Proctor, of the British army. We have seen with how much sympathy these young men came together; and we may add that not a single selfish feeling was at work, in either bosom, to impair the friendship thus quickly established. Our quondam loyalist repeated his injunctions to his friend, to be wary and patient in his encounters with his subtle enemy, Vaughan, whose equal coolness and lack of principle were subjects of sufficient apprehension to his mind. But we have no need to renew his counsels and exhortations. It is enough, that the friends separated with real feelings of sympathy and interest, and that the advice of Singleton, well-meant and sensible, was such as Proctor promised to observe and follow. Then they parted with a warm shake of the hand; Proctor returning to "The Oaks," and Singleton, as loyalist captain of rifles, pushing over to Dorchester, where he was to join the train of wagons under the escort of Lieutenant Meadows, who brought him letters both from Balfour and Williamson. Those from the latter were of a character to keep up the *ruse* which had been agreed upon between himself and our partisan. They were written to the old acquaintance of Williamson in the interior, and were ostensibly designed to bring them over to the king's allegiance. We may add that they had been submitted to Balfour's inspection, as a matter of policy. Williamson had no real notion that his letters would ever reach their destination, or, if they did so, that they could ever possibly help the British cause.

We shall not endeavor to detail the hourly progress of the detachment and train under the charge of Lieutenant Meadows, pursuing the well-known military route to Camden *via* Nelson's Ferry. They moved slowly; the events occurring were few and of little interest. Except at well-known places of rest, and in some few places where the labors of a plantation were still imperfectly carried on with a few slaves, the country seemed almost wholly abandoned. Singleton was rather pleased than otherwise to find in Lieutenant Meadows a very sublime specimen of the supercilious John Bull; a person of more decided horns than head, mulish, arrogant, cold, inflexible; one who had religiously imbibed, as with his mother's milk, all the usual scornful prejudices of his tribe toward the provincials, and who, accordingly, encouraged no sort of intimacy with the supposed captain of loyalists. This relieved our partisan from all that embarrassment which he might have felt, with regard to his future operations, had the lieutenant been a good fellow, and had he shown himself disposed to fall into friendly intercourse. But let us hurry to the event.

It was toward the close of the second day after the departure of the cavalcade from Dorchester, that Meadows had the first intimation of probable danger from an enemy. His warning, however, only came with the blow, and quite too late to allow him either to evade the danger or properly to guard against it. Singleton had galloped off to the front, and was pursuing his way entirely alone, some two hundred yards in advance of the party. He had reason to anticipate that the moment drew nigh for the encounter with his followers, and he preferred to withdraw from close proximity with one who was not only indisposed to show himself companionable, but who might, by possibility, discover in the struggle much more of the truth than it was desirable for our partisan — still as Furness — that he should know. The whole train, with its escort, nearly equally distributed in front and rear, had entered a long, close, circuitous defile in a thickly-set forest, when Singleton was apprised, by a well-known whistle, that the moment was at hand for the attack. He was, accordingly, not a whit startled at the wild yell and the sharp shots with which the onset was begun.

"Marion's men! Marion's men! Hurrah!" was the slogan which startled suddenly the great echoes of the wood, and caused an instant sensation, only short of utter confusion, in the ranks of the British detachment.

But Meadows, with all his faults of taste and temper, was something of a soldier, and never lost his composure for a moment. He hurried forward, with the first signal of alarm, and shouted to his men with a cheerful courage, while he sought to bring them to a closer order and to confront the enemy, who were yet scarcely to be seen. Singleton, meanwhile, wheeled about, as if suffering greatly from surprise, yet drawing his sword, nevertheless, and waving it above his head with the air of a person in very desperate circumstances. He was then distinctly seen to rush boldly upon the assailing Americans, who had now completely interposed themselves between him and the British.

It will not need that we should follow *his* particular movements. It will be quite as easy to conjecture them. Let us give our attention wholly to the affair with the detachment, which was short and sharp as it was sudden. They were assailed equally in front and rear. At first, as he beheld the cavalry of the partisans, and heard their bugles sounding on every hand, Meadows conceived himself to be dealing wholly with that description of force. He, accordingly, commanded his wagons to wheel about and throw themselves across the road at both extremities, thus seeking to close all the avenues which would facilitate the charge. But he reckoned without his host. His operation was only in part successful; since, before the movement could be fully made, the troopers were already cutting down his wagoners. But this was not all. The rangers of Singleton began to show themselves, darkly green, or in their blue uniforms, among the trees which occupied the intervals, and every sharp crack of the rifle brought down its chosen victim. Meadows himself was already slightly wounded in his bridle-arm, and, wheeling about his steed in the direction of the shot, he found himself confronted by a group just making their way out of cover, and darting boldly upon him.

He clapped spurs to his steed and met the leader of the assailants, who, on foot, had reached the open road-space, and was entirely withdrawn from the shelter of the thicket. This person was no other than our epicurean friend, Lieutenant Porgy, who, with an audacity quite inconsistent with his extreme obesity, advanced with sword uplifted to the encounter with the British lieutenant. A single clash of swords, and the better-tempered steel of the Englishman cut sheer through the inferior metal of the American, sending one half of the shattered blade into the air and descending upon the cheek of Porgy, inflicting a slight gash, and taking off the tip of his ear. Another blow might have been fatal. Meadows had recovered from the first movement, and his blade was already whirled aloft for the renewal of the stroke, when Porgy, drawing a pistol from his belt, shot the horse of his enemy through the head. The animal fell suddenly upon his knees, and then rolled over perfectly dead. The sword of Meadows struck harmlessly upon the earth, he himself being pinioned to the ground by one of his leg, upon which the dead animal lay. In this predicament, vainly endeavoring to wield and to use his sword, he threatened Porgy at his approach. The latter, still grasping his own broken weapon, which was reduced to the hilt and some eight inches only of the blade, totally undeterred by the demonstration of the Briton, rushed incontinently upon him, and, in a totally unexpected form of attack, threw his gigantic bulk over the body of the prostrate Meadows, whom he completely covered. The other struggled fiercely beneath, and, getting his sword-arm free, made several desperate efforts to use his weapon; but Porgy so completely bestraddled him that he succeeded only in inflicting some feeble strokes upon the broad shoulders of the epicure, who requited them with a severe blow upon the mouth with the iron hilt of his broken sword.

" It's no use, my fine fellow ; your faith may remove mountains, but your surrender only shall remove me. You are captive to my bow and spear. Halloo ' 'nough !' now, if you wish for mercy."

And, stretching himself out on every hand, with arms extended and legs somewhat raised on the body of the dead horse,

Porgy looked down into the very eyes of his prisoner; his great beard, meanwhile, well sprinkled with gray, lying in masses upon the mouth and filling the nostrils of the Englishman, who was thus in no small danger of suffocation.

"Will nobody relieve me from this elephant?" gasped the half-strangled Meadows.

"Elephant!" roared Porgy. "By the powers, but you shall feel my grinders!"

His good humor was changed to gall by the offensive expression, and he had already raised the fragment of his broken sword, meaning to pummell the foe into submission, when his arm was arrested by Singleton, now appearing in his appropriate character and costume. Meadows was extricated from horse and elephant at the same moment, and by the same friendly agency, and rose from the ground sore with bruises, and panting with heat and loss of breath.

"It is well for him, Colonel Singleton, that you made your appearance. I had otherwise beaten him to a mummy. Would you believe it?—he called me an elephant! Me! Me an elephant!"

"He had need to do so, lieutenant; and this was rather a compliment than otherwise to your mode of warfare. He felt yours to be a power comparable only to the mighty animal to which he had reference. It was the natural expression of his feelings, I am sure, and not by way of offence."

"I forgive him," was the response of Porgy, as he listened to this explanation.

"Colonel Singleton, I believe, sir?" said Meadows, tendering his sword. "The fortune of the day is yours, sir. Here is my sword. I am Lieutenant Meadows, late in command of this detachment."

Singleton restored the weapon graciously, and addressed a few courteous sentences to his prisoner; but, by this time, Porgy discovered that his ear had lost a thin but important slice from its pulpy extremity. His annoyance was extreme, and his anger rose as he discovered the full nature of his loss.

"Sir—Lieutenant Meadows," said he—"you shall give me personal satisfaction for this outrage the moment you are ex-

changed. You have done me an irreparable injury! You have
marked me for life, sir — given me the brand of a horse-thief —
taken off one of my ears! One of my ears!"

"Not so, my dear lieutenant," said Singleton. "Only the
smallest possible tip from the extremity. Once healed it will
never be seen. There is no sort of deformity. You were rather *full* in that quarter, and could spare something of the development."

"Were I sure of that!"

"It is so, believe me. The thing will never be observed."

"To have one's ears or nose slit, sir"—to the Briton—"is,
I have always been taught, the greatest indignity that could be
inflicted upon a gentleman."

"I am sorry, sir," said Meadows—"very sorry. But it was
the fortune of war. Believe me, I had no idea of making such
a wound."

"I can understand that, sir. You were intent only in taking
off my head. I am satisfied that you did not succeed in that
object, since, next to losing my ear, I should have been particularly uncomfortable at the loss of my head. But, if my ear
had been maimed, sir, I should have had my revenge. And
even now, should there really be a perceptible deficiency, there
shall be more last blows between us."

The British lieutenant bowed, politely, as if to declare his
readiness to afford any necessary satisfaction, but said nothing
in reply. Singleton suffered the conversation to go no farther;
but, drawing Porgy aside, rebuked him for the rude manner of
his address to a man whose visage he himself had marked for
life.

"You have laid his mouth open, broken his teeth, and injured
his face for ever; and he a young fellow, too, probably unmarried, to whom unbroken features are of the last importance."

"But my dear colonel, think of my ear; fancy it smitten in
two, as I did, and you will allow for all my violence. The
mark of the pillory ought to suffice to make any white man desperate."

It is probable that Meadows, when he became aware of the
true state of his mouth, and felt his own disfigurements, was

even more unforgiving than Porgy. But we must not, in this episode, lose sight of the field of battle. When our epicurean had secured the person of the British lieutenant, the affair was nearly over. The surprise had been complete. The conflict was as short as it was sharp. The ambush was so well laid as to render resistance almost unavailing ; yet had it been desperately made, and the victory was not won by our partisans without the loss of several gallant fellows. The followers of Meadows, taking the example of their leader, fought quite as long and as stubbornly as himself, without having the fortune to succumb to such a remarkable antagonist. A brave sergeant, with a small squad, made a fierce effort to cut through the partisan horse, but was slain, with all his party, in the attempt. This was the most serious part of the British loss. The detachment was so completely hemmed in on every side, that recklessness and desperation only could have found a justification for fighting at all. A prudent soldier would have been prepared to yield on the first discovery of his situation, and thus avoided any unnecessary effusion of blood. But Meadows was brave without being circumspect. His own account of the affair, as contained in a letter to Balfour, will answer in the place of any farther details of our own.

" To his Excellency, NESBITT BALFOUR, ESQ.

" SIR : It is with feelings of inexpressible mortification, that I have to inform you of the complete overthrow and capture of the detachment under my command, by an overwhelming force of the rebels under Colonel Singleton, of Marion's Brigade. We were met on the route to Nelson's Ferry, toward sunset of the second day after leaving Dorchester, and attacked in a close defile near Ravenel's plantation. We suffered no surprise, our advance feeling their way with all possible caution, and firmly led by Sergeant Camperdown, who, I am sorry to mention, fell finally, mortally wounded, in a desperate effort to cut his way through the ranks of the enemy. Several of my brave followers perished in the same desperate attempt. All of them fought steadily and bravely, but without success, against the formidable numbers by which we were surrounded. Many of the reb-

els were slain in the engagement, being seen to drop in the conflict; but I have no means of ascertaining their precise loss,
since they have studiously concealed their dead, having borne
them away for burial to the thickets. Our loss, I regret to say,
has been out of all proportion to our force; the desperate valor
of our men provoking the enemy to the most unsparing severity. Eleven of them were slain outright, and as many more are
likely to perish from their wounds. Three of the teamsters
were cut down by the rebels while calling for quarters. I myself am wounded, though not seriously, in my right shoulder
and face; and I am suffering severely from bruises, in consequence of my horse, which was killed, falling upon me. I greatly fear that Captain Furness, of the loyalists, is also among the
slain. I have seen nothing of him since the action, and the
enemy can give no account of him. He behaved very well in
the affair, and with a bravery not unworthy his majesty's regular service. He was exposed to particular peril, as, with great
imprudence, he persisted in riding in advance of the party, leaving a considerable interval between himself and the command.
He was thus cut off from all assistance. When last seen, he
was contending unequally with no less than half a dozen of the
rebel troopers, who finally forced him out of the field and into
the forest, where he was either slain or succeeded in making his
escape. It is my hope that he has done so. He is certainly
not among the prisoners. Colonel Singleton was not at the
head of the assailing party. He came up and took command
just as the affair was over. He treats us with a courtesy and
attention quite unusual with the rebels, and holds out to me the
prospect of an early exchange. He has already hurried off the
captured wagons, by the shortest route, to the Santee; though
I perceive that one of them has been sent off in the opposite direction. I trust that your excellency will believe that I have
been guilty of no remissness or neglect of duty. My conscience
acquits me, though unfortunate, of any culpable disregard to the
safety of my charge. I have the honor to be your excellency's
most obedient, humble servant,

" CH. MEADOWS."

This letter was written the day after the action. Of the rage and chagrin of Balfour, on receiving it, we shall learn hereafter. The reader will note that portion of its contents which describes the game—unsuspected by the Briton—which was played by the rebel colonel. When apparently forced from the field, he simply retired to a thicket, where he changed his costume, reappearing, shortly after, on the field in his own proper character. The alteration in his dress, speech, and general manner, was so thorough, as effectually to deceive the British lieutenant, who showed himself as respectful to the partisan colonel as he had been cavalier before to the same person in the character of a simple captain of loyalists.

The affair ended, Singleton proceeded to secure his captives, send off the captured wagons, and attend to the wants of his wounded and the burial of his dead. While engaged in this melancholy duty, he was suddenly called away by Lance Frampton, who conducted him into the adjoining thicket. The youth could scarcely speak from emotion, as he communicated the intelligence of the mortal hurts of Walter Griffin. The dying man was quite sensible as Singleton drew nigh. He lay beneath an oak, upon a heap of moss, which had been raked up hurriedly to soften that bed of earth, to the coldness and hardness of which he should be so soon utterly insensible. His friends were around him, satisfied, as well as himself, that assistance would be vain. As Singleton and Lance Frampton drew nigh, the youth went silently and took his place at the head of the sufferer. Griffin had done good service in the brigade. He was a great favorite with his superiors. Rescued by Singleton from the hands of a blood-thirsty tory, named Gaskens, who had made himself, his wife, and daughter, prisoners, and who was actually preparing to hang him on the spot, Griffin acknowledged a debt of gratitude to the partisan, which rendered his fidelity a passion. His words, on the approach of Singleton, declared his sorrows, not at his own fate, but that his services were about to end.

"I've fought my last fight, colonel; I've done all I could. If you say I have done my duty, I shall die satisfied."

"That I can safely say, Griffin. You have done more than

your duty. You have served faithfully, like a true man; and your country shall hear of your services. Can we do nothing for you, Griffin ?"

" I have it here, colonel—and here !"—his hands pointing to his side and breast. " Here is a shot, and here a bayonet stab; both deep enough. I feel that all's over; and all that I want is that you should send word to my poor wife and daughter. There's my watch, colonel—I've given it to Lance to carry to them—and two guineas in money. It's all I have—not much —but will help to buy corn for them some day in a bad season. Will you send Lance, colonel, and a letter, if you please ?"

" It shall be done, Griffin ; and I will add a little to the money, for the sake of your family. You've served long and well, like the rest of us, with little pay. The money-chest of the British that has just fallen into our hands makes us richer than usual. Your two guineas shall be made ten. Your comrades will see that your wife and child shall never suffer."

The poor fellow was much affected. He took the hand of Singleton and carried it feebly to his heart.

" I'm sorry to leave you, colonel, now, while every man is wanted. You will have years of fighting, and I sha'n't be there to help you. Yes! I will be there! Oh! colonel, if the spirits of the dead may look on earthly things, after the earth has covered the body, I'll go with you over the old tracks. I'll be nigh you when you are drawing trigger on the enemy; and if I can whisper to you where the danger lies, or shout to you when the bugle sounds the charge, you shall still hear the voice of Wat Griffin rising with the rest, " Marion's men, boys ! Hurrah ! Marion for ever !"

In a few hours after he was silent. He was buried in the spot where he died, beneath that great old mossy oak of the forest—buried at midnight, by the light of blazing torches ; and well did his comrades understand the meaning of that wild sob from Lance Frampton, as the first heavy clod was thrown into the shallow grave upon the uncoffined corse, wrapped only in his garments as he wore them in the fight.

The night was nearly consumed in this mournful occupation. British and Americans shared a common grave. The partisans

had lost several of their best men, though by no means the
large number which Meadows had assumed in his letter to Balfour. In silence, the survivors turned away from the cemetery
which they had thus newly established in the virgin forest, and
retired, each to his rude couch among the trees, to meditate
rather than to sleep. Two of the partisans, however, were
drawn aside by Singleton for farther conference that night.
These were Lieutenant Porgy and the young ensign, Lance
Frampton. To these he assigned a double duty. With a small
detachment, Porgy was to take charge of a wagon with stores,
designed for Colonel Walton, whom he was to seek out between
the Edisto and the Savannah. In order to effect his progress
with safety, he was specially counselled to give a wide berth to
Dorchester—to make a considerable circuit above, descending
only when on the Edisto. Singleton was rightly apprehensive
that the report of Meadows' disaster would set all the cavalry
of Dorchester and Charleston in motion. The wagon was to be
secured in the swamps of Edisto until Walton could be found ;
and, with the duty of delivering it into his keeping fairly executed, Porgy, with Frampton, was to seek out the dwelling of
Griffin's wife and daughter, who dwelt in the neighborhood of
the Edisto, conveying a letter from his colonel, and the little
treasure of which the poor fellow died possessed—Singleton
having added the eight guineas which he had promised to the
dying man ; a gift, by the way, which he could not have made
but for the timely acquisition of the hundred and fifty found in
the British money-chest.

The duty thus assigned to Porgy and Frampton was one of
interest to both parties ; though the corpulent lieutenant sighed
at the prospect of hard riding over ground so recently compassed which lay before him. At first he would have shirked the
responsibility ; but a secret suggestion of his own thought rapidly caused a change in his opinions. To Lance Frampton,
who stood in a very tender relation to Ellen Griffin, the daughter of the deceased, the task was one equally painful and grateful. To Porgy, the interest which he felt was due to considerations the development of which must be left to future chapters.

CHAPTER XX.

LOYALIST BEAUTIES IN CHARLESTON.

SINGLETON was compelled to forego the small but valuable successes which he had been pursuing, by a summons from Marion. The latter had, by this time, provoked the peculiar hostility of the British general. Cornwallis sent Tarleton in pursuit of him with a formidable force ; and the "swamp-fox" was temporarily reduced to the necessity either of skulking closely through his swamps, or of taking refuge in North Carolina. We shall not follow his fortunes, and shall content ourselves with referring to them simply, in order to account for Singleton's absence from that field, along the Santee and the Ashley, in which we have hitherto seen him engaged, and where his presence was looked for and confidently expected by more than one anxious person. He had made certain engagements with Williamson— subject always to the vicissitudes of the service—which required him to give that gentleman another meeting as soon as possible.

In the hope of this meeting, we find Williamson very frequently at the Quarter House, or at the tavern immediately above it, known as the Eight-Mile House. Sometimes he went alone on this pilgrimage, at others he was accompanied by companions whom he could not avoid, from among the officers of the British garrison. Most commonly, these visits were ostensibly for pleasure. Pic-nics and other parties were formed in the city, which brought out to these favored places a goodly cavalcade, male and female, who rejoiced in rural breakfasts and dinners, and gave a loose to their merriment in the wildest rustic dances. The damsels belonging to loyalist families readily joined in these frolics. It was a point of honor with the "rebel ladies" to avoid them ; a resolution which the British officers vainly endeavored to combat. Balfour himself frequently strove to engage Katharine Walton as one of a party especially devised in her honor, but without success.

It is time, by the way, that we should recall that young maiden to the reader's recollection. She was received into the family of the venerable Mrs. Dick Singleton, the aunt of her lover. This old lady was a woman of Roman character, worthy to be a mother of the Gracchi. She was sprung of the best Virginia stock, and had lost her husband in the Indian wars which ravaged the frontier during the last great struggle of the British with the French colonies. She was firmly devoted to the Revolutionary movement — a calm, frank, firm woman, who, without severity of tone or aspect, was never seen to smile. She had survived some agonies, the endurance of which sufficiently served to extinguish all tendencies to mirth. Her dwelling in Church street, in the neighborhood of Tradd, was a favorite point of re-union among the patriots of both sexes. Hither, in the dark days which found their husbands, their brothers, their sons in exile, in the camp, or in the prison-ship, came the Rutledges, the Laurens', the Izards, and most of the well-known and famous families of the Low Country of Carolina, to consult as to the future, to review their condition, consider their resources, and, if no more, " to weep their sad bosoms empty." Katharine Walton was not an unworthy associate of these. She was already known to the most of them personally, and by anecdotes which commended her love of country to their own ; and they crowded about her with a becoming welcome when she came.

These were not her only visiters. She was an heiress and a beauty, and consequently a *belle*. Balfour himself, though past the period of life when a sighing lover is recognisable, was pleased to forget his years and station in the assumption of this character. He was followed, at a respectful distance, by others, whom it better suited. There were the Campbells, the one known as " mad," the other as " fool," or " crazy" Campbell ; there was Lachlin O'Fergus, a captain of the guards, a fierce, young, red-headed Scotchman : there was the gallant Major

Barry, *le bel esprit* of the British garrison, a wit and rhymester; and his inseparable, or shadow, Capt. M'Mahon, a gentleman who, with the greatest amount of self-esteem in the world, might have been willing to yield up his own individuality, could he have got in place of it that of his friend. And Barry was almost as appreciative as M'Mahon. They were the moral Siamese of the garrison, who perpetually quoted each other, and bowed, as if through self-respect, invariably when they did so. There were others who, like these, with them and after them, bowed and sighed at the new altars of beauty which, perforce, were set up when Katharine Walton reached the city; and the house of Mrs. Singleton, from having hitherto been only the sad resort of the unhappy, who mourned over the distresses of the country, was now crowded, on all possible occasions, by the triumphant, whose iron heels were pressed upon its bosom. Nor could the venerable widow object to this intrusion, or discourage it by a forbidding voice or aspect. She had been long since taught to know that the "rebel ladies" were only tolerated by the conquerors, who would rejoice in any pretext by which they would seem justified in driving forth a class whose principles were offensive, and whose possessions were worthy of confiscation. She resigned herself with a good grace to annoyances which were unavoidable, and was consoled for her meekness as she discovered that Katharine Walton was as little disposed to endure her visiters as herself. She esteemed the tribe at its true value.

It was seldom that the "loyalist ladies" showed themselves in the circles of Mrs. Singleton. They were held to have lost *caste* by the position which they had taken, and, perhaps, felt some misgivings themselves that the forfeiture was a just one.— It was seldom that they desired to intrude themselves; or, rather, it was seldom that this desire was displayed. They held a rival set, and endeavored to console themselves for their exclusion from circles which were enchanted by a prescriptive *prestige* of superiority, by the gayety and splendor of their festivities. They formed the *materiel* and *personnel* of the great parties given by General Leslie, by the Colonels Cruden and Balfour, and by other leading officers of the British army, when desirous of conciliating favor, or relieving the tedium of garrison life.

As a ward of Colonel Cruden, and measurably in the power of Colonel Balfour, it was not possible for Katharine Walton wholly to escape the knowledge of, and even some degree of intimacy with, some of the ladies of the British party. A few of them found their way, accordingly, to Mrs. Singleton's. Some of these were persons whose political sympathies were not active, and were due wholly to the direction taken by their parents. Others were of the British party because it was the most brilliant; and others, again, because of warmer individual feelings, who had found objects of love and worship where patriotism—the more stately virtue—could discover nothing but hostility and evil.

Of these persons we may name a few of whom the local tradition still entertains the most lively recollections. Conspicuous among these damsels, known as "loyalist" belles of Charleston, during its occupation by the British army, were "the Herveys;" three sisters, all of a rich, exuberant, voluptuous beauty, and one of them, at least, the most beautiful of the three, of a wild and passionate temper. "Moll Harvey," as she was familiarly known, was a splendid woman, of dark, Cleopatra-like eyes and carriage, and of tresses long, massive, and glossily black as the raven's when his wing is spread for flight in the evening sunlight. A more exquisite figure never floated through the mazes of the dance, making the eye drunk with delirium to pursue her motion. She was of subtle intellect also, keen and quick at repartee, with a free, spontaneous fancy, and a spirit as bold and reckless as ever led wilful fancy wandering. She had been, for a long time, the favorite of Balfour. He had sighed to her, and followed her with addresses that only seemed to forbear the last avowal. But this, though still forborne, was still anticipated hourly by all parties, the lady herself among them. That Balfour still refrained was a matter of common surprise, and to be accounted for in two ways only. Though of the best family connections, she had no fortune. This might be a sufficient reason why he should forbear to unite himself irrevocably with her, or with any woman; for the commandant of Charleston was

notorious for his equal greediness of gain and his ostentatious
expenditure. There was yet another reason. Moll Harvey had
made herself somewhat too conspicuous by her flirtations with
no less a person than Prince William, then in the navy; better
known to us in recent periods as William IV., king of Great
Britain.* She might have been only vain and frivolous, but the
mouths of public censure whispered of errors of still graver character. She certainly gave much occasion to suspicion. That
the prince was madly fond of her is beyond question. It was
even said that he had proposed to her a secret marriage, but
that the proud, vain spirit of the girl would listen to nothing
short of the public ceremonial. Such was the *on dit* among
those most friendly and most inclined to defend her conduct.
This may have been wild and daring rather than loose or licentious; but a woman is always in danger who prides herself in
going beyond her sex. Enough, that public conjecture, seeking
to account for Balfour's reluctance to propose for her hand,
while evidently passionately fond of her person, was divided
between his known avarice, and his doubts of the propriety of
her conduct in the flirtation with his prince. Such were his
relations with Moll Harvey at the period when he first saw
Katharine Walton, and was struck with the twofold attractions
of her beauty and her fortune.

There were three other young ladies, belonging to the British
party, with whom Katharine Walton shortly found herself
brought occasionally into contact. One of these was Miss Mary
Roupell, who divided the sway over the hearts of the garrison
very equally with her competitors. She was the daughter of
George Roupell, a firm and consistent royalist, a man of worth
and character, who, before the Revolution, had been one of the
king's council (colony), and held the lucrative office of post-
master. Mary Roupell was a proud beauty, as haughty as she
was lovely, and particularly successful in the ball-room. It was
never her fortune, on such occasions, to remain unnoticed, a
meek, neglected flower against the wall.

Paulina Phelps was another of these loyalist beauties. She
was a lady of handsome fortune, and of one of the most respec-

* Traditional.

table families. With many admirers, she was particularly distinguished by the conquest of one of the most dashing gallants
of the garrison. This was Major Campbell—Major Archibald
Campbell, or, as he was better known, "Mad Archy," or "Mad
Campbell"—a fellow of equal daring and eccentricity; his dashing and frequent adventures of a startling nature securing for
him his very appropriate nickname. We shall have occasion
to record some of these adventures in the course of our narrative,
by which we shall justify its propriety.

There was still another damsel, ranked among the loyalist
ladies of Charleston, whom we should not properly style a *belle*,
since she was not acknowledged to possess this distinction. Yet
her beauty and grace were worthy of it. Ella Monckton was a
blonde and a beauty; but the eager impulse of her nature,
which might have carried her forward to conquests—at least
secured her some of the social triumphs in which her companions delighted—had been checked by the circumstances of her
condition. Her family was reduced; her mother lived upon a
pittance, after having been accustomed to prosperity, and her
brother, a youth a year younger than his sister, obtained his
support in the employment of Balfour, as his secretary. Ella
was just twenty years old, with features which looked greatly
younger, an almost infantine face, but in which, in the deep
lustrous depths of her dark blue and dewy eyes, might be read
the presence of the ripest and loveliest thoughts of womanhood
and intellect. She was quiet and retiring—sensitively so—shy
to shrinking; yet she united to this seemily enfeebling characteristic a close, earnest faculty of observation, a just, discriminating judgment, high resolves, deliberate thought, and a warm,
deeply-feeling, and loving nature. She was one of those, one
of the very few among the rival faction, who commended themselves, in any degree, to the sympathies of Katharine Walton.
Yet, properly speaking, Ella Monckton had no active sympathies with the British party. Her father had been a supporter
and servant of the crown, and she rather adopted his tendencies
tacitly than by any exercise of will. That her brother should
find his employment with Balfour, should be another reason for
her loyalty. There were yet other reasons still which we must

leave to future occasions to discover.   Shy and sensitive as was the spirit of Ella Monckton, she was singularly decisive in the adoption of her moods.   These were rarely changeable or capricious.   They grew out of her sympathies and affections; and she was one of those who carry an earnest and intense nature under an exterior that promised nothing of the sort.   Her heart, already deeply interested in the business most grateful and most important of all to the woman—her affections involved beyond recall—she was as resolute in all matters where these were concerned, as if life and death were on the issue.   And, with such a heart as hers, the issue could be in the end no other than life and death.   But these hints will suffice for the present, furnishing clews to other chapters.

CHAPTER XXI.

BROTHER AND SISTER.

It was late at night. The close of the day in Charleston had been distinguished by the return of Balfour from Dorchester. Waiting on his moods, rather than rendering him any required services, his secretary, Alfred Monckton, lingered until abruptly dismissed. He hurried away, as soon as his permission was obtained, to the ancient family abode, one of the remotest, to the west, at the foot of Broad street. The dwelling, though worn, wanting paint, and greatly out of repair, attested, in some degree, the former importance of his family. It was a great wooden fabric, such as belonged particularly to the region and period, capable of accommodating half a dozen such families as that by which it was now occupied. The Widow Monckton, with her two children, felt all her loneliness. She had waited for Alfred till a late hour, until exhaustion compelled her to retire; foregoing one of her most grateful exercises, that of welcoming her son to her arms, and bestowing upon him her nightly blessing. He was her hope, as he was her chief support. She well knew how irksome were his labors, under the eye of such a man as Balfour. And still she knew not half. But her knowledge was sufficient to render her gratitude to her boy as active as her love; and once more repeating the wish, for the third time, " How I wish that Alfred would come !" she left her good-night and blessing for him with Ella, his sister, who declared her purpose to sit up for him.

This, indeed, was her constant habit. It was in compliance equally with her inclination and duty. A tender and confiding sympathy swayed both their hearts, and the youth loved the sister none the less because love between them was a duty. She was his elder by a single year; and, shy and shrinking as was her temperament, it was yet calculated for the control of his. Yet he was quick and passionate in his moods, and it was only with the most determined reference to the condition of his aged mother, her dependence upon his patient industry and his submission, that he was able to endure a situation which, but too frequently, was made to wound his pride and outrage his sensibilities. Balfour was an adept in making all about him feel their obligations and dependence.

Alfred Monckton was of slight frame and delicate appearance. In this respect, he resembled his sister; but, otherwise, there was physically but little similarity between them. While she was a blonde, of a complexion as delicate as that of the rose-leaf, the crimson blood betraying itself through her cheeks at every pulsation, he was dark and swarthy, with keen, quivering black eyes, and hair of the blackest hue and the richest gloss. A slight mustache, little deeper than a pencil line, darkened upon his lip; but nowhere was his cheek or chin rendered manly by a beard. This description must suffice. So much, perhaps, is necessary in connection with the character which we propose to draw.

His sister received him with a kiss and an embrace

"You have been drinking wine, Alfred?"

"Yes, Ella. And I sometimes think that the liquor will choke me, as I drink at the board of Balfour."

"And why, pray?"

"He *bids* me drink, Ella; he does not ask. He *commands;* and you can scarcely understand how such a command should be offensive, when you know that I relish old Madeira as well as any one. But so it is. It is as if he would compensate me, in this manner, for the scorn, the contempt, the frequently haughty and almost brutal insolence of his tone and manner. How I hate him!"

"Bear with him, my brother, for our mother's sake."

"Do I not bear, Ella? Ah! you know not half."

"Nor would I know, Alfred, unless I could relieve you. But —he has, then, returned?"

"Yes; late this evening. He comes back in great good humor. He talks nothing now but of the famous beauty, Katharine Walton. She is his new passion; and Moll Harvey is in great danger of losing her ascendency. Miss Walton is wealthy as well as handsome. I have not seen her; but she is already in the city."

"In the city, Alfred?" was the inquiry, in tones singularly subdued and slow, as if they required some effort on the part-of the speaker to bring them forth.

"Yes. It appears that she arrived yesterday or the day before. But I heard nothing of it till he came. He has already been to see her. She lodges with her kinswoman, Mrs. Dick Singleton, where you may have an opportunity of meeting her."

"I do not care to meet her, Alfred," was the hastily-uttered answer; and the sounds were so sad, that the youth, placing a hand on each of her cheeks, and looking steadily into her large blue eyes, inquired, curiously and tenderly—

"And why, Ellen, my sister—why have you no curiosity to see the beauty whom the whole city will run to see!"

"That alone should be a sufficient reason."

"Ah! but there is yet another, my sister. Your voice is very sad to-night. Ella, my dear Ella, beware of your little heart. I am not a sufficient counsellor for it, I know; but I can see when it suffers, and I can give you warning to beware. You do not tell me enough, Ella. You do not confide sufficiently to your brother—yet I see!—I see and fear!"

"What do you fear, Alfred?"

"I fear that you are destined to suffer even more than you have done. I have other news to tell you, which, if I mistake not your feelings, will make you still more unhappy."

"Do not—do not keep me in suspense, Alfred."

"I will not. You will know it sooner or later, and it is best always, to hear ill news at first, from friendly lips. Major Proctor is disgraced, and that subtle, snake-like fellow, Vaughan, is now in command of the post at Dorchester!"

The maiden clasped her hands together in speechless suffering.

"Ah, Ella! I was afraid of this. I have seen, for a long

time, how much you thought of Major Proctor; yet you told me nothing."

"And what was I to tell you? That I loved hopelessly; that my heart was yielded to one who had no heart to give; that I had been guilty of the unmaidenly weakness of loving where I could have no hope of return; that, with the fondness of the woman, I lacked her delicacy, and suffered the world to see that passion which I should never have suffered myself to feel until my own heart had been solicited! Oh! Alfred, was this the confession that my brother would have had me make? You have it now! I have shown you all! Would it have availed me anything that I had told you this before?"

This was passionately spoken, and the girl covered her eyes with her hands as she made the confession; while an audible sob, at the conclusion, denoted the convulsive force of that emotion which she struggled vainly to suppress.

"Ah, my poor, sweet sister! It is what I feared. I have not studied your heart in vain. And, what is worse, I can bring you no consolation. I can not even give you counsel. Proctor, it is said, is devoted to Miss Walton. It is through his passion for her that he is disgraced. He is said to have helped her father in his escape at Dorchester, and is to be court-martialed for the offence. The charge is a very serious one. It amounts to something more than neglect of duty. It is a charge of treason, and may peril his life; at all events, it perils his reputation as a man of honor and an officer."

"And this is *all* the doing of that venomous creature, Vaughan! I *know* it, Alfred. This bold, bad man, has been at work, for a long while, spinning his artful web about the generous and unsuspecting nature of Proctor. Can nothing be done to save him?"

"I do not see how *we* can do anything."

"Do not speak so coldly, Alfred. Something *must* be done. You know not how much may be done by a resolute and devoted spirit, however feeble, where it honors—where it loves! The mouse may relieve the lion, Alfred."

"You speak from your heart, Ella, not from your thought."

"And the heart has a faculty of strength, Alfred, superior to any thought. *You* may do something, my brother. You *will* do something. If we are only in possession of the counsels of the enemy, we may contrive to baffle them. You will see — you will hear. You will know where Balfour and Vaughan plant their snares; and we shall be able to give warning, in due season, to the noble gentleman whom they would destroy."

"Ella, my sister," replied the other gravely, "you forget that I am, in a measure, the confidant of Balfour. It will not do for me to betray his secrets. I have hitherto withheld nothing from you. I have spoken to you as my other self; but, remember, these are not my secrets which I confide to you. They must be sacred. It is impossible that I should communicate to you the counsels of my employer, with the apprehension that you will use your knowledge to defeat them."

The warm, conscious blood rushed into the face of the maiden. She hesitated; she felt a keen sting of self-reproach as she listened; but, the next moment, she replied with an argument that has frequently found its justification in morality.

"But we are not to keep the counsels of the wicked. We are not to keep faith with those who aim to do evil. It is but right and just that we should seek to warn the innocent against the snare spread for them by the guilty."

Alfred Moncton was not equal to the moral argument. He waived it accordingly.

"But you forget, my sister, that the innocence of Major Proctor rests only on our assumption. Everybody believes him guilty. Of the facts we know nothing, except that they show against him. He has suffered a rebel to escape from justice even at the place of execution. He is reputed to be a devoted lover of this rebel's daughter. He was a frequent visiter at her residence, to the neglect of his duties in the garrison. The consequences are serious. All the loyalist families cry out against him; and the general impression of his guilt seems to be borne out by the facts and appearances."

"I will not believe it, Alfred."

"There, again, your heart speaks, Ella! Ah, my poor sister, I would that you had never seen this man!"

She exclaimed hastily, and in husky accents —

"Perhaps I too wish that I had never seen him. But it is too late for that, Alfred. I can not control my heart; and to you, I am not ashamed to confess that I love him fondly and entirely. You must help me to serve him, Alfred—help me to save him."

"And yet if he loves another!"

"Be it even so, Alfred, and still we must save him if we can. It is not love that for ever demands its recompense. It is love only when prepared for every sacrifice. I must seek to serve in this instance, though the service may seem wholly to be without profit to myself; and you must assist me, though, perhaps, at some peril to yourself. But there will be no peril to you really, as I shall manage the affair; and where the heart is satisfied in the service, it must needs be profitable. The love need not be the less warm and devoted, because felt for a being who is wholly ignorant of its existence. Let Proctor be happy with this rebel lady if he may. It is enough that he knows me not —that he loves me not! Why should he not love another? Why not be happy with her? The world speaks well of his choice. May they be happy!"

"It is not so certain that he loves hopefully, Ella. On the contrary, much is said against it."

"Ah, believe it not! She is sensible, they say; she will scarcely have listened to Proctor with indifference."

"You will call upon her, Ella?"

"No; that is impossible."

"How will you avoid it? She is the ward now of Colonel Cruden; and both Balfour and himself will expect all the loyalist ladies to do honor to one whom they have so much desire to win over to the cause. Besides, she lives with Mrs. Dick Singleton, and mother's intimacy with her—"

"Is not exactly what it has been. They still visit; but there is a spice of bitterness now in the eternal discussion of their politics; and they have tacitly foregone their intimacies. An occasional call is all that either makes. Still, mother will have to go; but there is no obligation upon me to do likewise."

"And have you really no curiosity to see this beauty!"

"No—yes! The very greatest. I would see, search, and

study every charm, and seek to discover in what the peculiar fascination lies which has won that cold, proud heart. But I fear—I tremble, Alfred, lest I should learn to hate the object that he loves."

"My poor Ella! what shall I do for you?"

"Do for *him*, Alfred. You can do nothing for me. I must do for myself. If I have been weak, I will show that I can be strong. I will not succumb to my feebleness. I will overcome it. You will do much for me, if you will assist me in saving Major Proctor from his enemies."

"And wherefore should I peril myself for one who has done you such a wrong?"

"There will be no peril to you, dear Alfred; and for the wrong, he has done me none. It is I, only, who have wronged myself."

"Ay, but there is peril—nay, little less than my sacrifice, Ella, which may follow from my helping you in behalf of Proctor. And I see not why *I* should risk anything in behalf of a man who will neither know nor care anything about the sacrifice we make. He has no claim upon *me*, Ella."

"Ah, brother, would you fail me?"

"What is this man to you or me? Nothing! And—"

"Oh, Alfred!—Proctor nothing to *me*, when he compels these tears—when, to mention his name only, makes my heart tremble with a mixed feeling of fear and joy! Oh, my brother, you are greatly changed, I fear!"

She threw herself upon the youth's bosom as she spoke these words of melancholy reproach; and his eyes filled with sympathetic drops as he heard her sobbing upon his shoulder.

"Alas! Ella!" he exclaimed. "You speak as if I had any power to serve or to save. You deceive yourself, but must not deceive me. I know my own feebleness. I can do nothing for you. I see not how we can serve Proctor."

"Oh, I will show you how!" she answered eagerly. "A just and good man need have no fear of open enmity. It is the arts that are practised in secret that find him accessible to harm. You shall show me how these spiders work, and where they set their snares, and leave the rest to me."

"Yes; but, Ella, you are not to betray any of my secrets. That would be dishonoring, as well as endangering me, Ella; and I much doubt if it would be of any service to the person you seek to serve. But I will help you where I can with propriety. If I can show you in what way you may avert the danger from him without—"

"Oh, yes! That is all that I ask, dear Alfred! That is all!"

The poor fellow little suspected to what extent the fond and erring heart of his sister had already committed both. He little knew that her secret agency—which might very naturally conduct to his—was already something more than suspected by the wily Vaughan.

CHAPTER XXII.

LOVE PLAYS THE SPY.

It was probably a week after this conversation, when, one night, Alfred Monckton returned home to his mother's dwelling at an early hour of the evening, and with a roll of papers beneath his arm. He was all bustle and weariness.

"Come with me, Ella, into the library," he exclaimed to his sister. "I have more work for you than ever."

Seated in the library, at the ample table which was usually assigned to his nightly toils as the secretary of the commandant —where, in fact, his labors as an amanuensis usually employed him, and, occasionally his sister, until midnight—he proceeded to unfold an enormous budget of rough notes and letters, to be copied and arranged. In these labors, Ella Monckton shared with a generous impulse which sought to lessen the burden of her brother's duties. She now lent herself readily to his assistance, and proceeded to ascertain the extent of the performance which he required.

"These are all to be copied and got in readiness by the morning, Ella, and I am so wearied."

"Let me have them, Alfred; show me what I am to do, while you throw yourself upon the sofa and rest yourself."

"There, that's a good creature. Copy me that, and that, and that. You see all's numbered; letter them thus, A, B, C, and so on, just as you find them on the scraps; only copy them on these sheets. Here's the paper; and the sooner you set to work the better. I will come to your help as soon as I have fairly rested. If I could sleep ten minutes only."

" You shall. Give me the papers, and let me go to work."

And she began to gather up, and to unfold, and arrange the several manuscripts.

" Stay! Not these, Ella. And, by the way, you are not to see these, though they would interest you much. They concern Proctor."

" Ah !"

" Yes; they are notes for his trial. There is to be a court of inquiry, and these are memoranda of the charges to be made against him, with notes of the evidence upon which they rest."

"And why am I not to see these, Alfred ?"

" Because I am positively forbidden to suffer them to be seen, Ella. Balfour seems a little suspicious, I think. He was most particular in his injunctions. The fact is, Ella, the allegations are very serious and the proofs are strong. If the witnesses be of the proper sort, they will convict and cashier Proctor. The worst is, that they will take him by surprise ; for, as it is to be a court of inquiry only, no specifications will be submitted, and he will scarcely anticipate these charges if he be innocent of them. There, I can't show them to you, so don't ask me."

" But, Alfred, will you really suffer me to do nothing—will you do nothing yourself—for the safety of a person against whom there is such a conspiracy ?"

" What can I do ? What should I do ? I have no right to anything which shall involve a breach of trust. You would be the last person, Ella, to expect it."

The poor girl sighed deeply and looked wistfully upon the mass of papers which he detached from the others, folded up, and put away in his escritoir. But she forbore all further entreaty, and, with a good grace and a cheerful manner, proceeded to the work assigned her.

" And news for you too, Ella," said the young man, now looking up from the sofa upon which he had just flung himself. " Proctor is in town. He came down yesterday, and was this morning to see Balfour. But he refused to be seen—was too busy. Such was his answer; though I knew he was only busy with his tailor, whom he frequently consults—perhaps quite as frequently as any other person. Proctor waited in my apartment. I am truly sorry for him. He is a fine manly-looking fellow, and wore so sad, yet so noble a countenance."

Another sigh from Ella—but she said nothing in reply; and, in a few moments, Alfred was asleep, fairly overcome by the toils of the day and the preceding night. She, meanwhile, urged her pen with a rapid industry, which seemed resolute, by devotion to the task immediately before her, to forget the exciting and sorrowful thoughts which were struggling in her mind. When her brother awoke, her task was nearly ended. But his remained to be performed; and, with assiduity that never shrunk from labor, she continued to assist in his. It was nearly midnight when they ceased.

"We have done enough, Ella, for the night, and your eyes look heavy with sleep. You are a dear girl, my sister, and I love you as brother never loved sister before. Do you not believe me? There, one kiss, and you must to bed. To-morrow night shall be a holiday for you. I mustn't receive assistance in that business of Proctor's, and that's for to-morrow. Good night, Ella; good night!"

They separated, and took their way to their respective chambers. When Ella Monckton reached hers, she threw herself into a chair, and clasped her hands in her lap with the air of one struggling with a great necessity and against a strenuous desire.

"I must see those papers!" she muttered, in low accents, to herself. "They may be of the last importance in *his* case. I can not suffer him to be crushed by these base and cruel enemies. Shall I have the means to save him from a great injustice—from a wrong which may destroy him—yet forbear to use them? There is no morality in this! If I read these papers without Alfred's privity, in what is he to blame? He betrays no confidence; he violates no trust; he surrenders no secret. I can not sleep with this conviction. I must see these papers!"

Where was the heaviness that weighed down these eyelids when her brother looked tenderly into her face at parting? He was mistaken when he ascribed their expression to the need for sleep. They were now intensely bright, and glittering with the earnestness of an excited will which has already settled upon its object. Her meditations were long continued, and, occasionally, broke out into soliloquy. Her mind was in conflict, though her will was resolute and fixed. But, with such a will, and goaded by the passionate sympathies of a woman's heart in behalf of the being whom it most loves, we can hardly doubt as to her final conclusion.

She arose, and left her chamber with the lightest footstep in the world; traversed the passage which divided her brother's chamber from her own, and listened at the entrance. All was still within, and his light was extinguished. She returned to her chamber with a tread as cautious as before; possessed herself of the lighted candle, and rapidly descended once more to the library. The escritoir was locked, but the key, she well knew, occupied the corner of a shelf in the library. Here she sought and found it. She paused when about to apply in to the lock, but recovered her resolution with the reflection, which she was scarcely conscious that she spoke aloud—

"It can't hurt Alfred; *he* violates no trust;—and I may save the innocent man from the snares of the guilty."

The moral philosophy of this speech was not quite satisfactory to the speaker herself. A moment after, and when the escritoir was laid open before her, and before her hands were yet spread forth to seize the papers, she clasped her palms together suddenly, exclaiming—

"Oh! Proctor, could you but know how much is the sacrifice I make for you!"

She sat down, covered her eyes with her hands, and the bright drops stole down between her fingers.

She did not long remain in this attitude. The night was going rapidly. She knew not the extent of the labor before her, but she felt that what was to be done should be done quickly. She unfolded the papers, which were numerous, consisting of letters, memoranda, and affidavits, and read with a nervous eagerness. Her heart beat more loudly as she proceeded. Her cheeks flushed, her eyes filled again with tears, as she possessed herself of the contents. The object of the papers was to show that the attachment of Proctor to the beautiful daughter of the rebel Walton had led to the escape of the latter ; that the former had frequently neglected his duties; had been a frequent visiter at " The Oaks," and had studiously forborne to see those signs of treason and conspiracy which he had been particularly set to watch.

It does not need that we should detail all the facts, as set forth in these documents against him. The nature of the charges we may conjecture from what is already known. The important matter in the papers was the sort of evidence, and the names of the persons, relied on to establish the accusation. The quick intelligence of Ella Monckton enabled her, almost at a glance, to see how much of this testimony it was important for Proctor to know, and to conceive how small a portion of it was possibly open to his conjecture. She shuddered as she reviewed the plausible array of circumstances by which he was enmeshed ; and, while her heart shrank from those particulars which showed the extremity of his passion for Katharine Walton, her mind equally revolted at the depth, breadth, and atrocity of the art, by which he was to be convicted as a criminal.

With a quick and vigilant thought, she determined to afford the victim an opportunity to encounter the enemy, who was evidently resolved upon surprising him by an ambush. She resolved to make a *catalogue raisonnée* of the charges, the specifications, and the evidence under them. Love lent her new strength for the task ; and she who had sat up till midnight copying for her brother now occupied the rest of the night in abridging the documents which threatened the safety of the one whom she so unprofitably loved.

The gray dawn was already peeping through the shutters of her chamber window, when she was preparing to retire. She had completed her task. Excluding all unimportant matter — all unnecessary preliminaries — she had made out a complete report of the case as it was to be prosecuted before the court of inquiry. She had copied so much of the testimony as was needful to cover the points made ; dismissing all surplusage, and confining herself to the absolute evidence alone ; and completed the narrative by a full list of all the witnesses who were relied on to establish the charges against the victim. With this evidence in his possession, and with ample time allowed him, it was in Proctor's power, if really innocent, to meet his enemies on their own ground; to encounter their witnesses with others, and rebut their allegations with all the proofs necessary to explain what was equivocal in the history of his unfortunate command at Dorchester. To cover the papers which she had copied out, in a brief note, and under a disguised hand to Proctor, was the completion of her task; and this done, and the packet sealed, poor Ella, doubtful of the propriety of what she had done, yet the slave of a necessity that found its authority in her best affections, retired to her pillow, with eyes too full of tears to suffer them to be quickly sealed by sleep.

The very next day, Proctor was in possession of the package from his unknown but friendly correspondent, and saw, with mingled feelings of consternation and relief, how large a body of evidence had been conjured up against him, and with how much subtlety and art. Yet, with the game of his enemies revealed to him, he also felt how comparatively easy it would be to defeat their machinations. But let us not anticipate.

It was with some surprise, the next evening, that Alfred Monckton heard his sister propose to her mother to accompany her on a visit to Katharine Walton. He looked up, at the moment, and caught her eyes, but said nothing. But, an hour after, when Mrs. Monckton had retired, Ella herself volunteered an explanation of the motives which had occasioned the change in her resolutions.

"If Colonel Balfour has set his heart upon this lady's being received into society, Alfred, it is particularly incumbent upon us to do what we can to please him. This will be the policy of most persons of the loyalist party in the city, and my refusal, or forbearance, to adopt the same policy would only subject me to suspicions. That my mother should go to see her, and not I, would certainly be suspicious."

She paused, and her brother met her glance with an equivocal smile. Her cheeks flushed, and then, with sudden energy of manner, she continued—

"And, the truth is, Alfred, I *must* see her. I shall never

sleep until I do. I will nerve myself for the encounter with my best strength, and endure the meeting with all the courage and philosophy I can master. The enemy is never more formidable than when at a distance ; and—and—I am not without hope that, when I see Miss Walton near, I shall find in her such qualifications of her beauty as will serve to excuse a lover for becoming cold in his devotions, particularly if—if—he has no longer reason to indulge in hope."

"Never hope it, Ella. Opinion seems to be too universally agreed on this subject. But I am glad that you have thus determined. The sooner we can reconcile ourselves to a painful subject, which we are nevertheless compelled to encounter, the better for our happiness. You will have to meet her, soon or late, for several balls in her honor are in preparation. Colonel Cruden has already resolved on making the Pinckney House a sort of Palace of Pleasure, and as their ward of the crown, Miss Walton is to be the queen thereof. He will be followed, as a matter of course, by the fashionable widow, Mrs. Cornelia Rivington, and she by a dozen others, all emulous, on a small scale, of working after her patterns. But I must to my task. These papers will keep me more than half the night. How I wish, Ella, that I could let you see them, but I dare not. Ah! if poor Proctor only had these papers !"

And the young man proceeded to his solitary labors. His sister dared not look up and meet his glance, while he spoke so innocently of the secrets in his possession. She blushed at the consciousness of the theft of them, which she had committed; her conscience not quite satisfied that, even with the most virtuous motive in the world, she was quite right in doing wrong.

CHAPTER XXIII.

FASHIONABLE SOCIETY IN GARRISON.

IT was eleven in the morning, by the massive mahogany clock that stood in the great entrance to the spacious dwelling at the foot of Broad street, which was occupied by the fashionable Mrs. Rivington. This lady was the widow of a wealthy planter, one of the king's former counsellors for the province, and, for a goodly term of years, the holder of an office of dignity and profit under that best tenure, *durante bene placito*, in a monarchy. The worthy widow, as in duty bound, shared in the unselfish devotion to the crown by which her lord and master was distinguished. She was naturally true to an old school in which, not only had all her lessons, but all her fortunes, been acquired. She was now, accordingly, a fiery loyalist, and the leader of *ton* with all that class in the good city of Charleston who professed similar ways of thinking. She cut most others with little hesitation. She turned her back, with a most sovereign sense of supremacy, upon the Gadsdens and the Rutledges—upon all those, in other words, whom she could not subject to her authority. Resistance to her sway was fatal to the offender. A doubt of her supremacy was a mortal injury to be avenged at every hazard. She aimed at such a tyranny in society—though just as little prepared to avow her policy—as the king of Great Britain was desirous to assert in government; and, for the brief period of time in which the British troops were in sole command of the city, she exercised it successfully. She was an important acquisition to the garrison. She had wealth, and the temper to employ it—was witty if not wise, and her suppers were unexceptionable. Fair, but not fat, nor much beyond the tolerated border line in widowhood, of forty, Mrs. Cornelia Rivington had as many admirers, of a certain sort, as any of the more legitimate *belles* within the limits of the garrison. Stout, red-faced majors of foot, who had impaired their lives in the free use of curry and Jamaica, who enjoyed the good things of this life without much regard to the cost, when the expense was borne by another — or to the evils, when the suffering only followed the feast and did not interfere with it — these were generally the most devoted admirers of the wealthy widow. They would have been pleased — a score of them — to persuade her out of her widowhood, at her earliest convenience ; but, with all her infirmities of wealth and vanity — both of which prompt, quite commonly, to put one's self into the keeping of another — she had, up to the present moment, proved inaccessible to the pleadings and persuasions upon the perilous subject of a second matrimony. Her life, as a widow, was more cheering and grateful, *sub rosa*, than she had found it when a devoted wife, subject to a rule at home, which had acquired its best lessons from an arbitrary official exercise of authority abroad. In brief, Mrs. Rivington's present mode of life was an ample revenge for her sufferings in wifedom. She had no notion of going back to the old experiences, and, perhaps, was by no means satisfied with the special candidates among the garrison who had sought, with bended bodies and fair smirking visages, for the privilege of *keeping* the soft hand, the touch of which, in the ordinary civilities of society, they professed to find so wondrously provocative of the desire for eternal retention. The widow smiled graciously enough upon her *blasé* admirers ; but her smiles led to no substantial results, and afforded but little encouragement. As Major Kirkwood sullenly exclaimed among his messmates, at Tylman's Club-House, on the Bay, near Tradd street —

" She's one of the few women I have ever met, who, with so much wealth, and not more than forty-five, had fairly cut her eye-tooth. She's not to be taken in by gammon. The fact is, boys, professions are of as little value in her eyes as in ours; and the whole game with her is one of a calculation too strict to suffer such nonsense as the affections to be taken into the account at all. What do you think she said to me, when I suffered myself to say some foolish, flattering nonsense in her ears?"

"You proposed to her, Osborne!" cried one of his companions with a shout.

"Devil a bit! unless she construed a very common speech of the mess into a meaning which none of us think to give it."

"But which *you* as certainly meant, major."

"Out with it, Osborne, and confess, you proposed. Your gills tell the story."

They were certainly red enough.

"Not so, I tell you, unless you find an avowal in a commonplace."

"What was it? The words—the words!"

The demand was unanimous, and, with an increasing redness of face and throat, the hardy major of sepoys admitted that he had suffered himself to say to the widow that he should be the happiest man in the world to take her widowhood under the shadow of the Kirkwood name.

"What," he added, "has been said by all of us, a thousand times, to a thousand different women, and without attaching any real meaning to the speech."

"Ha! ha! ha! That won't do, major. The speech is innocent enough, I grant you, at a frolic in the midst of supper, or while whirling through the ball-room. But time and place alter the thing very materially. Now, did you not say these innocent words in a morning call, and did you not entreat the meeting beforehand? The widow Rivington is not the woman to mistake a soldier's gallantry for a formal proposition. No, no! The whole truth, old boy. Confess! confess!"

"You push me quite too hard, Major Stock—quite too hard. I wonder where your accounts would stand, if you were scored in the same manner against the wall. But I frankly admit that it was in the course of a morning call that Mrs. Rivington construed my complimentary commonplace into a proposal."

"You die hard, Kirkwood," replied Stock. "But I have a reason for putting you to the torture, since, to anticipate detection, I am disposed to go to the confessional myself. The truth is, boys, I got an inkling of what Kirkwood intended. I had

not watched his play at the trout for nothing. It was at Vaux-
hall that I overheard him arrange to see her at her house the
next day. The hour and all was appointed, and a glance at
the widow's eyes, at the moment, showed me that Kirk was a
candidate for the ' back door out.' Half an hour after, I walked
with her ladyship myself. I, too, had set my heart upon this
same comely fish"—

"What, you, major ?" was the query from several voices.

"You've been on the sly, then ?"

" I confess it, boys, in the bitterness of my heart, and with a
sore conscience ; happy, however, that I am able to lay my hand
on another's shoulder and say, as the blind man said to the ass,
' there's a pair of us, brother !' "

"Well, what next ?" demanded Kirkwood himself, somewhat
impatiently.

" I'll make the story short for your accommodation. You arranged to call upon the widow at twelve. I entreated the privilege of seeing her just one hour later."

" The devil you did !"

" Yes, i'faith ; and I will venture a trifle that our answers
were both in the same language."

" Yes, perhaps, if the questions were alike," growled Kirkwood.

" Oh, mine was a regimental commonplace, pretty much as
yours. In plain terms, I did as you did, offered myself,
hand heart, and fortune—*pour passer le temps*—only, I assure
you."

" And her answer ?" quoth Kirkwood.

" What was yours ?" demanded Stock.

" I'd as lief tell it as not. It was a sly answer, such as she
would have made believing me to be in earnest."

" Or not believing it. But let's have it."

" ' Major Kirkwood,' said she, ' I've seen too many people
fresh from the blarney-stone, to allow me not to understand you.
It will be your fault if you do not understand me. Of course,
major, you mean nothing of what you say. If I could think
that you did, I should think as little of your understanding as I
should then believe you thought of mine. But, hereafter, even

in jest, do not let me hear you speak such nonsense. We are both too old to suffer from any innocent credulity.'"

"Ha! ha! ha! Ho! ho! ho! Hurrah for the widow. Rivington for ever! And your answer, Stock?"

"The same in substance, though not in words, but just as full of deviltry."

"Ha! ha! ha! What a widow! She'd kill off the regiment in short order."

"Well for us that precious few cut their eye-teeth so precociously," responded the good-humored Stock. "But you look sulky, Kirkwood. Don't harbor malice, my boy. The widow's suppers are as admirable as ever, and she smiles as sweetly as if she had never flung the blarney-stone in the face of either."

"Did she tell you of my visit?" growled Kirkwood, in painful inquiry.

"Not a syllable. I conjectured her answer to you from that which she made to me. Believing myself to be the handsomer, the younger, and the better man, and knowing her to be a woman of admirable taste, I naturally felt sure that you could not stand where I had fallen."

"Out upon you for a vain puppy!" cried Kirkwood, as the merriment of his comrades rang in his ears.

The laugh was against him, and he felt that any further show of soreness would only exaggerate his annoyances. With an effort, he succeeded in recovering his strength and composure of face, and the two baffled candidates, a few moments later, were agreed to call upon the heedless widow, availing themselves of a new privilege which she had just accorded to the fashionable world, by which an ante-meridian visitation would escape misconstruction.

Mrs. Rivington had just adopted a round of "mornings." Her rooms were thrown open at *eleven*, to remain open till *one*. Here she held *levées* for conversation wholly. The device was new —perhaps designed to legitimate such visits as those which Kirkwood and Stock had paid her. At all events, she made the visits unexceptionable, and found security in numbers. In a crowd she could escape the dangers of a *tête-a-tête* with *blasé* majors of foot, each fresh from kissing the stone of blarney.

The old mahogany clock that stood, "like a tower," in the great passage of the stately mansion of Mrs. Rivington, at the foot of Broad street, was, as we have said before, on the stroke of eleven, when the doors were thrown wide for the reception of company. And very soon they came. Mrs. Rivington was not the person to be neglected by the Charleston fashionables at that period, when the objection to the equivocal in place and birth was not so tenaciously urged as in modern times. The indulgent requisitions of that day insisted rather upon externals than the substance. In brief, wit and mirth, and good clothing, and manners *selons les règles,* satisfied the utmost demands of the nice and scrupulous, and nobody needed to boast of his grandmother to find his proper *status* on the floor. There were bores in those days as in ours, and strange to say, some of the most unexceptionable in point of quality and family belonged to this description. But worlds and cities are oddly made up ; and he who would be tolerant in building up humanity must not show himself hostile to any sort of blocks. Mrs. Rivington knew just as well as anybody else of what miscellaneous stuff society is made. She was indulgent in proportion to her experience.

"La, you there ?" she said to Penfield, who wrote gent. after his name, and had once been a lawyer in hope to be attorney-general of the province. He had turned up his aristocratic nose at some of the *oi poloi* of the saloon.

"La, you there, counsellor, and be merciful to yourself if not to me. Were we to admit the quality only, we should die of atrophy, or commit suicide, or some other less-dignified sin ; and were we not to suffer the *canaille,* our gentry would lack the only provocation that makes them endurable. You, for example, have scarcely had a word to say since your entrance, till you saw that long line of Smiths make their appearance, and since that moment your words and features have both been positively sublime. Shall I make the Smiths known to you ? They are really very clever people—good company enough for the summer."

"I thank you. But how is the name spelled ? With an *i* or *y* ?"

"What difference does that make?" inquired Mrs. Rivington.

"All the difference in the world, madam. The Smy/thes are not the Smiths are to be known in society. It is the former only which you will find among the noble families of England. Indeed, the Smiths have all snub noses, which, as my venerable grandmother always assured me, is a sign of low birth and doubtful origin. Excuse me; but as they are crossing here, I'd rather find my way to the opposite end of the room. These steel mirrors of yours exhibit the outline admirably. They are just at the proper hang. Ah, my dear Mrs. Rivington, could we only choose properly our guests!"

And, with a sigh, Penfield, *gent.*, crossed the apartment, while the Smiths, five in number, male and female, with a warm impulse, that betrayed freshness and exuberance, not the less grateful because vulgar, came forward almost at a bound, to acknowledge the presence of their hostess.

"You came but a moment too late, girls," said the widow. "I should otherwise have brought to your acquaintance the famous counsellor, Penfield, a man of talents, and connected with the oldest families of the country."

"Pooh! pooh! no such thing, my dear Mrs. Rivington," cried Mrs. Jeremiah Smith, the mother of the flock. "You never made a greater mistake in your life. Old Penfield, the grandfather of this young fellow, was a good man enough, and quite honest, I believe. He was a first-rate silversmith; and all of our plate—no great deal, I allow—bears his stamp and brand. My father used to say, in his praise, that you could rely upon his putting into his spoons all the old silver that you gave him. As for this youngster"—so she called a person of thirty-five— "he was spoiled by Sir Egerton Leigh, who, finding that he wrote a good hand, took him as his secretary, and afterward made something of a lawyer of him. And *that's* the true history. But I'll have a talk with him, and set him right in his genealogy."

"Do so, my dear Mrs. Smith, and you will be doing him a service. I really believe, if Mr. Penfield could learn the facts from a proper authority, it would be the making of him."

"Would he like it, think you, Mrs. Rivington?" whispered

10

the old lady, now, for the first time, having some doubts on the subject.

"Oh, surely, my dear madam; he is the most grateful being in the world to any person who will prove, unquestionably, the antiquity of his family."

And the mischievous widow turned away to the reception of other guests; but not losing sight of the Smiths, whom she saw in a drove, following in the wake of the mother as she waddled across the room, in full chase of Penfield, the gentleman.

The rooms were, by this time, filled with various groups of both sexes, civil and military. The British officers loomed out conspicuously in their scarlet, while, here and there, might be seen a loyalist captain or colonel, in the more modest green or blue of his own command. These persons were not prominent nor particularly popular, and it might be seen that they were not often sought out by the officers of the regular service. The ladies seemed inclined to give them the cold shoulder also, though this might be owing entirely to the fact that none of them had particularly distinguished himself by his services in the ranks of his majesty.

General Williamson, who made his appearance at this time, was rather more in favor. But he was a *general*, and something still was expected at his hands. It was the policy of the British officers to encourage this opinion, and to treat him accordingly. But even *his* star was on the wane. He felt it so, and rated the courtesies he received at their true value. He was not the person to figure in a saloon, and his appearance now was quite as much to prevent his absence being remarked, as to compel remark by his presence. Besides, Mrs. Rivington's reunions were of a sort to provide the *on dit* of the garrison, and note equally opinions and events. Williamson was too deeply involved in politics to find the scene an attractive one, and he lingered but a little while after showing himself to the hostess.

It was while he conversed with her, however, that the saloon was thrown into quite a buzz of excitement by the *entrée* of the famous belles, *par excellence*, the Harveys—the graces, as they were gallantly styled by the gallant Harry Barry. They were certainly beautiful girls; but the beauty, beyond comparison, of the three was Mary, the younger, lovingly and not irreverently called Moll Harvey. Beside her, all the other stars grew pale. Mary Roupell rapidly made her way to other groups in an opposite direction; the lively Phelps, more dignifiedly, followed this example; and other smaller lustres, fearing, in like manner, that their lesser fires would be entirely extinguished, left an open path for the advancing beauties to the presence of the hostess.

It will be enough if we confine our description of the beauty, on this occasion, to the one being whose possession of it was thus conclusively recognised by the spontaneous fears of every rival. Moll Harvey was of middle size and most symmetrical figure. Ease and grace were natural to her as life itself; but her motion was not that simply of grace and ease. There was a free, joyous impulse in her movements, an exquisite elasticity, which displayed itself in a thousand caprices of gesture, and seemed to carry her forward buoyantly as a thing possessing the infinite support and treasure of the air. As song to ordinary speech, such was the relation which her action bore to the common movements of her sex. A fairy property in her nature seemed to bring with her the spring and all its flowers where she came; and the loveliness which appeared to ray out from her person, as she walked or danced, compelled the involuntary homage of the eye, making the thought forgetful of all search or inquiry except through that single medium.

It was the day for buckram figures and starched pyramidal structures upon the head, reminding you of the towering temples of the goddess Cybele. But Moll Harvey had quite too excellent a native taste to sacrifice her genuine beauties to these monstrous excesses of fashion. A wood-nymph could not have attired herself much more loosely. She would have served admirably as the model for Moore's Norah Creina. A free, flowing skirt, the cincture by no means too closely drawn, sufficing to show that her figure needed no making. A silken cymar encircled, but did not enclose the bust, which, it must be confessed, was much more freely displayed than altogether suits the taste of the present times — so white, so full and exquisitely rounded.

Symmetry was the exquisite characteristic in the beauty of Moll Harvey. The white pillar of the neck, the skin softer and purer than ivory, delicately warmed by health and a generous blood, rose from the bust with a graceful motion that carried its expression also, and seemed endowed with utterance of its own. Nor was the head wanting to, nor the face unworthy of, the rest of our fair picture. A perfect oval, the brows rising up nobly and showing a goodly mass above the eyes; the eyes arched fairly, with brows of jetty black, not thick and weighty, yet impressive; the lashes long, the orbs full, but not obtrusive, lightening now, and now drooping, as with a weight of tenderness, changing with the rapidity of light in correspondence with emotions which were for ever quickening in her wild, warm heart; the nose and mouth both Grecian, of the most perfect cut and finish; and the chin sweetly rounded, to perfect the whole. When, over the white, full shoulders, you have thrown the happily disordered tresses, and when, upon the forehead, you mark the nice dexterity which has grouped the frequent locks in the most sweet and playful relationship, ready, like the silken streamers of the corn, to hold converse with every passing zephyr, you see the outline of look, face, form, feature, but lack still that inspiring presence, the life, the soul, which, like the aroma to the flower, proves the possession of a secret something to which these are but as the chalices that contain the essential spirit. See the life that lightens up the features into love, and gives a motion as of the first flights of a wanton bird, and you forget the external form in the real beauty of soul, and fancy, and feminine impulse, that animates it from within. Ah! too sadly left untutored, that wild and froward heart, that passionate impulse, that delirious glow of feeling, which now but too frequently usurp the sway and overwhelm the affections—never so happy as when subdued and patient—with fierce passions, that appeal ever to the last sad tyranny of self.

The beauties of Moll Harvey naturally provoked reflections in respect to her future fortunes. The crowd which gathered about her, and the few that retreated from her side, were all equally familiar with her career. They had censures, free enough, in regard to her intimacy with Prince William, then a lieutenant in the British navy. They knew how devoted had been the attentions of Balfour, and how undisguised was his homage; yet they well knew that he had kept himself from any absolute committals; and, knowing the humble character of her fortunes, and the selfish character of his ambition—his equal greed of wealth and power—they never doubted that the flirtation between the parties would never assume a more serious aspect, or, if it did, an aspect quite too serious to be grateful to the fame and future of the fairer and the weaker party. As the beauty swept by with her train, the whole subject was very freely discussed by all that class "who but live by others' pain." Our excellent Mrs. Smith, still followed by the clan of Smith, was the first to open the survey.

"Her nose is out of joint now, I reckon. This Miss Walton is not only as handsome as she—every bit—but she's a fortune besides, and everybody knows how much that makes in the scale in showing where beauty lies. After all, the commandant knows—no one better—that it isn't what beauty *shows*, but what it can do—what it can buy or what it can bring—that it is most valued and valuable. Yes, you may put it down as certain, that Moll's nose is for ever out of joint in that quarter."

Good Mrs. Smith had not seen—perhaps had not cared to see—that, while she was making this most consolatory speech, the subject of it was passing directly behind her, and must have heard every syllable. The eye of Moll Harvey flashed, her lips curled with pride, and her brow darkened, and she inly resolved, from that moment, that she would allow no longer the trifling of her lover. She would no longer permit his enjoyment of the *prestige* belonging to such a conquest as herself, without paying the proper price for it. *He* should submit to wear those bonds which the world assumed him to possess the power to place on *her* hands at any moment. She disdained to listen to the farther conversation among the Smiths and their companions, but swept out of hearing as rapidly as was consistent with her pride and dignity. Her absence caused no cessation of the fire.

"As for Miss Walton comparing with our Moll in beauty, that's all a mistake," said Miss Calvert, a spinster who had become an antique without arriving at the condition of a gem. "I've seen this Walton. She's quite too large for beauty— her features are all big; it is true they are somewhat expressive; but no more to compare with Harvey's than mine with Juno's."

"You've certainly gone to sufficient extremes for a comparison, my dear Miss Calvert," put in Major Barry, who at this moment joined the group, followed by his eternal shadow, Captain M'Mahon. Barry bowed and smiled the compliment, which his words did not convey. Miss Calvert's ears were thus taught to deceive her. She smiled in turn, and immediately responded to the dextrous little wit—the wit, *par excellence*, of the British garrison.

"Now, don't you agree with me, Harry Barry?"

"There is, perhaps, but a single respect in which we should not agree, Miss Calvert."

"And, pray, what is the exception?" demanded the lady, with some little pique of manner.

"Nay, nay," he answered slyly, "that confession must be reserved for a less public occasion. You were speaking of Miss Walton's beauty, and that of our Harvey. You are quite right about the former. She is large, but perhaps not too large for her particular style. She is evidently a fine woman—a magnificent woman, indeed—and, if to be styled a beauty, we may style her an angel of a beauty; but Moll Harvey is a love of a beauty, and is so much the more to my liking."

"I knew we should agree," said Miss Calvert, triumphantly, and flattered, she knew not well why.

"Ah!" put in Captain M'Mahon, "Miss Walton is certainly a fine woman, a real lady, and a beauty too. My friend Barry and myself called upon her yesterday, and, after a close discussion, we fully concurred in respect to her points."

"Egad, M'Mahon," cried Major Stock, "you speak of the lady as if you had trotted her out and scrutinized her with the eye of a jockey."

"What! does M'Mahon's pun escape you?" cried Kirkwood. "Do you forget that *points* is his word for *counters*. His image was taken from the whist table, not from the stables. He was thinking of the lady's *cash* when he discussed her *charms*. His idea of beauty—like that of most of us poor soldiers of fortune—must be built upon positive resources, such as tell just as seriously in a private bureau as in an army chest."

" I' faith, my friend M'Mahon is no more prepared to deny the soft impeachment than myself. The fact is, a mere beauty, however beautiful, is quite beyond the means of any of us. For myself, I confess to a preference for Moll Harvey, *per se ;* the beauty of the Walton is quite too stately, too commanding for me. It half awes and overpowers me. Still, the *argumentum ad crumenam* tells wonderfully in her behalf."

" Ah, my friend Major Barry always discriminates the point most admirably. You must let me repeat his impromptu, made this morning as we left the hairdresser's on this very subject."

" Nay, now, M'Mahon, my dear fellow, honor bright!" and the deft and tidy little major affected to be horror-stricken at the threatened exposure, while his little eyes twinkled with his anticipated triumph.

" Oh, but I must repeat, Barry."

" To be sure; repeat by all means.—Come, Barry, this affectation of modesty won't do. You have not a single article in all your wardrobe that sits so badly upon you."

" What! you out upon me also, Stock ?"

" I would save you from yourself, my boy, and from your own vanities, which will surely be your death the moment they assume the show of modesty. We have recognised you, by common consent, the wit and poet of the garrison. You have flung a thousand shafts of satire at the poor rebels and the rebel ladies: and we have applauded to the echo. Shall we be denied our proper aliment now ? No! no! Ah, my dear Mrs. Rivington, you are here in season. Barry has been doing a smart thing, as usual."

" In verse, of course. Are we to hear it ?"

" Are we to be denied ?—particularly when we are told that it relates to the rival beauties, the Harvey and the Walton ?"

" How can you compare them, major ?"

" I do not. I contrast them only. It is Barry's comparison that you are called to hear. His friend M'Mahon answers for it, and he is sufficient authority. We must have it."

"Certainly we must! Captain M'Mahon reads verses like an angel, I know; and, as *his friend* wrote them, he will be sure to read them, with the best affect."

"There's no resisting that, M'Mahon. Come, clear your throat and begin. You are as long in getting ready as was the inspired beast that waited for the blows of Balaam."

"What beast was that, Major Stock?" was M'Mahon's innocent inquiry.

"Oh, one whose voice was that of an angel, so that the comparison need not give you any shock. Come, the ladies wait. Positively, Mrs. Rivington, I never saw so much anxiety in any countenance as in yours. How any gentleman should tantalize a lady's curiosity to such a degree is astonishing!"

"If my friend, Major Barry, will only consent," said M'Mahon.

"I won't stay to listen, M'Mahon," cried Barry, trotting out of the circle, but immediately passing to its rear, where his short person might remain unsuspected; his ears, meanwhile, drinking in the precious streams of his own inspiration.

Thus permitted, as it were, M'Mahon, the centre of a group which had so greatly increased, placed himself in a stiff, schoolboy attitude, and, thrice hemming, extended his hand and arm, in a preparatory gesture, as if about to drag the pleiades from their place of shining. The painful parturition of his lips followed, and the mouse-like monster of an epigram came forth, head and tail complete; and this its substance.

M'Mahon recites —

"When bounteous Fate decreed our Harvey's birth,
We felt that heaven might yet be found on earth;
But when the Walton to our eyes was given,
We knew that man might yet be raised to heaven.
Indulgent Fates, one blessing more bestow —
Give me with Harvey long to dwell below;
And when, and last, ye summon me above,
Then let the Walton be my heavenly love!"

"Bravo! bravo! Harry Barry for ever, and his friend M'Mahon!" cried Major Stock, and the circle echoed the applause.

"And he did it. my friend Barry," said M'Mahon, with the sweetest simplicity of manner—"he did it in the twinkling of an eye, just as we left the hairdresser's. I was determined that it shouldn't be lost, and went back and wrote it down."

"You deserve the gratitude of posterity, Captain M'Mahon, and our thanks in particular," said the fair hostess, in the sweetest accents, and with a smile that did not wholly conceal the sarcasm in her thought.

"What," continued M'Mahon in his narrative, "could have put the idea into my friend Barry's head, at such a moment, I can not conjecture. It was as much like inspiration as anything I ever heard of."

"What put it into his head? Why the oil, the powder, the pomatum, and that picture of the Venus Aphrodite, rising in saffron from a sea of verdigris, which hangs up in the shop. Here's inspiration enough for a wit and poet at any time."

"Ah!" interposed Barry, now slyly pressing through the group, "I am always sure of a wet blanket at your hands, Stock."

"What! you there! And you have heard every syllable! Well, all I have to say, Barry, is this, that your modesty can stand anything in the way of applause, and take it all for gospel."

What further might have been said on this fruitful subject, must be left to conjecture; for, just at this moment, a smartly-dressed officer, of thirty, in the costume of a major, with a wild, dashing air, and long disheveled locks over a florid face, and a dark blue flashing eye, penetrated the circle with a cry of—

"Break off! break off! No more of your fun now; put on your gravest faces and rehearse for tragedy. Here's the commandant coming, all storm and thunder. There's the devil to pay, and no pitch hot."

"Why what's the matter now, mad Archy?" demanded Stock.

The new-comer was famous, after a fashion, in the circle. He was distinguished from a score of Campbells in the city, by the grateful *nom de guerre* of mad, or crazy Campbell. To the former epithet he submitted, rather pleased than otherwise at the imputation. The latter was commonly used in regard to him when he had left the circle.

"Matter enough! Meadows and his train have been cut off by Marion's men. Half of the escort cut to pieces, and the rest prisoners. The wagons all captured, with all the stores. Meadows himself is badly wounded, maimed, and disfigured for life—mouth and nose beaten into one by the butt of a rifle."

"Shocking!" was the cry among the ladies. "Poor, poor Charley! what a fright he must be!"

"He seems to have felt it so ; for so great was his fury that, even after the rebel who struck him was down—a monstrous fellow of twenty stone and upward—Charley's fury never suffered him to stop hewing at the fellow till he had smitten off both of his ears close to the skull, giving him the puritan brand for life."

Campbell's narration, received through third hands, is as we see, something imperfect. We are already in possession of the facts.

"And Balfour ?"

"He is even now coming in this direction, and in an awful fury. I pity all who vex him at this moment. It will need all the smiles of the fair Harvey"—bowing in the direction of the beauty, who had, by this time, joined the group—" and even these may not suffice, unless seconded by those of the fair Walton."

At this open reference to her rival's power, the imperious beauty bit her lips with vexation. Her eyes flashed with fires of scorn she did not seek to suppress, and she turned away from the circle as Balfour entered the apartment. But we need not linger for the tragedy. The farce is sufficient for our purpose.

CHAPTER XXIV.

REBEL LADIES OF CHARLESTON.

WE pass from scenes of frivolity to those of graver cares and objects. This is the true order of human events, and the transition is more natural from gay to grave than the reverse, as they have it at the theatre, and as the moral poet orders it. It is an extreme change from the lively and thoughtless mornings of Mrs. Rivington, to the gloomy evenings at Mrs. Singleton's—from the fashionable and frivolous seeker after motley, in talk and habit, to the serious questioner in the sad affairs of life and its necessities. The two ladies, it may be said, are both politicians; but of very different schools. Mrs. Rivington, the widow of a royal official, finds it pleasant to respect his memory by adhering to his faith, the more especially as his party is in the ascendant, and as she rejoices in the tributes of a brilliant circle in which loyalty commands all the voices. Her preferences will provoke no surprise among the great body of the people, since they represent a triumphant party and cause, and are themselves very agreeable social triumphs. Politics, in her circles, are not so much discussed as accepted; measures rarely command a single reflection, though our lady statesmen are as earnest in their declarations of fidelity to the reigning sovereign as ever were Madame Roland and her amiable associates, in respect to the abstract deities to which they offered their unavailing incense. At Mrs. Rivington's, you will hear as much said against rebellion as a provincial loyalism, ever solicitous to please, will always be found to say ; but the politics of her circle were not calculated to afford much assistance to the councils of Balfour. Nevertheless, he greatly encouraged them.

They had their uses in influencing, through the medium of society, the moods of all those doubtful, capricious, and unprincipled, of whom, perhaps, the greater number of mankind are composed. The youthful of both sexes were always sure to find principles at Mrs. Rivington's suited to their own desires, if not to the necessities of the race and family.

The politics at Mrs. Singleton's were of a different sort. Balfour more than suspected that the old lady was engaged in labors that were forbidden ; but he had been able to fasten upon her no specific cause of offence. Yet was she busy, with a restless interest, in the cause of liberty, that made her nights sleepless, and filled her aged head with vexing thoughts and subtlest combinations. Her house was a point of reunion with all those who, like herself, long for the overthrow of the existing *régime;* who yearn for the return of exiles, well-beloved sons of the soil, dear to their affections, precious to their hopes, the kinsmen of their blood. Hither came, almost nightly, those favoring the cause of the patriots, who, by reason of age, of sex, of feebleness, were suffered to remain within the city of the conqueror. What could these superannuated old men achieve or attempt, who might be seen at dusk, or after it, to enter the doors of the old-fashioned dwelling in Church street ? How should British lords and generals, captains and men-at-arms, apprehend anything from those ancient and well-bred ladies, or those fair and witty young ones, who showed themselves openly in this much-frequented domicil ?

Yet among these were many rare women, such as would have given strength to the Girondins, and armed them more ably for the work of their own and their country's safety. Mrs. General Gadsden, whose stately pride defied the sneer of the witling Barry ; the fierce, proud spirits of Mrs. Savage and Mrs. Parsons, whom the same wit described as tragedy queens, so noble was their spirit, and so well prepared for the extremest perils of humanity. The names of Edwards, Horry, and Ferguson, highly and equally endowed with grace and courage ; of Pinckney and the Elliotts, names immemorially allied with dignity and patriotism ; these were all to be found regular attendants at the " evenings" of Mrs. Singleton. And these evenings were not given to pleasure, as were the mornings of the dashing widow Rivington. Grave studies occupied her guests; work was to be done under counsel of studious and far-seeing heads. Their words went forth from the city with significance to the remote interior, and were frequently followed by large results. They gathered and reported the signs of the times; they conveyed intelligence, sometimes money, and sometimes ammunition— shot and powder—to their brethren in arms. They devised schemes by which to relieve the city from its thraldom. In brief, the dwelling of which Katharine Walton had become an inmate, was the place of frequent assemblage for a very active and sleepless circle of conspirators.

Several of these were present with Mrs. Singleton and Katharine Walton, on the evening of the day distinguished by the opening of the fashionable " mornings" of Mrs. Rivington. From without, silence and darkness seemed to brood over the habitation ; but there was an inner room, well lighted, around the centre table of which might be seen a group of heads which would have been held remarkable in any council or assembly. That of the venerable Mrs. Singleton was itself a study. Her thin, attenuated visage was elevated by a noble forehead, which the few stray gray hairs about her temples, and the sombre widow's cap which she wore, rather tended to ennoble than disparage. Her keen, gray eye and closely-compressed lips denoted vigilance, courage, and circumspection. It had all the fires of youth, burning, seemingly, with as much vigor as ever—the heart of the volcano still active, though in the bosom of the iceberg.

Katharine sat beside her, a steady observer, and mostly a silent one, of the group and the subjects which it discussed. Old Tom Singleton, the wit and humorist, as well as patriot, stood up in the circle, hat in hand, preparing to depart. We shall speak of him more fully hereafter. Behind him stood a boy, sharp-featured and intelligent, of whom the parties spoke sometimes as George, and sometimes as Spidell, the lad being afterwards well known by the people of Charleston, by the two names combined, as a worthy and respected citizen. He carried on his arm a basket, which the ladies had been filling with tapes, laces, linens, and other small articles of dress, designed for a peddling expedition. At the bottom of the basket, however, might have been found one or more packets, cleverly done up, and looking very innocently upon the outside, which a very quick-sighted royalist might have found to contain any quantity of treasonable matter.

The youth of the lad, and the seeming openness of his operations, however, were calculated to disarm suspicion. George Spidell, in fact, was under the active superintendence of Joshua Lockwood, one of the conspirators of the circle, employed constantly as a sort of supercargo in a large *periagua*, which was busily engaged in plying between the city and all the landings and inlets along shore to the Santee river. Stopping at certain well-known points, George was sent ashore with his basket in search of customers; But it was always understood that his visit was first to be paid to certain well-known dwellings. Here it was that the secret package at the bottom of his basket was invariably sought out and selected; and in this manner, Marion, and Horry, and Maham, and others of the partisan captains, contrived to receive weekly information of the condition of affairs in the city. Lockwood, the principal in these expeditions, and little George, his subordinate, suffered some narrow escapes in these innocent expeditions. But these must not beguile us into further digression.

"Let us be off, Lockwood," said old Tom Singleton; "we shall have little time to spare. The tide will serve at daylight, and George must have some sleep before he starts."

"He needs it, and deserves it," said the hostess, kindly, looking at the boy. "But have you eaten heartily, my son?"

The boy glanced at the plate, still remaining on a side-table, which exhibited very few fragments, but enough perhaps for a sufficient answer to the question.

"Thank you, ma'am, yes," he answered; "and I have this, too," he added, showing a huge triangular mass of cake, which he had deposited within his basket. The party smiled.

"George is seldom *off his food*," said Lockwood, "pursuing such a pleasant life."

"And he has learned one of the best lessons," said old Tom Singleton; "that of making provisions for the morrow : the

one great virtue which distinguishes the wise man from the fool.
Let us practise a little upon this lesson ourselves. It is under-
stood that nothing more remains to communicate to our friends.
You were speaking, Doctor——"

Singleton paused, his glance fixing upon one of the gentlemen
of the circle who had hitherto been silent. All eyes were turned upon this person with an expression of deference and esteem.
This was the celebrated David Ramsay, one of the first historians of the country, and a physician of high distinction. He
was then in the prime of manhood, and in the full vigor of his
intellect. In person he was about five feet ten, healthy and
somewhat athletic, but not stout. His countenance was by no
means a handsome one, but it was not an unpleasing one. A
blemish in one of his eyes, from small-pox, gave a slight obliqui-
ty to his gaze; but the entire character of the face was impressive and somewhat prepossessing. An earnest reflection and
cool, intrepid judgment, were clearly shown in the speaking
countenance and the eager and almost impetuous manner. His
utterance was vehement and rapid, but always clear and intelligible. Thus addressed by Singleton, his answer was prompt.

" We were speaking of Williamson. What you hear is no
doubt true. His situation is precisely as is described; and,
doubtless, he never really intended to betray his country or
himself. He was only too weak to be honest at a moment of
great external pressure. He has shrewdness enough to see that
his future situation is unpromising, and foresight enough to discover that Britain has exhausted her own resources, and must
now really rely on ours, if she hopes to continue the war. But
the partisan warfare has put an end to this hope with all persons
of sagacity. The partisans must increase in number daily, and
their frequent small successes will more than avail in keeping
up the popular courage against the occasional large victories of
the British regulars. Now I take for granted, from all I know
of the man, that this prospect has been fully presented to his
eyes. It will become more and more evident with every day.
But is this a reason that we should trust him with ourselves or
with our secrets, particularly as he has not yet so far committed
himself to us as to give us any proper hold upon him ? I sup-

pose that Colonel Singleton is in possession of a certain amount of proof—that Williamson has, in fact, given pledges of returning fidelity; but of the character of this proof and these pledges we know nothing; and they may be such as an adroit person might readily explain away. I am of opinion that we should, at present, make no use of this information. We should watch him, and when he can clearly serve us in any important matter, it will then be time enough to let him understand that we are in the same vessel with himself; but, with my consent, not a syllable before."

"You are right, doctor. Once a traitor, always a traitor. He may be useful—*would* be useful, if he could be true; if treacherous, he might sink our vessel in the moment when the gale was most prosperous, and when we are most richly freighted. Let Robert Singleton manage the matter with him wholly; he has coolness and sagacity enough for any purpose; and there seems to be no reason that we should mix in this business; at all events, not for the present. I confess that, to have any communion with Williamson at all, suggests to me the idea of that unhappy conference—the first on record—which our excellent, but too accessible grandmother had in Eden with the great sire of all the snakes!"

A laugh rewarded this speech, the sentiment of which was generally echoed by the company. The speaker was a lovely and spirited woman, the fairest among the Carolina rebels, the witty, wealthy, and accomplished widow of Miles Brewton, Esq. The father of this lady, Edward Weyman, was among the first of the Carolina patriots to declare himself under "Liberty Tree" in 1766. She inherited his patriotism; and Mary Weyman was, by training and education, well fitted to become the wife of Brewton, who was as strenuous in support of the revolutionary argument as ever was his father-in-law. By marriage with this gentleman, she became strengthened in her attachment to the cause. Her associations rendered it the prevailing sentiment of the household. Her husband was brother to the celebrated Rebecca Motte, and uncle of Mrs. Thomas Pinckney; and their decided sentiments in behalf of the *mouvement* party in America, even if her own had been inactive, would have sufficed to determine hers. But there needed nothing beyond her early training to bring about this result. She was not only a warm patriot, but a thoughtful and a witty one. While observing the utmost grace and delicacy in her deportment in the society of British and loyalists, not withholding herself from them — polite and even sociable with both — she was yet capable of uttering the most sharp and biting sarcasms with the most happy dexterity. Her mind was fresh, sparkling, and original ; her manners equally graceful and lively ; and she brought to the business of conspiracy a shrewdness and depth of opinion which appeared somewhat anomalous, though never unbecoming or out of place, in union with her pleasant wit and surpassing beauty.

"Why, Brewton," said old Tom Singleton, playfully, "you speak with singular feeling of your venerable grandmother's associates ; as if, indeed, you had some personal cause of complaint."

"And have I not ? Is it not sufficient reason for complaint that her weaknesses should have left us perpetually subject to the sarcasms of your pestiferous sex ; in which, though you always play the snake, you still chuckle at your capacity to take advantage of the woman ?"

"Well, the worst reason for your discontent still remains unspoken," said the other.

"Ah, what is that ?"

"Verily, that your complaints avail you nothing, nor your resolves either ; since you only murmur against a fate."

"Which means that, doomed to a connection with your sex, we are never secure against the snake finding its way into our garden. I suppose *that is* our fate ; but, at all events, there is no reason that we should not bruise his head with the hoe whenever we discover him. In the case before us, knowing the reptile, it is agreed we shall keep him at a distance. It will be no bad policy, whenever we do admit him, that we should first be careful to see that his teeth are drawn."

"I am afraid," said Singleton, "if you do that, you deprive him of all power of usefulness. But we need not discuss the matter further. It will be time enough to do so when we shall be perfectly satisfied that he has *cast his skin.* In the meantime, it is agreed that we leave him in the hands of Bob Singleton."

"Ay, ay," said the fair widow; "we may safely do so. *He* has quite enough of the family art to keep a menagerie, yet never fear the fangs or claws of its beasts."

The allusion was to a private collection of beasts, birds, and reptiles, which old Tom Singleton kept for his own amusement.

"Ah!" said the latter, who found something grateful in the allusion—"ah, Brewton, by the way, you are yet to make the acquaintance of my juveniles. I have added to my collection. I have a Rawdon and a Balfour; a young Bruin from Buncombe, one of the most surly of dignitaries, brown and bigoted; and a surprising dexterous monkey from Yucatan, who is a perfect model of an appropriator. In a week, I shall have them both in costume, and you must come and make their acquaintance."

"Present me to his lordship, at least. The bear, by all odds, is preferable to the ape."

"Look you, Singleton," said Lockwood, bluntly, "you will peril your neck always upon your tongue. I pray you, Mrs. Brewton, say not a word further, or you will keep Singleton here all night. We have much to do before midnight, and old Tom belongs to that class of lawyers who prefer to lose a case rather than a witticism. He is so far like your own sex, that a last word with him at parting is essential to his rest for the night."

"Good! very good!" responded Singleton. "We may now claim, between us, to have a power like that of Falstaff, and are not only witty ourselves, but the cause of wit in other persons. Ah, Josh, make your bow to Brewton. She has been to you what the angel was to that excellent beast which Balaam knew better how to beat than ride."

"Away with you!" cried the widow. "You are as inveterate as an ague, and cause shaking sides wherever you come. Hence contagion! Begone, before we have another fit."

The party were preparing to leave—old Singleton, at least, with Lockwood and Master George Spidell, who, by this time, had begun to munch upon the angles of his three-cornered cake;

but, at this very moment, the trotting of horses was audible from the street.

" Hark !" said Mrs. Singleton, " they approach."

The sounds ceased at the entrance, and the company rose in preparation, if not in apprehension. Frequent experience had made them instinctively conscious of danger.

" You can not go forth now," said Mrs. Singleton, " and must steal to your hiding-places. We are to have visiters. You, cousin Tom, and Mr. Lockwood, had better take the back-door into the garden, while you, doctor and Master George, will please step up stairs. Take the basket with you, George."

A heavy rap at the knocker, and the parties thus addressed hurried instantly out of sight, according to the given directions. In another moment, the doors were opened, and the British colonels, Balfour and Cruden, were announced.

CHAPTER XXV.

SHAFTS AT RANDOM.

KATHARINE WALTON would have left the room when these persons were announced, but Mrs. Singleton arrested her. Policy was in conflict with good taste at present.

"You must remain, Kate; it is a necessary ordeal. Have patience. We must submit with a good grace where resistance is without profit. Let us conciliate those whom we can not defy."

She was prevented, by the entrance of their guests, from further remarks of this nature. The ladies all had resumed their seats before the appearance of their visiters. Some were busy in needlework; one appeared to have been reading, her finger resting between the leaves of a volume that she held in her hand. The fair widow Brewton, alone seemed to be unemployed, as, perhaps, her more natural *rôle* lay rather at the tongue's, than the fingers' end. She occupied a venerable arm-chair, which might have dated from the time of Queen Elizabeth. In this she reclined rather than sat, the capacious seat giving full scope to her form, which was seen to the very best advantage. Thus reclined, with her head leaning over the side of the chair, rather than against its back, an arch smile playing on her features, and a world of mischief, concentrated and bright, looking forth from the half-shut eye, she encountered the first glance of the British dignitaries.

Balfour's hurried look around him took in the whole assembly. Mrs. Singleton rose at the entrance of the two—"*arcades ambo*"— and welcomed them to seats with a stately grace and a cold dignity that made itself felt, yet left nothing which could be complained of. Salutations were soon exchanged between the par-

ties. Balfour was quite ambitious of the character of the easy,
well-bred gentleman. He aimed at that pleasant exhibition of
haut ton which never forgets to show its consciousness of superiority.

"Mrs. Singleton, I am glad to see you looking so well. When
I last had the pleasure of calling, you were complaining. You
must give me credit for magnanimity, my dear madam, since
we might well be out of humor with one who has a kinsman
who proves so troublesome to us. I take for granted that you
are aware of the recent performances of Mr. Robert Singleton.
I could wish, for your sake, madam, if not his own, that this
young man had not so deeply involved himself. I am afraid
that he has passed that limit when it would have been the pleasure, no less than policy, of his majesty to hold out to him the
hopes of mercy."

"You are very good, Colonel Balfour; but I doubt if Robert
Singleton will easily be persuaded that this boon is so necessary
to his happiness."

"Ah, my dear madam, do I find you still incorrigible?"

"At my age, sir, change of principle and feeling is not easy.
You will give me credit, sir, for the frankness which has never,
from the beginning, attempted any disguise of sentiment."

"I regret to make the concession, madam. I sincerely wish
that it were otherwise. It is, perhaps, fortunate for all parties,
however, that the cause of his majesty renders necessary no
coercion in the case of your sex. We are content that time
shall do its work. Events that are inevitable will perhaps reconcile you to a condition against which you erringly oppose
yourself at present."

Mrs. Singleton bowed with a dignified gravity, but was silent.
Balfour now passed round the table and approached Katharine
Walton.

"And how is our fair captive?"

"Even as a captive should be, sir. I sigh for the green pas-
tures. I have lost my voice. I sing no longer."

"We shall recall it! We shall hear you again in song. You
will surely soon become reconciled to a captivity that brings you
security under loving guardianship."

" Never! never! I am not conscious of any better security here than at Dorchester, nor do I need any more loving guardianship than that which I have always enjoyed."

" Ah, I see that you are in the hands of erring counsellors. I am afraid, Mrs. Heyward, that something of this wilfulness is due to your ministry. Why is it that one so capable of devotion to a cause should yet be possessed of so little loyalty to her proper sovereign?"

" Meaning George the Third, Colonel Balfour?" replied the lady addressed, a very noble-looking lady, majestic in person, and of singularly fine features.

" Surely!"

" He is no sovereign of mine, sir!"

" My dear madam, will you never take warning from the past?"

" Would Colonel Balfour remind me of the assault upon my dwelling by a ruthless mob, when a dear sister lay dying in my arms? Would he force upon me the recollection of that dreadful brutality, which would have torn a woman to pieces because she refused to show pleasure in the misfortunes of her country? Really, sir, if this is the process by which my loyalty is to be taught, I fear that you will find me the dullest of your pupils."

Balfour's insolence, as usual, had made him blunder. The indignant feeling expressed by the lady was too natural and proper not to find the fullest justification in every mind. Mrs. Heyward's dwelling was assailed and battered by a mob, because she refused to illuminate in honor of the successes of the British.

The commandant of Charleston turned away to some of the other ladies. He was somewhat abashed, but not silenced. After certain speeches meant to be gallant, addressed to Mrs. Savage and Mrs. Charles Elliott, he approached the fair widow Brewton. He was rather afraid of the lady, whose readiness of retort, sufficiently experienced by all of the British officers, was of a sort which enabled her to shape every answer to a dart, and to find, in the most cautiously-uttered address, the sufficient provocation to a witticism.

" Have I found thee, mine enemy?" he said.

"Knowing me as such," she replied, "you have sought me out last. Shall I refer this to your gallantry or your caution? —to the sense of my weakness or your own?"

"To mine own, of course," he answered, bowing.

"The admission is an appeal to my magnanimity," said the widow; "and yet the foe who acknowledges his feebleness and entreats for mercy has no longer the right to entertain a hostile feeling. He must surrender at discretion, in order to obtain the boon which he solicits."

"Why, so I do! You have always found me at your feet."

"Yes; but with the spirit of one who was weaving snares for them all the while."

"Is the sex so easily enmeshed?" he answered, with a sneer.

"Good faith and innocence, which look upward always, are too frequently unconscious of the subtle enemy of whose existence they have no suspicion; since no feeling in their own bosom suggests its image, and they are too lofty in their souls to look *down* for objects of study and contemplation. But, when I spoke of the *snares* of the evil one, I said nothing of his *success*. We are told that the faithful and the true, the innocent and the good, shall always triumph in the end; we are equally assured that evil shall not always exist, and its triumphs shall be temporary. It is the special curse of sin that it must labor in the service of the devil, and without profit; must weave its snares with the toil and industry of the spider, day after day, only to be mortified constantly with the ease and freedom with which, at the proper moment, the supposed victim breaks through all the meshes woven about its feet. I assure you, colonel, when I behold you, and others in your livery, busily working, day and night, in this futile labor against the freedom of our people, I think of those long-legged gentry who congregate in the remote corners of the wall; and I look every moment for the approach of Molly with the house-broom."

"Still keen, sharp, piercing, and cutting as ever."

"How should it be otherwise, since, at every turning, we find the hone; the curious necessity of which seems to be to sharpen the instrument which shall finally separate it in twain."

"Nay, your metaphor halts. The stone may suffer abrasion and diminution from wear; but to be cut in twain by the knife it sharpens——" He paused.

"I suppose I must not complain that a soldier in the service of such a prince as George of Hanover does not readily recall the lessons of history. My metaphor lacks nothing. My allusion was to the case of the Roman augur, Accius Nævius. Your Livy will tell you all the rest."

"You gain nothing, Balfour," said Cruden, sulkily, "in a conflict with Mrs. Brewton."

"O, yes! I trust that both of you gain in proportion to your *need*. I shall suppose that to be far greater than I even regard it now, if, indeed, you do not profit in one respect. He who carries a weapon that he knows not well how to use, or encounters voluntarily with an enemy whom he can not overcome, is in a bad way, indeed, if he does not acquire some lessons of humility at least from such experience."

"Wisely said, that, Cruden. But, of a truth, we must, in some way, overcome an enemy so formidable as Mrs. Brewton. We must do this by love, by service, by devotion, such as the cavaliers of the Middle Ages paid to their chosen mistresses. We must woo and win, if we can, where we can not overthrow. How shall we do this, Mrs. Brewton? You are surely not insensible to the reputation you would enjoy, and the good that you would do, in making us worthy of your affections rather than your hostilities?"

Alas, sir! If it be not sin to venture any opinion as to God's hidden providence, I should say that he must find it easier to make a thousand new generations than to mend an old one. You must be born again, before anything can be done with you; and the fear is that, even then, the second childhood will find you quite as prone to perversion as the first."

"Mrs. Brewton, you are incorrigible!"

"I am as God made me, sir; and if it be a proof that I am incorrigible, that I refuse to submit to any but proper authority, I bless God that he has endowed me with this quality!"

"You got my invitation?" asked Cruden, abruptly.

"Yes, I did; this morning."

"Well, you are not too much of a patriot to come. Your stoicism and satire will hardly revolt at good fellowship?"

"Surely not. But I should accept your invitation from quite another motive."

"Ah, indeed! And pray what is that?"

"Patriotism is a gloomy virtue just now, and satire, in her circles, lacks all provocation. I shall go to yours in search of it. Of all medicines, I find the most perfect in being able to laugh at the follies of mine enemy."

"Well," said Cruden, doggedly, "I don't care on what footing you put it, so you come. I should rather you should laugh at us than be denied the pleasure of seeing you laugh at all."

"You improve decidedly in voice, as the fox said to the crow, whose cheese he envied. I shall surely look in upon you; but I warn you to do your handsomest. In entering the house you occupy, I shall be reminded of many a pleasant and joyous party in the circle of Cotesworth Pinckney; and though I can scarcely look to the British officers in Charleston to supply all of the essentials which made that circle a pride and a delight, yet, in mere externals, I take for granted, as you have all the means, you will not suffer yourself to be outdone."

"We shall certainly do our best to find favor with one whom we so anxiously desire to win," was the answer, with a bow.

In regard to this appointed *fête*, Cruden had already been speaking, though in under tones, with Katharine Walton. Balfour now made it the subject of remark to her.

"We shall have the pleasure of seeing you there, Miss Walton. You must not suffer yourself to adopt this ungenial humor of your associates. Nay, I would prefer that you should even put on the mocking spirit of my witty foe, Mrs. Brewton, and make your appearance, though it be only to find cause for sarcasm."

"Colonel Cruden requires my attendance, and I submit to his wishes," replied the maiden, calmly.

"Nay, I could wish that you recognised rather the requisitions of society than of authority, in this matter."

"It need not be a subject of discussion, sir, whether I obey my own will in this respect, or that of another. If not indis-

11

posed, I shall certainly be present. I have no wish to increase the animosities which exist between our friends respectively."

"A proper feeling, and one that might, with more profit, be entertained by all."

An interval ensued in the conversation, which we have only detailed in portions. On a sudden, the eye of Balfour caught sight of a pair of large gloves upon the table. He stretched out his hands and gathered them up.

"Are these yours, Cruden?" he asked.

"No. Mine are here."

He turned them over, and muttered—

"They are not mine, yet are they a man's."

Mrs. Singleton quietly interposed—

"They are probably Tom Singleton's. He was with us a while ago."

Balfour smiled skeptically. He had, in the meantime, while turning the gloves over, discovered the initials "D. R.," printed legibly within them. He said nothing, but threw them back upon the table. At this moment, a strange sound was heard from an inner passage conducting to the stairway. It was strange because of its suddenness, but of no doubtful character. Every ear at once distinguished it as issuing from a human proboscis—a most decided snore, such as might be expected naturally to issue from the nostrils of a lusty urchin after a supper in excess, and from sleeping in an awkward position. Balfour and Cruden smiled, and looked knowingly in the faces of the ladies. But Mrs. Singleton remained entirely unmoved, and the rest looked quite unconscious. The snore was repeated with renewed emphasis.

"Not a bad imitation of Tarleton's bugles," was the remark of Balfour.

"It reminds me very much of one of Knyphausen's," responded Cruden; "that of the little Hessian who had lost his nose by a sabre-cut. You remember him? When he blew, it was evidently the play of two distinct instruments, the one, however, clearly inferior to the other."

"Yet it *would* maintain the rivalry, and continued to do so to the last. The nostrils—all that remained of them—never

would give way to the bugle ; and 'Drick'—so they called him
—short for Frederick, probably—went on blowing a double
bugle, doing the service of two men, until a shot through his
lungs cut off effectually the supply of wind necessary for both
instruments."

The music from the interior audibly increased.

" That instrument might be trained to good service, like that
of 'Drick,'" continued Balfour, who was apt to pursue his own
jests to the death. " It has all the compass and volume, and
the blasts are quite as well prolonged, without subsiding into
that squeak or snivel, which rendered 'Drick's' music rather
unpleasant at the close. Pray, Mrs. Singleton, where were you
so fortunate as to find your bugler ?"

The old lady replied with most admirable gravity.

" Really, Colonel Balfour, but for the sex of poor Sally, she
should be at your service in that capacity. Kate, my dear, go
and wake up the girl, she is asleep on the stairs."

Katharine rose, and Balfour also.

" Suffer me, Miss Walton, to save you this trouble," said the
officious commandant, somewhat eagerly, advancing, as he spoke,
toward the door leading to the passage.

But it was not the policy of Mrs. Singleton that he should
find Master Spidell in her dwelling. Kate Walton hesitated.
The old lady spoke, coolly, deliberately, yet with a manner that
was conclusive.

" Thank you, Colonel Balfour ; but I prefer that you should
see Sally out of *deshabille.* I can't answer for the stupid creature's toilet at this hour. That she has so far forgotten herself
as to bestow her music on us from such near neighborhood,
makes me doubt how far her trespasses may be carried. Do *you*
see to her, Kate ; we will dispense with the commandant's assistance, even in a duty so arduous as that of routing up a drowsy
negro."

The last phrase forced Balfour once more into his seat. He
felt how greatly his dignity would suffer at being caught in the
proposed office. Had he any suspicions, they would have been
quite hushed in the consideration of his own *amour propre,* and
in the coolness and admirable composure maintained by Mrs.

Singleton. Her allusion to the possible *abandon* of Sally, in the matter of costume and toilet, which made the younger ladies cast down their eyes, was also suggestive, to the coarse nature of the commandant, of a sort of humor which is properly con-fined to the barracks. We will not undertake to repeat the sorry equivoques in which he indulged, under a mistake, natural enough to such a person, that he was all the while very mischiev-ously witty.

Kate Walton, meanwhile, had penetrated the passage and wakened up the sleeping boy. He had been doubled up upon the stairs, and a few more convulsions of the nostrils might have sent him rolling downward. Fortunately his shoes were off, and, roused cautiously, he was enabled to retrace his steps to the upper room, where Ramsay was impatiently—but without daring to move—awaiting the departure of the hostile guests.

This event was not long delayed after the occurrence de-scribed. Having exhausted his stock of flippancies, and suc-ceeded in whispering some soft flatteries into the ears of Katha-rine, Balfour turned to Mrs. Brewton, reserving his "*last words*" for her. He said something to this effect, spoke of his testamen-tary addresses; and the retort, quick as lightning, sent him off in a jiffy.

"Ah, Colonel Balfour, were they indeed your '*last words*,' you know not how gladly we should all forgive your offences— nay, with what gratitude we should accept the atoning sacrifice, as more than compensative for all the evils done in your very short life!"

"Confound her tongue!" exclaimed the enraged commandant to his companion, as they left the house together. "It is all Tartar! What a viper she has at the end of it! But I shall have my revenge. She is at mischief, and shall pay for it. These people are all conspiring; those gloves were Dr. Ramsay's; and you heard the old woman admit that Tom Sin-gleton had but lately left them. The hag said the gloves were *his*, not dreaming that I had seen Ramsay's initials in them. I have no doubt that both are in the house at this moment. They will emerge probably very soon after they hear us ride away. Now let us see if we can not detect them. By occupying the opposite corners, we can readily see all who pass, and, ten to one, we find Ramsay, Singleton, and others whom we do not suspect, who have been at this secret meeting, I only want a pretext for putting them all in limbo. There is more confiscation to be done, Cruden."

"All's grist that comes to my mill," was the response of Cruden, with a hoarse chuckle, as he mounted his horse.

A groom, in the undress costume of a soldier, stood in waiting, his own steed beside him, as he brought up that of Balfour. To him the latter gave his instructions, and the party divided in opposite directions, moving off at a moderate canter.

The sound of their departing footsteps brought the male conspirators from their several places of hiding. Tom Singleton and Lockwood looked in from the garden impatiently, summoning Ramsay and the boy, George, from the interior. Meanwhile, the unlucky gloves were once more brought upon the *tapis*. Mrs. Brewton had remarked the peculiar smile upon Balfour's visage as he turned them over and heard them ascribed to Singleton, and her curiosity was awakened. The moment he had gone, she darted from her seat, and hastily snatching up the gloves, discovered the two capital letters conspicuously printed within the wrist.

"Now, out upon the man," she cried, indignantly, " who must set his sign-manual upon all his possessions, however insignificant, as if he for ever dreaded robbery!—who must brand ox, and ass, and everything that is his, with his proper arms and initials! Oh, doctor"—turning to him as he entered, and holding up the gloves, big with his initials, before his eyes—"for a wise man you do a great many foolish things! Look at that! See the tell-tales you carry with you wherever you go!"

"Ah, Brewton, this was certainly a childish folly. But wisdom affords few impunities, since, in due proportion with our knowledge, is the conviction we feel of the vast possessions that we can never acquire. I shall take care of this hereafter. In the meantime, has any mischief been done?"

"Balfour has read the initials."

"He knows, then, that I have been here. But this is nothing."

"Much to him; regarding you, as he must, with suspicion."

"Besides, it was unlucky," said Mrs. Singleton, "that, supposing them the gloves of Cousin Tom, I admitted that *he* had
just left us also. To know that you both were here, and with
us, all of whom are looked upon with evil eyes, is to set his suspicions at work. We must move more cautiously."

"Right!" said Singleton and Lockwood, in a breath. "And,
to do this, the sooner we *move off* together the better, the tide
will soon serve for George."

"He has given us proof to-night," said the widow, "that he
will never want a wind."

A laugh followed this, and poor George hung his head, inwardly swearing vengeance against his own unlucky nose, that
had so greatly exposed and almost betrayed him. He seized
his basket and moved toward the door. Ramsay was moving
in the same direction, when Tom Singleton interposed.

"Look you, doctor, you certainly don't mean to take Church
street? That won't do! If Balfour has the slightest reason
to suppose that we have been here to-night, and have been so
much hurried as to leave our gloves, he will naturally suppose
us here still, and will set a watch for us. We must take the
back track, scramble over the fences, and find our way out upon
the Bay."

"That is awkward," said Ramsay, hesitatingly.

"So it is, doctor; but advisable, nevertheless."

Some preliminaries were discussed, and the plan was settled
upon. Hurried partings were interchanged, and, stealing down
through the garden, the four, including the boy George, prepared to climb the fence, which was a high, ragged breastwork
of half-decayed pine plank. Tom Singleton went over first,
followed by the boy George; but the worthy doctor hung in
mid-air for a season, his skirts having caught upon a huge spike
in the fence, which had not been perceived, and which narrowly
grazed the more susceptible flesh. Singleton and Lockwood
both were employed in his extrication, which was only effected
by increasing the rent in the changeable silk breeches of the
worthy doctor. The scene provoked Singleton, whose risibles
were readily brought into play, into insuppressible merriment.

"I do not see what there is so ludicrous in the matter," said Ramsay, almost sternly.

"Indeed, but there is," was the answer; "when we reflect upon the predicament of the future historian of America, skewered upon a rusty nail in an old wall, and as incapable of helping himself as was Absalom caught by the hair."

Ramsay's intention of writing a history of the whole country was already known to his friends. Singleton continued—

"It would make a glorious picture for the book, doctor, to have you drawn on the fence-top, with Lockwood and myself tugging at your skirts."

"This is no time for nonsense, Singleton: let us go on," was the doctor's somewhat surly reply.

The party, in silence, then pursued a somewhat circuitous route, which, under Singleton's guidance, familiar equally with the highways and byways of the town, promised to be a safe one. Crossing several fences, in which toil the historian suffered no further mishaps of habiliment, they at length found themselves in a well-known enclosure, near the corner of Tradd street and the Bay. The region, at that period, presented an aspect very different from its appearance now. The Bay was then, instead of a well-paved avenue, a mere quagmire in wet weather. The sea penetrated it in numerous little indentations, which left the passage exceedingly narrow when the tide was high; and the chief obstruction to its constant invasion was the various bastions and batteries which looked out upon the harbor; though, even in the rear of these, the water occasionally formed in pools that might be called lakelets.

Before reaching this limit, our fugitives held a hurried consultation under a group of guardian fig-trees that occupied the lot, now covered by stately buildings of brick, which still interposed between them and the thoroughfare. Finally, it was agreed that Lockwood and George should go forth first, making their way upward to the place of concealment for their boat, which lay not far distant from the Governor's bridge; while Singleton and Ramsay, after a certain interval, were to pursue their homeward course, singly, and with all possible circumspection. These arrangements brought them late into the night.

The morning star saw Lockwood and George passing over
Deadman's Ground and into the shadowy gorges of the Wando
river; while Ramsay, safe in his own chamber, was curiously
inspecting the serious hurts which his changeable silk small-
clothes had suffered from his unwonted exercises. The whole
party escaped the *surveillance* of Balfour, who, after the delay
of an hour, impatiently consumed in watching, rode back to the
house of Mrs. Singleton only to find it all in darkness. He
naturally concluded that the prey had escaped before his visit.
Let us change the scene.

CHAPTER XXVI.

THE REBEL'S MENAGERIE.

WE have seen Major Proctor in possession of all the materirials which the hatred of Vaughan, his cunning, and that of Balfour, were preparing to adduce against him for his destruction. Thus warned, he was measurably armed. He had no reason to doubt the testimony thus put into his hands; though still ignorant of his secret friend, and totally without clews which might lead to her discovery. He was now, however, better prepared than before, to believe in the conjecture of Furness, that his correspondent was really a woman. In the haste with which Ella Monckton had abridged, or copied the documents which she had sent him, she had somewhat forgotten her former caution. She had commenced her work in the stiff, feigned hand which she had formerly employed in communicating with him; but, as she proceeded and grew more and more absorbed in her labors, her artifices were neglected, and the greater portion of the manuscript was evidently not only in a female hand, but in a *natural* one; written hurriedly, and exhibiting a singular contrast between the style of penmanship with which she had begun and that with which she finished. Still, the hand was totally unknown to him, and he brooded over it with an interest greatly increased in the writer, moved equally by curiosity and gratitude. He could only content himself with the reflection that, with the *natural* handwriting in his possession, his prospects, hereafter, of discovering the fair unknown were something better than before; and, if the truth were told, he now began to feel quite as much interest in this new object as was consistent

11*

with the paramount necessity of using her information, with all despatch, for the purposes of his defence.

Here his difficulties began. It was now that he needed a friend, like Furness, present in the city, who would counsel with and assist him. Furness had promised to bring him to the knowledge of such a friend, and had furnished him with a note to one of the citizens of Charleston, premising, at the same time, that the person to whom it was addressed, though once an intimate with the father and family of the loyalist, was yet himself a warm supporter of the *mouvement* party, and had been active in the labors of the patriots. Proctor had put this note of introduction into his trunk, and had not looked at the superscription, except in the first moment when he received it. That moment was one in which his mind was busy with other matters. It was, indeed, the very moment of parting with his new friend, and the feelings natural to the occasion made him oblivious, even while he read, of the name which he beheld written on the envelope. He now took the letter from his trunk, and was quite surprised as he examined it.

" To THOMAS SINGLETON, ESQ., Charleston.
" By friendly favor of Major Proctor," &c., &c.

Old Tom Singleton, one of the rankest of the rebels of the city ; a man bitterly uncompromising in his hostility to the British cause ; a wit, a humorist, full of perpetual sneer and sarcasm at the expense of the invaders—how should Captain Furness, of the loyalists, be in communion with such a person ? A little reflection answered the question. The best friends, the nearest kindred in the colony, had been divided by this unnatural war. This was no reason for the disruption of all the ties of friendship and society. Besides, Furness had expressly announced Singleton as of the other party, but had still spoken of him as a friend of his family — as an honest man, and one of those shrewd, acute, penetrating persons whose counsels would be particularly useful in his emergency. That emergency was pressing upon Proctor now. The British interests no longer commanded his sympathy. Its leaders had wronged and were pursuing him with hatred and injustice. Why should he scruple to seek and accept the services of a friend who would serve his individual cause, without seeking to know, or feeling disquiet at, his political sympathies?

Proctor soon satisfied himself of the propriety—nay, necessity—of visiting the satirical graybeard, Tom Singleton, in his domicil in Tradd street. But he resolved, also, that he must move cautiously. He remembered the counsel of Furness, whose shrewdness he could not but acknowledge. He must do nothing rashly.—There was no need, for example, that his servant-man John, the traitor, still in his employment, should be able to report to Vaughan, or Balfour, that he followed him to the dwelling of a well-known rebel. He sent John, accordingly, out of the way, with a missive, quite innocent in its character, to a remote quarter of the city. There was as little need that *any* curious eyes should notice where he himself went. He chose, therefore, the night as the time for his purposed visit; and between eight and nine of the evening, traversing the unlighted streets, he soon found himself in front of the little old-fashioned brick building, of two stories, with tall, pointed roof, which old Singleton occupied. The door was promptly opened at his knock, and Singleton himself received him at the entrance of his parlor, opening directly on the street.

The old man seemed disappointed when, holding the candle to the face of his visiter, he discovered who he was. He had evidently expected a very different person.—He had seen Proctor before, but failed to recognise him. The British officer at once relieved his curiosity.

"Major Proctor, Mr. Singleton, late of the post at Dorchester."

"Ah! and to what, Major Proctor, am I indebted for the honor of this visit? I am not aware that it is just now in my power to be of any service to his majesty's cause in this province. These arms are no longer able to carry sword or musket; my wits are of little use even to myself, since Lord North has become the monopolist of all the wisdom in the united kingdom and its dependencies; and, for the matter of money, sir, why you will scarce believe me, but I now find it impossible to gratify my usual appetite for *whiting* and *cavalli*. To go to the fish market now-a-days, is only to provoke the most gnawing and painful sensations. In brief, sir, forced subsidies would scarcely disquiet me, since it would give me as much pleasure if our noble commandant of Charleston could find out my ways and means, as to find them out myself."

"Pardon me, Mr. Singleton, but I am here with no official object. At all events, the commandant of Charleston would be as little likely to employ me upon any service as to employ yourself."

"Ah, indeed!"

"Let me put this letter into your hands, sir, which will explain the true object of my visit, and probably furnish a sanction for this intrusion."

"Be seated, sir, Major Proctor," said Singleton, as he took the letter. Taking a seat himself without preliminary, and putting on his great gold spectacles, the old man, the light in one hand, the letter in the other, proceeded to master the contents of the paper. The name of "Furness," dubitatingly uttered, arose to his lips; but he soon discovered what, even had Proctor read the billet, he would not be likely to have seen, the two Greek letters which Robert Singleton usually incorporated with the flourish below his name. The letter was read with the greatest deliberation, then folded, then quietly passed into the flame of the candle, and the burning scroll deposited in the chimney-place. Fixing his deep gray eye upon the features of his visiter, old Singleton extended his hand.

"Major Proctor, I am glad to see you, and will be glad to serve you; though my young friend, Furness, entirely overrates my capacity to do so. But I consider it quite a compliment to my heart, if not to my head, that he has written and referred you to me. I need not tell you, sir, that I am quite of another way of thinking from himself. He has chosen to take up arms against his people, and I naturally feel some bitterness on the subject. But I knew and loved his father, sir; he entertained me in his mountain region with a warm hospitality, and when I lay for a month dangerously sick in his dwelling, his excellent wife nursed me with as much affection as if I had been her own brother. The young Furness, too, was a smart and proper boy, and promised to be a strong and thoughtful man. I love him for his parents' sake, and would be happy if he had suffered me to love him for his own. But he is wrong, sir; he has been dreadfully erring. You have *your* excuse in serving your sovereign in this war ; but what is the excuse for him who pleads duty in justification, while he cuts the throat of his kinsman and his neighbor ?"

All this calmly, sadly spoken, sufficed admirably to impress the British officer with the entire truthfulness of the whole narrative. Proctor said something by way of excuse for the young loyalist, but the other interrupted him.

" There is an argument, Major. Proctor, for every error, and poor Humanity will never want a lie to justify any of her failings to herself. But your matter is private. We are here upon the street. Come with me into my den, where we can speak in safety."

He led the way into an inner room, plainly furnished, and thence, by a back door, down into an apartment in the cellar— a low-ceiled vault, which had been fitted up with some care for comfort, if not display. The room was plastered and carpeted. There was no fireplace, and the wall against which it should have stood was covered with books. These were not seen, however, until a second candle had been lighted ; and then Proctor discovered enough to confirm the report, which he had heard before, of the eccentricity of old Tom Singleton. There were a pair of huge Angola cats lying with heads together beneath the table ; a cage of wire, suspended from the wall, contained an immense rattlesnake, whose eyes reflected the glare of the candles with the brightness of a pair of diamond lustres in the bosom of an Indian princess. On the floor, directly beneath the cage, was a large tub, in which an occasional plash was heard, as of a fish struggling for sea-room ; and all about the room might be seen frames of stuffed and cages of living birds. In a remote corner, covered with shelves, Proctor heard the frequent rattling of sheets of paper, and was occasionally startled at the whizzing of some small object close to his face, which he at one time fancied to be the sportive assaults of some enormous beetle, but which might have been a missile. He was soon informed of the source of his annoyance by the sharp accents of his host, addressed to an object which he did not see.

"To your sleep, Lord George, before I trounce you!" and there was a rustle again among the paper, as if the object addressed was preparing to obey. "You are in my den, Major Proctor, you will please remember—I should rather call it my *menagerie*—so you will please be startled at nothing."

"Do I hear the rattle of a snake?" said Proctor, with a shudder.

"Yes; I have a most glorious monster in that cage, with but seven rattles; he is fully as large as any I have seen with twice the number. He is harmless. I have drawn his fangs. That fish which you hear plashing in the tub is the torpedo. I paralyzed one of your dragoons the other day by a touch, which will make him careful never to grapple with fish again until he sees it fried and on table. The little monster which annoyed you by his dexterity of aim—your nose being between him and the light, he evidently strove to see how nearly he could come to the one without extinguishing the other—is a monkey, of which I have large expectations. I call him Lord George, after your famous nobleman, Germaine, who behaved so well upon the plains of Minden, and so bravely in the walls of Parliament house. You shall see Lord George."

The monkey was summoned from his perch, and, at the word, he leaped from the shelf where he harbored directly upon the table. The cats were awakened by the movement, and raised themselves quickly to their feet; hair bristling all the while, backs rising in anger, and tongues hissing and snapping at the annoyer, who had now approached the edge of the table and was looking down wickedly upon the apprehensive pair. To Proctor's surprise, and, we may add, indignation, the monkey was habited as a British general officer.

"Head up, Lord George," cried old Singleton.

The beast took an attitude of great dignity, head up, nose in air, and right hand upon his breast.

"Your sword, Lord George."

Off he sprang to a dark corner of the room, whence he returned instantly with the implement, which he waved aloft in the most threatening manner, marching across the table with an immense strut, and audaciously confronting the visiter. Proctor was half tempted to seize and wring the neck of the mocking little monster, whose antics and costume he beheld with a feeling of vexation, which he found it difficult to suppress.

"Do you not incur some peril, Mr. Singleton, in this caricature of the uniform of his majesty's service?"

"My dear sir, did you happen to see the corps of black dragoons sent off to Monk's Corner some weeks ago, in his majesty's uniform, and commanded by Captain Quash—the very picture of the Jack of spades done in scarlet? If you ever saw that troop, uniformed by Balfour himself, you will be satisfied that none of his majesty's officers have a right to quarrel with the costume of my Lord George here, or, if you please"—in lower terms—"Colonel Balfour."

Proctor was silent. He felt the sarcasm. Old Singleton addressed the monkey—

"Hence to bed; and no more noise, do you hear, or"—and he pointed threateningly to the tub where swam the torpedo.

The monkey shuddered, bowed gracefully to both the gentlemen, and disappeared in silence.

"I make one of my beasts the terror of the other. I threaten the cat with the monkey, the monkey with the fish, the snake with the eagle—"

"Have you an eagle?"

"A pair of them; but they are wretched things in a cage, like our poor people in this struggle. I shall set them free the very next victory which follows to our arms."

Proctor slightly smiled. Singleton saw the smile, but did not appear to notice it. He proceeded—

"I am strangely fond of beasts, otherwise outlawed, and I moralise upon them with a taste like that of Jacques in the forest. Thus, what a lesson against pomp and vanity are the egregious pretensions of my Lord George, the monkey! How my snake, venomous, but fangless, illustrates envy, malice, and all uncharitableness! My cats, snarling even when in clover, are fashionable married people, whose spite and bad humor are but natural consequences of a life of indolence. My spiritless eagles teach me the blessings of freedom; but, mark you, to those only who, from the first, have been endowed with the faculty of living in the eye of the sun, and bathing in the upper air. And my fish — but enough. I am an egotist when I moralize upón my beasts. I must apologize for not thinking of your affairs; but, in truth, you needed an introduction to my associates. It is one satisfaction that I feel in bringing you to know them, that not one of them will betray your secrets. You *have* secrets, it appears from the letter of — ah — Furness; and I am to assist you with my counsels. Major Proctor, I am a whig, and you a Briton. Command my counsels in anything not inconsistent with our respective politics, and I am yours."

Proctor took the extended hand, and thanked him with a warmth proper to the frankness with which the old man made his offer of service.

"My loyalty shall not seek to obtain any advantage over your patriotism, Mr. Singleton. My affair, though it brings me into collision with my superiors, is yet wholly personal."

With this introduction, Proctor proceeded to unfold the whole history, as already in our possession, of his conflict with Vaughan and Balfour, his exercise of command at Dorchester, his relations with Colonel Walton and daughter, and those subsequently which had made Furness interested in his affairs. Nor were the anonymous communications of his fair correspondent forgotten. His statement concluded with the exhibition of the whole body of documentary testimony which was preparing to be brought against him. This old Singleton examined curiously.

"The hand is unknown to me; but Furness is right. It is a woman's hand. His conjecture as to her interest in you is right also. These last papers might enable you to find out who she is, if that were an object.

"That *is* an object," said Proctor.

"But not necessary to your case."

Perhaps not; but the curiosity is natural and—"

"Justifiable. You certainly owe much to the lady. But now to the papers. These documents are derived from fountain-head. I have no doubt that they are genuine copies, and that they show truly what you have to guard against. It might be well, however, if we could arrive at the possible source of your information. Balfour has two regular secretaries, both mere lads; one named Monckton, the other Hesk. Do you know either?"

"I do not. But he has others occasionally."

"Are you intimate with them, or with any of his aids?"

"No."

"Nor his associates, Barry, Cruden—?"

"We have nothing in common. Colonel Cruden is my uncle; but he values the commissions on confiscated estates much more than any claims of kindred, and he is the ally of Balfour, as a matter of policy. As for Barry, he is a vain fopling, a small wit, who has no sympathies, no heart, no magnanimity—"

"Egad, you have learned to appreciate justly the dominant virtues of our conquerors. You have no clew, then, to this writing?"

"None but what I relate."

"We must leave that matter, then, for the present. And now for this body of evidence. On the face of it, you perceive that it is formidable. It makes out a strong case against you. Something will depend upon these witnesses, much upon such as you can bring to rebut them. The details of this testimony are all of a sort to be severally rebutted. Who is this Gradock?"

"A squatter in the neighborhood of Dorchester, who brought us supplies of game and fish; a poor, worthless fellow, claiming to be half Indian, but who is, probably, half mulatto. His character is notoriously bad. He is a great liar, and a wretched drunkard."

"Have you testimony to that effect? This Blonay—"

"Dead. A fellow of like description."

"Clymes, or Clymer?"

"Clymes?"

Proctor answered all the questions of old Singleton; and, in this way, the whole body of testimony was sifted. We need not pursue the details of the investigation. The result for the present may be given in the old man's language.

"It is clear that you must visit Dorchester and the neighborhood, with reference to all these witnesses. You must meet their testimony by that of other witnesses, or convict them out

of their own mouths. At all events, get sufficient proof of the
sort of people to be sworn against you. Do you know old
Pryor, of Dorchester?"

"He is, secretly, a rebel."

"But none the less an honest man. At this moment, it will
be wise, Major Proctor, to dismiss your prejudices as a British
officer. Pryor is a rough dog, scarcely civil of speech, but with
a man's heart; and he will serve you faithfully if you can persuade him to take an interest in your affairs. These witnesses
against you have, you think, been *bought* up by your enemies.
Old Pryor was once a sort of king over all the people in that
quarter. He can probably assist you in getting the truth out
of some of these hirelings. Gradock, you see, and Clymes are
the persons whose testimony is most likely to be troublesome.
These must be managed, and Pryor is probably the very person
to undertake this part of the business. He can do it for you, or
put you in the proper way to do it for yourself. At all events,
your policy is to proceed to Dorchester with all the despatch
and all the secrecy possible."

The whole process underwent examination between the parties. The details of the contemplated plan of action need not
be discussed further at this stage of our narrative. Enough,
that the shrewdness, good sense, acuteness, and rare knowledge
of persons, possessed by old Singleton, surprised Proctor, and
encouraged him to believe that he could meet all the difficulties of his case. At the close of their interview, Proctor requested him to take charge of his papers, referring to the secret
espionage of his servant, John, and the insecurity of his own
chambers.

"Do you keep that fellow still?" demanded Singleton.

"I was counselled to do so by Captain Furness. His opinion
was that any person whom I should get in his place would be
equally liable to be corrupted; while, by keeping *him*, I disarmed the suspicions of my enemies in regard to my knowledge
of their schemes; and, knowing John, I was better prepared to
guard against him."

"A sensible fellow is Furness. He is probably right. Well,
Major Proctor, I will be your depositary. You are probably

not unaware of the fact that my own position here is one of great insecurity. I am at any moment liable to be seized in my bed, and sent to *provost* or prison-ship, at the whim and mere caprice of your despotic commander. But I have places of hiding for your papers such as will be likely for some time to escape search. My rattlesnake shall take your secrets into keeping. Behold what a snug *escritoir* he has for the service of my friends."

This said, the old man touched a spring in the bottom of the cage in which the serpent lay coiled in repose. A false bottom was instantly revealed, showing a shallow drawer, which already contained sundry papers. The rattle of the snake was quickly sprung, and the burnished head of the monster was threateningly raised at the same moment.

" He is on the watch, you see. Few persons would prosecute a search in this quarter, with so vigilant and terrible a guardian of its secrets. Give me the papers."

" One recommendation, Mr. Singleton," said Proctor, " before I leave you. Your kindness to me and interest in my affairs will justify me in speaking of yours. Take your monkey out of his uniform ! Balfour would scarcely forgive you the caricature, particularly as you have caparisoned the beast in a costume very much like his own."

" Fashioned directly after it, I confess. And do you observe I have taught him the genuine Balfour strut and carriage ?" said the old man with a complacent chuckle.

" A dangerous experiment, which, if known, will be certain to get you lodgings in the provost."

" Poo ! poo ! my young friend, this alarms me nothing. What matters it upon what plea, whether of fun or patriotism, I get into limbo ? When it is needful to dispose of me, Balfour will never lack a pretext. In the meantime shall I be without my amusement ? In the ' durance vile' of my present condition, it is something when I can laugh at the antics of the enemy whose claws I have yet to fear."

Proctor shook his head. He saw that old Singleton was one of those men who never lose their joke in their perils, and he forbore all further exhortations, which he felt would be waste of counsel. They had much talk besides, but such as we may dispense with in this narrative. Returning to his lodgings, the Brittish officer found his man John returned, and looking very curious at his absence. But he gave him little heed, The next morning he was on his way to Dorchester; but not unattended!

CHAPTER XXVII.

CAPTIVITY.

BALFOUR was soon apprized, by the treacherous servant, of the absence of Proctor from his lodgings the night before; and the impossibility of accounting for it, as usual, led to the conjecture that John had been sent out of the way, simply that he might not follow the footsteps of the master. When, the next day, Proctor left the city, it was determined by the commandant, after a long conference with John, that the latter should pursue him, but in a disguise, and on a horse which Balfour furnished. Two hours, accordingly, had not elapsed, when the faithless servant was on the tracks of his master. The progress of Proctor was not so rapid but that he could be easily overtaken by an eager pursuer. Fifteen miles from the city the spy distinguished him about half a mile ahead. He maintained this distance for the rest of the journey.

Proctor reached Dorchester and proceeded to take lodgings at the house of Humphries, "The Royal George," the better to avoid suspicion. A rival tavern was kept by Pryor, but, as he was a suspected whig, he no longer received the public patronage. Even the patriots, in order to escape suspicion, avoided the dwelling of one with whom they yet thoroughly sympathized.

The spy, whom practice had made an adept, having ascertained the manner in which his master had disposed of himself, went at once to the post of Dorchester, carrying letters from Balfour to Vaughan. His horse groomed and stabled, he left the fortress under cover of the night, and established a watch upon the house of Humphries. After supper, Proctor came forth, and, as the localities were all well known to him, he took the direct route for the neglected hotel of Pryor. Thither the spy followed him; but, beyond the single fact that he saw his master enter this dwelling, he gathered nothing from his espionage. Pryor received his visitor at the entrance, and conducted him to an inner apartment, where in the course of an hour's conversation, Proctor unfolded all the difficulties in his case, and indicated the extent of service which the other might perform for him.

Though a blunt, rude man, and a fierce whig, Pryor was not hostile to Proctor. The latter, in command of Dorchester, had done his spiritings so gently as to have compelled the respect of the people generally. Besides, the service desired by him was one which aimed to defeat the machinations of Balfour and Vaughan, both of whom were hated, and was further commended to him by a brief letter from old Tom Singleton, whom our landlord well knew and greatly honored. The consequence was that Pryor took up heartily the cause of his visitor.

"It can be done, Major Proctor. It *shall* be done!" said Pryor with an oath. "I will do.it. I can manage Gradock and Clymes, but I must have money and my own way."

"You shall have both," was the prompt reply.

Twenty guineas were at once put into his hands.

"This will do," returned the landlord. "If more is wanted I will contrive that you shall know it. You shall hear of me through old Tom Singleton. He will tell you that your money will be safe in my hands."

Proctor quickly declared that he needed no such assurance.

"Nevertheless, major, it's in the way of business that you should have it. And now that we understand what's to be done, we don't need you any longer. You must be off with to-morrow's sun. You can be of no service in dealing with these people, and your presence here will only occasion suspicion, and make the affair difficult to manage. Of course, Balfour knows all about your coming here."

"Scarcely."

"Don't you believe it. He knows you've left the city. If he's busy, as you think, in this matter, and really desires to destroy you, and if your man John be in his employ, and is the rascal you think him—and which I verily believe—I never could bear the fellow—then, be sure, that he has sent a spy after you."

" I saw no one," replied Proctor, with rare simplicity.

" Oh, to be sure not! It is a spy's business to see and not to be seen. But do you so act as if you felt that every footstep which you take is watched. Go back to Humphries, and ask the old scoundrel all sorts of questions in regard to the affair of the rescue of Colonel Walton. Don't say a syllable of Gradock and Clymes. Talk only of Marion's men, and the goggle-eyed tory, Blonay! This will lead them off the scent. Set off with the dawn to-morrow, or an hour before it, and, by sunrise, I'll report everything to Vaughan, just as Humphries will be sure to do. This will save me harmless. Otherwise, I should be very apt to enjoy the bayonet pricks of a corporal's guard before I had fairly swallowed breakfast. We must be artful. We must fight fire with fire."

Satisfied that things were now in proper train in this quarter, Proctor left the shrewd old landlord and returned to play the game prescribed with the loyalist, Humphries. We need not dwell upon the details. The counsel of Pryor was closely followed, and the whole history of the rescue of Walton, by Marion's men, was deliberately discussed, point by point, in all its particulars, under the dubious lights accorded by the wit or wisdom of the tory landlord.

With dawn, Proctor was already crossing Eagle bridge, gazing sternly, as he passed, upon the little fortress in which his experiences for more than a year, had been those of unmixed trial and bitterness. His heart was filled with the maledictions which his lips did not utter, as he thought of his enemy, Vaughan; and his hand griped fiercely the handle of his sword in a mute but expressive thirst for the moment when he could close the account of enmity between them in the deadly arbitrament of fight. He little dreamed that his action was beheld, and its import properly divined. The traitor John was also in the saddle, and, from a neighboring covert, had him clearly in his eye. Proctor drove the spur into his steed and darted forward; and the other dogged resolutely after him, taking due care not to draw too nigh, yet as careful never long to lose his master from his sight.

The spirits of Proctor grew more elastic as he rode. There is something in the very effort to foil an enemy which contributes to the conviction that the thing may be done; and the exhortations of Furness, of old Singleton, and Pryor—their counsels, and the cool readiness with which their several faculties had been brought to bear, in the same manner, and upon the same game—seemed to relieve it from all its embarrassments. For a moment, it occurred to the British major as something singular that his two agents in the business should both be of the patriotic or rebel party; and that he should owe his acquaintance with Singleton to the interposition of a provincial loyalist—though sufficiently explained by the former—was yet a circumstance which continually occurred to his thoughts as something curious. Nor did it escape him, as also among the catalogue of things to occasion surprise, that Pryor should speak so confidently of communicating with old Singleton whenever the necessity for it should occur.

But Proctor had become quite too cold, as a subject of his royal master, and entertained quite too little sympathy with the existing powers in Carolina, to allow himself to meditate these doubts with his usual vigilance. If there was anything suspicious in the connection between these parties, there was no responsibility on his part, which required that he should investigate the matter. New thoughts and fancies, new conjectures, hopes, and fears, passed into his brain ; and he found himself busied in fruitless guesses as to the unknown, but, as he now believed, *fair* correspondent, to whom he was indebted for all the clews to his present inquiries.

Was she fair ? was she young and lovely ? and how, when, and where, had he awakened in her bosom the degree of interest such as her solicitude in behalf of his fortunes would necessarily show that she felt ? He was bound to believe her both young and fair. Common gratitude required nothing less, and it gave him pleasure to believe it.

His interest in the unknown continued to rise—it had risen prodigiously within the last few days—and his fancy began to frame a portrait of her to his eye, which might possibly become a fixed image in his heart. But of this Proctor had no misgivings. He felt grateful for the love which, unknown, had watched so faithfully over his fortunes ; and the sympathy which had been thus gratuitously shown, might, naturally, in the heart of one so much alone in the world, and so much assailed by enemies, provoke and deserve a warmer sentiment than simple gratitude.

It was while thus brooding over the services of the unknown damsel that our British major was suddenly, and somewhat roughly, brought back to more immediate interests by a stern command to halt, from unknown lips, and by finding the bridle of his steed in the grasp of an assailant. He looked up, to behold before him a sturdy forester, in the well-known blue hunting-shirt of the colonial rangers, one hand presenting a pistol, while the other bore heavily upon the bridle of his steed.

To clap spurs to his horse, to ride over the obstruction, and draw his own pistol from the holster, was the instant impulse of Proctor ; but his action and purpose were beheld in season for a warning, to which he was compelled to listen.

" It's useless, major. You're surrounded. You're a prisoner."

The man's tones were civil, but firm. His words were seconded by the appearance of three other persons in similar costume, each of whom presented his rifle as he drew nigh. The necessity was not to be eluded or escaped, and, submitting with a good grace to his captors, one of them led his horse by the bridle into the neighboring thicket. In ten minutes after, a similar party had taken like possession of the treacherous servant John. The whole affair happened within twelve miles of the city.

The captives were taken to the shelter of a dense forest growth which skirted the Ashley. Not a word was spoken during the progress. Proctor, staggered by the audacity of the proceeding, was yet comparatively resigned to the event. His mind was in a state which enabled him to look with something like indifference upon all the caprices of fortune. For the present, he made no inquiries, contenting himself with the reflection that the explanation would come quite soon enough.

12

He was permitted to throw himself at ease, where he would, among the trees; and his horse was properly cared for by a negro groom whose face Proctor fancied he had seen before; a conjecture which seemed to find encouragement in the broad grin that opened the fellow's countenance to barn-door dimensions, as he led away the steed. But the captive was permitted no words with him. He was vigilantly guarded, three or four riflemen constantly keeping him in sight.

Proctor was surprised at the numbers of these people. They were continually coming and going. He noted no less than forty different persons. All of them were well mounted and apparently well armed. The place had the appearance of being frequently used, as in the present instance, for the camp of the scouting party. The earth was well beaten by the hoofs of horses. The trees bore saddles and bridles; the cook-pot smoked constantly with wild cheer of the woods; and yet the whole party were within two miles of the Ashley Ferry road, then much more travelled than at the present day. Among all this motley and somewhat savage group, Proctor saw no officers beyond the grade of a sergeant; but the utmost order prevailed in the encampment. It was while he lay at ease in the shade that he saw another captive brought in as he had been. This was his man John. But the British major did not recognise him, and the prisoners were guarded separately, and at no time allowed to come together.

At noon, dinner was served him alone, and he was waited on with respect by one of the foresters. He was well known. The man addressed him by name.

"Who is your leader, sir?" was the question of Proctor.

"He must answer that question for himself," was the reply.

"When shall I see him?"

"To-night, I reckon."

It was an hour after dark, when a considerable bustle in the camp announced an arrival. Meanwhile, a fire had been built among the trees where Proctor had made his tent, and a couple of blankets were provided him, with a thick roll of black moss by way of pillow. He had supped; and while he lay at ease, with his feet to the fire, meditating the novel phase in his fortunes, a group approached him of three persons, the centre and taller figure of the party, to his great surprise, being masked. They stood on one side of the fire, while Proctor lay on the other. The masked figure began the conversation with asking the captive how he had been treated.

"As well as I could wish, sir, my captivity alone excepted. Am I to understand that I am a prisoner in the hands of the Americans?"

"You are! You will be treated well, Major Proctor, and with proper respect for your character and rank. Indeed, sir, you need not be a prisoner a moment longer. If you will give me your word, as a man of honor, that, for one week, you will say nothing of this adventure, nor make any report of the body of soldiers you see here, you shall be free to depart with the dawn."

"That is impossible, sir. I can make no such pledges. My duty, sir——"

"Enough, Major Proctor! It will be my duty then to keep you safely, at least for a few days. It will be our care that you shall have no reason to complain of anything but your detention. Our fare is coarse, and the couch assigned you is a hard one; but you are a soldier, sir, and can accommodate yourself to such small inconveniences."

"I am content, sir. But, Colonel Walton, your voice betrays you—I know you!——"

"You know too much for your own safety," cried one of the officers accompanying Colonel Walton, drawing a pistol from his belt, with the words, and presenting it at the head of the prisoner. But for the timely interposition of Walton, the rash subordinate would have drawn the trigger. The piece was already cocked.

"Pshaw! M'Kelvey!" cried Walton, arresting his arm. "He can do us no hurt. We have only to keep him safely. Put up your weapon. Let me see nothing of this."

"You are too indulgent, colonel," said the other. "You will pay for it some day. This man——"

"At least, let us do no murder! Major Proctor, have I your word that you will not endeavor to escape, until we release you?

This will be in a week, at the utmost. If you refuse, I shall
only be compelled to subject you to greater restraint—in fact,
to put you in irons."

"I can have no objection to make you such a promise, Colonel Walton, in the hope to escape such ignominy."

"It is then understood. Your range must be limited to the
hundred yards on either side of your present place of rest. To
attempt to pass beyond these limits will subject you to the
rough handling of your guards. Good night, sir."

With these words the party retired. Proctor, however, could
still hear, as they went, the expostulations of the angry officer
who had threatened his life, against the ill-advised mercy of his
superior. He congratulated himself upon his narrow escape
from a sharp and sudden death, and wondering at the nature of
the enterprise which brought the partisans so near to the city
garrison, he sank into slumbers not less grateful because of the
rough couch assigned him for their enjoyment. His fortune was
much better than that of his servant John. The treacherous
spy was hustled across the river that very night, his wrists folded together with bracelets of iron, and a determined trooper on
each side ready to shoot him down at the first sign of difficulty.
Let us return once more to the city.

CHAPTER XXVIII.

GRADUALLY DEVELOPING

WHILE these events were in progress in the career of Proctor, society in Charleston was not wholly stagnant. The undercurrents, which represent the moral influences of the social world, were in sleepless motion ; and the several parties to our history were more or less moved by their varying influences. The great ball at Cruden's was yet to take place, and was looked forward to with eager excitement, by hundreds of those who sought in society rather the passing delights than the substantial virtues which make society secure and permanent. The interval, meanwhile, was not unemployed by those who, without being able to emulate the splendor of the intended assemblage, were yet anxious to make some figure in the world corresponding with their proportions and resources. The days were, accordingly, consumed in *fêtes champetre*, and the nights in lively reunions. Parties for Haddrill's, Sullivan's, James', and Morris islands, were of constant occurrence, and drives into St. Andrews', Goose Creek, Accabee, and other contiguous places furnished employment and excitement to merry groups to whom the question of the Benzonian, " Under which king, &c. ?" never offered the slightest annoyance. These excursions were all taken during the daylight, for the autumn season, in the swamp regions of Carolina, did not suffer pleasure to sport with impunity along the water-courses, unless with the sanction of the daylight and the sun. At night, gay abodes in the city received and welcomed the butterfly tribes to whom life offered no aspects which rendered the economy of time desirable. Our excellent Mrs. Rivington had her " evenings" as surely as her

"mornings;" and there were a number besides, who, if individ-
ually less frequent in throwing open their saloons, were sufficiently numerous to suffer no night to pass without affording a
point of gathering for the light and motley multitude.

We will suppose some few days to have passed in practices
such as these, since our last meeting with the conspirators at
Mrs. Singleton's. The occasions were studiously contrived by
Balfour and his satellites to bring Katharine Walton into company. The policy of Mrs. Singleton encouraged her in yielding to this object, however little she may have relished it at
heart. But two results were aimed at in the concession. It
was only prudent not to offend authorities which had the parties
completely in their power; and quite as important, by conce-
ding thus much, if possible, to divert suspicion from the secret
toils of our feminine conspirators. Accordingly, Katharine Walton moved in a circle which in her heart she loathed, and received the devotions of those whose tributes revolted equally
her patriotism and pride. But she preserved her temper in the
calm control of her pure and proper thoughts, and if she was
not all that her suitors desired, she at least afforded them no
necessary cause of complaint.

In the meanwhile, she had met with and made the acquaintance of Ella Monckton. At first the two maidens were somewhat shy of each other. We are in possession of the sufficient
reason for this shyness on the part of Ella. Katharine's reluctance arose naturally enough : first, from the knowledge that
Ella belonged to the enemy—was of the loyalist faction; and,
second, because there was nothing either in what was said of
her by others, or in the *empressement* of her own manner, to enable her to fix or command the consideration or curiosity of our
heroine. But circumstances, and occasional communion, served
to break down the first barriers which natural restraints had set
up between them. A word, a tone, a look will suffice, where
hearts are ingenuous and young, to appeal to the affections;
and, very soon it was that, under a shrinking aspect, which the
vulgar might consider pride, but which is just as likely to be an
exquisite sensibility, Katharine Walton perceived that Ella
Monckton harbored the most delicate, pure, and generous of na-

tures. On the other hand, Ella, somehow, felt herself, in spite
of herself, drawn toward her rival, as by an irresistible attraction. At first, the language of her heart secretly said—

"I do not hate, but I fear her! She pains and distresses me,
though she does not offend."

Subsequently, it had another language.

"There is something very noble and commanding about this
lady! She *is* a lady; sensitive, yet firm; pure and chaste, yet
without any affectations of delicacy. She is gentle, too, and
sweet, and there is a wondrous strength and melody, mixed, in
the tones of her voice. I like her in spite of *him;* I like her,
and feel that I, too, could love her."

But there was a reserve even about the intimacy of the parties, which time alone could have broken down. Of course,
Katharine Walton was not aware of any interest which she
could have in the affairs of Ella; while the latter, on the other
hand, was restrained by an ever-present fear that Katharine
would decipher her secret interest in herself at every glance of
her eyes and in the tremulous tones of her every utterance.
The fear was idle. Katharine saw nothing in those eyes but
the expression of a rare tenderness and delicacy; and heard
nothing in her voice but a soft and touching harmony, which increased her interest in one in whom she never once thought to
find a rival. But the parties insensibly came together more and
more every day. The ancient intercourse between the widows
Monckton and Singleton was gradually resumed through the
growing intimacy between the two damsels. To spend a morning at the house of the latter was a not unfrequent thing with
Ella; while Katharine was easily persuaded to take her work,
or her book, to the house of Mrs. Monckton, and go into a sort of
temporary solitude in the sweet society of the widow and her
daughter, whither the crowd never came, and where she was
seldom exposed to the annoyances which elsewhere invariably
pursued her, of a misnamed gallantry, and a devotion which
suggested nothing grateful to her fancies.

It was one afternoon, while Ella Monckton was on a visit to
Katharine, that the gay widow Brewton joined the circle. In
the constantly increasing round of her social progress, this lady

was usually put in possession of the latest *on dit* of the city. She had been that morning at Mrs. Rivington's, where it seems that Proctor, and his command at Dorchester, had been the subject of conversation.

" There is evidently a determination, in high quarters," said the widow, " to destroy that poor fellow, Proctor."

The heart of Ella trembled at these words.

" I suspect, Kate Walton," she continued, " that you are to blame for it all."

" Me ! How ? Why ?"

" Ah ! do not feign ignorance. Barry, and his eternal shadow M'Mahon, were both in full cry against him for his presumptuous admiration of you. It was charged that you are the cause of all his neglect of duty ; and a great deal was said of a nature to lead me to suspect that great pains will be taken to establish the facts against him. But I did not so much trouble myself in relation to his case as to yours. The question was, in what degree you had given Proctor encouragement."

" I give him encouragement !"

" Come, come, Kate ! Do not put on that sublime look of indignation. Proctor is not a person to be despised. He is one of the noblest of all these British officers, and, by the way, one of the best looking. A maiden might well give him encouragement without intending it, and might just as easily forget to shield her own heart against his attacks. Mark you, I do not say that such has been the case with you ; but there were those present this morning, that did say so, and who brought forward a large number of proofs to conclude what they asserted."

" And what did *you* say ?" asked Katharine, with a smile.

" Oh ! you may guess. I asked, with no little scorn, if there was any one so stupid as to suppose that you were going to throw yourself away upon a red-coat ; and I turned to Major Barry, and remarked in these very words ; ' Undoubtedly, major, you are among the handsomest, the bravest, and the wittiest of all your crew — perhaps the very Magnus Apollo of the tribe. Now, pray you, think of Miss Walton, of her mind, her person, and, last and least of all, her fortune ; then, be pleased to wheel about and confront your own image in that grand mirror of Mrs. Rivington's. Having done so, and having brought all your well-known self-esteem to bear upon the question, then ask yourself what would be the amount of claim and attraction which you might urge, if seeking the hand of Katharine Walton.' "

"Oh, Mrs. Brewton!"

"I did; and, positively, a miracle! The little fellow blushed! Blushed, until nobody thought to look at the scarlet of his regimentals. And Captain M'Mahon, looking in his face, blushed also—by reflection, I suppose; and for a moment the whole squad was silenced. But, with a sort of desperation, they renewed the fire, as much, it would seem, to please that brazen beauty, Moll Harvey, as with any other object. The argument was that you were quite too deeply involved with Proctor ever to escape; that Balfour, accordingly stood no chance; that whatever might be done against Proctor was to him a matter of perfect indifference, so long as his life remained untouched; that he was already prepared to abandon the British for the American cause; and that your love, of which he was secure, was sufficiently compensative for all his losses and privations."

Poor Ella felt as if she could have buried her face in the earth—as if her heart were already buried there.

"What a farrago of absurdities!" exclaimed Katharine.

"Nay, Kate, upon my soul, I don't see that. I give you my word for it they made a very plausible story among them. Somebody did say something about your once having drawn trigger upon Proctor, as a proof of your dislike; but the story was positively denied by others, and Proctor's own words quoted in denial."

"It was nevertheless quite true," said Katharine, gravely.

"True!" exclaimed Ella, with a convulsive shudder.

"All true," answered Katharine, with increasing gravity. "It is one of those things of which I do not care to speak. I revolt at myself when I think of it; and no doubt Major Proctor denies it, with an honorable disposition, to relieve me from the odium of having attempted such a crime. But it was in a moment of desperation, almost of madness, that the thing was done; and having told you thus much, I must tell you all, by way of

12*

explanation; but I entreat you, Mrs. Brewton, and you, Ella, to keep the matter secret. My dear cousin, Emily Singleton, was dying in our house : her brother, Robert, was with us, concealed, a fugitive, about to receive her last breath. At that awful moment, Major Proctor entered the dwelling, followed by his troops. I arrested him at the door of my cousin's chamber, from which Robert made his escape by the window. Major Proctor approaching with the resolution to enter, though I had forbidden it, I seized one of my cousin's pistols, and fired, fortunately, without effect, for I had no aim! I knew not what I did!"

A deep sigh struggled forth from the breast of Ella Monckton.

"Why, what a desperado you are, Kate!" exclaimed Mrs. Brewton. "I thought I had wickedness and wilfulness for anything; but I never once dreamed of the possibility of my ever attempting to shoot down a British major. How did you feel, child, when you were doing it? when you pulled the ugly little crooked iron they call the trigger? when you heard the sudden bam! bam! and saw the flash? Did you tremble? Did you faint? Did you not feel like going off into hysterics? Bless me, you are, indeed, a heroine! and how the thing was hushed up!—for the person—who was it?—that mentioned it this morning, gave it only as a rumor, and was easily silenced!"

"It was too true! I knew not what I was doing—this must be my apology. I owe much to Major Proctor for his forbearance."

"And will pay him with your heart."

"Never! never! Let me tell you further, and thus silence *your* doubts for ever, Mrs. Brewton—I am the betrothed of my cousin, Robert Singleton; Major Proctor can never be anything to me but a gentleman of worth, whom I very much esteem."

Could Katharine Walton have seen the bright but tearful eyes of poor Ella at that moment! With what a bound her little heart rose to her mouth, and fluttered there like some captive bird, deluded for a moment with a dream of escape from prison!

Mrs. Singleton entered the apartment at this moment. She heard the revelation of Katharine, and spoke rebukingly.

Katharine, my child, this should not have been told. It is our policy to keep it secret. If known abroad, it may be fatal to your fortunes. Balfour's forbearance is due entirely to his doubt of your engagement. He has, thus far, no reason to believe it. Let him suppose that the affair is irrevocable, and the commissioner of sequestrations keeps no terms with you, and you lose everything."

"Be it so, my dear aunt," replied the other; "but, believe me, I should rather lose all than deserve the reproach of holding out any encouragement to others, which may mislead."

"You are quite right, my dear," cried the widow Brewton. "I much prefer the manly course myself."

"Nay, she is quite wrong, and *you* are quite wrong, permit me to say," responded Mrs. Singleton, with great gravity. "You are only asked, my child, to keep a secret which peculiarly concerns yourself, and which nobody has a right to seek. In doing so, you hold forth no encouragement to others, so long as your deportment is that of a lady. The presumption which takes for granted its own merits as too potential to be withstood, must pay its own penalties, and is not particularly a subject of commiseration or concern. If these people assume your freedom, let them do so; if they presume upon it, there will always be a season to interpose and check them, either by simple rejection of their civilities, or by showing, if you think proper, that you are no longer your own mistress. In your present circumstances, there is no impropriety in that reserve which simply keeps from one's neighbor a private history, which is especially one's own; and every motive of policy insists upon the reserve."

"My dear aunt, my secret will be perfectly safe with Mrs. Brewton and Ella."

The ladies thus mentioned hastened to give their assurances to this effect.

"No doubt, no doubt, my dear; but without my warning, you would probably, under the same provocation, have revealed yourself in like manner to anybody else."

"It is very like I should. I have been always accustomed to this freedom; and I confess to a feeling nowise agreeable in yielding to the reserve which you call policy, but which certainly seems to me to lead necessarily to false notions of one's situation."

"Not so; nobody ought to suffer because a lady keeps the secret of her betrothal. The gentleman who seeks a lady must feel his way cautiously. His first approaches, met properly by the lady, are his last, and there's an end of it. Everything depends upon herself. If she trifles with her situation, that is quite another thing. In your case, my dear, there can be no fears of this sort."

The entrance of another visiter changed the subject. Mrs. Ingliss, who now joined the party, was a genuine patriot, and at present under special annoyance. She had some of the more foppish of the British officers billeted upon her, among whom was the famous wit of the garrison, so often mentioned, Harry Barry, Esq., Major, &c. But the annoyance was not greatly regretted by her friends, since her patriotism enabled her upon occasion to turn it to excellent use. Keeping her own counsels, and studiously forbearing to offend the prejudices of the enemy, she inspired them with a certain degree of confidence, and they spoke very freely before her. By this means she gathered many items of intelligence, which found their way to our circle of female conspirators, and were by them conveyed to the partisans. Something was due to this lady, accordingly, and it became the policy of our patriots to afford every possible countenance to her mode of housekeeping. She visited the ladies of both parties, and they did not withhold themselves from her assemblies. Her present visit was to Katharine Walton. It was the usual formal initial call preparatory to an invitation; and the customary preliminaries being dismissed, Mrs. Ingliss solicited the presence of our heroine at her house on the ensuing evening. Finding Katharine hesitate, Mrs. Brewton interposed:

"Of course she will come, Mrs. Ingliss; we will all come. We know what is due to you, and we shall enjoy ourselves rarely with your lodgers. Barry, you know, is my delicate aversion. I approach him as I would Tom Singleton's monkey, with the mood to torture him into the antics, without which the beast has no qualities. We will come, of course."

Mrs. Singleton gave a similar assurance, and the consent of

Katharine followed. Mrs. Ingliss did not linger long after this; and when she departed she was accompanied by the lively widow. Ella Monckton still remained, her heart filled with inexpressible emotions. She had spoken little during the conference between the parties, but her interest had been lively enough in all that had been said. There was nothing now wanting to confirm that warm feeling of sympathy which she had begun to cherish for the character of Katharine. That the heart of the latter was quite free in respect to Proctor—that there was no possibility that the parties should be ever more nearly connected with each other than they were at present— was a conviction too firmly established in her mind, from what she had heard, to suffer any future doubts or misgivings from that source.

The poor girl was, for the time, unreservedly happy in this conviction. When she was about to go, to the surprise of Katharine, she threw her arms abou: the neck of the latter, and passionately kissed her cheek. The proceeding was so unusual —so unlike everything that had hitherto marked their intercourse—that for a moment Katharine absolutely recoiled. But, in the next instant, as she saw the face of Ella covered with blushes, while her eyes, gleaming with a most unusual brightness, were yet filled with the biggest drops, she took the tender girl fondly in her arms, and returned her kisses with a tenderness only less warm than her own. She could only account for the unwonted warmth of her companion by giving her credit for a heart of very great sensibilities, which society had not yet tutored into reserve and caution. But the scene, almost without words, united the two maidens in a tie very superior to that which ordinarily brings persons of their age and sex together.

CHAPTER XXIX.

SWEETHEART AND STEED AT STAKE.

Our scenes are required now to change with almost panoramic rapidity. The night of the day on which the proceedings of our last chapter took place was distinguished by a grand ball at the well-known dwelling of Mrs. Tidyman, in Ladson's court, then occupied by Biddulph, the paymaster of the British forces in Carolina, a person of showy and expensive habits, who lived in great style upon the profits — since vulgarly styled "pickings and stealings" — for which his office afforded him such excellent facilities.

The court was lighted up with great splendor, and every apartment of the house was filled to overflow. Hither came all the select of the garrison, all of the loyalists, male and female, and a very few of the whigs, but those only who were too timid to refuse an invitation which might reasonably be construed into a command. There was one exception, among those who did attend, to this general classification of the whigs present. This was Mrs. Brewton, whose talents for repartee usually saved her from any annoying assaults on the score of her patriotism, and who found these assemblages very favorable to her desires, which at once aimed to conceal her purposes, and to afford them opportunities. It was a profound policy which prompted her desire to acquire the reputation of a mere lover of pleasure; while the boldness with which she declared her whigism aloud was almost a guarantee to the enemy that they had nothing to fear from her secret machinations.

Here she met General Williamson, and, to her surprise, was

drawn aside by him from the press, and sounded upon various matters which only did not openly trench upon the actual issues between the parties. She observed that he was curious and anxious, and that, though possessed of little ingenuity in conversation, he yet contrived, through the very necessity in which he stood, to throw out sundry remarks, which, had she been disposed, might have conducted to an interesting *éclaircissement*. She had only to seize, with a bold assumption, upon one of the two susceptibilities contained in some of his equivoques, to have found the way clear to a complete development. So, at least, she thought. But, predetermined that he was not to be trusted, and loathing his character as she did, she availed herself of none of the opportunities which he really desired to afford her. It was while they spoke together, however, that a young officer of the guards, named Sadler, approached them, and, addressing Mrs. Brewton, mentioned that he was ordered to Camden, and should leave the city in two days. He politely offered to take letters for her to Mrs. Motte (her late husband's sister—afterward famous in story for confiding to Marion the bow and arrows by which her mansion-house was destroyed) or for any other of her friends in the neighborhood. She replied in her usual spirit—

"I thank you, lieutenant; I should very much like to write, but really I have no wish to have my letters read at the head of Marion's brigade."

"Do you really mean, Mrs. Brewton, that I am in danger of falling into the hands of the rebel?"

"Would you have me prophesy more clearly, sir? The thing is inevitable. It is your fate. I see it as clearly in your face as if I read it in your palms. Persuade the commandant to send somebody else. His destiny may be otherwise written."

Sadler turned off in a huff. But we may venture to pause in our narrative to anticipate the rest of the story. Poor Sadler was really captured by Singleton, of Marion's brigade; and, in two weeks after, he returned to Charleston, and called immediately upon Mrs. Brewton to thank her for his disgrace. He fully believed that she had contrived to convey intelligence of his route and progress to the partisans. This event was one of several which finally provoked the British authorities to expel the lady from the city.

When Sadler had retired, Williamson, with evident eagerness, remarked—

"You speak with confidence of the whereabouts of Marion's brigade. Is your confidence the result of shrewd guessing, or do you know——"

She interrupted him quickly.

"It is prophecy, sir. I am another Cassandra—doomed to tell the truth, and not to be believed when I do so. This poor lieutenant only goes to be taken. When I say so, I obey an irresistible impulse, which I certainly believe."

"Ah! the days of prophecy are not ours! We should half suspect you of knowing well what you prophesy so boldly. Now, my dear Mrs. Brewton, it concerns me something to know how far you speak from a knowledge of the fact. It will materially affect my habits if I could suppose you knowing rather than prophetic. I propose, for example, to take my usual weekly ride, the next day, or the day after, into the country, and——"

He paused, and looked exceedingly sagacious and encouraging. She replied quickly—

"General Williamson, I do not prophesy for everybody. I can only say in your case that, should you be taken by Marion's men, your chance of being kept long in captivity would be infinitely less than that of this beardless lieutenant."

For a moment the significance of this answer did not seem to strike her companion. When, however, the full meaning flashed upon him, his face blackened to a thunder-cloud.

"Madam—Mrs. Brewton!" he exclaimed—then stammered and grew silent. He rose abruptly from his seat, and then returned to it, his features somewhat more composed. Looking at her with an earnest glance, he resumed—

"It is evident, Mrs. Brewton, that you do not know me. You still regard me as an enemy. You will do me more justice hereafter."

"Nay, General Williamson, if you think that I do not desire, from the bottom of my soul, to see justice done to *you*, you do not know *me*."

This was as bad as before. He turned away quickly, saying—

"Very well, madam, very well! But you will yet repent these expressions!"

She hummed gayly, as he went, the refrain of an old ballad, then quite popular—

> "And they bore away my bonny boy,
>   And they bore him away to the fatal tree;
> Brief space they gave him then to pray—
>   But his latest breath it was breathed for me."

"Jezabel!" was the single word of Williamson, as he heard the words, and disappeared in the crowd. The widow saw no more of him that night.

Meanwhile, the dancing had begun, and the gayly-caparison-ed knights and damsels whirled about the apartment, subject to frequent concussion with the densely-packed groups that looked on the while. Mrs. Brewton became the centre of one of these inactive groups ; but it was no silent one.—The events of the evening had vexed others as well as Williamson. One of these outraged persons was the somewhat famous Archibald Camp-bell, better known as Mad Archy, or Crazy Campbell, a wild, reckless, harem-scarem soldier, who united a most irregular in-tellect to a most daring courage—if, indeed, we may consistent-ly discover, in a deficient mind, the fine moral virtue which is described as courage.

Archy Campbell was famous for doing desperate things. He was vain, rash, headlong, and presumptuous, and much feared as a fire-eater. The arguments upon which he relied, in all dis-cussions, were the bet and the duello. To stake life and mon-ey, equally, on his sentiments and opinions, was his favorite mode of proving himself right, and making himself so. He had his virtues, however—though, by the way, the former were not always considered vices or even defects of character. The women rather favored him, possibly because the men feared him. He was handsome and generous, and *kept a gig*, which was one of the most showy of all the garrison. To drive out a favorite damsel of an afternoon to the " Quarter" or " Eight-

Mile House," or beyond, to Goose Creek—making his trotter do his ten miles by the hour—was with him a sort of triumph which made him indifferent to the capture of posts or armies. His great ambition was social conquest. To come, see, and conquer, in a sense somewhat different from that of Cesar, was his daily aim. And he fancied himself always successful.

This easy assurance led him, on the present occasion, into an error in which his presumption was duly mortified. We have spoken elsewhere of Paulina Phelps, as one of the loyalist *belles* at that time in the city. She was a very pretty girl, lively and intelligent; her charms being duly increased in public estimation by the fact that she was the heiress to a very handsome fortune. Mad Archy was not so far demented as to be insensible to this consideration. He was accordingly her avowed suitor and constant attendant. She did not discourage his attentions, as she was not the person to be regardless of the devotion of a young, handsome, and high-spirited gallant. Whether she encouraged them beyond proper limits is a question. It is certain, however, that he construed her good humor and indulgence into something more significant. On this occasion, just before the dancing had commenced, and while she was interested in the conversation of a very graceful gentleman, one Captain Harley, who had recently arrived from New York, Mad Archy broke in upon the party with a bound.

" Come, Paulina, Miss Phelps," he cried; " your arm, they are about to dance."

The lady drew up, offended with this freedom, and somewhat disdainfully answered—

" You mistake, Major Campbell; I am not engaged to dance with *you*."

" Eh!—no!—what!" he replied, astonished. " Not dance with me!"

" No, sir."

You refuse me, Paulina! You are capricious, Miss Phelps!"

" And you presumptuous, Major Campbell!"

" The devil you say!" cried Campbell, abruptly; and, turning with a rude stare to Harley, he cried aloud—

"Well! Let me see the man who will dance with you to-night."

At these words, with great ease, dignity, and self-possession, Captain Harley said—

" May I have the honor of being your partner in this dance, Miss Phelps ?"

The lady, still smarting under Campbell's insolence, instinctively rose and took the arm of the other. The action confounded Mad Archy, who, for a moment, knew not what to say. It was in this mood that he was joined by the professed mischief-makers of the garrison, Major Stock and others.

" Done for, Archy !" cried Stock, with a grin. " Clearly cut—made dog's meat of, and no burial service."

" I'll punish her !" exclaimed Archy with an oath. " And as for Harley, I'll teach him such a lesson as will cure his love for dancing from now to doomsday. Look you, Stock; you will take my message to him in the morning."

" You will do no such thing, Major Stock," said the widow Brewton, who had overheard every syllable. " If Archy Campbell will be a fool, with malice prepense and aforethought, as the lawyers say, there's no reason that you should prove yourself an accessory, either after or before the fact."

" 'Pon my soul, madam, you are bold," cried Campbell.

" What ! to brave such a fire-eater as yourself ? Look you, Major Campbell, if you are so totally without friends as to be able to hear the truth from none but a woman's mouth, hear it from mine. Let me tell you that there is no extraordinary renown in being considered the madman, *par excellence*, of a very silly garrison of foot and horse. Remember, moreover, that no degree of folly and madness will excuse brutality."

" Brutality, madam," cried Campbell, fiercely.

" Even so, sir. There is no other word half so appropriate to our present uses. You have been guilty of a great offence against all the proprieties, and must not make your offence still more enormous. You have outraged the sensibilities of a lady whom you profess to admire, and have presumed upon those very weaknesses of her sex which should have been her securities against offence. You must not proceed farther—you *shall* not—in the same erring direction. You can not quarrel with Captain Harley without adding still farther to this brutality.

He could do no less than he has done under the circumstances ; and, if you can not emulate, at least learn to respect his deportment."

" Upon my soul, Mrs. Brewton, you queen it most royally ! You say I *shall* not, and I *must* not ; but madam, suppose I say, in answer, that I *will !*"

" Why, then, sir, I shall only have mistaken the nature of the animal that I have sought to tame."

" Well, madam, and pray what animal was that ?"

" A lion, sir ; at worst a royal tiger—"

" Well, madam ?—"

" And not a bear—not an—"

She paused. He spoke—

" Not an ass, you would say !"

" Really, sir, your instincts are sufficiently good, whatever may be the condition of your wits."

" By Jove, Mrs. Brewton, you are too hard upon me ! But you have courage, madam, and courage is a virtue—and I like you nevertheless. But I can't submit to this ; and I beg that you will interfere no farther. I will shoot this fellow, Harley, or pink him—"

" No you won't, unless you really have resolved to give up the lady."

" How ?"

" Take another step in this business, and you lose her for ever. Behave like a man of sense and proper feeling, and if you ever had a chance of success you will certainly increase it. Go to her—seek your opportunity—become the penitent—show that you regard her feelings as well as your own—that you are prepared to sacrifice your feelings for hers—and you will make a more favorable impression on her than you ever made before."

He hesitated, and shook his head.

" Do you really love the lady ?"

" Yes, Mrs. Brewton, as the apple of my eye !"

" Then, do as I tell you, even though you should lose the apple of your eye. Proceed to bully her, or her present attendant, and, if she have any spark of feeling or of spirit, she will spurn you with loathing from her sight. Go, now, seek your opportunity — do not despair if you make no progress to-night — better, indeed, not try to-night, but be sure you seek her and make amends to-morrow; and, by the way, it would be well to make gentlemanly terms with this Captain Harley—"

"Oh! by Jove, I can't do that! but I thank you, Mrs. Brewton, for your counsel, I do! By the Eternal! madam, you have the soul of a war-horse; and I honor you, madam, though I'm afraid of you!"

"And *because* of it," she answered, quietly.

Major Stock had heard the better part of this conversation, though pulled this way and that by some old ladies who wished for refreshments.

"Well," said he, when Mad Archy had joined him, "so the widow takes your case in hand. It will be well peppered. But she counsels rightly. You can't call out this fellow Harley, who has only played handsome at your expense. You *will* run your head against it, Archy! It's unfortunate. I think there's no chance with the Phelps, after this! You've lost her, my boy, for ever."

"What'll you bet I don't dance with her to-night?"

'Five guineas on it!"

"Done! Now for another; what'll you bet I don't marry her?"

"Fifty guineas against your trotter."

"It's an even go. Now look to it; for, as sure as thunder, I shall have both the girl and the guineas."

"Get the one and you get the other," cried Stock, and the parties separated, each seeking different avenues among the crowds.

CHAPTER XXX.

CARTEL.

THE equally restless and benevolent spirit of Mrs. Brewton was not satisfied to administer to mad Archy Campbell alone the counsels necessary to propriety. At an early hour, after the interview with him, she sought out the fair object of his temporary resentment.

"Paulina, my dear," she began, "you have greatly irritated Archy Campbell."

"Well, he deserves it," was the reply.

"I think it very likely; but are you prepared for all the consequences of his anger?"

"I don't see how it is to affect *me*."

"Well, in regard to yourself I can say nothing. I know not in what degree you are interested in him. It is very certain that he is greatly interested in *you*, and I much fear that any unusual harshness on your part will only drive him into mischief. I am afraid that he will force a duel upon this newly-come gentleman, Captain Harley."

"God forbid!" exclaimed the other.

"Let me beg that *you* will forbid also. I am sure, unless you are at some pains to be civil to your suitor, that such will be the event. You may be quite civil, and disarm his anger, without committing yourself in any way."

The result of the conversation, thus began, was satisfactory; and, whether Paulina really felt an interest or not in Campbell, she determined to adopt a course less calculated to provoke his irritable nature into excess and violence. The consequence of this interposition was made apparent to Mrs. Brewton within the next half hour, when Major Stock approached her, with no little ill humor, and pointing to Campbell and Paulina, engaged in the mazes of the dance, said—

"I owe it to you, Mrs. Brewton, that I am five guineas *minus* to-night."

Both Stock and Mrs. Brewton remained long enough to discover that Campbell was restored to his usual good humor; the behavior of Paulina being such as to encourage him in the highest hopes for the future. He had won his first bet; that was grumblingly acknowledged by Stock.

"But don't deceive yourself," said the latter. "You owe this only to the good nature of the girl. She saw that you were in a devil of a sulk, and knowing what a mad beast you are when in an ill humor, she was afraid that you'd be venting your fury upon her new favorite. Mrs. Brewton did this for you. I overheard her. But I shall have your trotter for all that. If ever woman was taken with a fellow, she is with Harley."

"Do you think I fear him?" cried Campbell, exultingly. "I'll have her in spite of all the Harleys in creation. Will you go another fifty guineas on it?"

"No," was the reply. "I don't know where you'd find the money. The horse will be loss enough for you at present—and the disappointment."

With a great oath, Campbell broke away to escort Paulina to her carriage. He returned, after a few moments, in increased spirits, and in good humor with all the world—being particularly civil to Harley himself, whom he found conversing with Stock and others over the decanters. Harley was quiet, dignified, and reserved, in his deportment. It was observed that he evaded a good-humored remark made him by Campbell, contriving to answer somebody else at the moment.

"You design no quarrel with this man, Harley?" said Stock to Campbell, as they left the house together.

"No. Why should I?" was the response. "The fellow was right enough; and if anybody had cause of offence he was the person. I threatened all the world, and looked into his face while I did so."

It was while Stock was busy over a late breakfast, the next morning, that mad Archy bounced in upon him.

"Look at that!" said he, throwing down a billet.

"Eh! by the powers!" exclaimed Stock, reading the billet. "This is bringing the mill to the grist!"

It was a *cartel* from Harley. The tables were turned.

"Prompt and cool, eh?" said Campbell. "Who'd have thought it? The fellow has blood, that's certain."

"By Jove, yes! A positive demand; no sneaking invitation to the pacific. Well, what have you done?"

"Referred his friend to you. Major Ponsonbly acts for him."

"Then it is business. Well, what will you have?"

"The small-sword, and as soon as you please; but not within the next three days."

"How! It will get abroad. Why not this afternoon or to-morrow? The sooner the better!"

"All true; but I require two days, at least, for my marriage."

"Pshaw! are you so absurd as to dream of that?"

"Absurd! Do you suppose I mean to lose my trotter, or to forego your guineas? No! no, Stock! I shall have my girl and your gold, or hold me a spooney. After that shall Mr. Harley have his desires, not before."

"He will find his patience fail in waiting, if you hope for Paulina Phelps before you fight."

"Never you fear! Make your arrangements; but not to take effect before Saturday. I insist only on the small-sword. Make the arrangements accordingly—place and time, at his pleasure, or yours."

"Very good! You are only a shade madder than I thought you. Do you go to Mrs. Ingliss's to-night?"

"Where else? I dance with Paulina in the first quadrille."

"And her consent to this has led you to assume all the rest! What a vain dizzard you are!"

"Look you, Stock, get your guineas out of the pay-chest. I shall need them all in two days more. The money is mine, I tell you."

"Speak out honestly; has she consented to the marriage?"

"No; but *I* have!"

"Pshaw! Get you gone, and see Francisco at the guard-room. You may need a little exercise with the weapon."

"Not a bit of it. I shall touch no sword, and think of no fight, until I am a married man."

"Hark! there's a rap. No doubt our customer. Begone!"

A servant entered at this moment, and announced "Major Ponsonby."

"He's prompt. That's handsome!" said Campbell. "Good by, Stock, and see that you get the guineas."

Campbell and Ponsonby passed each other at the entrance with a bow and a smile; and the former had scarcely rounded the next square, before the two seconds had arranged the meeting for the ensuing Saturday, at five in the afternoon, swords the weapons, the place a well-known grove, just without the lines, on the banks of Cooper river.

13

CHAPTER XXXI.

BARRY, AS A SCULPTOR.

THAT night both the principals were to be seen at the party of Mrs. Ingliss, as cool and happy as if their immunities of life were insured in the book of Fate for the next hundred years. It was observed that they treated each other with especial good humor and courtesy. But Harley bit his lip when he beheld his rival leading out the fair Paulina the first into the ring; and his vexation was not a whit lessened to perceive the smiling grace with which the damsel welcomed the attentions of her gallant. Mad Archy could not forbear, in the exultation of his spirit, casting a mischievous glance of triumph at his disappointed enemy. Harley saw and understood the meaning of the glance, and he resolved to be as merciless in the duel as his rival was in the dance. He soon sought his present consolations in another quarter of the apartment, and being as cool and courteous as brave—affecting, indeed, something of the *preux cheva-lier*—he very quickly joined in the measured mazes of the whirling parties, coupled with a partner whose bright eyes kept his own too busy to suffer him to see the happiness which he envied in his neighbors.

The scene of festivity on this occasion, the dwelling of Mrs. Ingliss, is yet conspicuous, a fine, airy mansion, scarcely looking so antique as lofty, in Queen street, directly opposite Friend, in the venerable city of Charleston.* It was illuminated for the occasion from top to bottom. The region west and north of it held but few houses, and an ample garden, in both these quarters, was richly lighted up also, cressets and lamps being sprinkled

* Now in the possession of Mr. William Enston.

quite freely among the shrubs and orange-trees. Beyond this garden, on the south, the view was almost unbroken to the river; a smooth esplanade spreading down to the green skirts of salt marsh which bordered the Ashley on the east. The whole scene was one of great beauty, and the soft airs from the southwest played deliciously among the chambers, in grateful unison with the moonlight and fragrance which surrounded them. The company was not in the mood to suffer these luxuries to escape them. They gave themselves up to unreserved enjoyment, or at least seemed to do so; the secret care at the hearts of many being hushed into repose, or disguised beneath that social mask which so frequently shelters the wounds of sensibility and the volcanoes of passion. The lower apartments and the piazza were yielded up to the dancers. The graver persons of the party were grouped here and there among them, as spectators, or congregated in the upper rooms. Some dispersed themselves about the garden, and love and sentiment, and mere humor and politics, found each some fitting place or subject for exercise.

Leaving the gay groups below, let us ascend to the front or southern apartment in the second story. Here we find Mrs. Ingliss with her more ancient guests. With these are Mrs. Singleton and Katharine Walton, both quietly seated, the latter with an admiring circle, small, but dutiful, in close attendance. Here was to be seen Colonel Cruden, as her guardian, dignified and complacent. Balfour, to the surprise of all, failed to make his appearance. Here, too, at intervals in the dancing, Major Barry was most obsequious in his service; and passing from chamber to chamber, the gay groups loitered with that restless feeling, a pleasant sort of discontent, which, perhaps, at places of this sort, furnishes the best stimulus to pleasure and excitement. We shall certainly not seek to detain the reader with such general descriptions as he may readily imagine for himself, but shall detach, for his benefit, from the events of the evening, such as bear more or less directly upon the progress of our history.

We have glanced at Major Barry among the guests. It must not be forgotten that the house of Mrs. Ingliss was his place of lodging. In the distribution of abodes for the British officers, after the conquest of the city, he had been billeted upon her. This lady, as we have seen, was a good patriot; but she was treated civilly by Barry, and his harmless vanity, and almost unvarying good humor, inclined her in his favor. She rather liked him than otherwise, though she never spared her censure of his conduct whenever it deserved rebuke.

It happened, at one of these pauses of the dance this evening, that Barry drew nigh to the group about Mrs. Ingliss, with whom we found Mrs. Singleton and Katharine Walton. He was then officiating as one of the numerous *cortège* of the fashionable widow Rivington. Hither, also, drew nigh our other famous widow, Mrs. Brewton. Close behind her followed Captain M'Mahon, Barry's shadow, who was, or affected to be, very earnest in supplicating Mrs. Brewton for some favor or some act of forbearance. But she was obdurate, and broke into the circle of which Barry, though quite *petite* of person, was the somewhat conspicuous object.

"Major Barry," observed Mrs. Brewton, "you must positively cut Captain M'Mahon."

"Fie! Mrs. Brewton!" implored M'Mahon.

"Why?" was Barry's inquiry.

"He is no friend of yours."

"I no friend of Major Barry! I am the only friend he has in the world."

"Heaven help him, then! The sooner he hangs himself the better. But I speak the truth. He has proved it to me most conclusively."

"And how, Mrs. Brewton?" was the inquiry of Barry, beginning to be quite curious,

"In striving to hide your light under his bushel."

"In plain terms," said Major Stock, "standing with his big head between you and the candle."

"Something worse than that," responded the widow. "We all know that Major Barry is both wit and poet. He is continually doing something very brilliant and grateful to Apollo. A true friend would be anxious that the world should be put in possession of these good things; yet here is Captain M'Mahon studiously suppressing them—"

"Which means," said Stock, "showing them to everybody under an injunction of secrecy."

"Precisely. Now this is treachery to one's friend and treachery to the public."

"To be sure," said Stock; "particularly as the friend knows all about it, and the world don't care a button to know."

"Oh, what a malignant!" cried Mrs. Rivington.

Mrs. Brewton continued—

"You are mistaken quite, Major Stock. The world *does* care to know. At all events, it should be protected from painful surprises. Now, if Major Barry's friend would honestly publish his good things in the 'Royal Gazette,' I could read them or not, at my pleasure; but when his friend makes me a sort of confidant, and forces upon me a secret, there is a double injury done to me and to the public. The possession of a secret, to a woman, is a sort of temptation to sin; and I will not be forced to keep that of Captain M'Mahon or his friend, Major Barry. Here, now, is a new epigram of the major's," holding up a paper.

"Read it!—read it!" was the cry from a dozen voices.

"Oh, don't!" appealed the author, in feeble tones.

"Oh, don't!" echoed M'Mahon, in tones quite as feeble.

"It appears," continued the widow, "that Major Barry has been honored with the gift of a pair of slippers, wrought by the fair hands of—— but that is a lady's secret, and must not be revealed by one of her sex. His acknowledgment for this gift is contained in the following very felicitous verses."

"Buzz! buzz! buzz!" went round the circle, Barry and M'Mahon both striving, but very inadequately, to increase the confusion.

"Oh, I won't read till we have perfect silence," said Mrs. Brewton.

And, with the words, our two Arcadians were the first to stop. With clear tones, and mock heroic manner, she then read the following—epigram, we suppose, it must be called:—

"To Miss Phebe ——, in compliment for a pair of slippers, wrought by her own hands:—

> "Woman, of old, with wondrous art,
> Was still content to snare the heart;

> But now her more ambitious goal
> Is conquest o'er the very soul (*sole?*):
> No more, with *understanding* sure,
> Man walks the earth he ruled of yore;
> On humbler *footing* now he stands, —
> His *footsteps* taken through her *hands.*
> His *sole* (soul?) enmeshed, her happy snares
> At least protect from toils and tears (*tares?*)
> Nor all forgot her ancient art,
> Still through the soul o'ercomes the heart."

"Is that all?" demanded Stock, as the lady paused.

"All!"

"Certainly that mountain suffered grievously from that mouse!" cried Stock. "Positively, there should be some enactment, some heavy penalty against this cruel repetition of ancient puns. I am against you, Mrs. Brewton. If you can really satisfy me that M'Mahon honestly desired to keep secret these verses when he communicated them, then shall I aver that he was a better friend to Major Barry than Barry himself."

"Oh hush!" cried Mrs. Rivington. "You are too barbarous for a critic, Major Stock."

"Grant you, ma'am; but not too much so for a friend."

"Cynic!—but here come the waiters. We have need of cordials and comfits to take the bitter from our mouths."

And, with these words from Mrs. Rivington, the assault temporarily ceased upon Barry. The circle opened to receive the servants, bearing splendid and massive silver trays and salvers containing refreshments. These consisted of jams and jellies, pines, bananas, and other West India fruits, cordials and lemonade; and sundry more potent beverages for the stronger heads of the military. It would surprise a modern assembly, in the same region, to behold, in the centre of such a service, an immense bowl of punch, the chief ingredients of which were old Jamaica rum and cogniac, of nearly equal virtue.

While the gentlemen served the ladies, without finally forgetting themselves, the eyes of the company were directed, by some remark of Mrs. Rivington, to a good-looking young negro boy of sixteen, in the livery of Barry—a blue ground, with scarlet facings.

"By the way," said the fashionable widow, quite abruptly, "where did you pick up that clever boy, Major Barry?"

The question was so sudden, and Barry's consciousness at the moment, so quick, that he answered confusedly—

"Me, Mrs. Rivington?—that boy—where did I get that boy? Why, I made him."*

A solemn hush succeeded this strangely equivocal answer. The elderly ladies looked grave, and the younger vacant. A boisterous laugh from Stock added to the confusion.

"A better piece of work, by all odds, than the epigram. I should greatly thank you to make me a hundred or two of the same animal, out of the same sort of ebony."

Barry had, by this time, recovered himself. The little wit found it necessary to put a bold face on the matter, and to exercise his ingenuity for his escape from his blunder.

"And there would be no great difficulty in the matter if you have the necessary amount of faith. Faith is the great essential. The fact is that, some time ago, happening to be in the neighborhood of Monk's Corner, I thirsted for a draught of cool water from a neighboring brooklet. But I did not wish to wet my feet in getting at it, so I looked about me; and just before me noted a tract of the bog of the most ivory smoothness and as black as jet. 'Now,' said I, 'will I see what faith will perform.' I scooped up some of the earth, which was soft and pliant. I moulded it into the form and features of a handsome boy. I then devoutly concentrated my will upon it, and I said—repeating the abracadabra, and other potent formula of ancient magic— 'Rise up, Cæsario!' and thereupon he rose, a good-looking lad enough, as you see him now, and quite creditable to me as a sculptor."

"A round about way," said Mrs. Ingliss to Mrs. Singleton, in tones almost audible to the circle, "of telling us he stole him somewhere near Monk's Corner."

"There's no end to Barry's sorceries. Captain M'Mahon, your friend needs a new title."

* This answer was really given by Barry. The scenes of this story, which occur in Charleston, were mostly of real occurrence, as the parties were mostly real and well-known persons.

"Ah! What, major?"

"Henceforth let him be known as the Ethiopian Prometheus."

The name stuck to the major for a long time afterward—certainly as long as the negro did.

A crash of plates and glasses interrupted the scene, and furnished an excuse to Barry for leaving the circle. His newly-created servant, Cæsario, not being bred to his vocation, had allowed the heavy silver tray to slip from his grasp, emptying the entire contents into the lap of the excellent Mrs. Smith, who, it was thought, had caused the accident by bearing with too much stress—under a mistake as to the character of its contents, of course—upon the punch bowl. There was great clamor, in the confusion of which, Katharine Walton, taking Ella Monckton by the arm, escaped into the garden. Let us leave them for a season, while looking after certain other interesting parties to our story.

CHAPTER XXXII.

BRIGHT AND DARK.

WE left mad Archy Campbell in the full whirl of a most delirious and grateful excitement. Whether it was that Paulina Phelps really gave him a preference in her affections, or was afraid of giving provocation to his anger, it would not be easy to determine. Certain it is that she treated him with all the considerate solicitude of one who claimed a large portion of her favor. And, to do him justice, he now seemed properly careful to deserve it. His behavior was unwontedly gentle, modest, and devoted. He studiously avoided the language and manner of passion and excess. The coarse phraseology in which he was too much disposed, ordinarily, to indulge, was carefully made to give way to a dialect better fashioned to persuade the sentimental nature; and it really seemed as if the effort to appear more amiable had taught the lips of mad Archy an unusual eloquence. He was evidently laboring at an object—evidently to us.

It was doubtful if the fair Paulina beheld any other art in her gallant than that which should properly distinguish every lover. From the dance, he beguiled her to the garden, and she was pleased to be so beguiled. She forgot the more sedate attractions of the new-comer, Captain Harley, and, sitting with Archy Campbell in the subdued moonlight, which fell in softest droplets through the leaves and branches of the sheltering orange, the natural language of the occasion was of flowers, and hearts, and sentiments, all of the brightest and sweetest character. After much harmonious conversation, which seemed like musing and revery rather than discourse, Archy led his companion down the slope of the garden to a spot where the umbrage was

13*

less close and massive. The green plain stretched away to the river, the lines which bordered the green marsh not concealing the bright and glittering mirror of the wave from the spot on which they stood. Beyond were the dense groves of St. Andrews, the great pines mingling with brooding oaks, and looming out, grandly solitary, in the embracing moonlight.

"Oh, how delicious is the picture!" exclaimed Paulina. "One feels anxious to escape to it, and be at peace for ever. I detest the crowd, this perpetual hum of tedious voices, that speak nothing to the heart, and leave us perpetually wearied even of our pleasures. Give me loneliness rather—give me the sad, sweet woods of autumn—the ground strewn with brown leaves, and the winds sighing gladly over their perishing beauties."

"And now is the time to see the woods in the very perfection of their beauty. I drove out the other day to Goose Creek church, and I was charmed into forgetfulness at every step. Suppose you let me drive you out to-morrow. I have the most famous trotter in the world, and my gig is as easy as a cradle. But you know them both. Take a seat with me to-morrow, and you shall enjoy the luxury of the woods in their fullest sweetness."

"I will!" was the prompt affirmative. "Do you know I've never seen the church at Goose Creek?"

"Is it possible? Oh, you will be delighted! The region is a perfect fairy land. But who comes here?"

"Miss Walton, the new beauty, I think, with Ella Monckton. Do you think her so very, *very* beautiful?"

"I might think her so if I did not find a much superior beauty elsewhere," was the reply, the gallant Archy looking tenderly, as he spoke, into the bright eyes of his companion. He offered her his arm at this moment, and they turned upward once more to the shelter of the garden and its protecting bowers; neither being in the mood, apparently, to receive any addition to their company. The spirits of Mad Archy were greatly increased; but he kept a strong rein upon his impulses. We may add that he never once, by any indiscretion of look or word, forfeited the favor which he seemed to have gained that evening, and the last words which Paulina spoke on his leaving her, as he es-

corted her home that night, reminded him of the engagement
for the morrow.

The eyes of Katharine Walton and her companion, like those
of Paulina and her lover, were turned longingly to the fair
stream before them, and the silent forests that spread away
beyond it. They, too, had yearnings which carried them away
into the solitude and from the crowd.

"Oh, how these woods recall to me my home! the sweet, safe
thickets, the venerable shade-trees under which I played when
a child, and where I first learned to weep and sorrow as a
woman. Would I were among them still! I feel as if all my
days of pleasure—nay, of peace and hope—are gone from me,
now that I have left them. I feel, Ella, as if I were destined
to some great and crushing calamity. My thoughts by day are
full of presentiments, and by night my dreams are of evil
always. Would I were away, afar, safe from all these bewildering sights and sounds, which speak to me of danger and deceit
rather than of merriment or love!"

"And why is this! Why is it that you, young, and so beautiful, wealthy and so beloved"—

"Hush! hush!"

"Yes; why should you be unhappy?"

"Ah, you see not! You know not what I dread and what I
deplore."

"Indeed, I know not. Before me the prospect appears very
bright. Yet a few days ago it was not so."

"It is because you hope. I fear! You look forward. It is
upon the past only that I cast my eyes with any satisfaction.
The future wears nothing but doubts and clouds upon its face.
God forbid, Ella, that it should ever seem to you what it now
seems to me!"

"Ah, Katharine, *but for you*, mine would have been such a
prospect,"

'But for me?"

Yes! But I dare not tell you now. I must reserve the
confession for another time, when I have more courage. You
little know how much I owe you."

Katharine expressed her surprise and curiosity; but, though

trembling to unfold her heart to her companion, Ella found herself unable to approach more nearly the subject which made her tremble. Thus musing together, and contrasting the bright and cloudy in their several horizons, the two maidens continued their walk until they were again shrouded among the groves of the garden. Here they paused, and seated themselves in an arbor sheltered by thick vines and the dense foliage of the lemon, the orange, and the gardenia. While they sat, speaking occasionally only, and then in such subdued accents as could reach no other ears, voices were suddenly heard approaching them, and entering an adjoining copse.

"It is Balfour," said Katharine, in sterner tones than was her wont. "Let us go to the house."

"Stay!" replied Ella, in a whisper. "We can not now move without being detected."

Meanwhile, Balfour and Cruden entered the grove, only separated from the two maidens by a clump of bushes of the gardenia and the rose. They seated themselves directly opposite, and proceeded to converse as if upon a subject already fully broached. Balfour, it may be said, had only just reached Mrs. Ingliss's. He had been delayed by business. His manner was still hurried, and his tones indicated some excitement.

"Well," said he, "of *her* we can speak hereafter. She shall not always avoid me! But what of your loving nephew? Have you heard nothing recently of Major Proctor?"

"Nothing. What of him?"

"Do you not know that he has disappeared?"

"Disappeared! I have not seen him for a week. He would take none of my counsel, so I let him take care of himself."

"That is right. You can neither serve nor save him."

"But what do you mean by disappeared?"

"He has left the city suddenly. Gone to Dorchester, it appears, where we have the last traces of him."

"How do you know that he went to Dorchester?"

"I sent his man, John, after him."

"What! As a spy upon his master?"

"How can you suppose it? But, hearing that he went off

suddenly and strangely, I thought it best that the servant should attend the master, and gave him permission to do so."

"Balfour, this was not right. You should give my nephew fair play."

"Pooh! pooh! It was only a measure of proper precaution. If I had been disposed to deny him fair play, he should have been closely in ward, well secured in irons, until his trial."

"And why has not his trial taken place?"

"For the very reason that I wished to give him fair play, and waited for the arrival of new officers from New York—persons who know nothing of the affair, and have no interest in the case one way or the other."

"Well, and what do you hear of my nephew since he left the city?"

"That he went to Dorchester, and made inquiries of old Humphries and Pryor in regard to the escape of Colonel Walton. It appears that he could get nothing satisfactory out of either of them, and the moment he turned his back they denounced him to Vaughan."

"You hear all this from Vaughan, and Vaughan is his enemy."

"Pshaw, Cruden, men are their own enemies. They will do well enough if they never have any worse than themselves. Dismiss this notion from your mind. The result of all is this, that Proctor left Dorchester the next day, and has not since been heard of."

"Indeed!"

"Even so! And this makes the case look worse than ever. My purpose was to put him on trial as soon as he returned to the city. The charges were all prepared. He has probably taken the only mode of escaping conviction."

"How! What do you suspect?"

"That he has fled to the enemy!"

Katharine Walton felt her hand convulsively grasped in that of Ella.

"Impossible! I will never believe it!" exclaimed Cruden.

"I am afraid you will find it true. The strangest part of the affair is that his servant John is also missing."

"Well, should that surprise you?" retorted Cruden, with a

sneer. " Is it anything strange that so faithful a servant should cling to the fortunes of his master ?"

" Come, come, Cruden, that won't do. We know each other too well for sneers of this sort. There is no denying that John was in my pay, and I feel sure that we should have had his report before this but for the fact that he has been made away with. He has, perhaps, attempted to arrest his master in his flight, and has been shot down for his pains."

" Monstrous! What do you take John Proctor to be ?"

" A traitor to his king and country, and a fugitive in the camp of Marion or Sumter ! Such is the appearance of the case. Despairing of defence, he has fled, and has probably put to death my emissary."

" And rightly enough. The dog deserved a dog's death.

" Very like ; yet *we* must not say this."

" What is to be done ?"

" Nothing ! Let him go. You will believe me, Cruden, when I say that I do not desire to bring *your* nephew to disgrace ; still less to see him shot as a traitor. I prefer that he should fly. He saves both of us some shame and trouble. There is only one thing to be said. We must see that Katharine Walton does not escape also. She may or may not like him. I can not yet fathom *that*. But *he* likes *her ;* and both together in the rebel camp, a mutual liking might not be so difficult, the fellow being good-looking enough, and—not unlike his uncle.

The smile which accompanied this sentence might have been a sneer. Balfour continued—

" To render this impossible, I must thrive in my own wooing, and you must give me more help than you have done. I have some plans by which to secure opportunities, of which you shall know hereafter. Enough for the present. Let us now go to the house. I must play the gallant, and do the amiable to her, with all the grace and spirit I can muster."

In silence sat the maidens till the two had walked away. Both of them had heard much to deepen and occasion anxiety.

" Do you wonder now," said Katharine, " that my future should seem so gloomy to my eyes ?"

"No! no!" replied the other; "and my star has also grown dim all of a sudden."

They returned to the dwelling, but only to endure two hours of mortal weariness, surrounded by music and revelry which inspired loathing only, and pressed with the attentions of those whom they equally dreaded and despised.

CHAPTER XXXIII.

IN THE TOILS.

St. Michael's was just pealing the eleventh hour, when Major Stock opened his eyes listlessly, and, after a few preliminary yawns of more than ordinary duration, rang for his servant. The fellow had been waiting in the passage, and appeared almost instantly.

"Who has been here, Paul, this morning ?"

"Nobody, sir."

"Have you seen Archy Campbell ?"

"Oh! yes, sir; he passed in his chair more than an hour ago, driving a lady, and going off at full speed. He looked up at the windows, sir, but did not stop, and went by without a word."

"A lady! Hum! Who could it be ?—not that girl, surely; —not Paulina!

This was said musingly, but the servant answered it; and nowise to the satisfaction of his master.

"It was Miss Phelps, sir, I'm thinking."

"Well, sir, and what has your thinking to do with it; and who asked you to do any thinking; and what if it were Miss Phelps, sir? Do you suppose that riding out together makes them man and wife ?"

"Oh! no, sir; not by no means, sir; I beg pardon, sir; I did'nt mean to be thinking, sir; but it did look, sir, as if they was pretty thick together."

"Thick! do you say! Certainly, the plot seems to thicken! Can she be such a fool! Can it be that Fortune takes such pains to spoil such a bruin as Archy Campbell ? I must see into it! I saw but little of them last night. I must—ah!

(yawns) Paul, get me the hot water ! That I should have risked my guineas upon the impossibility of a conjunction between a crack-brain and a chit !"

Major Stock was unusually rapid in making his toilet that morning. He scarcely gave himself time to discuss his toast and chocolate, when he departed on his rounds, anxious, by inquiries in the proper quarters, to relieve himself of his doubts with regard to the safety of his guineas. For the present, we must keep him and the reader equally in suspense. He learned but little that was satisfactory in relation to the matter, and the hour of *one* found him at the widow Rivington's, still urging his inquiries. He ascertained that Miss Phelps *had* ridden out of town with her suitor, but such drives were frequent enough, and no person seemed to attach any ulterior importance to the affair. Leaving him still in a state of much disquiet, and still at the fashionable widow's, let us take the road also.

Mad Archy Campbell kept quite a showy establishment, and his trotter, as he boasted, could show a clean pair of heels to any four-legged beast in Charleston. Paulina Phelps was quite as delighted to see him whirl like lightning over the sandy tracks, between the city and the Four-Mile Post, as was any of the spectators. Just beyond this point, the pair came up with General Williamson, jogging slowly, on horseback, in the same direction. The general was accompanied, or rather followed, by a couple of dragoons, assigned him by Balfour, as much, perhaps, by way of guaranty for his return to the city, as a guard of honor.

" Clear the track, general ;" was the cry of Mad Archy, as, with a wild flourish of the whip, he scored the flanks of his trotter, and passed through the opening files of the horsemen. The next moment he had left the latter far behind him. Gayly he sped from sight, leaving to the more soberly-paced Willamson to proceed at leisure to the Quarter House. Hither he came soon after, and, without looking at his watch, to see that it was legitimately twelve o'clock, he ordered a bowl of milk punch, and retired to a chamber.

The day was quite warm, and the general threw off his coat, and vest, his cravat, and sword, boots, and spurs, and settled down at length upon his couch, having prepared himself duly for this attitude, by quaffing, at a single draught, one half at least of the foaming noggin which he had ordered. The residue was placed beside the bed, upon a small table, upon which lay his watch, sword, and cravat.

Meanwhile, his escort of dragoons were not unmindful of what was due to the comforts of the subordinate. Their horses were fastened in front of the dwelling, under the shelter of some China trees, and, by turns, the riders penetrated to the hospitable bar-room, satisfied with draughts of a liquor which, if less elegant and fashionable than milk-punch, was quite as potent. They strolled about the grounds, paraded before the house, lounged to and fro between their horses and the woods, and, finally, threw themselves lazily at length upon the benches which graced the piazza of the rude hotel, with a sense of luxury quite as lively as that of their superior.

Thus disposed, our vigilant dragoons saw but little of the world around them. It was not long before they were seized with a certain degree of drowsiness, to which the potent influence of the Jamaica which they had taken, the warmth of the day, and the slumberous waving of the foliage, shading the couches which they occupied, equally contributed to incline them. They did not know, or suspect, that, a few hundred yards below, and as many above, the Quarter House, there might be seen, stealing from tree to tree, and covering the road, as well from the city, as from Dorchester, certain wild-looking foresters, well armed with rifle and pistol, who seemed to be singularly alert, and who were gradually contracting themselves about the point which the two occupied so pleasantly. As little did they fancy that, closely harbored within the woods, not half a mile away, were fifty stout cavalry steeds, bitted and bridled, and awaiting to bear away, in fleet career, as many well-armed riders.

In fact, one of our dragoons was wrapt in a slumber quite as profound as ever hushed the cares of an infant. The other was not so fortunate, but was just in that condition, betwixt sleeping and waking, which leaves the sense doubtful of what disturbs it —which feels but can not fix the disturbance—and mingles the *real*, which assails the external consciousness, with the dreaming method which employs it. A trampling of the horses at the tree, and the whinnying of one of them—an old dragoon charger, which took as much heed of all causes of disquiet as ever did his rider—at length roused up the half drowsy soldier.

He raised himself upon his elbow suddenly, and caught glimpses of a human figure, darting into the shadows of the wood opposite. This roused him, and, without waking his companion, he left the piazza and went out to his horse, which, with ears erect, and eyes keenly fixed upon the thicket in which the stranger had disappeared, was giving our dragoon as full a warning of danger as was possible to his vocabulary. Half dubious that mischief might be brewing, yet not willing to show unnecessary alarm, the soldier was meditating a call to his comrade, when his movements were decided by the sudden appearance of full half a dozen persons from the woods below, accoutred in the well-known blue hunting-shirts of the Carolina rangers. To disengage the bridle of his horse from the swinging limb to which it was fastened, to leap upon the animal, to draw the pistol from his holster and discharge it in the faces of the enemy, were all movements of a single moment, and in obedience to a single impulse. To shout to his comrade, and then clap spurs to his steed in flight, was the work of another instant. He saw that there was no chance of conflict; that he was about to be overwhelmed by numbers, and that his escape to the city was cut off.

He wheeled about, thinking of Dorchester; but, to his consternation, a group of rangers were approaching him rapidly from this quarter also. To dart for the Goose Creek road was the only remaining resource, and no time was allowed him for hesitation. Throwing to the ground the pistol which he had discharged, he drew the other, and, pointing it backward as he fled, gave free reins to his horse, and applied the spur without commiseration.

He was not instantly pursued; no horses of the enemy were visible; and, to his surprise, though he saw many rifles among his assailants, not one was discharged. There was a reason for this forbearance, which we may conjecture. He escaped, in the direction taken some two hours before by Mad Archy Campbell and the fair Paulina Phelps. But he had not yet gone from sight before he saw his comrade in the hands of the rangers. The poor fellow, aroused by the shot of his associate, only opened his eyes to see the butt of the huge horseman's pistol, by which he was knocked down, descending wildly in the heavy hands of a man looking as savage as an Indian, and as well bearded as a Cossack. How had Mad Archy been suffered to escape, was the reflection of our fugitive dragoon? We may be permitted to say that it had been just as easy to have arrested the one party as the other. But the ambush had been specially ordered to suffer the lover and the lady to pass.

" He is not *our* man!" said one who wore the manner of a leader. "We must make no unnecessary alarm, lest we lose the object we aim at. Besides, this officer is protected by the lady. Let them go. If they stop at the ' Quarter,' we shall probably have to seize them, if only to make all things sure ; and, if they go beyond, we are equally satisfied ; they will be out of our way."

It was for these reasons that Mad Archy and his companion went by with impunity. Let us see to other parties.

We left General Williamson "taking his ease at his inn." But ease and repose on this occasion, and with him, did not imply sleep. His milk-punch had not produced oblivion. He was deep in thought and expectation. Events had been ripening with him for some time past. He had been in communication with Singleton, and now expected to meet him, still in the character of Furness. He had much to communicate, which was of importance to the partisans, and to the future objects of the continental army of the South ; and his anxieties were in due degree with the sense of the weight of that intelligence which he brought, and which, in war, derives its value chiefly from the adaptation of the time to the tidings.

He was destined to be disappointed. Singleton's employments had delayed him in his purpose of meeting Williamson. It was a double misfortune to the latter that he was fated to meet with another of the partisans, who had no sort of suspicion of the new *rôle* which the general had assumed.

It was while Williamson was musing the condition of his own and the public affairs, almost as deeply abstracted from the world about him, in consequence of the pressure of his thoughts, as if he had been asleep, that he was slightly conscious of some disturbances without; but he gave them little heed. Soon after came a shot, the hurried treat of a horse, a struggle in the piazza, a groan, and then the rush to the interior of a score of feet. He immediately threw himself from the bed, and, in the same moment the door of the chamber was burst open, and the room instantly filled with a dozen rangers.

Well did he remember the costume. He had led a thousand such fellows on an Indian campaign. He had gained all of reputation that he enjoyed, while in the confidence of this people. He had deserted his trust, had failed in his faith, was now odious in the eyes of those who lately followed him with respect, if not admiration, and his heart misgave him as he beheld their swarthy faces, and dark eyes glaring upon him—arms in their hands, and he alone and almost weaponless. He had seized his sword as he leaped from the bed, and bore it, stretched nakedly and threateningly, with point to the intruders.

" Put down your weapon!" said the stern voice of a noble-looking gentleman. " It can be of no service. You are General Williamson ?"

" I am, sir !"

" You are my prisoner?" was the stern response.

" Who are you?

" Col. Walton, of the state line of South Carolina. Give me your sword, sir !"

" Let me know first——"

" It is enough, sir, that you know that we are here, in numbers, able to put you to death in a moment; that your dragoons are taken, and that you have no alternative ! What more would you know ?"

" Do *you not* know *why* I am here, Col. Walton? Have you seen Col. Singleton ?—have you heard nothing from him ?—are you not despatched to meet me here ?"

These questions were hurriedly put, and in husky accents. If Col. Walton indeed, knew nothing of Williamson's previous conference with Singleton, the renegade was in a perilous case. He was in the hands of men whom he had abandoned ; with the danger of doom at the drumhead for his treachery. The answer of Walton was equally prompt and unpleasant.

"Sent to meet you, sir ! No ! And how should I know *why* you are here—and what have you to do with Col. Singleton ? Your questions are without significance in my ears, General Williamson. It is enough that you are my prisoner. I have planned this enterprise, solely, to take you prisoner. I had heard of your frequent visits to this place, and knew not that you had any deeper purpose in coming here than the enjoyment of such pleasures, as, it appears, you have not forgotten this morning."

The finger of Walton pointed to the empty punch-bowl. The face of Williamson was suffused. But his voice grew firmer.

"I will not yield, sir ! I will perish first !"—and he thrust his weapon full at Walton's breast. But the other was not unguarded. His own sword was instantly crossed in air with the steel of the assailant; with quick strokes the opposing blades flashed above their heads, and finally lay together for a moment, lapped in a close buckle, until that of Williamson flew to the opposite quarter of the room. He was disarmed. He folded this hands with dignity upon his breast, and looked steadily in the face of the visiter, as if inviting the *coup de grace.*

"Secure him !" was the brief, stern command of Walton; and his subordinates rushed in. The captive was fast fettered, and conducted instantly to the opposite woods. He was mounted on a powerful steed, and escorted by two determined fellows on each hand. Walton then gave his orders :—

"And now, men, with all speed across the Ashley. If we delay, these woods will soon be too hot for us ; not a moment is to be lost."

"What is to be done with Major Proctor?" demanded M'Kelvey.

"We must take him with us ! we dare not let him off just yet. He would reach Charleston in an hour and alarm the garrison. Has the dragoon been pursued who made off ?"

"He has Brace and Kirby after him. They will skirt the

road till sunset, if they do not overtake the fellow, and at least keep the officer and the lady from reaching town before dark. They have their orders."

"That will serve. We must push for the Edisto with all despatch. Take the head of the command, M'Kelvey."

No sooner said than done. Williamson was immediately sent forward under guard; while Col. Walton, bringing up the rear, once more penetrated the thicket assigned to Proctor, and announced the necessity of keeping him in durance a little longer. The latter was too much relieved by finding himself once more on horseback, to feel any great concern as to the route he was pursuing.

CHAPTER XXXIV.

HOW MAD ARCHY CAMPBELL DROVE.

NEVER was heart of young damsel more free and buoyant than that of Paulina Phelps, while speeding over the deeply-shaded roads of Goose Creek, borne in a vehicle so easy, and by a trotter of such admirable speed and vigor. The day was a fine one; a little warm perhaps; but the heat was scarcely felt by our fair one, going at such a rate, a breeze playing around her as she flew, and mad Archy Campbell in the best of all possible humors. Never, in fact, did he so excellently reconcile his *riant* mood with so much grace and amenity. There was a reckless buoyancy in his words and manner, a playful humor, a wild but not irreverent freedom in what he said, that had an inexpressible charm for his thoughtless companion. She was, as may be supposed, a creature of extreme levity. She was playful and capricious, and somewhat wilful. It was one of her weaknesses to aim at being considered strong. Her ambition was to exhibit a strength beyond that usually accorded to her sex—a dangerous ambition always—which, perhaps, proves nothing more certainly than the real weakness of the party. But for this, she had never committed the indiscretion of taking such a drive, with such a gallant, and without any other companions.

It is possible that mad Archy calculated on these particulars; but it is just as possible that, in what he thought and resolved upon, his reference was rather to his own character than to that of the lady. He was just the person to conclude according to his own desires, without considering their propriety, or in what degree they might be acceptable to other persons. To *dare,* where most others would be inclined to doubt—to *do*, simply because it was the opinion of others that the thing should not or could not be done—to startle the sober moods of thought or policy, with a splendid audacity—this was his delight, if not his ambition. He had conceived one of these schemes for achieving the impossible; his mind had matured its purpose, and, with a method, which always improved his madness, when his design had taken the shape of a will, he had made all his preparations.

This done, he was assured. He had no misgivings, either of his own failure, or of the defeat of his purpose, and, thus assured, there was nothing of moodiness in his words or manner. His mind was not one to brood upon its objects, however grave their character, or extreme the exigencies which they might involve. His conspiracies never kept him wakeful. You would suppose him never to entertain a single thought beyond the moment. Gay as a bird in summer, he was garrulous in a capricious utterance of the most sportive and thoughtless fancies, as if life had no object beyond the momentary flight or song. Such a random, headlong couple never sped away together on such a flight, and with so little seeming purpose, or with so little regard to the judgments of the considerate and grave.

They were soon beyond the range of Izard's camp. Archy Campbell had his remarks in passing.

"Fine place for deer, that! I have hunted there frequently, and with success always. Went out last with old Stock, and killed a couple of does myself. Five deer were killed among the party. I roasted Stock that day, famously."

"*Roasted* him! How, pray?"

"*Stuck* him, that is to say."

"I am no nearer your meaning yet."

"How ignorant you girls are! But beauties are allowed to be so. *Roasting* and *sticking* are the most sensible words in a *better's* vocabulary. We bet on the first shot, which I got. I *stuck* him for two guineas there. Our next bet was on the first bagging."

"*Bagging!* And, pray, what's that?"

"Pshaw! I shall have to get you a sportsman's dictionary.

14

To bag the game, is the proof that you have shot or captured it. I bagged my deer first, and *stuck* the old major there, also, to the tune of three guineas more. He lost every bet, and was thus *roasted, done down*, as they say of roast beef when it is *done up*."

" I declare you have the most mysterious mode of speaking. What now do you mean by *done up?*"

" 'Pon my soul, you need teaching! Why, what should *done up* mean but *undone?* The sportsman's language is the most expressive in the world."

" It may be, when you can get the key to it. But it might as well be Egyptian for me! But, hold up ; whose charming place is that on the right?"

" Charming! Pretty enough, but not absolutely charming in my eyes, unless, indeed, you were the charmer at the window, instead of that blowsabel you see there. That's one Daniel Cannon's—one of the rebels of the city, who forgot to count the cost of his patriotism before he adopted the expensive habit. That a man should adopt an unprofitable sentiment! He has paid for it! Have you seen enough of the charming settlement? My trotter, you see, has no sympathy with you, and is anxious to be off."

" Let him go. He is certainly a splendid creature."

" Is he not! What a skin he has! Did you ever see a more perfect purple bay in your life? It is like a velvet silk, only richer ; and what legs!"—touching him slightly with the whip over his flanks, and shaking out the reins—" now shall you see him fly!"

" Nay, do not push him. The sand is heavy."

" He scorns sand! He is of the genuine Arabian stock, to whom sand is nature. How he speeds! and you scarcely feel the motion. What a pity to lose such an animal; and yet—"

" What! Why think of losing him?"

" Ha! ha! Paulina; to think that that heathen Turk, Stock, should have set his eyes on the beast, that he should hanker after such a creature, and really fancy that he was the man to get him. I'd sooner cut his throat, than he should have him ; and yet—"

" Yet what ?"

" We have a bet upon his performances to-day."

" Indeed !"

" Yes! the trotter is staked against a purse of guineas; fifty yellow hammers against my purple bay! Which shall fly, Pauline? The birds or the beast? Eh! It would be a pity to lose such a creature."

" I would not lose him for the world."

" What would you do to keep him ?"

" What would I *not* do ?" answered the lady.

Mad Archy chuckled, and with a sly glance at his companion—

" I must win the bet, of course !'

" Surely ; if you can !"

" Ah! there's the rub ! *If I can !* I must do my best for it—leave no means untried for it—eh ?"

" Certainly not !"

" Leap, fly, overturn fences, break through farm-yards, laugh at the laws, if necessary, the church ?—"

" All! all!" cried the gay damsel, with a merry laugh ; " anything rather than lose so beautiful and fine a horse. But you have not told me what the bet is ? There is no secret about it ?"

" Ah! but there is !—for the present at least ; but you will be the first to know it, I assure you. I am resolved to win it, and will! If I had entertained any doubts before, your encouragement has settled them. But I may call upon you for assistance. Indeed, to confess the truth, the bet is of such a nature, that, without your help, I shall lose it. May I count upon you?"

" Oh! to be sure ! But you rack me with curiosity. How can you do so ? Do you forget that I am a woman ?"

" Heaven forbid ! It is as a woman only that your assistance will be valuable. But, rest in patience for a season. In truth, the secret will be worth nothing to you at present. It is one of those which can have no interest, but in the moment of its discovery ; and that discovery, I promise you, shall be first made to you."

" And to-day ?"

"Before the day is out; nay, possibly, in the course of a very few hours. But here is Garden's. You know the doctor and his place, 'Otranto'?"

"Yes; shall we stop?"

"By no means! we should suffocate! Don't you suffer, at this distance, from the perfume of his favorite flowers—to which his name is given—the Gardenia?"

"I see none of them."

"But you scent them?"

"I can't say I do."

"It don't matter, we are safely past. Go it, Turcoman—go it, Arab! You know not (but you should know, O! most royal beast) what a burden of beauty it is that you carry! You know not, oh! bird-eyed deserter, that upon your legs depends the happiness which you enjoy, in the possession of such a master; nay, the happiness which your master enjoys in the possession of such a beauty. You shall help him to get more exquisite joys, my sleek-skinned Arabian! This day shall be marked with a white stone in our calendar! You shall feed on silver oats hereafter; you shall sleep in a stable of swan's down; and there shall be a page, night and morning, to sprinkle you with rose-water, ere you come forth, as a fleet hippogriff, bearing the lady of my love to pleasure."

Speaking this extravagance, which he concluded with a wild whistle, our harem-scarem cavalier touched gracefully and lightly the purple flanks, now slightly flecked with froth, of the high-spirited animal; who went off with increasing impulse at an application which rather showed than enforced the desire of his master.

"Why, you are quite poetical!" exclaimed Paulina.

"Should I be otherwise? I have a champagne exhilarance working in brain and bosom! I feel that I have wings. I am on my way—better mounted than ever was Mahomet, when he rode Alborak, the mule—to something more certain to give me happiness than any of his seven heavens! And did you note that my noble Arabian understood every word I said?"

"I can't say that I did!"

"Indeed; where could you have been looking all the while?

Did you not see how he threw up his head; how his ears were erected; with what an air he set down his feet, and stepped off as if he knew there was nothing but air to receive him? He understood me, be sure, every syllable; and that whistle which I gave"—here he repeated it—"do you see what a glorious bound he takes, as if with the view to leaving the shafts behind him? But he shan't do that! How we spin—how we fly—even as the fairies do! Do you believe in fairies, Paulina?"

"To be sure I do! Not your masculine fairies, they are too coarse a creature. Your Oberon is a sort of monster, for·example;—but I have no doubt about Titania, and Loline, and Nymphalin, and the rest of the tender sex. I would not give up my faith in the *female* fairies for all the world."

"As if these could be tolerable, even to themselves, without a just proportion of the other sex! How we go! That I should give up such a horse as this! It was a great rashness to make such a bet; but, with your encouragement, Paulina, may I be utterly consumed in bitumen, if I lose him! You say I shall not—and I *will* not. Paulina, you do not know me."

"What do you mean? I know that you are Mad Archy Campbell!—"

"Ah! but not *fou* Archy Campbell! You shall see! You know me! Well, I suppose you do, in some respects. You know me as your most devoted worshipper. That I take for granted; but you little know that I can set fire to the very temple in which I worship! By Jupiter Ammon, to employ Balfour's most expressive oath, I am capable of a devilish sight of things of which you have no conception!"

"You wish to scare me, do you? But you're mistaken. I know enough of you to fear you nothing!"

"Ah! Eh! Do you say so! Well, do you see that hog trying to make his way into that cornfield? a huge beast, such as they would have hunted with dog, and cry, and bow-spear, in the forest of Ardennes. You see how he rears himself against the fence, absolutely bent to send it down by mere force? Now shall you see me put one of these wheels over his back before he or you can cry out—'Cha!'"

"For Heaven's sake, Archy Campbell, don't think of such a thing! Do you see the ditch? We shall be upset."

"Not a bit of it! Through the ditch we go! Ha! Smack!" and the whip was now laid on with unction. "Bravo! beast of mine; across him for a thousand!"

A jolt—a bound—the ditch is crossed, and, even while the hog, with forefeet erect, is pressing all his weight against the worm-fence, which he had already half shaken from its propriety, the obedient horse took the irregular motion which had been prescribed to him, and the vehicle rose in air, upon the hog's quarters, and hung in this manner for a perilous instant. A scream from the lady was nothing to the wild succession of screams that issued from the throat of the porker. Down rolled the beast into the ditch; down, for an instant, settled the wheels upon him; another jolt of the vehicle, and the ditch was recrossed; the wheels recovered their balance, and off bounded the good Arabian, seemingly as heedless as his master, of the condition of the hog. Before Paulina had recovered, Mad Archy spoke:—

"By Jupiter Ammon, it was almost a hang! I knew that there was some peril in it from the first, Paulina, and but for your assurance that nothing could scare you, I should never have tried it. You are a fearless creature—not once to cry aloud—not once to tremble."

Then, looking round with a mischievous smile, into her face—"Not the slightest change in your color or feature! Ah! Paulina, you are worthy to be a soldier's wife. *You have* courage, indeed!"

This novel sort of flattery did not soothe the lady very materially. If not absolutely scared, she was bewildered and confounded. She felt that a mocking devil was in the smile which beheld her features. She knew that they were pale. She felt that her heart and lips were equally trembling. She knew that she had screamed in her momentary terror, and was as perfectly satisfied that he had heard her scream. She spoke nothing. She began now to feel all the imprudence of which she had been guilty in riding with such a companion. Was he mad or not? He was rapidly, to her mind, realizing the propriety of the epithet which had hitherto been conferred upon him in jest. His recklessness was assuming an aspect quite as uncomfortable, to her, as his madness would have been. He did not allow her apprehensions to subside.

"You say nothing, Paulina? Perhaps, you wonder that I should suppose it a meritorious show of courage, on your part, to feel no fear at such a small adventure. But I can assure you that most of your sex would have felt or expressed some alarm. You do neither. Ah! it is delightful to drive such a woman! One is annoyed at the petty feminine fears which see danger in a straw. Now, do you see yonder pines growing upon the old track? I'll venture a guinea that there is scarcely a lady in Charleston who would not be disquieted at my driving between them!"

"For Heaven's sake, sir, do not attempt it!" cried the damsel, now seriously alarmed, and all over in a tremor, catching his arm as she spoke.

"Ah! child Paulina, this apprehension is expressed for me! You feel none yourself. You dread that I will falter at the proper moment, and disgrace my driving. But I will show you that I am as cool and firm of nerve as you are. I have been through that grove before! I led the way for Barry and M'Mahon. I drove old Stock, and the old fellow hadn't a word to say! By that I knew his nerves were disquieted. We went through at a bound. We measured it afterward, and there was but an inch to spare on each hand. Then I shouted to Barry to come on; and he did—after a fashion! He soon saw sights! The trees, he swore, came out into the path. The left wheel struck, locked, was torn out, and ran a hundred yards, more or less. Barry went out on one side, as if making his way to Cooper river; while M'Mahon, for the first time taking a different direction, bounced upward, on his way to Dorchester. We picked them both up with bloody noses. Ha! Smack! Turcoman! Now for it, and oh! villain, if you swerve under the riband, I'll roast your flanks for you!"

With a long whistle, our Jehu gave the animal the whip, threw his head forward, slightly increased his grasp upon the reins, and, in a moment, Paulina was conscious of the passage

between the trees. The wheels rolled on a root, and the slight
shock, in her nervous condition, persuaded her that the vehicle
had gone to pieces. A deep sigh escaped her, and when Archy
looked round upon her face again, with that half diabolic smile,
the madman felt that he had conquered. She was powerless.
The lustre had left her eyes. Her cheeks were pallid! The
gaze with which she met his own, was that of a subject. The
fair coquette, so boastful of her strength and courage, was absolutely speechless; but she could still appreciate the danger of
a philosophy so wild as that with which her companion continued to regale her senses.

"Talk of driving!" said he. "There's no driving where
there's no danger! Where's the merit of doing that? A cat
may drive a blind horse over a beaten track, and safely keep
the centre; but it is a man only that can scrape the edge of a
precipice with his wheel, yet never cease to whistle while he's
doing it! I could take you now, Paulina, full speed, among all
the tombs and vaults of the Goose Creek churchyard, chip the
corner of every tombstone, whirl three times round the church,
leaving but an inch to spare between the corners and the wheels,
and haul up at the altar place, cool enough for the marriage
ceremony! There's the church, now!"

And he touched the flanks of the trotter with his whip, and
began to whistle.

"Oh! for Heaven's sake, Mr. Campbell, don't think of it."

The poor girl found her voice in anticipation of new and
greater danger.

"Don't think of what?" he demanded.

"Driving among the tombstones. It can't be done with
safety."

"Can't be done! What will you bet on it? I'll show you.
Such an imputation on my skill in driving! Ah you think I
fear? You would test my courage — my nerves — in every way!
You are a fearless creature; but you shall see that I have as
firm a heart as yourself."

"Oh! I do not mean that, Mr. Campbell. I am not firm. I
am fearful — very fearful. In fact, I feel quite sick. I must
have some water."

"It is this cursed beast! He goes so slowly! He creeps as if he had the gout! We have been a tedious time on the road, and you are naturally tired out. I could cut the rascal's throat. Water! we will get it at the parsonage. We will drive there first; after that we can visit the church. It is one of the prettiest of the antiquities in all the low country. Fine tesselated aisles—fine mahogany pews—carved work in abundance, and —but," looking round upon the pale face of his companion, "but for the parsonage, now! You know the rector, Ellington?"

"Oh! yes, yes! go to the parsonage."

"Phew!"—a shrill prolonged whistle, and artistlike flourish of the "persuader," as he styled his whip, and the vehicle was soon whirled up at the door of the parsonage.

14*

CHAPTER XXXV.

HOW MAD ARCHY CAMPBELL WON HIS BRIDE.

I⊤ is probably very well known by our readers, that the establishment of the English church was that which generally prevailed before, and during the Revolution, throughout all the *parish* country of South Carolina. Hence, indeed, the *parochial* divisions which exist in the same region to this day, occasioning something like a political anomaly in the distribution of civil power throughout the state. The church establishment, at that period, was a highly respectable one. Great Britain had a reasonable sense of what was due to externals, at least in matters of religion ; and the temples which she raised for worship were strong, fair-proportioned brick fabrics. Good dwellings, near at hand, were provided for the rectors, and the incumbent was usually one of those " sleek, oily men of God," who show themselves duly sensible of the value of an arrangement which so happily unites the state with the church.

In South Carolina, the English church was probably quite as well served by its priests as in any other of the colonies—perhaps better than in most. It possessed a very fair amount of education, talent, and good manners. The reverend Edward Ellington, the rector at Goose Creek, was a very respectable clergyman—a man of good looks, easy, pleasant address, and fair ability. There are those living who have listened to and been greatly edified by his preaching. As far as we can learn, though an honest man, and laboring properly in his vocation, he did not suffer his zeal to distress his nervous system—was of a gentle and easy disposition—not at all favorable to martyrdom ;

and, probably, was much more accessible to turtle-soup and Madeira.

We do not blame him for this. Men must live and toil according to the endowments of their nature. The phlegmatic temperament may be united to a very excellent head and a good Christian disposition, without feeling at all anxious to enjoy the distinctions of John Rogers; indeed, without any feverish zeal to vex and goad their neighbors into the way of peace. Mr. Ellington was a priest after this order. He was mild, and meek, and indulgent; no fierce reformer; and perfectly satisfied with a flock which betrayed the least possible distrust in regard to their situation as well as his own. It was seldom that flock or pastor disturbed the quiet of one another, or suffered from any spasmodical excitements to which they could give the name of religion. Whether they were worse or better than their neighbors, in consequence of this easy mode of encountering the flesh and the devil, is a question which it does not become our province to discuss.

Our pastor was taking his ease on the shady side of his piazza as Mad Archy Campbell and the fair Paulina drove up to his entrance. The shade-trees received them, and a servant in a neat livery promptly made his appearance, to whom Campbell threw his reins; then, jumping out with an easy bound, he assisted his companion, trembling all the while, to the solid earth, her heart beating almost audibly with the sense of a danger hardly yet escaped. The worthy pastor arose from the cot of canvass, on which he had been soliciting his siesta, and partly descended the flight of steps leading to the piazza, to receive and welcome the parties, both of whom he slightly knew.

With a somewhat boisterous courtesy Mad Archy responded to the gentle salutation of the rector, who, giving his arm to Paulina, assisted her into the dwelling. She sank feebly into the first chair that presented itself in the piazza, and faintly called for a glass of water, which was immediately brought. Mr. Ellington soon perceived that her nerves were somewhat discomposed, but he was too phlegmatic to conjecture the full extent to which they had been tried. Besides, Mad Archy gave him little leisure for meditation or scrutiny.

"We are out of breath, parson! Such a horse! Look at the creature! Hardly ruffled; never a stain upon his skin; and just enough moisture to increase the beauty of his purple. You'll hardly think it, but we have reached you in less than two hours from the city."

The preacher looked incredulous; turning his eyes from one to the other of his visiters, with a doubtful inquiry in his glance.

"By Moses and Aaron, parson, but what I tell you is the truth," was the irreverent response. The rector looked a becoming gravity as he replied—

"Swear not at all!"

"Oh! psho! Parson, you don't call that an oath? I only appealed to such witnesses as I thought you might believe in. Now, Moses and Aaron ought to be good evidence with you, and if you have any mode of communicating with them, you can soon learn that what I tell you is solemn, hard-favored fact. Don't you see that Miss Phelps has not yet recovered breath. In truth, we flew rather than rode. It is a beast among a thousand, that of mine! Pity to lose such a beast, eh, Paulina? But you say we must not lose him, and we will not. Parson, if you have no objection, we will let him pick from that grass plat on the left; there, under those oaks, where he will find both shade and substance."

The rector was evidently bewildered by his visiter, but he consented to the arrangement; and, with a few words to the ostler, the horse was stripped of his furniture. In the meanwhile, ranging the piazza with the air of Sultan Solyman, Mad Archy divided his attention between the rector, the lady, and the Arabian. The gig was suffered to remain beneath the shade trees at the entrance.

"You have a world to yourself, Mr. Ellington," was the condescending remark of Campbell. "Can be happy here as the day is long. But your world would not suit me. Peace is not my element. Repose does not refresh me. I prefer a storm any day to a calm; and if I were doomed to such a life as yours, I should burn down the parsonage first, and then the church, if it were only to have the trouble of rebuilding them. Did you ever in your life enjoy a bit of fun, parson? Were you ever in a row ?   When you were a boy, for example, did you ever knock down a watchman, or upset his box ?"

"Never, sir," said the parson meekly.

" At college, however, you have taken the road as a whip ? You have rode steeple chases ;—you have torn off the gown of an official, of a dark night, and met his eyes innocently in the morning ?"

"I am glad to say that I have never done any of these things."

"Glad to say ?   I don't see why it should make you glad ! But you are fond of cards, I am certain."

"I acknowledge that I find pleasure in a rubber of whist, with shilling points."

" Shilling points !   Silver !   There is no dignity in such play. What think you of fifty guineas on a cast ?"   Then, without waiting for an answer : " Now, pray, look at that beast of mine. His fate depends on his and my performance to-day.   He has done his part thus far, with very excellent success.   I must not neglect mine.   Do you know Stock, Major Stock, Mr. Ellington ?"

"I do not, sir."

" The last man in the world to do justice to a horse like that ! It is barely possible that he thinks to own him.   He has put fifty guineas on his head ; and it will soon be certain whether he or I shall have the felicity of flinging the ribands over him hereafter.   This day will decide it.   That warns me that no time is to be lost.   Paulina, my love, you have said that we must not lose the horse ; and you are right !   Pray, rise, my charmer.   Parson, we have come to be married ; will you make the ceremony as short as possible ?   We must take our dinner in town to-day !"

The parson looked more bewildered than ever.   The lady stared aghast, her eyes ranging from one to the other gentleman.   Both the persons addressed were silent.   Campbell grew impatient.

" Zounds !   parson—don't you hear ?—don't you comprehend ?   we are come to be married."

"Are you serious, Mr. Campbell ?"

"Serious! Do I look like the man to jest when my happiness is at stake? Is not happiness one of the most serious interests in this life? Have we ridden up to you for any less object? I tell you, sir, that Miss Paulina Phelps and myself have come hither to be married. We know the pleasure that you feel in bringing hearts together, and we entreat this office at your hands. Will you not rise, my Paulina? I know that you are fatigued, but the church requires that we should be married in a standing posture, with head uncovered; unless, indeed, one is too sick to rise, and suffers from a bad cold; then some allowance is made for the suffering party. But we can make no such plea. Come, sweetheart! It will occupy but a few moments."

The lady remained seated and silent, but looked more terror-stricken than ever. The rector beheld the expression of her face, and it suggested to him the answer to Campbell's demand.

"I will cheerfully marry you," he said, "if the lady consents to it."

"If the lady consents to it! And what right have you to suppose that the lady will not consent to it? For what purpose has she come hither? Do you question my word? Should I not know? What! She says nothing herself! Well, sir, and does not a lady's silence mean consent? Are you capable of making no allowance for the delicacy of feelings which would rather have you understand them, without absolutely forcing the tongue to speak! Sir, I'm shocked and surprised at you. Learn better, hereafter, how to appreciate the nice feelings of the sex."

"But, sir—Mr. Campbell——"

"No unnecessary words, Mr. Ellington—we are in haste. We must be in town for dinner. The sooner, therefore, you officiate, the better. We are both of marriageable years, and should know what we desire."

"You speak for yourself, Major Campbell."

"Zounds, man, I speak for the lady also."

"She does not say *that!*" turning and looking at Paulina. The poor girl caught his hand and looked appealingly into his face.

"But she says nothing against it," replied Campbell.

"That will not suffice, Major Campbell. She must speak for

herself!" replied the rector, taking an accent and aspect of more decision.

"Ha! do you say that!" exclaimed Campbell, in subdued tones, his eye resting upon the face of the pale and trembling Paulina—"Do you say that? You are not satisfied with what I tell you! Now, by Jupiter Ammon, you marry us instantly, or I will blow your brains out! It is an oath!"

With these words drawing a pair of pistols from his coat, he clapped one of them to the head of the rector, cocked it quickly, and repeated the oath.

"We are come hither to be married! Either you marry us, or I put a brace of bullets through your brains. Paulina, fear nothing, my love; he shall do as I command. I will sooner shoot both of us, than see you disappointed."

Ellington looked into the face of the madman, and read there a degree of desperate resolution, under which his firmness succumbed. He had met the eyes of a master. He felt that the person with whom he had to deal was capable of any excess or violence. He reasoned rapidly with himself under the exigency of his situation.

"It is true," he said, "that the lady seems paralyzed with terror, and evidently appeals to me for protection from this man; but why has she intrusted herself to him! Unless marriage was her purpose, why consent to such a hair-brained expedition as the present—one which should seriously involve her reputation? To perform this office will really be to save this reputation; and if the lady does not know her own mind, it is high time she had somebody to teach her all necessary lessons in future."

Such were the rapid conclusions of the rector, under the coercive terrors of Campbell's pistols. The latter gave him but little time. He saw that the parson was alarmed and prepared to yield. He had no doubt of the pliant nature of the lady.

"Hark ye, Mr. Ellington, I am willing to reason with you, even though I shoot you. Shoot you *I will*, and shoot her, and shoot myself, rather than go back to the city to be a finger point for every d——d blockhead in the garrison! Now, look you, to what is the common sense of the subject. Do you suppose

that Miss Phelps rode out with me to Goose Creek—with me
alone—unless she understood that my purpose was honorable
marriage? You can not surely suppose her a simpleton. What
then? Shall I disappoint her reasonable calculations? Will
you contribute to this result, at the manifest risk of this lady's
character? By ——, sir, you shall not! We shall both perish
first. Rise, Paulina, my love. Mr. Ellington sees the justice
and propriety of all I say."

Campbell took the lady's hand as he spoke, and looked into
her eye, with that mixed smile of deviltry and affection which
he had shown her in the maddest moments of their morning
drive. She rose as if unconsciously—passively yielding at his
will—and, in this action, she afforded to the rector an opportunity of complying with the demand which his courage did not
allow him any longer to oppose. He conducted the couple into
the parlor, and prepared his books. We may pass over a brief
period of delay consumed in preliminaries, which greatly increased the impatience of Campbell. His madness had so much
method in it, as never for a moment to allow him to lose anything that he had gained. He still continued, by words and actions, to keep up the apprehensions of the rector and the terror
of the damsel. To the latter he said, while the former was making his preparations—

"It is a sublime thing to perish with one that we love! I
have always thought well of French passion, from the frequency
of this habit among that people. A couple, truly devoted, will
say to each other other—'We are happy—why should we endanger our love by exposing it to the vicissitudes of time? We
might change—a terrible caprice might endanger both hearts—
and familiarity produces coldness, and age neglect. Better escape this peril. Now, that love is secure, let us die together!'
And they agree, and suffocate themselves with charcoal, dying
together in the sweetest embrace; or, they drown together, and
are taken up locked in each other's arms; or, the man shoots
the woman, and taking her upon his bosom, in this attitude
shoots himself! This is love—this is to be beloved!"

And, thus speaking, he kissed the pistol in his grasp, with the
air of one who embraces a benefactor. Poor Paulina had not a

word to utter. When the rector prepared to officiate, Campbell still kept one of the pistols in his grasp, and, sometimes, as if unconsciously, would point it, taking aim the while, with a nice precision, at the mirror, or the pictures against the wall, or through the windows. To the ceremonial requisitions, Paulina nodded droopingly ; — an action that the rector preferred to construe into a proof of modesty rather than of fear. But the ceremony was performed ; and, flinging a purse containing ten guineas into the hands of the parson, Campbell exclaimed—

"We have saved the horse, Paulina ; I knew we should : but it is at the peril of Stock's life. By Jupiter, but he will swear !"

We must do our madman the justice to say that he closed the ceremony by most affectionately kissing the bride, and by wrapping her in an embrace, as fervent as was ever yet vouchsafed by a devoted lover. Then, leaving her with the. rector, he sallied forth to give orders for the harnessing of his trotter to the vehicle.*

"This is a strange proceeding, Mrs. Campbell ;" remarked the rector.

"Very, sir," cried the newly-wedded wife, clasping her hands with strong emotion ; — "but what *could* I do ?"

Further explanations were, perhaps, fortunately arrested at this moment, by a clamor and a loud shouting, which sounded from the road without. The rector moved to the entrance, followed by Paulina, and there discovered a British dragoon, riding at full speed up to the dwelling. Meanwhile, the horse was harnessed to the gig of Mad Archy, and that worthy, more magnificent than ever in his carriage, was just about ascending the steps of the piazza, when arrested by the appearance of the dragoon.

This dragoon, as the reader will readily conjecture, was the fugitive who had succeeded in making his escape from the

* It may be a proper precaution only, to assure the reader that the marriage thus described, did actually take place, under these very circumstances, and between these very parties ; the Rev. Edward Ellington officiating as above. He, himself, subsequently reported all the particulars. We may add, that long after, Mrs. Campbell admitted that she had been surprised and terrified into the act ; that she had never seriously thought of Archy Campbell for a husband.

"Quarter House," and from the grasp of Walton's partisans, at the moment when his companion was taken. He had been pursued, for several miles, very closely by a couple of Walton's troopers; but, through the merits of his stout English dragoon horse, had been fortunate enough to leave them behind him. That they still pursued, he had no reason to question, and a certain urgent conviction of his danger, led him very readily to place himself entirely under the direction of Mad Archy. He had almost unconsciously followed the track of Campbell's wheels, and now only drew his breath with ease, when he found himself in the presence of so famous a fire-eater!

CHAPTER XXXVI.

HOW BALFOUR SPEEDS IN HIS WOOING.

IF anything moved by what he heard, the feelings of Campbell, as he listened to the narrative of the dragoon, were rather of a sort to welcome the tidings with delight, than to recoil from them with apprehension. Strife, tumult, the hazard of the die, the rare provocation to wild adventure, were things grateful to his impulsive temper. But he subjected the fugitive to close and sensible cross-examination. From him, however, he gathered little beyond the simple facts detailed at his first entrance. How he and his comrade had been surprised by a goodly host; the latter knocked down and taken, and himself pursued till within three miles of the parsonage;—this was all that he could tell. Of the captivity of Williamson he knew nothing. Campbell readily conjectured it; and, assuming this to be the object of the expedition of the partisans, he at once conceived the full danger of the captive. He was also persuaded, from what he heard, that they had disappeared from the scene of action as soon as they had secured their victim. He reasoned for their policy with reference to their necessities, and reasoned justly. A squad of fifty light-horse were not likely to linger long in a neighborhood so near to the city garrison after such an adventure. His decision was taken almost instantly.

"Paulina, my love, let us be off! We must push with all speed for the city! Not a moment to spare. Parson Ellington, a thousand thanks, for the spontaneous manner in which you have complied with my wishes!"

This was spoken with a delightful grin, that caused a deep

suffusion upon the cheek of the rector. But the disquiet which he felt did not prevent him from expostulating with the husband upon the peril of taking his wife with him upon such an adventure, threatened, as he was, with enemies upon the road.

"You will surely leave Mrs. Campbell in my protection, until——"

"Devil a bit will I! In *your* protection, forsooth! As well ask me to employ the wolf to keep my flocks. Ho! ho! reverent sir. He who has but a single diamond, and that so precious, will do well to keep it in his single bosom only. Shall I just get a wife to part with her so soon? I were as mad as my worst enemies are pleased to consider me, were I to do so ridiculous a thing; and, suffer me to say, meaning no particular personal disparagement to yourself, Mr. Ellington, that I have no such faith in your cloth, as to leave to any of the brotherhood the keeping of my ewe lamb. She goes with me. She is a soldier's wife. We will encounter the danger together. You shall carry one of my pistols, Paulina! You shall! They are both charged with a brace of bullets! And when I say the word, look you, then shall you thrust out the weapon thus, full in the face of the assailant, and, keeping your eye open all the time, you will pull tenderly upon this little bit of curved iron, do you see, and leave the rest of the affair to me!"

Campbell suited the action to the word, while giving these instructions. The rector was too much disconcerted by his speech to expostulate any further, and the bold-hearted Paulina was as much subdued as if she had been caged for six months on bread and water.

"See to your pistols!" said Campbell to the dragoon, as he lifted the passive wife into the vehicle. "We shall have a glorious day of it, Paulina. By my soul, you *are* a heroine! There, my angel, I put one of these bull-dogs behind you. He shall give tongue at a moment's warning. You do not fear, eh?"

"No!" was the faint response.

"I thought not!—Good-by to ye, parson! We shall pay you another visit at seed-time and harvest!—There, my lad!" throwing the servant a couple of shillings. "And now, my blood, my beauty, now that I have saved you from the rapacious grasp of Stock, show your gratitude by showing your best heels. Phew!"—a wild whistle, followed by a flourish, smack, and sharp application of the whip, and the goodly trotter went off at a bound that soon left the parsonage out of sight behind them.

"Now am I the happiest of living men, Paulina! I have the best horse and the loveliest wife in the country! I shall mark this day with a white stone in my calendar. How that mameluke, old Stock, will growl! By Jupiter, a treble triumph! I have not only won you, but conquered him, and saved Bucephalus! My precious! what say you; shall we make the drive to Charleston in an hour? We can do it!"

"It will kill your horse!"

"Very likely! But I feel happy enough to be killing something, and if these d—d rebels do not give us a chance at them, I shall be wolfish before we get in town. Hark you, my good fellow," to the dragoon, "how many pursued you, do you say?"

"Two, major, that I saw close after me. There were many more at the 'Quarter.'"

"How many?"

"More than fifty."

"But only two pursued you? Why the d—l didn't you show fight, when you had drawn them out of the reach of their comrades? You were well armed, had your sabre and pistols?"

"One of them I had already emptied, major."

"Well! the other was enough; the sword for one of the rebels, and the pistol for his mate. Look you, my good fellow, if you show no better spirit while with me, I'll shoot you myself; nay, my wife shall do it! Look you, Paulina, use your pistol upon this brave dragoon the moment that you see him disposed to skulk. That she may be able to do it cleverly, my good fellow, do you ride on the left; keep just five paces ahead of the chair, that you may be within easy range; and see that you keep up. I warn you that you will have to gallop like thunder if you expect to do so; but if you do not keep up the Philistines will be upon you! Phew!" and the usual whistle concluded the speech, and was followed by a smart flourish and smack of the whip.

The dragoon obeyed orders; placed himself on the left of the vehicle, and rode under the constant terror of the lady's pistol. The speed of Campbell's trotter kept the dragoon's charger at a strain, and, as he had been compelled to tax his utmost strength and spirit in his flight from the partisans, Mad Archy was soon forced to see that if he did not relax in his requisitions, the poor beast of the dragoon would be dead-foundered and broken-winded.

"Ho! there! It's a bore to hold him; but, d—n your beast, I must not kill him, if I kill my own, and to leave you, without the protection of myself and wife, would be pretty much to kill you too. The rebels would swallow you at a mouthful. So hold up, and let the elephant creep awhile in these sandy places."

The dragoon was very well pleased to do as he was commanded. He had an affection for his charger, which, pressed much longer as he had been, would, he well knew, be very soon in a condition rendering him fit for dog's meat only. The progress of both horses subsided for a while into a walk, Campbell taking advantage of every piece of hard ground, to make up by an increased speed for lost time. In this way they reached the "Quarter House" without encountering any interruption.

They saw no enemies. It is probable that the partisans of Walton, finding the pursuit of the dragoon unavailing, and content with having driven him off sufficiently far, wheeled about and took the route back, as instructed by their superior. It is possible only that they lurked in concealment on the road-side, and forebore the attack upon a party of which one of the number was a woman. At the "Quarter House," Campbell obtained full particulars from the hostess, of the seizure of Williamson. He also discovered by whom he had been made captive. Charged with these particulars, he pushed with all speed for the city, leaving the dragoon to follow at his leisure, the road thence being considered safe from the partisans.

We pass over unnecessary details. The reader will suppose the newly-married wife, "so wildly wooed, so strangely won," to have been safely and quietly disposed of at her own habitation. Mad Archy then hurried away to Balfour's quarters, where he found the usual guard at the entrance. But Balfour

himself was absent, and our Benedick proceeded to seek him at
his usual haunts. But he failed in the search at Barry's domicil in Queen street; failed equally at the house of the beautiful
Harvey in Beaufain; and, after vain inquiries here and there,
he at length obtained a clew which conducted him to the dwelling of Mrs. Singleton, in Church street. But, before reaching
this point, he contrived, in passing, to stop at Stock's quarters,
and report events, which he could scarcely hope to make so
gratifying to the old major as they were to himself. He found the
major engaged at his toilet for the evening. A few words sufficed
to empty his budget of the matter most interesting to himself.

"Those guineas, Stock; they are now absolutely necessary
to my establishment."

"What do you mean, fool?"

"Mean! That I am married, and to Paulina Phelps. The
Sultana is mine, and that saves me the Sultan."

"Don't believe a word of it," said Stock.

"Very likely; but you will have to believe in fear and trembling — and pay for your slow faith in the bargain. We were
hitched for life, man and wife, this very day, at the Goose Creek
parsonage, Ellington, the rector, presiding, and your humble
servant submitting. You will hear all soon enough. I don't
want your guineas until you are satisfied; but that will be to-
morrow. Meanwhile, there's news — work on hand — and a
very great mischief. General Williamson has been captured by
the rebels. Please prepare accordingly."

"Begone with you for a madman, as you are. The thing's
impossible."

"I grant you; but nevertheless quite true."

"If it be so, by all the powers, I shall pray thàt Harley
may make you quite indifferent to your wife and my money.
I'll help him to cut your throat; by G—d, I will!"

"I think your malice may lead you to it, very nearly. But,
talking of throat-cutting, reminds me that General Williamson
is in danger of a short-cord, and five minutes only to say grace
in it. He was captured to-day, by Colonel Walton, with a
party, at the Quarter House. I am now looking for Balfour to
give him the tidings."

"Well; he will be grateful for them, no doubt. Seek him at the widow Singleton's. He is there now pretty constantly. The star in the ascendant is Walton's daughter. He will be delighted to show her how many are the obligations he owes to the family."

Leaving the old major in no good humor, Campbell immediately proceeded to the designated dwelling, where he found Balfour in no pleasant humor at the interruption. But, when he heard the intelligence brought by Mad Archy, he was aghast. It took him no long time to learn all the particulars, and to anticipate all the consequences."

"Great God!" said he, "Walton will hang him!"

"Very likely," was the cool reply. . . . "When a man turns traitor to his colors, hanging forms a part of the understanding. It is the peril always incurred in such cases."

"But we must save him if we can!"

"If they mean to hang him at all, it is probably too late. Rope and tree are too convenient in our forests, to render much delay necessary."

"They may delay with the view to a formal trial. A provincial colonel will seldom venture on any such decided measure as execution without trial."

"According to all accounts, Walton is an exception to this rule. The surprise and capture show boldness enough, here, within five miles of the city; and why this audacity, unless they designed to make an example of the captive?"

"Granted; but a hurried execution will afford no such example as they require. They will aim at an ostentatious exhibition of their justice. In that is our hope. We must move promptly. Campbell, do you get your command in readiness. Go to Major Fraser, instantly, and let him call out *all* the cavalry of the garrison. To horse *all of you*, and scatter in pursuit. There is no time to be lost."

His commands were instantly obeyed; and, stripping the city of all its horse, Major Fraser led his forces that very night in pursuit of our partisans. Mad Archy was hurried away with his squadron, with a moment only allowed him for leave-taking with his wife. He bore the necessity like a philosopher of the stoic order. Folding the lady in an embrace rather more fervent than scrupulous, he bade her be of good cheer, and show the courage proper to a soldier's wife.

"These rebels shall pay for our privations, Paula-Paulina! I almost wish that I were a Cherokee, that I might be justified in bringing you a score of scalps for your bridal trophies! But, if there be any sooty captives to be taken, you shall have spoil enough. There, my beauty! One more smack! Remember, if I perish, Stock has no claim upon my Arabian, and you *have* a claim for fifty guineas upon him. I may die in *your* debt, Paula-Paulina, but not in his. There! another! smack!"

And with this characteristic speech and parting, mad Archy hurried from the dwelling, leaving his wife quite unprepared to determine whether his death in battle would really be an evil or a blessing. We must in charity conclude that her reflections were finally put at rest by conclusions favorable to their mutual fortune.

We must not forget what took place between Balfour and Katharine Walton, when, after the departure of Archy Campbell, he returned to the apartment where he had left her. He had been, as we may conjecture, urging indirectly a suit which her reserves had too much discouraged to suffer him to pursue a policy more frank. He had been doing the amiable, after his fashion, for a good hour before Campbell had appeared. In this aspect, his deportment had been forbearing and unobtrusive; his solicitude had been as gentle and delicate as was possible to his nature; marked, indeed, by a degree of timidity which had been steadily on the increase from the moment when his interest first began, in the lady and her fortunes. The controlling dignity of her character had sensibly coerced and checked the presumption natural to his, and he was thus, perforce, compelled to submit to an influence which he felt as a curb, from which he would have found it a real pleasure to break away, if, in doing this, he should not thereby forfeit other objects even more grateful to him than the license which he loved. On the present occasion, the tidings brought him of Williamson's capture, and of Walton's agency in that event, were suggestive to his mind of a mode of accounting with the daughter of the rebel, in such

15

a way, as not to compromise his own suit, yet to enable him in some degree to exercise his freedom.

"Miss Walton," he said, with serious countenance, "my esteem for you comes greatly in conflict with my duty."

"How so, sir?"

"You can not know how indulgently I have forborne in your case already, to the great annoyance of all the loyalists in the garrison. But I have just received intelligence which makes it almost criminal for me to regard any of your name with favor."

"Indeed, sir?" curiously, but with a smile.

"Yes, indeed, Miss Walton. Your father—"

"Ah! sir: what of my father?" more anxiously.

"He seems resolute to deprive his friends of all power of saving him, or saving his daughter."

A pause. He was answered only with a smile.

"You do not seem curious, Miss Walton?"

"Well, sir—since you desire it—what of my father?'

"He has done that, Miss Walton, which, in the case of any other rebel, would conduct all his connections to the provost, and work a complete forfeiture of all their possessions, and of all hope of the future favor of our sovereign. He has audaciously surprised and captured General Williamson; almost within sight of the garrison."

"General Williamson was a traitor to his country! I see nothing in this but the act of an open enemy, and such my father has frankly avowed himself to your sovereign and his armies."

"Very true; but General Williamson, if a traitor to the rebel cause, is true to that of his sovereign. If a hair of his head suffers at the hands of your father, I fear, Miss Walton, that his pardon will be impossible."

"It will be time enough, Colonel Balfour, to think of his pardon, when the attitude of my father shall be that of supplication."

The maiden answered proudly. Balfour's reply was made with a deliberate gravity which had its effect on his hearer in her own despite.

"And you may very soon behold him in that attitude, Miss

Walton; needing and entreating mercy without finding it. I have been compelled to order out my entire cavalry in pursuit. They will spare no speed—they will forego no efforts, for the recapture of General Williamson, and the destruction of the rebel squadron. Should they succeed, which is highly probable —should your father fall into their hands, I shall not be able to answer for his life. It will need all my efforts, and I shall labor in the very teeth of duty, if I strive to save him from his fate. What shall move me to these exertions—why should I so labor in his behalf? There is but one consideration, Miss Walton, but one! Your hand, your heart, your affections, in return for those which I now proffer you."

He took her hand as he spoke these words, but she instantly withdrew it from his grasp.

"Colonel Balfour, let me entreat you to be silent on this subject, and at such a moment as the present. You describe my father to be in a situation of great danger. I am not prepared to believe in this danger. But if your report be true, it is neither a proof of your affection nor your magnanimity that I should be addressed to this effect, and at this juncture. Let me beg your forbearance. You have given me sufficient cause for sad thought; for apprehensions which forbid all consideration of the subject of which you speak."

"But you do not forbid the subject?" he asked eagerly.

"And of what avail that I should? I have already, more than once, entreated your forbearance. If I could hope that my command would be regarded, when my entreaty is not, the word should be spoken. Is it not enough that I tell you that the subject is ungracious to me, that you only give me pain, that I can not see you in the character which you assume?"

"It is no assumption. It is felt, it is real! Miss Walton, I love you as fervently as man ever yet loved woman."

He threw himself at her feet, and again endeavored to possess himself of her hand. She rose calmly, and with dignity.

"Colonel Balfour, this must not be! I must leave you. I can not entertain your suit. That you may be sure that I am sincere, know that my affections are wholly given to another."

"What!" he cried, with an impatience almost amounting to

anger, which he did not endeavor to conceal; "what! is it then true? You are engaged to that rascally outlyer, Singleton?"

"Enough, Colonel Balfour; this was not necessary to satisfy me of your character, and to teach me what is due to mine. I leave you, sir. In future, I shall much prefer that we should not meet."

"You will repent this haste, Miss Walton!"

"I may suffer for it, sir!"

"By the Eternal, but you *shall* suffer for it!"

She waived her hand with dignity, bowed her head slightly, and passed into an inner apartment. The lips of Balfour were firmly set together. He watched with eyes of fiery hostility the door through which the maiden had departed; then, after the pause of a few seconds, striking his fist fiercely upon the table, he exclaimed—

"She *shall* pay for this, by all that's damnable!"

In the next moment he darted out of the dwelling, and made his way, with mixed feelings, which left him doubtful where to turn, toward the residence of *la belle Harvey.*

CHAPTER XXXVII.

WALTON'S CAMP.

THE stir and excitement in the good city of Charleston, now, had scarcely been equalled by any event occurring since its conquest by the British. The loyalists were everywhere in alarm, dreading that every moment's intelligence would bring them accounts of the summary execution of Williamson; and in his fate, they perceived lowering intimations of their own, at the hands of the patriots, should the events of war throw them into the same predicament. For the same reason, the patriots in the city were in a high state of exultation. The avenger was at work to redress their grievances, and to exact bloody atonement for the wrongs, the insults, the injuries, which they had been made to suffer. The exertions of the officers in garrison, had set the entire cavalry of the British in motion, soon after the commands of Balfour had been given; and that very night, as we have seen, Major Fraser, with an ample force, set forth in pursuit of Walton. Of course both parties were in a state of equal excitement for the result of this expedition. Fraser obtained his clews *en route*, and was soon across the Ashley. Our acquaintance, mad Archy Campbell, we may mention, conducted one of the strongest of his detachments, which were all soon dispersed in several directions, as the whole of them approached the Edisto. Leaving them to hunt out their game as they best could, let us once more join the partisans.

Walton had selected, for his temporary camp, a very pretty spot on the east bank of the Combahee. His own quarters were taken up in the dwelling-house of the plantation which his troops occupied—an airy, comfortable habitation, the proprietors of which were in exile. His sentinels and videttes were so placed as to secure all the avenues to the place, and his scouts ranged freely for a considerable distance around it. With ordiry vigilance on the part of the subordinates to whom these duties were assigned, there could be no possible danger of surprise ; and the commander of the party, feeling himself secure, was enabled to bestow his attention upon his several prisoners. Major Proctor was one of these prisoners, but he was held in no duresse beyond that of courtesy ; his word being taken that he would make no endeavor to escape, if subjected to no bonds but those of honor. Even these were to be released, now that an interval, supposed to be sufficient for safety, had been thrown between the partisans and all pursuers from the city. It was at dinner that day that Colonel Walton was pleased to say to his guest, or prisoner, that he should be free in the morning to depart.

"You will need," said he, "less than two days' easy riding to reach town, and may as well remain till to-morrow, and take an early start with the sun. I trust, Major Proctor, that you will have seen in your detention thus far nothing less than an absolute necessity, which I could not escape."

"I have nothing, Colonel Walton, of which I could possibly complain. You have treated me with great courtesy and kindness, and the release which you grant me, without any equivalent, is a debt which I shall always cheerfully acknowledge and requite."

While dinner was under discussion, a sergeant made his appearance at the door of the apartment, and summoned M'Kelvey, one of Walton's officers, away from the company. He returned a moment after with the tidings that one of the prisoners had somehow succeeded in making his escape.

"It appears, by the way, Major Proctor," said M'Kelvey, "that the fellow was a servant of yours. This I have just ascertained. He was taken about the same time with yourself, while returning from Dorchester."

"Ha !" exclaimed Proctor, with surprise. "Is it possible? *He* taken ?"

"Had you mentioned him, major," said Walton, "I should have placed him in your hands."

" It is, perhaps, better that you did not. Had you done so,
I had most probably shot him. He is a scoundrel. If taken
following me from Dorchester, he was a spy upon my actions,
commissioned by my enemies. And he has escaped?'

" Within an hour," replied M'Kelvey.

" You will do well to pursue him," said Proctor. " He is
a consummate scoundrel, and will bring your enemies upon
you."

" Scarcely, for we shall be away by sunset, leaving you in
possession of the mansion. We can spare no time, now, for pursuit, and the fellow is not worth the trouble. Had we known
his relations to you before, we might have prevented this; but
—fill, Major Proctor ; do not let it annoy you. This is choice
old Madeira, such as seldom honors our camp."

Proctor filled the glass mechanically ; his brow contracted
with thought, and his imagination readily suggesting to him that
circumstances had, strangely enough, woven around him a web
of increasing meshes, rendering his case more than ever com-
plicated. With an effort, he shook off this mood, and abruptly
addressed Colonel Walton in reference to his more distinguished
captive.

" Pardon me, Colonel Walton, but you have another prisoner.
Pray tell me what is your design with regard to General Williamson?"

" He is a traitor, Major Proctor, to our cause!" was the stern
reply.

" Yes, but——"

" There is but one fate for such."

" But *you*—*you* will not be the voluntary instrument of punishment?"

" I would not if I could escape it. If it were possible to convey him to the hands of Marion or Greene, I would gladly do
so, but——"

" There is no need of this, Col. Walton, said M'Kelvey impatiently ; " I know not any right that we have to shuffle off an
unpleasant duty upon others. It is our duty to try this traitor,
or it is not. He deserves punishment, or he does not. He is
in our hands, and the blood of our fathers, hung at Camden and

other places, by Cornwallis and his tory allies, demand that he shall not be suffered to escape without his deserts. I am for doing *my* duty. If we delay, we may lose him. We ought not to risk the chances of securing justice, by any wild attempt to convey such a prisoner quite across the country, from the extreme south to extreme north, from Combahee to Lynch's Creek, only that he may be tried and punished for an offence of which he is notoriously guilty, and upon which we have the right to sit in judgment and to execute. Had you suffered me, he should have been swinging to the highest tree on the high road to Charleston, in twenty minutes after he was taken."

"I am glad you did not consent to so summary a procedure," said Proctor to Walton.

The latter said gravely, answering M'Kelvey:—

"Do not reproach me, Captain M'Kelvey. I have no desire to escape my duties when I clearly recognise them to be such. As for this man, Williamson, we have ordered him for examination this afternoon, and my decision will depend upon what shall be then educed in evidence. I hope to prove myself neither blood-thirsty nor weak. If his death can be shown as likely to promote our cause, he shall die, though I myself become the executioner. If this can not be shown, then shall he live, though I myself perish in defending him. In this reply, Major Proctor, you too are answered. As you remain here this afternoon, you will please be present at his trial. I prefer that you should be able, as an impartial witness, to report truly what we do."

"This privilege, Colonel Walton, determines me to remain. But for this, I should have entreated your permission to depart for the city instantly. It is, indeed, quite important to my own interests that I should be there. You are, perhaps, not aware that I too labor under suspicions which seriously threaten my safety; and that I momently expect to be brought to trial for something like treason to my sovereign. It is but natural, therefore, that I should sympathize with another in a like danger, though, perhaps, under circumstances exceedingly unlike."

"Yes, indeed: there can be no comparison in the facts of

your case and those in the case of Williamson. But what are your offences?"

"A supposed participation in your escape at Dorchester—"

"Good Heavens! Is it possible?"

"And other treasonable conduct evinced during my command of that post, particularly in my visits and supposed intimacy with yourself and family."

"But my testimony would acquit you of all these absurd charges!"

"Yes, perhaps; if your testimony would be received. But you forget the position which you yourself occupy in the eye of the British authorities."

"True! true! But can I do nothing for you?"

"Nothing that I can see. Yes, perhaps! Be merciful to this unfortunate man in your custody."

Walton grasped the hand of Proctor, as the parties rose from the table. He made no other reply. M'Kelvey was not thus silent.

"Mercy to ourselves and to our people, deny that so great a traitor should have mercy!"

This was said aloud, and, as he left the room, he muttered audibly: "Would that I had run him up to the first oak before we left the Ashley."

"He is not the proper person to sit on this trial, Colonel Walton," said Proctor, referring to the last speaker.

"At all events, Major Proctor, I shall exercise the discretion of a supreme judge in this case. I do not say that we may not find it imperative to condemn this man to instant execution; but I can assure you, that I shall feel a real satisfaction in escaping from such conviction."

Nothing more was said upon the subject. Proctor was left for awhile to himself, and employed his solitude in becoming meditations of his own future and affairs. He had enough to make him gloomy and apprehensive. The intelligence of the espionage of his man John—for such it evidently was—of his capture and escape, showed him the probability of new and unexpected involvements, making his case more suspicious in character and more difficult of defence. It was only with a desperate effort, finding his head to ache under the embarrassments of his thought, that he succeeded in giving a new direction to his meditations.

Meanwhile, Walton had ascertained the particulars of the escape made by Proctor's servant. The fellow had been gone fully three hours when his absence was first discovered. A woman, bringing in fruits and vegetables to the camp, had met him several miles on the road below, and described his person exactly. By what means he had escaped the vigilance of the sentinels could not be ascertained; but that he had thus succeeded, counselled Walton to a strengthening of his guards, which accordingly took place. Having given orders to his officers to have their men in readiness for moving across the Combahee by sundown, Walton prepared for the examination of Williamson. The great hall of the mansion was assigned for this purpose, and the unfortunate prisoner, conscious equally of his degradation and danger, in the eyes, and at the hands, of his old associates, was brought manacled into the centre of a group, in whose stern faces he read no sympathy, and from whose harsh judgments he could possibly entertain no hope. At the very moment that he was thus brought up for trial, with a penalty the most fearful in his eyes, the runagate servant of Proctor was encountered by the British detachment under the command of Mad Archy Campbell. He was brought before that dashing officer, and his examination may well precede that of Williamson.

"What! John, is that you? Where the devil have you been? Where's your master?"

"Ah, sir; your honor, I've been in bad hands; I've been a prisoner to the enemy. They're only seven miles, here away, a matter of fifty horse or so, under the command of Colonel Walton."

"Beelzebub! Do you say? Walton; and but fifty men; and I have sixty! Push forward with the advance, Captain Auld; but seven miles! We must have a grand supper on steel to-night!"

"If you'll move cautious, major, you'll surprise 'em. They don't look for you or any of our people. They're very loose about the sentinels; that's how I came to get away. Most of their parties are busy looking for fruit about the farms, the regular grub being pretty scarce in those quarters."

"A good notion! Better to surprise than be surprised, and an ambuscade is an inconvenient thing. Hold up your men, captain, while we discuss this matter. I say, John, you are quite sure of what you say?"

"Oh! yes, sir, it's as true as the Book."

"It is Walton's party, and he has but fifty men, and his sentries are careless."

"All true, sir."

"Has Colonel Walton any prisoners—your master?"

"Why, major, my master's *with* Colonel Walton's party; but whether he's a prisoner or not, it's not for me to say."

"Why, you d——d Trojan, what do you insinuate?"

"Well, major, I don't insinuate nothing, only I can't help seeing for myself. I followed my master from Dorchester, and they put me in ropes, and let him go free."

"Why, you booby, did you think that they would tie up a gentleman like a blackguard! They could rely on your master's word of honor, fool; but who could rely on yours?"

"Yes, sir, I know that, but——"

"But what?"

"I don't think that Major Proctor's been a prisoner at all. I've a notion that when he went into Colonel Walton's camp, he know'd pretty much where he was going. He's been free ever since. I never heard that they watched him at all; and, indeed, the people told me that he had gone over to the rebel cause."

"Silence, you d——d heathen! That a fellow should suspect his own master! Where do you expect to go when you die, Philistine? Say no more of your master! But tell me if General Williamson is still a prisoner with Colonel Walton."

"Fast, sir, and they do say that they mean to hang him. There was something said this very morning of a jury to be set upon him."

"It is not too late! We must push forward quickly, but cautiously, Captain Auld. This fellow will be your guide. Take him to the front, and follow his information; but, if he shows any trifling, cut him down as you would a cabbage. Do you hear that, John? do you understand it? Very well; I see you do; and you know that there's no jest in it! Now, go forward, lead us faithfully, and, if we succeed in surprising the rebels, you shall have five guineas. If you fail us; if you show treachery, or even lie in this business, you are only so much dog's meat to the sabre."

"Thank your honor," said John, lifting his hat, and referring wholly to the five guineas. "If they ain't moved from the camp, you'll be sure to catch 'em in it."

"Reasonable logic; away!" cried Mad Archy, and the party disappeared from sight under the guidance of the fugitive.

He led them unerringly. Unhappily for our friends, his report of the remissness of Walton's sentries was much too true. Newly-raised militiamen, not yet subdued by training, and far from systematic in their military habits, they were quite too prone to assume their position to be secure, without making it certainly so. Without dreaming of any movement from the garrison, they did not anticipate one. Pinched by hunger, or lured by the love of fruit, the sentinels had wandered off, in most cases, from the posts assigned them, and were busied in deserted orchards, thrashing the peach-trees for their late and unripe harvest.

While thus occupied, the British troopers stole within the line of sentries. One incident will serve to illustrate the fate of these unfortunate wretches, in their miserable neglect of duty. On the edge of an old orchard, which was bounded by an open tract of pine forest, a young woman was seated upon a fallen tree, peeling peaches, and chipping them up into small pieces, evidently meant for a pot which stood near her, in which a few quarts of water was simmering above a slow fire. At the side of the woman, lay a man upon the ground, his head leaning upon the log. He was sleeping. He was garbed in the usual costume of the rangers, with a light-blue hunting shirt fringed with cotton, and with falling cape similarly ornamented. At the end of the fallen tree, leaned against some of the upright branches, was the rifle which he carried. With the exception of a *couteau de chasse*, stuck in his belt, he wore no other weapon. His coonskin cap had fallen from his head while he slept, and now lay on the other side of the log.

On a sudden, the young woman raised her head and seemed to listen. She resumed her occupation after a moment's pause, as if satisfied; but again, after another brief interval, she put on the attitude of a listener, and at length, with some anxiety in her manner, she laid her hand on the arm of the sleeping man.

"Joel, Joel," she cried, "wake up: I hear horses from below."

"Eh! ah!" sighed the sleeper—slowly comprehending her —and opening his eyes vacantly.

"I hear horses from below, Joel."

"Ah! some of our scouts I 'spose."

"It sounds like a troop, Joel; better get up."

"Oh! Sall, it's only jist that you wants to be talking to me; that's it."

"No! I declare! Don't you hear them, Joel?"

"Why, yes I do; but it's only a few of the scouts got together, and a riding into the camp."

"There's a great many on 'em, I reckon by the sound."

"So there is," cried the fellow, rising slowly to his feet, and looking curiously about him.

Beginning to perceive something unusual in the approach of such a body of horse as he now distinctly heard, the sense of vigilance was not sufficiently habitual to move him to an instant decision for his own safety, or the performance of his duties. Had he then seized his rifle, prepared to discharge it as soon as thoroughly certified of an enemy, and dashed for the thickets a moment after, he would have saved himself, and advised the camp of the approach of danger. But he stood gazing at the wood from which the sounds continued to approach, his rifle still leaning among the branches twenty feet from him and more.

On a sudden, he was brought to the fullest conviction of his folly and his danger, as a group of three British horsemen dashed out of the wood, within less than fifty yards distant. Their scarlet uniforms at once opened his eyes to his true situation. To bound forward to the place where stood his rifle, was the first instinct, but it lay between him and the approaching enemy. He hesitated. Sally cried to him, catching his arm as she did so, and pushing him toward the thicket—·

"Run, Joel. Take the bushes—that's your only chance."

But the manly instinct, tardy as it was, interposed to prevent his adoption of this now judicious advice. He flung her off, and rushed for the rifle. But his haste, and the fact that, while seeking it with his hand, his eye was kept upon the enemy, caused a momentary embarrassment, some of the dead branches of the tree catching the lock of the weapon. When, at length, he drew it out, one of the three horsemen was upon him, and within a few paces only. The whole proceeding had occupied but a few seconds. The rifleman, in a moment, perceived that, to prepare his weapon, turn upon his assailant, take aim and fire, would be impossible where he then stood. His object was to secure a little space which would give him momentary safety. To leap the massive shaft of the tree, and throw its branches between himself and the horseman, was the obvious plan for safety; and he attempted it; but too late. Even as he leaped, the sabre of Mad Archy—for he was the foremost enemy—made a swift bright circle in the air, and, striking with horizontal edge, smote sheer, slicing off completely the coronal region of the unfortunate man. He fell across the tree, prone, without a struggle.

"Uneasy lies the head that wears a crown!" cried the reckless trooper in a quotation from Shakspere, shouted rather than spoken. He added, making the sentence significant—"Yours, my good fellow, has no such impediment to sleep hereafter."

The horrors of the scene seemed only to enliven the mood of the desperate soldier. His eye glared with that rapture of the strife, which made the Hun so terrible in battle, and which forms the vital passion of the Birserker of the northern nations. Mad Archy Campbell belonged to this order of wild and terrible spirits. His sword was still uplifted, when the young woman rushed toward the body of her late companion, her arms extended, her face wild as that of a maniac.

"Out of the way, woman!" he cried aloud as he beheld her movement, and sought to draw his steed aside from her path.

"Out of the way, I say! A woman is never in more danger than when she would run over a horseman."

She did not heed him at all; but, tottering forward, fell down by the side of the murdered man. Clapping spurs to his horse, Campbell went over her at a bound, clearing, and without touching, the unhappy creature. For a moment the fierce horseman thought it possible that his wild blow had cut asunder some dear and very precious, though very humble human affection; but unhappily such performances lay within the province assigned him, and he had still other and like duties to perform. He looked not even back upon the mixed group, the living and the dead; but, joined by others of his squad, bearing swords already dripping like his own, he hurried forward to the surprise of the rebel camp.

CHAPTER XXXVIII.

LIFE OR DEATH.

WE have seen Walton and his officers assembled for the trial, or examination, of the prisoner, Williamson. Major Proctor was present at the proceedings, a curious and somewhat excited spectator. Walton presided, grave, stern, commanding, and resolute to do his duty, and that only. Williamson looked weary, but his carriage was not undignified. He noticed the presence of Proctor with looks which seemed to betray dissatisfaction. Knowing, as we do, his secret, the presence of the British officer was necessarily a restraint upon him. How could he declare, in his hearing, that he was actually playing the part in the British garrison, as an emissary of Marion and Green? Yet, to establish this fact, to the satisfaction of his present judge, was the only hope left to him of safety.

Every form common to such trials was rigidly adhered to. The officers of the court were sworn. The prisoner was duly arraigned. The charges and specifications were then stated by a judge advocate, by whom a list of witnesses was submitted, upon whose testimony he relied to establish the truth of the charges made. Upon these charges he dilated in a speech, which reviewed the whole career of Williamson, from the first period of his public life, when he did good service to the state against the Indians, passing to that when he strove honorably in the cause of the patriots; and showing, in contrast with these honorable histories, his supposed unhappy falling off from sworn faith and country. To all this matter the arraigned person was permitted to reply.

Williamson was not an orator, not a speaker at all, not even a tolerably-educated man. He was absolutely illiterate; but by no means wanting in intelligence. He had mother-wit and shrewdness in considerable share; was sensible and thoughtful; had lived too long by his own efforts, and among intelligent and accomplished men, not to have acquired a considerable degree of readiness, and, indeed, a certain share of grace. He rose to reply to the charges made against him, and which, we need not say, were proved by several credible witnesses. He reviewed the history which had been just given of his career. He did not complain of any injustice, until the period was reached which described him as deserting from the cause of his country, and taking sides with her enemies. To this point he answered in some such language as the following : —

"This alleged desertion from the cause of my country consists in my having taken a British protection, even as you, sir, have taken a British protection——"

This was addressed to Colonel Walton. His brow was warmly flushed, as he replied—

"When I took a British protection, sir, I was under *duresse*, a prisoner, in fact, and in a situation well known to the country; and the protection which I took, under protest all the while, was urged upon me by my friends as absolutely unavoidable in my situation, and absolutely necessary to the safety of my family no less than my own. But *I* am not under trial, sir : — when it becomes necessary for me to answer to my country, I trust that I shall not find it difficult to meet all the charges made against me."

"Pardon me, sir," replied Williamson, modestly. "In referring to the protection taken by yourself, I meant only to indicate the true character of that compromise which the necessities of the time forced so many of us to make. Until Buford's defeat, I appeal to all the world to say, if I did not honorably and truly maintain my allegiance to the revolutionary party. But in the defeat of Buford went down all organized opposition in the state. It was supposed, on all hands, that the contest was at an end, so far as South Carolina and Georgia were concerned. The regular troops of both were defeated and mostly in captivity. In the fall of Charleston, five thousand of our disposable troops were taken from the field. The defeat of Buford disposed, in like manner, of all our Virginia allies. The continental army was a skeleton, and continental money had ceased to be a tender. Without means, or men, or money, I called my officers together. My command of rangers was almost the only one in the state which had not been dispersed ; and, after deliberate consultation, it was agreed that the contest was hopeless. I declared my determination to abide by their decision, and the result of our deliberations was that we should abandon the field and disperse."

"But not surrender to the enemy"—said the judge advocate —"not join his forces, not give him aid and comfort."

"I did neither," was the somewhat hesitating reply of Williamson.

"It is unfortunate for you," said the advocate, "that your correspondence with Richard Pearis, Robert Fletchall, and others, is on record, and in our hands."

"All these letters can be explained, and shown as innocent. Besides, when they were written, I can show that I too was under *duresse*."

"Yes : but it was of your own seeking. You had voluntarily thrown yourself into the city of Charleston."

"What was to be done ? Of all the acknowledged leaders of the state, not one was to be found. Some were in captivity ; others had fled. General Moultrie was a prisonor-of-war; so was General Gadsden; it was not known what had become of Colonel Marion; and General Sumter and Governor Rutledge had both fled the state."

"Fled only to North Carolina, and thither only to find recruits in order to renew the struggle," answered the judge advocate.

"I grant, sir," continued Williamson, "that I might have done the same : I confess my regret that I did not. I now see, by what Marion and Sumter have done, what might have been done by many others ; but I must plead ignorance of our resources, or my own resources; and not wilfulness or a treacherous purpose, when, forbearing to follow the example, which as yet had not been shown, I yielded up a seemingly hopeless struggle. I followed, indeed, a very frequent example, in taking British protection, as entirely hopeless of any other."

"The charge is not simply that you disbanded your command, and submitted to the enemy; it is that you joined them, and took sides against your friends. I herewith submit to the court your intercepted letters to certain notorious royalists of the back country, and your letters to certain patriots of the same region, urging upon them the necessity of going over to the British cause. If you deny your agency in these letters, we are prepared to prove your signature."

"I am very far from denying these letters. I freely confess them; but look at the dates when they were written, and you will discover that they were written at the moment when I myself took the protection of the British, and embodied simply the arguments by which I was influenced; showing, indeed, the exigency which, as I supposed, prevailed throughout the state. Nobody then believed, or appeared to believe, that we had anything to hope for. Congress, it was understood, scarcely able to maintain its ground in the north, was prepared to abandon the extreme south to its fate. That Marion, Sumter, and others, should subsequently take the field, and with so much success, was nowhere anticipated; and that they have done so, affords me a satisfaction quite as great as that which any of you feel."

A smile of derision lightened up the faces of several members of the court at this assertion. Walton regarded the speaker with a grave sorrow of countenance. The judge advocate indulged in a bitter sarcasm; and Captain M'Kelvey, striking impatiently upon the table, exclaimed—

"Upon my soul we have too much talking by half. What need of it? The prisoner confesses the charges against him. He admits the letters, and they prove everything. That he should try to explain them away is absurd. His crime is acknowledged. I don't see why we should not proceed to judgment. I say, for one, that he is a proven traitor, and deserves the death of one; and I move you, Mr. President, that we take the vote on the question."

"Ay, ay! the vote: guilty or not guilty?" was the echo from several other voices. Williamson became fearfully agitated.

" Is this a trial, Mr. President ?"

" Be patient, sir," answered Walton.

" It is a more formal and regular trial, by far, than Rawdon
and Balfour accord to the whigs, our brethren," was the angry
reply of the judge advocate.

" Ay, indeed, 'Rawdon's mercy,' and 'Tarleton's Quarters,'
are rare sorts of trials !" cried M'Kelvey.

The feeling was rising. The court was becoming momenta-
rily more and more irritable and boisterous. " Death to the
traitor !" was audibly announced.

" Mr. President," said Williamson, " it is surely clear to you
that I can not have justice at this board, with such a temper
prevailing among its members."

" Silence the traitor !" muttered several voices ; " we have
heard quite enough !"

" The vote, Mr. President," cried M'Kelvey.

" I do not see why the question should not be taken, Mr.
President," pursued the judge advocate. " Every substantial
fact is admitted by the defendant. He is guilty, by his own
confession, of going over to the enemy — of corresponding with
the blood-thirsty tories who have been rioting in the spoils of
our people upon the borders ; — he admits that he has written
these letters to our friends, seeking to seduce them from their
allegiance ; asserting the inevitable ascendency and success of
the British. He lives within a British garrison, and is, as we
can also show, the trusted counsellor of Balfour and Rawdon.
Is anything more necessary for his conviction ?"

The excitement increased with this speech. Williamson
eagerly and urgently entreated to be heard ; renewed his arguments and explanations ; and was with difficulty secured a hearing. It was evident that a vote taken in regard to his guilt,
and decreeing summary and extreme punishment, would be
almost, if not quite, unanimous ; and the defence of the prisoner,
as made by himself, was now of a sort rather to provoke than
conciliate hostility. His agitation, and the exhibition of some
temper, were at variance with all prudence and good policy.
Proctor could no longer restrain himself. He rose from his seat,

passed to that of the president, and placed before him a paper on which he had pencilled these words—

"For God's sake, for your own sake, Colonel Walton, do not suffer these men to decide this case! They are resolute to have this man's blood, and the circumstances of the case, and the condition of the country, neither call for, nor will sanction its shedding. Let me entreat you, as a man of honor and a Christian, to interpose!"

Walton wrote at the bottom of the paper—

"At the right moment, I will. Fear nothing. I will adjourn the court and refer the case to General Greene, and a board of superior officers."

This episode had not taken place without causing a new emotion in the assembly. There were audible murmurs about the court in regard to the impertinence of one prisoner taking part for another. These murmurs were silenced by the judge advocate, who, in a whisper to the most turbulent said—

"All's right; Proctor's come over to us. He has no more love for the traitor than we. Be still!"

Whether be expressed his own conjecture, or repeated only what he had heard, can not be said; but Williamson appeared to regard the interposition of Proctor with a mind suspicious that it augured him no good. With a somewhat violent manner, he exclaimed—

"This is unwarrantable, Mr. President. I protest against any interference, in this case, on the part of a British officer and an enemy. This court is not in the temper for the just trial of my case. It is full of my enemies."

"Does General Williamson appeal from this court? His appeal will lie to General Marion, or to General Greene?"

The suggestion was eagerly seized by the accused.

"I do appeal," he cried; "but in the meantime, I have that to say to the president, if allowed to speak with him in private, which, I think, will satisfy him of my innocence, and, that I ought to go free from trial altogether."

"Ha! ha! ha! Very good!" was the response of M'Kelvey. Walton gravely spoke:—

"Gentlemen, with your permission, I will accord to General

Williamson the private interview he seeks. This can do no harm; particularly, since his appeal will render delay inevitable."

"If allowed," cried the judge advocate; "but I see not why it should be allowed."

"It must be, if urged," answered Walton; "our jurisdiction is not final."

"It ought to be," muttered the judge advocate; and audible murmurs around the board showed how intractable were the wild spirits whom the president was required to control. Walton did not seem to heed these murmurs, but, rising from his seat, said to Williamson—

"Now, sir, if you have anything to communicate, we will retire to the adjoining chamber. I would not do you injustice, General Williamson; nay, would save your life if this be possible."

"I will show you good reason why you should," answered Williamson, eagerly, as the two left the room together. A noisy discussion among the heated bloods of the court, followed the departure of the president and the prisoner. It was now very evident, to Proctor, that, but for Walton, Williamson would, long ere this, have expiated his offences, real or supposed, on the nearest tree. His reflections assured him that, according to the mode of judgment in these times, such a summary execution would have been perfectly justified by the circumstances, assuming them to be true. Of course, he knew nothing of the secret relations between Williamson and Colonel Singleton.

While the officers around him continued in noisy discussion of the matter, our Englishman rose and went to the window. He gazed out upon a once lovely lawn, now in ruins. The shade trees, in front of the house, had shed numerous branches, which were unremoved, and the undergrowth was gross and matted; all was significant of the wild and vexed condition under which the land was groaning. Broken and decaying fences, right and left, and the slender skeleton stalks of the cornfields of previous years, looked equally mournful; while the silence, that spread everywhere without, was singularly expressive of the real desolation of the country.

While Proctor gazed and mused, the silence was suddenly

broken by the sound of pistol-shots. These seemed to command no attention among the assembly within. Proctor thought the event worthy of remark, as it would have been in any well-ordered encampment; but he reflected upon the loose habits, and frequent disorder among the militia, and he concluded this to be nothing more than one of their ordinary violations of discipline.

But, even as he looked out, he caught a glimpse, at a distance, beyond the open cornfield, of three of the rangers, running confusedly from one side of the field, as if seeking a cover in the woods beyond. A few moments after, he descried the flashing of scarlet uniforms among the trees in the opposite woods. This unfolded to him the true history. He, at once, felt for the officers around him, and for Walton; all of them wholly unconscious of the apparent danger. With a generous impulse, he turned to the company, still eagerly clamorous in respect to Williamson.

"Gentlemen, lf I mistake not, your camp is in danger of surprise, if not actually surprised. I have heard pistol-shots, and have just now caught glimpses of the British uniform among the pines in that wood upon the southeast."

The whole party rushed to the window. By this time, other pistol-shots were heard. Soon, others of the riflemen, scattered, and in evident flight, were seen to hurry for the woods along the edge of the cornfield, and, at length, a group of dragoons, in the rich uniform of the British army, suddenly appearing, left the event no longer doubtful.

"Great God! we are surprised! They will be soon upon us!" cried more than one of the officers.

"These d——d videttes and sentries!" cried M'Kelvey; "that the lives of brave men should rest upon such rascals! To horse, men, and let us see what can be done."

"Nothing remains to be done now," remarked Proctor, quietly, "but to fly! Your people are evidently dispersed."

M'Kelvey gave him a fierce look, and glanced upon him with angry eyes; but, without a word, darted to the chamber where Walton and Williamson were in conference. He knocked with the hilt of his sword upon the door, which he vainly attempted to open, crying out the while —

'The enemy are upon us, colonel; you have not a moment to lose."

The door was instantly thrown open, and Walton came forth eagerly, followed by Williamson.

"The enemy! where? And no alarm?"

"None! The sentries have been asleep, d——n 'em, and our men are probably all dispersed."

"We must see to that," cried Walton, preparing to go forth.

"It is too late, Colonel Walton, to look after your men," said Proctor, approaching. "Fly, while time is allowed you. The dragoons are, even now, speeding across the cornfield, directly for the house."

"Too true!" cried M'Kelvey, who had been looking; "we must take the back track, colonel, for the swamp. Fortunately, our horses are just behind the house."

Walton looked out, and saw a squad of Campbell's dragoons, headed by that impetuous captain, in full speed for the dwelling, and scarcely three hundred yards distant. "*Sauve qui peut!*" was the counsel of every instinct. The back door of the house was already open, and the party rapidly descended from the piazza to the horses. Looking back, just as he was mounting, M'Kelvey saw Williamson at the entrance, watching every movement with great appearance of anxiety.

"Shall the d——d traitor escape after all?" he cried, fiercely. "Not, by Heavens, while I have a bullet!"

He drew a pistol from his holster at the word, but Walton caught his arm.

"Stay!" said he; "you know not what you do! Let the man alone. He better serves us in the British garrison than he did when he was ours. Spurs, gentlemen, and scatter for the swamp!"

Walton saw his officers off at different points, making for the ricefields beyond which lay the thickets, which, once reached, would afford the most ample refuge. With a courteous wave of the hand to the balcony, where Proctor and Williamson stood, he gave spurs to his own splendid charger, a black, which had never before failed him. M'Kelvey kept beside him, a fierce but devoted follower; and they were rapidly approaching the rear fence which separated the house enclosure from the abandoned ricefields, when the British dragoons, Campbell at their head, burst into the yard. They never noticed Proctor or Williamson; but, with the fugitives full in view, dashed pellmell upon their tracks. Meanwhile, Walton, as M'Kelvey and himself approached the fence, gave way to the latter, crying—

"Go ahead, captain, and take the leap; the causeway will suffer but one horseman at a time."

This was a generous suggestion, for the horse of Walton was in the lead. It was an unwise decision made at that moment, since, to enable M'Kelvey to go ahead, it was necessary that Walton should curb the impulse already given to his horse. M'Kelvey, to do him justice, growled audibly at the idle courtesy, but felt that it was not a moment to dispute the privilege. He drove the rowel into his lighter-made steed, and the animal went clear. Walton was less fortunate. The track grew slippery as he descended the bank. He felt the beast falter slightly, and, in fact, trip, just before the fence was reached. But, giving him spur and rein at the right moment, he, too, went over, but fell prone to the earth, as leaping beyond the horse of M'Kelvey, he stumbled upon a break in the rice-dam. Walton was thrown completely over his head, and lay stunned for a moment.

In that moment the British troopers passed. M'Kelvey, beholding the danger of his superior, wheeled about, and dashed back, sabre uplifted; and, with all the recklessness of a knight errant, rushed headlong to meet the enemy. He was cut down in the conflict with two of the dragoons, and, when Walton's eyes opened upon the scene, the last struggles of his brave lieutenant were at an end.

He opened his eyes only to find himself a prisoner. Mad Archy, with a score of dragoons, stood over him, effectually precluding every thought of conflict. Stunned and bruised, and scarcely conscious of his situation, he was taken by his captors back to the dwelling, where mad Archy was enabled to realize the full extent of his successes. There he found both Williamson and Proctor. The former, though by no means a favorite with Campbell, he congratulated upon his escape—having been already taught how imminent had been his danger. Williamson

16

very properly omitted all reference to the inteview which he had had with Walton, in which, by the way, he had shown to the latter what all-sufficient reasons there were, why, if to be hung by anybody, he should suffer that fate by the hands rather of the British than the American.

To Proctor, the manner of Archy Campbell was marked by great gravity and coldness.

"Your servant is here, Major Proctor. To him we are indebted for guidance to the rebel camp. Perhaps you will do well to set him right as to the true circumstances in which he left you here. I have only to say to you, that his report shows him to entertain very equivocal notions of your present relations with the enemy."

"My servant is a scoundrel, Major Campbell," was the stern response of Proctor.

"I think it very likely," was the indifferent answer; "and shall beg you to take charge yourself of his correction and reform. I have but to pay him five guineas, and we are quits."

CHAPTER XXXIX.

WIDOWS THE BEST MATERIAL FOR WIVES.

IT was noon of the day which has thus been distinguished by the rescue of Williamson and the capture of Colonel Walton, when two horsemen might have been seen slowly riding in a southerly direction, on the route between the Edisto and the Combahee rivers. They were both well mounted and armed; the one who seemed the leader carrying sword by side, and pistols in his holsters; the other, in addition to pistols, having a neat, well-polished, and short rifle, lying across the pummel of his saddle. In the portly person and fresh, florid features of the former, we recognise Lieutenant Porgy, of Singleton's command: in the latter the young ensign, Lance Frampton.

If the reader has not forgotten some former passages in this true history, he will find it easy to account for the presence of these two personages in this neighborhood, at the present juncture. It has probably not been forgotten, that, soon after the defeat which Singleton had given to Lieutenant Meadows, and the capture of that officer and of his convoy, the former commissioned these two officers, Porgy and Frampton, to convey a baggage-wagon, with supplies, to the camp of Colonel Walton. As this camp was known to be erratic — as was usually the case among the partisans of any experience — the duty thus assigned them implied delay, difficulty, a tedious search, and the exercise of a constant caution. Lieutenant Porgy was instructed to take his wagon with as much despatch as was consistent with secresy, to the cover of the swamps of the Edisto, on the west side of that river; to leave it there in concealment, with a portion of his detachment, and then, himself, with Frampton, to proceed in search of the squadron of Walton. There was yet another duty, if we recollect, which was assigned, at the same time, to this officer and his young companion. This was to seek out the widow of Walter Griffin, one of the soldiers of Singleton, who had fallen in the engagement with the troop of Meadows, and to convey to her and her daughter the tidings of his death and burial, together with his effects, and a certain amount in English guineas, which Singleton was fortunate enough to gather from the treasure-chest of Meadows, and which he promptly shared among his followers.

This latter duty was properly confided in part to Frampton. He might now be considered almost a member of Griffin's family ; the tender interest which he felt in Ellen, the fair daughter of the latter, having received from Griffin, while he lived, every sanction, and being generally supposed equally agreeable to the young damsel herself. The melancholy part of his task, therefore, was not without its compensative considerations, and no one could better express the language of sympathy and regret than one who was thus necessarily a sharer in the misfortune. Nor, according to his own notions, was Lieutenant Porgy himself improperly assigned a portion of this duty. This excellent epicure had his own secret. He had a selfish reason for his readiness to undertake a search like the present, which, but for this reason, would have brought him annoyance only. But we must leave it to himself and the sagacity of the reader to unfold this secret motive as we proceed.

We need not very closely follow the footsteps of Porgy and his party, from the moment when they left Ravenel's plantation on the Santee, and proceeded to the Edisto. Porgy was a man nearly as full of prudence as plethora. He was luxurious, but he was vigilant; fond of good things, but neglectful of no duty in seeking them. He succeeded in conveying his baggage-wagon in safety to the spot destined for its hiding-place, in the swamp-thickets of the Edisto. Here he left it in charge of Lieutenant Davis, a shrewd and practised ranger. This done, he set out, as we have seen, with Ensign Frampton, with the twofold object of finding Colonel Walton and the widow Griffin. Of the former, the party had been able to hear nothing by

which to guide their progress. He was supposed to be ranging
somewhere between the Salkehatchie and the Savannah. In
the route now pursued, they had the widow Griffin in view,
rather than the partisan. Frampton knew where she dwelt,
and it was hoped that, on reaching her abode, some intelligence
might be obtained from her of Walton. The two had accordingly taken a bee line from the swamps of Edisto for the humble farmstead of the widow, and at noon of the day in question
might probably be some ten miles from it. But they had ridden fast and far that morning, and when, after crossing a brooklet, or *branch*, which gushed, bright and limpid, across the
high road, Frampton exclaimed—"It's only nine miles and a
skip ; we could make it easy in two hours, lieutenant ;"—
the other answered with a growl that singularly resembled
an imprecation. "Only nine miles !" repeated Frampton, urgently.

"And if it were only three, master Lance, I would not budge
a rod farther until I had seen our wallet emptied. No, no !
young master, you must learn a better lesson. Never do you
hurry, even if it be on the road to happiness. No man enjoys
life who gallops through it. Take it slowly ; stop frequently
by the way, and look about you. He who goes ahead ever,
passes a treasure on both sides which he never finds coming
back. By pausing, resting, looking about you, and meditating,
you secure the ground you have gained, and acquire strength
to conquer more. Many a man, through sheer impatience, has
swam for the shore, and sunk just when it rose in sight. Had
the fool turned on his back and floated for an hour, the whole
journey would have been safe and easy. If you please, master
Lance, we'll turn upon our backs for an hour. I have an appetite just now. If I fail to satisfy it, I lose it till to-morrow, and
the loss is irretrievable. There is some jerked beef in your
wallet, I think, and a few biscuit. We will turn up this branch,
the water of which is cool and clear, put ourselves in a close,
quiet place in the woods, and pacify the domestic tiger."

The young ensign, eager, impatient, and not hungry, was
compelled to subdue his desire to hurry forward. He knew
that argument, at this hour, and under these circumstances, with

his superior, was vain. He submitted accordingly without further expostulation, and with a proper grace ; and, riding ahead, ascended a little elevation, which led him, still following the winding of the creek, to a cool, shady, and retired spot some two hundred yards from the roadside. He was closely followed by his more bulky companion ; and, dismounting, stripping their horses, and suffering them to graze, they prepared to enjoy the frugal provision which was afforded by the leathern wallet which the young man carried. This was soon spread out upon the turf ; and, letting himself down with the deliberation of a buffalo about to retire for the night, Lieutenant Porgy prepared for the discussion of his dinner.

It was scarcely such as would satisfy either the tastes or appetites of epicurism. Porgy growled as he ate. The beef was hard and black, sun-dried and sapless. The biscuits were of corn-meal, coarse, stale, and not palatable even to the hungry man. But the tiger was earnest, and the food rapidly disappeared. Frampton ate but little. His heart was too full of excited hopes to suffer his appetite to prevail. It would be doing injustice to Porgy to suppose that he was glad to behold this abstinence. Though fully equal, himself, to the consumption of the slender provision before them, he was sincerely urgent that the youth should feed.

"Why don't you fall to, boy ! Do you suppose there's not enough for both ? Eat, I say ! You've done nothing worth the name of eating since last night. Eat ! I know I'm a beast, seeking what I may devour, but understand, that I regard you as one of my cubs, and will see you feed, even before I do myself. Take that other biscuit, and there's the beef. Cut, slash —it will need a sharp knife, and sharper teeth to get at the merits of that bull's quarter."

Frampton complied, or seemed to comply with the command. Meanwhile, Porgy ate on, growling all the while.

"This is life, with a vengeance, and I *must* be a patriot if I stand it much longer ! Nothing seems to agree with me ! Hand me the bottle, Lance, and run down to the branch with the cup. I believe I should perish utterly, but for the little seasoning of Jamaica which is left. Ah !" looking at the small remains of the liquor in the bottle, "it is now only what the poet calls the drop of sweetening in the draught of care."

"But if it be a draught of care, lieutenant," said Lance archly, taking up the cup, and moving toward the branch, "why do you drink of it so often?"

"So often! When, I pray you, have I drank of it before, to-day?"

"Only three miles back, at the Green Branch."

"Oh! I drank three miles back, at the Green Branch, did I? Well, it was the cup of Lethe to me, since I certainly forgot all about it."

"There couldn't have been much bitterness in the draught, lieutenant, or the taste would still be in your mouth. But, have you forgotten the other cupful at Swan's Meadows, about nine miles back?"

"Do you call that a draught, you ape of manhood, when you know that the Jamaica was just employed to precipitate the cursed clayey sediment of that vile mill-pond water? Get you gone, and bring the water. This *is* good water, and I will have a draught now, a genuine cupful; since the others were only calculated to provoke the thirst and mortify the desire. Away!"

The boy soon returned with the water. The worthy epicure refreshed his inner man; threw himself back upon the green turf, under the pleasant shade-trees, and seemed deeply engaged in meditating the merit of his performances. Lance Frampton crouched quietly on the opposite side of the tree, and, for a little while, neither party spoke. At length Porgy, with whom taciturnity was never a cherished virtue, broke the silence.

"Lance, my boy, you are beginning life monstrous early."

"How so, lieutenant?"

"When do you propose to marry this little girl, Ellen Griffin?"

"Well, sir, I can't say. It's as she pleases."

"Pshaw, fool, it's as *you* please. When a girl consents to be married, she's ready to be married. Lay that down as a law. The consent to marry implies everything; and all then depends upon the man."

"Perhaps——"

"Perhaps! I tell you it *is* so, and more than that, I feel

pretty sure that unless you are picked up by a British bayonet or bullet, you'll marry before the war is over."

"I should like it, I own, lieutenant."

"No doubt; no doubt; and you are right. I begin to think that marriage is a good thing. I have wasted many years unprofitably. How many women might I have made happy had my thoughts led me this way before. But I may yet do some good in this behalf before I die. I must marry soon, if ever."

"You, sir!" with something like surprise.

"Ay, to be sure! why not? am I too old, jackanapes?"

"Oh! not a bit, lieutenant!"

"Well! what then? what's to prevent? You don't suppose that I'm fool enough to think of marrying a slight, fanciful, inexperienced thing, such as you desire. The ripe, sir, not the green fruit, for me. I require a woman who has some knowledge of life; who is skilled in housekeeping; who can achieve successes in the culinary department; who knows the difference between hash and haggis, and can convert a terrapin into a turtle, by sheer dexterity in shaking the spice box. There is another quality which a woman of this description is likely to possess, and that is a due and reverent sense of her husband's authority. It is because of her deference for this authority that she acquires her art. She has learned duly to study his desires and his tastes, and she submits her judgment to his own. She waits to hear his opinion of the soup, and is always ready to promise that she will do better next time. I feel that I could be happy with such a woman."

"No doubt, sir."

"The difficulty is in finding such. There are precious few women who combine all the necessary qualities. They are not often native. They come from training. A wise father, or a wise husband, will make such a woman; she can not make herself. Were I, for example, the husband of a girl such as your Ellen — "

"My Ellen, sir!"

"Oh! don't be alarmed, boy; I have no idea of such a folly! But were I the husband even of such a young and inexperienced creature, and did we live together but ten years; were I then to die, she would be a prize for any man. She should be as absolutely perfect as it is possible with one of a sex, a part of whose best merits depend very much upon their imperfections. Now, this leads me to the reflection that, perhaps, widows are, after all, the best materials out of which to make good wives; always assuming that they have been fortunate in the possession of husbands like myself, who have been able to show them the proper paths to follow, and who have had the will to keep well them always in the traces. I am clearly of the opinion that widows afford the very best material out of which to manufacture wives."

"Indeed, sir."

"Yes indeed! my widow would be a treasure for any man; and if I could only find the widow of a man who in some respects resembled myself, I should commit matrimony."

"Commit!—when you said that, lieutenant, I thought murder was to be the next word, instead of matrimony."

"Did you! You are getting humorous in your old age, my son."

There was a pause, after this, of several minutes: but Porgy resumed, apparently taking up a new topic entirely.

"Poor Griffin! What a loss he must be to his wife! Poor woman! I do pity her! I liked Griffin, Lance. He was very much a person of my own tastes; not so refined, perhaps, not so copious or various, but with an evident tendency my way. Nobody in camp relished my terrapin soup half so well, and, for an ordinary stew, he was admirable himself. We once compared notes for our dressings, and it surprised us both to discover that our ingredients and the quantities were, almost to a fraction, the very same. I liked the poor fellow from that very hour, and he, I think, had quite a liking for me."

"That he had, lieutenant!"

"I am pleased to think so, Lance. Many of his other qualities resembled mine. He was generous, and spent his property in too great a hurry to see which way it went. He was a man of character, and detested all hypocrisy. He was a man of will, and when he put his foot down, there it stuck. It was law. I

16*

have not the slightest doubt that poor Mrs. Griffin is an admirably-trained woman."

There was a pause, in which Porgy himself rose, took his cup and bottle and went down to the brooklet, saying—"Thinking of poor Griffin, I will drink to his memory."

He soon returned and resumed the subject, somewhat, we should fancy, to the annoyance of his companion.

"I am of opinion, Lance, that Mrs. Griffin, when a girl, must have greatly resembled your Ellen. She has exactly the same eyes and hair, the same mouth and chin, and, allowing for the natural portliness of a woman of thirty-five, very much the same figure. She is a fine-looking woman now; and in her you will be gratified to see what her daughter will be twenty years hence. If she has trained her as she herself has been trained, you will have every reason to be satisfied. Did you ever observe, when Mrs. Griffin was in camp with us on the Santee, how frequently I dined in Griffin's mess? Well, it was in tribute to her excellent merit in preparing the dinner. Her husband shared the labor, it is true, and I sometimes contributed my counsel as an amateur. This, no doubt, helped her very much; but that should not be allowed to disparage her real merits, since, to be satisfied to submit to good counsellors, shows a degree of wisdom, such as ordinary women seldom arrive at. Poor woman! how I pity her! How such a woman, so meekly dependent upon her husband, can endure widowhood, is very problematical!"

There was another pause, Lance Frampton being heard to turn uneasily behind the tree, when Porgy resumed—

"Yes! the truth is not to be denied. I have been quite too selfish! I might have made many a woman happy—I might have carried consolation to the heart of many a suffering widow! I have lived thus long in vain. I must make amends. I must sink self, in the sense of duty!—Come, Lance, saddle the horses, lad, and let us be riding."

CHAPTER XL.

GRIEF — BACON AND EGGS.

IN less than two hours, our companions reached the humble farmstead which the widow Griffin occupied. The dwelling was a poor cabin of logs, with but two rooms, such as was common enough about the country. The tract of land, consisting of two hundred acres, was ample for so small a family. This property, with a few head of cattle, a score of hogs, several of which lay grunting in the road in front of the entrance, and other trifling assets, were the bequest of a brother, a cripple, who died but a few months before, and whom Mrs. Griffin, with her daughter, had gone from the camp of Marion to attend in his last illness. The place had a very cheerless aspect. The fences were dismantled, the open spots of field grown up in weeds, and some patches of corn, from which the fruit had been partially stripped already, stripped, indeed, as it ripened — added rather to the cold and discouraging appearance of the place.

Our companions did not, at once, and boldly, ride up to the habitation. They were too well practised as partisans for such an indiscretion. When within half a mile of the dwelling, they turned into the woods, made a partial *detour*, and while Porgy remained under cover, Lance Frampton stole forward, on foot, to reconnoitre. The horses, meanwhile, were both fastened in the thicket.

Lance was absent about a quarter of an hour only, but long enough to make his superior quite impatient. The youth, though eager to gain the cottage, was yet too well trained to move incautiously. He had carefully sheltered himself in his approach, as well as he could, by the cover of contiguous trees. These had been allowed to grow almost to the eaves of the building, in front and rear, affording an excellent protection from the sun, which, as the house was without a piazza, was absolutely necessary for comfort in such a climate.

The door was open in the rear of the building, and the first glimpses of it showed Lance the person of his pretty sweetheart, sitting just within it, busily engaged with the needle. The youth, his heart beating more than ever quickly, glided forward with increased stealthiness of tread, in the hope to surprise her. To creep beside the building, until he had nearly reached the doorway, and then, with his cheek against the wall, to murmur her name, was the simple art he used. She started, with a slight cry, at once of pleasure and astonishment, and exclaimed—

"Oh! Lance! Is it you? How you scared me!"

"I did not mean to scare you, Ellen."

"To surprise me so," continued the girl: "and I without stockings on;" and with a blush, she drew the delicately-formed white feet beneath her dress, but not before the eye of the youth had rested upon their whiteness.

"And how's father? where did you leave him?"

Lance was silent. The gravity of his face at her question did not escape her. She spoke eagerly—

"He's well, Lance, ain't he?"

"Where's your mother, Ellen?"

"In the room." She pointed to the chamber.

"Well, I must go and report to Lieutenant Porgy. *He's* here. He's got letters for your mother. There's been no British or tories about?"

"Yes: they've been about, I hear. Some passed up yesterday, by the other road. But all's safe hereabouts now, I reckon."

"I'll run, then, and bring the lieutenant. He'll be mighty tired of waiting."

"But you haven't told me about father, Lance."

"No!" said he, hesitatingly, "the lieutenant will tell you all."

"But he's well, Lance—he's well? You haven't had any fighting, have you!"

"Wait awhile, Ellen," he answered as he hastened away, and

his evasion of the inquiry at once alarmed the quick instincts of the girl. She called immediately to her mother.

"Oh! mother, there's news from camp, and I'm afeard it's bad news."

"Bad news! Ellen," answered the mother, coming forth.

"I'm afeard; for Lance has just been here, and, when I asked him about father, he would tell me nothing, but has gone off to call Lieutenant Porgy, who is here too in the woods."

"Lance wouldn't bring bad news, Ellen."

"Not if he could help it, mother; but why didn't he answer me when I asked after father; and why did he say that Lieutenant Porgy would tell us all?"

"Lieutenant Porgy—he's here too?" said the mother, smoothing her cap and apron. "If it was bad news, Ellen, we'd hear it soon enough. It's never slow to travel when it's bad."

"I'm sure father's hurt; something's the matter. They've had a battle; and why didn't he write?"

"Well, I don't know; but maybe he did write."

"But, if he did, wouldn't Lance have brought the letter the first thing?"

"Maybe the lieutenant's got it! Don't be foolish, Ellen. I don't think Lance would be the one to come with bad news."

"Oh! I know he'd be sorry to do so; but, mother, he looked sorry enough when I asked about father, and he spoke so little."

"Come, child, you're always thinking of the cloud before it comes! That's not right. Go, now, and look up something for Lance and the lieutenant to eat. I reckon they'll be precious hungry. Put on a pot of *hominy* at once, and kindle up the fire, and get down the gourd of eggs, while I slice off some of that bacon. I don't think there's any bad news. I don't feel like it! God knows we've had sorrow enough to last us now for a long time, and I ain't willing to believe that we're to suffer any more on a sudden. Come in, Ellen, and stir yourself; that's the way to lose the feel of trouble. Don't be looking out for *them*"—meaning the men—"it don't look quite proper for a young girl, Ellen."

"Oh! mother, how can you——"

The sentence remained unfinished.　The girl obeyed, and was soon busied with the domestic preparations which the mother had suggested.　The pot of hominy was soon upon the fire, the eggs laid out upon the table, and Mrs. Griffin herself, with a somewhat unsteady hand, prepared to cut from the shoulder of bacon the requisite number of slices.　She was interrupted while thus employed, by the arrival of the expected guests. Her agitation, when she received them, was not less great, though less conspicuous than that of her daughter.　The poor woman seemed to fancy that a certain degree of hardihood was essential to proper dignity.　It is, indeed, a characteristic of humble life among the people of the forest country of the south and southwest, to assume an appearance of stoicism under grief, in which they resemble the Indian; appearing to consider it a weakness of which they have reason to be ashamed, when they give vent to their natural emotions under affliction.　In like manner, it is their habit to suppress very much their show of impatience, particularly when they are conscious of an active and growing curiosity.　Mrs. Griffin felt fully the anxieties of her daughter, but her training was superior to the nature which strove within her.　She met her visiters with the air of one who had nothing to fear; and, that she really felt anxiety, was to be seen entirely in the measured and cold manner with which she welcomed them.

"I'm glad to see you, Lance.　I'm sure you're welcome, lieutenant; sit down.　You must be mighty tired with your long ride in this hot weather."

"Tired and hungry, and thirsty and sleepy, all together, Mrs. Griffin, I assure you.　And how is Miss Ellen? has she no welcome for an old friend?" was the reply of Porgy.

The girl, who had hitherto hung back, now advanced and put her hand shyly within his grasp, but said nothing.

"Ah! you are still as bashful and still as pretty as ever, my little damsel.　Don't be shy of me, my dear creature.　I need not tell you that I am old enough to be your father; and I feel that I could love you like a father.　You would hardly think, but I have a heart full of the milk of human kindness.　It might have been better, perhaps, for me, in a mere worldly point of view, had I less. But I am content. The feelings which I possess are more precious to me than vaults of gold and wagons of silver." He released her hand as he spoke this, and, addressing Mrs. Griffin, proceeded as if the girl were no longer in hearing.

"Ah! madam, what a treasure to you to have such a child as that. She is all gentleness and sweetness, and all duty, I am sure."

"She is, indeed, a blessed child. There are few like her, Lieutenant Porgy."

Ellen stopped not to listen to her own praises thus began, but stole out, closely followed by Frampton. Porgy, obeying the repeated request of his hostess, proceeded to take a seat, while the good woman, having finished slicing her bacon, and thrown it into the frying-pan, laid the implement upon the table conveniently beside the eggs, and, having looked at the pot of hominy, given it a stir, and pushed up the brands beneath it, drew a chair near the fireplace, and, folding her hands in her lap, assumed, unavoidably the look of a person in waiting and expectation.

The lieutenant surveyed her curiously as she sat thus, her eyes bent upon the ground, and only raised occasionally to look at the fire. Mrs. Griffin was a comely woman, not much beyond the middle period of life, and, as thus she sat, plainly, but neatly dressed, with a face smooth yet, and fair, and with the bloom of health upon her cheeks, our lieutenant inwardly said—

"Verily, the woman is well to look upon."

His conviction took a somewhat different shape when put into words.

"Mrs. Griffin, you are very comfortable here; that is, you might be, with health and youth, and a pleasant abode—one that may be made so, certainly—but, don't you find it very lonesome?"

"I'm used to it, lieutenant."

"Yes, indeed; and that is fortunate. To be accustomed to lonesomeness is to be independent, in some degree, of the changes of life. Solitude, once familiar to the mind, ceases to be oppressive; and who is sure against solitude? We may have a large number of relatives and friends, but what is to secure us against the chance of losing them? We may have a full house to-day, and all shall be silent and cheerless to-morrow. Such are life's vicissitudes. It is fortunate, therefore, when one has been prepared already for such privations. Misfortune, then, can do us little evil, and should death steal into the household——"

"Death! Lieutenant Porgy?"

"Yes, Mrs. Griffin, death. We must all die, you know. One will be taken away, and another will be left, and the survivor will have need——"

"Lieutenant, a'n't you just from the camp?"

"Not very long, ma'am."

"And my husband—didn't he write—didn't he know that you were coming into these parts?"

"Why, no, ma'am, he didn't write—he didn't know—he—"

"Lieutenant, there's something you've got to tell!" interrupted the woman. "Speak to me, now that Ellen's not here. Let me know if there's anything the matter with my husband."

"Well, Mrs. Griffin, I'm sorry to say that something is the matter," replied Porgy, seriously—the earnest, sad, almost stern manner of the widow impressing him with solemnity, and compelling him, by a natural intuition of what was proper, to forego all the absurdities and affectations of speech which a long indulgence had rendered, in great degree, habitual. He continued—

"You are a strong woman, Mrs. Griffin; you have seen much trouble and sorrow, and you must be prepared for more."

"Tell me!" she exclaimed, clasping her hands and bending toward him. "Tell me! Don't keep me in this misery."

"We have had a battle, Mrs. Griffin." Here he paused.

"And he was killed!—he was killed!" was her cry.

Porgy was silent. His eyes were cast upon the floor.

"Walter Griffin! Oh, my God! my poor, poor Walter! He is dead—he is dead! I shall never see him again!"

The head of the woman fairly dropped upon her knees, while strong, deep sobs broke from her breast, with occasional ejaculations.

"Walter, Walter, my poor, poor Walter!"

Porgy did not reason unwisely when he forbore all effort at consolation. He took the opportunity, now that she seemed to be in full possession of the fact, to relate the particulars.

"He died like a brave man, Mrs. Griffin, in battle against the enemies of his country!"

"Ah! I know'd he would. Walter was a true man. He had the heart of a lion in him!"

"That he had, indeed, Mrs. Griffin. I will bear witness to his courage and his manhood. He was a brave, generous, whole-souled fellow—a good companion and an excellent friend."

"Oh! yes! Poor, poor Walter! But you don't know half what he was to me, when there was nobody and nothing!—ah! how could you know? And what is to become of us now!— my child—my poor Ellen, fatherless here, in these cruel times, and in these lonesome woods."

"Ah! Mrs. Griffin, remember you are a Christian. Trust in God brings with it the best of promises. He tempers the wind to the shorn lamb. You will never want a protector, I am sure, and your sweet and gentle daughter will surely find a father and many friends."

"Oh! I don't see *where*, lieutenant; we are very poor, and very unbefriended. If the war was over, and the people would come back to the settlements!"

"The war will be over before very long; the people will surely come back to the settlements. You will have many and kind neighbors; and I can promise you, Mrs. Griffin, one among them, who will be as true a friend to you as he was to your husband. Let peace be restored to us, and if my life is spared me, I mean to live in this parish. I will be your friend. I will protect your daughter. I will be a father to her, out of the love I bore to her father."

"Oh! lieutenant, I thank you for your kindness, from the bottom of my heart. I reckon you will be as friendly as any-body in the world; but there's no such thing as replacing the husband and the father, and making us feel as if we had never known the loss. Oh! Walter Griffin, I was dubious always that you would be killed by the enemy! I know'd how ven-turesome he was, lieutenant. I told him he ought not to be rash, for the sake of his wife and daughter; and it's all turned out as I warned him. My God! what are we to do now, here in this lonesome wilderness! I don't see! I don't see! I feel as if I could lay right down and die."

"Don't give up, Mrs. Griffin. There's no help in despair. Death must come, at last, to all of us. It might be Griffin or it might be me. It might be on the field of battle, or it might be here in bed. We can't know the moment when the summons must be heard, and we must resign ourselves with philosophy, to a fate from which there is no escape. There's no use in sorrow."

"Oh! but who can help it, lieutenant! I know there's no bringing Walter back; but that don't make me feel easier because he's gone. If I did't cry, my heart would be sure to burst."

Her speech throughout, was broken by continual sobs and wailing. The evidences of real feeling were quite too conspicuous to suffer Porgy to indulge in any follies, and what he said, by way of consolation, was respectfully and kindly said, though as usual in such cases, of no value. At length, he bethought him of Singleton's letter, and the money intrusted to his care.

"It ought to be a great satisfaction to you, Mrs. Griffin, that Walter had so completely won the love of everybody in camp. I've seen the colonel himself standing over him, with the big tears gathering on his cheek, as he listened to his last words. The colonel has written to you in this letter."

"God bless him! Colonel Singleton is a good man, and Walter loved him very much. Read the letter for me, lieutenant, for I'm too blind to see the writing."

The letter of consolation was read accordingly. It set the stream of tears flowing anew.

"Really," thought Porgy as he watched her, "a most exemplary woman. It is pleasant to think that we shall be thus wept and remembered when we are no more."

This reflection led to another. "What a profitless life is mine! Were they to assign me my last tenement to-morrow, I doubt if a single eye would give out water; unless, indeed, this youngster, Lance, and possibly, Tom, the cook! Verily, this thing must be amended. This poor woman is the very person to whom I must administer consolation, and from whom I must receive it. But, not now! not now! We must give ourselves time. She feels her sorrow, that is clear, and does not merely feign it; but the stream flows too freely to last over long; and the fountain that exhausts itself quickly, will soon feel the need of new supplies."

Such was the unspoken philosophy of our epicure. He really persuaded himself that the sort of consolation, which he proposed ultimately to offer to the widow, was the proof of a certain virtue in himself. He congratulated himself with the conviction, that he was about to do a charitable action. An interval in the grief of Mrs. Griffin allowed him to place in her hand the ten guineas which had been sent her by Singleton, Griffin's watch, and some other trifles which he brought. She gave them little heed, emptying the gold upon the table, and putting the watch into her bosom. Then, as if Singleton's letter had yet to be read, she turned it over, and appeared striving to possess herself of its contents. But she handed it, a moment after, to Porgy, saying—

"I can't see the letter!" What does the colonel say, lieutenant?"

He again commenced the perusal of the letter, but had scarcely compassed a sentence, when hasty feet were heard at the entrance without, and, in the next moment, Ellen Griffin and Lance hurriedly entered the apartment. Both seemed very much agitated. The eyes of the girl were red with weeping, and the big drops yet stood upon her cheeks. But there was little time allowed for observation.

"The red-coats, lieutenant—the British!"

"Where?"

"Not a quarter above, coming down at a walk, dragoons, more than fifty that I see! We must cut for the bushes. We'll have time, if we move at once, but we must run for it."

"The devil! run! as if I had not an infirmity in my heel, like that of Achilles!"

"Shut the front door, Ellen," cried the prudent Mrs. Griffin.

"Better gather up these guineas, Mrs. Griffin," cried Porgy,

" or the British will swear to the stamp. Lance, my boy, can
we find cover all the way back ?"

" Pretty much ! There's a bend in the road above, just here
at the corner of the cornfield, where there is a piece of woods
that screens us for awhile, and if we get beyond that, we're in
the thicket. But we must put out at once."

" To be sure we must ! Mrs. Griffin, with your permission
we'll withdraw the temptation of this bacon and these eggs from
the eyes of these rapacious red-coats. We must not feed, or
give comfort in any way to the enemy. Lance, tumble these
eggs into the frying-pan—it already contains the bacon, and
take it on your shoulder. I will take possession of the pot of
hominy."

" But I have my rifle, lieutenant."

" What of that ! carry both, can't you ? I have my sword,
do you see ; yet, I mean to take the pot also."

" We must be in a hurry, lieutenant," said Lance, swinging
the frying-pan, laden with eggs and bacon, over his left shoulder, and grasping his rifle in his right hand.

" Oh ! yes ! better go !" cried Ellen, entreatingly, who divided her time between a watch through the cracks of the door
and her lover. Wiping her eyes with her apron, Mrs. Griffin
hurried their departure also.

Porgy had already seized upon the hangers of the hominy
pot, and was unbuckling his sword, to carry in his hand, that it
might not embarrass him in walking. The sounds of the approaching horse were beginning to be faintly heard, as the two
partisans stepped out of the door in the rear of the building,
each armed after the fashion described, and stealing away under the shelter of the trees.

It required no extraordinary haste, for the British came slowly down the road. This was fortunate, since Porgy was not the
man to fatigue himself in flight. He would much prefer to encounter odds in conflict at any time. His portly figure presented quite a picture, such as Cruikshank would have painted *con
amore*, rolling, rather than striding, away beneath the trees, his
sword in one hand, thrown out at right angles with his body,
the better to preserve that balance which was necessary to his

carrying the hominy-pot at a proper distance from his breeches. Mrs. Griffin and her daughter watched the two from the back door for awhile ; then, as the nearer approach of the British was heard, closing the entrance in the rear as well as the front, and they prepared within for the possible necessity of receiving unwelcome visiters. The money, just received, and watch, with certain other portable treasures, were dropped down within a secret hollow in the floor ; and, with a hope that the enemy would pass by without pausing, the widow and the daughter both sat down, seemingly busied in knitting and needle-work.

But they were not thus destined to escape. The dragoons in advance stopped at the entrance of the dwelling, and, as the several divisions came up, they paused also. There was some delay, during which all was anxiety in the hearts of the widow and her daughter. A knock followed at the door, and a voice of authority demanded entrance. It was immediately thrown open by Mrs. Griffin herself, while her daughter sought shelter in the chamber. Let us leave the widow with her unwelcome guests while we follow the footsteps of our lieutenant and ensign into the forest.

CHAPTER XLI.

PORGY PROVES POT-VALIANT ONLY.

THE two partisans, laden as they were, the one with the pot of hominy, the other with the frying-pan, made their way to the woods with all despatch, and without detection. Fortutunately, as we have said, the forest cover extended almost to the cottage. Our fugitives soon satisfied themselves that they were in a place of security, though but a few hundred yards from the dwelling. They were in a tolerably close covert, on the slope of a moderate hill, at the foot of which stole off a slender brooklet, the child of a great bay or wooded pond, that covered a hundred acres, more or less, a quarter of a mile distant. Here Porgy paused. He had found his pot of hominy, precious as it was, an incumbrance. He laid it upon the ground, cast down his sword beside it, drew a long breath, and wiped repeatedly the perspiration from his brows. Lance Frampton followed his example; and the youth, at the bidding of his superior, proceeded to strike fire in his tinder-box, which he brought from his horse furniture; the two steeds being fastened still farther in the woods, where, still bitted and saddled, they were allowed to nibble the grass, which was now tolerably rank. The fire kindled, and the pot set to boiling anew, Frampton proposed that he should take an observation—in other words, see how the land lay with the enemy.

"Ay, do so, lad. You are of no use here. You have no merits in the kitchen. I will do the cooking, for which I flatter myself I have a native faculty, and, if you do not stay too long, you will find your share of the dinner in waiting for you. And look ye, Lance, boy—don't forget your business, in your anxiety to have a chat with Ellen. Many a poor fellow's heart has been pampered at the cost of his head. Be on the lookout, for if caught, you will be trussed up to the first tree, hung against all odds, as no better than a spy ; and I sha'n't be there to hear your last confession. Be off, at once, and show yourself back again as soon as possible."

The lad promptly acted on this permission. He sped away with the lightness of a deer, though with the cunning and caution of a much smaller animal. Porgy, meanwhile, went on cooking. In this province he was at home. His pot began to boil ; with the aid of his *couteau de chasse* (vulgarly Jack-knife), which the partisans all wore as habitually as the sailors, he converted a bit of cypress clapboard, which he found convenient to his hand, into a *hominy-stick* (an article of which our northern friends know nothing, unless, perhaps, as a *baster* or *paddle*, as a substitute for school-birch, when an unruly urchin is to be admonished) with which he stirred the simmering grist, and occasionally drew it up for inspection. His eggs and bacon, meanwhile, lay ready in the frying-pan, to be clapped on the fire the moment that the hominy had reached the proper consistency. In these operations, our *cuisinier* was singularly deliberate. He knew what a good supper required, and he had no fear of the enemy. His calculations were that the British, on their way to Charleston, had made but a momentary pause ; and as they had no suspicions, so far as he knew, of the proximity of any of the Americans, he saw no reason to suppose that they would penetrate the wood sufficiently far to disturb his operations. Besides, Lance was out upon the scout, and of his vigilance, Porgy had sufficient experience. During all these operations and calculations, the soliloquies of our lieutenant were frequent and prolonged. Had we leisure, it would be easy, from his own lips, to prove him equal epicure and philosopher. He mingled his philosophies with his occupations, and dignified the latter with all the charms of sentiment. He was indeed a rare compound of the sensual and the sentimental philosopher.

His hominy was about to assume the degree of consistency which rendered it fit for use, and he was engaged in hauling away the fire from beneath it, in order to set on the frying-pan, with its contents of eggs and bacon, when Lance Frampton reappeared. The youth was all consternation.

"Oh! Lieutenant, would you believe it? they've got Colonel Walton a prisoner!"

"The d——l they have!"

"Yes! I've seen him myself, sitting in a chair in the hall, under a guard of six dragoons with their pistols cocked and watching every movement. I counted more than seventy dragoons, and I reckon there's quite a hundred. How could it have happened? What's to be done? We ought to be doing something to get him clear!"

"Doing something, boy! What the d——l would you do with seventy dragoons or more? If we save our own bacon, it's as much as we can hope to do. Did the enemy look as if they were suspicious? Do they show any signs of stopping long?"

"Not that I see! They have only stopped to rest and refresh. They've been off to the spring and got some buckets of water for themselves, and most of them are leading their horses to the spring, and rubbing them down. I saw several of them out in the bushes, here and there, but they did not straggle far from the house. But what's to be done for Colonel Walton?"

"What can be done? He's a prisoner, and must wait for his exchange, I suppose, with what philosophy he may."

"Oh, Mr. Porgy, I'm afraid of something worse. I am afraid they'll not treat him as a common prisoner. You remember that they were going to hang him when our colonel rescued him before."

"That's very true," replied Porgy, with increasing gravity; —"that's very true. I had not thought of that. But, whatever may be their purpose with him, we have no power to serve or save him. We must only be on the lookout to see that we ourselves are not gobbled up by these scarlet-bodied dragoons— whether, indeed, they should not be called *dragons* rather than *dragoons*?"

"Lieutenant," said the youth quickly, as if with the resolution suddenly made, "I must hurry off to camp and let our colonel know all about it."

"Why, boy, Singleton's on the Santee by this time."

"Yes, sir, I reckon, but I'll find him."

"What good in that? Before you find him these dragoons will have their prisoner in the provost in Charleston. There would be some use in it, if there was time enough to enable Singleton to dash between and cut them off before they could get to the city, but that is impossible; and to know that Walton is in the provost, will be only annoying information, quite as pleasant to learn a month hence as now."

"I don't know, Mr. Porgy! Our colonel has a good many strings to his bow. I know he has working friends in the city, and has got some plans going on for getting up an insurrection there. Now, he ought to know of this capture, and if I set off at once, by hard-riding, I may give him the information much sooner than he would even hear of it from Charleston. I must go, lieutenant."

"You shan't go till you have eaten, boy."

"I don't want to eat, lieutenant; I'm not at all hungry."

"You are a fool! Not eat! defraud the docile animal that walks, rides, toils, fights, for you! send it supperless to bed, when its work is done! That won't do, boy. You shall eat before you ride. As for riding with you, helter-skelter to the Santee, and at this moment, I don't do it, for all the Waltons and Singletons between this and Huckleberry Heaven! You may go by yourself, if you choose; perhaps it's just as well that you should; for, as you say, Singleton has his plans, and conspiracies, and agents, everywhere, and he may do something to extricate his kinsman. But you sha'n't depart till you have eaten. Indeed, you can not expect to go till the enemy have disappeared."

"I can take the back track, lieutenant; steal off in that direction, going upward and westward, and then wheeling about and pushing for some of the upper fords on the Edisto."

"Yes, and defeat your own subject; lose half a day's time or more in this *roundabouting;* when, by waiting quietly and lying close, for an hour, you may be able to start off on the direct road, without an enemy in the way. Quiet, boy, and eat before you ride. I sha'n't go with you, mark that. I shall cer-

17

tainly stay to-night at the house of our friend. I have much to communicate—much to say, in the way of consolation, to this amiable and lovely widow. You may tell the colonel that I shall devote myself to the task, now that Colonel Walton is taken, of saving my little party, and our wagon of stores. My object will be to find Colonel Harden and furnish his command with all that is necessary, rather than risk everything by returning with such an incumbrance. Push up those brands, boy, and turn that bacon. Our mess will soon be ready. What a savory odor! Heaven send that it penetrates no worse nostrils than our own."

The boy did as he was directed, turned over the slices of bacon in the pan with an air of resignation, while Porgy gave the hominy a finishing stir, and drew the pot from the fire, to enable it to cool. He was thus busied when he heard Lance Frampton give a slight cry, and was astounded to see the youth leap away, at a couple of bounds, putting the brooklet and the bay between them. Just then, a harsh voice, just above him, in the direction of the house, cried out—

"Hoo noo! wha' would ye be after there, you overgrown divil that ye are!"

Porgy, the *pot-hooks*, with pot depending, still in one hand, and the hominy stick in the other, looked up only to discover a dragoon leisurely marching down upon him, and but a few steps off. He cast his eyes about him for his sword, but it lay where he had been sitting, to the windward of the fire, fully ten paces off. Here was a quandary. The dragoon was in the act of picking his teeth when he first saw him; he was now deliberately drawing out his sabre. Porgy's glance at his sword, and a slight step backward, moved the Scotchman to suspect him of flight; to prevent which, the latter rushed directly upon him, his weapon now flourishing in air.

The bulk of Porgy, the nearness of the enemy, and the distance at which his own sword lay, forbade the hope of his recovering it in season for his defence, and as the dragoon darted on him, obeying a first impulse, our epicure raised the pot by the hangers, with his left hand, caught one of its still burning feet in the right, and, with a desperate whirl, sent the entire contents of the vessel, scalding hot, directly into the face of his assailant.

The effect was equally awful and instantaneous. The dragoon dropped the uplifted sabre, and set up the wildest yell of agony, while he danced about as if under the direct spells of Saint Vitus. The hominy stuck to his face and neck like a plaster, and the effort to remove it with his hands, only tore away the skin with it. Porgy was disposed to follow up his success; and, knocking the fellow on the head with the empty vessel, was a performance which was totally unresisted. In the agony of the dragoon, his approach for his purpose was totally unseen. Down he rolled, under the wild shock of the iron kettle; and our hero, congratulating himself with his narrow escape, seized upon the frying-pan, not disposed to lose his bacon as well as his bread, and was wheeling to make off for the woods, when another dragoon made his appearance on the brow of the hill, making swift tracks in pursuit.

"D——n that fellow, Lance," muttered Porgy to himself, " he has left me to be butchered!"

He gathered up his sword, as a point of honor, but still held a fast gripe upon the frying-pan. There was but one dragoon in chase, and if he could draw him yet further into the woods, the noise of the strife would probably alarm no other—that is, if the howlings of the first had not given the alarm already.

Our epicure, as we know, had little speed of foot, and with his impediments of sword and frying-pan in his hands, he made very awkward headway. The pursuing dragoon gained upon him; and Porgy was already preparing to wheel about for the purpose of defence, when his feet tripped in some roots that ran along the surface, and over he went, headlong, the contents of the frying-pan flying forward in all directions. In another moment, and when only half recovering—on his knees still, and painfully rising to his feet—the dragoon stood above him.

" Surrender, ye d——d ribbel, or I shorten you by the shoulders."

Furious at the loss of both meat and bread, Porgy roared out his defiance.

" Surrender be d——d ! Do I look like the man to cry *peccavi* to such a sawney as you? Do your best, barelegs, and see what you'll make of it!"

With unexpected agility, unable to rise, he rolled over at these words, and now lay upon his back, his sword thrust upward, and prepared to parry that of the assailant, after a new fashion of defence. In this situation, no defence could well be made. The exhibition was, in fact, rather ridiculous than otherwise. The abdomen of Porgy rose up like a mountain, seeming to invite the attack. The dragoon, however, did not appear to see anything amusing in the spectacle. He showed himself in sober earnest. His brother soldier groaned hideously at this moment, and he had no reason to doubt that his hurts were mortal. He straddled the prostrate Porgy, and, in reply to his defiance, prepared to strike with his broad claymore at the head of the epicure. His sabre was thrown up, that of Porgy thrown out to receive it, when, suddenly the dragoon dropped lifeless upon our partisan, and the next instant the report of a rifle was heard from the neighboring wood.

"Ah!" cried Porgy, throwing off the incumbent body of his assailant, "that dog Lance; he has not abandoned me; and I should have known that he never would. The rascal—how I love him!"

The next moment Lance Frampton rushed in.

"Up, lieutenant, we have not a moment to lose. That shot will bring all the dragoons down upon us, and we don't know how nigh they are. The horses are ready, not thirty yards off. They've rested well and eaten, and we can soon leave these heavy English drags behind us."

"You're a lad among a thousand! I love you, Lance, by all that's affectionate!"

Then, as he bustled up, with Frampton's help, seeing the scattered eggs and bacon strewed upon the ground, he fairly groaned aloud in the tribulation of his spirit.

"I must lose my dinner after all! And that hominy was as good a pot as was ever boiled. It served a purpose, however; never, in fact, boy, did pot of hominy do such good service before."

But there was no time for trifling. This was said while our

corpulent professor, hurrying off under the guidance of his ensign, was making such headway as, in later days, was quite new to his experience. They were both in the saddle, and in full retreat, when the British trumpets, sounding the alarm, faintly echoed through the forest.   Pursuit was fruitless.

CHAPTER XLII.

CUTTING THE CARDS.

THE night appointed for the great ball of Colonel Cruden at length came round, and at a tolerably early hour in the evening —for great parties, in that day, convened some hours sooner than at present—the guests began to crowd the spacious and well-known mansion of General Pinckney, on East Bay. This venerable and stately dwelling still stands, one of the many memorials which the city of Charleston has to show, in proof of the troubles and changing scenes of that period of revolution. As we have already mentioned, it had fallen to the lot of Colonel Cruden, who fondly anticipated such a permanence of title as no caprices of revolution could disturb. The dwelling, on the occasion referred to, was splendidly illuminated "from minaret to porch." The spacious gardens were draped with lights, which were multiplied and reflected a thousand times at the extremity of each avenue, from pyramidal lustres of shining steel, bayonets, burnished muskets, and sabres grouped in stars and crescents.

The *fête* was the great display of the season. It was attended, accordingly, by all who felt a becoming loyalty, and by many who only sought to display it. There were others, besides, whom policy, or the love of pleasure, drew to the assemblage, but who did not sympathize with the common sentiment of the company. In the former category, hither also came Mrs. Singleton and Katharine Walton, governed, in doing so, by considerations of prudence, which were greatly in conflict with every political and social sentiment which filled their bosoms. They were not without countenance from others, their friends and relations. Witty and mischievous as ever, Mrs. Brewton was the life of the circle whither she went, and made merry with the spectacle which she had not the stoicism to avoid.

Balfour quickly attacked himself to Katharine Walton, in spite of the angry glances cast upon them both by *la Belle Harvey*, who looked her loveliest that night, and seemingly looked in vain. Balfour was in the best spirits, though it was remarked that the subdued and grave features of Katharine promised him no encouragement. She had evidently come with the determination to endure passively a certain degree of annoyance in regard to certain leading necessities; and her air was that of a resignation, where will, though sufficiently determined, was yet held in abeyance. Her passiveness of temper decided Balfour. He regarded her seeming submission as an indication in his favor, when greater privileges were to be implored; and his satisfaction in this conviction, almost rendered him gallant. It was in the midst of his attentions, promenading one of the several thronged apartments, that he was passed by *the* Harvey. She was walking with Major Stock. She caught the eye of Balfour, and her eye flashed with increasing fires. As they passed slowly, restrained by the crowd, she whispered him—

"It is war, then, between us?"

"Why should it be?"

"Who is not *for* me is *against* me!" She answered through her closed teeth. "Beware, Colonel Balfour!—I always told you that your danger was from a woman. You shall pay for all this!"

He laughed—full in her face—he laughed; and the next moment the crowd separated them. She regarded his retreating form but a moment, and with a glance full of malignant passions that might have taught even a bolder nature than Balfour that her threat was something to be feared. But he was one of those men whom good success and prosperity make forgetful of all prudence. He was quite too much enamored of Katharine, to care a straw what were the feelings of vexation, disappointment, baffled love or hate, in the bosom of his former mistress.

"What had you to whisper so lovingly to Balfour?" demanded Stock of his companion. "It seemed to amuse him wondrously?"

"I *did* whisper him lovingly, and that is reason good why I should not tell you what was spoken. He is a person to be loved, is he not?" She did not wait for the answer, but continued thus—"But might he not have shown a much better taste in the selection of his new flame? She positively is not even good looking."

"Is it possible you think so?" asked Stock curiously—"You once thought otherwise."

"Yes, in truth!—But such a stiff, starched, cold, no-meaning sort of person as it is now, as if there were no more blood in her veins than in those of an icicle—is enough to change my opinion. And they speak of her as a very paragon of virtue, a sort of Una, as if it were any merit in ice not to burn."

"My dear Harvey: let me differ with you! You are a beauty in *your* way—indeed, very brilliant and very beautiful; but, by Jove, don't deny that the Walton is a beauty also. You, at least, are bound not to deny it."

"Why, indeed!"

"From policy! Utter such an opinion to other ears than mine, and you will be set down as envious of a rival, and trembling for the loss of empire. Now, Harvey, believe me, *you* can well afford to give the Walton as much credit as anybody else."

"Look you, Stock, I don't care *that*" (snapping her fingers) "for anybody's opinion. I repeat that she is positively homely."

"Now, my dear child, don't be wilful; you must not say so, for another and a better reason. People, then, will be quite as apt to decry your lack of taste as of generosity! But let us on! I have a sneaking notion that a tumbler of punch will be particularly grateful at this moment."

They passed into the adjoining apartment; while, pursuing another route, Katharine Walton—never dreaming that she formed the subject of Miss Harvey's criticism—passed into an opposite room, still attended by Balfour. Let us follow Stock and his companion.

That rousing bowls of punch should be conspicuous objects at a mixed party of males and females, in that day, will something shock the sensibilities of ours. Yet the fact is not to be denied. Major Stock made his way with the fair Harvey into the midst of a circle surrounding a table upon which stood a richly enamelled vase, holding several gallons of this potent beverage. In goodly-sized cups of filagreed china, the liquor was served out. Filling one of the smallest of these for his companion, Stock provided himself with another of more ample dimensions; the providence of the host always remembering that the capacity of endurance was mnch greater in some persons than in others. Thus armed, the two made their way to one of the ample windows, at which stood—the centre of a devoted group—the lovely Mary Roupell, another of the loyalist belles of Charleston, of whom we have already spoken. She half sat upon and half reclined against the open window, the sash of which, it so happened, was sustained by a dragoon's sword; the button which usually supported it, having been broken off during the evening.

Stock was a rough and somewhat awkward gallant. He contrived in some way to jostle the sabre, and elbowed it out of the place. The heavy sash fell upon the wrist of Miss Roupell, who screamed violently, and under the extreme anguish of the hurt, fainted. Great was the confusion. The crowd was such as to render the place excessively warm; and the extrication of the lady was, for the time, impossible. In the emergency, greatly excited, and before any one could interfere, our excellent major, seizing upon the mammoth bowl of punch, incontinently discharged its voluminous contents, with admirable dexterity, over her face and bosom. With another scream she came to herself only to swoon again at the condition in which she found her person—saturated with Jamaica, and redolent of sweets that very soon substituted a swarm of flies for a swarm of courtiers. A more considerate friend bore her out of the circle, and, as she recovered, into her carriage. As we may suppose, she never forgave the major. Nor did he escape that evening. Barry's muse was instantly put in requisition for an epigram.

"Ha! ha! ha! decidedly the best thing that I ever heard in all my life," said M'Mahon, breaking into the circle of which Mrs. Rivington was the centre. "My friend, Major Barry, is a most wonderful genius. Here it is!"

17*

And he repeated : —

> "When fair Roupell lay fainting in her pain,
> 'Oh! what,' cries all, 'will bring her to again?'
> 'What! what!' says Stock, 'but punch — a draught divine;
> ''Twill ease her pain — it always conquered mine!'"

The company cheered and applauded.

"But that's not all," continued M'Mahon. "My friend, Major Barry had another arrow in his quiver. Listen to this —

> "Stock, to the lady dearest to his breast,
> Gave the sweet beverage that he loved the best,
> Yet mourned the fault committed in his haste,
> Such goodly physic doomed to such a waste;
> And prays his friends, should fainting be his case,
> They'll fill his throat and leave unsoused his face;
> A natural error 'twas, that what is good,
> Taken internally for flesh and blood,
> More grateful, too, than any dose beside,
> Should still be good externally applied."*

The laugh was too great for Stock to withstand. He disappeared by the back stairs, and found his way alone into the garden which, like the dwelling, was brilliantly illuminated But he was followed by the merry crew whom he thought to baffle, and, unequal to the encounter with them, he darted once more into the dwelling, and hurriedly made his way through the lobby and into the front portico, resolved on flight to his own lodgings. But he was prevented. At that moment rode up a couple of officers, who proved to be Mad Archy Campbell and one of his lieutenants.

"You, Stock?" asked Campbell.

"Yes, what they've left of me! I've been doing a d——d stupid thing, and shall never hear the end of it."

"Well," said Campbell, "it will keep, then; and I will permit myself to hear it another time. I need you, now. Go and bring Balfour out into the garden. I've news for him — matters which must be seen to at once."

"Get in yourself, then, and see him."

"Nay, that's impossible. I'm covered with mud and dust,

---

* This incident really occurred to Miss Roupell at the ball in question.

and something of a darker stain than either. I've had a sharp brush, and have brought in certain prisoners."

" Have you saved Williamson ?"

" Yes ; but take my message, and laugh at the laughers. I suppose it's no one worse than Barry."

" D—n him for the meanest of all doggrelists !" was the surly answer, while the major was disappearing. A groom, meanwhile, took Campbell's horse and he glided through the wicket gate into the garden.

Balfour very unwillingly left the side of Katharine Walton, at the instance of Major Stock ; but the revelations of Campbell in the garden reconciled him to the interruption of a *tête-à-tête* which seemed to promise him every encouragement.

" Walton here, and my prisoner ? Then *she* is in my power! But what did you say of Proctor ?"

Campbell, with a gentlemanly reluctance, related this part of his history ; that portion of it, in particular, which he had derived from the revelations of the treacherous serving-man.

" Enough ! enough !" exclaimed Balfour, " and *he*, too ! Ha ! ha ! Campbell, you are a bird of bright omen. What a lucky cast of your net this has been !"

Cruden was now summoned to secret conference by Balfour.

" It is all as I told you, Cruden. The very worst is true of Proctor. He has gone over to the rebels, was privy to the capture of Williamson, privately whispered his counsels into the ear of Walton, when they were actually trying the general for his life, and has now been captured with Walton. Taken in the very act. Nothing now can save him. He must be tried for his life."

" I know not that, Balfour," said Cruden, somewhat sullenly, " I know you hate him ; but he must have fair play. The trial must be had, of course ; he himself will desire it ; but I trust, for my sake, you will subject him to no indignity."

" He is under guard ; he ought to be in custody."

" No ! no ! I will be his surety that he will not seek to escape."

" Beware ! you undertake too much."

" I would undertake nothing if I could avoid it. But he is

my sister's child, Balfour, and I must not abandon him without an effort."

"Make your effort, but see that it does not involve you in any embarrassments with our superiors; particularly as you will scarcely serve him, however much you may sacrifice yourself. But to another matter. You perceive that this capture of Walton places Katharine completely in my power. You will not forego any opportunity of impressing this upon her."

"Truly not: but what is the process?"

"We shall try him for his life, if need be, as a traitor to his majesty's cause, and a spy of the enemy. For that matter, according to Rawdon's maxim, we need not try him at all. We have only to identify his person, and hang him to the nearest tree."

" It certainly is a most fortunate event."

"Yes, indeed! It makes her mine, if there had been any doubt about it before. I am now the master of her fate!"

They left the garden together, having discussed sundry other matters in detail, which need not concern us. Scarcely had they gone, when Moll Harvey rose from the deep thicket of a bower, where she had been crouching, and where she had heard every syllable. Her features were greatly inflamed, and she spoke in a brief soliloquy, but with accents of concentrated bitterness.

" So! thus the land lies, Signior Nesbitt Balfour! and thus I am to be sacrificed! But we shall see! There shall be another party to this game, or the soul of woman never knew the passion of revenge, and never had the courage to enjoy it. We shall see; you may shuffle the cards after your own fashion; but I will cut them after mine."

CHAPTER XLIII.

BALFOUR TRIUMPHS.

In less than twenty minutes after this conversation, Mrs. Singleton hurried Katharine Walton away from the assembly, though without giving her the reason which prompted her somewhat precipitate withdrawal. She reserved the painful communication for a situation of greater privacy. She was in possession of the evil tidings, which had been brought by Mad Archy Campbell; the patriots, in Charleston, being almost as well served with information as their temporary masters.

Balfour, it may be mentioned, had left Cruden's house, immediately after the conference just reported. He withdrew with Campbell; the circumstances of the case calling for his immediate absence. Cruden returned to his guests, with a bow somewhat graver than before, but without betraying any knowledge which might cause a sensation among the company. He did not oppose the departure of Katharine Walton, and immediately perceived, from the countenance of Mrs. Singleton, that she was in possession of the secret. When the two reached home, Katharine for the first time, remarked in the face of the latter, a stern and melancholy gravity, which struck her as significant of something evil.

"You have heard something—something that concerns me. What is it?"

"I *have* heard something, my child, and something that seriously concerns your peace of mind. Katharine, my child, you have need of all your courage. Read that; your father is in the hands of the enemy!"

Katharine clasped her hands together, and gazed with a wild vacancy of look in the face of the venerable woman.

"God be merciful!" was her only exclamation, as she took the little billet, which had been brought her by the boy George Spidell, written by old Tom Singleton, and which, in a single sentence, contained the whole painful information.

"He is in the provost;" such was the fact contained in the note. "Oh! madam, you will go with me at once."

"It is midnight, Katharine."

"Day and night are the same;" answered the other vehemently. "He is in bonds and shall I sleep—in sorrow and humiliation—perhaps, covered with wounds, and shall I not console and minister to him?"

"I doubt if they will give us admission at this hour."

"Oh! madam, no doubts, unless you would drive me mad. How can they deny the father to the child?"

"We shall need to see Balfour first, to obtain permission."

"Is this necessary?"

"I take that for granted. They would scarcely admit us at any hour without this permission."

"Then let us go to him at once."

"It might be more prudent to wait till morning; but be it as you say. The carriage is not yet put up. We can have it ready in a moment."

A few moments sufficed for this, and the two ladies were driven at once to Balfour's quarters. Two sentries guarded the entrance, who gave surly answers to their application to see the commandant. They were denied, and told that he was absent. He had not returned from Cruden's party. Back to Cruden's the carriage was driven. There the merriment still continued; gay crowds were passing and repassing, in quick succession, beneath the shining chandeliers and cressets. The garden was now, also, full of crowds. The sight of all this gayety seemed to sicken Katharine.

"Ask quickly, quickly if you please."

Cruden was sent for, and came out to the carriage.

"The commandant, is he here still, Colonel Cruden?"

"He is not, madam; he left us nearly an hour ago, on receiving some important intelligence."

"You know it then, sir," exclaimed Katharine—"my father."

" I have been informed, Miss Walton."

" And where shall we find Colonel Balfour ?" asked the damsel impatiently.

" Most probably at his own house."

" We have been there. He is not there."

" Then I know not, unless at the provost. But would it not
be well to wait till morning, ladies ?"

" Wait ! wait. How can I wait ; and he a prisoner ?—my
father in bonds—perhaps wounded, ill and suffering."

" Nay, I can relieve you on that score. Your father is un-
hurt. He is not sick, he has received no wounds, and, except-
ing a few bruises, he has no cause of suffering."

" I must see him, nevertheless, as soon as possible. Oh !
madam, will you let them drive to the provost ?"

" Surely, my child, we will go thither ;" and the carriage was
driven off accordingly. They reached the guarded entrance of
the gloomy edifice at the eastern extremity of Broad street—
" where now the merchants most do congregate"—and were
doomed to another disappointment. Balfour was not here, nor
could they obtain direction where to find him.

" But you will suffer me to see my father, sir ?" said Katharine to the officer on duty, and who treated the ladies very respectfully.

" I am sorry, Miss Walton, that I am not permitted."

" What ! not permit the child to see the father ?"

" It would give me pleasure to comply, Miss Walton, if this
were possible ; but the commandant has strictly enjoined that
the prisoner is to be seen by nobody."

" Ah ! he has been here, then," she exclaimed with bitterness. " He is merciful ! It is his humanity that would not
have the eyes of the daughter behold the chains about the neck
of the father."

" Your father is not in chains, Miss Walton ; he is strictly
guarded, but subjected to no indignities. Colonel Balfour has
said nothing about excluding you in particular. He has only
commanded that *nobody* shall be suffered to visit the prisoner,
unless with his permit. I presume that you will find no difficulty in obtaining this permit during proper hours, in daytime."

"Then we must wait, I suppose ; and yet,.my dear madam, if you would consent once more to drive to the commandant's quarters."

"Cheerfully, my dear child ; cheerfully."

"Thank you, thank you," cried the maiden eagerly, the big tears rolling from her eyes, and falling rapidly upon her hands, which were now clasped upon her knees. A few moments sufficed to bring them once more to Balfour's dwelling, which, as before described, was that fine old mansion at the foot of King street, now in the possession of the Pringle family. The visit was again fruitless. The commandant had not yet returned. They received the same answer as before. In silent despair, Katharine gave up the effort for the night.

"We must wait till morning, my child," said Mrs. Singleton. She was answered by an hysterical sobbing, which lasted painfully, for several minutes, to the great anxiety of the venerable widow. A free flood of tears at length came to the relief of the sufferer, and she appeared patiently to resign herself to a disappointment, for which there was no apparent remedy. The parties reached their abode, and Katharine retired to her chamber, but not to sleep. The rest of the night, indeed, was a long vigil. Slumber never, for a moment, visited the sad eyes of that suffering daughter, and as soon as she could reasonably insist upon another visit to the commandant, she did so. But it was no part of Balfour's policy that she should see him *yet*. He well knew that her excitement would be intense, and that she would be an early petitioner for his indulgence. He determined to avoid her.

"She shall *feel fully* that I am the master of her fate. She shall sue for the smallest privileges, and be made to understand that every concession must have its price. I shall concede nothing too quickly. She shall pay well for every favor."

With this policy he kept out of her way. It was easy to do so ; and, hour after hour during that long first day of her father's captivity, did she haunt every abode in the city where it was possible to find the person who kept the keys of his dungeon. It was only at the close of the day, when Balfour well knew that she was half distraught, that he suffered himself to receive her.

When he did so, at his quarters, in the afternoon, his countenance boded no favorable auspice. His words were equally discouraging.

"Miss Walton," said he, "for the first time since I have known you, do I regret to see your face."

"Do not say, do not look thus, Colonel Balfour; you will not deny that I should see my father."

"I know not how I should consent, Miss Walton."

"Not consent—not suffer the daughter to console the father in his bonds!"

"Were these simple bonds, Miss Walton, were his an ordinary case——"

He paused with well-studied gravity of visage.

"What mean you, Colonel Balfour?"

"Is it possible you do not remember, that you do not comprehend?"

"What should I remember? what should I comprehend? My father is a prisoner, taken in battle, the victim of the chances of war, and must remain in captivity until exchanged; as soon as General Greene, or General Marion, can affect his exchange, I have no doubt——"

He shook his head with great solemnity. She paused.

"Miss Walton, your father is not simply a prisoner-of-war. He is regarded as a fugitive from justice, as one under condemnation of a competent tribunal, against whom judgment of death stands on record."

"Death! Death! Judgment of death!" she cried wildly, almost fiercely; "Colonel Balfour, you can not mean this! You do wrong, you are cruel, sir, thus to trifle with the feelings of a daughter!"

"I have found no pleasure in speaking that, Miss Walton, which you will be compelled to hear from others. But I can not shrink from a duty, however painful."

"But you will suffer me to see him?"

"Even this would be an indulgence, which, under present circumstances, I should very reluctantly accord; and, perhaps, make myself liable to much reproach in doing so. His majesty's government is in possession of facts which go to show that an insurrectionary spirit is at work within this city, that a conspiracy has been for some time on foot, and that Colonel Walton has been privy to the secret workings of this nest of traitors. My duty forbids that I should suffer them in any way to commune with one whose boldness and daring may give them any counsel or encouragement."

"Oh! Colonel Balfour, I'm no conspirator! I will promise you to take no part with any traitors, or share in any treason. It is the child that seeks her father, to console with him, attend upon him, weep over his captivity, and succor him with love and duty only. I give you the word of one who has never wilfully spoken falsely, that I will convey no message of treason—that I shall in no way partake in any plots of any conspirators."

"Your assurance, Miss Walton, might well satisfy me, as a mere individual. As Nesbitt Balfour, my dear Miss Walton, it would not need that you should give them. Nay, it would not need that you should ask for the sympathy and favor which my heart would rejoice to offer you unasked. But I am not permitted to forget that I am here in charge of my sovereign's interest. I know not the extent of our danger, nor the degree to which these conspirators have carried their designs. Caution becomes necessary to our safety. Distrust of all is now a duty; and you and yours, it is well known, are the undeviating enemies of my sovereign."

Mrs. Singleton, who had said little before, now interposed.

"Colonel Balfour, the hostility of Katharine Walton and her father, to say nothing of myself and all my kindred, has been an openly avowed one, to your king and his authority. That it has been always thus openly avowed should be a sufficient guaranty for the assurance that we make you now, that Katharine Walton will not abuse the privilege she solicits, of seeing and being with her father. Her claim, indeed, is the less questionable, since you proclaim the painful and perilous situation in which he stands. The policy, real or pretended, which should deny her the privilege of consoling him in his dungeon, would be an outrage to humanity."

"So would his death, madam, under a lawful judgment; but humanity is thus outraged daily for the maintenance of right and justice. But I am not disposed, Miss Walton, to incur your reproaches, however little I may shrink at those of other persons. I will grant your petition; preferring to incur any risk rather than see you suffer where I have the power to prevent it. The order shall be made out that you shall see your father."

"Oh! thank you! thank you!—And shall I have it now?" Katharine asked eagerly.

"On the instant;" and with the word he hastened to the table and wrote.

"This order," he said, will secure you admission at any hour of the day, between nine in the morning and six in the afternoon. You will have something over.an hour in which to spend with him to-day."

"Oh! thanks, Colonel Balfour—believe me, I am very grateful."

He smiled with a peculiar self-complacence, which did not escape the eyes of Mrs. Singleton; and taking the extended hand of Katharine, carried it to his lips, before she was aware of his purpose. She hastily withdrew it, while her cheeks reddened with shame and annoyance. He laughed quietly as he perceived her disquiet—a low sinister chuckle which might have been construed to say—"You are coy enough now, my beauty; but there shall be a season which shall find you more submissive." But his lips said nothing beyond some idle words of courtesy and compliment, and as the ladies prepared to depart, he gave an arm to each and assisted them to the carriage. When they had whirled away, he rubbed his hands together exultingly.

"Now, let no lurking devil at my elbow dash the cup from my lips, and mine shall be a draught worthy of all the gods of Olympus! Let her refuse me, and the father dies—dies by the rope! Will she suffer this? Never! She will yield on these conditions: she dare not incur the reproach, even if she had not the strong attachment for her father, of suffering him to perish by a shameful death, when a single word from her would save his life!—And what is the sacrifice? Sacrifice, indeed!"— He passed the mirror with great complacency while he said this.—"Sacrifice, indeed! She will perhaps be not unwilling to find an excuse for a necessity which gives her such a good-looking fellow for her lord."

"How now?"—aloud—to young Monckton, who suddenly entered the apartment—"what do you wish, Monckton?"

"Major Proctor, sir, was here repeatedly to-day, and seemed very urgent to see you. He came, at last, and brought this letter, requesting that it should be placed in your hands the moment you came in."

"Ha! Well! Lay it down. I'll see to it."

The secretary disappeared.

"Proctor, eh! Well! we have him, too, in meshes too fast to be broken through."

He read the epistle, which, as we may suppose, gave a detailed account of Proctor's captivity, and, of what he saw while in the camp of the partisans.

"Pshaw!" said he, "that bird can never fly—that fish can never swim—that story can't be swallowed."

He was interrupted by the entrance of Cruden.

"Balfour," said the latter, "I have seen Proctor. He has been to me—he has been to see you also, a dozen times, he says, but without finding you. He explains all this matter, and very satisfactorily."

"I have his explanation here," was the answer, "and I'm sorry, for your sake, to say, that there's nothing satisfactory about it. His revelations are all stale. He makes them only when he can't help himself; when he knows that Williamson has told the story, and Campbell has told the story, and his own fellow, John, has told the story. They all agree in most particulars, and Proctor supplies nothing which we have not from another quarter, in anticipation of his account. They are all before him."

"But, Balfour, that is not his fault; he sought for you last night and repeatedly to-day."

"How idle, Cruden! Campbell sought for me last night, and so did Williamson; they could find me. Why did not Proctor come to your house in search of me, last night?"

"He did so, and you were gone."

"He was unfortunate; but, in truth, Cruden, his narrative is without weight, unless supported by other testimony than his own. Look at the facts. He leaves the city without beat of drum. His objects were then suspected, and I sent his man, John, after him. He leads John into an ambush, where the fellow is laid up neck and heels, hurried across the Ashley and the Edisto, with his legs fastened under the belly of a horse; his master meanwhile, with sword at his side and pistols in holster, rides in company with the rebel leaders, Walton and others, and actually takes part in the deliberations which they hold upon the fate of Williamson."

"Does Williamson say this?"

"Swears to it. John, the servant, contrives to escape from his bonds; but Proctor the master, when found, is in the rebel camp and under no restraint."

"But Proctor explains all this."

"Pshaw, Cruden, leave it to the criminal to say, and he will always explain away the gallows. Come in with me, and you shall see all the affidavits."

CHAPTER XLIV.

THE PRICE OF LIFE.

PERMISSION had no sooner been granted to Katharine Walton, then she flew to visit her father. In an agony of tears she threw herself into his arms, and, for a long time, no words were spoken between them. Colonel Walton was the first to break the silence.

"Nay, my child! Kate, my dear, exercise your firmness. There is really no necessity for tears. I am a prisoner, it is true. I am in the hands of the enemy, useless to my country, when every soldier is needful to her cause. This is a great grievance, I confess; but I shall be exchanged as soon as our people shall find a British captive of rank equal to my own."

"But, is this true, my father? Is it certain that you will be exchanged? Is it sure that you will be regarded only as a prisoner-of-war?"

"And why not? Where is the reason to think otherwise, my child?"

"Oh! if you were sure; but——"

"But what? Wherefore do you hesitate? Who has led you to suppose that such will not be the case?"

"The commandant, Balfour! He tells me that you are to be tried as a fugitive from justice—as a——"

"As a what, my child? Speak fearlessly."

With choking accents, she answered—"As a traitor and a spy?"

"Ha!"

Walton's brows were clouded for a moment, but he shook off the sudden feeling which had oppressed him, and answered:

"It was base and unmanly that he should seek to alarm you thus! He has some vicious purpose in it. Even were it true, my child, which it can not be, he should have said nothing of the sort *to you*. He should have felt how cruel was such a statement to a woman and a child."

"No, no! If it be true, my father, I thank him that he has told me all. Better that I should hear the whole danger at the outset. But you tell me that it is not true. You are sure? You know? Do not *you* deceive me, my father. Let me know all the danger, that we may labor in season to save you from these people."

"And what can you do, my daughter?"

"Oh! much can be done in all dangers, by love and courage. Devotion, armed with a resolute will, can move the mountain. We are feeble, I know; I know that I am good for little; but you have friends here. There are wise and virtuous citizens here, busy always day and night, in planning measures for the rescue of the country. What they can do for you I can not say; but they will strive to serve you, I am certain. Do not deceive me, therefore; do not suffer me to remain in blind ignorance of the truth until the bolt falls, and it is too late to save you."

"Be of good cheer, Kate. Dismiss these apprehensions. I have heard nothing yet which should lead me to apprehend that Balfour really designs what you mention. I suspect that he only aimed to impress upon you the great value of his favor, in permitting you to visit me. There is no denying that the British authorities have a sufficient pretext for bringing me to trial; but there would be no policy in doing so. They would gain nothing by it but discredit to their cause. I see no room for fears at present; of one thing, Kate, be sure, that should I ever feel that I stand in danger, you shall be the first to know it."

"Oh! thanks for that, my father. Do not underrate my strength for endurance. Believe me, I can die with you if I can not save you."

The father pressed her to his bosom.

"You are the same noble, fearless, loving child, my Kate, that I have ever known you. Believe me, I do not feel or fear the danger that you speak of; yet I do not doubt or deny that, if the policy of the British authorities lay in putting me on trial for my life—nay, putting me summarily to death—at this moment—there would be sufficient pretext, and no law of right or reason would be respected by them. But their policy, at present, is forbearance, toleration, and a mild government. Revenge or cruelty would only embitter the public feeling, and arouse a spirit in the country such as they could never hope to allay. Enough now, my child, on this subject. Have you heard anything lately from Robert?"

She told him the history of the *ruse de guerre* by which Lieutenant Meadows had been defeated by the *soi-disant* loyalist, Furness; at which he laughed heartily.

"But, of course, you keep this to yourself, my child. I presume it is known to you only. Furness did not appear in the business, except as a loyalist, and if I know Robert Singleton truly, he will not abandon a character so long as it will serve a good purpose. We shall hear more of this Furness, be certain. You have not heard directly from Robert since you parted with him at the 'The Oaks?' "

"*Of* him, but not *from* him. We were told——"

"Hush! some one approaches."

It was the officer on duty. The evening had closed in, and the time had come for Katharine's departure. She would have lingered—she clung to her father's neck with a renewal of her tears, and it was with some effort that he put her away. When the officer reappeared at the entrance, she met him with dried eyes and a calm exterior, which greatly astonished him. An hour after her departure, Colonel Walton was honored with another, but less welcome visiter. This was Balfour.

"Colonel Walton," said the intruder, in mild and gravely sympathizing accents, "I am truly sorry to find you in this situation."

"As the sentiment honors your magnanimity, Colonel Balfour, at the cost of your policy, I am bound to give you credit for sincerity. I certainly find it irksome enough just now, to be a captive; but it is the fortune of war; it is one of the incidents of our profession, and not the worst."

"But, my regret, Colonel Walton, has its source in the peculiar condition which you occupy as a prisoner. You can not be insensible to the fact that his majesty's government regards you in quite another character than that of mere prisoner-of-war."

"Indeed, sir; well!"

"When rescued at Dorchester, you were under sentence of death. That sentence has never been revoked."

"But was that the sentence of a proper tribunal, Colonel Balfour? Was it not a denial of the right which I had to a proper trial by my peers? Was it not the exercise, by Lord Cornwallis, of a despotic will, in which he sacrificed law and justice to arbitrary authority?"

"I have no right to discuss this question with you. His majesty's officers here are not prepared to oppose their superiors in matters in which the responsibility is theirs alone. It is the expressed opinion of Lord Rawdon, for example, that all that is necessary, is to indentify your person, and immediately carry out the sentence of Lord Cornwallis."

"I am truly obliged to his lordship, Colonel Balfour. He does not mince matters with us poor provincials. Well, sir, am I to understand that you concur with him? That you are prepared to carry out his opinion into performance? If so, sir, I have but to spare you the trouble of all investigation, by assuring you that I am the real Richard Walton, colonel in the state line of South Carolina militia."

"It is my wish, Colonel Walton, to save you. It is therefore that I am reluctant to recognise the opinion of Lord Rawdon. I should much prefer an investigation—that you should have a regular trial, as if no decree from Earl Cornwallis had gone forth; in fact, sir, I am anxious to give you time, that you may reconcile yourself to his majesty's government, and make your peace with the powers you have so grievously offended. They are not vindictive, and, in the case of one whose private character they have so much reason to respect, they would prefer to be indulgent."

"No doubt of it, sir; no doubt. Hitherto, they have proved their indulgence in a thousand cases, as well known to you, sir, as to me. Was it an instance of this regard to our sensibilities,

Colonel Balfour, that you should deliberately communicate to my daughter the peril in which her father stood—that you should speak of me as a fugitive and spy, and point, as it were, to the ignominious gallows in which I was to be justified as such?"

The face of Balfour paled at this address. His heart and eyes sank together under the stern questioning of Walton. He spoke stammeringly—

"I had to excuse my reluctance, sir, at suffering her to visit you in prison."

"And whence this reluctance? Suppose me the condemned criminal, convict, and doomed to the fatal tree; even in such case what ground would there be for refusing the visits of a child to a parent. At such a time, and under such circumstances, she had an especial claim to make them, if, indeed, you recognise humanity as having a claim at all."

"But, Colonel Walton, you do not know the circumstances; you do not know that there are traitors in this city—an organized conspiracy, including wealth and numbers, who are forever plotting against the peace of his majesty's government."

"In spite of all its indulgences and humanities!"

"Yes, sir; in spite of all! These conspirators would like nothing so well as your extrication from bonds."

"I should be grateful to them for it."

"No doubt, sir; and what would be my answer to his majesty's government, if, knowing these things, and knowing how many women are concerned among these conspirators, I afforded them such facilities of communicating with you, through your daughter, as to enable you to make your escape?"

"A subtle difficulty, Colonel Balfour, but the plea is without substance. All captives will desire to escape from captivity, and all true friends will help them to do so. It is for the jailer to see that they do not succeed; not, sir, by a denial to humanity of what it may justly claim, but by vigilance that never sleeps or tires. Sir—Colonel Balfour, you have done a very cruel thing in speaking to my daughter as you have done."

Balfour by this time had recovered his native effrontery. He felt his power, and was disposed to assert it. The tone of superiority which Walton employed annoyed his *amour propre*, and he answered somewhat pettishly—

"I am willing to think, Colonel Walton, that I may have erred. I certainly have no desire to object that *you* should think so. The error, however, must be imputed to the head only. I had no desire to make Miss Walton unhappy."

"Let us say no more of it, Colonel Balfour."

The lofty manner in which this was spoken had in it an appearance of disgust which increased Balfour's irritation. He was doubly vexed that, resist it as he would, he felt his resolution quite unseated in the conference with his prisoner. It was with something of desperation, therefore, that he proceeded to resume the conversation, taking a higher attitude than before; in fact, determined on making Walton fully feel and (as he hoped) fear his situation.

"Colonel Walton," he said, "I must tell you that you do not pursue the right course to make friends. This tone of yours will never answer. Here you are in our hands, a prisoner. By the decree of our highest local authority your life is forfeited. You are a recovered fugitive from our justice. You are told what is said of our power, having identified you, to subject you, *instanter*, to the doom of death, from which you were once so fortunate as to escape. Yet you take a tone of defiance which rejects the help of those who would befriend you, alleviate your situation, and, perhaps, help you to elude its dangers. Is it wise, sir, or prudent, that you should act thus?"

"Colonel Balfour, I take for granted that you have some meaning when you speak thus. You mean to convey to my mind, in the first place, that you yourself are friendlily disposed to me."

"Undoubtedly, sir; you are right."

"Well, sir, a profession of this kind from you, sir, in your position, to a person in my circumstances, would seem to say that something may be done—that, in fact, my case is not entirely desperate."

"I certainly mean to convey that idea."

"Well, sir, now that we understand each other on this point, may I ask in what manner you propose to exercise this friendly feeling toward me ! Clearly, Colonel Balfour, my object is to escape from captivity and death, if I may do so. That I am legitimately a prisoner, I admit ; but only a prisoner-of-war. That I am lawfully doomed to die, I deny ; yet I do not profess to think myself safe because I am innocent. I frankly tell you, sir, that I do not doubt the perfect coolness and indifference with which the present authorities of the country will commit a great crime, if it shall seem proper to their policy to do so. I am perfectly willing to deprive them of any excuse for the commission of this crime, in my case, if you will show me how it is to be done ; and if, in its performance, I am required to yield nothing of self-respect and honor—"

" Oh ! surely, Colonel Walton, I am bound to do so. I would not, for the world, counsel you to anything at all inconsistent with either. I have too high a respect for your name and character—too warm an admiration for your daughter——"

" Ah !—"

" Yes, sir, for your daughter, whom I esteem as one of the most amiable and accomplished, as she is one of the most beautiful women I have ever seen."

" I thank you, Colonel Balfour, but I, who know my daughter well, can readily dispense with this elogium upon her."

Balfour bit his lips, replying peevishly—

" Colonel Walton, you carry it quite too proudly. I would be your friend, sir—would really like to serve you.—"

" Well, sir ;—proceed—proceed !"

" Thus, then, Colonel Walton—having endeavored to show you perfectly your situation, and the danger in which you stand, I declare myself friendlily disposed, and willing to assist you. Your case is a bad, but not exactly a desperate one ; that is to say, it may be in the power of some persons, so to interpose between the justly-aroused anger of our sovereign, and the victim, as to save him from his punishment."

" In other words, sir, you, Colonel Balfour, can exercise a sufficient influence with Lord Cornwallis to relieve me from his sentence."

" Precisely, my dear colonel ; that is exactly the point. I may venture to affirm that, besides myself, and possibly Lord

Rawdon, there is no other man or set of men, in South Carolina, to whom this thing is possible."

" I think it very likely."

" And I am disposed, Colonel Walton, to use this influence in your behalf."

" I am very much obliged to you, Colonel Balfour, as I have said ; I think it very probable that you may interpose, as you have said, successfully, for my safety, and that no other person that I know, is likely to do so. But, sir, you will suffer me to say, that I am too well aware that I have no personal claim upon you for the exercise of this act of friendship. I certainly can not claim it on the score of former sympathies, or even by a reference to your recognition of my individual claims as a man of worth and character."

Balfour winced at this. He felt the latent sarcasm. Walton proceeded :—

" It is clear, therefore, that I can not expect you thus to serve me, without some special acknowledgments. There must be a consideration for this. The *quid pro quo*, I understand, is not to be overlooked in anything that may be determined upon."

" Really, Colonel Walton, you relieve me very much," answered Balfour. " As you say, you have no personal or particular claims upon me, except, generally, as a man of worth. There have been no previous relations of friendship existing between us. If, therefore, I am moved to serve you, it must evidently be in consequence of certain considerations, personal to myself, which—ah !"

Here he faltered for a moment. The stern but calm eye of Walton was upon him. His own wavered beneath the glance ; but the recollection of the vantage ground which he held, restored his confidence, and he assumed a tone somewhat foreign to his spirit, when he resumed what he was saying.

" In short," said he, " Colonel Walton, I can save you from this danger, and I alone : and I will save you sir, upon one condition, and one only."

" Name it, Colonel Balfour," answered Walton calmly.

" Your daughter, sir, Miss Walton——"

" Ah !"

The brow of Walton grew clouded. The air of Balfour became more desperate, as he added—

" Yes, colonel, your daughter ! I acknowledge her virtues and her beauties. They have subdued a heart which has never yet trembled at the smile or power of woman. Sir — Colonel Walton, give me the hand of your daughter, in honorable marriage, and you are saved. I pledge my life upon it."

Walton started to his feet with a burst of indignation which he could not repress. He confronted the commandant with a stern visage, and a voice that trembled with passionate emotion.

" What, sir, do you see in me to suppose that I would sell my blood to save my life ! That I would put the child of my affections into bonds that I might break my own ! Colonel Balfour, your offer is an insult. You owe your safety to the fact that I am your prisoner !"

" You will repent this violence, Colonel Walton," said Balfour, rising, and almost white with rage. " You are trifling with your fate, sir. Be warned ! Once more I repeat the offer I have made you. Will you give me your daughter's hand in marriage, and escape your dangers ?"

" Never ! Let me rather die a thousand deaths ! Sell my child — yield her to such——"

" Beware, Colonel Walton ! You are on the precipice. A single word — a single breath, and you go over it !"

" Away ! sir ; away, and leave me !"

" Very well, sir ! if the daughter be no wiser than the father, look to it ! Your doom must be spoken by *her* lips, if not by your own. That is your only chance !"

Balfour gave the signal at the close of this speech, to the keeper of the door without, and as soon as it was opened to him, he rushed out with feelings of fury and mortified vanity, such as he had not often endured.

" He means to offer this alternative to my child — this dreadful alternative ! But no ! she shall never be made the sacrifice for me ! Richard Walton can not accept the boon of life, however precious, at the peril of his child's peace, and to the ruin of her best affections !"

Such was the stern resolution of Walton, spoken aloud, after

Balfour had retired. He felt that his peril had greatly increased in consequence of the passion which the latter declared for his daughter. He now well understood his game. The danger lay in the bad character of the commandant, and the general irresponsibility of the British power, at present in the state, the recklessness of its insolence, and the conviction which its representatives generally felt, however blindly, that there was no fear to be entertained that they were destined to any reverses. Walton's mind promptly grasped all the circumstances in his case, and he deceived himself in no respect with regard to the extremity of his danger; but the result only found him more resolute in the determination he had formed so promptly, to perish a thousand times rather than suffer his daughter to make such a cruel sacrifice as that which was required as the price of his deliverance.

CHAPTER XLV.

ULTIMATUM.

WHEN, the next day, Katharine Walton presented herself in her father's dungeon, he had reached the course which he had resolved to pursue by which to defeat the desires of Balfour.

"Kate, my child," said the father, as he pressed her affectionately to his bosom, "there is a matter upon which I must speak with you in advance of all others. You are engaged, I know, to Robert Singleton. But ties of this sort, unless the heart really furnishes the cement between the parties, are perhaps better broken than maintained."

"Broken, father! You surely would not have me break faith with Robert!"

"By no means, my child, if you really feel that you love him beyond all other men, and if your confidence in his judgment and honor be such as to enable you to repose with perfect reliance upon his bosom. It is this very question which I desire to urge. Are you as quite satisfied this hour with the engagement made to Robert as in the hour when you first consented to it? Is there no falling off of faith — no coldness, no indifference, no distrust between you?"

"None, father. But wherefore do you ask? Surely, you do not hold me so fickle as to—"

"No! no! Kate, my precious! I have no such suspicions; and your answer, as it concerns yourself, is perfectly conclusive. And now tell me of Robert. Are you quite satisfied with him? Is he still, so far as you know, as faithful, as devoted to you as you feel yourself to him? Have you no neglect, no coldness to complain of? Does he still appear to you the man of honor, of character, and of high sentiment that we have hitherto always thought him?"

"I have never once fancied that *he could* change, my father. Robert has always been, to my mind, the ideal of a noble and faithful gentleman."

"Enough, then, on that subject. My opinion and estimate of Robert Singleton have long been the same as yours. Your feelings remain the same as ever: your engagement must be equally obligatory. And now, Kate, assure me on your sacred word—nay, I must have it on the sacred volume, my child—that, while Robert Singleton lives and continues true to his pledges, you will never wed with any other man!"

"Say this—*swear* to this, my father! Oh, how can it need that I should do so? Can you, indeed, require that I should take such an oath?"

"Kate, my child, I am but taking a precaution against events. There are some things which, as yet, you do not know, and which I shall be the last person to unfold to you. I do not doubt your affections, my child, or your principles; but I see certain contingencies ahead, which, but for the support I desire to give you by the oath which I now propose to administer, might find you feeble, and seem to force you to a faithlessness which your own heart would abhor. You might find it necessary to rupture your ties with Robert, and, perhaps, give your hand to another person."

"Never! never! Oh, my father, how can you so think of me? What contingencies can possibly occur to make me so base and so faithless to Robert!—so false to my own heart as well as pledges?"

"As I have said, Kate, I foresee that which you do not suspect. I foresee trials of which you have no fears. I do not question your faith, your love, your sense of duty, your principles. Your truth is one of the most precious convictions in my heart. But I distrust your *strength* under certain circumstances, and would wish to give it succor at the moment of your trial. The process for doing so is the one that I have resolved upon. Do not you doubt me, my child, or question if I have sufficient

18*

reason for what I do. If still devoted to Robert Singleton, preferring him to all the world of men, and still confident of his integrity and nobleness, it can not give you pain to renew to me, in the most solemn manner, in his behalf, the pledges already made to him. Submit to me, my child, and believe me that there *are* necessities for this proceeding of which I may not speak to you. This Bible which you have brought me is your dear mother's. She has kissed it a thousand times. Take it to your own lips while I adjure *you*, and you promise me, that, so long as Robert Singleton lives and without loss of character, you will wed no other man, no matter what events may happen to make it appear politic to do so; though death, though danger, though wrong, contumely, and murder even, should threaten yourself and others most dear and precious to you! Swear to me, my child, and remember all my words, for there may come a moment when you may discover that the very meanest of them has a value. Will you not do for me what I require, my child?—what I entreat?"

The maiden took the sacred volume in her hands. She looked bewildered and confused; but she spoke—

"I will do as you require, my father. I should be wretched, however, to suppose that you doubt my faith, and deem it necessary thus to make it steadfast."

"I do not doubt your faith; but you little dream in what manner it is to be assailed. I would really seek to strengthen *myself* in the conviction that nothing which may happen shall prevail to separate you and your cousin."

"And nothing shall, my father, while Robert remains faithful to his pledges. I will take the oath which you propose. It is sworn. I have pressed my lips on pages which my dear mother has made doubly sacred by the frequent pressure of hers. I solemnly vow that no other man shall have the hand which I have given to Robert Singleton."

"I am satisfied, my child. You have relieved me of a dreadful apprehension. But of this I must say nothing. I will not shock your ears by a revelation which I fear that you will be compelled to hear from less scrupulous lips. Be firm in what you have promised, for you are destined to be terribly tried.

And remember that, whatever may happen, your mother and your father, the one a pure spirit, the other a still suffering mortal, are the witnesses of a pledge that they will both expect you to redeem with all your heart, with all your soul, and with all your strength."

We need not linger now with our captive in his dungeon. Throughout the long day it was relieved of its gloom, if not made cheerful, by the fond and unwearied attentions of his daughter. Her food was brought her also in his prison, and it was only at nightfall, when required to depart, that she consented to tear herself away. She returned to her home that evening to gather, for the first time, an inkling of the purpose of her father in the solemn requisition which he had made upon her.

Scarcely had the tea-service of Mrs. Singleton been removed, when Colonel Balfour was announced. He was promptly conducted to the parlor, when he desired the servant to say that his visit was made to Miss Walton. Katharine did not long delay in presenting herself.

Balfour was profound in his courtesies. He rose at her entrance, conducted her to the sofa, and seated himself beside her. We dismiss, without notice, the preliminaries, the civil inquiries after her own and the health of other parties, his remarks upon her good looks, and all those usual phrases with which the veteran politician would naturally strive to qualify the effect of more annoying matter. Balfour's hardihood was too great, however, his anxieties too urgent, his consciousness of power too complete, to allow of much delay in approaching the more serious object of his visit.

"Miss Walton," said he, after finishing his prefaces, "I surely need not now inform you that, since I have known you, I have entertained the warmest sympathy for you, and the most earnest desire to see you happy."

The face of Katharine wore its most vacant expression, yet she steadily met his glance. He continued —

"You will do me the justice to admit that, from the moment of your arrival in this city — since, in other words, you have become a ward of the crown — you have been honored with the most respectful attentions. Your health, happiness, and comfort, have been equally cared for, and your slightest wishes considered, where these did not conflict with the rights of his majesty."

"Colonel Balfour, I do not know what is the nature of the acknowledgment which you desire to extort from me by this speech. It may be enough, perhaps, to say that I have no complaint to offer. I do not acknowledge that my happiness or desires have been at all an object of the solicitude of his majesty's government, as these can not well be consulted in a condition of captivity such as mine."

"Captivity, Miss Walton! Surely not!"

"Surely yes! I regard my situation as one of captivity, the severity of which has been modified only with reference to my sex. Were it left to me, sir, the mountains of North Carolina or Virginia should environ me, rather than the walls of a British garrison."

"I am sorry to hear you speak thus, Miss Walton. I had hoped that the kindness with which you have been welcomed everywhere in Charleston, the respectful devotion of all in garrison, the indulgence—"

"No more, Colonel Balfour. Is it not enough to say that I have no complaints? I utter no reproaches."

"No, Miss Walton; let me say that this is not enough, when it is remembered how small was the claim upon his majesty's indulgence which could be urged by any of your name, or any of your connections. We find them all against us, all hostile in sentiment, and most of them in arms against their legitimate sovereign."

"I am willing to admit all these alleged offences, Colonel Balfour; but whither do your charges tend? I am your captive —my father is in your bonds. Our humiliations have kept pace with our supposed offences. What farther admission would you have me make?"

"Your father's situation, Miss Walton, should surely convince you of our power."

"It is not denied. We are *in* your power."

"We! You! I would it were so! We shall see. Your father *is;* and you must be sensible in what danger. I have spoken of this matter already."

" Yes, Colonel Balfour, you have; and I trust that it is not for the renewal of that communication that you seek me now. I can not believe that, in your calmer and cooler moments, you mean to urge so cruel a subject."

" But if it be true? If it be that your father is in peril of his life—is—"

" It is not true! It can not be true! I can not doubt that there is humanity enough in the British authorities in this state —magnanimity, perhaps, I should say—to arrest all such murderous purposes, such as you yesterday expressed."

Balfour shook his head.

" Suppose I tell you, Miss Walton, that you hope against hope? Are you prepared to listen to the whole truth, and without looking with hate and horror on him who speaks it?"

" I know not, sir!—I know not! But, at all events, speak the truth, the whole truth, whatever be the consequences. Have no fears for me. If what you propose to tell me be the truth, it is just as well that *you* should declare it as another. Only let it be *the truth* that you speak, and without any such exaggerations of its mischievous import as the *very generous* of your sex too frequently employ when they would impress the fancies or the fears of ours. If the truth is to be borne, I must bear it and prepare for it as I may."

" You are sarcastic, Miss Walton—very bitter—"

" Bitter, you say! Certainly a very unnatural savor in the case of one with such a prospect of sweets before her."

" The prospect is dark enough, I grant you; but not without its light. If I show you the threatening tempest, it is possible that I may also show you the blue sky and the harbor of refuge beyond. Be patient with me, I entreat you, while I do so. I have to speak of gloomy and terrible things; but you shall see that I can point you out the little gleam of light which comes up out of the darkness. What I said to you yesterday was quite true. Your father has nothing to hope but from the mercy of his majesty's representatives in Carolina. He is a doomed man, as he himself must feel; one who, whether justly or unjustly, is sentenced to a forfeiture of life. That sentence might, from the nature of the case, be carried into effect by any British officer who found himself in the possession of Colonel Walton's person. He is in *my* possession. I hold this authority to execute the decree of Lord Cornwallis; and what prevails to prevent that I should do so ?"

"You will prevent ?"

"Ah! You shall hear yet further. We regard these states of Carolina and Georgia as already conquered. Your continentals are even now flying before Cornwallis in Virginia, and Rawdon holds undisputed authority within the interior. Marion, and Sumter, with their ragged followers, will soon share the fate of your father's command. The southern states will all fall into our hands one by one. The New England states no longer supply the armies of Washington and his generals. From the moment that the war was withdrawn from their barren domain, they abandoned the contest. The destruction of a French fleet will effectually cut of another of the allies of rebellion; and your states of the south will perish under the natural exhaustion which is sure to follow from such an unequal conflict. It is mere desperation to hope that anything can be done for saving those states of which we have possession. The struggles of your father and such men are simply suicidal."

"You will not convince *him* of that."

"That is *his* misfortune. But we must bring him to this conviction, as one of the means of saving him. We must persuade him to renounce the conflict and accept the mercy of his majesty."

Katharine shook her head mournfully.

"He will never prove false to his country."

"We shall not ask him to take up arms. We shall simply require him to lay them down, and resume the neutral attitude which he kept until, in evil hour, beguiled to take the field at Camden."

"And if he consents — should we persuade him to this."

"Something then will have been gained toward restoring him to the favor of his majesty; and, upon certain other conditions being complied with, I think I might venture to say that his mercy —"

"Ah, there are other conditions !"

" Yes, Miss Walton ; but such as, I trust, will not be found too difficult for compliance. In fact, my dear Miss Walton, the rest will depend on yourself."

" On me, sir !" with unfeigned astonishment.

" Yes, on you, and you wholly ! The fact is, my dear Miss Walton—I need not perhaps, tell you that, to my discretion, Sir Henry Clinton has confided the whole government of affairs in this section. Mine is the power to bind and loose, to save or execute. The life of your father is in my hands. My voice, my will, can save him ; and the question is, what shall be the influence by which I am to be moved to exert this voice and will ?"

" Oh, sir !—Colonel Balfour—humanity alone—"

" Won't do for me ! I confess to being a rather selfish man ; and when I see before me a great treasure, which I fondly believe I may attain through the exercise or the forbearance of the power I possess, of life or death, I tell you frankly that my selfishness rejects all minor considerations, and insists wholly on the treasure for which it thirsts. Do you not understand me ?"

" I confess, sir, I do not."

" My dear Miss Walton, you have already heard me declare the admiration which I felt for you, and the passion which sought you as its first and only object. You have treated this passion with scorn, unwisely ; for I am not the man to suffer tamely. I gladly forget your scorn. I renew my vows of devotion. Once more I fling myself at your feet."

And the action was suited to the word.

" Rise, sir—rise, Colonel Balfour ! I can not suffer this !"

Katharine herself rose ; but he seized her hand.

" Nay, my dear Miss Walton, it is thus that you *must* hear me —that I *must* make my confession, and declare the love that I feel for you, and the desire that I cherish to make you mine !"

" Rise, sir ! It is impossible !"

He rose, reluctantly.

" Nay, do not say impossible. Do not be rash. Remember all the circumstances in your condition. You must feel the necessity of finding friends at this juncture—of finding such a friend as myself; one who has the power to destroy; but who may be persuaded to spare and save. Believe me, you have but to say the word, and all the power I possess shall be subject to your will."

"You do but try me, Colonel Balfour. I can not believe so harshly of you as to suppose that you will make a father's life depend upon a daughter's favor. You say you have the power to save him. I believe it. I rely upon you—your sense of justice, your humanity, the obligations that you owe to the people over whom you rule, the policy which becomes the sovereign that you represent. You will not outrage all of these by an extreme exercise of power—by the cruel murder of a noble gentleman, from whom his enemies always found humanity and mercy."

"You plead eloquently, my dear Miss Walton, but the selfishness of my passion will not allow me to listen to your plea. I love you too earnestly not to take every advantage of the circumstances in which you are placed. I can not afford to be magnanimous. I see before me a treasure, the loveliest and most precious that ever blessed mortal eyes, or was intrusted to mortal keeping; and I feel that by the exercise of a certain resolution, that treasure *must* be mine. I can not venture to be generous. I can not fling away, perhaps, the only hope upon which I build for the attainment of this treasure. You must be mine, Katharine Walton, if not through the love you bear to me, through that which you bear your father."

"Oh! Colonel Balfour, this is terrible—it is cruel, it is unmanly—and when you know that it is impossible——"

"I know nothing of the sort! Nay, Katharine Walton, let me tell you freely, I know that there is nothing impossible in a situation like yours. Your father's life hangs upon a thread, as fine, as easily sundered as that by which the spider hangs against the wall. You love your father—I know how precious is the tie between you. Will *yours* be the hand to smite that thread which is his only hold upon life? Will yours be the stern voice which dooms him to a premature and shameful death?"

"No more, Colonel Balfour! You have no right to torture me thus! I will carry the tidings of this wanton cruelty, this profligacy and tyranny, this equal abuse of power and humanity, to Lord Cornwallis, to Sir Henry Clinton, to the foot of the throne itself! and you shall feel and be made to tremble, in your turn, at a power to which all that you may boast is but a breath, an echo, without either strength or substance. Release my father from this danger, consent to his exchange with some loyalist captive of his own rank, or I expose you to your own superiors !"

" And is it thus, my lovely Katharine, that you defy me, and oppose your feeble strength to mine ? You will expose me to Cornwallis and Clinton—you will carry your plaint to the foot of the throne itself ! One would suppose, my fair enemy, that you Americans had already sufficiently experienced the unprof-itableness of petitions at the foot of the throne and elsewhere. Will you learn nothing from experience ? But why should I argue ? With the endeavor to convince ? The result must prove itself. Miss Walton, the case of your father will undergo investigation within the next three days. When the decision of the court is made, I shall again seek you. Meanwhile, let me commend you to a calmer view of the whole subject. Katharine Walton, you can only escape me at the peril of the loss of all that you most value. On the word of a soldier and a man, your father's life hangs entirely upon your speech."

" You are neither a soldier nor a man, sir, to speak to me in such language. Go, sir; I will not believe you! I will not suffer myself to think that the British authorities will so trample upon all that is precious in humanity, in order that the passions of one bad man shall triumph."

Balfour smiled bitterly.

" You will recall these words. You will repent that you have spoken them. When you rest in my arms, as my lawful wed-ded wife, Katharine, you will blush for these reproaches, and ask yourself with wonder, how was it that you should have de-nied soldiership and manhood to your lord; how you should have applied the epithet of *base* to one whose name you bear."

Katharine rose to her full height.

" Enough, sir; I have no more epithets for you! May I hope that you will leave me now ?"

This was spoken with a rare mildness of tone and manner. It impressed her visiter. His accents were changed and apologetic.

"You provoke me unreasonably, Miss Walton, and mine is a temper not too placable. It would always yield to you. I will not trespass longer. You have heard me. What I have said is earnestly and truly said. The facts are all as I have stated them. The danger is precisely what I have shown it. The remedy, I repeat, is in your own hands. Think upon it calmly, for you may be assured of this, that I have declared the only conditions upon which your father's safety depends; and, as I live, I will relax in nothing of what I ask! I love you too passionately to forego a resolution through which only may I hope to bend your stubborn heart to my desires."

With these words he left her, miserable enough.

"This, then, was the secret of my father's purpose. Can it be that this base, bad man revealed to him his cruel calculations? But, he dare not—he dare not! Rawdon would not suffer it, nor Cornwallis, nor Clinton. I have but to declare the facts in this interview to shame him before the world."

Poor Katharine—she little fancied how little responsibility the world feels in such matters—how quietly it submits to the wrong-doing that trespasses not upon its individual limbs or pockets. Still less did Katharine, in her rare simplicity of heart, comprehend the degree of independence enjoyed by British officers when three thousand miles from the throne, or how intimate was the alliance between these worthy agents in Carolina when victims were to be chosen and spoils were to be appropriated.

CHAPTER XLVI.

DUELLO.

EVENTS began to move with unwonted rapidity among all parties in Charleston. Proceedings were initiated against Colonel Walton as a rebel and a spy, and a court of inquiry was designated for an early investigation of his case. Similar proceedings, under charges which were studiously rendered vague, were also appointed for the consideration of another court, soon to be convened, in regard to the case of Major Proctor. He remained still under a nominal arrest only; a forbearance due chiefly to the desire of Balfour to conciliate Cruden and save appearances. But the wily commandant only waited the moment when his game was quite sure, to convert the nominal into an actual arrest, made certain with bolts and fetters.

In the meanwhile, the patriots and friends of Walton were busy, day and night, in studying how to meet his danger, or effect his deliverance. Meetings took place nightly at old Tom Singleton's, and other places. But the consultations of the conspirators only showed them their weakness; and at length, their whole hope of rescuing Walton was based upon a plan for corrupting the keepers of his person. In this work, Mrs. Brewton took an active part, and made the greatest progress of any of her associates. Between herself and Tom Singleton two of the guards were bribed; but these successes proved delusive, the corrupted parties being removed the very night after they had sold themselves.

The game had to be begun anew, and with increased caution. It was evident that the vigilant eyes of Balfour were upon all

their movements, and the zeal and activity of Mr. Brewton soon
drew down upon her the especial attentions of the commandant.
She was congratulating herself one morning upon the considerable progress which she had made in the favor of a British
sergeant, in whom the officers placed considerable confidence,
when she was surprised by a visit from Balfour. He was
smiling and very courteous, and these, with him, were always
suspicious appearances. He did not leave her long in doubt as
to his purpose.

"My dear Mrs. Brewton," said he, "I am sorry to perceive
that the atmosphere of Charleston does not quite agree with you
this season. Everybody remarks how much flesh and color you
have lost within a month. My anxiety in your behalf makes
me resolute that you shall change the air. I have brought you
a passport, accordingly, giving you permission to retire to the
country, whither you will please depart within the next twenty-
four hours. You had better go to the Congarees—anywhere not
within eighty miles of the city."

The beautiful widow, for once, was overwhelmed.

"What do you fear?" she at length demanded, impetuously.

"Your health, your beauty, your spirits, all of which are in
peril while you remain here."

She would have expostulated and argued, even promised and
pleaded, for she was willing, at this moment, to submit to some
sacrifices, to make some concessions of pride and spirit, but in
vain! The petty tyrant was not to be moved, and, with a
Parthian arrow, she prepared for her departure.

"I could have looked for nothing less from such as you. The
want of gallantry and grace is always the sure sign of an equal
want of character and courage. Colonel Balfour, I am encouraged by your fears, since these alone expel me from your garrison. Well, sir, the fortress which thus apprehends danger
from a woman must surely first have become conscious of the
worthlessness of its men."

"Ah! madam, you will then give me no credit for the sympathy and care which are thus mindful of your health. We
shall greatly miss you from the garrison, but shall find consola-

tion in the fact that when you come back to us, you will have
recovered all your bloom and beauty. Good morning! An
escort shall attend you to the 'Four-mile House.'"

Her departure was a loss to our conspirators, and somewhat
discouraged their hopes and efforts. Several of them, that
night, were assembled in consultation at old Tom Singleton's
when Proctor suddenly presented himself. Singleton received
him alone, in an upper apartment, and did not now take him
down to the vaulted chamber whither we accompanied him on a
previous occasion. The old man received him hurriedly, and
reviewed his case with some abruptness. Proctor had seen him
repeatedly, we may here mention, in interviews which we have
not been required to report. The two spoke, accordingly, with
reference to foregone conclusions, which the reader must take
for granted.

"Prior," said Singleton, "has done all that he could for you.
I have the affidavits which he has procured, and the witnesses
are all forthcoming. But, from all that I can see and hear, Major Proctor, they will avail you nothing. It is evident to me
that Balfour means to destroy you, and he is well seconded by
that insidious scoundrel, Vaughan. What they alleged against
you in the affair of Dorchester, might be met and refuted, were
that alone the difficulty; — but your capture by Walton, the unhappy combination of circumstances which marked your detention, the evidence of Williamson and of your servant John, all
together, persuade me that you can do nothing better than make
your way from the garrison, and cover yourself amòng the
mountains of North Carolina."

"What! sir, and not face the enemy—not stand this trial?"

"By no means."

"Impossible! my honor!——"

"Can not counsel you to surrender yourself, bound hand and
foot, into the hands of your enemy."

Proctor shook his head mournfully, and being provided by
Singleton with the papers for which he came, and finding the
manner of the latter rather hurried and impatient, he prepared
to take his departure; but, before he could do so, both parties
were suddenly surprised by the appearance, even as the door

was unclosing for the egress of Proctor, of his supposed loyalist acquaintance, Furness.

Proctor was really rejoiced to see him, and old Singleton disquieted. A squeeze of the hand with the latter, and a word or two, as it were, to remind him that he was *young* Furness, son of *old* Furness, whom he ought to know so well, and the partisan turned away with Proctor, saying to Singleton that he would see him again within the hour. The old man replied, gruffly —

"Better see your friend out of the city, and take care, both of you, that no one sees your backs unless beyond cannon distance."

With these words, he closed the door upon them, and returned to his guests in the cellar.

Furness, or rather Singleton, soon told his story to Proctor, as he had, within two hours, told it to Balfour. He professed to have been taken by Marion's men at the defeat of Lieutenant Meadows' escort, and had just succeeded in making his escape from captivity.

Such was the substance of his narrative. Of course, he revealed as little as possible to his companion, being more anxious to hear him speak than to say anything himself. The details given by Proctor, in answer to his inquiries, unfolded fully the condition of affairs in the city, his own approaching trial, with that of Colonel Walton, and the charges brought against both. Singleton soon gathered from the statement, in Proctor's own case, that he stood in an attitude of serious danger. He did not hesitate to give him the same counsel which had been given by old Tom Singleton. Proctor was unwilling to see the matter in so gloomy a light; but was evidently deeply oppressed by what he heard.

"In a few days," said Singleton, "I hope to leave for the mountains myself, as soon as I shall have procured some new supplies from the commandant; and if you will only steal away before that time, and meet me on the road, we can find a safe tetreat for you until you can be sure of a proper tribunal and honest judges. Think of this matter to-night, and do not deceive yourself. There is evidently a secret and strong purpose, on the part of Balfour, to destroy you; and, unfortunately, circumstances have given him all the advantage in the game. I will see you soon to-morrow—nay, if you will give me a part of your bed, I will sleep with you to-night, for, as yet, I have sought no quarters."

"Gladly," was the reply; and Proctor gave him instructions where to find him. They separated, and Singleton immediately hurried back to his kinsman. He conferred with him for ten or fifteen minutes, heard all that had been done, and all that was doing, and then proceeded to see Katharine, whom he yet dreaded to encounter. She threw her arms about his neck as she recognised him, and exclaimed—

"O, Robert! you peril everything for me—for him! Tell me, can you save him again?"

"I have come to see and try, Katharine. God alone knows yet what we may achieve. As yet, I know but little of his condition and his dangers. Sit, dearest, and you shall tell me all."

She did so—all that she knew, felt, and feared. Mrs. Singleton did the same. Our partisan shuddered as he beheld the prospect. It was no longer one in which a troop of desperate horsemen could achieve deliverance. But he did not suffer his gravity to appear conspicuous.

"Cheer up," said he. "It is a sad affair; but I have struggled through worse. We must not despond, since that will make us feeble. I must hurry off at once, and see Uncle Tom again. I must learn some other particulars before I can hope to do anything. I will try to see you in the morning; but must move cautiously. You remember that I am still Captain Furness, of the loyalists."

This, for the time, ended their conference; and the indefatigable partisan hurried off once more to see his ancient kinsman. We need not ask what subjects they discussed, as, for the time, the discussion was without result. Enough, that the more our partisan became aware of the true nature of the case in the affair of Walton, the more did its dangers loom out upon his imagination. When old Singleton apprized him of the terms offered by Balfour for the safety of Walton, he was stricken as with a bullet. These had been suppressed by Kate.

"Can it be true!" he exclaimed, when he recovered speech. "Then, if we fail to rescue him, Katharine will consent."

"Never!" cried the old man, fiercely.

"She *must!* She can not avoid it!" was the mournful reply of Robert Singleton. "I shall deplore the necessity more than all, perhaps, but it will be a necessity, nevertheless."

When told of the oath prescribed by Walton to his daughter, he exclaimed—

"Ah, the same magnanimous spirit and true heart! But, should the last necessity occur, even that oath will not, and ought not to bind her."

"Would you have her marry that scoundrel?"

"She must save her father, even at that sacrifice!"

"Never!"

"Hush, sir! Hush! This is all idle."

We need not pursue the unprofitable dialogue. It was late when the parties separated; but Singleton, or Furness now, found Proctor waiting him with anxiety. They sat up late together, these young men, making their mutual revelations, and "chewing the cud of sweet and bitter thought." Our partisan continued to persuade his companion to a secret and swift departure from the city; but with no success.

"No!" was the reply of Proctor. "Though I perish, I will never, by such a flight, give countenance to the slander that assails my honor."

Early next morning, both of them were abroad. Soon after breakfast, Furness found his way to the presence of Balfour. We have already mentioned his communication with the latter the day before. It will suffice to say that he gave the commandant a full and satisfactory account of all his adventures, as a loyalist, from the moment when he set out with the escort of Meadows. Balfour had no complaints of Furness in this business. On the contrary, basing his judgment upon the favorable, but singularly mistaken, report of Meadows, he was pleased to bestow a high compliment upon the fidelity and desperate courage which the former had displayed. In fact, the loyalist captain was in a fair way to become a favorite with Balfour. The profound deference of the provincial was particularly grateful to the self-esteem of the puffed-up *parvenu*. He freely spoke to him of his own and public affairs, until, at length, the affair of Walton was brought upon the carpet. Having stated the full particulars of his case to a very attentive auditor, who found it exceedingly difficult to restrain the exhibitions of his emotion and keep them within the limits of simple curiosity, Balfour suddenly clapped Furness on the shoulder, exclaiming—

"By the way, captain, you are the very man to serve me in this business!"

"Anything that I can do, colonel?"

"You can do much. You shall visit Walton in the provost. You shall let him know how hopeless is the chance for rebellion in the back country. You shall report all the dangers of his case, and persuade him of the necessity of full submission. He doubts me—he distrusts me—and will doubt all the British officers; but one of his own people, who knows the interior, and can report truly how little he has to build on, will probably be listened to. The object is fully to alarm his fears and those of his daughter, and to reconcile him to such concessions as I shall require in return for his pardon. I am not successful in showing him these things. I provoke his anger, and become angry myself. Now, you shall see and show that I do not seek his life; but that I *will* use my power *and take it*, unless he consents to my demand! You will report to him also that to-morrow is appointed for his trial. Succeed in what I desire, Furness, and I am your friend for life. You are in the way of promotion."

Singleton had great difficulty in suppressing the shows of eagerness and joy, when told that he was to see Walton in his dungeon.

"I will do it, colonel! I will do what you require. That is, if I can; but I am afraid that Colonel Walton will be as little likely to listen to me, a loyalist, as to the British officers. Besides, I am—"

"Pooh! pooh! You distrust yourself, Captain Furness. You are only too modest. You have better abilities, my young friend, than you yourself suspect; but I have pierced your depths, and see what can be made of you. You will do this business well, I feel very certain. Here, let me write the order

19

for your admission to Walton. You will go to him to-night, after his daughter shall have left him, or to-morrow night—that will be better, when he shall have undergone his trial, and been made aware of his sentence. To-morrow evening dooms him to the gallows—you will insist upon the only measure by which to save him from it. Do you understand?"

"Perfectly. I will see him to-night and prepare him for the danger, and to-morrow, when what I have predicted shall have been realized, he will, perhaps, be better able to appreciate his situation."

"Meanwhile, I shall work upon the daughter. Do your part faithfully, and it is odds but we carry the game. But where are you lodging?"

"Nowhere, exactly. Last night, Major Proctor, whom I met at Dorchester, gave me a bed at his lodgings."

"Ha! Beware of him! He is a traitor!"

"He! Major Proctor!"

"What! You have not heard? He is about to be tried, also, for offences which will drive him from the army or hang him. Beware of him; but continue to lodge with him, if he will suffer you. You can keep an eye on him. Eh? You understand?"

"I do! I see! It shall be done!"

"What are you doing with yourself to-day? Nothing? Then drive out at twelve o'clock to Hampstead—the 'field of honor;' anybody will tell you where to find it. There is to be a duel to-day between two hot bloods of the garrison, about a lady's favors; Mad Archy Campbell, who captured Colonel Walton, a regular dare-devil, and Captain Harley, of the rifles, who is said to be a fire-eater. They fight with the small-sword. It will be a pretty passage, and you will be delighted. Your presence will be no objection. There will be several spectators."

"But do you suffer such affairs?"

"I do not *see* them. I hear of them only when all's over, and then arrive at nothing positive. I only see when I am not disposed to suffer them. In this case, there are reasons why I *should not* see. Do you go, and report to me the affair."

"I shall be there, colonel. I shall be pleased to see."

" Should the passage be a short one, drive round, after it, to Mrs. Rivington's, whose 'mornings' take place at 'one.' You will see everybody there. I have *carte blanche*, and you will find yourself at home there, at that hour, any day in the week."

Singleton gladly availed himself of Balfour's suggestion to see the duel. He rode out with Proctor, who procured for him a horse; our hero having made his appearance in the city without one. His precaution had stabled his own steed, with the horses of those of his best troopers, and in their keeping, within six miles of town, in a close thicket, not far from the Goose Creek road.

A score of spectators were already upon the ground. The spot chosen in that day for such purposes was but a little way beyond the lines of the garrison, amid a clump of mingling pines and oaks that covered a small headland on the banks of the Cooper. Hither soon came the two combatants, attended by several friends, a couple of assistants, and as many surgeons. Dueling was then as now, in the same region, a recognised social institution. But it was then an affair of *honor*, and not, as too frequently now, an affair of malice. The solicitude was the *point of honor* simply — to maintain the social attitude. Malice, rage, vindictiveness, would have been held qualities entirely inconsistent with the grace and chivalry of a passage at arms between gentlemen; and to waive all advantages, in favor of an opponent, was always a struggle, gracefully, but tenaciously urged between the parties, even after weapons had been crossed.

Singleton observed the scene with much interest. He prided himself upon his own swordmanship, and anticipated, with some eagerness, the event. The parties were both fine-looking men. Archy Campbell was in the best of spirits, smiling and satisfied, habited in a sort of military undress, in the most gentlemanly fashion of the time. Stock, his second, was sulky and satirical. Harley, his opponent, was cool, courteous, and rigid as a martinet. The time was come, and, under the direction of Stock, Campbell threw off his coat, vest, *chapeau bras*, and cravat. The spectators became as eager for the issue as ever were the gamesters of the cockpit, largely betting on a favorite main. But they were all destined to disappointment. The "point of

honor" in that day did not deny such a conclusion to the affair
as that which followed. When all was expectation, the friend
of Harley stepped forward and demanded of Stock, loudly
enough for everybody to hear—

"Is it true, Major Stock, that your principal is married?"

"The devil! Yes! But what a question! True, to be sure
it is"—then, *sotto voce*—" and the worse for me ! But"—aloud
—"what has this marriage to do with the business?"

"A great deal, sir," replied the other, "as we will show you
hereafter. One other question : Is it true that your principal is
married to Miss Paulina Phelps?"

"Certainly, sir. It is to Miss Paulina Phelps that Major
Archibald Campbell is married."

"Then, sir, we withdraw our invitation to the field. It is not
our policy or principle to fight with a gentleman on behalf of
his own wife; and, indeed, we conceive that, in marrying the
offender, she has preferred a mode, and perhaps the best, of
punishing him for his offences to herself. We repeat that our
challenge is withdrawn upon the original grounds; but without
the assertion of any claim on our part that the duel should not
go on. It is with the defendant to say whether he will suffer
us to quit the field."

This was said with a profound gravity, and with the stateli-
ness of a *diplomate*. A hearty laugh followed from Campbell.

"To be sure," said he, "I consent; but on one condition,
that Captain Harley and his companions dine with me and my
wife to-day. Expecting to be hurt in the encounter with so
keen a swordsman, I ordered a good dinner, in order that my
friends should not behold my sufferings without some consolation."

The parties embraced; and thus ended an affair of honor of
the eighteenth century. Stock seemed the only person not
satisfied with the arrangement. He said, with an affectation of
disappointment—

"It's too provoking! I was in hopes that Harley would have
given you your quietus, and then I should have saved my
guineas."

"Not so," cried Campbell. "I prepared against that, and

left proofs of the debt in the hands of my wife, who is the very woman to prosecute the claim, if only that she might have in her power so rare a gallant."

"I am reconciled to your escape and safety," retorted Stock. "I have too sensible a fear of the tender mercies of a creditor among the sex."

CHAPTER XLIX.

THE PLOT.

THE rest of the day was employed by Singleton, the partisan, with the assistance of tried friends in the city, in procuring certain implements for the use of Colonel Walton in prison. The permit which enabled him, as Furness, the loyalist, to have free access to the prisoner, offered him an opportunity quite too important to be foregone. He accumulated files, acids, and a rope-ladder, and took them to him that very night, after Katharine had left the prison. We may take for granted that he urged none of the arguments to Walton which Balfour had put into his mouth.

The next day Walton's trial came on—if that may be called a trial which examined no witnesses. Conviction and sentence were things of course; and the prisoner was remanded to his dungeon with the assurance that he would, in four days, expiate his offences to the crown upon the gallows. He heard his doom with a calm and fearless spirit, indignantly protested against the mockery of justice which he had just gone through, and appealed to the arms of his country for the punishment of those who should shed his blood under such a sentence. Scarcely was the examination over, when Balfour again waited upon Katharine. He was the first to report the decision of the court.

"Your father's life is in your own hands, Miss Walton."

"Mercy! mercy!" she shrieked, falling before him.

"Boon for boon, prayer for prayer, mercy for mercy—love for life!"

She held up her hands, pleading dumbly.

"As we both live, Katharine Walton, these are the only conditions!" he answered, sternly.

She sank forward gasping, and lay without sign of life upon her face. He raised her up in alarm, and called for Mrs. Singleton. She hurried in and relieved him of his burden.

"Why do you linger, sir?" she asked. "You have done your work effectually, for the present, at least. Leave us now, sir, if you please. It will take some time before I can recover her."

An oath rose to Balfour's lips, which he found it somewhat difficult to suppress. He seized his *chapeau bras* and hastily disappeared, without saying a word. Hurrying to the provost, he left instructions there that Miss Walton should *not* that day be admitted to see her father. This was on the plea of tenderness for her feelings, and sympathy with her situation. But, in truth, the policy was dictated by a desire to work upon her anxiety and fears—to make her feel, in every possible way, how arbitrary and entire was his power. Meanwhile, the native citizens of the place were moving. A memorial, in behalf of Colonel Walton, was prepared and signed by all the chief people among the whig inhabitants. Several of the loyalists signed it also, and the signatures of the ladies were numerous. A committee of these presented it, and the petition was enforced by the personal entreaties and tears of those presenting it. It was without effect. The answer of Balfour was a cold one. It is to the credit of General Williamson that he earnestly added his efforts to those of the citizens.

"What!" said Balfour. "You, too, general! Do you so soon forget your own recent escape from the clutches of this insolent rebel?"

"No, sir: and it is this recollection that now prompts my entreaty. I cannot forget that, but for the interposition of Colonel Walton, which saved me from the tender mercies of his subordinates, I should certainly have tasted of the terrible doom which now threatens him."

"And which he *must* suffer!" was the conclusive reply. "The public safety requires this sacrifice. We must rebuke rebellion by the punishment of some of its conspicuous leaders."

That day Balfour took his dinner alone at his quarters, dining at a late hour, and after many fatigues and excitements which, to a mind like his, were not unmixed with pleasure. He was rioting in power. He was not without a hope of realizing his most selfish objects. At length, he had persuaded the people of Charleston, and Katharine Walton in particular, of the earnest purpose which he entertained. She, at length, felt that her father's life was really in danger. She had already begun to seek and to sue, in tears and gloomy apprehension. She had paid him a visit, in order to obtain permission to see her father again; a privilege which, as we have seen, he had that day denied. He had avoided her, and he conjectured the extent of her agony. Gloating over his convictions, he drank freely of his Madeira, and was already at the close of his feast, when Alfred Monckton made his appearance from the adjoining room where he wrote, and communicated the arrival of Major Vaughan from Dorchester. He had been summoned down to attend the trial of Proctor, which was assigned for the ensuing day.

"Send him here," said Balfour, and Vaughan was instantly ushered into the presence of the potentate.

"You are welcome, Vaughan, doubly welcome at this moment. Sit, and fill yourself a glass. We are at the harvest time at last."

"Yes, colonel, and a full harvest shall we have of it. I bring you news which shall strengthen the evidence against this arch-traitor."

"Ah, indeed! The more the merrier, though we scarcely need it. We have quite enough in this late affair, for his full conviction. But what's your news?"

"Such as will startle you. You remember the fellow that palmed himself off upon you as Captain Furness of the loyalist rifles?"

"Yes. Well, was he not what he called himself?"

"No, indeed! He was no other than the rebel, Colonel Singleton, of Marion's brigade!"

"What!" cried Balfour starting to his feet. "How know you this?"

"By the true Captain Furness himself, who has just escaped from the guard assigned for his safe-keeping among the rebels. He made his way to the post at Dorchester, and has come with me to town. I have brought him here, and only wait the word from you to introduce him."

"Bring him in! By the Lord Harry, but this is excellent! And Proctor knew him at Dorchester?"

"Intimately!"

"And they are intimate together here, at this moment, and occupy the same lodgings."

"Indeed! then we have them! *Here*, do you say?"

"Here! here! and the rebel has imposed upon me thrice. Shall he not swing? But bring in the genuine Furness. Are you sure of him?"

"Quite sure! His proofs are beyond question, and he brings a great deal of intelligence."

"Bring him in, bring him in! Singleton! Ha! ha! *Her* lover, *her* betrothed! The audacious rebel! Well! the vengeance shall be sweet in degree with the insolence! Nothing shall save *him!* She shall pray for *him* in vain. She can purchase but the life of one, and her choice must be her father. Ha! well. He is here."

Vaughan returned, bringing in the true Furness. He was a man very much in size and person like the bold rebel who had assumed his character, but wanting the noble bearing, the high tone, the eagle eye and aspect. He was seated, and the wine poured out, and the impatient Balfour summoned him to a narrative of all the particulars relating to his capture, detention, and escape. The commandant was very soon convinced that he had been egregiously deceived hitherto; and his mortified vanity, at the deception, made him doubly vindictive in his determination. He recalled all the dialogues between himself and Singleton, in the assumed character of the latter; how freely he had unfolded himself to the supposed loyalist; and bitterly reflected how much material for secret scorn and laughter his confidence must have afforded to the partisan. His cheeks flushed with the reflection of a deeper red than could be given by the ruddy juices which he drank, and, striking his fist heavily down upon the table, he exclaimed, in a voice of thunder—

"Shall he not swing for it!—swing on a gallows as high as that of Haman!"

"And you say that he is here—here now, within the city?" demanded Vaughan.

"Ay, indeed! and a lodger with that other traitor of our own, John Proctor!"

"Then we have them both!"

"Ay, indeed! in the same net! They shall pay for their audacity."

"Should you not seize them at once, colonel?"

"Ay, indeed!"—rising—"I will see to it. Here, Mr. Monckton."

The secretary appeared at the entrance.

"But, no!" said Balfour, resuming his seat, and filling his glass anew. "You may go," said he to Monckton. "Pass the bottle, Major Vaughan, to Captain Furness. I have a better plan for making this arrest. We are probably watched. Any movement, at this moment, were I to send a guard to Proctor's lodgings, and Singleton not happen to be there, might only give him warning, and enable him to make his escape."

"How can that be? Issue orders, in advance, that no one leave the city, and strengthen the guards along the lines."

"Ah! Vaughan, that would only make the matter worse. The city is full of traitors. They have their emissaries everywhere, and communicate with the enemy by means of the winds, I believe, for there's no finding out the process exactly. But it is fortunate that my very confidence in this rebel Singleton gives me the means for securing him, if we make no stir, and do not alarm his apprehensions. He is to visit Walton to-night, at eight o'clock, in the provost. *There*, we have him. He will scarcely fail to be there; *was* there last night, and made me quite a glowing report, this morning, of what he had done toward convincing Walton of the necessity of making submission, and doing what is required of him."

"What is that, sir?"

"Oh, sir, a matter of state, which"—looking askant at the loyalist—"need not be dwelt upon. It is enough that the rebel will seek Walton again to-night in his dungeon. I am now satisfied that he will do so with the view of facilitating his escape. Against that we will guard. But we will take him in the toils. We have this fellow of Proctor's, John, constantly on the heels of his master. I will have *him* here, and command his watch upon both, and, to-night you shall be ready, with a guard, to arrest him in Walton's dungeon. How do you relish the service?"

"Command me, sir," eagerly.

"And you, Captain Furness, will have no sort of objection to change places with your late captor—to assist in putting him into limbo?"

"Not a bit, colonel!"

"Very good! Let us make our arrangements."

The plan was devised. The details, which were fully adequate to the object, need not concern us. Enough that Balfour, Vaughan, and the loyalist, were all warmed with a tiger appetite for the blood of the victim, which could scarcely be restrained by the policy which determined not to move until it could move with certainty. We may add that Proctor's treacherous servant, John, was soon put in requisition, and counselled to report equally all the movements of Singleton as well as those of his late master. When, at the close of the conference between the parties, Alfred Monckton was again called for, he had disappeared.

"Gone to dinner, sir," was the answer of the other secretary, who had just returned from his.

CHAPTER XLVIII

THE COUNTER PLOT.

BALFOUR, filled with excitement and wine, had spoken in louder accents than were necessary, and Monckton heard every syllable. He was at once struck with the importance of the new danger, not only to Proctor—with whose fate he deeply sympathized on account of his sister—but to Singleton, in whose behalf he felt a rising interest, in consequence of his intimacy with Kathatine Walton, which had duly ripened with that of Ella Monckton. We have seen how large was the influence which his sister possessed over him, and how small was that of Balfour. The latter he regarded with positive antipathy, the consequence of the tyrannous and wanton insolence of the commandant, which he seldom forbore to exercise. Should he suffer these two noble young men to become his victims ? Should he refuse to the sister whom he loved that intelligence, the timely use of which might save them—a result so precious to her desires and best affections? He had not strength for this. His conscience reproached him with the betrayal of his employer's secrets ; but his will was not sufficiently potent to suffer him to keep them when the safety of such dear interests counselled their revelation. The struggle in his mind was a very brief one. With eager agitation, he revealed the whole affair to Ella, with all the resolutions which had been adopted by the commandant, and the particular means to be employed for the capture of Singleton. She was overwhelmed at the danger which threatened the man she loved and the lover of her friend.

"Alfred," said she, "you must go to Kate this very moment and tell her every syllable."

"Impossible! I must hurry back this very moment, or as soon as I have swallowed my dinner. I am wanted; and if not absolutely called for before I return, it will be only because Balfour has started another bottle."

"Then I must do it myself!"

And, with that calm, but unyielding energy which was characteristic of her affections, the noble girl at once hurried off to the dwelling of Mrs. Singleton, while her brother, trembling with a secret consciousness of wrong, hastened back to the weary toils of his secretaryship.

Kate Walton was absent; and, in an agony of apprehension, Ella related her discovery to Mrs. Singleton. The old lady was seriously alarmed.

"They must be found!" said she; "Robert must be advised of this new danger in season to prevent it. Yet where to find him at this moment! There is but one hope. Write, my child — write all that is necessary to be said — to Tom Singleton. Fortunately, little George Spidell is here preparing for his trip to-night. He will find him, and carry the letter safely. This is our only chance."

Ella sat down to the table and penned the hasty billet, giving all the substantial details in respect to the impending danger. George was called up and despatched upon his errand; while Ella hastened home, in order to provoke as little suspicion at this moment as possible.

Let us now proceed to the lodgings of Proctor. Here, Singleton and himself were just sitting down to a late dinner. The former had only a moment before made his appearance. Both of them were gloomy enough, and but little inclined to eat. Their disinclination was increased by the sudden appearance of old Tom Singleton. The apology was brief which took our partisan away from the table to a corner of the room. Here, the billet of Ella Monckton was thrust into his hands. The moment he had possessed himself of its contents, he turned to Proctor.

"What would you do?" demanded Tom Singleton.

"What I should! Proctor, I have deceived you. Read that!"

He displayed the billet to the eyes of the astonished Briton, who had scarcely glanced at the paper before he exclaimed —

" Who does this come from ? Whose handwriting is it ?"

" What matters that ?" demanded Tom Singleton. " Enough that it comes from a true friend. It is all the truth."

" Pardon me," said Proctor, " that, seeing the handwriting, I did not consider the contents. You will see that it is from the same pen that wrote me the anonymous warning of danger."

" Then I congratulate you, Major Proctor, on having found interest in the heart of one of the noblest young creatures in the city," answered Tom Singleton.

" Who ?" demanded Proctor, eagerly.

" Miss Monckton—Ella Monckton ; as sweet a girl as I ever knew. But of this hereafter. What is to be done ?"

" Proctor," said Robert Singleton, I am in your power. I throw myself on your generosity. You see how I have deceived you !"

"And can you doubt me, Singleton ?" The young Englishman extended his arms, and the two were at once locked in a fast embrace. Old Tom Singleton looked on silently for a moment. At length he spoke —

" All very well, and very grateful, young gentlemen ; but you are neither of you out of the halter yet. The question is, what is to be done ? Now, if you will listen to me —"

" Speak, sir."

" Well, briefly, then, the house is watched at present. Your fellow, John, is on the lookout somewhere. He has seen me come in. He must see me go out. And the next question is how to get Bob Singleton out without his being seen by the same rascally eyes. Now my notion is, Major Proctor, that, if we two go forth together, we shall certainly draw this spy after us. We may go forth to a certain distance and then separate. When we have thus drawn off the spy, our kinsman here can take his departure and shape for himself another course. To do anything for *his* safety, we must first cut the clews of the spy. I will give Robert directions whither to go ; and, when I separate from you, I will seek for him. The rest hereafter. Are you prepared to lose your dinner ?"

Proctor caught up his hat on the instant, and old Singleton, after a few words to our partisan, went out with the former.

Having allowed a reasonable time after their departure, Robert Singleton went forth also; and, obeying the instructions of his kinsman, took his route in a northeastern direction, gradually inclining to the Governor's Bridge.

The streets were generally quiet. He met but few persons, and but one or two of the military. The day was quite warm, and it was just that time of the day when, dinner being over mostly in every quarter, the great body of the people were in the full enjoyment of the customary *siesta*. Singleton provoked little notice, and congratulated himself with the belief that he had been seen by no one likely to give him trouble. Thus advancing, he at length reached the eastern margin of the city, and but a short distance below the lines which divided it in that quarter from "The Neck." The tide was low. An old hulk lay stranded beside the wharf, which, at this point, was a rude fabric of palmetto logs, clumsily thrown together and very much in decay. On one side the logs were partially rotted out, leaving a space sufficiently large for the entrance of an able-bodied man. Singleton loitered awhile about the old hulk, then, as his eyes took in the neighboring places, and he fancied himself unseen, he quietly passed over the sides of the hulk and stole into the openings of the wharf. Here he was in a sort of cavern. The space between the logs had never been filled in, and, while the tide was low, his territory was ample for all reasonable exercise. At ordinary tides, he could still have kept his head out of water, yet kept within his cavern. Looking about him, he discovered within the recess, also, the well-kept boat of Master Lockwood and his efficient second officer, Master George Spidell. Another chasm in the wharf, on the northern side, afforded the little craft the means of egress; and quietly throwing himself down in the bottom of the vessel, Singleton yielded himself up to meditations, the nature of which, as we may readily suppose, were anything but agreeable.

Meanwhile, old Tom Singleton and Proctor pursued their way together in a westwardly direction, finally passing into Broad street.

"I am greatly concerned about your kinsman's safety," said Proctor. "What plan will you adopt for it?"

"Better that you should *not* know," said the old man; "the more ignorant you are, on this subject, the less embarrassment to you if called upon to answer. Do not be displeased. If you could really assist in his escape, I should tell you freely what I purpose."

"And if you need the help of a weapon, sir, I beg you will think of mine."

"No! no! Proctor, we must keep your enemies in the wrong. It will be of no service on your trial, even if you could prove it so; but it is something also to suffer with a pure heart, and a fearless conscience. Had you taken the counsels of this dear girl in season!"

"What do you know of Miss Monckton?" demanded Proctor abruptly.

"Know her! I know everything of her—knew her from an infant—know her mother, and very intimately knew her father."

"She is of good family?"

"One of the best in the country."

"She is not beautiful?"

"No! but very sweet, and very true, sir—and there's a world of beauty in her heart. You do not ask if she is rich!"

"I did not think of it."

"Humph! a very singular omission. And now, sir, as I take for granted that your scoundrelly servant has his eyes upon us, and that Robert Singleton has made off in the opposite direction, it may be just as well that we should separate. We are now within a hundred yards of the widow Monckton's dwelling. An old house, sir—lacks paint, you see. The widow is rather needy."

The old man wheeled off without any adieus. Involuntarily, Proctor turned about in the same direction. But a moment's reflection taught him that, with the eyes of the spy in all probability upon him, his better course was to continue onward. As he did so, his eyes caught again the venerable outlines of the widow Monckton's mansion. Instantly a new impulse fastened upon his mind. He did not soliloquize, but the thoughts, fashioned somewhat in this manner, passed through his brain.

" It may be that I am at the end of my career, and, at this moment, the only two persons who have manifested any interest in my fortunes, and who have striven to avert my fate, are those whom I have never sought. Here is a noble rebel against whom I have fought. He has taught me to understand the full beauty of that friendship of which we read in the history of David and Jonathan. I could freely die in battle for that man! —And here is one—a woman—young, devoted!—I will see her! I will speak to her the thoughts—the gratitude that fills my heart! She, perhaps, of all this city, would feel a pang at my death. Her hands, alone, might plant some sad flower upon my grave!"

He looked round in search of Tom Singleton. The retreating form of the old man was nearly out of sight. Proctor went forward. A few moments brought him to the door of the widow's dwelling. He raised the antiquated knocker, and was scarcely conscious of the heavy reverberations which followed from the stroke. He asked to see Miss Monckton, and was instantly admitted.

CHAPTER XLVIII.

THE DOVE'S CONQUEST, AND THE ADDER'S RAGE.

SHOWN into the parlor of the ancient mansion of Mrs. Monckton, and left alone by the servant, Proctor, for the first time, began to reflect coolly upon the motive of his visit. He had simply obeyed an impulse. But that impulse, when he appealed to his deliberate thought, he soon discovered to spring from a just recognition of his duty. In his mind, he ran over very rapidly the whole history of that grateful interest which (he now knew) Miss Monckton had taken in his fortunes. The discovery which had just been made furnished the clew to a long train of services which he owed to that lady, and revealed her to him as a being of generous and noble nature, whose devotion to his safety and honor, so long and delicately concealed, was significant of warmer feelings than those of mere generosity. He recalled hurriedly what he knew of her personally — what he had heard her say — her looks, tone, and general manner; and his interest in her person and character sensibly increased in consequence of this review. When, again, he remembered his own isolation, the absence of all relationships on which he could rely in his emergency, the indifference and selfishness of his kinsman, and the hostility of his superiors, his heart warmed more than ever to the young and gentle creature whose preferences, so secret and so useful to him, had been so generous and decided. When, at length, Ella Monckton entered the apartment, he was prepared, though unconsciously, to do justice not only to her devotion, but to her affections. A warm suffusion covered her face and neck as she appeared before him; but her eye was tremulously bright, and her heart was glowing with emotions which might have had their birth in hope. As she appeared, he advanced impetuously, and, under another warm impulse of gratitude, he extended her his hand. Silently, she yielded her own to his grasp, which was accompanied with a warm pressure; and he scarcely suffered himself to conduct her to a seat, before he declared his knowledge of all that she had wrought in his behalf.

"Miss Monckton, I can not do justice to my gratitude by words. I have only lately become aware of what you have done for me. You have found me alone, cheerless, hopeless, struggling against many and powerful enemies. You have, like an unseen angel, whispered to me in counsels and warnings which I have not sufficiently heeded. It is now, perhaps, too late for safety—not too late for acknowledgment and gratitude. Would that I could requite such kindness, such generosity! But you have my prayers, my thanks, my best thoughts and fondest remembrances."

He carried her hand to his lips. A deep sigh escaped her. It was her only answer. He continued:—

"Had I but known in season! Had I but suspected the source of these secret intimations of my guardian angel, which would have taught me of my secret dangers! Had I but given them the heed which they deserved! Regret is hopeless now; my enemies are about to triumph; I am in the toils; they will conquer; I see no process of escape. But, if I perish, Miss Monckton, believe me, the thought of your interest in my fate, the feeling of a most devoted gratitude within my soul, will be the last consciousness which will leave my spirit."

She murmured, rather than spoke—

"Oh! do not speak thus—do not speak of perishing. Surely, surely, Major Proctor, you have means of escape!"

"No!" he answered gloomily—"my trial takes place to-morrow. My enemies are prepared to destroy me. Circumstances of the most cruel sort combine against me, and afford proof which will be conclusive to any court of what will be declared my guilt and treason. They will find me guilty, and shame will fasten upon my name, even if the tyranny under which I suffer shall forbear my life."

" But you may escape. You are still free. You will fly from the city and avoid this trial !"

" That will be as fatal to my fame as if I were to linger here and perish. That is what my enemies desire. It is for this reason that, charged as I am with the most criminal offences, Balfour leaves me out of bonds. He pretends to ascribe this forbearance to a due regard to my uncle, and to the hope that I will free myself from these imputations. But he knows his power to convict me, and only affords me these opportunities of flight that I may convict myself. I dare not avail myself of this opportunity. I must face my enemies—and must perish!"

Ella Monckton covered her face with her hands. A slight sob escaped her, and Proctor beheld the glistening tears stealing through her fingers. He was seated beside her on the sofa Unconsciously, his arm encircled her waist.

" You weep for me, Miss Monckton ! Ah, these are precious tears ! So strange to me, and doubly precious for this reason. I could die for such ! I could almost dare to live for them !"

" Oh, live ! live !" she exclaimed impetuously. "Let me implore you to fly from this danger, and from these merciless enemies. If they convict you, as you say they will—nay, as I know they will—it is shame, and perhaps death also. It can not be worse if you fly ; and time will then be allowed you to refute these charges—to fasten the shame upon these hateful and treacherous people."

In thus speaking, she had removed her hands from her face, and her eyes had resolutely sought his own. The big drops yet stood upon her cheeks, and the soft suffusion yet hung upon and fell from her lids. But the animation of glance which seconded her appeal made her very beautiful in the eyes of Proctor. How had he failed before to discover so much loveliness ? His heart was deeply touched by her warm sympathies.

"Alas !" he exclaimed, " I can not hear you. I must not listen to such counsel. No, my dear Miss Monckton, I have been trained in a school which teaches that such a flight would be unmitigated dishonor. I must brave and face the danger, even though I foresee that it will overwhelm me. Whither should

I fly? To the rebels! Safety I might find among them—no doubt would; but a safety found in shame would make life intolerable. I must not contemplate such a prospect. Where else could I fly? To no region covered by our arms could I retire, without the double danger of disgrace and death. The fates surround me with a wall of fire I can not break through. I must encounter all that they threaten."

She answered him with new entreaties and arguments; but he mournfully checked her pleadings.

"It is all in vain. To this fate I must yield. I can pursue no such course, not even though life were certainly safe, and shame were equally certain not to follow. Had I listened sooner to the sweet but unknown voice that counselled me at a season when I was deaf and blind to the danger which hunted at my heels! Ah! had I known you then, Miss Monckton, as I know you now! Hear me!" he exclaimed, passionately— "hear me, Miss Monckton, if it be not worse than madness to listen to such a declaration from one who, like myself, stands upon the brink of the precipice, with the terrible fate towering above and preparing to hurl him down the steeps! Hear me at the last moment, when life is without hope and love dreams of no fruition; hear me in the wild declaration that I would gladly live, if it were only to offer you a heart which now enshrines your image as its most precious treasure!"

Her head rested upon his shoulder. A deep-drawn convulsive sigh and sob spoke more than any words, the passionate delight with which her heart received a declaration which was not the less grateful because it came with the assurance that it was made hopelessly and in vain. He continued—

"I feel that I do not deceive myself, Miss Monckton. I feel that I do not make you an idle assurance. You have not shown this long-continued and devoted interest in my fortunes without being conscious of nobler and warmer sympathies than belong simply to humanity and friendship. In giving you my heart, Miss Monckton, do I deceive myself—have I not yours also? Ah!"

She threw herself with a wild cry upon his breast, and he held her there, closely pressed with emotions such as seemed to

kindle a new being in his breast. They were thenceforth
united.

"It is not vain!—it is not vain, this precious consciousness,
even though I die to-morrow!"

"You must not die!" she said, in quick but whispered accents.
"You must *live* now—you *will* live"—the rest of the sentence
was spoken in a whisper—"if not for yourself, for *me!*"

She buried her blushing face in his bosom. A new necessity
became apparent to him. Whatever he should finally determine, she at least must be spared every unnecessary pang. She
must be encouraged for the present with a hope, even if he indulged in none himself. And he promised—he knew not exactly what—to fly, to live—to preserve a life which had acquired a new value to both in that passionate, but fleeting interview of bliss. He promised her to elude the mockery of a trial
which he well knew was but designed as furnishing the sanction
to a brutal and selfish crime; though without really entertain-
ing such a purpose. But her tears, and his own tenderness of
mood, made him readily yield to an entreaty which he could
find no other way to answer.

Why linger upon the scene? Enough that Proctor tore himself away from the maiden whom he had made happy and
wretched in the same moment—happy in the sweet response to
a sympathy which can live on nothing else; and wretched with
fears that threatened to dash the cup of joy from her lips in the
very moment when its delicious waters had been only tasted.
Proctor had been gone but fifteen minutes. Ella Monckton
was on her knees, before the sofa on which he had left her,
when she was startled by a loud and sudden rapping at the
door. It was opened by the servant, and the visiter, without a
word, pushed into the passage, and darted at once into the parlor, the way to which he seems to have well known. Ella looked up to behold in the intruder the person of Major Vaughan,
the enemy of Proctor, if not her own!

"How now, sir!" she exclaimed, starting to her feet, her face
all flushed with indignation. "You here! By what right, sir,
do you presume thus to intrude upon me?"

His eyes searched the room. He did not instantly answer,

and her question was repeated with increasing indignation.   It was evident that he was disappointed—that he did not expect to find her alone; but he put on an air of confidence, and the sneer that mantled his lips was of the most provoking insolence.

"He has gone! he has escaped; but only for the present. Did you suppose, Ella Monckton, that it was on a mission of love that I sought your dwelling?"

"If it were, no one should better know than yourself that such a mission was in vain."

"Ah! is it so? But I will spoil the love of others! It was *hate* that brought me to your presence. It was for the purpose of a long-delayed vengeance that I came! If I can not find the way to *your* heart, no other shall!"

"In that I defy you, sir! You are too late!" This was said with all the exultation of a heart for the first time secure in a requited affection.

"I know it *now!* But your triumph shall be a short-lived one. Look! I hold in my hands the authority for the arrest of your minion. He shall be in bonds before the night is over. To-morrow brings his trial as a traitor, and in twenty-four hours he dies an ignominious death. Ha! do you *feel*—do you *fear* me now?"

"I loathe—I scorn you! Hence, sir, and leave me. You have no right here—none to insult me with your language or your presence. You may triumph in your hate, but you shall have no triumph over *me*. Were I myself decreed to perish, instead of *him*, my last words should be those of loathing and of scorn for you."

With a grin of bitter malice, he shook the warrant at her, as he cried—

"Know, at least, that your faithlessness to me, and your silly passion for him, have doomed him. You could lure me to your feet *once*. Could you now prostrate yourself to mine, it would be unavailing for his safety. The gallows shall clip the neck that your fair hands have striven to environ!"

"Liar and craven! I deny that I ever offered a lure to your affections. Your vanity alone, confounded the courtesies of a lady with another feeling. Begone! Were you not utterly base, you would seek your enemy with your sword, and not with the wretched artifices with which you have striven to destroy him."

" And were he not already *convict,* I should seek him now with the sword. But that were a poor revenge for me! No! Ella Monckton, I shall not now balk the sweets of a perfect vengeance by giving him an honorable death."

"Away! and meet him if you dare! You but cloak your cowardice under this miserable plea of vengeance!"

With a lurid grin that lighted up his features with a Satanic expression, he once more shook the order for arrest before her, and, striking it with his hands, exclaimed—

" When *this* has done its work, Ella Monckton, you may look for another visit from the man whose affections you have outraged. Till then, I leave you to your very pleasant meditations."

Once more, the maiden was left alone. Let us drop the veil for the present over her sorrows.

CHAPTER XLIX.

FINAL ISSUES.

THE secret of Vaughan's sudden appearance at Mrs. Monckton's is easily made known. The treacherous servant of Proctor had tracked the latter to the spot. Vaughan had instructed him to communicate *to himself*, in particular, whatever movements Proctor might make ; and the spy, having seen him safely housed, had hurried off to his employer with his information. Vaughan, in his long interview with Balfour, had drunk freely. Though ordinarily a temperate man, cold and circumspect, he had been taken off his feet by the peculiar influences working upon his feelings. He was about to enjoy a long-delayed and vindictive passion. The prey was almost in his grasp, and the doom was about to be spoken. This conviction greatly excited him, yet this was not the sole cause of excitement. He was still unsatisfied. He would obtain revenge—he would atone to wounded pride ; but there was a lurking sense of shame and baseness which left his pride in need of far other sorts of soothing. Besides, Ella Monckton, the object, at one time, of far more grateful emotions, was as far removed from his attainment as ever. There was one thing which promised consolation. It was in the belief that, as yet, the feelings with which Ella regarded his enemy, were totally unknown to the latter, and locked up from all knowledge except his own, in the single bosom of the maiden herself. But even this assurance was about to be taken from him. He had just left Balfour, and returned to his own lodgings, inflamed with wine and gnawing passions, when the traitor, John, made his appearance hurriedly, and in-

20

formed him of Proctor's appearance at the residence of Mrs. Monckton.

Thoroughly roused by the information, in his excitement he lost his coolness and circumspection; and, congratulating himself on the precaution which had provided him with Balfour's warrant for the arrest of Proctor, he hurried in search of him, with the hope to take him in the very presence of his mistress. His evil passions rendered him insensible to the brutality of such a proceeding. We have seen the results in his temporary disappointment. The event of the interview did not greatly improve his temper or his prudence. When he emerged from the dwelling of Mrs. Monckton, he found the spy in waiting with a couple of Hessians, who had been brought for the purpose of taking the prisoner into safekeeping. Vaughan was not willing to forego their services.

"You must recover trail, John," he said to the spy.

"Must have time for it, major. We must get back to his lodgings and see if he's gone back there; I left a pair of eyes on the lookout in that quarter, and can soon know. But it won't do to be going in a crowd. These men can follow us at a distance without appearing to follow, and you had better keep a good bowshot behind me. These rebels have their spies out as well as ourselves, and they whisper, from wall to wall, who's coming."

"As you will," said Vaughan—"only hasten! We must have him by the neck and heels before night!"

The party distributed by the spy pursued their way, but with considerable intervals between the several divisions. They reached, at length, the neighborhood of Proctor's lodgings. There they ascertained from the subordinate who had been left to watch the premises that he had reappeared, entered, and again gone forth, not ten minutes before. The direction which he had taken was pointed out, and the pursuers again resumed the chase.

For a long time they found it fruitless. Proctor, it seems, had set out to seek for Singleton, alias Furness. His mind had taken a new direction since his recent interview with Ella Monckton. Strange to say, the feeling of despair, and complete resig-

nation to his fate, which had weighed him to the earth not an
hour before, had given way entirely to a new sentiment of hope
and life. He scarcely yet grasped fully the vague intimation of
his thought; but, for the first time, he felt how much wisdom
there was in the counsel of his friend, which warned him to fly
from a trial in which he was already unjustly condemned.
Proctor had not yet fairly determined to adopt this advice, but
the earnest desire to see and talk with Singleton once more
vaguely contemplated this very necessity, and the means for
employing it. Besides, we must do him the justice to say that
a very considerable feeling of anxiety for the safety of the latter entered into the desire which he felt in respect to his own
affairs.

But how to seek the fugitive was the question! Old Tom
Singleton had, very properly, given him no clew; being very
conscious that if, as he knew, Proctor was under espionage, it
would only conduct the pursuers on Robert Singleton's track to
suffer the former to find him out. We have seen where the latter had found shelter. It was sunset, and the dusk was rapidly
approaching, when Tom Singleton left Conover's Hotel, in
Queen street, and pushed up East Bay. He was suddenly encountered near Colonel Cruden's (Pinckney) residence by Proctor, the last man he desired to see. The latter would have
stopped him, but he pushed by him, saying abruptly, as he
passed—

"Major Proctor, if you would not do mischief, walk over to
Ashley river, and forget that you have seen me."

"But I would see my friend Singleton—I have something to
say to him of very great importance."

"Say it to your looking-glass! Dig a hole in your garden,
as the barber of Midas did, and bury your secret from the winds.
I tell you, sir, that you will mar everything—that you will only
bring the enemy upon our footsteps."

Proctor paused, half piqued at the rudeness of the old man,
and half impressed by the reason of his suggestion. He stood
aside, accordingly, and suffered him to make his way as he
pleased. Old Singleton pushed forward, and, for a moment,
Proctor watched him. The old man looked back, and seeing

that he was watched, darted aside into Pinckney street, pursuing a due-west direction. Proctor continued up the Bay, walking slowly, and fast forgetting the external world in his inward meditations. On a sudden, however, he was startled by the reappearance of Tom Singleton, who crossed the Bay from one of the streets at right angles with it, and hurried rapidly down to the wharves. Proctor's desire to see and speak with Robert Singleton was immediately revived within him. He looked back upon his own footsteps. He saw nobody, and the dusk had now so thickened that he could distinguish objects only at a small distance.

"This old man," he said to himself, "exaggerates the danger. There is no one after us now; and if there were, he could see but little."

He came rapidly to his determination, his desires prompting him to make light of all causes of apprehension; and, wheeling down the wharves also, he kept old Singleton's retreating figure constantly in his eye. He little thought that, when he wheeled from the Bay into another street, he placed himself under the very espionage which he flattered himself he had eluded, and which indeed, had failed, up to this moment, to come upon his tracks. It was in this very street that the keen eyes of his treacherous servant, John, still followed by Vaughan and the Hessians, had caught sight of old Singleton. The same treacherous scoundrel now instantly detected a something in the air and gait of the new-comer which reminded him of his master; but the dusk was now too great to enable him to reduce this to certainty, unless by a nearer approach, which, as he knew his master's temper, he was careful not to make alone. He waited accordingly, till Vaughan came up, when he expressed his belief that Proctor was just before them, a space of not more than fifty yards."

"Why, then, do you stop?" demanded Vaughan, eagerly. "Why did you not dart upon him?"

"He will fight like a devil, major."

"Push on with me!"

"Hadn't we better hold on till the Hessians come up?"

"He is alone, you say?"

"Yes, sir; but old Singleton was ahead of him."

"And he is too old to give us any trouble. But do you run back and hurry on the Hessians. I will push on and keep our man in sight."

He was obeyed. Alone, he pressed forward, and with such speed as brought Proctor again in sight. The route led to a lower wharf—that in which we have seen Robert Singleton concealed. Something which Vaughan could not see, prompted Proctor suddenly to increase his pace. It was now growing difficult to distinguish objects at thirty yards. Vaughan's impatience would not allow him to delay. He knew but of the single enemy before him, and reasonably calculated that all that was necessary was to retard his flight for a few moments until the arrival of the spy with the Hessians. He quickened his walk, already hurried to a run, and suddenly found himself almost at the head of the wharf, with a group of shadowy figures upon it and a boat on one side, in which several persons were to be seen. Proctor was speaking with one of the persons in the boat. The sound of his voice was enough to bring out all the vindictive animosity of his pursuer. He pushed at once for the group, which opened as he drew nigh, leaving Proctor conspicuously before him, but with his back toward him. Vaughan seized upon his arm, exclaiming, as he did so—

"You are my prisoner, Major Proctor! Here is the order for your arrest from Colonel Balfour."

Proctor wheeled about, shook himself free, and with a sudden blow of the fist, delivered fairly in the face of his assailant, he sent him staggering back. But Vaughan instantly recovered himself, drew his sword, shouted to the emissary, John, with his Hessians, whom he supposed to be close behind him, and rushed with mortal fury upon his enemy. At this moment, Singleton's voice was distinctly heard to say—

"This determines it, Proctor; you have no alternative."

Proctor had drawn his sword the moment he had given Vaughan the blow. Their weapons now crossed; and the group on the wharf, seeing the approaching Hessians, with the spy, disappeared over the sides, completely concealed in the shadows of the wharf, and on the old hulk that lay there in the marsh.

Vaughan heard the cry of the treacherous servant announcing his approach, and he called to him while still fighting with Proctor—

"Seize the boat! The rebel, Singleton, is in it!"

The Hessians, with the spy, at once jumped upon the hulk, to the stern of which the boat was fastened. Scarcely had they done so, when the two former were seized by unseen enemies and violently thrown down upon the deck. John, the spy, however, continued to seize the fasts of the boat, and, stretching over, laid his hand upon the prow. A single blow from Robert Singleton with an oar, which he caught up suddenly, delivered roundly upon the head of the fellow, stunned him, and falling between into the dock, he went down like a stone, and never reappeared. Meanwhile, the contest between Proctor and Vaughan was continued with fearful violence. Both of them were wounded, though not dangerously, and Vaughan, aware in some degree, of the capture of the Hessians, and no longer hearing the voice of the spy, was losing all his caution in the fear of losing his prey. Proctor was never cooler in his life. The desperateness of his situation seemed to bring out all his character. Meanwhile, Singleton leaped ashore.

"We must put an end to this, Proctor. Lights are moving down toward us, and they are waving torches upon the eastern bastion. We can take and tie this worthy gentleman, and either leave him on the wharf or take him with us."

"A moment!—only a moment more!" was the reply of Proctor, who felt his advantages. It scarcely needed so much. Almost while he was speaking, a desperate lunge of Vaughan threw wide his guard, and the prompt weapon of Proctor found its sheath in his bosom. He leaped up as he received the thrust, and fell forward upon his enemy, the sword breaking off short at the hilt. Singleton stooped to the body, which was utterly lifeless.

"It is done! And your flight is decided," said he. "You have resisted the arrest of your superior, and your fate is sealed if you remain!"

Proctor offered no resistance; but silently suffered himself to be led away to the boat. It was pushed off the moment he was seated. The inmates were six in number: Singleton, himself, Lockwood, the boy George Spidell, and two faithful negroes. The last four took the oars; but of these little use was made, except to direct the course of the vessel, as the tide, now nearly at the flood, bore it in the required direction.

"These stars are shining out too brightly," said Lockwood, and may give those fellows on the bastion a glimpse of us. We must strike over for Haddrill's until out of sight, then take the tide for the marshes of Town Creek. You persist, Colonel Singleton, in going on the west side of the river?"

"Yes, certainly. My horses are hidden this side of the 'Quarter,' and such a course will be totally unsuspected. They will naturally expect us to strike over for Haddrill's."

"Oars, boys," said Lockwood; "we must use them for awhile, at least, till we get fairly beyond the range of sight from that bastion. They are waving torches. They see something, that is certain."

"Yes, indeed; and design to make us see something, too," said Singleton, as the roar of a twenty-four pounder shook the welkin. The grape, a thick shower, hustled over the heads of the fugitives.

"A civility designed for us! They evidently see us."

"They will not see us long," answered Lockwood. "One or two more lusty pulls, my good boys, and they must aim at random."

Another and another shot followed; but they were now quite wide of the object.

"Enough, boys; that will answer. They see us no longer, and we may leave everything to the tide. All that need be done now may be left to that paddle. Hand it me, George."

The night deepened, and under its shadows the little boat once more approached the western banks of the Cooper. The channel called Town Creek received them, and they were already within the gorges of the marsh when they saw the lights of numerous boats setting forth from the city in pursuit, and all taking the route for Haddrill's.

'Safe for the present, colonel," said Lockwood; "and the

sooner we part the better. You wish no other help? I can put
you higher up if you desire it."

"No! no! take care of yourself now. I trust you will find
that easy. For me, nothing is more so. I have horses at hand,
such as none in garrison could overtake, unless, perhaps, Archy
Campbell's, and no one will look for us in this quarter. What
will you do, Lockwood?"

"Give yourself no concern about me. Daylight will probably
find us up the Wando."

The parties separated; and, before dawn, Singleton and
Proctor, with a few followers, were rapidly approaching the
heads of Cooper river.

CHAPTER L.

CONCLUSION.

We may imagine the fury of Balfour at the events of the night. Two of his victims had escaped, and one of his allies had perished in the very moment that he deemed his vengeance certain. But there was one victim still in his hands, and perhaps two. At all events, the commandant of Charleston was resolved that the fate of Colonel Walton should be sealed beyond redemption, unless with the sacrifice of his daughter. We have already mentioned that the trial of Walton had taken place. The whole proceeding was a miserable mockery of justice. The witnesses were unsworn, and the charges according to the plea put in for Walton, were denied to furnish just grounds for a criminal prosecution. He denied the jurisdiction of the court, and offered a protest against its proceedings, which was not received. His appeal lay to his country only, and the patriots fighting her battles to do justice to his memory and avenge his cause. He was found guilty, as a matter of course, and condemned, within twenty-four hours, to expiate his alleged treason upon the gallows. The citizens of Charleston were overwhelmed with consternation and surprise. They scarcely could believe that anything more was designed by the commandant and his court than simply to occasion a wholesome sentiment of terror. They proceeded, as we have said, by memorial, to implore the mercy which they did not doubt would be accorded them. They were to be terribly undeceived in this expectation. The ladies presented this petition in person, and were repulsed with austerity. The venerable men of the city, including numerous loyalists of rank, among whom was ex-governor Bull, a

20*

public character greatly esteemed by all parties, renewed the petition, and all without success. In Balfour's dwelling Katharine Walton threw herself at his feet in a vain entreaty for her father's life.

"It is in your hands," was the only reply — "*you* have but to speak to save him. You know the conditions! By the God of heaven, Miss Walton, you shall have no other!"

She was taken away swooning.

The day came assigned for the execution. Colonel Walton was taken from the vaults of the provost, and carried up stairs, in the same building, to the northeast chamber, in the second story, where he was permitted to see his friends, and to habit himself properly for his painful public exhibition. Hither his daughter found her way at the earliest possible moment. There was a sense of utter desolation in her grief that left her almost speechless. But we shall not attempt to describe the agony, which needed not, and was indeed superior to the necessity for, any words to declare its intensity and extremity. There are some sorrows, over which the judicious painter always draws the veil, despairing to depict them. Such is our policy and necessity. At length, the moment came for parting. At this moment, Balfour appeared in the dungeon. He approached Katharine.

"It is not too late!" he whispered in her ears. "You have yet time! You may yet save him!"

The voice of Walton immediately followed the whisper of Balfour.

"Katharine!"

She looked up through her tears.

"Remember, my child! your oath! your oath!"

She sank down at her father's feet.

"Colonel Balfour," said Walton, "this is very unmanly. Do you not see the misery which you inflict? You embitter the last moments of my life."

'I would *save* your life!" was the answer.

"You can not do it by this process."

"There is then no other!" was the savage reply, and with these words, Balfour left the chamber. As he was about to depart, Katharine half rose with the purpose of arresting him, but her father grasped her by the arm.

"My child, my Kate, remember! Do not think to save the short remnant of my life by the sacrifice of your own. Remember your oath! It is my last command, my child, that you never wed this man!"

We forbear the rest of the scene. The moment came for separation, and with one agonizing embrace, one convulsive kiss upon her quivering lips, Walton tore himself away from his swooning daughter. For a moment after, she lay unconscious in the arms of her venerable kinswoman. Then, as she heard the roll of the melancholy drum without, signalizing the movement of the sad procession, she started to her feet.

"Let us go," she cried, "I can not endure this agony and live! I must go to *him*! to *him*!"

"To whom, my child?"

"To Balfour! My father *must* be saved!"

Mrs. Singleton did not oppose her. It was impossible to do so. The two hurried to the carriage, which was in waiting, and it was driven with all speed to Balfour's quarters. Katharine, leaving Mrs. Singleton in the vehicle, hurried into the house. Without noting who was present, she exclaimed, as she entered the room in which hitherto she had found the commandant—

"Spare him, save him, Colonel Balfour—I consent to all you require!"

She was answered by Alfred Monckton—"Colonel Balfour is not here, Miss Walton."

"Oh! My God, do not tell me so! Where is he?"

"I have to go to him, even now, upon business," was the reply—"I will conduct you to him."

"Thanks! thanks! But hasten, or we shall be too late."

The young man assisted her into the carriage, and took a seat on the box. He ordered the coachman to drive at once to Miss Harvey's, whither Balfour had ordered him to bring certain papers. The horses were put to their speed, and were soon at the residence of that rival beauty whose charms had only failed with the commandant when Katharine Walton entered upon the scene.

Balfour, after leaving the provost, had hurried to his residence, full of rage and disappointment. Here he had left a few
orders; then, mounting his horse, he had galloped up to the
dwelling of the beauty he had so much neglected of late, seeking that consolation from the one damsel which he had failed to
obtain from the other whom he most affected. His steed was
fastened at the entrance, and he entered the house. As he did
so, Moll Harvey cried out from the upper story, bidding him
take a seat in the parlor, and promising to be down directly.
She had not made her toilet; and now proceeded to this pleasant duty with a full sense of the situation of affairs, and a full
determination to make herself as irresistible as possible.

It was while she was engaged in this employment that she
heard the carriage which bore Kate Walton drive up to the
door. Looking through the lattice, she saw her alight and enter. The servant conducted her into the parlor, whither she
was followed by Alfred Monckton. Mrs. Singleton remained
within the carriage. The moment Kate appeared, Balfour saw
that he had conquered. He hastily took the papers from Monckton, and told him to wait in an adjoining room. The hurried
words of Katharine, meanwhile, had announced her resignation
to her fate.

"I consent, Colonel Balfour—only save him—hasten, before
it is too late!"

"You will be mine, Katharine?"

Yes! O yes! anything—only do not waste these precious
moments."

Meanwhile, Moll Harvey had descended to the lower story.
She was standing beside the half-closed door as the words were
spoken. She heard all that was said. She knew all that was
determined upon. Through the crack of the door, she saw Balfour approach a table, and, with a pencil, hastily pen a few
words on a scrap of paper; then, as he came toward the passage, she drew back and sheltered herself within a closet. Balfour came out, entered the adjoining room, and putting the paper into the hands of Alfred Monckton, bade him take his horse
and gallop off, with all haste to the scene of execution. He was
ordered to put the paper into the hands of Major Frazer, com-

manding the detachment. This done, Balfour returned to the apartment where he had left Katharine Walton.

Alfred Monckton had already left the house, and was about to mount the horse of Balfour, when Moll Harvey ran out to him. She carried a folded paper in her hands.

"Mr. Monckton," she cried, "approaching him, "Colonel Balfour sends you this. He says you must send him back the other paper. This is more satisfactory. Now hurry, as fast as you can, or you will be too late." The exchange was effected. Monckton could have no misgivings, and he immediately put his horse to the top of his speed for the scene of execution. Moll Harvey re-entered the house through the gate and garden. She stole silently up the back steps, and once more to her chamber. There she read the billet which she had taken from Monckton; the order to Major Frazer to "suspend the execution, and to conduct the prisoner, under a strong guard, to his (Balfour's) quarters." A bitter smile, full of triumphant malice, covered the face of the lovely traitoress, as she tore the scrap to atoms. She only said—"Wretch! I have baffled him at last!"

Colonel Walton was attended to the place of execution by Dr. Ramsay and other friends, and by the Rev. Mr. Cooper, an ecclesiastical clergyman. He walked; preferring this to the degrading progress in a cart. The military detachment assigned as his guard consisted of equal bodies of British and Hessian troops. These formed a hollow square at the place of execution; the Hessians on the right and left, the British in front and rear. Crowds were in attendance, but of foreigners only. The natives kept their houses, which were closed in mournful silence as the procession was in progress. It had already reached the scene of appointed sacrifice, a place beyond the fortifications, well known in that day as Radcliffe's Garden, before Alfred Monckton made his appearance. The preparations were all complete, when the courier, spurring onward, "hot with haste and fiery red," made his way to the presence of Major Frazer, and handed him the billet as from Colonel Balfour. Frazer opened it, turned it over, and exclaimed—

"What means this? There is nothing here! Are you sure, sir, that you have given me the right paper?"

"Quite sure!" was the answer; but the youth was greatly bewildered as he examined the seeming billet and found it a blank envelope only.

"I understand!" muttered Frazer. "It is just like Balfour. It was only to get rid of some importunate petitioners that he has sent this empty paper. I could have wished it otherwise, gentlemen," he remarked, turning to Ramsey and the other anxious frends of the condemned. "But it only rests with me to do my duty."

They expostulated with him, and insisted upon the evident intentions of Balfour in sending a messenger in such hot haste; the blank paper was evidently some mistake. But Frazer shook his head mournfully, but firmly.

"Gentlemen, this blank paper means everything! It especially commands me to do my duty, and shows me that no orders are designed to arrest it. Let the prisoner prepare himself. The minutes are nearly exhausted."

When Balfour, having despatched Monckton with the billet, returned to the parlor, he found Katharine Walton with her face covered by her hands, and leant upon the arm of the sofa. She was silent, but, at slow intervals, drew long convulsive sobs. Balfour undertook the work of soothing; but such a task required the agency of finer sensibilities than any in his possession. He either annoyed the sufferer, or failed to make any impression on her senses. When, however, his pertinacity fixed her attention, she hastily started up and exclaimed—

"Let me go now, Colonel Balfour, my aunt is in waiting, and I—I—should be at home. I am very sick and very weary."

"Mrs. Singleton has already gone home, dear Miss Walton, having left the carriage for you."

"Gone! gone! and I am here alone!" she exclaimed, with some surprise and annoyance.

"And why not, my dear Miss Walton? You are not alone. Who should better assert the right to protect and comfort you than he to whom you have given so precious a claim?"

"Comfort! comfort! Oh God, have mercy upon me! My father, when will he return?"

"Now, very soon."

"Ah, thanks! thanks!"

It will not task the imagination to conceive the sort of comfort and consolation, mixed with bald professions of affection, which Balfour *would* attempt to bestow upon his companion; nor will it be hard to understand with what annoyance Katharine Walton heard them all. But she had adopted her resolution, and she submitted with resignation to his declarations, his soft tones, and honeyed assurances of love. Only, when he would have encircled her waist with his arm, did she revolt and resist. She could not, at such a moment, bring herself to submit to this —not so soon, at least.

We pass over an interval of time, which she felt to be equally tedious and full of anxieties. It was in a moment when Balfour was most pressing and solicitous that both the parties were suddenly startled by the sullen roar of a heavy cannon. Balfour started to his feet.

"Ha, that cannon! What can it mean?"

Katharine looked up with sudden terror.

"It is a signal!" she exclaimed. "Tell me—tell me, Colonel Balfour. Can it be—can it be that"—

She could say no more. Breathless, with hands extended, she advanced toward him, while, evidently annoyed and confounded, he approached the window and threw it open. His evident disquiet increased that of Katharine, who now impetuously appealed to him in respect to her father's safety.

"He is safe!" he answered. "Quite safe, dear Miss Walton. He will be here directly."

At this moment, Moll Harvey threw wide the door, and, dressed in the most splendid style, suddenly appeared before them.— Katharine looked up at her, but without any feeling of interest or surprise—with eyes, indeed, of vacancy. Balfour recoiled from the unexpected vision. Moll Harvey addressed herself to her unconscious rival. Her accents were full of scorn and fire.

"He tells you that your father is safe—that he will be here

directly! He tells you what is false! He is himself a living falsehood! Your father is dead—he will be here only in his coffin! That cannon announced the moment when the executioner did his work!"

With one wild scream, Katharine Walton sank senseless.

"Fiend!" cried Balfour, "what have you done?"

"Spoken the truth! I have saved *her*, and punished *you!* You wonder that Walton perishes. Know that when you gave your order for a respite to Alfred Monckton, I exchanged it for one in blank, professing to do so by your orders."

"Woman, you have been guilty of murder!"

"Hang me for it, if you dare! I overheard your bargain with this poor creature, and I determined to save her from such a monster!"

"Yet you would willingly surrender your own charms to such a monster!" he answered, with a sneer.

"Not *now*, Nesbitt Balfour!" she answered, sternly. "You might have said *that* an hour ago. Now! No! no! Never! I have too much pride for that: too much scorn of so base a spirit as that which you bear, to link myself with it for life. I would sooner link myself to a carcass! And she, the unhappy minion whom I have saved from this doom—she will loathe you now as much as I do. If I mistake not, your bargain is void. I have spoiled that very pretty arrangement. I avow the deed. If mine is a crime which merits punishment, inflict it if you dare! I defy you, and challenge you with all your power!"

"You are a devil, Moll Harvey! But keep your secret. You have done mischief enough. For this poor girl, you have killed her."

"No! no! no! I have *saved* her! She will do well enough now. Had you succeeded, *you* would have killed her by a thousand tortures; for I know that she loathes you. I saw that in the choking accent which declared her compliance, and I resolved, from that moment, that she should not be sacrificed. From that moment, I pitied her from the bottom of my heart. Away now, and leave her to me. I will recover her. I will see that she is restored to her haughty but honorable kinswoman. And, Balfour, in leaving this house, see that you do not enter it again, unless you desire that I should spit upon you. I have been weak—vicious, perhaps; and know that I deal with passions which are quite too powerful for me. They will destroy me yet. That I know; but destruction—death itself, for and with one whom I could honor as well as love—nay, shame itself with such a one—I should not dread to welcome. But with you! No! no! Nesbitt Balfour—impossible!"

Balfour evidently quailed in spirit before that of the fierce woman whom he had roused to fury. There was a story and relations between them, of which we have not heard. They gave her the vantage-ground in the struggle. She probably had good reason for the scorn which she expressed. Balfour strove to make light of it.

"Pshaw! Harvey, this is sheer nonsense. You will grow wiser by to-morrow. But, just now——"

"Why will you linger? You certainly have no longer any hope of succeeding with Miss Walton? As for me, if you are so confident of *me*, brave me' to-morrow, if you will—if you dare! *Now*, begone, and let me tend to her. I am only fit for curses while you remain."

Colonel Walton met his fate with courage and a manly firmness. His daughter, with Mrs. Singleton, obtained permission to leave the city for the interior, a few days after. Balfour could not venture to outrage public decency so far as to deny this permission. She ultimately became the wife of Robert Singleton. Under their auspices, Major Proctor, at the close of the war, married Ella Monckton. The descendants of both parties are now to be found among the most noble citizens of the great southwest. Three nights after Walton's execution, Dr. Ramsay, old Tom Singleton, with thirty-eight others, suspected citizens of Charleston, were seized in their beds, and sent off in a prison-ship to St. Augustine, where they were kept as hostages.

We have but to speak of mad Archy Campbell. He was killed, some time after, at the battle of Videau's Bridge. He fell a victim to his own restless nature and headstrong will. At the opening of the action, the Americans having the advantage,

Campbell was taken prisoner, disarmed, and placed under the guard of Nicholas Venning, of Christ Church parish, who was ordered to kill him if he attempted to escape. In a little while after, the fortune of the day began to change ; the Americans were about to be repulsed ; and, seeing this, Campbell became so impatient and so insubordinate that, after repeated threats and warnings, Venning put his orders into execution, and slew him. Here ends our chronicle.

It may be well to mention that, in our progress, we have dealt largely with real historical personages. Our facts have mostly been drawn from the living records. Our dialogues, our incidents, our portraits, have mostly a traditional, if not an historical origin. We may add that many of the details in the narrative of Colonel Walton have been borrowed from those in the career of the celebrated Colonel Hayne. It was Hayne who took Williamson prisoner, as described in our story. He himself was captured under the very circumstances given in the case of Walton ; and the details of the execution are gathered from the lips of living witnesses.

THE END.

From the S. Lewis engraving, Plate VIII of the Atlas accompanying
John Marshall's *The Life of George Washington* (1807).

EXPLANATORY NOTES

by

Elisabeth Muhlenfeld

These notes are intended to identify persons, places, events, quotations and obscure or archaic words and terms in the text of *Katharine Walton*. Special emphasis has been placed upon the Revolutionary War history in this novel, including, when possible, the identification of Simms' sources and his departures from them.

1.2 "Hon. Edward Frost": Edward Frost of Charleston was a judge of the court of appeals and the court of errors of South Carolina, and active in the state legislature throughout his career. His retirement in 1853, to which Simms refers, was made voluntarily and was considered an admirable and unusual step by his friends, among them Simms and Benjamin Franklin Perry.

1.12 "'Content . . . your own ground'": Alexander Pope, "Ode on Solitude," stanza 1.

2.9 "Burleighs of society": Reference to John Balfour, 17th century Baron of Burleigh (d. 1688). Colonel Nesbit Balfour, a major character in *Katharine Walton* (see note 7.13), was his grandson.

2.12 "Scott and Cooper": Sir Walter Scott and James Fenimore Cooper, well-known authors of historical romances.

2.13 "Bracton and Fleta, Littleton and Sir Edward Coke": Classic legal authorities. Henry de Bracton was a mid-13th century medieval English jurist, author of *De Legibus et Consuetudinibus Angliae*; Sir Thomas Littleton wrote *On Tenures* (c. 1481), the first important English legal text not in Latin. Coke, author of *Institutes of the Lawes of England* (1628-1644), was known for his defense of the supremacy of the common law against the claims of the royal prerogative. Fleta, though apparently used here as a personal name, was actually the title of a text of English law, c. 1290.

2.34 "third of a trilogy": *Katharine Walton* was probably originally conceived as the second in a series of three novels about the Revolution,

477

the first to be *The Partisan* (1835) and the third to be *Woodcraft*, published as *The Sword and the Distaff* in 1852. By the time *Katharine Walton* was published, Simms had written *The Partisan* and its sequel, *Mellichampe* (1836), and thus *Katharine Walton* became the final volume in a trilogy centering around the exploits of Robert Singleton. Another Revolutionary novel, *The Scout*, published in 1841 as *The Kinsman*, had no direct connection with the trilogy.

3.4 "discoveries to our people": Several romantic novels set in Revolutionary times had appeared before *The Partisan* was published, but Simms was a pioneer both in the high degree of historical accuracy the novels reflect and in their focus on the civil war character of the Revolution in South Carolina and on the role of the partisan in the conflict.

3.6 "clews to the historian": Simms was the first writer-intellectual of any stature in the South to turn his attention to the local history of the Revolution. He was in contact with a large number of historians and antiquarians, his own work frequently serving as an inspiration for these others, and his knowledge and experience used freely to guide and assist their researches. Among those works which Simms had some hand in beginning or directing are Joseph Johnson's *Traditions and Reminiscences* (1851), Elizabeth Ellet's *The Women of the American Revolution* (1848-50) and *Domestic History of the American Revolution* (1850), Robert Wilson Gibbes' *Documentary History of the American Revolution* (1853-1857), William Bacon Stevens' *History of Georgia* (1847, 1859) and Albert James Pickett's *History of Alabama* (1851). As editor of the *Magnolia* from 1842-1843, Simms sought and published articles on local Revolutionary lore from such authors as B. F. Perry and John Belton O'Neall.

3.15 "nothing latent": Although it is difficult to document such a statement, it is clear that Simms was distressed by the remarks made by some of his friends in reviews of *The Partisan*. For example, one review which Simms attributed to his friend Henry William Herbert but which was actually written by Park Benjamin said "the story lacks excitement; the actors interest, identity, and spirit" (*The Letters of William Gilmore Simms*, Odell, Oliphant, Eaves, eds., I, 85).

3.25 Ashley, Santee, Wateree: The Wateree River flows south from North Carolina through the center of the state and converges with the Congaree to form the Santee which enters the Atlantic south of Georgetown. The Ashley (first named the Keawah) and the Cooper (Etiwan) join at Charleston.

3.28 Charleston or Charles Towne (until 1783) was the major city of the South at the time of the Revolution. Of utmost strategic importance to the British, it was finally taken in May 1780 and held by them until it was evacuated on 14 December 1782.

3.35 "sources as unquestionable as abundant": Simms used both published and unpublished accounts of occupied Charleston as resource material for *Katharine Walton*. David Ramsay's *History of the Revolution of South Carolina* (1785), Moultrie's *Memoirs of the American Revolution* (1802), Alexander Garden's *Anecdotes of the Revolutionary War in America* (1822) and *Anecdotes of the American Revolution . . . Second Series* (1828), Ellet's domestic histories, Henry Lee's *The Campaign of 1781 in the Carolinas* (1812) and the revised edition of 1824, and Banastre Tarleton's *A History of the Campaigns of 1780 and 1781* (1787) are among Simms' most frequently used published sources. Also available to him were tales told by his grandmother, Mrs. Jacob Gates, who had been in Charleston during the siege and occupation, and by other people still living who had witnessed the events which he describes. Simms actively sought to interview such people and to record their impressions. Several scenes in *Katharine Walton* are based on incidents which are also reported by Simms' close friend, Joseph Johnson, in *Traditions and Reminiscences* (1851), published the year after *Katharine Walton*.

4.8 "another romance": Simms refers here to *Woodcraft* (see note 2.34) in which Porgy, Lance Frampton, the Griffins and Dennison were to appear.

4.22 "'A spirit, yet a woman too!'": Wordsworth, "She was a Phantom of Delight," stanza 2.

4.35 "Woodland": After his marriage to Chevillette Roach in 1836, Simms lived at Woodlands, one of twin plantations on the South Edisto near Orangeburg, belonging to his wife's father, Nash Roach.

5.10 "In previous narratives": I.e., *The Partisan* and *Mellichampe*, which deal with events immediately prior to and after the first battle of Camden (16 August 1780).

5.12-21 "the events following": The bombardment of Charleston by the British began on 13 April 1780 in one of the largest military operations of the war. The British force under Clinton eventually grew to more than 11,000 men against a garrison of less than 6000 American troops in the city under General Lincoln. Lincoln was forced to surrender on 12 May 1780, yielding all public property to the British. Continental troops were designated prisoners. 1500 militia troops were allowed to leave the city as prisoners-on-parole, and all remaining persons including noncombatants were also considered prisoners-on-parole. A month after the fall of Charleston, there were almost no Continental or militia troops remaining in South Carolina. The British devoted their energies to increasing loyalist support, both by promising protection to all who abandoned resistance and by denial of legal rights and confiscation of property for those who resisted.

Occasional partisan successes by Thomas Sumter near the North Carolina line and by Francis Marion in the eastern part of the state kept alive the patriots' hopes. In July, General Horatio Gates, then famous for his defeat of the British at Saratoga, New York, in the fall of 1777, took command of the Southern armies, consisting almost entirely of 1400 Continental troops from Maryland and Delaware and an equal number of untried militia from North and South Carolina. His first and only major encounter with the British under Lord Cornwallis occurred at Camden on 16 August 1780. The battle was devastating to the Americans. More than 2000 troops were killed, wounded or captured, and all artillery and supplies were seized. Perhaps equally important, the Americans were demoralized by the way in which the militia, ill-fed and untrained, had thrown down their rifles and fled, and by Gates' hasty retreat to North Carolina.

5.22 "Many of their prisoners": Simms' fictionalized account of the executions at Camden in *The Partisan* (p. 476) follows those of earlier historians except for William Johnson who, in his *Sketches of the Life and Correspondence of Nathanael Greene* (1822), I, 300, states that the victims were not prisoners taken at Camden but rather some of Sumter's men captured by Tarleton at Fishing Creek on 18 August, brought to Camden and tried in a British effort to coerce submission.

6.6 "Colonel Richard Walton": See *The Partisan* note 117.1-16 for full annotation of Walton as he is presented in *The Partisan*. In *Katharine Walton*, Walton's personal and family life are largely fictional, but his military career and death follow that of Isaac Hayne (1745-1781), who was a planter and lived at "Hayne Hall" in Colleton District near Jacksonboro. About thirty at the beginning of the Revolution, he served as an officer in a Colleton County regiment. Hayne had a partnership with William Hill in a large iron works near the North Carolina line which was destroyed by a British and loyalist force under Captain Huck in June 1780. Before beginning *Katharine Walton*, Simms inquired (see *The Letters*, V, 322) about the background of George Walton (1741-1804), a Georgia signer of the Declaration of Independence who, though he fought briefly during the Siege of Savannah in 1778, spent most of the war years in various political offices. Simms' inquiry was perhaps to verify that his fictional Walton in no way resembled George Walton.

6.10 "British protection": Clinton offered this protection on 22 May 1780, issuing a similar, more strongly worded proclamation on 1 June. Although Walton has, in *The Partisan*, taken the protection to secure his property, Isaac Hayne was forced to sign because his wife and children were terminally ill, and in order to leave the city and return to them, he had to declare his neutrality. Hayne was very careful to stipulate that he did so for this reason only, and asked David Ramsay to bear witness to his reluctance.

6.21 "by proclamation": On 3 June, Clinton abolished the status of prisoner-on-parole for all but those within the Charleston garrison. Holders of protections were given until 20 June to declare allegiance to the king, after which time all who refused would be considered enemies.

6.24 "Cornwallis": Lord Charles Cornwallis (1738-1805), commander-in-chief of the British forces in the Southern Department, subsequently surrendered at Yorktown on 19 October 1781.

6.30 "foot of the gallows": This fictional rescue occurs in *The Partisan*, pp. 528-529.

6.32 "Major Singleton": Robert Singleton is a fictional character but may have been based on one or more of Simms' own ancestors. Simms was descended from a Charleston branch of the Singleton family. His grandfather, John Singleton (Mrs. Gates' first husband), and two great-great uncles, Ripley and Bracey, served under Marion. Another branch of the family lived in the High Hills of Santee (now Sumter County); of this branch, Matthew Singleton and his son John also served under Marion. Robert was a family name—Matthew's second son by the name was considerably younger than the fictional Singleton at the time of the Revolution. See *The Partisan* notes 46.21.

6.36 "Dorchester": Located nineteen miles northwest of Charleston on a bend of the Ashley River, Dorchester was settled in 1696 by Congregationalists from Massachusetts and was, at the time of the Revolution, the third largest town in South Carolina. By 1788, it was virtually abandoned. Walton's rescue and the burning of Dorchester are fictional.

7.13 "Colonel Balfour": Nesbit (Nisbet) Balfour (1743-1823) was of noble Scots descent. He was wounded at Bunker Hill, and saw action at Long Island and Brooklyn. About 1777 he became friendly with Lord Cornwallis and Lord Rawdon, and was promoted to lieutenant colonel shortly thereafter. He received praise from his superiors when, as commandant of the fort at Ninety Six, he raised 4000 loyalists to serve as militia, after which he was appointed commandant of Charleston. After the war, he served as aide-de-camp to the king, as a member of Parliament, and as a general in France.

7.18 *"otium cum dignitate"*: Latin: leisure with dignity.

7.28 "Rawdon": Lord Rawdon, later Earl of Moira and Marquis of Hastings (1754-1826), only twenty-six or twenty-seven and a lieutenant colonel at the time of *Katharine Walton*, was in command of the British forces in South Carolina outside Charleston after Cornwallis left the state in January 1781.

7.33 "Marion . . . upon the Santee": Francis Marion (1732-1795), famous whig partisan leader, commanded the 2nd South Carolina Regiment of the Continental Army in the early years of the war. After the fall of Charleston, he was made a brigadier general of militia and waged a brilliant guerrilla war against the British. At Nelson's Ferry on 19 (20?) August 1780 in his first encounter after Charleston, Marion met a British guard with a large body of prisoners taken at Camden, and was successful in retaking all the prisoners. Ironically, of the 150 Continentals thus rescued, only three agreed to ride with Marion, the rest so demoralized by Gates' defeat that they felt the whig cause was hopeless.

8.33 "vigor of his years": The physical description of the thirty-nine year old Balfour is accurate.

9.18 "never distinguished himself": Simms errs here (see note 7.13), having taken his description from Ramsay. See note 9.38.

9.21 "second in command": In his 1813 letter to Henry Lee, Rawdon protested that he had been junior to Balfour. Balfour outranked Rawdon, but his job as commandant of Charleston was one of support and organization, while Rawdon's was one of direct military operations. In fact, Rawdon is repeatedly referred to as Commander-in-Chief or Supreme Commander in proclamations and dispatches of the day.

9.28 "Howe": Sir William Howe (1729-1814) took command of the British forces in October 1775. He resigned in 1778.

9.33 "Sir Pertinax MacSycophant": A hard, worldly old character in Charles Macklin's *Man of the World* (1781).

9.38 "'By the subversion . . .'" Ramsay, *History of the Revolution of South-Carolina*, II, 264.

10.21 "Lothario": A young seducer in Nicholas Rowe's tragedy *The Fair Penitent* (1703).

10.28 "Mark Antony": (83?-30 B.C.) Roman general, friend of Caesar, member of the second triumvirate and rival of Octavian.

10.30 "rods, like those of Aaron": Numbers 17:6-10.

11.1 "that noble old mansion. . . . of Miles Brewton": Miles Brewton was a member of the Provincial Congress in 1775, and the most conservative member of the Council of Safety. He and his family left Charleston for Philadelphia in 1775, but the ship never reached port.

The Brewton house, #27 King Street, is one of the most magnificent in Charleston. During the occupation, it was Balfour's headquarters. It was bought by Colonel William Allston who, though very young at the time of the Revolution, served under Marion as a captain, and was a long time friend of Thomas Jefferson. At his death in 1838, the house passed to his youngest daughter, Mrs. William Bull Pringle. It is still a private residence.

11.22 "Colonel Cruden": John Cruden, commissioner of sequestered estates, was charged with managing all properties under sequestration, including slaves. See note 44.4-23.

12.1 "Laurens": Henry Laurens served as president of the Continental Congress from November 1777 to December 1778. See note 156.3.

12.12 "Cotesworth Pinckney . . . the finest house": Built by Charles Pinckney about 1740 at a cost in excess of $40,000, the "Mansion House" closely resembled that of Miles Brewton. It occupied an entire square on East Bay above Market Street, and commanded a magnificent view of the harbour. Charles took his family to Europe in 1753, and the house was leased to a succession of governors. When Charles died in 1758, the house was left to his son Charles Cotesworth, then a boy of thirteen. Charles Cotesworth remained in England at school, and the house was not lived in by Pinckneys until his return in 1769. It was destroyed by fire in 1862.

12.23 "take the field": After the Battle of Monmouth in June 1778, no significant battles occurred in New England or the middle colonies.

12.25 "the colonies of Great Britain": In the summer of 1780, a report that Congress intended to negotiate a peace with Great Britain by ceding the southern states to her caused consternation among the American troops and prisoners of the British. The report had some basis in fact—such a suggestion was actually debated in Congress. On 25 June 1780, however, Congress issued a resolution disavowing any such intention and affirming their commitment to the southern colonies.

12.28 "*uti-posidetis* principle": A principle in international law which holds that at the conclusion of a war, each side has legal claim to the territory under its actual control, including goods in its possession.

14.9-10 "Kitty Harvey. . . . Moll": The Harvey sisters are apparently fictional. There were Harveys both on the whig and loyalist side, and a Harvey estate southwest of Charleston towards the Stono River. An Alexander Harvey of Charleston was an addressor of Sir Henry Clinton in 1780. He was banished in 1782 and his property confiscated.

15.11 "the stud of this rebel": Hayne, the character on whom Walton is based, was known for his fine stables. The cavalry of Banastre Tarleton (1754-1833) had lost all their mounts at sea and restocked in part from the stables of wealthy whigs.

15.23 "to spoil the Egyptians": Exodus 12:36.

16.9 "the 'Citadel,' in Charleston": This building still stands, facing Marion Square at Hutson and Meeting streets.

16.20 "'Up the path'": A commonly used local expression which referred to the old Indian path, predecessor of Highway 17 leading north out of Charleston.

16.25 "the 'Neck'": That portion of the peninsula of land between the Ashley and Cooper rivers above Charleston.

16.25 "of the leaguer": Clinton's army landed on the Neck after crossing the Ashley on 29 March 1780.

17.2 *horn-work*": An addition to a fortification.

17.5 "fraised, picketed": Fraized: covered with pointed stakes projecting from the ramparts in a horizontal or inclined position. Picketed: strengthened by soldiers placed before the fortifications to warn of enemy advance.

17.8 "field-works": Temporary fortifications.

17.9 "Beyond them" and ff.: Charleston was besieged by the British from February to May of 1780. Clinton's army landed at John's Island on 11 February and proceeded very cautiously from island to island, finally landing on the peninsula on 29 March. Lincoln had positioned his troops within the city, and spent the period of Clinton's advance strengthening its fortifications which ran across the Neck approximately where Calhoun and Vanderhorst streets stand today. Clinton constructed redoubts and trenches (or parallels) successively closer and closer to the American fortifications and bombarded them from 13 April until 11 May, by which date the British had crossed a wet ditch dug by the defenders in front of their fortifications, and stood within twenty-five yards of the American lines. The fate of the Americans and Lincoln had been obvious long before the siege started: the city could not be defended by a garrison; it was vulnerable on the north by land and on all other sides by water. Fort Moultrie guarding the harbour had surrendered on 7 May without firing a shot—the British had simply not stopped to engage the Americans. Those within the city had repeatedly pled with Lincoln to surrender; thus, he was in no position to extract good terms from the British. The articles of surrender were signed on 12 May.

17.19 "abbatis": Abatis: an obstacle of logs with bent or sharpened branches directed toward the enemy.

17.20-24 "the 'Broadway,' . . .": Now King Street. John Archdale was appointed colonial governor of South Carolina in 1695. This is a quote from his "A New Description of that Fertile and Pleasant Province of Carolina, with a Brief Account of its Discovery and Settling and the Government thereof to the Time, with Several Remarkable Passages of Divine Providence during My Time" (London, 1707), reprinted in 1836 in B.R. Carroll, *Historical Collections of South Carolina*, II, 95.

18.12 "'What bloody scene hath Roscius now to act?'": "What scene of death hath Roscius now to act," Shakespeare, 3 *Henry VI*, V, vi.

19.13 "usual permit to depart": In the early months of the occupa- tion, travel to and from the city was relatively easy. By 1781, as the British grew more desperate and their intelligence network was nearly destroyed by Marion and Sumter, permits to leave the city became more difficult to obtain.

19.34 "General Williamson": Andrew Williamson was the leading whig in Ninety Six District at the opening of the war, and distinguished him- self in campaigns against the loyalists in 1775 and the Cherokees in 1776. At the time of the surrender of Charleston, he was the highest ranking officer in the state not a prisoner, but he retired from the field (see note 354.7), took a "protection" and eventually moved to Charles- ton, where he was accused of aiding the British.

20.7 "his correspondence": History does not support this statement. However, in a letter to Cornwallis, Lord Rawdon wrote on 24 June 1780, "I have had several private conversations with Williamson . . . and if I am not much deceived indeed [he] will be infinitely useful here, if properly treated" (quoted in George Smith McCowen, Jr., *The British Occupation of Charleston, 1780-82* [1972], p. 67), indicating that the British intended to use Williamson in some way similar to this.

20.8 Ninety Six; Congarees: These names refer both to districts and specific locations. Ninety Six District, in the central and western part of the state, included the town of Ninety Six, a loyalist stronghold about fifty miles northeast of Augusta. Congarees refers to the district near present day Columbia, along the Congaree River. Fort Granby, located just below present day Columbia, was often called "The Congarees" or "Congaree Fort."

20.10 "'Quarter's House'": About five and one-half miles north of Charleston at Ashley Road.

21.11 "the conquest of New York": In late August and September 1776, Howe's army defeated Washington at Staten Island, Long Island and Manhattan, forcing Washington to retreat to New Jersey.

23.14 "seventy-six men in garrison": No sources have been found detailing the number of British at Dorchester in late 1780 or early 1781, but by December 1781 there were 550 troops garrisoned there.

23.32 "Blonay": Blonay is a major character in *The Partisan* and in *Mellichampe*.

24.31-35 "Lord Rawdon . . . in any quarter": Simms errs here. Ninety Six was under the command of Colonel Cruger rather than Colonel Stuart. Orangeburg, Fort Motte, Fort Watson, Monck's Corner and Fort Granby (apparently Simms errs in calling this "Quinby," a bridge which was the site of a later battle) were small forts strategically placed by the British to protect lines of communication and supply between Charleston and their troops in the up country. Proctor's statement that his scouts brought no news of the enemy reflects the fact that after the Battle of Camden, Marion so successfully cut off the lines of communication between Charleston and Camden that Rawdon was forced to dispatch Tarleton to find him and drive him out.

28.3 " 'The Oaks' ": Walton's plantation was probably modeled after two plantations connected with the Izard family: Fair Spring and Newington, both located near Dorchester, both originally properties of provincial nobility, and both approached by a long avenue lined with oak trees. See *The Partisan* notes 117.1-16 for complete documentation.

29.1 "as quick with the pen as with the sword": Probably an allusion to "The pen is mightier than the sword," in *Richelieu*, II, ii (1838), by Edward Bulwer-Lytton.

30.37 "*chevaux de frize*": probably *cheveux de frisé*, French, meaning curly hair.

32.33 "Sir Henry Clinton": (1738?-1795) Commander-in-Chief of the British forces in North America. Balfour refers here to the proclamations of 20 May, 1 June and 3 June.

33.4 "Portia. She comes to the point manfully": Heroine of Shakespeare's *The Merchant of Venice*, Portia disguises herself as a young doctor of laws to plead mercy for Antonio.

33.13 "general terms of the British regulation": As set forth in Cornwallis' proclamation of 16 September 1780, which announces the sequestration of estates, real and personal, of "wicked and dangerous traitors."

33.34 "money chest of Marion": Because of the depreciation of Continental money, plate and jewels were used both for the purchase of goods and occasionally as payment for officers. Women sympathetic to the whig cause frequently gave up their pewter plate to be made into bullets.

35.12 Many of the details of Chapters III and V may have been suggested by an anecdote recounted in Johnson's *Traditions*, pp. 559-562, in which a Mrs. Slocomb received Tarleton at her home. When asked if her husband was a rebel, she replied, "No, sir, he is in the army of his country, and fighting against our invaders, therefore not a rebel." Mrs. Slocomb treated Tarleton with great dignity (much as Katharine treats Balfour here), and when he announced that he would quarter in her house, she said "We are your prisoners." She fed the enemy a large dinner (as Katharine does in Chapter V), and while Tarleton was quartered there, his troops were attacked by a party led by her husband, much as the Oaks is visited by Walton in the night in Chapter IX.

37.9 "Captain Furness, of the True Blue Rifles": An apparently fictional person and troop. The role of Captain Furness assumed here by Singleton well illustrates the independent, sincere back country loyalist —a type portrayed by Simms nowhere else.

37.23 "Tom Sumter": Thomas Sumter (1734-1832), an early whig leader and member of the Provincial Congresses, refused British protection after the fall of Charleston and instead led a partisan campaign against the British. Colonel Thomas Taylor joined Sumter, and both men successfully staged the raid described here, at Camden Ferry about a mile from Camden, on the Wateree, on 15 August 1780, the day before the Battle of Camden.

38.4 "supplies sent after them": Tarleton pursued Sumter and Taylor, and routed them completely at Fishing Creek on 17 August, destroying Sumter's troop. Taylor and his brother were captured, but later escaped. Simms' chronology is confused here. Walton's rescue took place several days after the Battle of Camden, and Balfour's visit to the Oaks several days after that. Thus he would undoubtedly have been aware of Tarleton's success. Tarleton's letters to Balfour are apparently fictional.

41.17 "a territory no less": According to Johnson, Mrs. Slocomb's guests (see note 35.12) discussed how property captured during the war would be divided, with Tarleton commenting, "officers . . . will undoubtedly receive large possessions of the conquered American provinces . . . this beautiful plantation will be the ducal seat for us" (p. 562).

44.4-23: "To distress the enemy": Clinton remarked about his policy of confiscation, "This I looked upon as a most prudent measure," intended to prevent underhanded doings among the patriots (quoted in McCowen, p. 54). A policy of confiscation in the Revolution was by no means a British invention. The South Carolina constitution of 1776 proclaimed the right to confiscate the property of all those who refused to take an oath of loyalty to the state. The practice of sequestration differed somewhat from that of simple confiscation, in that the wives of the owners of the estate thus seized were to receive one-sixth of the profit from the estate or, if minor children existed, one-fourth. The estate was theoretically held by the Crown until such time as it was no longer needed, or until the traitor was persuaded of the error of his ways. The first sequestrations by the British in South Carolina were ordered by Cornwallis after Camden, and were begun in September 1780. Over one hundred estates and more than 5000 Negroes were taken during the occupation of Charleston. The British hoped that the plantations could produce such supplies as were needed by the garrison at Charleston, that the Negroes not actually needed on the estates could be used on civic projects, and that profits would remit to the king. The task of operating the sequestered estates proved nearly impossible for the British: often the lands were in disrepair due to the absence of their owners, and as the strength of the partisan militia increased, frequent raids resulted in recapture by the whigs.

44.23 "We have no 'pickings,' sir": An incident related in Alexander Garden's *Anecdotes of the Revolutionary War* (1822) may have been the inspiration for this scene. "A blundering Refugee, one of a number who gave a dinner to Lieutenant Colonel Provost, on his arrival in London with dispatches, relative to the repulse of the French and Americans at Savannah, said to him, on being presented, —'Well, Colonel, you have had a peep at Charleston, and given a terrible fright to the Rebels. 'Tis true, that on your expedition you gained but few laurels, but you made a devilish good trading voyage, plundering, as we are credibly informed, all the Islands on your retreat.' 'Sir,' said the Colonel, with the benignant smile of innocence, 'you are misinformed. His Majesty's troops never plunder'" (pp. 263-264). However, an estimated £300,000 sterling was systematically plundered from the patriots and distributed among the British officers: "Commissioners of captures administered the plunder and assigned it by rule. The quota of a major-general approached four thousand guineas, but individuals often secured in addition by private plunder more than their allotment from the commissioner" (David Duncan Wallace, *South Carolina: A Short History* [1951], p. 294).

44.32 "The laborer is worthy of his hire": Luke 10:7.

45.7 "the up country": Though the phrase was often used synonymously with "back country" in the 18th century, Furness refers here to the section of South Carolina generally north and west of Columbia.

46.4 "Forks of Edisto": About twenty miles southeast of Orangeburg, the north and south forks of the Edisto merge and flow southeast. Many Germans settled in this region, although Cammer is apparently a fictional character.

46.12-15 "no annihilation": It is difficult to prove the truth of Furness' statement because of the difficulty of dating his appearance at "The Oaks." Although there were several skirmishes immediately after the first battle of Camden in which the partisans had some success, they showed only limited strength until later in the fall of 1780.

48.3 "can't they get it there?": Johnson in his *Traditions* (p. 298) says of the Madeira in South Carolina wine cellars, "Such wine could not be imported, it could not be bought, but it might be plundered."

48.10 "my Altamira": Balfour's reference here is muddled: Altamira refers to some caverns in northern Spain in which a rich archive of pre-historic drawings were found.

49.5 "small-pox": There was a smallpox epidemic in Charleston during the spring and summer of 1780.

49.20 "That was the reason": When the British Army landed within thirty miles of Charleston in February 1780, prior to laying siege, Governor Rutledge commanded the militia to move into the city, but with little effect. They feared both yellow fever and smallpox.

54.9 "the old tabby walls": Many of the fortifications in Charleston were constructed of a mixture of oyster shells and lime, originally called *tapis*, later corrupted to "tabby."

55.2 "Old French War": Simms refers here to the French and Indian War which, in South Carolina, culminated in the Cherokee War of 1760-1761.

56.2 "Was it not thence": The destruction of the Singleton plantation on the Santee and Emily Singleton's flight to "The Oaks" and her subsequent death are reported in *The Partisan*.

56.12 "Were the French to help": In the spring of 1781, the French did send the long hoped for fleet to Yorktown, Virginia. The British, expecting it to land at Beaufort, South Carolina, abandoned their interior posts to concentrate on the southern coast of South Carolina.

56.14 "an efficient general": General Nathanael Greene (1742-1786) was appointed to succeed Gates as commander of the Southern armies in October 1780, and assumed command on 4 December.

56.17 "a Fabian war": A war in which victory is obtained by delay and harassment rather than by a decisive battle.

57.7 *"petit maitre"*: An insignificant but self-important person.

57.8 "Harry Barry": Henry Barry (1750-1822) served as aide-de-camp and private secretary to Rawdon and probably saw action at Bunker Hill, Brooklyn, White Plains and Fort Clinton. He was appointed deputy adjutant general under General Alexander Leslie by Cornwallis on 24 December 1780. Leslie's troops were not headquartered in Charleston until November 1781, however, so Barry's presence in *Katharine Walton* is anachronistic. He was known for his skill at doggerel. (Johnson, for example, quotes a satirical letter by him in *Traditions*, pp. 278-279.) Mad Campbell, or Mad Archy, was an actual British captain in Charleston known for his violent temper during the occupation. Fool or Crazy Campbell appears in traditional accounts of occupied Charleston, but it is not clear if he was indeed a different person.

60.2 "Father Mathew": Theobald Mathew of County Cork, Ireland, was one of the most famous temperance missionaries of the 19th century, and was widely acclaimed in Ireland and England in the 1840's. He made a trip to the United States in 1850, the year *Katharine Walton* was written.

60.17 "'Milk for babes, but meat for men'": Hebrews 5:12-13.

60.27 "too many of the American generals . . .": Though it is difficult to determine how many American generals overindulged with liquor, it was apparently customary for officers to drink heavily. Wallace (*A Short History*, pp. 195-196) cites large importations of liquor as evidence of the pattern of the day.

61.10 "his countrymen": The Scots.

62.30 "'Drink deep' . . . Twickenham": "Drink deep, or taste not the Pierian Spring," Alexander Pope, *An Essay on Criticism*, I, 215.

62.36 "André did some rhyming": Major John André was the principal contact between the British and Benedict Arnold (see note 156.32). In the guise of Mr. John Anderson, he arranged the surrender of West Point. André was captured and the plot was uncovered; he was court-martialed, convicted of spying and executed on 2 October 1780. Johnson's *Traditions* (pp. 204-206) quotes his poem on a duel between William Howe and Christopher Gadsden.

63.1 "M'Mahon": There was a Captain McMahon in the British garrison at Charleston, but any close association he might have had with Barry is unknown.

63.11 "Sufficient for the day is the plunder thereof": "Sufficient unto the day is the evil thereof," Matthew 6:34.

64.26 "You look as surly as Sir William": Perhaps a reference to Sir William Howe, under whom Balfour had served in the early days of the war.

65.23 "gowned inquisitor of . . . Westminster": Balfour's drunken allusion confuses the promulgators of the Spanish Inquisition with the British Parliament.

68.14-22. landgrave; landgravinoes; cassicoes; palatinos: When Charles II granted lands for a colony in South Carolina in the 1660's, the Lords Proprietors to whom this grant was made, among them Anthony, Lord Ashley-Cooper, later Earl of Shaftesbury, devised a code of laws which provided for a nobility consisting of landgraves, cassiques, and barons—titles conferred upon those who made large purchases of land. The oldest proprietary lord was granted the title of Palatine, and was given royal privileges by the king, to act in his stead in the province.

68.25 "Prince Macklevelly": Machiavelli's *The Prince* extolled the expedient and advocated the use of craft to maintain authority.

69.30 "my Bellamira": A frequent heroine in 17th century drama. See, for example, *Bellamira, her Dream* by Thomas Killigrew and *Bellamira, or the Mistress* by Charles Sedley.

70.2 "queen of Sheba": I Kings 10:1-13.

73.20 "Saint Absalom": An apparent confusion of the biblical Absalom and St. Andrew, the patron saint of Scotland. II Samuel 18:9 describes the death of Absalom who, while riding a mule, got his hair caught in an oak, thus allowing his enemies to kill him with arrows. St. Andrew was crucified upside down.

73.26 "Ishmael": Son of Abraham and Hagar, both he and Hagar were cast out of Abraham's family by Sarah, Genesis 16:11, 12. The epithet "Son of Ishmael" was used in the 19th century South to mean Negro.

73.28 "the cream of Potosi": Potosi, a city in Bolivia, was an extremely rich silver-mining center.

74.21 "you irreverent Ichabod": Ichabod was the infant son of Phineas, I Samuel 4:21, and was also the name of the schoolmaster in "The Legend of Sleepy Hollow" by Washington Irving, included in *The Sketch Book* (1820). However, Simms may also have had in mind a poem by John Greenleaf Whittier, "Ichabod!," which was published in *National Era*, an abolitionist newspaper, in May 1850, and which attacked Daniel Webster for his support of the Compromise of 1850.

74.22 "Bull Apis": In ancient Egyptian religion, Apis was a sacred bull worshiped at Memphis and identified with Ptah and later Osiris.

74.24 "Grand Turk": The Ottoman sultan.

75.38 "buff": Military clothing.

76.4 "the rod should be put in pickle for awhile": Balfour's pun on rod is a double-entendre; rod-in-pickle was a term used to describe the punishment of a mischievous child, but "in pickle" also meant venereally infected.

77.25 "as Michael Angelo painted": Balfour refers here to Michaelangelo's statue of the seated Moses on the Julius tomb, c. 1513-1515.

78.27 "few boots in the camp of Marion": Johnson's *Traditions* (p. 68), for example, relates an eyewitness account of one of Marion's men at Videau's Bridge stealing boots from a dead British soldier.

82.16 "Hanover turnip": A reference to George III of the House of Hanover, who enjoyed farming, and was at the same time inclined to plumpness.

85.1 The incident related in this chapter may also have been suggested by the adventure of Mrs. Slocomb recorded in Johnson's *Traditions* (see notes 35.12 and 41.17). After dinner, a small band led by Slocomb, the master of the house, surprised the British. When Tarleton asked his officer "What force attacked you?", the man replied "I cannot tell, but I suppose an hundred men," whereupon Tarleton remarked, "We saw but some half dozen, and five of you were running from three men and a boy" (p. 565).

85.21 "the seven sleepers": The seven sleepers were seven mythical youths of Ephesus said to have hidden in a cave during the Decian persecution and to have slept there for several hundred years.

90.21 "Major Tatem": Although numerous atrocities committed by the loyalists are recorded in contemporary accounts, no such man or action has come to light.

100.14 "state of feeling in the back country": In the fall of 1780, the British had good reason to be concerned with the back country, or that portion of the state more than about thirty or forty miles from the coast. In spite of the fact that the fall of Charleston and the loss at Camden had temporarily destroyed the regular American forces and that the proclamations of Clinton and Cornwallis had persuaded many to turn loyalist, the partisan effort was becoming increasingly effective. British communication lines were harassed, and the defeat of Ferguson at King's Mountain in October 1780 and of Tarleton at Cowpens on 17

January 1781 testified to the increasing strength of the whigs. The back country throughout this period was characterized by extremely bitter civil war.

101.11 "Eight-Mile House": One of a series of public houses along the road to Goose Creek.

116.13 "the positive instructions . . .": Simms may refer here to the policy expressed in Lord Howe's proclamation to the Colonies, from Boston in 1776: "I do therefore hereby declare, that due Consideration shall be had to the Meretorious Service of all Persons, who shall aid and assist in restoring the public Tranquillity in the said Colonies, or in any Part or Parts thereof; that Pardons shall be granted, dutiful Representations received, and every suitable Encouragement given, for promoting such measures as shall be conducive to the Establishment of legal Government and Peace, in pursuance of His Majesty's most gracious Purposes aforesaid" (*Yearbook—1882: City of Charleston*, pp. 357-358).

118.1 "*passa-tèmpo*": Italian, *passatèmpo*: pastime, sport. Proctor's remark puns on the fencing term tempo, meaning to take care never to thrust unless sure of the mark, and the musical a tempo.

120.6 "*perdu*": Hidden.

122.13 "the British army . . . by favor": Simms' assessment here is perhaps overstated, but is basically an accurate description of the promotion practices of the British army in the 18th century.

124.3 "She is already almost exhausted": George III had severe financial problems which were debated in Parliament as early as 1777. In 1778, war was declared with France. There is no doubt that Great Britain was indeed sick and tired of the rebellion in the colonies. Nevertheless, Simms' statement here, made in late 1780 or early 1781 (the dating of the events in *Katharine Walton* is imprecise), is premature in regard to England's state of exhaustion.

124.10 "they have taken up": In the early days of the war, most loyalists seem to have been appalled at the idea of taking up arms against the king. Many had serious reservations about American independence in spite of their love for their homeland. Nevertheless, Proctor's statement here is true for the period immediately after the fall of Charleston, during Clinton's policy of pardons and "protections," and Cornwallis' subsequent sequestrations. Many loyalists seem to have been motivated entirely by the need to protect their property. It was not uncommon for a man to vacillate from side to side through the war depending on which way the tide turned.

124.16 "Already they begin": Again, Simms here expresses his own opinion, which is a debatable one. Most of the effective actions carried on by the British were those of regular soldiers, but notable exceptions include the Battle of King's Mountain, the second battle of Camden (Hobkirk's Hill) and the defense of Ninety Six. Further, the marauding actions of loyalists in the back country did much to maintain British authority in the state.

125.4   "The American loyalists": Proctor's prediction here proved accurate. In January 1782, South Carolina voted to expel or fine all who had sided with the king and to confiscate all their properties. Illustrative of the antipathy against the loyalists a half-century after the war is Johnson's delicate suppression of the name of a loyalist, "as the family still live in the State, and some of them are said to be respectable" (*Traditions*, p. 561).

125.9   "the greater number": Most loyalists, especially in the South, were native Britons, either English or Scots.

126.27   "exchange the service": Lord Charles Greville Montagu, former Royal Governor of South Carolina, arrived in Charleston after its fall and set about raising a regiment by attempting to persuade the prisoners to change sides. He enlisted 530 men by promising them that they would serve in the West Indies rather than against their neighbors.

127.36   "from the Cypress": The Cypress Swamp begins a few miles north of Dorchester, and extends in a mile-wide stretch along the Ashley River.

128.3   "Bacon's bridge": Crosses the Ashley River northwest of Dorchester about five miles.

130.6   "According to his letters . . .": This quotation, apparently from Greene's correspondence, has not been located.

130.24   "the Pedee": The Pee Dee and the Little Pee Dee rivers flow southeast across the northeast section of the state to the coast sixty miles north of Charleston.

131.5-9   "the Carolina partisans . . . immediate vicinity of Charleston": Simms accurately describes here the kind of partisan activity which distressed the British garrison at Charleston. Isaac Hayne himself, as captain of the Round O Company of the Colleton County regiment, is said to have led such actions during the Siege of Charleston.

131.25   "tupelo": The black gum tree, native to the swamps of South Carolina.

133.13   "The employment . . .": There is no evidence that the whigs used the bow and arrow as a regular weapon.

134.6 "Lance": Lance Frampton, who first made his appearance in *The Partisan*, is apparently fictional, though Frampton is a common name in the low country. William Dobein James in *The Life of Francis Marion* (1821), p. 94, tells of a young boy named "Gwyn" in Marion's band who was an excellent shot, and on whom the character of Lance may be based.

134.13 "Barnett": A man named Joel Barnett actually served in the militia, though nothing is known about his exploits.

135.15 "Lieutenant Porgy": Simms' most famous character, Porgy is unquestionably fictional. One possible source, however, appears in Major Alexander Garden's *Anecdotes* (1822), pp. 135-139. Garden describes a Dr. Skinner who looked like Sancho and would "at any time rather have risked the loss of his friend, than the opportunity of applying a satirical observation in point." Very eccentric in his dress, Skinner also had an eye for ladies and, writes Garden, "I have seldom met with a man more fond of good and dainty cheer, or a more devoted idolater of good wine; but when they were not to be met with, the plainest food, and most simple liquor, were enjoyed with the highest relish" (p. 136). Several of the remarks attributed to Dr. Skinner by Garden are highly reminiscent of statements made by Porgy throughout the Revolutionary novels. Skinner, a native of Maryland, served as surgeon of the infantry in Lee's legion.

135.30 "the Zincali of Iberia": The Gitanos, or gypsies, of Spain call themselves Zincalis.

140.11 "The French and Spanish narrative": The particular document to which Simms refers has not been identified.

141.28 "a Parthian": Parthia was an ancient country in western Asia (now part of N.E. Iran) whose cavalry shot arrows while in real or feigned flight.

142.16 "three rounds to the man": Simms' source here is Moultrie, *Memoirs*, II, 223.

142.23 "On the Edisto": If the scenes early in the novel take place within ten days of the Battle of Camden, as they would seem to in reference to *The Partisan*, then Simms is in error here, for Marion in a letter to Colonel Peter Horry of 27 August 1780, stated that he was on Lynch's Creek encamped at Britton's Neck, a strip of land just above the junction of the Pee Dee rivers. If, on the other hand, the events take place after Cornwallis' 16 September proclamation regarding sequestration, then Marion may well have been on the Edisto.

142.27 "Aaron . . . must have fallen into the hands": Policy dictated that slaves belonging to "unfriendly persons" became public property, were placed under the supervision of John Cruden, commissioner of sequestered estates, and were put to work on the estates in the hands of the British or on civic projects. They were promised their freedom at the end of the war. In truth, however, slaves who either fell into the hands of the enemy or, spurred by the promise of freedom, delivered themselves up to the British, often suffered greatly. Thomas Jefferson, writing several years later, said *"the State of Virginia lost, under Lord Cornwallis's hand . . . about thirty thousand slaves; and that, of these, twenty-seven thousand died of the small-pox and camp-fever; and the rest were partly sent to the West Indies, and exchanged for rum, sugar, coffee, and fruit"* (George Livermore, *An Historical Research Respecting the Opinions of the Founders of the Republic on Negroes as Slaves, As Citizens, And as Soldiers* [1863], pp. 137-138). Wallace (*A Short History*) reports that the British fleet left Charleston after the evacuation with 5333 Negroes.

142.30 "Lieutenant Davis": Possibly Captain W. R. Davis, remembered for his sacking of Georgetown in July 1781 at the direction of Sumter.

143.24 "Izard's camp": Adjacent to the Quarter House, north of Charleston on the road to Goose Creek.

146.9 "we who get no pay at all": Like the historian Edward McCrady, Simms felt that the patriotism of the militia, which fought without pay (see Simms' *The Life of Francis Marion* [1844], p. 141) was greater than that of the Continentals, who were on regular payrolls. Wallace *(A Short History*, pp. 283-284) takes issue with this point, and notes that the Continentals "were not only without pay, but were also without sufficient food and even without clothing sufficient to prevent actual suffering or indecent exposure in many cases for long periods, whereas the militia, after a few days' service, returned home to eat and rest." In fact, both militia and regular soldiers fought under circumstances of extreme privation.

149.24 "*escritoir*": Writing desk. In this case, a small box that served as both valise and desk.

151.18 "would serve two masters": Matthew 6:24.

155.19 "General Williamson" and ff.: Simms' description of Williamson and the details of his career is accurate, except where otherwise noted.

156.1 "certain local rivalries": It is not clear why Williamson sided with the whigs. He was a major of militia at the post of Ninety Six in 1775. William Henry Drayton made a tour to the Ninety Six District in August 1775 to persuade the leading men of the up country to take the whig side, but apparently at this time Williamson was already in the whig camp. Edward McCrady in *The History of South Carolina in the*

Revolution (1901) reports that Drayton ordered Williamson's force of three hundred men to march to Snow Hill in late August, and that Drayton conferred with Williamson and others regarding the course to take with Robert Fletchall, an influential back country loyalist (I, 46-47).

156.3 "Laurens": Henry Laurens, of Charleston, probably South Carolina's leading patriot, was president of the Council of Safety at the time Williamson sided with the whigs. Laurens was subsequently president of the Continental Congress, and was later captured by the British while en route to a diplomatic post in Amsterdam, and was imprisoned in the Tower of London. Exchanged for Lord Cornwallis at the close of the war, he, with Benjamin Franklin, John Adams and John Jay, signed the peace preliminaries in Paris on 30 November 1782.

156.32 "The affair of Arnold": General Benedict Arnold was, at the beginning of the war, a distinguished patriot, but grew dissatisfied with Congress because of several altercations over promotion and finances. In 1779 or 1780, he secretly turned traitor and began to provide the enemy with valuable information. When in command of West Point, his treachery was uncovered. He fled, fought for a year in this country for the British and sailed for England in December of 1781.

159.3-4 "Colonels Fletchall, Pearis": Colonel Thomas Fletchall had been a colonel in the provincial militia from the Saluda area in 1775. He was considered an important man by Drayton and the patriots, who made an effort to win him to the whig side. Fletchall was an ineffectual leader, and virtually betrayed his army by signing a peace treaty with Drayton which was favorable only to the whig side. He later deserted the army to hide from a strong whig force, was captured and taken to Charleston. After the fall of Charleston, he served in the British army and, in 1782, his estate was confiscated by the Jacksonborough Assembly. Colonel Richard Pearis fought with Drayton early in the war, but became dissatisfied with promotion and changed sides, becoming an influential loyalist in the up country. He was captured with Fletchall, and later served under Clinton.

159.11 "Nelson's Ferry": Crossed the Santee between Orangeburg and Sumter counties about one mile from Eutaw Springs.

159.36 "Waters, Caldwell" et al.: A John Waters, a militia officer on parole in Charleston, was seized on 17 May 1781 and imprisoned on the schooner *Pack-Horse*. John C. Caldwell of Saluda was designated by the Provincial Congress as a captain in the 3rd Regiment (Rangers) in 1775. In October of that year he charged a loyalist, Robert Cunningham, with "seditious words" and had him arrested. Colonel Benjamin Roebuck of Pickens' militia brigade served at Cowpens and the Battle of Mud Lick in March 1781. Colonel John Thomas of Fair Forest in what is now Spartanburg County also served in Pickens' brigade, and was among the earliest whigs to take up arms. During much of the war, he was a prisoner. His son was also an influential patriot, and served in the Jacksonborough Assembly. A Samuel Miller was being held on the prison ship *Torbay* in May 1781.

160.21 "The provincials are not properly esteemed. . . .": Williamson's summary of British error in the treatment of the loyalists is historically sound. Loyalists in arms were rarely promoted above the rank of major. Few were chosen to lead significant encounters, and it was unusual for a loyalist to be welcomed into British social circles in the Charleston garrison.

160.34 "When I first left": There is no evidence that Williamson wrote such letters. However, a letter from Lord Rawdon to Cornwallis of 24 June 1780 states "I have had several private conversations with Williamson, who has every appearance of candour; & sincerely wishing to remain under the British Government, he has a strong sound understanding and if I am not much deceived indeed will be infinitely useful here, if properly treated" (in Cornwallis papers, quoted in McCowen, p. 67).

163.8 "Beaufort was cut to pieces": Lieutenant Colonel Abraham Buford was, on 29 May 1780, overtaken and defeated by Tarleton in the Waxhaws (now Lancaster County near the North Carolina line). English and American accounts of the battle differ radically, but historians agree that the British showed extreme cruelty, and when asked for quarter proceeded with an outright slaughter, by some accounts continuing to slash at the whigs for fifteen minutes after none were left standing. Tarleton reported 113 whigs dead, 150 wounded and left at the scene and fifty-three prisoners capable of moving. The British loss was five dead, twelve wounded. Most of the American wounded died later at Waxhaw Church.

163.36 "Unless you make terms . . . the forfeit": See note 44.4 for discussion of confiscation on both sides. In January 1782, at the Jacksonborough Assembly, an act of expulsion and confiscation was passed which declared that all who had fought against their country or had given voluntary aid to the enemy were subject to banishment and their property belonged to the state. Gadsden, Marion and Charles Pinckney, among others, opposed the measure, and Edward Rutledge, author of the bill, suggested moderation, but the confiscation of loyalist estates soon got out of hand and most were treated very badly. Though some were banished, many had their estates restored after they were amerced either 30% or 12%, depending on the extent of their offenses against the state.

    In September 1781, John Rutledge had issued a proclamation granting pardon to all who had taken protection provided they declared their loyalty to the Americans in thirty days. (The penalty for not so declaring was banishment and confiscation.) However, certain classes of Loyalists were exempted from this pardon, and Williamson would probably not have qualified.

164.5 "Mrs. Thompson and her daughter": This incident is based on a tradition that Mrs. Thompson, the wife of Colonel Thompson of Orangeburg, had permission to visit friends in Charleston, and came to that city bringing her six year old daughter. She went out, leaving the child alone with orders "to do anything that a gentleman should tell her. In a little while a gentleman appeared, who put a letter into the bosom of the child's frock, charging her not to show it or speak of it to any one until an officer should ask for it." After he left, the mother returned, asked no questions, and went directly to General Greene's camp, where Greene asked for the message (Mrs. St. Julien Ravenel, *Charleston: The Place and the People* [1906], pp. 304-305).

164.17 "it comes from General Marion": There is no hard evidence that Williamson was actually made such an offer. However, Simms' *Life of Marion* quotes a letter from Greene to Marion written the day after his arrival at Charlotte: "Spies are the eyes of an army, and without them a general is always groping in the dark. . . . At present, I am badly off for intelligence. It is of the highest importance that I get the earliest intelligence of any reinforcement which may arrive at Charleston. I wish you, therefore, to fix some plan for procuring such information and conveying it to me with all possible dispatch. . . . It will be best to fix upon somebody in town to do this, and have a runner between you and him to give you the intelligence; as a person who lives out of town cannot make the inquiries without being suspected" (pp. 190-191).

165.4 "You will remember": Robert Cunningham (1739-1813) was a prominent judge of Ninety Six District when war broke out. In 1775, he was arrested by the whigs and imprisoned at Charleston. Released from custody in 1776, he subsequently served as brigadier general in the loyalist forces in South Carolina. After the war, his estate was confiscated and he retired to Nassau. Singleton's reference to his confrontation with Williamson is historically accurate.

165.28 "the commandant has already": Simms errs here as to Balfour's consideration of the use of black troops in the fall of 1780 or early 1781. Clinton had issued a proclamation printed in Rivington's *Royal Gazette* in New York on 3 July 1779 calling for Negroes to join his army, and Lord Cornwallis then issued a similar proclamation. In a February 1781 letter to Washington, Greene states that the British had begun to form two regiments of Negroes, but such an order would have come from Rawdon via Cornwallis rather than from Balfour. Balfour did endorse the proposal made by Lord Dunmore (see note 255.6) in early 1782.

168.3 "to pay the piper": From the Pied Piper of Hamelin of medieval legend.

168.10 "Ben Mosely"; 168.28 "Stokes . . . Ike Waring": None of these members of Singleton's partisan troop have been positively identified, but Simms has been careful to use surnames identified with the whig side in South Carolina. The Warings, for example, came from the Goose Creek/Dorchester area.

171.19   "Tagliona": Maria Taglioni. The Taglionis were a family of famous ballet masters and ballerinas during the early and mid-19th century.

171.24-30 *Continental* money": The value of depreciated Continental money in late 1780 and early 1781 varied from region to region, and from city to back country, but Simms' estimate of the cost of a pair of shoes is not exaggerated. An officer's journal of the time quotes the cost of a pair of gloves at $118, and a shirt at $150. Ramsay states that by 1 June 1780, paper currency had depreciated 8114%, and by the summer of 1781, it ceased to be worth anything, by "common consent" (II, 96-97).

173.9   "halbreds": halberds, 15th and 16th century weapons which combined the battle-ax and the pike.

174.31-175.27   Dennison's ballad: No historical incident has been identified as the source for this ballad of Dennison, the poet who first appears in *The Partisan*. Possibly, Simms is here commemorating the victory of Marion on 14 September 1780 at Black Mingo, a deep creek flowing into the Black River northwest of Georgetown. Marion attacked a party of loyalists under Captain John Ball at midnight, forcing them into the swamp. High losses were suffered on both sides, partly because Marion had failed to muffle the hooves of his men's mounts before they crossed a plank bridge, thus giving warning of their approach.

177.2 "Walter Griffin": No Walter Griffin who served in the Revolution has been identified, though Griffin is a common name in South Carolina Revolutionary War records.

179.11   "John Bull": I.e., typical Englishman, from *The History of John Bull* by John Arbuthnot (1712).

184.30   "Ravenel's plantation": Wantoot, near the head of the Cooper River in Berkeley County.

189.4 "Cornwallis sent Tarleton": Because of repeated incidents very like the one described by Meadows in Chapter XIX, Cornwallis ordered Tarleton to find and destroy Marion's camp and disperse his men, in order to protect the British lines of communication. Tarleton pursued Marion into Clarendon County, and on 10 November 1780 awaited his attack, but Marion, realizing that the British outnumbered his own troop two to one, retreated down the Black River. Tarleton reportedly said in disgust, "Come, my boys! let us go back, and we will soon find the game cock (meaning Sumter) but as for this d--d *old fox*, the devil himself could not catch him" (James, p. 63).

190.8 "Mrs. Dick Singleton": Apparently a fictional character, but see note 6.32.

190.16 "Her dwelling": The house here described as Mrs. Singleton's was actually that of Tom Singleton (see Ravenel, *Charleston*, p. 304). According to Ravenel, Tom Singleton's house functioned in the occupied city as does Mrs. Singleton's here, "being a great meeting place for the rebels" (p. 303).

190.21 "Rutledges, the Laurens', the Izards": Three leading Revolutionary families of South Carolina. Three Rutledges, John, Thomas and Edward, had been members of the first Provincial Congress in 1775. At the time of the novel, Edward was a prisoner in St. Augustine, Florida, and John was governor of the state, with "dictatorial" powers in the absence of any formal standing legislature. Henry Laurens (see note 156.3) was in the Tower of London; his son, Colonel John Laurens, made a prisoner at the fall of Charleston, was about to embark on a diplomatic mission to France. The Izards had loyalist connections as well as whig. Sarah Izard married Lord William Campbell, the last Royal Governor of South Carolina. Though her father Ralph Izard was not a tory, he and his family loved England and had lived there since 1771; he had taken a diplomatic appointment to Tuscany, and his son Ralph Jr. was in the militia.

190.24 "'to weep their sad bosoms empty'": Shakespeare, *Macbeth*, IV, iii.

190.38 "Major Barry": Harry Barry (see note 57.8) was a captain rather than a major during the occupation of Charleston.

191.37 "General Leslie": General Alexander Leslie commanded the royal forces in South Carolina at the time Charleston was surrendered to the Americans in December 1782. However, as he had not taken command in Charleston until 7 November 1781 (when he arrived with a corps of artillery to defend the city against General Greene), Simms is probably incorrect in calling him a great party-giver at the time of this novel.

193.3 "her flirtations with . . . Prince William": William IV (1765-1837) ascended the throne on the death of his brother George IV in 1830. In June 1778, at the age of fourteen, he shipped aboard the *Prince George* with Captain Robert Digby. In March and April 1782, he made a trip to New York, but there is no evidence that, in 1780 or 1781, the fifteen year old prince was in Charleston, or that he carried on a flirtation with any local belles. At that time he was serving in Spanish waters, when not in England.

193.26 "Miss Mary Roupell": Simms here means Polly Roupell, the "chief Royalist belle" (Ravenel, *Charleston*, p. 296).

193.28 "George Roupell": Of Scottish descent, he was banished in 1775 and apparently went to London but returned after the fall of Charleston. He lived at the corner of Tradd and Friend.

193.26 "Paulina Phelps": A death notice in the *Royal Gazette* of 5 January 1782 suggests that the lady was Margaret Philp, daughter of Robert Philp, a Charleston merchant and one of the addressors of Sir Henry Clinton. See note 329.36; see also Johnson's *Traditions*, p. 67, and Ravenel's *Charleston*, p. 297.

194.13 "Ella Monckton": Although fictional, she represents a group of loyalist ladies whom Garden (1822) describes as honorable and worthy of admiration (pp. 243-245). One such lady may have inspired Simms' portrait of Ella: "There was another lady, whose name circumstances of peculiar delicacy compel me to withhold. . . . Led, from the political creed of her friends and family, to favour the British interests, it never caused her, for an instant, to cherish illiberal animosity. . . . If she engaged in scenes of gaity, it was evident from the calm tenor of her conduct, that it was more from necessity than choice. . . . when the noble Hayne became a victim of political animosity, she wept his fate as she would have done that of a martyr" (p. 244).

201.8 "It is not love that forever demands its recompense": Possibly a paraphrase of Shakespeare's Sonnet 23, line 11.

208.23 "*catalogue raisonnée*": A descriptive or analytical list.

211.7 "*durante bene placito*": At the pleasure or at the discretion [of the king].

211.12 "*ton*": Style.

216.1 "clock that stood, 'like a tower'": Milton, *Paradise Lost*, Book 1, 591.

216.11 "*selons les règles*": Selon les règles, French, meaning according to the rules.

216.25 "*oi poloi*": Hoi polloi, Greek, the general populace.

216.37-38 "With an *i* or *y*?": In September 1780, a number of Smiths were willing to accept the oath of allegiance, among them George Smith, Thomas Bradford Smith and Peter Smith. Alexander, William and Nicholas Smith were all addressors of Clinton at the fall of Charleston. There were also a good many Smyths in loyalist Charleston, including James Smyth and John Smyth. (The latter typified the

Charleston loyalist; he was an addresser of Clinton and a petitioner to be armed in the Crown's defense. He was banished in 1782 and his property—along with that of many other loyalists—was confiscated.)

217.30 "Sir Egerton Leigh": Leigh was attorney general and surveyor general of South Carolina. He was of Scots ancestry, and his father had been Chief Justice of the colony. He rose rapidly in social and legal position, and was extremely influential. In his early thirties, he became a baronet (see note 68.24) and married the niece of Henry Laurens, then president of Congress. In the late 1760's, he became involved in a lengthy and serious legal controversy with Henry Laurens which, combined with a scandal, rendered him ineffectual in the state during the early years of the war, but after the British occupied the city, he served on the Board of Police, a powerful position. Garden (1822) says that "The character of Sir E. LEIGH, is so well known in Carolina, that it is sufficient to establish the infamy of a Court, to say that he presided at it" (p. 225).

219. 27 "the towering temples of the goddess Cybele": Cybele, in Greek myth, was the mother of the Olympian gods.

219.32 "Norah Creina": The Maclise 1845 engraved edition of Thomas Moore's *Irish Melodies* contains an illustration which corresponds to this description of Nora Creina, a figure in the poem "Lesbia Hath a Beaming Eye."

219.35 "cymar": A robe or loose light garment for women.

223.10 *"argumentum ad crumenam"*: Argument made by her wealth.

224.7 "the inspired beast": Balaam's ass, Numbers 22:23-28, patiently awaited the blows of his master.

225.32 "the devil to pay, and no pitch hot": A nice mess. A phrase used by sailors in the late 18th century, which comes from the smearing of a ship's bottom, or devil, with pitch to stop a leak.

225.36 "a score of Campbells in the city": Johnson's *Traditions*, pp. 65-70, mentions several Campbells who served in the British forces in South Carolina.

225.37 *"nom de guerre"*: Simms here combines the characters of Mad Campbell and Fool or Crazy Campbell. See note 57.8.

226.12 "twenty stone": 280 pounds.

226.14 "the puritan brand": The cutting off of an ear was a common punishment for minor crimes in 16th and 17th century England and New England.

227.21   "Madam Roland and her amiable associates": Madam Roland
was the leading figure in a French salon which served as headquarters of
the republicans and the Girondists during the French Revolution.
Madam Roland was guillotined in 1793, reputedly crying as she went to
her death, "O Liberty! What crimes are committed in thy name."

228.29   "Mrs. General Gadsden": Anne Wragg was the third wife of
Christopher Gadsden (1724-1805), a leading merchant of Charleston
who had been a leader of the radicals in South Carolina in the Stamp
Act Congress, a delegate to both Continental Congresses, and a soldier.
At the time of the narrative of *Katharine Walton*, he was a prisoner in
St. Augustine.

228.31   "Mrs. Savage and Mrs. Parsons": Probably Mrs. Thomas Savage,
whose husband was among the first prisoners-on-parole to be arrested,
imprisoned in the Provost, and eventually sent to St. Augustine. His
estate was sequestered by Cruden on or about 30 December 1780. Mrs.
Parsons is probably the wife of James Parsons, a member of the first
Provincial Congress and subsequently a lieutenant colonel of militia
who died in 1779, apparently broken in spirit by the invasion and capture of Savannah.

228.34   "Edwards, Horry, and Ferguson": Simms is here listing leading
whig families in Charleston. John Edwards, who was esteemed for his
work in the first Provincial Congress and for his bitter opposition to the
surrender of Savannah, was at present a prisoner-on-parole, and would
subsequently have his estate sequestered and be imprisoned on the
schooner *Pack-Horse* in May 1781. It was to his wife, Mrs. John
Edwards, that Isaac Hayne directed his personal record of his case be
sent after his execution. Thomas Ferguson, a self-made man and son of
ferry keepers, had risen to prominence as a landowner and patriot. He
was exiled to St. Augustine. There were three Horrys in the first Provincial Congress, Daniel, Elias and Thomas. The brothers Hugh and Peter
Horry both fought under Marion. Peter commanded Marion's mounted
troops, and Hugh, the foot soliders.

228.36   "Elliotts": Moultrie lists three Elliotts, Barnard, Benjamin and
Charles, in the first Provincial Congress, and the name continued to be
associated with patriotism throughout the Revolution. Mrs. Barnard
Elliott is said to have presented Moultrie's regiment with colors after
the Battle of Fort Sullivan in 1776 just before the Colonies declared
independence, and it was her husband who read the Declaration of
Independence to Charlestonians.

229.11   "active and sleepless circle of conspirators": A group very like
the one described here was active in Charleston, with Tom Singleton's
house as one of its frequent meeting places; see note 190.16.

229.29   "Old Tom Singleton": Simms' great grandfather, Thomas Singleton, was originally from Virginia, was a rich tobacco planter and merchant and owned the land which today comprises Marion Square and the old Citadel.

229.31 and 230.9   George Spidell, Joshua Lockwood: The details of the messenger service run by George Spidle and Joshua Lockwood are recorded in Johnson's *Traditions*, pp. 279-280. Simms follows this source very closely, but since *Traditions* was published after the writing of *Katharine Walton*, we can assume that Simms heard the story either from Johnson or from Spidle himself, whom Johnson says had related it before his death. According to Johnson, George Spidle was often an unconscious agent, delivering bundles and parcels which he did not know contained information for Marion.

230.10   "*periagua*": or periauger, a large open boat used in marshes and creeks.

230.18   "Maham": Colonel Hezekiah Maham, who often fought with Marion's brigade, was most famous for his invention of a log tower erected in the night from which Marion's soldiers could shoot with protection into an otherwise unassailable fort. The device was first used successfully at Fort Watson in April 1781, and again at the sieges of Augusta and of Ninety Six.

231.8   "David Ramsay": Author of *History of the Revolution of South-Carolina*, and later histories of the Revolution and of South Carolina. Only twenty-five at the beginning of the Revolution, he was a physician and statesman. In the fall of 1780, he was banished to St. Augustine and exiled there for eleven months. After the peace was signed, he took the place of John Hancock, then ill, as president pro tem of Congress, a position under the Articles of Confederation equivalent to President of the United States. The physical details of his description here appear in Johnson's *Traditions*, complete even to the blemish in his eye from smallpox.

232.26   "widow of Miles Brewton, Esq.": Simms errs here both in asserting that the famous widow Brewton was the wife of Miles Brewton (who had been lost at sea with his wife and family in 1776) and in declaring Miles Brewton "strenuous in support of the revolutionary argument." Brewton supported the colonists in their grievances, but opposed independence and therefore left South Carolina. Miles Brewton's wife had been one of the Izard daughters, sister to Lady Campbell (see note 190.21). Simms has confused Miles Brewton with his half-nephew, Robert, whose widow was indeed a famous patriot in Charleston. Ravenel writes of her, "she even dared to tease the dreaded Moncrieff, the commissioner of captures" (*Charleston*, p. 303). Edward

Weyman was an upholsterer, and had declared himself a patriot as early as 1766. He was exiled to St. Augustine. See note 11.1.

232.28   "'Liberty Tree'": A large oak on Alexander Street near Charlotte, in the northeast section of the city under which patriotic meetings were held by Weyman, Daniel Cannon, Christopher Gadsden and others, first in protest against the Stamp Act in 1766.

232.35   "Rebecca Motte": Mrs. Brewton's cousin by marriage, Rebecca Motte, widow of Jacob Motte and sister of Miles Brewton, encouraged Lee to burn her home on 12 May 1781, when it became evident that in no other way could the British be driven out of the house which had been converted into a fort. She provided the arrows for the occasion, and Simms paid tribute to her heroism in *Mellichampe*, where the incident furnishes the basis for the burning of the Berkeley mansion.

232.36   "Mrs. Thomas Pinckney": Daughter of Rebecca Motte, and wife of Major Thomas Pinckney, who was wounded and taken prisoner by the British at the Battle of Camden (an incident Simms relates in *The Partisan*).

232.37 *"mouvement"*: Revolutionary.

234.6   "a private collection of beasts": Tradition relates only that Singleton had a pet monkey. See note 254.18.

234.12   "Buncombe": Simms uses a word meaning "nonsense" for the name of a country.

234.28   "Falstaff": A character in Shakespeare's 1 and 2 *Henry IV* and *The Merry Wives of Windsor*.

234.30   "what the angel was to that excellent beast . . .": Numbers 22: 23-34. Balaam's ass saw an angel and, in order to save Balaam, refused to go as his master directed him.

236.15   "Queen Elizabeth": Reigned 1558-1603.

238.5   "Mrs. Heyward": Mrs. Thomas Heyward, wife of a signer of the Declaration of Independence.

238.25   "Mrs. Heyward's dwelling": This incident is recorded in Garden's *Anecdotes* (1822), pp. 227-228.

238.32   "Mrs. Charles Elliott": Wife of Charles Elliott (see note 228.36) and daughter of Thomas Fergusson (see note 228.34).

238.38   "'Have I found thee, mine enemy?'": "I did find him still mine enemy," Shakespeare, *As You Like It*, I, ii.

240.7 "the case of the Roman augur": Livy (*History of Rome*, I, xxxvi) tells the story of the soothsayer Attus Navius, who opposed a military decision of Tarquin on the grounds that he had not consulted the necessary auguries. When Tarquin ridiculed the art of divination, Attus Navius demonstrated its power by cutting a whetstone in two with a razor, thus suggesting symbolically that the troops with which Tarquin proposed to strengthen his force would prove powerless.

242.32 "Knyphausen's": General Knyphausen took over command of British troops at New York in December 1779 from Sir Henry Clinton. Whether he had a Hessian bugler with a slit nose is not known.

246.22 "the Bay": Charleston Bay, at the confluence of the Ashley and Cooper rivers.

247.7 "Ramsay's intention": Ramsay's two volume *History of the Revolution of South-Carolina* was published in 1785. Garden (1822) confirms that he was carefully preserving documents and materials for a history during the war (p. 180). The effort must have been known to his friends, for Isaac Hayne took care to discuss his case with Ramsay. See note 438.13.

247.34 "the Governor's bridge": Crossed Market Street just north of St. Phillip's Church. What is today Market Street was a creek at the time of the Revolution.

247.38 "Wando river": A short river with headwaters northeast of Charleston; it flows into Charleston Bay at Haddrill's Point.

250.27 "The best friends, the nearest kindred": The Pinckney family provides a good example. Eliza Pinckney, by the time of the war quite elderly, and her sons Thomas and Charles Cotesworth were ardent patriots. Thomas was wounded at Camden; both sons were members of the Jacksonborough Assembly which reconvened state government and drafted the confiscation act. Eliza's son-in-law Daniel Horry, as well as her cousin Daniel Huger and her husband's nephew Charles Pinckney, took protection. Similarly the Middleton family was divided: Henry Middleton, once president of the Continental Congress, sided with the Crown; his son Arthur, a signer of the Declaration of Independence, was sent to St. Augustine. His stepson Thomas Drayton joined Marion; his son-in-law Charles Drayton vacillated between whig and loyalist sentiments. Two other sons-in-law were Charles Cotesworth Pinckney and another prominent patriot, Edward Rutledge.

251.5 "his domicil": Tom Singleton's house still stands on Church Street, below Tradd. See note 190.16.

251.33 "Lord North": Lord Frederick North (1732-1792) was head of the king's cabinet during the Revolutionary War.

254.18   "Lord George": Lord George Germaine (1716-1785) during the Battle of Minden, 1 August 1759, put off advancing until too late because he said his orders were not sufficiently clear. He subsequently went to great lengths to obtain a court-martial to clear his name, for many broadsides and pamphlets of the day called him a coward. He was eventually convicted of disobeying orders and his name was erased from the privy council books in 1760.

Ravenel (*Charleston*, p. 304) relates the story of Singleton's "large pet baboon" uniformed "in an exact reproduction of the commandant's regimentals" and says that he always addressed the monkey by Balfour's name and title.

255.6   "the corps of black dragoons": This reference cannot be authenticated. History records no Captain Quash and no corps of black dragoons at Monck's Corner in 1781, though a mounted black troop from New York did appear in the Dorchester area in April 1782. General Greene, in a letter to Washington dated 28 February 1781, says that the "enemy have ordered two regiments of negroes to be immediately embodied" (Livermore, *An Historical Research*, p. 139), but apparently these regiments were not actually formed. However, extensive use of slaves was made during the Revolution on both sides. Between 8000 and 10,000 Negroes served in American armies, but only about 5000 of these as regular soldiers.

In South Carolina, Negro soldiers had been used in the Yemassee War, on ships against the Spaniards in 1742 and occasionally thereafter. The Provincial Congress of South Carolina voted on 20 November 1775 to allow military officers to use slaves as "pioneers and laborers" (Livermore, p. 99), their masters to be paid a set fee for this use. On 26 September 1775, Edward Rutledge moved to discharge all Negroes in the army, but the motion was defeated. In November 1775, Lord Dunmore, the Royal Governor of Virginia, attracted many runaways by issuing a proclamation which promised freedom to any slave enlisting in the British army. Several regiments of black soldiers were effective in the North during the first years of the war. Henry Laurens and his son John were ardent supporters of the idea of enlisting slaves, and urged Congress to enact the necessary legislation, but Washington objected, fearing that it might cause the Negroes thus enlisted to rebel against their masters: "I am not clear that a discrimination will not render slavery more irksome to those who remain in it. Most of the good and evil things in this life are judged of by comparison; and I fear a comparison in this case will be productive of much discontent in those who are held in servitude" (Livermore, p. 131). Despite Washington's objections, Congress voted to arm 3000 Negroes, but the South Carolina legislature in 1779 rejected the proposal. In 1780, though the need for manpower had become greater, the South Carolina house rejected General Lincoln's request to arm blacks (to which James Madison had replied that those Negroes who served as soldiers should be set free), but allowed 1000 to be used to fortify against the British: "No slave was excused unless his owner had produced a written exemption from the governor" (McCowen, p. 98).

In a long letter dated 5 January 1782, John Cruden wrote to Lord Dunmore from Charleston suggesting a plan for recruiting and implementing 10,000 blacks. Dunmore forwarded the plan to Sir Henry Clinton, recommending approval, and suggested that the loyalist officers garrisoned in Charleston be chosen to command the troops. On 24 January 1782, General Greene similarly suggested to Governor Rutledge that blacks be used to fill the vacant places in his regiments, recommending freedom, "without which they will be unfit for the duties expected from them" (Johnson, *Life of Greene*, II, p. 274). Nothing came of either of these plans, as the war quickly drew to a close. At the end of the war, many of the Negroes who had served in various capacities obtained their freedom (by law, in Virginia), usually by individual petition to the various legislatures. Examples of these petitions can be seen in Livermore, *An Historical Research*, p. 153, and in Herbert Aptheker, ed., *A Documentary History of the Negro People in the United States* (1951), pp. 12-14.

255.30 "a taste like that of Jacques in the forest": Jaques is a cynical, philosophical character in Shakespeare's *As You Like It*.

259.2 "liable to be seized": Singleton himself was exiled to St. Augustine in August 1780, along with many other most prominent patriots of the city. Other patriots were imprisoned in the Provost, under the Exchange Building at the east end of Broad Street, or were detained on the prison ships *Torbay* and *Pack-Horse*.

259.33 "'durance vile'": Imprisonment.

261.19 "A rival tavern was kept by Pryor": A "Prier's" Tavern was situated above Dorchester on the "Broad Path" or public road, and the grave of a Seth Prier still exists in the graveyard of St. George's Church at Old Dorchester. Simms' statement here that Pryor's Tavern was still in operation conflicts with *The Partisan*, in which Pryor burns his own tavern in the effort to rescue Walton (*The Partisan*, p. 527).

263.25 "Eagle bridge": Across Eagle Creek, which flows into the Ashley below Dorchester.

263.26 "little fortress": The tabby fort at Dorchester was built in 1757 on a bluff overlooking the river below the town, as a defense against the Indians. During the early years of the Revolution it was repaired and equipped with a powder magazine by the Americans, and later occupied by the British.

266.17 "Ashley Ferry road": Branches off the main road from Charleston (to Goose Creek) about six miles north of the city, and continues into St. Andrews parish on the southwest side of the Ashley.

267.32 "M'Kelvey": Although a real William McKelvy fought during the Revolution in South Carolina, this character is probably based on Lieutentant Colonel McLauchlan, who was Isaac Hayne's second in command and was killed at the capture of Hayne.

269.15-17 "Haddrill's . . .": Simms' list of places popular as excursion spots during the Revolution includes Haddrill's Island, just east of Charleston across the mouth of the Cooper River; Sullivan's Island, site of Fort Moultrie, at the east side of the mouth of Charleston Bay; James Island, which forms the southwest side of Charleston Bay; Morris Island on the southwest side of the mouth of the bay at the eastern tip of James Island; St. Andrews, a settlement in St. Andrews parish just across the Ashley at Ashley Ferry; Goose Creek, a town in St. James Goose Creek parish about sixteen miles north of Charleston on Goose Creek; and Accabee Plantation, located on a curve of the Ashley south of Ashley Ferry and north of Charles Towne Landing which, during the Revolution, was owned by Barnard Elliott.

276.10 "Mrs. Ingliss": This is probably the wife of loyalist Alexander Inglis, who was killed in a duel in Charleston in 1791.

278.4 "Mrs. Tidyman, in Ladson's court": Mrs. Tidyman has not been positively identified, though Ravenel assigns her house to Number 2, Ladson Street. She may have been Hester Rose, born in 1755, who married Phillip Tidyman, a silversmith from England. This Tidyman, however, had a lot on Tradd Street and a house on Broad Street, but no record exists of any property he held on Ladson. There is a Tydiman estate on the south Santee near the Horry estates about fifteen miles from the coast.

279.15 "Sadler": Although Sadler is a fictional character, the incident related here is alleged to have happened to Mrs. Brewton much as Simms tells it. See Garden's *Anecdotes* (1822), p. 233.

280.1 "This event was one of several": Mrs. Brewton had been present at the firing of Rebecca Motte's house, and is said by some accounts to have taken part in the firing. Further, she was known throughout Charleston for her quips and caustic remarks to British officers. Several of these are reported in Garden's *Anecdotes* (1822), pp. 230-234. Mrs. Brewton was exiled to Philadelphia in July 1781, by order of Balfour, and left the colony on or before 1 August. See note 232.26.

280.19 "usual weekly ride": Although history does not verify that Williamson rode weekly beyond the city, it was the custom for officers to ride beyond the fortifications up the Neck daily, and the Quarter House was the most frequent destination for these morning rides.

282.23 "Captain Harley": Ravenel records that the officer who challenged Mad Archy's suit was from Philadelphia (*Charleston*, p.

297), but this source is inaccurate in several respects regarding Margaret Philp, and may be in error here.

284.20 "pink him": Draw blood.

288.13 "small-sword": A light tapering sword for thrusting used chiefly in dueling and fencing.

290.22 "the dwelling of Mrs. Ingliss": This house has not been identified.

292.30 "In striving to hide your light": Allusion to Matthew 5:15.

293.10 "Royal Gazette": The *Royal Gazette* was published by John Wells for his father Robert Wells from 3 March 1781 to the close of 1782, at number 71 Tradd Street. The paper was an organ for the British. Gibbes' *Documentary History* (III, 72) quotes a letter from Harry Barry, acting as secretary and deputy adjutant general, in which he tells the publishers to insert a notice in the paper.

293.33 "mock heroic manner": A manner burlesquing the heroic epic.

294.13 "mountain suffered grievously from that mouse!": "The mountain labored and brought forth a mouse." Aesop's *Fables*, "The Mountain in Labor."

295.36 [note] "This answer was really given by Barry": Has not been identified. Much of the factual information in *Katharine Walton* detailing the social life of the British garrison may have come from Simms' interviews with eyewitnesses, or from diaries and similar sources which have since been lost.

298.15 "Goose Creek church": St. James Episcopal Church, Goose Creek, still stands about a mile beyond Otranto in Goose Creek (see note 269.15-17). Services are held there annually on the Sunday after Easter, though weekly services were discontinued in 1808.

304.1 "St. Michael's": St. Michael's Episcopal Church, at 78 Meeting Street, was built in 1752. Its "tower holds a four-faced clock that has marked Charleston's time since 1764, and chimes that have crossed the ocean five times . . . their mellow tones still sounding the hours" (*South Carolina: A Guide to the Palmetto State* [Writers Program, WPA, 1941], p. 192).

305.21 "Four-Mile Post": Four miles up the Charleston Neck was Four Mile House Tavern, on the road leading north out of the city.

307.17 "well-known blue hunting-shirts of the Carolina rangers": Because of the scarcity of replacement uniforms, American regular and militia troops often fought in work and hunting clothes. So prevalent was the practice that Washington suggested that the hunting shirt be made the standard dress for the American soldier. Blue was adopted as the official Continental Army uniform color in October 1779.

307.29 "Goose Creek road": Goose Creek Road extended northwest from the Six Mile House Tavern (six miles north of Charleston) to Goose Creek.

308.22 "taking his ease at his inn": "Shall I not take mine ease in mine inn?" Shakespeare, 1 *Henry IV*, III, iii.

309.8 "threw himself from the bed": Simms, in this fictionalized account of the capture of General Williamson, has chosen to ignore the possibly fallacious legend that Williamson was taken while in bed with a prostitute, was given no time to dress and was thus captured in his shirt, as Johnson says, "in a situation not creditable to him as a man of family" (*Traditions*, p. 361). Williamson was actually captured on the Dorchester road, within about five miles of the city, by Isaac Hayne on 5 July 1781. Williamson's capture here at the Quarter House may also be based on a raid made by Colonel Wade Hampton, on 15 July 1781. Hampton encountered a small patrol of Royal South Carolina Dragoons, whom he made prisoners. Several loyalists from Charleston were also spending the morning at the Quarter House; some escaped, others were taken and paroled. Hampton's raid, following so closely on that of Hayne, greatly alarmed the garrison. "The bells were rung, the alarm guns were fired, and the whole city was under arms" (McCrady, II, 329).

309.11 "He had led a thousand": Williamson led a campaign against the Cherokees from July to October 1776. At the beginning of the campaign, his force numbered only forty men, but by October, more than 2000 were under his command. His campaign, brilliantly successful, was the first major military effort of the newly formed Commonwealth of South Carolina, acting independently of and in opposition to the British.

309.27 "of the state line": Of the militia.

310.3 "doom at the drumhead": A summary or battlefield court-martial.

313.7 "method . . . madness": Shakespeare, *Hamlet*, II, ii.

313.30 "*Stuck*": Cheated.

314.4 "*done down*": Cheated.

314.16 "Daniel Cannon's": One of the earliest patriots in Charleston, he was one of the group who met frequently at the Liberty Tree in 1766, and a member of the first Provincial Congress in 1775. Johnson says he was a house carpenter, the "oldest and most influential mechanic in Charleston," and was later called Daddy Cannon (*Traditions*, p. 34).

315.4 "fifty yellow hammers": Fifty gold sovereigns.

315.15 "Ah! there's the rub!": Shakespeare, *Hamlet*, III, i.

316.2-7 "Garden's": Dr. Alexander Garden (1730?-1791), Scottish born, came to South Carolina about 1754. He became a fashionable doctor, and through his interest in botany developed a correspondence with Linnaeus and scientists around the world. The British naturalist John Ellis was a special friend, and named the Gardenia in his honor. A loyalist, Garden congratulated Cornwallis after Camden. In 1782, he was banished and his property confiscated, and though it was later returned, he never returned to America. His son, Alexander Garden (1757-1829), was born in Charleston, and served in Lee's legion in Greene's army, eventually acting as Greene's aide-de-camp. His father never forgave him for his whig sentiments. Garden the son wrote *Anecdotes of the Revolutionary War in America* (1822) and *Anecdotes of the American Revolution . . . Second Series* (1828), both of which Simms used extensively. Otranto lies about one and a half miles south of Goose Creek. Apparently during the war it belonged to the son, for it was not amerced though the elder Garden's properties were.

316.18 "marked with a white stone": Allusion to Revelation 2:17.

316.35 "seven heavens": The seven heavens of Muslim and cabalist doctrine.

317.11 "Oberon": King of the fairies in medieval folklore, and a character in Shakespeare's *A Midsummer Night's Dream*.

317.12 "Titania": Queen of the fairies in Shakespeare's *A Midsummer Night's Dream*.

317.19 "consumed in bitumen": Bitumen is a kind of pitch traditionally associated with the lake of Sodom and with Hades.

317.23 *"fou"*: Mad, insane.

319.36 "Jehu": II Kings 9:20.

321.9 "rector, Ellington": Reverend Edward Ellington was elected rector of St. James Goose Creek Church in January 1775, "at that time . . . probably the best clerical appointment in South-Carolina" (Johnson's *Traditions*, p. 382). He continued there until 1793, when he retired to Savannah.

322.4 *"parish* country of South Carolina": The Church Act of 1706 divided the colony of South Carolina into ten parishes, subdivisions for both ecclesiastical and political government in the low country. The parishes remained as election districts in the low country until after the Civil War. In 1785, the up country was divided into new counties for the purpose of political representation, but because the low country kept the parish divisions, it continued to have a majority in the House and Senate, a circumstance which caused political dissension periodically throughout the state until the state constitution was revised.

322.13 "'sleek, oily men of God'": "A little, round, fat, oily man of God." James Thomson, *The Castle of Indolence* (1748).

322.20 "The reverend": Simms' description of Ellington here is accurate as recorded in Johnson's *Traditions*, pp. 382-383.

323.7 "John Rogers": Rogers was an English Protestant clergyman who, in 1537, published Matthew's *Bible*. He was tried as a heretic during Mary Tudor's reign for preaching against Roman Catholicism and was burned at the stake in 1555.

324.4 "in less than two hours": Goose Creek Church lies sixteen miles from Charleston.

324.11 "'Swear not at all'": Shakespeare, *Romeo and Juliet*, II, i.

324.27 "Sultan Solyman": Sultan Suleiman, a Turkish ruler at the height of the Turkish empire (1520-1566).

329.36 "He . . . reported all the particulars": Johnson's *Traditions*, p. 67, relates the story of Mad Archy and Paulina Phelps. Johnson contends that Ellington himself told it frequently in society, and that Johnson had heard it from a lady who was still living during the writing of *Traditions* (1851). An article by Samuel W. Ravenel in *Southern Bivouac*, n.s.1 (December 1885), pp. 444-445, asserts that the marriage between Mad Archy and "Paulina" as related by Ellington and later by Simms and Johnson is largely fiction. Ravenel says that the family tradition of Margaret's descendants holds that she and Campbell had the consent of her father, but that the delay requested by Mr. Philp seemed intolerable to the young couple. Campbell therefore staged a prearranged ambush of the Philp carriage when Margaret and her mother were riding in the vicinity of Goose Creek Church, and he and Margaret were indeed married by Reverend Ellington, who performed the service at gunpoint.

335.1 "Benedick": A character in Shakespeare's *Much Ado About Nothing*.

335.4 "Beaufain": No historical basis has been found for a Harvey house on Beaufain Street, though in the mid-18th century there was a Harvey house on Broad Street.

335.18 "in fear and trembling": Philippians 2:12.

336.30 "Major Fraser": Major Fraser in *Katharine Walton* seems to be a combination of two brothers, Major Charles Fraser, the head of military police in Charleston or "the town Major," and Major Thomas Fraser, who conducted the British cavalry against Colonel Hayne. It was Charles Fraser who signed the various orders summoning Hayne to appear before a court of inquiry, and who signed the verdict and sentence. Johnson (*Traditions*, pp. 362-363) describes Thomas Fraser as being a rather brutal soldier who, after the Revolution, remained in South Carolina, eventually becoming a merchant in Charleston. The capture of Williamson occasioned both horror and indignation within the garrisoned city; Hayne's exploit was vivid proof that the British were not safe from attack, and could not adequately protect the loyalists. Accordingly, Fraser was sent with ninety dragoons (rather than cavalry) to rescue the prisoner.

341.23 "Combahee": The Combahee River flows southeast to the coast about forty miles below Charleston.

341.23 "His own quarters": Like Walton, Hayne had taken up quarters at a plantation, Mrs. Ford's north of Parker's Ferry on the Edisto. Hayne was thus separated from his troop which was encamped at Horse Shoe in Colleton County.

343.32 "Marion or Greene": It is impossible to verify where Marion or Greene would have been at the time of the fictional Williamson capture, because the time scheme of the novel is very vague. On page 422, at the trial which takes place on the same day, Williamson says that the Continental Army is "even now flying before Cornwallis in Virginia," which indicates that Simms intends for the events at the end of the novel to correspond with those of the capture and execution of Isaac Hayne. If this is the case, then, in early July 1781, Greene and Marion were both engaged in the Orangeburg area, pursuing Lord Rawdon as he moved south from Ninety Six.

344.6 "Lynch's Creek": Lynch's Creek flows south past Camden and about twenty miles to the east, then flows east to join the greater Pee Dee. Where the two streams join was Marion's most famous camp, Snow's Island.

350.25 "Uneasy lies the head that wears a crown": Shakespeare, 2 *Henry IV*, III, i.

352.14 "Every form common to such trials": Although trials such as the one Simms here records were not uncommon throughout the Revolution, there is no historical basis for the assumption that Williamson was tried by Hayne's troop. In a letter to John Dickinson, John Rutledge wrote that Williamson was treated well and that Hayne "immediately gave him his parole to Charles-town" (quoted in David Bowden, "The Execution of Colonel Isaac Hayne: Its Implications and Aftereffects" [M.A. thesis, University of South Carolina, 1974] , p. 24).

353.31 "Buford's defeat": Williamson's statement that he remained an honorable patriot until Buford's defeat is correct. See note 163.8.

354.7 "deliberate consultation": An account which is of questionable reliability, that of Colonel Samuel Hammond, who claimed he was present at these deliberations, suggests strongly that Williamson after the fall of Charleston did not want to lay down arms and tried to talk his officers out of such a course, but was outvoted. Hammond claims that Williamson was wrongly maligned by public opinion and cites the facts that he never bore arms against the whigs after taking protection and that he apparently helped Greene by sending intelligence from Charleston (Johnson's *Traditions*, pp. 149-154).

354.16 "Richard Pearis, Robert Fletchall": History does not support the assertion that there was correspondence between these men and Williamson. See note 159.3-4.

354.25 "General Moultrie . . .": General William Moultrie (1730-1805), one of South Carolina's most prominent soldiers, had been captured in the fall of Charleston and imprisoned on Haddrill's Point. Christopher Gadsden (see note 228.29) was eventually made a prisoner in August 1780 and sent to St. Augustine. At the time Williamson took protection, Gadsden was a prisoner-on-parole in Charleston.

356.6 " 'Rawdon's mercy,' and 'Tarleton's Quarters'": The phrase "Tarleton's Quarters" arose from the Buford massacre (see note 163.8) when Tarleton refused quarter to the defeated whigs and slaughtered them. "Rawdon's mercy" probably refers to his instructions to Colonel Rugely after the first Battle of Camden: "I will give . . . ten guineas for the head of any deserter belonging to the volunteers of Ireland, and five guineas only if they bring him in alive" (Ramsey, II, 134).

356.21 "the blood-thirsty tories": Walton's troop is indignant over the brutal treatment which whig families received at the hands of marauding loyalist bands throughout the back country from the late fall of 1780 and continuing until the end of the war in South Carolina in 1782. Simms was interested in depicting this civil strife, and portrays many such incidents in his later novels *The Forayers* (1855) and *Eutaw* (1856). Whigs were often as brutal as loyalists, however, and the desire of Walton's men to execute Williamson without a fair trial shows the brutality which Simms felt the war had engendered on both sides.

360.18 "*Sauve qui peut!*'": French: save (himself) who can.

360.36 "own splendid charger": Hayne's own capture on 8 July 1781 parallels that of Walton closely. Hayne rode his favorite horse, "Herod" or "King Herod," which had been a magnificent charger, but which had become fat and sluggish during its master's inactivity.

361.24 "M'Kelvey": M'Kelvey's death is perhaps based on that of Lieutenant Colonel McLaughlan. See note 267.32. Historians disagree as to who captured Hayne himself. Most attribute the deed to Mad Archy Campbell, though Walton seems simply to have been pursued by Campbell's troop. Balfour, in a letter to Clinton on 21 July 1781, wrote: "By avoiding the main Roads, Major [Thomas] Fraser was enabled to surprize Col. Haynes's Comp. of Colleton County Militia, where he was informed Gen'l Williamson then was, and coming upon it suddenly, killed a Lt. Col. McLoughlan, with ten or twelve others, made Col. Haynes a Prisoner and retook Gen'l Williamson" (quoted in Bowden, p. 24). Probably, the actual capture was made by Mad Archy, riding in Major Fraser's troop.

365.2 "Salkehatchie": The two forks of the Salkehatchie River flow southeast roughly parallel to and between the Edisto and the Savannah. The Salkehatchie forks converge and form the Combahee River.

380.35 "Cruikshank": George Cruikshank (1792-1878) was a British artist and caricaturist who illustrated the works of Dickens, among others.

386.6 "Colonel Harden": Colonel William Harden, active under General Bull in the first years of the war, had joined Marion after the fall of Charleston. On 18 April 1781, he wrote to Marion that he was anxious to convince Hayne to resume arms, stating that if Hayne forsook his oath, many neighbors would follow his example (Gibbes, *Documentary History*, III, 53-55). Harden, at the time of Hayne's capture, was in camp at Horse Shoe on the Ashepoo River, and it was from this camp that Hayne left to capture Williamson. It was Harden who informed General Greene of Hayne's execution.

390.5 "General Pinckney": Simms errs in calling Charles Cotesworth Pinckney a general; he was a colonel in 1781.

391.23 "'Who is not *for* me is *against* me!'": Matthew 12:30.

392.13 "Una": "Lovely Ladie," the personification of truth in Edmund Spenser's *The Faerie Queene*.

393.18 ff. "The heavy sash . . .": This incident happened, according to tradition, as it is told here. Miss Polly Roupell never married, and lived to be an old lady, respected by Charlestonians. Ravenel remembers her riding around in an ancient coach in the 1840's.

396.12 "Rawdon's maxim": In August of 1780, the patriots had intercepted a letter from Cornwallis to Cruger which described the action at Camden, in which Cornwallis wrote, "every militiaman who has borne arms with us and afterwards joined the enemy shall be immediately hanged" (McCrady, I, 710). This practice of execution without trial was followed by Rawdon, who also initiated other measures, including imprisonment, to insure that all the inhabitants of the Camden area would take up arms against the whigs. His policy had the opposite effect, and is credited with causing much disaffection among the local people.

399.16 "the guarded entrance": Hayne was, like Walton, imprisoned in the Provost, in the basement of the Exchange Building, still standing in Charleston.

399.18 "'where now the merchants most do congregate'": Shakespeare, *The Merchant of Venice*, I, iii.

400.9 "that fine old mansion": The Pinckney house; see note 11.1.

401.24 "He is regarded": It should not be overlooked that such treatment was practiced by both sides. Governor Rutledge, known for his kindness, directed Sumter on 6 October 1780, that any person who had voluntarily aided the enemy should be held for trial by civil court for treason.

406.9 "I shall be exchanged": Although the practice of exchanging prisoners was common in the early years of the war in New England and the middle states, and continued to be accepted as policy, in fact, prisoners were less often exchanged in the Southern Department. McCrady writes, "The large number taken by the British at Charlestown and Camden in 1780 had rendered them indifferent in the matter—if indeed it was not against their policy to enter into any agreement looking to the release of the Continental officers and soldiers they held in Christ Church Parish and on the prison ships, as well as the distinguished exiles in Florida" (II, 344). A large exchange was negotiated in March 1781, but worked to the Americans' disadvantage: the exchanged British prisoners went back to the ranks, but most American prisoners went home as their period of service had expired (Johnson, *Life of Greene*, I, 470-471).

419.4 "with all your heart, with all your soul": Deuteronomy 6:5.

422.7 "Your continentals": Balfour's discourse on the state of the war is, of course, entirely false. By the summer of 1781, all of the British outposts in the back country had been abandoned, Sumter, Marion and Lee were moving against Rawdon, and Greene was in camp in the High Hills of Santee. The events of this section of the novel probably can be dated in relation to Hayne's trial and execution as in late July 1781.

422.15 "The destruction of a French fleet": Miscalculations about the French fleet had plagued the British from 1780, when they determined to take Charleston to prevent the French from basing a fleet there. See also note 56.12.

428.1 "activity of Mrs. Brewton": Mrs. Brewton (see note 280.1) was exiled to Philadelphia, not to the Congarees. There is no evidence as to whether she made any efforts in behalf of Hayne, though she would have been likely to sign the petition (see note 439.16) of the whig ladies.

432.20 "chewing the cud": Shakespeare, *As You Like It*, IV, iii.

434.24 "Hampstead—the 'field of honor'": Presumably a meadow or field in the northeastern or Hampstead section of the city.

435.18 "Dueling": Wallace in *South Carolina: A Short History* says, "Dueling seems to have grown worse as the eighteenth century advanced. The men of the Proprietary period quarreled abundantly, but not with such deliberate deadliness. Ramsay thought . . . that the Revolution strongly encouraged dueling" (p. 196). See Johnson's *Traditions*, pp. 45-47, for a typical account of a duel caused when one man called the other a liar.

436.31 "The parties embraced": No historical reference to this duel has been found.

438.13 "Walton's trial came on": The details given here of the last few days of Walton's life, the trial and the execution, parallel closely those of Colonel Isaac Hayne except for the inclusion of Balfour's pursuit of Katharine, which is entirely fictional. Hayne's death has been well documented, primarily because Hayne himself carefully preserved all of the materials relating to his case, recorded his own position and actions and gave all these papers to his son immediately before his death. Too, Dr. David Ramsay was a confidant of Hayne, an eyewitness to the execution (having but recently returned from his exile in St. Augustine), and was much affected by it. Simms was very interested in the Hayne affair, and included accounts of it in his *History of South Carolina* and *Life of Nathanael Greene*. An early extended account of the Hayne affair which Simms may have used as a source was "The

Execution of Colonel Isaac Hayne" by Hayne's descendant, Senator
Robert Y. Hayne, in the first issue of *The Southern Review*, February
1828. The documents relating to the trial and execution may be found
in Gibbes' *Documentary History of the American Revolution*. David
Bowden in "The Execution of Colonel Isaac Hayne: Its Implications
and Aftereffects" (Master's thesis, U.S.C., 1974) provides the fullest
account to date of Hayne. Almost every history and memoir of the
time commented on the affair. General Greene issued a proclamation
signed by every one of his officers except Lee, who was out of the area
at the time, declaring that he would retaliate on the next high ranking
British officer made prisoner. Both Lord Rawdon and Earl Cornwallis
were considered by Congress as possible subjects for retribution, but
with the war drawing to a close, no retaliation was ever officially taken.
Lord Rawdon, after his return to London, found himself severely cen-
sured for the affair—which received considerable debate in Parliament.
(Parliament voted against official censure.)

   Although Walton was tried a few days after his capture, Hayne was
actually held for several weeks until Rawdon returned to Charleston.
Hayne was never officially tried, but rather stood before a court of
inquiry which heard no witnesses and in which the testimony was not
sworn. Though Walton was told that he would die on the gallows,
Hayne apparently did not know the means by which he would be put
to death until the last minute. He had hoped to die a soldier's death
rather than that of a spy. Walton was told from the first that he would
die in four days, but Hayne was originally sentenced to die on the day
he learned of his sentence, requested a delay that his family might be
brought to Charleston so that he might take leave of them, and was
eventually granted two forty-eight-hour delays through the offices of
those who pled for his life.

439.16   "the native citizens": Hayne's sentence excited widespread
indignation in Charleston, and several petitions were written, one signed
by the ladies of the town said to have been authored by Mrs. Charles
Elliott and addressed to Lord Rawdon (Garden's *Anecdotes* [1822], p.
236). Hayne's wife's sister, Mrs. Peronneau, took his children with her
to Col. Balfour to plead for his life, but without effect. There is no evidence that Williamson signed any petitions.

439.35   "The public safety": There is no record of Balfour's having
made any such statement. Historians have not agreed as to whether the
blame for the Hayne affair ought to fall on Balfour or Rawdon, though
most agree that Rawdon should be named the real villain. For a full
discussion, consult the sources listed in note 438.13.

441.37   "Haman": An enemy of the Jews hanged, according to the book
of Esther, for plotting their destruction.

447. 13 "the lines which divided it": The lines of fortification which had been used in the Siege of Charleston (see note 17.9). Singleton reached the Bay just south of Calhoun Street.

463.9 "Town Creek": A creek flowing along the east side of the Charleston peninsula between Charleston and an island in the Cooper River. It is now spanned by the Cooper River bridge.

463.18 "twenty-four pounder": A large cannon, so called because its shell weighed twenty-four pounds.

465.12 "offered a protest": See Gibbes' *Documentary History* (III, 109-111) for Hayne's letter of protest to Rawdon and Balfour.

465. 26 "The venerable men of the city": William Bull (1710-1791), a native born American, was acting Royal Governor of South Carolina until he was replaced by Lord William Campbell in 1775. That he was highly respected is evidenced by the fact that after the war his estates were not confiscated. Nevertheless, he went to London in 1782 and remained there until his death. Robert Y. Hayne in "The Execution of Colonel Isaac Hayne" (p. 34) states: "we have it on the authority of an old and most respectable inhabitant of this city, now alive, 'that Governor Bull caused himself to be carried in a litter to the quarters of Lord Rawdon, in order personally to intercede for the pardon of Colonel Hayne: that on his return home, the dejection of his countenance too plainly spoke the ill success of his interference.'" Other petitioners included Major Fraser, who had been present at the capture of Hayne, and Harry Barry. Bull, according to Rawdon's 1813 letter to Lee, first said he would sign the petition only if Sir Egerton Leigh did (see note 217.30), but when Leigh replied *"that he would burn his hand off rather than do an act so injurious to the king's service"* (Lee, p. xxxix), Bull apparently relented; his personal intervention was responsible for the granting of one forty-eight-hour reprieve to Hayne. Tradition holds that Campbell, who had captured Hayne, was indignant over his treatment, and that he repeatedly said "that if he could have supposed it, he would rather have killed Colonel Hayne in the pursuit, that he might have died the death of a soldier" (Johnson, *Traditions*, p. 69).

468.38 "Major Frazer, commanding": It has not been verified who commanded the detachment, but it would have been the duty of Major Charles Fraser, "the town Major" (see note 336.30).

469.20 "Colonel Walton was attended": This description comes almost entirely from manuscript notes of an interview Simms had with an alleged eyewitness of this event. Radcliffe's Gardens was at the corner of Pitt and Vanderhorst streets. The Reverend Robert Cooper had served for sixteen years as the rector of St. Michael's, but had been

dismissed in 1776 for praying for the king. Refusing to take an oath of
loyalty to the American cause, he had left Charleston in 1777, but
returned to become rector of St. Phillip's in 1781.

469.33 "'hot with haste and fiery red'": "Bloody with spurring, fiery-
red with haste." Shakespeare, *Richard II*, II, iii.

473.29 "Three nights after": Singleton (see note 259.2) could not have
been present during Hayne's execution (4 August 1781); he had just
been sent to Philadelphia from a year-long exile in St. Augustine. For
an account of an exiled patriot being "seized in his bed," see Garden's
Anecdotes (1822), p. 239.

473.36 "Archy Campbell": Johnson's *Traditions*, p. 68, relates how,
during the Battle of Videau's Bridge in St. Thomas parish on 2 January 1782, Campbell became unhorsed in an encounter with Marion,
and was forced to surrender. He was ordered to sit on the root of a tree,
and a sentinel, Nicholas Venning of Christ Church parish, was set to
watch him. Though told not to stir or he would be shot, Campbell
became impatient, attempted escape and was killed.